CHERRYH   Cherryh, C.J.
           Cyteen

DATE DUE			
JUL 1 4 '88			
OCT 1 3 '88			
OCT 3 1 '88			
JAN 2 7 '89			
MY 1 2 '95			
AG 2 8 '96			
JUN 1 6 2004			
JUL 1 3 2004			
NOV 1 4 2006			
AUG 2 2 2007			
AUG 1 8 2009			

CYTEEN

C.J.CHERRYH
CYTEEN

WARNER BOOKS

A Warner Communications Company

Copyright © 1988 by C. J. Cherryh

Warner Books, Inc., 666 Fifth Avenue, New York, NY 10103

A Warner Communications Company

Printed in the United States of America
First printing: May 1988
10 9 8 7 6 5 4 3 2 1

Library of Congress Cataloging-in-Publication Data

Cherryh, C. J.
  Cyteen.

  I. Title.
PS3553.H358C98   1988   813'.54   87-29985
ISBN 0-446-51428-4

Book design: H. Roberts

CYTEEN

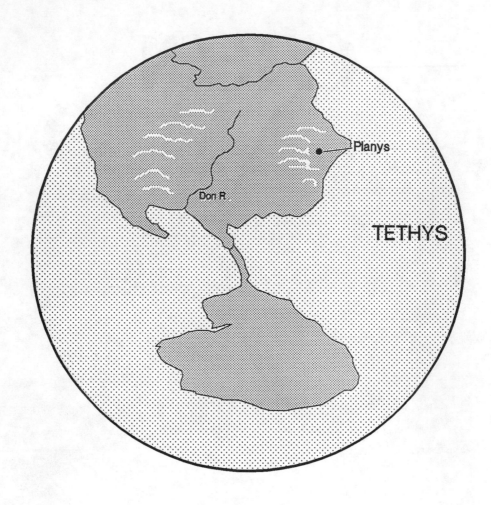

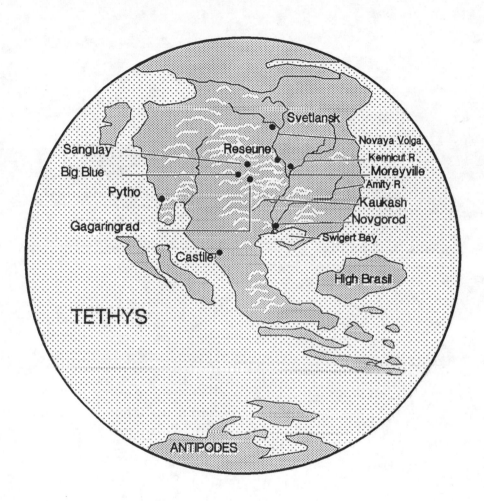

Svetlansk

Novaya Volga

Kennicut R.

Reseune

Moreyville

Sanguay

Amity R.

Big Blue

Kaukash

Pytho

Novgorod

Gagaringrad

Swigert Bay

Castile

High Brasil

TETHYS

ANTIPODES

Verbal Text from:
THE HUMANE REVOLUTION
"The Company Wars": #1

Reseune Educational Publications: 4668-1368-1
approved for 80+

Imagine all the variety of the human species confined to a single world, a world sown with the petrified bones of human ancestors, a planet dotted with the ruins of ten thousand years of forgotten human civilizations—a planet on which at the time human beings first flew in space, humans still hunted a surplus of animals, gathered wild plants, farmed with ancient methods, spun natural yarns by hand and cooked over wood fires.

Earth owed allegiance to a multitude of chairmen, councillors, kings, ministers and presidents; to parliaments and congresses and committees, to republics, democracies, oligarchies, theocracies, monarchies, hegemonies and political parties which had evolved in profusion for thousands of years.

This was the world which first sent out the starprobes.

Sol Station existed, a much more primitive Sol Station, but altogether self-sustaining; and favored with a system of tax remission in return for scientific benefit, it launched a number of ambitious projects, including the first large-engine starprobe, and ultimately the first crewed pusher-ship cluster toward the near stars.

The first of the pusher-modules was of course the venerable Gaia, which was to deliver the Alpha station-component at the star known at that time as Barnard's, and leave thirty volunteer scientists and technicians in what in those days meant inconceivable isolation. They would build their station out of the star's expected system-clutter of rock and ice, perform scientific research and maintain long-distance communication with Earth.

The first concept had been disposable pushers, hardly more than robotic starprobes; but human passengers mandated an abort-and-return capacity which, considering all the possibilities for disaster, was negotiated finally to mean a full-return capacity. That led to the notion of a crewed pusher-module to stay at Barnard's should the star prove impossibly deficient in raw materials necessary for self-sufficiency of the Alpha module, in which event Gaia might remain for a number of years, then strip the station to the essential core and return the mission to Earth. If the star proved a viable home for the station, Gaia would remain only a year or so until the Alpha Station module was fully functioning and stable in its orbit. Then it would return to Sol with its tiny complement of crew and surrender the Gaia module to a second mission, which would, after refitting, go out again with such supplies as trace minerals and materials which the infant station might not have available. Equally important with the supplies, those early pioneers theorized, was the human link, the reassurance of face-to-face contact with other human beings across what in those days was an inconceivably lonely expanse of space.

Earth, with years' advance warning via the constant data-flow from Gaia and Alpha Station that the mission was abundantly successful and that Gaia was returning, trained a replacement crew and dutifully prepared the return mission.

But the crew of Gaia, subject to relativistic effects, running into an information stream indicating greater and greater changes in the Earth they had left, had become more at home in the ship than in the mainstream of a Terran culture gone very alien to them. Their sojourn on Sol Station was intensely unhappy, and they re-occupied Gaia by a surprise move which immensely disconcerted station authorities, but which finally won them their ship and relegated the replacement crew to waiting on the next pusher-craft.

Other crews of further missions reached the same decision, regarding themselves as permanent voyagers. They considered their small ships as home, had children aboard, and as star stations and attendant pushers multiplied, asked of Earth and the stations only fuel, provisions, and the improvement of their ships with larger compartments, more advanced propulsion—whatever had become available since their last docking.

Star-stations at half a dozen stars linked themselves by the regular passage of such ships. But in the isolation of those days in which messages traveled at mere light-speed and ships traveled slower still, every station was at least four or five years time-lagged from every other human habitation, be it ship or station, and learned to exist in these strangely fluxing time-referents which were impossibly alien to the general population of Earth.

The discovery of intelligent life on the planet at Pell's Star, the star Earth once called Tau Ceti, was more than ten years old by the time the word of it reached Earth. The dealing of human beings with the Downers was more than two decades advanced by the time Earth's elaborate instructions could arrive at Pell; and it was much longer before Terran scientists could reach Pell, up the long route that led them station by station into a human culture almost as foreign to them as were the Downers.

As it is difficult from our viewpoint to imagine Earth of that time, it was virtually impossible for Earth to comprehend the reasoning of spacers who refused to leave their ships and who, in their turn, found the (to them) teeming corridors of Sol Station chaotic and terrifying. It was virtually impossible even for Sol Station to understand the life of their contemporaries in the deep Beyond—contemporaries whose culture was built on history and experiences and legendry that had much more to do with the hardships of life in remote stations and famous ships, than with events in a green and chaotic world they saw only in pictures.

Earth, beset with overpopulation and political crises largely attributable to its ancient rivalries, had nevertheless flourished while it was the focus of human development. The unexpected rush of stationers to new construction at Pell, following the prospect of abundant biostuffs, a native population primitive and friendly, and exploitable free-orbiting resources, became a panic flood. Stations between Earth and Pell shut down, disrupting the trade of the Great Circle, and creating economic chaos on Earth and Sol Station.

Earth reacted by attempting to regulate—across a ten-year time lag: Terran politicians could not readily conceive of the economic strength the remaining stations might achieve, given the unification of population that rush to Pell had created. The concentration of population and the discovery of vast resources combined with the psychological impetus to exploration . . . meant that Earth's now twenty-year-old instructions arrived in a situation in such rapid flux even a month's lag would have been significant.

Earth found itself increasingly isolate, subject to internal pressures from a faltering trade system, and in a desperate and ill-advised action imposed a punitive tariff which led to smuggling and an active black market; which in turn led to a sudden fall-off of trade. Earth's response was the declaration of most-favored-status for certain ships; which led in turn to armed hostilities between ships from Earth and ships which had not been built by Earth and which did not hold any allegiance to its convolute and wildly varying politics.

Further, Earth, convinced that emigration of scientists and engineers from Sol System was feeding the spacer cultures with the best and brightest and robbing Earth of its best talent, slammed down an emigration ban not only on travel from Earth and Sol Station, but on further moves of citizens in certain professions from station to station.

Gaia made her last trip to Earth in 2125, and left, vowing never to return.

A general wave of rebellion and mutiny swept through the stars; stations were mothballed and deserted; probes and missions sought further stars not only with economic motive now—but because there were more and more people anxious to move outward, seeking political freedom before restrictions came down.

Viking Station and Mariner sprang into existence as stationers found even Pell too vulnerable to Earth's influence and as Pell's now established economy afforded less opportunity for highly profitable initial-phase investment.

By 2201 a group of dissident scientists and engineers sponsored by financial interests on Mariner founded a station at Cyteen, about a world vastly different from Pell. The brilliant work of one of those scientists combined with the economic power of Cyteen's new industries sent the first faster-than-light probe out from Cyteen in 2234, an event which altered the time scale of spaceflight and forever changed the nature of trade and politics.

Cyteen's early years were characterized not only by a burst of growth and invention unparalleled in human history, but, ironically, by the resurrection of long disused technologies out of ship archives: combustion engines, gravity-dependent processing, all to save soft-landing the enormous mass-requirements of a full-scale terrestrial development. In addition, there were new on-planet technologies specific to Cyteen, to create pockets of breathable atmosphere in the otherwise deadly environment—all this effort because Cyteen represented a major biological opportunity for the human species. It had no intelligent indigenes. It did have a varied and entirely alien ecosystem—virtually two ecosystems, in fact, because of the extreme isolation of its two continents, differing significantly from each other but vastly different from Earth and Pell.

It was a biologist's paradise. And it offered, by its absence of intelligent life, the first new cradle of terrestrial human civilization since Earth itself.

It was not politics alone which led to the Company Wars. It was the sudden acceleration of trade and population mobility, it was the stubborn application of outmoded policies by Terran agencies out of touch with the governed, and finally it was the loyalty of a handful of specially favored Terran merchanter captains attempting to maintain a fading trade empire for a motherworld which had become only peripheral to human space.

It was a doomed effort. Cyteen, no longer alone in the Beyond, but motherworld itself to Esperance, Pan-paris, and Fargone Stations, declared its independence from the Earth Company in 2300, an action which, reported now with the speed of the Faster-Than-Lights, prompted Earth to build and dispatch armed FTLs to bring the dissident stations back into line.

Merchanters quickly fled the routes nearer Pell, thus reducing the availability of supplies, while Earth itself, even with FTL technology, was by no means able to supply the mass requirement of its fleet over such distances. Over a span of years the Earth Company fleet degenerated to acts of piracy and coercion which completely alienated the merchanters, always the Earth Company's mistake.

The formation of the merchanters' Alliance at Pell established the second mercantile power in the Beyond and put an end to Earth's attempt to dictate to its scattered colonies.

Surely one of the more ironical outcomes of the War, the Treaty of Pell and the resulting economic linkages of three human societies, drawing on three vastly different ecosystems, now exist as the driving forces in a new economic structure which transcends all politics and systems.

Trade and common interests have proven, in the end, more powerful in human affairs than all the warships ever launched.

CHAPTER 1

It was from the air that the rawness of the land showed most: vast tracts where humanity had as yet made no difference, deserts unclaimed, stark as moons, scrag and woolwood thickets unexplored except by orbiting radar. Ariane Emory gazed down at it from the window. She kept to the passenger compartment now. Her eyesight, she had had to admit it, was no longer sharp enough, her reflexes no longer fast enough for the jet. She could go up front, bump the pilot out of the chair and take the controls: it was her plane, her pilot, and a wide sky. Sometimes she did. But it was not the same.

Only the land was, still most of the land was. And when she looked out the window, it might have been a century ago, when humankind had been established on Cyteen less than a hundred years, when Union was unthought of, the War only a rumbling discontent, and the land looked exactly like this everywhere.

Two hundred years ago the first colonists had come to this unlikely star, made the beginnings of the Station, and come down to the world.

Forty-odd years later the sublight ships were coming in, few and forlorn, to try to convert their structure and their operations to faster-than-light; and time sped up, time hurtled at translight speeds, change came so fast that sublight ships met ships they took for alien—but they were not: it was worse news for them. They were human. And the game was all changed.

The starships went out like seeds from a pod. The genetics labs upriver at Reseune bred humanity as fast as it could turn them out from the womb-tanks, and every generation bred others and worked in labs breeding more

5

and more, till there were people enough, her uncle had said, to fill the empty places, colonize the world, build more star-stations: Esperance. Fargone. Every place with its own labs and its own means to breed and grow.

Earth had tried to call her ships back. It was all too late. Earth had tried to tax and rule its colonies with a hard hand. That was very much too late.

Ariane Emory remembered the Secession, the day that Cyteen declared itself and its own colonies independent; the day the Union began and they were all suddenly rebels against the distant motherworld. She had been seventeen when the word came down from Station: *We are at war.*

Reseune bred soldiers, then, grim and single-minded and intelligent, oh, yes: bred and refined and honed, knowing by touch and reflex what they had never seen in their lives, knowing above all what their purpose was. Living weapons, thinking and calculating down one track. She had helped design those patterns.

Forty-five years after the Secession the war was still going on, sometimes clandestine, sometimes so remote in space it seemed a fact of history—except at Reseune. Other facilities could breed the soldiers and the workers once Reseune had set the patterns, but only Reseune had the research facilities, and it had fought the war in its own dark ways, under Ariane Emory's directorate.

Fifty-four years of her life . . . had seen the Company Wars over, humanity divided, borders drawn. The Earth Company Fleet had held Pell's Star, but the merchanters of the newly formed Alliance had taken Pell and declared it their base. Sol had tried to ignore its humiliating defeat and go off in another direction; the remnant of the old Company Fleet had turned to piracy and still raided merchanters, no different than they had ever done, while Alliance and Union alike hunted them. It was only hiatus. The war was cold again. It went on at conference tables where negotiators tried to draw lines biology did not, and make borders in boundless, three-dimensional space—to keep a peace that had never, in all Ariane Emory's life, existed.

All of that might not have been yet. It might have been a hundred years ago, except that the plane was sleek and fine, not the patch-together that had run cargo between Novgorod and Reseune: in those days everyone had sat on bales of plastics and containers of seed and whatever else was making the trip.

Then she had begged to sit by the dusty windows and her mother had said to put her sunscreen on, even so.

Now she sat in a leather seat with a drink at her elbow, in a jet snugly warm inside, immaculately maintained, with a handful of aides talking business and going over their notes, a noise just barely enough to get past the engines.

No traveling nowadays without a clutter of aides and bodyguards. Catlin and Florian were back there, quiet as they were trained to be, watching her back, even here, at 10,000 meters and among Reseune staff whose briefcases were full of classified material.

Much, much different from the old days.

Maman, can I sit by the window?

She was anomalous, child of two parents, Olga Emory and James

Carnath. They had founded the labs at Reseune, had begun the process that had shaped Union itself. They had sent out the colonists, the soldiers. Their own genes had gone into hundreds of them. Her quasi-relatives were scattered across lightyears. But so were everyone's, these days. In her lifetime even that basic human thinking had changed: biological parentage was a trivial connection. Family mattered, the larger, the more extended . . . the safer and more prosperous.

Reseune was her inheritance. Hence this jet, *not* a commercial airliner. No hired plane, either, and no military jet. A woman in her position could call on all these things; and still preferred mechanics who were part of the Household, a pilot whose psych-patterns she was sure of, bodyguards who were the best of Reseune's designs.

The thought of a city, the subways, life among the clerks and techs and cooks and laborers who jostled one another and hurried about their schedules to earn credit . . . was as frightening to her as airless space. She directed the course of worlds and colonies. The thought of trying to buy a meal in a restaurant, of fighting crowds to board a subway, of simply being on a topside street where traffic roared and people were in motion on all sides—filled her with an irrational panic.

She did not know how to live outside Reseune. She knew how to arrange a plane, check out the flight plans, order her luggage, her aides, her security, every little detail—and found a public airport an ordeal. A serious flaw, granted. But everyone was due a phobia or two and these things were far from the center of her worries. It was not likely that Ariane Emory would ever face a Novgorod subway or a station's open dock.

It was a long, long while before she saw the river and the first plantation. A thin ribbon of road, finally the domes and towers of Novgorod, a sudden, remarkably sudden metropolis. Under the jet's wings the plantations widened, the towers of electronic screens and precipitators shadowed the fields and traffic crawled along the roads at ground-bound pace.

Barges chained down the Volga toward the sea, barges and pushers lined the river dockage past the plantations. There was still a lot of the raw and industrial about Novgorod, for all the glitter of the new. This side of it had not changed in a hundred years, except to grow bigger, the barges and the traffic becoming ordinary instead of a rare and wonderful sight.

Look, maman, there's a truck.

The blue of woolwood thicket blurred by under the wing. Pavement and the end-stripes of the runway flashed past.

The tires touched smoothly and the jet came rolling to a stop, for a left turn toward the terminal.

A little panic touched Ariane Emory at this stage, despite the knowledge that she would never get to the crowded hallways. There were cars waiting. Her own crew would handle the baggage, secure the jet, do all these things. It was only the edge of the city; and the car windows would permit vision out, but none in.

All those strangers. All that motion, random and chaotic. In the distance she loved it. It was her own creation. She knew its mass motions, if not its individual ones. At a distance, in the aggregate, she trusted it.

At close range it made her hands sweat.

Cars pulling up and a flurry of hurrying guards in the security entrance of the Hall of State said that it was no mere senatorial arrival. Mikhail Corain, on the balcony outside the Council Chamber, flanked by his own bodyguards and aides, paused and looked down on the echoing stone lower floor, with its fountain, its brass railings on the grand stairway, its multiple star-emblem in gold on the gray stone wall.

Imperial splendor for imperial ambitions. And the chief architect for those ambitions made her entrance. The Councillor from Reseune, in company with the Secretary of Science. Ariane Carnath-Emory with her entourage, late, dependably late, because the Councillor was damned confident of her majority, and only deigned to visit the Hall because the Councillor had to vote in person.

Mikhail Corain glared and felt that speeding of his heart that his doctors had told him to avoid. Calm down, they were wont to say. Some things are beyond your control.

Meaning, one supposed, the Councillor from Reseune.

Cyteen, by far the most populous of the entities in the Union, had consistently managed to capture *two* seats in the executive, in the Council of Nine. It was logical that one of them was the Bureau of Citizens, which meant labor and farming and small business. It was not logical that the electors in the sciences, far and wide across the lightyears Union reached, with a dozen eminently qualified potential candidates, persisted in returning Ariane Emory to the halls of government.

More than that. To a position which she had held for fifty years, *fifty damned years*, during which she had bribed and browbeaten interests on Cyteen and every station in Union and (rumored but never proved) in Alliance and Sol as well. You wanted something done? You asked someone who could get the Councillor of Science to arrange it. What were you willing to pay? What would you take in trade?

And the damned Science electorate, made up of supposed intellects, kept voting her in, no matter what the scandals that attached to her, no matter that she virtually owned Reseune labs, which was legally equal to a *planet* in Union's government, which did things within its walls that countless investigations had tried (and failed, on technicalities) to prove.

Money was not the answer. Corain had money. It was Ariane Emory herself. It was the fact that most of the population of Cyteen, most of the population of Union itself, had come in one way or another from Reseune; and those who did not, used tapes . . . that Reseune devised.

Which that woman . . . devised.

To doubt the integrity of the tapes was paranoid. Oh, there were a few who refused to use them; and studied higher math and business without them, and never took a pill and never lay down to dream what the masses clear across Union dreamed, knowledge pouring into their heads, as much as they could absorb, there in a few sessions. Drama—experienced as well as seen . . . at carefully chosen intensity. Skills—acquired at a bone and nerve level. You used the tapes because your competition would, because you had to excel to get along in the world, because it was the only way to know things fast enough, high enough, wide enough, and the world changed and changed and changed, in any human lifespan.

The Bureau of Information vetted those tapes. Experts reviewed them. There was no way any subliminals could get past them. Mikhail Corain was not one of the lunatic fringe who suspected government com-tapping, Alliance poisoning of cargoes, or mind-enslaving subliminals in the entertainment tapes. That sort of purist could refuse rejuv, die old at seventy five, and live off public works jobs because they were self-taught know-nothings.

But damn it, *damn* it, that woman kept getting elected. And he could not understand it.

There she was, getting a little stoop to the shoulders, allowing a little streak of gray to show in the black hair, when anyone who could count knew she was older than Union, on rejuv and silver-haired under the dye. Aides swarmed round her. Cameras focused on her as if there was no other center to the universe. Damn bony bitch.

You wanted a human being designed like a prize pig, you asked Reseune. You wanted soldiers, you wanted workers, you wanted strong backs and weak minds or a perfect, guaranteed genius, you asked Reseune.

And senators and Councillors alike came to bow and scrape and mouth politenesses—Good God, someone had brought her flowers.

Mikhail Corain turned away in disgust, plowed himself a way through his aides.

Twenty years he had been sitting as head of the minority party in the Nine, twenty years of swimming against the tide, gaining a little now and again, losing all the big ones, the way they had lost the latest. Stanislaw Vogel of the Trade electorate had died, and with the Alliance violating the treaty as fast as they could arm their merchant ships, the Centrists ought to have been able to carry that seat. But no. The Trade electorate elected Ludmilla deFranco, Vogel's niece. Moderate, hell, deFranco was only steering a careful course. She was no less an Expansionist than her uncle. *Something* had changed hands. Someone had been bought, someone had tilted Andrus Company toward deFranco, and the Centrists had lost their chance to install a fifth member in the Nine and gain the majority of the executive for the first time in history.

It was a crushing disappointment.

And there, there in the hall downstairs, in the middle of the sycophants and all the bright young legislators, was the one who had pulled the strings money could not pull.

Political favor, then. The unprovable, untraceable commodity.

On that, the fate of the Union hinged.

He entertained the most terrible fantasy, not for the first time, that somehow, on the steps outside, some lunatic might run up with a gun or a knife and solve their problem at one stroke. He felt a profound disturbance at that thought. But it would reshape the Union. It would give humankind a chance, before it was everlastingly too late.

One life—weighed very little in those scales.

He drew deep breaths. He walked into the Council chambers and made polite conversation with the few who came to commiserate with the losers. He gritted his teeth and walked over to pay his polite congratulations to Bogdanovitch, who, holding the seat of the Bureau of State, chaired the Council.

Bogdanovitch kept his face absolutely bland, his kindly, white-browed eyes the image of everyone's grandfather, full of gentility and civility. Not a trace of triumph. If he had been that good when he negotiated the Alliance settlement, Union would own the codes to Pell. Bogdanovitch was always better at petty politics. And he was another one who lasted. His electorate was all professional, the consuls, the appointees, immigration, the station administrators—a minuscule number of people to elect an office which had started out far less important than it had turned out to be. God, how had the framers of the Constitution let themselves play creative games with the political system? The 'new model,' they had called it; 'a government shaped by an informed electorate.' And they had thrown ten thousand years of human experience out the hatch, a damned bunch of social theorists, including, *including* Olga Emory and James Carnath, back in the days when Cyteen had five seats of the Nine and most of the Council of Worlds.

"Tough one, Mikhail," Bogdanovitch said, shaking his hand and patting it.

"Well, will of the electorate," Corain said. "Can't quarrel with that." He smiled with absolute control. "We did get the highest percentage yet."

Someday, you old pirate, someday I'll have the majority.

And you'll live to see it.

"Will of the electors," Bogdanovitch said, still smiling, and Corain smiled till his teeth ached, then turned from Bogdanovitch to Jenner Harogo, another of that breed, holding the powerful Internal Affairs seat, and Catherine Lao, who held the Bureau of Information, which vetted all the tapes. Of course.

Emory came sailing in and they left him in mid-sentence to go and join her claque. Corain exchanged a pained look with Industry, Nguyen Tien of Viking; and Finance, Mahmud Chavez of Voyager Station, Centrists both. Their fourth seat, Adm. Leonid Gorodin, was over in a grim confluence of his own uniformed aides. Defense was, ironically, the least reliable—the most prone to reassess his position and shift into the Expansionist camp if he conceived near-term reasons. That was Gorodin, Centrist only because he wanted the new Excelsior-class military transports kept in near space where he could use them, not, as he put it, 'out on our backside while Alliance pulls another damn embargo. You want your electorates hammering at your doors for supplies, you want another hot war, citizens, let's just send those carriers out to the far Beyond and leave us depending on Alliance merchanters. . . .'

Not saying, of course, that the Treaty of Pell, which had agreed that the merchanters' Alliance would haul cargo and build no warships; and that Union, which had built a good many of those haulers, would maintain its fleet, but build no ships to compete with the merchanters . . . was a diplomatic buy-off, a ransom to get supply flowing again. Bogdanovitch had brought that home and even Emory had voted against it.

The stations had passed it. The full General Council had to vote on it, and it got through by a hair's breadth. Union was tired of war, that was all, tired of disrupted trade, scarce supplies.

Now Emory wanted to launch another wave of exploration and colonization out into the deep Beyond.

Everyone *knew* there was trouble out there to find. What Sol had run into on the other side of space proved that well enough. It had brought Sol running back to the Alliance, begging for trade, begging for markets. Sol had neighbors, and its reckless poking about was likely to bring trouble in the Alliance's back door and right to Union space. Gorodin hammered on that point constantly. *And* demanded a larger share of the budget for Defense.

Gorodin's position was weakest. He was vulnerable to a vote of confidence. They could lose him, if he failed to get the ships the Fleet wanted, in the zones that mattered.

And the news from the Trade electorate was a blow, a severe one. The Centrists had thought they had won this one. They had truly thought they had a chance of stopping Emory, and all they could do now was force a point of order, persuade the Council that no vote ought to be taken on the Hope project, since it involved ship appropriations and a major budget priority decision, until deFranco could get in from Esperance and assume her seat.

Or . . . they could break the quorum and send it to a vote in the Council of Worlds. Emory's cabal would flinch at that. The representatives were far more independent, especially Cyteen's large bloc, who were mostly Centrist. Let them get their teeth into a bill of this complexity not already hammered out by the Nine, and they would be at it for months, sending up changes the Nine would veto, and round and round again.

Let Gorodin have another try at persuading the Expansionists to delay the vote. Gorodin was the one on the fence, the one with the medals, the war hero. Throw him at them, see if he could swing them. If not, the Centrists would walk, all four of them. It had political cost, profound cost, to break the quorum and close the meeting.

But time was what they needed, time to get to key lobbyists, time to see if they could pull a few strings and see if deFranco, when she arrived, could be persuaded to be the moderate she proclaimed herself—or at least tilt to the Centrist side on a bill that critical to her constituency. She might, *might*, vote to table.

Councillors drifted toward their seats. Emory's group came up last. Predictably.

Bogdanovitch rapped with the antique gavel.

"Council is in session," Bogdanovitch said, and proceeded to the election results and the official confirmation of Ludmilla deFranco as Councillor for the Bureau of Trade.

Moved and seconded, Catherine Lao and Jenner Harogo. Emory sat expressionless. She never made routine motions. The bored look on her face, the slow revolutions of the stylus in her long-nailed fingers, proclaimed a studied patience with the forms.

No discussion. A polite, pro forma round of ayes, officially recorded.

"Next item of business," Bogdanovitch said, "acceptance of Denzill Lal voting proxy for sera deFranco until her arrival."

Same routine. Another bored round of ayes, a little banter between Harogo and Lao, small laughter. From Gorodin, Chavez, Tien, no reaction. Emory noticed that: Corain saw her laugh shortly and take in that silence with a sidelong glance. The stylus stopped its revolutions. Emory's glance was wary now, sharp as she glanced Corain's way and gave a slow, slight smile, the kind that might mitigate an accidental meeting of eyes.

But the eyes were not smiling at all. *What* will you do? they wondered. What are you up to, Corain?

There were not that many guesses, and a mind of Emory's caliber would take a very little time to come up with them. The stare lingered, comprehended, threatened like a blade in fence. He hated her. He hated everything she stood for. But, God, dealing with her was like an experience in telepathy: he stared flatly, returning the threat, quirked a brow that said: You can push me to the brink. I'll carry you over it. Yes, I will do it. Fracture the Council. Paralyze the government.

The half-lidding of her eyes, the fondness of her smile said: Good strike, Corain. Are you sure you want this war? You may not be ready for this.

The fondness of his said: Yes. This is the line, Emory. You want crisis, right when two of your precious projects are coming up, and you can have it.

She blinked, slid a glance to the table and back again, the smile tight, the eyes hooded. War, then. A widening of the smile. Or negotiation. Watch my moves, Corain: you'd make a serious mistake to make this an open breach.

I'll win, Corain. You can stall me off. You can force elections first, damn you. And that will waste more time than waiting on deFranco.

"The matter of the Hope Station appropriations," Bogdanovitch said. "First scheduled speaker, sera Lao. . . ."

A signal passed between Emory and Lao. Corain could not see Lao's face, only the back of her blonde head, the trademark crown of braids. Doubtless Lao's expression was perplexed. Emory signaled an aide, spoke into his ear, and that aide's face tightened, mouth gone to a thin line, eyes mirroring dismay.

The aide went to one of Lao's aides, and Lao's aide went and whispered in her ear. The move of Lao's shoulders, the deep intake of breath, was readable as her now profiled, frowning face.

"Ser President," Catherine Lao said, "I move we postpone debate on the Hope Station bill until sera deFranco can take her seat in person. Trade is too profoundly affected by this measure. With all respect to the distinguished gentleman from Fargone, this is a matter that ought to wait."

"Seconded," Corain said sharply.

A murmur of dismay ran among the aides, heads leaning together, even Councillors'. Bogdanovitch's mouth was open. It took him a moment to react and tap the gavel for decorum.

"It has been moved and seconded that debate on the Hope Station bill be postponed until sera deFranco takes her seat in person. Is there discussion?"

It was perfunctory, Emory complimenting the proxy, the gentleman from Fargone, agreeing with Lao.

Corain made the request for the floor solemnly to concur with Lao. He might have made some light banter. Sometimes they did, Expansionists with Centrists, with irony under it, when matters were settled.

This one was not. Emory, damn it, had stolen his fire and his issue, given him what he demanded, and looked straight at him when he had uttered the tedious little courtesy to Denzill Lal, and taken his seat.

Watch me closely, that look said. That will cost.

The vote went round, unanimous, Denzill Lal voting proxy in the vote that took the Hope appropriations bill out of his hands.

"That concludes the agenda," Bogdanovitch said. "We had allotted three days for debate. The next bill on the calendar is yours, sera Emory, number 2405, also budget appropriations, for the Bureau of Science. Do you wish to re-schedule?"

"Ser President, I'm ready to proceed, but I certainly wouldn't want to rush a measure through without giving my colleagues adequate time to prepare debate. I *would* like to move it up to tomorrow, if my distinguished colleagues have no objection."

A polite murmuring. No objections. Corain murmured the same.

"Sera Emory, would you like to put that in the form of a motion?"

Seconded and passed.

Motion to adjourn.

Seconded and passed.

The room erupted into more than usual disorder. Corain sat still, felt the weight of a hand on his shoulder and looked up at Mahmud Chavez's face. Chavez looked relieved and worried at the same time.

What happened? that look said. But aloud: "That was a surprise."

"My office," Corain said. "Thirty minutes."

Lunch was a matter of tea and sandwiches couriered in by aides. The meeting had grown beyond the office and filled the conference room. In a fit of paranoia, the military aides had gone over the room for bugs and searched other aides and the scientists for recorders, while Adm. Gorodin sat glumly silent through everything, arms folded. Gorodin had been willing to go along with the walkout. Now things had slid sideways, and the admiral was glowering, anxious, silent, as it developed they had cornered Emory on the Hope corridor budget and might have an ultimatum on their hands.

"It's information we're after," Corain said, and took a glass of mineral water from an aide. In front of him, in front of all of them and most of the aides, eight hundred pages of exposition and figures that constituted the Science budget, in hard-copy, with certain items underlined: there were Centrists *inside* the Science Bureau, and there were strong rumors of sleepers in the bill. There always were. And every year no few of them involved Reseune. "The damn place doesn't *ask* for budget itself, the only thing we've got on it is the gross tax returns, and why in hell does Reseune want to get Special Person status for a twenty-year-old chemist on Fargone? Who in hell is Benjamin P. Rubin?"

Chavez sorted papers on his table, took one that an aide slid under his hand and gnawed at his lip, following the aide's finger down the paper. "A student," Chavez said. "No special data."

"Is there any way it's part of the Hope project? By any stretch of the imagination?"

"It's at Fargone. It's on the route."

"We could ask Emory," Chavez said sourly.

"We damn well may have to, on the floor, and take whatever documentation she comes up with."

There were dour looks all around. "We're beyond jokes," Gorodin said.

Lu, the Secretary of Defense, cleared his throat. "There is a contact we might trust, at least a chain of contacts. Our recent candidate for Science—"

"He's a xenologist," Tien objected.

"And a personal friend of Dr. Jordan Warrick, of Reseune. Dr. Warrick is here. He came in as part of Councillor Emory's advance staff. He's asked, through Byrd, for a meeting with, mmnn, certain members of Science."

When Lu spoke with that much specificity, he was often saying more than he could officially say in so many words. Corain looked straight at him, and Gorodin was paying full attention. The admiral had come in from military operations, would go back to military operations and leave the administrative details of the Bureau of Defense to the Secretary and his staff: it was axiomatic—Councillors might be the experts in their respective fields, but the Secretaries ran the apparatus and the department heads knew who was sleeping with whom.

"Byrd among them?"

"Very likely," Lu said primly, and shut his mouth.

Mark that one down, Corain thought.

"Is that an old friendship?" Tien asked in a low voice.

"About twenty years."

"How safe is that for Warrick?" Gorodin asked. "What are we jeopardizing?"

"Very little," Lu said. "Certainly not Warrick's friendship with Emory. Warrick himself has his own offices, rarely enters hers, and vice versa. In fact there's considerable hostility there. He's demanded autonomy inside Reseune. He has it. There *are* no Centrists in Reseune. But Warrick is—not an Emory partisan. He's here, in fact, to consult with the Bureau on a transfer."

"He's one of the Specials," Corain said, for those not from Cyteen, and not, perhaps, entirely aware who Warrick was. A certified genius. A national treasure, by law. "Forty-odd years old, no friend of Emory's. He's had a dozen chances to leave and found his own facilities, and she keeps blocking it in the Bureau, cut him off at every turn." He had made a personal study of Reseune *and* Emory. It was only reasonable. But some pieces of information were not as available as others, and Lu's tracing of connections was one of them. "Byrd can contact him?"

"Schedules have gone amok," Lu said softly, in his scholarly way. "Of course things have to be rearranged all along the agenda. I'm sure something can be done. Do you want me to mark that down?"

"Absolutely. Let's break this up. Get the staffs to working."

"That leaves us meeting in the morning," Tien said.

"My staff will be here," Corain said, "very late tonight. If anything comes up that we have to—" He shrugged. "If anything comes up, of the nature—you understand, something of a need to know nature—" *Walk-out* was not a word they used openly, and not all the staff present knew that that was in the offing, particularly the clerks. "My staff will contact you directly."

And quietly, catching Gorodin and Lu as the rest of them drifted out to offices and staff meetings in their own Bureaus and departments:

"Can you get Warrick?"

"Lu?" Gorodin said, and Lu, with a lift of clerkly shoulders:

"I should think."

ii

He was an ordinary enough man who showed up in the Hall of State conference room, wearing a brown casual suit, carrying a briefcase that looked as if it had been sent through baggage once too often. Corain would not have picked him out of any crowd: a brown-haired, handsome, athletic sort, not looking quite his forty-six years. But bodyguards would have attended this man until military police took him under their own wing, and very likely servants had all but dressed him and staffers attended him on ordinary business. By no means would Jordan Warrick have come by commercial carrier or a baggage department gotten its hands on that briefcase.

Emory was a Special. There were three at Reseune, the highest number at any single installation. One was this man, who devised and debugged psych tape structures, so they said, in his head. Computers ordinarily did that kind of work. When an important enough tape program had to be built or debugged, they gave it to Jordan Warrick's staff, and when a problem was more than any or all of them could handle it went to Warrick himself. That was as much as Corain understood. The man was a certified genius and a Ward of the State. Like Emory. Like the other dozen Special Persons.

And presumably if Emory wanted to accord that status to a twenty-year-old chemist on Fargone, and, the rumor said, open an office there to attach him to Reseune staff, *and* seemed to imply she attached a priority to that project that made it worth something in the scales right along with her cherished colonial push, there was a damned good reason for it.

"Ser Lu," Warrick said, shaking Lu's offered hand. "Adm. Gorodin. A pleasure." And a worried look but an overall friendly one as he looked toward Corain and offered his hand. "Councillor. I hadn't expected you."

Corain's heart did a little skip-and-race. Danger, it said. Warrick, he reminded himself, was not one of those bright types who operated in some foggy realm of abstract logic completely detached from humanity: he was a psychsurgeon, manipulation was his work, and he was quite in his element stripping people down to their motives. All this lay behind that sober pleasantness and those younger-than-forty eyes.

"You may have guessed," Lu said, "that this is more than I told you it would be."

A little alarm registered on Warrick's face. "Oh?" he said.

"Councillor Corain very much wanted to speak with you—without public attention. This is political, Dr. Warrick. It's quite important. Certainly if you would rather get on to your other meeting, for which you will otherwise be perhaps ten minutes late—we will understand that you don't want to involve yourself with our questions, and I hope you'll accept my personal apologies in that case. It's my profession, you understand, a disposition to intrigue."

Warrick drew a breath, distanced himself the few paces to the conference table, and set his briefcase down on it. "Is this something to do with Council? Do you mind explaining what, before I make any decision?"

"It's about the bill coming up. The Science appropriations bill."

Warrick's head lifted just the little bit that said: Ah. A small smile touched his face. He folded his arms and leaned back against the table, in every evidence a relaxed man. "What about the bill?"

"What's in it," Corain asked, "—really?"

The secret smile widened and hardened. "You mean what's it covering? Or something else?"

"Is—what it's covering—in any way connected to the Hope project?"

"No. Nothing in that budget to do with it. Nothing I'm aware of. Well, SETI-scan. But that's fairly general."

"What about the Special appointment? Is Reseune interested?"

"You might say. You want to know about Fargone in general?"

"I'm interested in whatever you have to say, Dr. Warrick."

"I can spare the ten minutes. I can tell you in less than that what's going on. I can tell you in one word. Psychogenesis. Mind-cloning, in the popular press."

It was not the answer Corain had expected. It was certainly not what the military expected. Gorodin snorted.

"What's it covering?"

"Not a cover," Warrick said. "Not the process in the popular press. Not exact duplicates, but duplicate capabilities. Not real significant for, say, a child trying to recover a lost parent. But in the case of, say, a Special, where the ability is what you want to hang on to— You're familiar with the attempt to recover Bok."

Estelle Bok. The woman whose work led to faster-than-light. "They tried," Corain said. "It didn't work."

"Her clone was bright. But she wasn't Bok. She was a better musician than she was a physicist, and desperately unhappy, thanks to all the notoriety. She wouldn't take her rejuv for days on end, till the effects caught up with her and she'd have to. Wore herself down that way, finally died at ninety-two. Wouldn't even leave her room during the last few years of her life.

"What we didn't have then was the machinery we have now; and the records. Dr. Emory's work in the war, you know, the studies with learning and body chemistry—

"The human body has internal regulating systems, the whole complex that regulates sex and growth and defense against infection. In a replication, the genetic code isn't the whole game. Experience impacts the chemical system the genetic code set up. This is all available in the scientific journals. I could give you the actual references—"

"You're doing quite well," Corain said. "Please."

"Say that we know things now that we didn't when we cloned Bok. If the program does what Dr. Emory hopes, we can recover the ability in the same field. It involves genetics, endocrinology, a large array of tests, physiological and psychological; and the records have to be there. I don't know all of it. It's Dr. Emory's project, it's secret, and it's in a different wing. But I do know that it's serious and it's not extremely far off the present state of the art. A little speculative, perhaps; but you have to understand, in our science, there's a particularly difficult constraint: the scientist himself has to live long enough to draw his conclusions; and Dr. Emory is not young. Every azi experimentation takes at least fifteen years. The Rubin project is going to take at least twenty. You see the difficulty. She has to take some small risks."

"Health problems?" Corain said quietly, recollecting the subtle change in skin tone, the loss of weight. Rejuv lasted an unpredictable number of years. Once it started to lose its effect—problems started. And aging set in with a vengeance.

Warrick's eyes left his. He was not going to answer that question frankly, Corain reckoned before he said anything. He had pressed too closely.

"Mortality is an increasing concern," Warrick said, "for anyone her age, in our field. It's what I said: the *time* the projects take."

"What's your estimate of this project?" Gorodin asked.

"It's very, very important to her: all her theories, understand, all her personal work, her work on endocrine systems and genetics, on psych-structures—lead toward this."

"She's a Special. She can requisition damn near anything she needs—"

"Except the Special status that would protect her subject from what happened to Bok. I agree with her on the matter of *not* using someone inside Reseune. The clone will be at Reseune, but not Rubin. Rubin is young.

That's a prerequisite. He's brilliant, he was born on a station, and every move he's ever made down to buying a drink out of a machine is there in station records. He was also born with an immune deficiency, and there are extensive medical records that go back to his infancy. That's the most important part. Ari can do it without the Council's approval; but she can't keep Fargone's local government from doing something that might compromise her results."

"Is Rubin supposed to be aware of this?"

"He'll be aware he's a blind control on an experiment at Reseune. More significantly, his clone won't know Rubin exists until he's the same age Rubin is now."

"Do you think it's a valid project?" Corain asked.

Warrick was silent a moment. "I think whether or not one equals the other, the scientific benefits are there."

"You have reservations," Lu said.

"I see minimal harm to Rubin. He's a scientist. He's capable of understanding what blind control means. I would oppose any meeting of the two, at any future date. I'll go on record on that. But I wouldn't oppose the program."

"It's not yours."

"I have no personal work involved in it."

"Your son," Corain said, "does work closely with Dr. Emory."

"My son is a student," Warrick said, expressionless, "in tape design. Whether or not he'll be involved is up to Dr. Emory. It would be a rare opportunity. Possibly he might apply for the Fargone office, if it goes through. I'd like to see that."

Why? Corain wondered, and wished he dared ask it. But there were limits with a hitherto friendly informant, and there were persistent rumors about Emory that no one proved.

"Student," Lu said, "at Reseune, means rather more than student at the university."

"Considerably, yes," Warrick said. All liveliness had left his face. It was guarded now, extremely careful of expressions and reactions.

"How do *you* feel about the Hope project?" Corain asked.

"Is that a political question?"

"It's a political question."

"Say that I avoid politics, except as a study." Warrick looked down and up again, directly at Corain. "Reseune no longer depends on the azi trade. We could live quite well off our research, whether colonies go out or not, —there'll be a need for what *we* do, never mind the fate of the other labs— who couldn't undercut us. We have too great a head start on other fields. We wouldn't be as rich, of course. But we'd do quite well. It's not economics that troubles me. Someday we should talk."

Corain blinked. That was not what he expected, a feeler from a Reseune scientist. He put his hands in his coat pockets and looked at the others. "Can Dr. Warrick miss that meeting—without it leaking?"

"No difficulty," Lu said; and added: "If Dr. Warrick wants to miss it."

Warrick drew a long breath, then set the briefcase on the floor and pulled a chair back at the conference table. "I'm willing," he said, and sank into the chair.

Corain sat down. Gorodin and Lu took the chairs at the end.

Warrick's face held no expression still. "I know these gentlemen," he said with a slide of the eyes toward the military. "I know your reputation, Councillor Corain. I know you're an honest man. What I'm going to tell you could cost me—considerably. I hope you'll use this—only for what it contains, and I hope you won't lay it to personal dislike. Dr. Emory and I have had our differences. You understand—working at Reseune, you have to make a lot of critical decisions. Our material is human. Sometimes the ethics of a situation are—without precedent. All we operate on is our best estimation, and sometimes those estimates don't agree.

"Dr. Emory and I have had—more than the average number of confrontations. I've written papers opposing her. We have a conflicting view of— certain aspects of her operations. So if she finds out I've been talking to you, she'll believe I've tried to do her damage. But I hope to God you give her this program at Fargone. It doesn't cost the government anything but that Special—"

"It creates a dangerous precedent, to create a Special just to satisfy a research project. Just to keep a subject in your reach."

"I want myself and my son transferred out of Reseune."

Corain stopped breathing a moment. "You're a Special, the same as she is."

"I'm not political. I don't have her pull. She'll claim I'm essential, under the very terms that make me a Special—I'm bound to stay where the government needs me. And so far it arranges to need me at Reseune. Right now my son is working in her program for two reasons: first because it's his field and she's the best; second, because he's my son and Ari wants a hold on me, and in the politics inside Reseune, there's nothing I can do about that. I can try again to get myself out of there, and if *I'm* out from under her direction, I can request my son over to the other project on a personal hardship transfer. That's one reason I'm anxious to see this Fargone facility built. It would be the best thing for the state. It would be the best thing for Reseune. God knows it would be the best thing for Reseune."

"Perhaps some things would come out. Is that what you're saying?"

"I'm not making any charges. I don't want to go public with any of this. I'm saying that Ari has too damn much power, inside Reseune and out. There's no question of her scientific contributions. As a scientist I have no quarrel with her. I only know the politics inside the house and politics outside it is the only way I see to get free of a situation that's become increasingly— explosive."

One had to be careful, very careful. Corain had not spent twenty years in government to take everything at face value. Or to frighten a cooperating witness. So he asked softly: "What do you want, Dr. Warrick?"

"I'd like to see that project go through. Then I'm going to transfer. She's going to try to prevent that. I'd like support—in my appeal." Warrick cleared his throat. His fingers were locked, white-edged. "The pressure at Reseune is considerable. A move would be—everything I want. I'll tell you, . . . I'm *not* in agreement with this colonization effort. I agree with Berger and Shlegey, there *is* harm dispersing humankind to that degree, that fast. We've just finished one social calamity; we're *not* what left Earth, we're not what left Glory Station, we're not going to be what our founders anticipated; and if we make this further push there's going to be a critical difference between us and our descendants—there's no miracle, no Estelle Bok, no great invention going to close up this gap. That's my view. I can't express that from Reseune."

"Dr. Warrick, are you telling me your communications are limited there?"

"I'm telling you there are reasons I can't express that view there. If you leak this conversation to the press I'll have to take Reseune's official position."

"Are you telling me, Dr. Warrick, that that transfer is what you're holding out for?"

"The transfer, Councillor. Myself. And my son. Then I would have no fear of expressing my opinions. Do you understand me? Most of us in the field that could speak with authority against the Hope project—are in Reseune. Without voices inside Science, without papers published—you understand that ideas don't gain currency. Xenology is strongly divided. The most compelling arguments are in our field. You do *not* have a majority in the nine electorates, Councillor. It's Science itself you have to crack, Ari Emory's own electorate. *This*, this psychogenesis project is very dear to her heart—so much her own, in fact, that she doesn't let her aides handle it. It's the time factor again. On the one hand, there's so very little in a lifetime. On the other—a process that involves a human life has so many hiatuses, so many periods when nothing but time will produce the results."

"Meaning we'll still have her to deal with."

"As long as she lives, definitely, you'll have her in Council to deal with. That's why the Fargone project is an advantage to both of us. I'd like to take a public position, on your side. An opposition from inside Reseune, as it were, particularly from another Special—would have considerable credibility in Science. But I can't do it now, as things are."

"The important question," Gorodin said, "aside from that: *is* the Rubin project likely to work? Is it real?"

"It's very likely that it will, Admiral. Certainly it's a much more valid effort than the Bok project was. You may know, we don't routinely create from the Specials' genesets. Even our genetic material is protected by statute. On a practical level, it's the old 'fine line' business—genius and insanity, you know. It's not total nonsense. When we create azi, the Alpha classes take far more testing and correction. Statistically speaking, of course. What went wrong with the Bok clone was what could have gone wrong with Bok, give or take her particular experiences, and influences we don't have record of. Our chances of recovering a currently living Special are much better. Better records, you understand. Bok came here as a colonist, her records went with her ship, and it was one of the de-built ones: too much was lost and too much just wasn't recorded. I'm not sure we ever will get Bok's talent back, but it certainly won't be in the present project. On the other hand—recovering, say, Kleigmann . . . who's, what?—pushing a century and a half . . . would be a real benefit."

"Or Emory herself," Corain said under his breath. "God. Is *that* her push? Immortality?"

"Only so far as any human might want progeny like himself. It's not immortality, certainly no sense of identity. We're talking about mental similarity, two individuals more like each other than identical twins tend to be, and without a dominant twin. Essentially the recovery of an ability latent in the interface between geneset and what we call tape in an azi."

"Done by tape?"

Warrick shook his head. "*Can't* be done with tape. Not by present understanding."

Corain thought it through again. And again.

"Meaning," Gorodin said, "that with our lead in genetics and reconstructive psych, we might replicate living Specials as well as dead ones."

"That is a possibility," Warrick said quietly, "if certain laws were changed. Practically—I'd speak against that. I understand why they're starting with one. But the potential for psychological trouble is very strong, even if the safeguards keep the two from meeting. Even dead ones— If I were such a subject—I'd worry about my son, and that individual—who would not, in any meaningful sense, be his brother; or his father. Do you see, it's very complicated when you're dealing with human lives? The Nine took a strong interest in the Bok case. Too strong. In this much I agree with Dr. Emory: only the Bureau of Science, in specific, only Reseune ought to have any contact with the two subjects. That's what she wants on Fargone. We're not talking about an office or a lab. We're talking about an enclave, a community Rubin will not leave except as I leave Reseune: rarely and with escorts for his protection."

"My God," Gorodin said, "Fargone will veto it."

"A separate orbiting facility. That's what she's had to promise Harogo. A compartmentalized area. Reseune will pay the construction."

"You know, then, what deals she's made."

"I happen to know that one. There may be others. That's a fat contract for certain construction companies at Fargone."

It rang true. All the way down. Corain gnawed his lip.

"Let me ask you a difficult question," Corain said. "If there were other information—"

"I would give it."

"If there were other information yet to come—"

"You're asking me to be an informant."

"A man of conscience. You know my principles. I know yours. It seems there's a great deal in common. Does Reseune own your conscience?"

"Even the admiral hasn't been able to requisition me. I'm a ward of the state. My residencies have to be approved by the Union government. That's the price of being a Special. The admiral will tell you: Reseune will call me essential. That's an automatic five votes of the Nine. That means I stay in Reseune. I'll tell you what I'm going to do, Councillor. I'm going to slip Adm. Gorodin a request for transfer, *just* as soon as that Special status is voted for Rubin, *before* the appropriations vote for the Hope Station project. Officially—that's when it will happen."

"God! You think you're worth a deal like that?"

"Councillor, —you can't win the Hope Station vote. DeFranco is in Ari's pocket. Or her bankbook, via Hayes Industries. The arrangement is—deFranco's going to try to abstain, which at least is going to show a little backbone for her constituency. Forget you heard that from me. But if you *don't* throw the vote into a tie and send the business into the General Council, it's inevitable. You buy me *and my son* out of Reseune, Councillor—and I'll start talking. I'll be worth far more—outside her direct surveillance, in the Reseune facility on Fargone. She might get Hope Station. But she can be stopped, Councillor. If you want a voice inside Science, I can be that."

It was a moment before Corain felt in command of his breathing. He looked at Lu, at Gorodin, suddenly trying to remember how Lu had maneuvered him into this meeting, suspecting these two dark eminences among the Nine, who played behind a screen of secrecies.

"You should go into politics," he said to Warrick then, and suddenly remembered to his disturbance who he was talking to: that this was a Reseune psychmaster, and that this mind was one of those twelve Union considered too precious to lose.

"Psych is my field," Warrick said, with a disturbing directness to his gaze, which no longer seemed ordinary, or harmless, or average. "I only want to practice it without harassment. I'm fully aware of politics, Councillor. I assure you it never leaves us, at Reseune. Nor we, it. Help me and I'll help you. It's that simple."

"It's not simple," Corain objected, but to Warrick it was. Whoever had drawn him into this meeting—be it Lu, be it Gorodin—be it Warrick—

He was not sure, suddenly, that it was not Emory. A man could grow insane, dealing with the potential in the Specials, especially those Specials who dealt with perception itself.

One had to trust someone sometime. Or nothing got done.

---

iii

"The first bill on the agenda is number 2405, for the Bureau of Science. Ariane Emory sole sponsor, regarding the regular appropriations for the Bureau of Science, under the provisions of Union Statute 2595, section 2. . . ."

Emory looked Corain's way. Well? that half-lidded stare said. Will you defy me, over something so routine?

Corain smiled. And let the bitch worry.

The gavel hammered down, again early: "We are in recess," Bogdano-vitch said. The murmuring in the Council chamber was subdued.

Ariane Emory drew a whole breath, finally. The first stage was passed. Rubin had his status, barring a veto from the Council of Worlds, and there would be none. Corain might orchestrate a double-cross, but he would save it for something important. Something *Corain* considered important. The Hope Station project could serve as a decoy until then. DeFranco might want to abstain. But she would not, when the heat came on.

Aides surged doorward, accompanying their Councillors. The press was, thank God, held downstairs, away from the chamber as long as there was no adjournment. A two-hour lunch and consideration of the dispensa-tion of the rest of the Science permissions afterward, a tedious long list of permissions which, in the way of a good many things in a government which had started small and cozy and grown into an administrative monster within a single lifespan, the executive Nine were supposed to clear, but which in fact had devolved to the Secretarial level and which had become routine ap-proval.

Still, she would not breathe easy until that clearance was given—until the obfuscated facts of permission to use a geneset from a living Special went through in the list of Reseune projects that required routine permissions.

There had been, each year, an attempt to cancel the whole Science per-missions grant from the floor of General Council. Every year the Abolitionists or some other lunatic group got up a proposal to outlaw azi and to outlaw hu-man experimentation. Every year the Council of Worlds sensibly voted it down. But there was that lunatic element, which the Centrists could in some attempt to exert leverage against the Hope project—use against the Science bill. If the fringes and the Centrists *did* combine on an issue in that body, it came dangerously close to a plurality against the Expansionist party.

She was worried. She had worried ever since her informers told her that the Centrists were talking walk-out. Corain's sudden willingness to deal both-ered her.

And if it would not have raised the issue of an unseemly haste, she would gladly have urged the chair to put the Science bill up before noon. As it was, obstacles were falling too fast, things were going too well, everything was slid-ing on oil. What had looked to be a lengthy session would end in a record three days, sending the Nine back to their civilian lives for at least another six months.

It had been intended as a means to speed up government, that the Nine would meet and pass all measures that impacted their various spheres of inter-est, then leave the staff of the Bureaus and the elected representatives of the Council of Worlds and the various senates and councils to handle the routine and the ordinary administrative detail.

In fact, the Nine, being top professionals, were very efficient. They met briefly, did their job, and went away again to be what they were—but some of them exerted an enormous control over the Bureaus they oversaw, wielding power that the framers of the constitution had not entirely foreseen, no more than they had foreseen Reseune's work in the war, or the fact that population would become what it was, or the defection of Pell from both Sol and Union, and the developments that had entrained. The Bureau of State had been conceived as carefully controlled by professionals in diplomatic service; but distances pushed it into greater and greater dependency on the Defense Bureau's accurate reporting of situations it was not there to see.

The Bureau of Science, considering the discovery of alien life at more than Pell's Star, had to take on diplomatic functions and train potential contact specialists.

The Bureau of Citizens had become a disproportionately large electorate, and it had elected an able and dangerous man, a man who had still the sense to know when he was trapped.

Possibly Corain did not know that deFranco was solidly hers. That would explain his willingness to risk his political life on a walk-out. Surely he did not think he had any hope of swinging the Pan-paris trade loop, which Lao dominated. He could do nothing but cost the government money, with which other interests would not be patient. It was certainly not likely that he would create any objection on the Science bill.

Surely.

"Dr. Emory." Despite her aides and her bodyguards a touch reached her arm, and Catlin was there too, instantly, her body tense and her expression baffled, because the one who had touched her was no one's aide, it was Adm. Gorodin himself who had just brushed by Catlin's defense. "A word with you."

"I'm on a tight schedule." She had no desire to talk to this man, who, already with an enormous share of the budget at his disposal, with sybaritic waste in his own department, argued with her about the diversion of ten ships to the Hope project; *and* sided with Corain. She had other contacts inside Defense, and used them: a good section of Intelligence and most of Special Services was on her side, and a new election inside the military might unseat both Gorodin and Lu: let Corain consider *that* if he wanted a fight.

"I'll walk with you," Gorodin said, refusing to be shaken, his aides mingling with hers.

"One moment," Catlin said, "ser." Florian had moved in. They were not armed. The military were. But it did not prevent them: they were azi, and they answered to her, not to logic.

"It's all right," Ariane said, lifting a hand in a signal that confirmed what she said.

"An inside source tells me," Gorodin began, "you've got the votes on the Hope project."

Damn. Her heart raced. But aloud, with a stolid calm: "Well, then, your source might be right. But I don't take it for granted."

"Corain's upset. He's going to lose face with this."

What in hell is he up to?

"You know we can stall this off," Gorodin said.

"Likely you can. It won't win you anything. If you're right."

"We have a source on deFranco's staff, Dr. Emory. We are right. We also have a source inside Andrus Company; and inside Hayes Industries. Damn good stock buy. Are they finally going to get that deep-space construction?"

My God.

Gorodin lifted a brow. "You know, Hayes has defense contracts."

"I don't know what you're getting to, but I don't like to talk finance anywhere near the word *vote*. And if you've got a recorder about your person, I take strong exception to it."

"As I would to yours, sera. But we're not talking finance. As it happens, I set my people to talking to people in Hayes when we heard that. And we know very well that the Reseune extension is connected to the Rubin bill, *and* when my staff spent last night investigating the Reseune Charter, a very helpful young aide came up with a sleeper in the articles that gives Reseune the unique right to declare any subsidiary facilities part of its Administrative Territory. That means what you're going to build at Fargone *won't* be under Fargone control. It's going to be under yours. An independent part of Union. And Rubin has something to do with it."

This is more than he could come up with on his own. Damn, but it is. Someone's spilled something and he keeps naming Hayes and Andrus. That's who I'm supposed to blame.

"This is all very elaborate," she muttered. They had reached the intersection of the balcony and the hall to the Council offices, where she wanted to go. She stopped and faced the admiral. "Go on."

"We find this of military interest. A Reseune facility at Fargone poses security risks."

For a moment everything stopped. It was not from the direction she had expected. It was not sane. It *was*, if one was worried about merchanter contacts.

"We're not talking about labs, admiral."

"What *are* we talking about?"

"Rubin's going to be working there. Mostly it'll be his lab."

"You have enormous faith in this young man."

Trap. My God, where is it? "He's a very valuable young man."

"I'd like to discuss the security aspects of this. Before the vote this afternoon. Can we talk?"

"Dammit, I've got a luncheon appointment."

"Dr. Emory, I honestly don't want to send this to committee. I'm trying to be cooperative. But I feel this is going through much too fast. I have other concerns that I *don't* think you want me to mention here."

Someone's talked. He's gotten to someone.

But aloud, to Florian: "Tell Yanni I'm caught in a crisis. Tell him to sit in for me. I'll get there when I can." She looked at the admiral, calmer, reckoning that it sounded like bargaining, not a torpedo from the flank. "Your place or mine?"

"Thank you," Ariane said, taking the coffee from Florian, who knew how she liked it. It was her office, her conference room, and her bodyguards present, the military aides staying outside, the admiral's own offer.

Conciliation, perhaps.

The admiral took his coffee black. Most did, who got a taste of it on special occasions. It was rare and real, imported all the way from Sol, Earth's southern hemisphere. It was one of Ariane's cultivated vices. And she took hers white. Real milk. A second extravagance.

"AG is still working on this," she said. "Someday." Cyteen had been a silicate-polluted hell when they started agriculture in the low-lying valleys, where domes and the precipitators could create mini-climate.

Another small flash: so much brown, so much blue-green on the hills. The lines spun above the valley like a webfly's work. The big mirrors caught light from space and flung power down from the hills. And the weathermakers in orbit raked the land with storms, terrible storms— *We're safe, Ari,* maman would say. *It's only noise. It's weather, that's all—*

Leonid Gorodin sipped his coffee with a tranquil look. And smiled. And said: "The rumor inside the Bureau is that this Rubin project is yours. Personally. There's nothing you do that doesn't change the balance between us and Alliance, us and Sol. I've talked to Lu. We have a lot of anxiety about this."

"We manage our own security. We've always managed it."

"Tell me this, Dr. Emory. Is the project you're undertaking . . . going to have any strategic significance?"

Trap. "Admiral, I suspect the development of a new toilet seat has strategic significance with some of your advisers."

Gorodin chuckled politely, and waited.

"That's fine," she said calmly. "We'll appreciate a vote of support from your Bureau. You want us to move the facility, we'll move it, even to Cyteen Station. We're very accommodating. We just don't want to lose Rubin."

"That important?"

"That important."

"I'll make a proposition to you, Dr. Emory. You've got an agenda. You want it passed. You want these things to go through, you want them to go through with a clean bill from Finance, you certainly don't want any long delays. You want to get back to Reseune. I want to get back to my command. I've got business out there, and between you and me, I'm allergic as hell to something around here and I hate the socializing."

"I'm also anxious to get home," she said. It was a dance. It would get where it was going in Gorodin's own time.

"You level with me," Gorodin said, "about the Fargone project."

"Say it's genetics. It's experimental."

"Are you going to have advanced labs out there?"

"No. Medical wing. Analysis. Administrative work. None of the classified equipment."

"Meaning you're following-up, not creating."

"In practical terms, yes. No birth-lab."

Gorodin looked at the empty cup, and at the two azi, and held his out.

"Florian," Ariane said, and the azi, with a quiet nod, took the pot from the sideboard and filled it. Gorodin followed Florian's moves with his eyes, thoughts proceeding.

"You can rely on their discretion," Ariane said. "It's quite all right. They're not sensitive to discussion. Reseune's best work. Aren't you, Florian?"

"Yes, sera," Florian said, preparing her second cup. He offered it.

"Beauty and brains," Ariane said, and smiled with the mouth, not the eyes. "Alliance *won't* develop birth-labs. They have no worlds to fill."

"Yet. We have to think about that. —Who's going to manage that facility at Fargone?"

"Yanni Schwartz."

Gorodin frowned, and sipped slowly at the incongruously tiny cup.

Ah, Ariane thought. *Now, now, we get closer to it.*

"I'll tell you, Dr. Emory. A lot of my people rely on the psych hospital at Viking. For reasons which are only politics—I'd like to have a facility a lot closer to that Hope Station route you're promoting. I'd like to have a place to send some of my worse cases—where Cyteen *won't* take them through the station facility."

"Any particular reason for that?"

"We're talking about special operations. People whose IDs change. People whose faces—you understand I don't want seen. These are people who live anxious lives. They feel exposed at the big stations. They'd feel a hell of a lot better if there were a way to get to a Reseune facility—not on Cyteen."

Ariane frowned, not bothering to hide her perplexity. It sounded halfway sane.

"What I want," Gorodin said, "is access. A facility where my people feel—safe. Where I know they are. I want to throw some of the covert budget in there. Some of my staff."

"No military."

"We're talking about unanimous support for that facility. I can deliver that."

"No military. Reseune staff. And it better be a damn large contribution. You'll force a redesign. I'm not having my project compromised by your people strolling through Reseune boundaries. There'll be a total separation between any military hospital and our offices."

"We can go with that. But we want a liaison between our side and yours that we have confidence in. Someone we've worked with."

The thought hit like ice water. It was hard not to react, to keep the fingers relaxed on the fragile handle of the cup. "Who did you have in mind?"

"Dr. Warrick. He designed the training tapes. We want him, Dr. Emory."

"Does he want you?" Calmly. Very calmly.

"We can ask him."

"I think I know your source, admiral. I'm damned sure I know your source. What else did he tell you?"

"I think you're jumping to conclusions."

"No, I'm not. I was afraid of something like this. You want him, do you? You want a man in charge of your highest security operations, who quite readily betrayed my interests."

"I've told you my sources."

"Of course you have. You're quite willing to have some Hayes employee's head on the block, some poor sod of an engineer, no doubt, that they'll find a way to blame if I come down on them. You want Jordan Warrick. Did he tell you why?"

"He didn't tell me anything."

"Admiral, you're a damn good poker player, but remember how I make my living. Remember how he makes his. What's he done? Offered to go public with his opinions? Is that how you'll guarantee me Corain?"

"Dr. Emory, you know I can deliver what I promise."

"Of course you can. And Jordan Warrick promises you my head on a platter. He promises you he can swing votes in Science. I'll tell you what I'll do. You can have him. I'll transfer him and his whole damned staff. If you want to put him over a top-secret facility, go right ahead. If he wants to make speeches and write papers against my policies, fine." She set the cup down. "Do we have a deal, admiral? We can get out of this damned city days early, if that's the case. You support me in a request to let us leave sealed ballots on the Hope bill, and if you can guarantee they'll be unanimous, none of us will have to show up here to call a question. Deal?"

"I think we can go with that."

She smiled. "Excellent. If you want Warrick's wing at Fargone, that'll have to be written up. I'll trust your staff for that. Mine's busy. But it'll wait on the establishment of a secure facility. And I do trust you know how to lay your hands on Warrick to get his signature on the request."

Gorodin swallowed his coffee in some haste and set his cup down. "Thank you, Dr. Emory. I'm sure this will work to everyone's good." He rose and offered his hand.

Ariane rose and reciprocated a strong handshake. And smiled at him all the way to the door.

The azi Catlin closed it then, her face as blank as any soldier at attention. Florian picked up the cups, trying not to look at her either.

They knew when to be afraid.

Verbal Text from: PATTERNS OF GROWTH A Tapestudy in Genetics: #1 "A Reseune Calendar: 2396"

**Reseune Educational Publications: 8970-8768-1
approved for 80+**

BATCH AL-5766: FOUR UNITS:

The technician begins a routine procedure at Reseune, the transfer of genetic material already replicated. Ten units of AL-5766 remain unused in the genebank, standard operating procedure for commercial and experimental materials.

AL-5766 is female, Alpha class. Alpha, the highest intelligence in the A-Z non-citizen classifications, ranges upward from 150 on the Rezner scale, to a current known high of 215. AL-5766 is 190, which verges on genius. Alphas are generated only rarely except for specific executive assignments, experimental studies or colonial operations in which there is minimum population density and considerable latitude for independent judgment. Alphas without early socialization are prone to personality disorders: the best successes in non-social Alphas have been achieved with positive feedback in early training and an accelerated early tapestudy consisting of world awareness, reading, and mathematics skills, with minimal intervention except for reward. The most reliably successful Alphas are those given to human parentage from the moment of birth: in such cases the behavioral and social statistics follow the same profile as citizen-born individuals of equal Rezner values. It should always be remembered that an azi geneset's traits and to some extent, classification, are determined by the tape designed specifically for that geneset; and that the primary failing with Alphas seems to be in tape design.

AL-5766 has shown developmental patterns in human parentage situations which are within acceptable ranges, but which indicate a propensity toward aggression. Within azi communities the AL-5766 statistics are wholly unacceptable, involving violent behaviors, moodiness, and abnormal and irrational anxieties.

AL-5766 disorders once manifested find no amelioration through tape, and only rarely find relief through interventive counseling, although some salvage has been effected on two occasions by transfer to military situations where hardship and physical challenge is extreme.

Neither case, however, has utilized the high potential of the AL-5766s in mathematics, and not even experimental use has been made of the AL-5766 geneset since 2353. Now, however, Reseune believes it has a tape-fix for the problem, of interest since AL-5767 proved out as Beta-class, lacking the traits which made 5766 both brilliant and troublesome.

There are four sets in this group because a tape-design team has come up with two fixes, subtly different. Two each will provide adequate comparisons for a first run. There is no need of a control using the original tape: AL-5766s have forty-six years of data behind them, and no one needs to prove that the old tapes were faulty.

The eggs lack a code of their own until they receive the full diploid set of AL-5766. This is standard, for azi and citizen replications.

The womb into which each egg goes is bioplasmed and contractile, the whole environment closely duplicating a specific natural pregnancy which has served Reseune for forty-nine years: it replicates all the movements, the sounds, the chemical states, and the interactive cycles of a living womb.

BATCH EU-4651: TEN UNITS:

The AL-5766 units are a day along, four motes of life with identical genetic codes busily dividing and growing in the dark of the wombs. The EU-4651s, male, have an identical start; and there are the usual ten units left in the genebank.

EU-4651 is an old type, Eta-class, between 90 and 95 on the Rezner scale and outstandingly stable, one of the most successful Etas in industrial and military fields, and not restricted to Cyteen, but patented in all its sets and derivative sets. Ordinarily Reseune would have simply sold the requisite eggs in whatever number the purchasing lab requested, but this is a new application for the EU-4651s, most of whom are in military service. An EU-4651 has shown an uncommon and late-developing aptitude under an emergency situation which might mean reclassification and upgrading of the type if a tape program could take advantage of it either in existing individuals or in future EU-4651s.

BATCH RYX-20: TWENTY UNITS:

This set is Rho-class, Rezner 45 and below. Rho is the last of the azi classes which Reseune deliberately engineers on a commercial basis. Rho-class azi perform very well with positive feedback and minimal intervention, having little inclination to deviate from program. Their ability to rebound from mishandling and so-called bad tape makes them valuable initial test subjects in any new tape structure, which, along with general labor, will be the usefulness of these twenty azi in Reseune. Because they are prone to physical strain during their lives they are, like classes N through Ps, generally not given rejuv, which of course does little to alleviate skeletal damage; but they are given a value structure which provides great satisfaction in continuance of the genotype.

BATCH CIT-*-**-**-**-****: ONE UNIT:

CIT--**-**-**-**** goes directly from processing to cryogenics, flown via company jet to a courier service in Novgorod, to make the scheduled shuttle lift on the weekend, weather permitting.*

Reseune maintains a special service to the general public, whereby it receives certain tax exemptions and utilizes equipment during its slack hours.

CIT--**-**-**-**** is from a tissue sample of a seven-year-old child from ***, who suffered a fatal fall. The release form has advised the mother there will be no identity transference: the replicate by law must have special counseling, but at the will of the parent, the clone may bear the name and must bear the citizen number of the deceased, being a posthumous replicate of the child, beloved daughter of Susan X. (Actual name and numbers withheld.) The embryo will develop in ***'s lab, indebted only with the minimal freight charge so tiny a canister requires on a scheduled military transport. In due course she will be delivered from the womb-tank into her genetic mother's arms.*

BATCH CIT-*-**-**-****PR: ONE UNIT:

Cloning individuals who want a personal twin instead of a genetically mixed offspring has become a lucrative business for the ordinary lab, since the cost runs upward of 500,000 credits; but Reseune, as a research and development laboratory, has no interest in this practice, sometimes called vanity cloning, except for the rare genotype Reseune finds of commercial or experimental interest. This is such a case, a fetus near term. In fact, Reseune has absorbed all cost on this replication, whose designation is CIT--**-***-****PR: the parent-subject is uniquely talented, willing to trade genetic uniqueness for one replicate, and willing to sign a release opening all informational records of applicable interest to Reseune: Reseune will store that data for future development of the geneset, but will not release the geneset for commercial use until fifty years after the decease of parent and replicate.*

*Reseune puts ten genesets in storage as A**-1.*

BATCH AGCULT-789X: ONE UNIT:

A day along, in a womb-tank in a large building somewhat downhill from the last facility, is AGCULT-789X. AGCULT-789X, experimental as the X-designation indicates, closely resembles the RYX-20s or the EU-4651s, except that the genetic codes of the RYX-20s and the EU-4651s indicate two feet while that of AGCULT-789X indicates four, and the RYX-20's and the EU-4651's codes indicate smooth skin, while AGCULT-789X's indicates a sleek bay hide and a superlative ability to run.

AGCULT-789X is exceedingly rare material, Terran in origin, another attempt at a species with which Cyteen has had limited success. The AGCULT pro-

grams, involving not only animal species, but also botanical studies, have had far more success with the algae and with the lower end of a food-chain which may one day support the descendants of Terran species. In a much-heralded gesture toward peace, Earth has provided Cyteen with genesets and data on the whole range of Terran species, with particular emphasis on the endangered or extinct, along with human genesets which may contain genetic information missing from Union and Alliance genepools.

Reciprocally, Union has released representative genesets of Union populations to Terran genetic archives, in an exchange program designed to provide a valuable comparison between the two populations, and to provide a reference in event of global catastrophe or unforeseen lapse in contact.

Of the two worlds presently supporting human colonies, one, Downbelow, is, of course, a protectorate, and there is no question of changing the environment to any extent that would wipe out the indigenes. Humanity remains a visitor to Downbelow.

Cyteen, far less hospitable, harboring no species more advanced than the various platytheres and ankyloderms, was far more suitable for radical terraforming, and Cyteen's ability to store genetic material against irrevocable climatic and atmospheric change at least raises hopes of selective recoveries in specific protected habitats should changes exceed their intended limits.

Terraforming, while wreaking havoc on many native species, has provided a unique opportunity to study interface zones and compare adaptive changes in Terrene and indigenous species, advancing our understanding of catastrophic changes which have impacted Terrene species over geologic time, and of the degree of change facing the human species in its radical changes of habitat.

Understanding that genetic changes are inevitable but not always desirable, Earth has begun to look on Cyteen as a repository for genetic information on species threatened with extinction. Some of the more ambitious projects involve large-mammal habitat, from the bottom of the food-chain up. Ironically, the experience in terraforming Cyteen, destructive as it has been of Cyteen's indigenous life, is making possible the recovery of certain threatened ecosystems on Earth, and the establishment of more fragile systems on Mars, fourth planet of Sol system.

Certain of the proposed future exchanges are quite ambitious.

Earth is particularly anxious for the success of cetaceans and higher primates on Cyteen. It has proposed a joint study program as soon as the cetacean project is viable, for the study of cetacean development and the comparison of whalesong on Cyteen and on Earth.

Cyteen finds such projects of interest too, for the future. But the present emphasis in terraforming and recovery is far more concerned with the immediate problems in large-scale atmospheric changes, and the problems of interface zones, high salinity, and trace minerals in Swigert Bay, at the delta of the heavily-colonized Novaya Volga, which offers the most favorable conditions for large-scale marine aquaculture . . .

CHAPTER 2

Reseune from the air was a patch of green in the deep valley of the Novaya Volga, a protected, low-lying strip stretching yearly longer on the riverside, white buildings at the last, and the AG pens, the barracks, the sprawling complex of Reseune proper spread out under the left-side window that was always hers. Ariane Emory latched up her papers, quite on schedule as the gear came down and Florian appeared beside her seat to take temporary custody of her personal kit.

She kept the briefcase.

Always.

The jet touched down, concrete coming up under the delta wings; it braked, taxiing to a gentle stop at Reseune terminal as ground crews swung into action, personnel transport, baggage crews, cleaning crews, mechanics, a crisp and easy operation from decontamination to docking that matched anything Novgorod could muster.

They were all azi, all staff born to Reseune. Their training went far beyond what Novgorod counted sufficient. But that was true of most Reseune personnel.

They were known faces, known types, and everything about them was in the databanks.

For the first time in days Ariane Emory felt herself secure.

The Security hand-off had gone smoothly enough, control passing to Reseune offices the moment the word reached Giraud Nye's office that

33

RESEUNE ONE had left the ground at Novgorod—with no more than an hour's advance warning. Ari's movements were usually sudden and unscheduled, and she did not always give advance notice even to him, who was head of Reseune Security—but this was a record suddenness.

"Advise the staff," he had told Abban, his own bodyguard, who did that, quickly, seeing to the transfer of logs and reports. *He* called his brother Denys, in Administration, and Denys advised Wing One as soon as the plane was on final approach.

The last was routine, the standard procedure on Ariane's returns, whenever *RESEUNE ONE* came screaming in and Ariane Emory settled into the place that was hers, in her wing, in her residency.

The word had come on yesterday's news that the Hope project had been tabled, and the stock market had reacted with a shock that might well run the length and width of space, although analysts called it a procedural delay. The good news was a tiny piece following, with biographical clip provided from Science Bureau files, that an obscure chemist on Fargone had been afforded Special status: *that* bill, at least, had gone through. And the Council had wrapped up in a marathon session that had extended on into the small hours: more ripples in the interstellar stock market, which loathed uncertainties more than it disliked sudden reverses of policy. The news bureaus of every polity in Union had held a joint broadcast of commentary and analysis, preempting scheduled morning broadcasts, senior legislative reporters doing their best to offer interpretations, frustrated in the refusal of even opposition Councillors to grant interviews.

The leader of the Abolitionist faction in the Centrist coalition had granted one: Ianni Merino, his white hair standing out in its usual disorder, his face redder and his rhetoric more extreme than ever, had called for a general vote of confidence of the entire Council and threatened secession from the Centrist party. He did not have the votes to do the one: he might well do the other, and Giraud Nye had sat listening to that, knowing more than the commentators and still wondering along with the news bureaus just what kind of deal had been struck and why Mikhail Corain had been willing to go along with it.

A triumph for Reseune?

A political disaster? Something lost?

It was not Ariane's habit to consult back during the sessions in Novgorod except in dire emergency, certainly not by phone, not even on Bureau lines; but there were staff couriers and planes always available.

That she had not sent—meant a situation under control, despite that precipitate adjournment—one hoped.

The social schedule had been thrown into utter confusion, the Councillors had canceled meetings right and left, and the Councillors from Russell's and Pan-paris had sped back to Cyteen Station to make passage on a ship bound for Russell's Star, departure imminent. Their Secretaries had been left to sit proxy, one presumed, with definite instructions about their votes.

It was more than protocol that brought Giraud Nye and his brother

Denys to meet the small bus as it pulled up in the circle drive at the front of Reseune.

The bus door opened. The first one down was, predictably, the azi Catlin, in the black uniform of Reseune security, her face pale and set in a forecast of trouble: she stepped down and reached back to steady Ari as Ari made the single step—Ari in pale blue, carrying her briefcase herself as usual, and with no visible indication of triumph or catastrophe until she looked straight at Giraud and Denys with an expression that foretold real trouble.

"Your office," she said to Denys. Behind her, exiting onto the concrete with the rest of the staff, Giraud saw Jordan Warrick, who was not supposed to be with that flight, who had flown out five days ago on *RESEUNE ONE* and was supposed to come back at the end of the week, on a RESEUNEAIR special flight.

There was trouble. Warrick arriving in Ari's company was as great a shock as Centrists and Expansionists suddenly bedding down together. Warrick's staff was not with him, only his azi chief-of-Household, Paul, who followed along with a sober, anxious look, carrying a flight-kit.

Abban might collect gossip from the staff, the ones who were Family, and free to talk. Giraud gave Abban the order and fell in with Ari and Denys, silent Florian heading off to the left hall the moment they cleared the doors, Catlin walking along behind with Denys' azi Seely.

Not a word until they were inside Denys' inmost office, and Denys turned on the unit that provided sound-screening in the room. Then:

"We've got a problem," Ari said, opening the briefcase very carefully, very precisely on the expensive imported veneer of Denys' desk.

"Hope's in trouble?" Denys asked, accepting the fiche she handed him. "Or is it Jordan?"

"Gorodin is promising us unanimous approval for Hope—if Jordan gets a liaison post at a Fargone military psych facility *we're* going to have hidden in our budget."

"God," Giraud said, and sat down.

"You tell me how you buy Mikhail Corain's vote, and why Jordan Warrick's transfer has to be part of Gorodin's bargain."

Giraud had no doubts. It was certain that Ari had none.

"He's become a problem," Ari said.

"We can't touch him," Giraud said. Panic welled up in him. Sometimes Ari forgot she *had* limits, or that prudence did.

"He's counting on that, isn't he?" So, so quietly. Ari settled into the remaining chair. "It still has to be voted. It doesn't need to be voted until the facility exists. And we just got the appropriation."

Giraud was sweating. He resisted the impulse to mop his face. The sound-screening tended to make his teeth ache, but at the moment the discomfort was mostly in his gut.

"Well, it's not that bad," Denys said, and tilted his chair back, folding his hands on his ample stomach. "We can map this out. Jordie's being a fool.

We can merge his wing right back into Administration, absorb his staff and his records, that for a start."

"He's not a fool," Ari said. "I want to know if we're missing files."

"You think he's left something in Novgorod?"

"What's ever stopped him?"

"Dammit," Giraud said, "Ari, I warned you. I warned you."

Ari tilted her head, regarding him sidelong. "I'll tell you one thing: even if he goes, son Justin won't."

"We've got five more years of budget to fight through! What in hell are we going to do when Jordie's out there in front of the cameras?"

"Don't worry about it."

"What do you mean, don't worry about it?"

"He's here, isn't he? Left his aides, his staff, everyone but Paul in Novgorod. I didn't confront him about the leak. I just sent Florian to advise him he was wanted. He's well aware what he's done and that I know he's done it."

"If you touch him— Listen to me. He won't have done this without advance preparation. God knows what kind of harm he can do us. Or what kind of information he's smuggled out of here. My God, I didn't see this coming."

"Jordan and his little feuds. His requests for transfer. His bickering on staff. Oh, we're still friendly. We have our little policy debates. We had one on the way home. And smiled at each other over drinks. Why not? There's always the chance I *believed* Gorodin."

"He knows damn well you didn't!"

"And he knows that I know that he knows, round and round. So we smile at each other. I'll tell you something: I'm not worried. He's sure I won't move until I know what he's got. He's manipulating the situation. Our Education Special thinks he's the best there is. He's gambling everything on things going the way he predicts. He'll make me a counter-offer soon. And I'll make mine. And that's how we'll pass the months. He's sure he can match me move for move. We'll see. I'm going to my apartments. I'm sure Florian's run his checks by now. I'm going to have a shower, put my feet up a while, and read the logs. *And* have a decent meal. *Formal* dinner tonight. It's a session-end, isn't it? Catlin can approve the menu."

"I'll tell the staff," Denys said. The thought of food turned Giraud's stomach.

"It's not a total disadvantage," she said. "Have you seen the news? The Centrist coalition is showing seams this morning. Corain's made Ianni Merino very, very upset. An old hand like Corain—this is moving much too fast for him. Corain had his people ready to walk, now he shifts stance on them—the Abolitionists will suspect a sell-out . . . won't they? Let the Abolitionists peel off and start talking about dismantling the labs again. It's bound to make the moderates a little anxious."

"That's where Jordan can do us the most damage! If he goes to the press—"

"Oh, you don't think the Abolitionists are going to credit a voice out of Reseune."

"If he's saying the right things they damn well will."

"Then we have to do something about his credibility, don't we? *Think* about it, Gerry. Corain's going to end up acquiescing—no, *voting for*—the establishment of a Reseune lab right on the Hope colony route. The Abolitionists haven't gotten saner, just quieter; and we have our own sleepers in their rank and file. Keep Corain quite busy putting out fires on his own decks. Gorodin may find the whole noise a bit more than he wants: there are always deals we can offer him: he always stands with his feet either side of the line. Lu is the problem, that double-crossing bastard. But we can persuade him. This facility is exactly the kind of thing that may do it. I want you to look into these things, I don't need to tell you how discreetly. Use your military contacts. The Science Bureau is dispatching a ship to notify Rubin of his status. They're also going to take measures to establish him a protective residency in Fargone Blue Zone: the team is on its way Sunday, when *Atlantis* pushes off for Fargone."

"Harogo's going to be aboard?" Denys asked.

"Absolutely. There's not going to be a hitch. He'll get our staff right through customs, and *Atlantis* is running light."

"Military can beat her."

"A worry. But Harogo's a much higher card, on his own station, and he's bringing home the second biggest construction project Fargone's ever lusted after. *First* being the Hope corridor, of course. There won't be a hitch. If the Centrists try anything with Rubin, Harogo can fry them, no question. We'd love that kind of ammunition. Did you see the clip? Rubin's a wide-eyed innocent. Pure science and total vulnerability. I thought that came across rather well."

"They can throw that back at us too," Giraud said.

"We can rely on Harogo, I think. At certain times, you have to let a thing go."

"Even Warrick?"

"If they want him by then."

ii

Ari smiled gently across the table, across the salad with vinaigrette, product of their own gardens, and dusted it liberally with a spoonful of Keis, synthetic cheese, a salted yeast, actually: spacer's affectation. Her mother had used it. Ari still liked the tang of it, and imported it downworld at some little trouble.

Most of the Family abhorred it.

It was the formal dining hall: one long table for the Family, and a large U-shaped table around the outside for the azi who were closer than relatives, and somewhat more numerous, about two to one.

Herself at the head: that had been the case since the day uncle Geoffrey died. To her right, Giraud Nye, to her left his brother Denys; then Yanni Schwartz rightside, left again, his sister Beth; and across from her, Beth's son by Giraud Nye, young Suli Schwartz, long-nosed and thin-faced, and looking preoccupied as usual: sixteen and bored; left next, and right and right again, Petros Ivanov and his two sisters Irene and Katrin, then Katrin's current passion the dark-skinned Morey Carneth-Nye; old Jane Strassen looking like a dowager empress in black and an ostentatious lot of silver; daughter Julia Strassen in green, a truly amazing decolletage; dear cousin Patrick Carnath-Emory, who was *far* more Carnath than Emory, and absolutely butterfingered—he was already mopping his lap; Patrick's daughter Fideal Carnath, olive-skinned and lovely, and her thirty-two-year-old son Jules who they had thought was Giraud's until they ran the genetics and found it was, of all people, Petros'. Then Robert Carnath-Nye and his daughter young Julia Carnath; *and* of course, endmost, Jordan and Justin Warrick, who looked exactly like father and son, unless you had known Jordan thirty years ago and knew that they were twins.

Vanity, vanity.

Jordan had had his passages. (Who had not?) But when it came to bestowing his heredity he had not trusted nature. Or women. It was the temptation to godhood, perhaps. Or the belief that he, being a Special, was bound to produce another.

A replicate citizen was not azi. There were considerable legal differences between young Justin, say, and elegant, red-haired Grant, at the second rank of tables, so, so close in all respects . . . born in the same lab, an insignificant day apart. But Justin, dark-haired, square-jawed, and, at a handsome, broad-shouldered seventeen, so very much Jordan's younger image . . . was CIT 976-88-2355 *PR*, that all-important Citizen prefix and that expensive Parental Replicate suffix—replicate except for the little accidents like the break in Jordan's nose, the little scar on Justin's chin, and oh, indeed, the personality, *and* the ability. When Justin was a mote in a womb-tank, the Bok project had already failed—but (Ari was amused) Jordan had entertained notions that his tapes and his genes could overcome all odds.

The lad was bright. But he was not Jordan. Thank God.

Grant's number, on the other hand, was ALX-972, experimental: a design of her own, aesthetic in the extreme, and with an excellent antecedent—another Special geneset, but, for certain legal reasons, she had corrected a genetic fault, incidentally expressing a few aesthetic recessives, to an extent that the legitimate descendants of a certain slightly myopic, brown-haired, unathletic biologist with a heart defect . . . would find astounding.

Neither was Grant a biologist. An excellent student in tape-design, an Alpha capable of working on the structures which had made him what he was—structures wherein lay the legal difference, *not* in the substitution of certain sequences in the geneset, *not* in the wombs which gestated them.

One infant had gone to a father's arms, to lie in a crib in the House, to hear—nothing, at times; or to deal with the fact that Jordan Warrick might be busy at some given time, and a meal might be late, or a noise startle him—

The other had gone to a crib where human heartbeat gave way at intervals to a soothing voice, where activity was monitored, crying measured, reactions clocked and timed—then extensive tape and training for three years until Ari had asked Jordan to take the boy in, nothing unusual: they fostered-out the suspected Alphas, as a rule, and in those days her relations with Jordan had been stormy but professional. A member of the House with a son the same age was a natural thought, and an Alpha companion was a high-status prize for a household, even at Reseune.

I have every confidence in Justin, she had said that day to Jordan. It's such a natural pairing. I'm perfectly willing to let that happen, on a personal basis, you understand, as long as I can continue my tapes and my tests with Grant.

Meaning that the azi as he grew might pass into Justin's care, become his companion—which implied her faith that young Justin would be in that small percentage licensed to work with Alphas—that Justin's own scores would be Alpha-equivalent.

Not entirely to her astonishment it had worked out very well. The correction was a routine one, minor, not likely to affect the azi's intelligence, . . . although, within certain parameters, that had not been a primary concern in creating the set.

So, so convenient to have a link to troublesome Jordan in those years, not informational, since there was hardly anything a ten , a thirteen year old azi knew in the House that *she* did not.

But one never knew—when it might be of use.

She finished the salad, chatted with Giraud while the serving staff took away the plates and brought in the next course: a fine ham. Terrestrial pigs thrived at Reseune, on the residue of the gardens, in sufficient numbers to provide seed stock for several other farms. Pigs and goats, humankind's oldest and hardiest foodstock, with sense enough not to poison themselves on a stray sprig of native shrubbery.

Horses and cattle had the damnedest self-destructive bent.

"Do you know," she said, over the dessert, a simple ice, tangy and pleasant. "We are going to have to make some far-reaching adjustments in staff."

Amazing how many ears were pricked at table, and how quiet a room could get, when she was only speaking to Denys.

"I really don't anticipate any difficulty with the Hope bill." They were all listening now, not pretending to do otherwise. She smiled at her family, put down the spoon and picked up the little cup of strong coffee. "You know how to read that. No difficulty. Forget the news reports. Everything is proceeding tolerably well on schedule, and we have a very exciting prospect in front of us . . . certainly a very exciting prospect, a military psych facility at Fargone—in addition. Which is going to make a real difference in operations here. You can congratulate Jordan for laying the groundwork—really, just everything that may put the Hope route in our laps; *and* the new labs; everything. *That's* what's going on. Jordan should have a lot of the credit for that."

Jordan's face was absolutely devoid of expression. "Let's drop the pretense. We're *home*, we're not in front of the cameras."

Ari flashed a smile. "Jordan, I don't bear you the least ill will. I'm sorry if that offends you, but you've done Reseune—and me—a great favor. I truly don't begrudge you the rewards of it."

"The hell!"

Ari laughed gently and took another sip of coffee. "Jordie, dear, *I* know you'd like to have upstaged me with this; but as it happens, Gorodin came to *me*, and I'm going to give you everything you asked for, on a platter. You'll *get* that long-awaited transfer, you and anyone in your wing who wants to go to Fargone, just as soon as the official request for military liaison comes down the tubes."

"What *is* this?" Yanni Schwartz asked.

"I don't say it'll be a bad thing," Ari said quite honestly, still smiling. "I'm not pulling surprises on you, Yanni—Jordan pulled this one on me. I think everyone should think about it, those who'll prefer to go out to the frontier, those who'd rather stay with the comforts of Reseune—God *knows*, some of us would miss ham and fresh fruit. But the opportunities out there are worth thinking about." Another sip of coffee, slow and thoughtful, watching Jordan's eyes like a fencer. "The Educational wing here will continue, of course. There are some of you we can't transfer, you understand that. We'll have to restructure here, rather well replicate the whole wing—" A little wider smile. It was a joke. Suli Schwartz woke up, a quick look around to see if people were supposed to laugh. "Jordie, you'll have to lay out some recommendations."

"Of course," Jordan said. "But I'm sure you'll use your own list."

She laughed, to keep it polite. "You know damn well I will. But I really will respect your choices wherever I can—after all, I'll assume anyone on your list *wants* to transfer, and I'll assume you want them. Yanni, you can deal with Jordie on that."

There was a growing wariness behind the attentive faces. Young Suli finally seemed to have understood what was going on, perhaps to have figured out for the first time in his life what it was to sit in this room on Family Occasions, and not with the juniors down the hall. No one moved, not the Family, not the azi at the tables round about.

A sonorous clearing of the throat from Denys. "Well," he said, "well, Ari, after all—" Another clearing of the throat. "I don't suppose we could have some of those little cookies we had last night, hmmn?" Wistfully.

"Yes, ser," a server said, close by the door, and slipped out, while Denys ladled sugar into his coffee.

"Hum. The essential thing is Reseune, isn't it? Ari, Jordie, Yanni, really, we all have the same thing at heart, which is the freedom to do our work. We all hate these administrative messes, we all do, it's such a damned waste of our time and there's so much more important on our desks than a lot of little regional authorities bickering away in Novgorod. I'm sure it's important whether station administrators can or can't hold stock in their own stations, but it's just not the kind of thing that *we* ought to have to sit through— I mean, the whole idea of the Bureaus was never meant to take valuable people completely away from work. Council's certainly no great inconvenience to Corain, or Chavez, or, God knows, Bogdanovitch, but it's not really productive to have Gorodin on a short string, and Science, my God, Science is an absolute tragedy—I mean, really, Ari, it's a dreadful waste of your time and energy—"

"I don't know why," Jordan said from his end of the table, with a wry lift of his wine-glass, a rivalry old as their existence in Reseune, dinner witticisms, "since Ari just considers the whole damned universe her province."

Ari laughed, pro forma. Everyone was relieved. Everyone laughed, because to do other than that was an Incident, and no one wanted it, not even Jordan.

"Well, you'll have your chance, won't you?" she said. "The whole Hope route right off Fargone, and you'll be working with old friends, so it's not like you'll be out there alone. If I were younger, Jordie, damned if I wouldn't jump at it; but Denys is right. The politics is done, the whole course is laid, and I'm sure I'm anxious to get on about my work, you're anxious to get yours underway. I hate like hell to drop another administrative job in your lap, but I really want your expertise. You've got to set us up another Educational wing here, really, really an opportunity for you to hand us on a legacy, Jordie, I'm very serious—"

"I left that in cryogenics," Jordan said. Another small round of anxious laughter. "Do you want another sample?"

Ari chuckled and took a sip of her coffee. "What? Jordie, I thought you went the other way. But we do have a second source."

Justin blushed. People turned to see if he had. There was another laugh, much too thin.

"I'm sure Jordie will cooperate," Denys said, intervening before the knives came out: it was the ancient rule in this room—nothing unpleasant. One retaliated with wit here, nothing else, and not too far.

"I'm sure," Ari said. And seriously: "We do have restructuring to do. I'm going to be doing some of my Council work by proxy, figuring it's going to be a little tamer now we have the major projects mapped out. There really shouldn't be any difficulty. I suppose I can fly down if they need me, but Denys is very right: I'm a hundred twenty years old—"

"You've got a few more," Denys said.

"Oh, yes, but I see the wall—true." The room was quiet again. "The Rubin project will take a great deal of my time. I'm not getting morbid. But you know and I know that there's not an infinite amount of time for getting this thing moving. I'll leave most of the Fargone set-up to you, Yanni. I'll be asking data from this department and that. I'll be wanting to oversee the process myself—just a desire to have hands-on again. Maybe a little vanity." She chuckled softly. "I'm going to be writing on my book, doing a little side research—preparation. Retirement, I suppose."

"The hell," Jordan said.

She smiled, covered her cup with her hand when the server wanted to pour more coffee. "No, dear, I've caffeine enough to see me to my rooms. Which is where I ought to go, figuring that the floor is still going up and down—we had a bitch of a lot of turbulence over the Kaukash, didn't we? And I don't think I really slept in Novgorod. Catlin?"

A chair moved, and Catlin was there, and Florian with her. Catlin drew her chair back for her.

"Good night, all," she said; and to Florian, quietly, as chairs went back and people began leaving: "Tell Grant I'm reclaiming him."

"Sera?"

"I need him," she said. "Tell him I've filed a new assignment for him. Jordan never did have legal custody of him. He surely realizes that."

---

iii

"A moment," the azi Florian said, when Justin and Grant started out the door after Jordan and Paul, in the general mill of family and azi headed their separate ways.

"Later," Justin said. His heart began to pound, the way it did anytime he came near Ari or her bodyguards on anything but coldest business, and he took Grant by the arm and tried to get him out the door as Florian blocked Grant's path.

"I'm very sorry," Florian said, looking as if he were. "Sera has said she wants Grant. He's assigned to her now."

For a moment Justin did not realize what he had heard. Grant stood very still in his grip.

"He can retrieve his belongings," Florian said.

"Tell her *no*." They were blocking the Schwartzes from exit. Justin moved confusedly into the hall, drawing Grant with him, but Florian stayed with them. "Tell her—tell her, dammit, if she wants my cooperation in anything, he stays with me!"

"I'm terribly sorry, ser," Florian said—always soft-spoken, soft-eyed. "She said that it was already done. Please understand. He should get his things. Catlin and I will watch out for him the best we can."

"She's not going to do this," Justin told Grant, as Florian slipped back into the dining hall, where Ari delayed. He was cold through and through. His supper sat uneasy at his stomach. "Wait here." His father was waiting with Paul a little down the hall, and Justin crossed the distance in a half-dozen strides, face composed, showing no more, he hoped, than an understandable annoyance; and please, God, not as pale as he was afraid it was. "Something's come up with a project," he told Jordan. "I have to go see about it."

Jordan nodded, had questions, perhaps, but the explanation seemed to cover it; and Justin walked back again to the doorway where Grant stood. He put a hand on Grant's shoulder in passing, and went inside where Ari lingered talking to Giraud Nye.

He waited the few seconds until Ari deliberately passed her eye across him, a silent summons; she seemed to say something dismissing Giraud, because Giraud looked back too, then left.

Ari waited.

"What's this about Grant?" Justin asked when he was face to face with her.

"I need him," Ari said, "that's all. He's a Special geneset, he's relevant to what I'm working on, and I need him now, that's all. Nothing personal."

"It is." He lost control of his voice, seventeen and facing a woman as terrible as his father. He wanted to hit her. And that was not an option. Ari, in Reseune, could do anything. To anyone. He had learned that. "What do you want? What do you really want out of me?"

"I told you, it's not personal. Nothing like it. Grant can get his things, he can have a few days to calm down— You'll see him. It's not like you're not working in that wing."

"You're going to run tape on him!"

"That's what he's for, isn't it? He's an experimental. Tests are what he pays for his keep—"

"He pays for his keep as a designer, dammit, he's not one of your damn test-subjects, he's—" *My brother*, he almost said.

"I'm sorry if you've lost your objectivity in this. And I'd suggest you calm yourself down right now. You don't have your license to handle an Alpha yet, and you're not likely to get it if you can't control your emotions better than this. If you've given him promises you can't keep, you've mishandled him, you understand me? *You've* hurt him. God knows what else you've done, and I can see right now you and I are due for a long, long talk—about what an Alpha is, and what you've done with him, and whether or not you're going to get that license. It takes more than brains, my lad, it takes the ability to think past what you want, and what you believe, and it's about time you learned it."

"All right, all right, I'll do what you want. He will. Just leave him with me!"

"Calm down, hear? Calm down. I'm not leaving him with anyone in that state. Also—" She tapped him on the chest. "You're dealing with *me*, dear, and you know I'm good at getting my own way: you know you always lose points when you show that much to your opposition, especially to a professional. You get those eyes dry, you put yourself in order, and you take Grant home and see he comes with everything he needs. Most of all you calm him down and don't frighten him any further. Where are your sensibilities?"

"Damn you! What do you *want?*"

"I've got what I want. Just go do what I tell you. You work for me. And you'll show up polite and respectful in the morning. Hear me? Now go take care of your business."

"I—"

Ari turned and walked out the door that led to the service area and a lift upstairs; Catlin and Florian barred his way, azi, and without choice.

"Florian," she called from some distance, impatient, and Florian left Catlin alone to hold the doorway—the worse, because Catlin had no compunction such as Florian had, Catlin would strike him, and strike hard, at the next step beyond her warning.

"Go the other way, young ser," Catlin said. "Otherwise you'll be under arrest."

He turned abruptly and walked back to the other door, where Grant stood, very pale and very quiet, witness to all of it.

"Come on," Justin said, and grabbed him by the arm. Ordinarily there would be a slight, human resistance, a tension in the muscles. There was none. Grant simply came, walked with him when he let him go, and offered not a word till they were down the hall and in the lift that took them up to third level residencies.

"Why is she doing this?"

"I don't know. I don't know. Don't panic. It's going to be all right."

Grant looked at him, a fragile hope that hit him in the gut, as the lift stopped.

Down the hall again, to the apartment that was theirs, in a residential quiet-zone, only a handful of passersby at this hour. Justin took his keycard from its clip on his pocket and inserted it with difficulty in the slot. His hand was shaking. Grant had to see it.

"No entries since last use of this key," the monitor's bland voice said, and the lights came on, since that was what he had programmed his Minder to do for his entry at this hour, all the way through the beige and blue living room, to his bedroom.

"Grant's here," he mumbled at it, and more lights came on, Grant's bedroom, visible through the archway leftward.

"I'll get my things," Grant said; and, the first sign of fracture, a wobble in his voice when he asked: "Shouldn't we call Jordan?"

"God." Justin embraced him. Grant held on to him, trembling in long, spasmodic shivers; and Justin clenched his own arms tight, trying to think, trying to reason past his own situation and the law inside Reseune which said that he could not protect the azi who had been a brother to him since he could remember.

Grant knew everything, knew everything that he knew. Grant and he had no difference, none, except that damning X on Grant's number, that made him Reseune property as long as he lived.

She could interrogate him about Jordan, about everything he knew or suspected, test systems on him, put him under tape with one structure and another, put sections of his memory under block, do any damned thing she wanted, and there was no way he could stop it.

It was revenge against his father. It was a hold on him, who, the same way Grant had just been transferred, had been Aptituded into Ari's wing. Let her, he had said to his father. Let her take me into her staff. Don't contest it. It's all right. You can't afford a falling-out with her right now, and maybe it's a good place for me to be.

Because he had had a notion then that his father, harried with plans (again) for getting a transfer, could lose too much.

You tell me, Jordan had said with the greatest severity, you tell me *immediately* if she makes trouble for you.

There had been trouble. There had been more than trouble, from his second day in that wing—an interview with Ari in her office, Ari too close and touching him in a way that started out only friendly and got much too personal, while she suggested quietly that there was more reason than his test scores that she had requisitioned him into her wing, and that he and Grant both could . . . accommodate her, that others of her aides did, and that was the way things were expected to be on her staff. Or, she had hinted, there were ways to make life difficult.

He had been disgusted, and scared; and worst of all, he had seen Ari's intention, the trap laid—slow provocations, himself the leverage she meant to wield against Jordan, a campaign to provoke him to an incident she could use. So he had gone along with it when she put her hands on him, and stammered his way through reports while she sat on the arm of his chair and rested her hand on his shoulder. She had asked him to her office after hours, had asked him questions, pretending to fill out personnel reports, and he mumbled answers, things he did not dwell on, things he did not want even to remember, because he had never even had a chance to do the things she asked him about, and never wanted in his life to do some of the things she talked about; and suspected that without tape, without drugs, without anything but his own naivete and her skill, she was in the process of twisting his whole life. He could fight back—by losing his capacity to be shocked, by answering her flippantly, playing the game—

—but it was her game.

"I'll think of something," he said to Grant. "There's a way out of this. It'll be all right." And he let Grant go off to his rooms to pack, while he stood alone in the living room in the grip of a chill that went to his bones. He wanted to phone Jordan, ask advice, whether there was anything legal they *could* do.

But it was all too likely Jordan would go straight to Ari to negotiate Grant free of her. Then Ari might play other cards, like tapes of those office sessions—

—O God, then Jordan *would* go straight to the Science Bureau, and launch a fight that would break all the careful agreements and lose him everything.

Query the House computers on the law—but there was nothing he dared use: every log-on was recorded. Everything left traces. There was no way that Reseune would not win a head-on challenge. He did not know the extent of Ari's political power, but it was enough that it could open new exploration routes, subvert companies on distant star-stations and affect trade directly with old Earth itself; and that was just the visible part of it.

Beyond the archway, he heard the sounds of the closet door, saw Grant piling his clothes onto the bed.

He knew suddenly where Grant *was* going—the way they had dreamed of when they were boys, sitting on the banks of the Novaya Volga, sending boats made of old cans floating down to Novgorod, for city folk to marvel at. And later, on a certain evening when they had talked about Jordan's transfer, about the chance of them being held until Jordan could get them out.

It was that worst-case now, he thought, not the way they had planned, but it was the only chance they had.

He walked into Grant's room, laid a finger on his lips for silence, because there *was* Security monitoring: Jordan had told him it went on. He took Grant's arm, led him quickly and quietly out into the living room, toward the door, took his coat from the closet—no choice about that: it was close to freezing outside, people came and went from wing to wing in the open, it was ordinary enough. He handed Grant his, and led him out into the hall.

Where to? Grant's worried look said plainly. *Justin, are you doing something stupid?*

Justin took his arm and hauled Grant along, down the hall, back to the lift.

He pushed T, for the tunnel-level. The car shot downward. God, let there be no stops on main—

"Justin—"

He shoved Grant against the wall of the lift, held him there, never mind that Grant was a head taller. "Quiet," he said. "That's an order. Not a word. Nothing. *Hear?*"

He did not speak to Grant that way. Ever. He was shaking. Grant clamped his jaw and nodded, terrified, as the lift door opened on the dingy concrete of the storm-tunnels. He dragged Grant out, backed him against the wall again. Calmer this time.

"Now you listen to me. We're going down to the Town—"

"I—"

"Listen to me. I want you to go null. Deep-state, all the way. Right now. Do it. And stay that way. That's an order, Grant. If you never in your life did exactly what I said, —do it now. Now! Hear me?"

Grant took a gulp of air, composed himself then, expressionless in two desperate breaths.

No panic now. Steady. "Good," Justin said. "Put the coat on and come on."

Up another lift, to the Administration wing, the oldest; back to the antiquated Ad wing kitchens, where the night shift staff did dinner clean-up and breakfast prep for the catering service. It was the escape route every kid in the House had used at one time or another, through the kitchens, back where the ovens were, where the air-conditioning never was enough, where staff from generation to generation had propped the fire-door with trash-bins to get a breeze. The kitchen workers had no inclination to report young walkthroughs, not unless someone asked, and Administration never stopped the practice—that routed juvenile CIT truants and pranksters past witnesses who would, if asked, readily say yes, Justin Warrick and his azi had gone out that door—

—but not until they were missed.

Shhh, he mimed to the kitchen azi, who gave them bewildered and anxious looks—the late hour, and the fact they were older than the usual fugitives who came this way.

Past the trash-bin, down the steps into the chill dark.

Grant overtook him by the pump shed that was the first cover on the hill before it sloped rapidly to the road.

"We're going down the hill," Justin said then. "Taking the boat."

"What about Jordan?" Grant objected.

"He's all right. Come on."

He broke away and Grant ran after him, pelted downslope to intercept the road. Then they strolled at a more ordinary pace down through the floodlit intersections of the warehouses, the repair shops, the streets of the lower Town. The few guards awake at this hour were on the perimeters, to mind the compound fences and the weather reports, not two boys from the House bound down toward the airport road. The bakery and the mills ran full-scale at night, but they were far off across the town, distant gleam of lights as they left the last of the barracks.

"Is Jordan getting hold of Merild?" Grant asked.

"Trust me. I know what I'm doing."

"Justin, —"

"Shut *up*, Grant. Hear me?"

They reached the edge of the port. The field lights were out right now, but the beacon still blipped its steady strobe into the dark of a mostly vacant world. Far off, the freight warehouses and the big RESEUNEAIR hangar showed clear, brightly lit, night-work and maintenance going on with one of the commercial planes.

"Justin, —*does he know?*"

"He'll handle it. Come on." Justin set out at a run again, leaving Grant no breath for questions, down the road that passed the end of the runway to the barge-dock and down across the concrete bridgeway to the low-lying warehouses at the edge of the river.

No one locked the doors down here at the small boathouse. No one needed to. He pushed at the door of the shabby prefab, winced at the creak of the hinge. Inside, an iron grid whispered hollowly under their feet. Water splashed and slapped at the pilings and buffers, starlight reflecting wetly around the outlines of the boats moored there. The whole place smelled of river-water and oil and the air was burning cold.

"Justin," Grant said. "For God's sake—"

"Everything's all right. You go exactly the way we planned—"

"*I* go—"

"I'm not leaving. You are."

"You're out of your mind! Justin!"

Justin clambered aboard the nearest boat, opened up the pressurized cabin door and left Grant nothing to do but follow him aboard with his objections.

"Justin, if you stay now, they can arrest you!"

"And if I take you out of here there's no way in hell I'll ever get certified to be near you, you know that. So I'm not down here tonight. I don't know a thing about this. I just go back up there, say I never left my room, how am I to know where you went? Maybe a platythere ate you and got indigestion." He flipped the on-switch, checked the gauges, one toggle-switch and another. "There you go, everything's full, batteries all charged. Wonderful how the staff keeps things up, isn't it?"

"Justin." Grant's voice was shaking. He had his hands in his pockets. The air was bitter chill near the water. "Listen to *me* now, let's have some sense here. I'm azi. I was listening to tape in the cradle, for God's sake. If she runs something on me I can handle it, I can rip the structures apart and tell you if there were any bugs in it—"

"The hell you can."

"I can survive her tests, and there's no way she can axe my Contract, there's no axe-code. I know for a fact there's not—I *know* my sets, Justin. Let's just forget this and go up the hill and we'll figure out another way. If it gets bad, we always have this for an option."

"Shut up and listen to me. Remember how we mapped this out: first lights you see on your right are still Reseune: that's the number ten precip station, up on the bluffs. The lights on your left two klicks on will be Moreyville. If you run completely dark you can pass there before Ari gets wind of this, and it's a clear night. Remember, stay to the center of the channel, that's the only way to miss the bars, and for God's sake, be careful of snags. Current comes from the left when you get to the Kennicutt. You turn into it, and the first lights you see after that, two, maybe three hours on, that's Krugers. You tell them who you are and you give them this—" He turned on a dim chart-light and scribbled a number down on the pad clipped to the dash. Under the number he wrote: MERILD. "Tell them call Merild, no matter the hour. You can tell Merild when he gets there—tell him Ari's blackmailing Jordan through me, dammit, that's all he has to know. Tell him I can't come until my father's free, but I had to get you out of there, you're one more hostage than Jordan can cope with. Understand?"

"Yes," Grant said in a faint voice, azi-like: *yes*.

"The Krugers won't betray you. Tell them I said sink the boat if they have to. It's Emory's. Merild will handle everything else."

"Ari will call the police."

"That's fine. Let her. *Don't* try to go past the Kennicutt. If you have to, the next place on down the Volga is Avery, overnight, maybe more, and she *could* intercept you. Besides, you'd get caught up in Cyteen-law and police down there, and you know what that could be. Krugers is it. It has to be." He looked back at Grant's face in the faint glow of the chart-light, and it struck him suddenly that he might not see him again. "Be careful. For God's sake, be careful."

"Justin." Grant embraced him hard. "You be careful. Please."

"I'll push you out of here. Go on. Dog the seals down."

"The other boat—" Grant said.

"I'll take care of it. Go!" Justin turned and ducked out of the door, hopped up on the deck and onto the echoing grating. He cast off the ties then, threw them aboard, shoved the big boat back with his foot and with his hands till it drifted clear, scraping the buffers.

It swung round sideways, inert and dark, then caught the current off the boathouse and drifted, following the sweep of the main channel, turning again.

He opened up the second boat and threw up the cover on the engine.

The starter was electronic. He pulled the solid state board, dropped the cover down, closed the hatch behind him, and dropped the board into the water before he made the jump between the boat and the metal grid of the dock.

In the same moment he heard the distant, muffled cough of Grant's engine.

Solid then, chugging away.

He cleared the boathouse, latched the door and ran. It was dangerous to be down here on the river-edge, in the dark, dangerous anywhere less patrolled, where something native could have gotten in, weed in the ditch, stuff carried in the air—God knew. He tried not to think about it. He ran, took up on the road again, walking as he caught a stitch in his side.

He expected commotion. He expected someone on night shift at the airport to have seen the boat, or heard its engine start. But the work at the hangars was noisy. Maybe someone had had a power wrench going. Maybe they thought it was some passing boat from Moreyville or up-Volga, with a balky engine. And they had the bright lights to blind them.

So far their luck was a hundred percent.

Till he got to the House and found the kitchen door locked.

He sat down a while on the steps, teeth chattering, trying to think it through, and gave it a while, time for a boat to get well on its way. But if he sat there the night, then it was unarguable that it was conspiracy.

If he gave them evidence of that—

It would land on Jordan.

So there was nothing to do finally but use his key and trip the silent warnings he knew would be in place by now.

Security showed up to meet him in the halls by the kitchens. "Ser," the azi in charge said, "where are you coming from?"

"I felt like a walk," he said. "That's all. I drank too much. I wanted some cold air."

The azi called that in to the Security office; Justin waited, expecting the man's expression to change then, when the order came back. But the azi only nodded. "Good evening, ser."

He walked away, weak-kneed, rode the lift up and walked all the lonely way to the apartment.

The lights came on inside. *"No entries since the last use of this key,"* the dulcet voice of the Minder said.

He went into Grant's room. He picked things up and hung them back in the closet and put them in drawers. He found small, strange things among Grant's belongings, a tinsel souvenir Jordan had brought back from holiday in Novgorod, a cheap curio spacer patch of the freighter *Kittyhawk* that he had brought back from Novgorod airport, for Grant, who had not been allowed to go. A photo of the pair of them, aged four, Grant pale-skinned, skinny, and shockingly red-haired, himself in that damned silly hat he had thought was grown-up, digging in the garden with the azi. Another photo of them, at a mutually gawky ten, standing on the fence of the livestock pens, barefoot, toes curled identically pigeon-toed over the rail, arms under chins, both grinning like fools.

God. It was as if a limb had been cut off, and the shock had not quite gotten to the brain yet, but it had hit his gut, and it told him it was going to get worse.

Ari would call him now, he had no doubt.

He went back to the living room, sat down on the couch, hugged his arms about himself and stared at the patterns in the veneer of the table, anything but shut his eyes and see the boat and the river.

Or think of Ari.

Only Grant? Merild would ask, when he got that phone message. Merild would take alarm. Merild might well call Reseune and try to talk to Jordan; and he could not afford that: he tried to think what he would say, how he would cover it. Grant could tell Merild enough, maybe, to set Merild working on a rescue of some sort; but, oh, God, if something got to Jordan about Ari and him, either from Grant, from Merild, or from Ari—and Jordan blew up—

No. Jordan was too cagy to do something without thinking it out—

The time passed. The air of the apartment felt cold as the chill outside; he wanted to go in to his own bed, and pull the covers about him, but he asked the Minder for more heat and kept to the living room, fighting to stay awake, afraid he would sleep through a Minder call.

None came.

Small boats went out of one port and never got to another, that was all. It happened even to experienced pilots.

He thought about every step he had taken, every choice he had, over and over again. He thought about calling Jordan, telling him everything.

No, he told himself. No. He could handle it with Ari. Jordan needed help, and Jordan *not* knowing was the only way it worked.

----------------------- iv -----------------------

A plane flew over. Grant heard it even above the steady noise of his own engines, and his hands sweated on the wheel as he ran down the clear middle of the river, his meager speed boosted by the current. He had no lights on, not even the small chart-light on the panel, for fear of being spotted. He did not dare increase the speed of the engines now, for fear of widening the white boil and curl of wake that might show to searchers.

The plane went over and lost itself in dark and distance.

But in a little time it circled back again: he saw it coming up the river behind him, a searchlight playing over the black waters.

He put the throttle up full, and felt the easy rock of the boat become an increasing vibration of waves as the bow came up. To hell with the wake, then, and with the floating snags that had sunk many a boat in the Novaya Volga.

If they had sent boats out from Moreyville, or from the other end of Reseune, and if someone on those boats had a gun, shots could go through the cabin, breach the seals fatally even if they missed him, or go through the hull and maybe hit the fuel tanks—but they had rather put a hole in the boat and slow it with waterlogged compartments. They would not, he was sure, want him dead if they had a choice.

He did not intend to harm Justin, that was his first determination: not to be used against Justin, nor against Jordan. And beyond that, even an azi had a right to be selfish.

The plane roared directly over him, throwing the decks into bright light, blinding glare through the cabin windows. The beam passed on a moment, leaving him half blind in the sudden dark. He saw it light the trees on the far side of the river, pale gray of native foliage against the night.

Suddenly the bow fell off to starboard and that floodlit view of the bank turned up off the bow, not the beam. In a moment's fright he thought the propeller might have fouled, and then he knew it was current he had run into—the Kennicutt's effluence into the Volga.

He put the helm over, still blind except for the fleeting glimpse the searchlight had shown him of the wooded ground on the far side. He could run aground. He dared not turn the lights on.

Then he saw the shadow of the banks, tall trees black against the night sky on either side of an open space of starlit water.

He drove for it; and the boat shuddered and jolted to impact along the keel, scrape of sand and a shock that threw him violently as the boat slewed out of control.

He caught himself against the dash then, saw a black wall in front of him and swerved with everything the boat had.

Something banged against the bow and scraped portside. Snag. Sandbar and snag. He heard it pass aft, saw the clear water ahead of him and hoped to God it was the Kennicutt he was in after that sort-out and not the Volga. He could not tell. It looked the same as the other, just black water, glancing with starlight.

He risked the chart-light for a second to sneak a look at the compass. Bearing northeast. The Volga could bend that much, but he thought it had to be the Kennicutt. The plane had not come back. It was even possible that the maneuver had confused it, and he was not, God knew, running with the Locator beacon on. Ari's power was enough to get Cyteen Station in on the hunt, and that plane's beacon could guide the geosynchronous surveillance satellites to a good fix, but so far as he knew there was no strike capacity on the Locators, and he could still, he hoped, outrun any intercept from Moreyville or further down the Volga.

First lights after that, Justin had said. Two, maybe three hours further on, up a river that *had* no further development on its banks. Krugers' Station was a mining outpost, largely automated, virtually all related to each other: what azi they brought in all got their CIT papers within the year, and a share of Kruger Mines on top of it—a dream of an assignment, the kind of place azi whispered among themselves did exist, if one were very, very good—

And if one's Contract was affordable.

Nothing like that existed for a seventeen-year-old azi with an X on his number, and all the political sense a boy could gain, living in Reseune and in the House, advised him that Justin had done something for his sake desperate beyond all reason—

Advised him that the Krugers might well have welcomed a Warrick with an azi he had a valid Contract for, but that there were good reasons they might not welcome that azi by himself.

God knew.

He was, the more he had time to think about it, a liability on all accounts, except for what he knew about Reseune, Ari, and Warrick business, which people might insist he give up; and he had had no instructions on that. He was Alpha, but he was young and he was azi, and all that he had learned only told him that his responses were conditioned, his knowledge limited, his reasoning potentially flawed— (Never worry about your tapes, Jordan had told him gently. If you ever think you're in trouble, come to me and tell me what you think and what you feel and I'll find the answer for you: remember I've got your charts. Everything's all right—)

He had been seven then. He had cried in Jordan's arms, which had embarrassed him, but Jordan had patted him on the back and hugged him the way he hugged Justin, called him his other son and assured him even bornmen made mistakes and felt confused.

Which had made him feel better and worse, to know that born-men had evolved out of old Earth by trial and error, and that when Ari had decided he should exist, she had done something of the same thing. Trial and error. Which was all the X on his number meant to a seven-year-old.

He had not understood then that it meant Jordan could not deliver what he promised, or that his life was Reseune's and not Jordan's. He had clutched that 'my other son' to him like daylight and breath, a whole new horizon of being.

Then he had grown enough, when he and Justin were twelve and Justin discovered girls, to know that sex made things very different.

"Why?" he had asked Jordan; and Jordan had walked him into the kitchen, his arm about his shoulders while he explained that an Alpha was always mutating the instructions the tapes gave him, that he was very bright, and that his body was developing and that he really should go to the azi who specialized in that.

"What if I make somebody pregnant?" he had asked.

"You won't," Jordan had said, which he had not asked about then, but he knew later he should have. "You just can't mess around with anyone in the House. They aren't licensed."

He had been outraged. And thought there was a kind of irony in it. "You mean because I'm an Alpha? You mean whoever I go to bed with—"

"Has to be licensed. You don't get a license at your age. Which lets out all the girls your age. And I don't want you sleeping with old aunt Mari, all right?"

That had been halfway funny. At the time. Mari Warrick was decrepit, on the end of her rejuv.

It had gotten less funny later. It was hard to stay cool while a Carnath girl put her hands where they did not belong and giggled in his ear; and to be supposed to say: "I'm sorry, sera, I can't."

While Justin, poor Justin, got girlish giggles and evasions, because *he* was Family; and Justin's azi was fair game—or would have been, if he had only been Beta.

"Lend him, can't you?" Julia Carnath had asked Justin outright, in Grant's presence, when Grant knew damned well that Justin was courting Julia for himself. Grant had wanted to sink through the floor. As it was, he had gone blank-faced and proper, and kept very quiet later when Justin sulked and said that Julia had turned him down.

"You're better-looking," Justin had complained. "Ari made you perfect, dammit. What chance have I got?"

"I'd rather be you," he had answered faintly, realizing for the first time that was the truth. And he had cried, for the second time in his life that he remembered, just cried for no reason that he could figure out, except that Justin had hit a nerve. Or a tape-structure.

Because he was made of both.

He had never been sure after that, until Jordan had let him see the structures of his own tapes when he was sixteen and starting into advanced design studies. He had figured out enough of his tape-structures on his own that Jordan had opened the book for him and let him see what he was made of; and so far he had not traced any lines that could lead to fear of sex.

But Alphas mutated their own conditioning, constantly. It was a constant balancing act, over an abyss of chaos. Nothing could dominate. Balance in everything.

Or the world became chaos.

Dysfunction.

An azi who had become his own counselor was begging for trouble. An azi was so terribly fragile. And so very likely to get into a situation he could not handle, in a larger game than anyone had bothered to tell him about.

Dammit, Justin!

He wiped his eyes with his left hand and steered with the right, trying to watch where he was going. He was, he told himself, acting the fool.

Like a born-man. Like I was like them.

I'm supposed to be smarter. I'm supposed to be a damn genius. Except the tapes don't work that way and I'm not what they wanted me to be.

Maybe I just don't use what I've got.

So why didn't I speak up louder? Why didn't I grab Justin and haul him off to his father if I had to hit him to do it?

Because I'm a damn azi, that's why. Because I go to jelly inside when some-one acts like they know what they're doing and I stop using my head, that's why. Oh, damn, damn, damn! *I should have stopped him, I should have dragged him aboard with me, I should have* taken *him to the Krugers and gotten him safe, and then he could have protected both of us; and Jordan would be free to do something. What was he thinking of?*

Something I couldn't?

Dammit, that's the trouble *with me, I haven't got any confidence, I'm always looking to be sure before I do anything, and I don't do a damn thing, I just take orders—*

—because the damn tapes have got their claws into me. They never told me to hesitate, they just make me do it, because the tapes are sure, they're so damned fucking sure, *and nothing in the real world ever is—*

That's why we never make our own minds up. We've known something that has no doubt, and born-men never have. That's what's the matter with us—

The boat hit something that jolted the deck, and Grant threw the wheel over and corrected furiously, sweating.

Fool, indeed. He suddenly arrived at the meaning of it all and damned near holed his boat, which was the kind of thing that happened to born-men, Justin would say, just the same as anybody else; which was how things worked—a second cosmic truth, in sixty seconds. His mind was working straight or he was scared into hyperdrive, because he suddenly had a sense what it was to be a born-man, and to be a fool right on top of understanding everything: one had to swallow down the doubts and just go, how often had Jordan told him that. *The doubts aren't tape. They're life, son. The universe won't break if you fuck up. It won't even break if you break your neck. Just your private universe will. You understand that?*

I think so, he had said. But that had been a lie. Till now, that it jumped into clear focus. *I'm free,* he thought. *Out here, between here and the Krugers, I'm free, on my own, the first time in my life.* And then he thought: *I'm not sure I like it.*

Fool. Wake up. Pay attention. O my God, is that the plane coming back?

As a light showed suddenly behind him.

A boat. O God, O God, it's a boat back there.

He shoved the throttle wide. The boat lifted its bow and roared along the Kennicutt. He turned the lights on. They shone on black water, on water that swirled with currents, on banks closer than the Volga's, banks overgrown with the gangling shapes of weeping willies—trees that tended to break as they aged and rot worked on them, trees which shed huge gnarled knots of dead wood into the Volga, navigation hazards far worse than rocks, because they floated and moved continually.

The lights were less risk now, he figured, than running blind.

But there would be guns back there, maybe. Maybe a boat that could overpower the runabout. He would be surprised if Moreyville had had something that could outrun him; damned surprised, he thought, with a cold knot of fear at his gut, watching the light wink out around a turning of the river; and then reappear in his rearview mirror.

A boat out of the precip station, maybe; maybe that end of Reseune had boats. He had no idea.

He applied his attention forward after that brief glance; center of the channel, Justin had warned him. Justin at least had taken the boat back and forth to Moreyville and down to precip ten; and he had talked to people at Moreyville who had gone all the way to Novgorod on the river.

Justin had done the talking; and Grant had paid attention mostly to the Novgorod part, because that had been what he was curious about. He and Justin—talking together about taking a boat that far someday, just heading down the river.

He steered wildly around a snag floating with one branch high.

A whole damned *tree*, that one. He saw the root-mass following like a wall of tangled brush in the boat's spot; and swerved wider, desperately.

God, if one of those came floating sideways—if the bow caught it—

He kept going.

And the light stayed behind him until he saw the lights Justin had promised him shining on the right, out of the dark— Ambush, he thought in the second heartbeat after he had seen them, because everything had become a trap, everything was an enemy.

But they were too high, they were too many: lights that twinkled behind the screen of weeping willies and paperbarks, lights that were far too high for the river, lights blinking red atop the hills, warning aircraft of the obstacles of precip towers.

Then his knees began feeling weak and his arms began shaking. He missed the light from behind him when he looked to see; and he thought for the first time to put Justin's note in his pocket, and to take the paper that had been under it, in the case someone returned the boat to Reseune.

He throttled back, seeking some dockage, alarmed as the spotlight showed up a low rusty wall on the riverside, and another, after that—

Barges, he realized suddenly. Kruger's was a mining settlement. They were ore barges, not so big as the barges that came down from the north; but the whole place was a dock; and there was a place for a little boat to nose to, there was a ladder that went up from a lower dock to an upper one, which meant he was not in the wild anymore, and he could breach the seals: but he did not do that. He did not think he ought to use the radio, since Justin had not told him anything about it; and he was not sure how to work it in any case. He just blew the horn, repeatedly, until someone turned the dockside lights on, and people turned out to see what had come to them from the river.

V

"You have a phone call," the Minder said, and Justin started out of what had become sleep without his knowing it, lying as he had all night curled up on the living room couch; the sound brought him up on his elbow and onto his arm and then, as the Minder cut in and answered it, to his feet— "I'm here," he said aloud, to the Minder, and heard it tell the caller:

"Justin is in. A moment, please."

He rubbed a face prickly with the faint stubble he could raise, eyes that refused to focus. "I'm here," he said, his heart beating so hard it hurt, and waited for bad news.

"Good morning," Ari said to him. *"Sorry to bother you at this hour, Justin, but where is Grant?"*

"I don't know," he said. *Time. What time?* He rubbed his eyes and tried to focus on the dim numbers of the clock on the wall console. *Five in the morning. He's got to be at Kruger's by now. He's got to.* "Why? Isn't he there?" He looked beyond the arch, where the lights were still on, where Grant's bed was unslept-in, proof that everything was true, Grant *had* run, everything he remembered had happened.

We can't *have gotten away with it.*

"Justin, I want to talk with you, first thing when you get in today."

"Yes?" His voice cracked. It was the hour. He was shivering.

"At 0800. When you get in. In the Wing One lab."

"Yes, sera."

The contact went dead. Justin rubbed his face and squeezed his eyes shut, jaw clamped. He felt as if he was going to be sick.

He thought of calling his father. Or going to him.

But Ari had given him plenty of latitude to do that; and maybe it was what he was supposed to do, or maybe it was Ari trying to make him think it was what he was supposed to do, so that he would shy away from it. Trying to out-think her was like trying to out-think his father.

And he was trying to do both.

He made himself a breakfast of dry toast and juice, all he could force onto his unwilling stomach. He showered and dressed and paced, delaying about little things, because there was so much time, there was so damned much time to wait.

It was deliberate. He knew that it was. She did everything for a reason.

Grant might be in the hands of the police.

He might be back at Reseune.

He might be dead.

Ari meant to drop something on him, get some reaction out of him, and get it on tape. He prepared himself for anything she could say, even the worst even-tuality; he prepared himself, if he had to, to say: *I don't know. He left. I assumed he was going to you. How could I know? He's never done anything like this.*

At 0745 he left his apartment and took the lift down to the main hall; passed Wing One security, walked to his own office, unlocked the door, turned on the lights, everything as he usually did.

He walked down the corridor where Jane Strassen was already in her office, and nodded a good morning to her. He rounded the corner and took the stairs down to the lab-section at the extreme end of the building.

He used his keycard on the security lock of the white doors and entered a corridor of small offices, all closed. Beyond, the double doors gave onto the dingy Wing One lab, with its smell of alcohol and chill and damp that brought back his early student days in this place. The lights were on. The big cold-room at the left had its vault door standing wide, brighter light coming from that quarter.

He let the outer doors shut and heard voices. Florian walked out from the vault-door of the lab.

Not unusual for a student to be here, not unusual for techs to be in and out of here: Lab One was old, outmoded by Building B's facilities, but it was still sound. Researchers still used it, favoring it over the longer walk back and forth to the huge birthlabs over in B, preferring the old hands-on equipment to the modern, more automated facilities. Ari had been down here a lot lately. She kept a lot of her personal work in the old cold-lab, as convenient a storage for that kind of thing, he had figured, as there was in Wing One.

Rubin project, he thought. Earlier her presence down here had puzzled him, when Ari did not need to do these things herself, when she had excellent techs to do the detail work. It no longer puzzled him.

I'll be wanting to oversee the process myself—just a desire to have hands-on again. Maybe a little vanity. . . .

It was also private, the kind of situation with her that he had spent weeks trying to avoid.

"Sera is expecting you," Florian said.

"Thank you," he said, meticulously ordinary. "Do you know what about?"

"I would hope you do, ser," Florian answered him. Florian's dark eyes said nothing at all as he slid a glance toward the cold-lab door. "You can go in. —Sera, Justin Warrick is here."

"All right," Ari's voice floated out.

Justin walked over to the open door of the long lab where Ari sat on a work-stool, at a counter, working at one of the old-fashioned separators. "Damn," she complained without looking up. "I don't trust it. Got to get one out of B. I'm not going to put up with this." She looked up and the hasty lift of her hand startled him as his hand left the vault door. He realized he had moved the door then, and caught it and pushed the massive seal-door back, steadying it in frustration at his own young awkwardness, that rattled him when he most wanted composure.

"Damn thing," Ari muttered. "Jane's damn penny-pinching—you touch it, it swings on you. *That's* going to get fixed. —How are *you* this morning?"

"All right."

"Where's Grant?"

His heart was already beating hard. It picked up its beats and he forced it to slow down. "I don't know. I thought he was with you."

"Of course you did. —Grant stole a boat last night. Sabotaged the other one. Security tracked him to Kruger's. What do you know about it?"

"Nothing. Nothing at all."

"Of course not." She turned on the stool. "Your companion planned the whole thing."

"I imagine he did. Grant's very capable." It was going too easily. Ari was capable of much, much more; of spinning it out, instead of going straight to the point. He held himself back from too much relief, as if it were a precipice and the current were carrying him too quickly toward it. Florian was still outside. There were no witnesses to what she said—or what she ordered. There was a lock on the doors out there. And there might well be a recorder running. "I wish he *had* told me."

Ari made a clicking with her tongue. "You want to see the security reports? You both went out last night. You came in alone."

"I was looking for Grant. He said he was going to borrow a carry-bag from next door. He never came back."

Ari's brows lifted. "Oh, come, now."

"Sorry. That's what I was doing."

"I'm really disappointed in you. I'd expected more invention."

"I've told you everything I know."

"Listen to me, young friend. What you did is *theft*, you know that? You know what happens if Reseune files charges."

"Yes," he said, as calmly, as full of implication as he could make it. "I really think I do."

"We're not Cyteen."

"I know."

"You're very smug. Why?"

"Because you're not going to file charges."

"Do you want to bet on that?"

He was supposed to react. He smiled at her. He had himself that far under control, not knowing, not at all knowing whether or not Grant was in her hands. "I'm betting on it," he said, and held his voice steady. "You've got me. You haven't got Grant. As long as things go right with me and my father, Grant keeps his mouth shut and we're all just fine."

"That's why you stayed behind."

That had bothered her. The irrational act.

He smiled wider, a thin, carefully held triumph, alone, in her territory. "One of us had to. To assure you we'll keep quiet otherwise."

"Of course. Did Jordan plan this?"

He did react then. He knew that he had. It was an unexpected and off-handed praise.

"No," he said.

"You did." Ari gave a breath of a laugh; and he did not like that, even when all the movements of her body, her rocking back against the back of the lab-stool, her rueful smile, all said that she was surprised.

Ari played her own reactions the way his father did—with all her skill, all the way to the end of a thing.

So must he. He gave a matching, deprecatory shrug.

"It's really very good," Ari said. "But you have to put so much on Grant."

He's dead, he thought, bracing himself for the worst thing she could say. *She might lie about that.*

"I trust him," he said.

"There's one flaw in your set-up, you know."

"What would that be?"

"Jordan. He's really not going to like this."

"I'll talk to him." His muscles started to shake, the cold of the cryogenics conduits that ran overhead seeming to leach all the warmth from him. He felt all his control crumbling and made a profound effort to regroup. It was a tactic his father had taught him, this alternate application of tension and relief she was using, watching cues like the dilation of his eyes, the little tensions in his muscles, everything fallen into a rhythm like a fencer, up, down, up, down, and then something out of the rhythm the moment he had discovered the rules. He saw it coming. He smiled at her, having gotten command of himself with that thought. "He'll be amused."

He watched a slow grin spread over Ari's face, either his point or a deliberate dropping of the shield for a moment to make him think it was.

"You really have nerve," Ari said. "And you aren't at all cocky, are you? Damn, boy, the edges are ragged, you're not real confident you've got all the pieces in your hands, but I'll give it to you, that's a damned good maneuver. Harder than hell to do twice, though."

"I don't need to leave till my father does."

"Well, now, that *is* a problem, isn't it? Just how are we going to disengage this little tangle? Have you thought it all the way through? Tell me how it works when it comes time for Jordan to go off-world. I'm interested."

"Maybe you'll make me an offer."

Ari flashed a bright smile. "That's marvelous. You were so quiet. What did you do, try to throw those test scores?"

"You're supposed to be able to figure that out."

"Oh, cheek!" She outright laughed. "You *are* bright. You've taught me something. At my age, I value that. You're very fond of Grant, to give up your camouflage for him. *Very* fond of him." She leaned against the counter, one elbow on it, looking soberly up at him. "Let me tell you something, dear. Jordan loves you—very much. Very, very much. It shows in the way you behave. And I must say, he's done a marvelous job with Grant. Children need that kind of upbringing. But there's a dreadful cost to that. We're mortal. We lose people. And we really hurt when they hurt, don't we? —Families are a hell of a liability. What are you going to tell Jordan?"

"I don't know. As much as I have to."

"You mean, as much as will let him know he's won?"

Break and reposition. He only smiled at her, refusing a debate with a master.

"Well," she said, "you've done Jordan proud in this one. I don't say it's wise. The plan was very smart; the reasons are very, very stupid, but then, —devotion makes us fools, doesn't it? What do you suppose Jordan would do if I charged you with this?"

"Go public. Go to the Bureau. And you *don't* want that."

"Well, but there's a lot else we can do, isn't there? Because his son really *is* guilty of theft, of vandalism, of getting into files that don't concern him— And there's so much of that that doesn't have to happen. Jordan can make charges, I can make charges; you know if this breaks, that appointment he wants won't make it, no matter what interests are behind it. They'll desert him in a flash. But you know all that. It's what makes everything work, isn't it—unless I really wanted to take measures to recover Grant and prosecute those friends of yours. That's what you've missed, you know. That I can do just exactly what you did, break the law; and if someone brings out your part in this, and if your father has to listen to your personal reasons, our little private sessions, hmmn? —it's really going to upset him."

"It won't do you any good if I go to court, either. You can't afford it. You've got the votes in Council right now. You want to watch things fall apart, you lay a hand on Grant—and I talk. You watch it happen."

"You damned little sneak," she said slowly. "You think you understand it that well."

"Well enough to know my friends won't use a card before they have to."

"What have you got on the Krugers, that they'd risk this kind of trouble for you? Or do you think the other side won't use you? Have you taken that into account?"

"I didn't have much choice, did I? But things ought to be safe as long as the deal for Jordan's transfer is going to hold up and you keep your hands off Grant. If they put *me* under probe they'll hear plenty—about the project. I don't think you want outsiders questioning anyone in Reseune right now."

"Damned dangerous, young man." Ari leaned forward and jabbed a finger in his direction. "*Did* Jordan map this out?"

"No."

"Advise you?"

"No."

"That amazes me. It's going to amaze other people too. If this goes to court, the Bureau isn't going to believe he didn't put you up to this. And *that's* going to weigh against him when it comes to a vote, isn't it? So we'll keep it quiet. You can tell Jordan as much as you want to tell him; and we'll call it stalemate. I won't touch Grant; I won't have the Krugers arrested. Not even assassinated. And yes, I can. I could arrange an accident for you. Or Jordan. Farm machinery—is so dangerous."

He was shocked. And frightened. He had never expected her to be so blunt.

"I want you to think about something," she said. "What you tell your father will either keep things under control—or blow everything. I'm perfectly willing to see Jordan get that Fargone post. And I'll tell you exactly what deal I'll strike to unwind this pretty mess you've built for us. Jordan can leave Reseune for Fargone just as soon as there's an office there for him to work in. And when he ships out from Cyteen Station, you'll still be here. You'll arrange for Grant to follow him as soon as the Hope corridor is open and the Rubin project is well underway. You can take the ship after his. And all of that should keep your father—and you—quiet long enough to serve everything I need. The military won't let Jordan be too noisy—They hate media attention to their projects. —Or, *or*, we can just blow all of this wide right now and let us fight it out in court. I wonder who'd win, if we just decided to pull Rubin back to Cyteen and give up the Fargone facility entirely."

I've fallen into a trap, he thought. *But how could I have avoided it? What did I do wrong?*

"Do you agree?" she asked.

"Yes. So long as you keep your end of it. And I get *my* transfer back to my father's wing."

"Oh, no, that's *not* part of it. You stay here. What's more, you and I are going to have an ongoing understanding. You know—your father's a very proud man. You know what it would do to him, to have to choose whether to go to the Bureau and lose everything over what you've done, or keep his mouth shut and *know* what you're involved in to keep that assignment for him. Because that's what you've done. You've handed me all the personal and legal missiles I need—if I have to use them. I've got a way to keep your father quiet, an easy way, as it happens, that doesn't involve him getting hurt. And all you've got to do is keep quiet, do your work, and wait it out. You've got exactly the position you bargained for—hostage for his release; and his good behavior. So what I want you to do, young man, is go put in an honest day's work, give me the BRX reports by the time your shift's over, and let me see a good job. You do what you like: call your father, tell him Grant's gone missing, tell him as much as you like. I certainly can't stop you. And you come to my Residency, oh, about 2100, and you tell me what you've done. Or I'll assume it's gone the other way."

He was still thinking when she finished, still running through all of it, and what she meant; but he knew that. He tried to find all the traps in it. The one he was in, he had no trouble seeing. It was the invitation he had dreaded. It was where everything had been going.

"You can go," she said.

He walked out past Florian in the outer lab, out into the hall, out through the security doors and upstairs into the ordinary hallways of Wing One operations. Someone passed him on the way to his office and said good morning to him; he realized it half the hall further on, and did not even know who it had been.

He did not know how he was going to face Jordan. By phone, he thought. He would break the news by phone and meet his father for lunch. And get through it somehow. Jordan would expect him to be distraught.

Ari was right. If Jordan got involved in it, everything that was settled became unsettled, and for all that he could figure, Jordan had no hand to play.

At best, he thought—go along with it till he could get control of himself enough to think whether telling Jordan the whole story was the thing to do.

Whatever the time cost.

vi

"What we did . . ." Justin turned the stem of his wine-glass, a focus to look at, anything but Jordan's face. "What we did was what we always planned to do, if one of us got cornered. Her taking Grant—was to pressure me. I know—I know you told me I should come to you. But she sprang that on us, and there wasn't time to do anything but file a protest with the Bureau. That'd have been too late for Grant. God knows what she might have put him through before we could get any kind of injunction, if we could get one at all—" He shrugged. "And we couldn't win it, in the long run, the law's on her side and it would foul everything up just after everything was settled on the Fargone deal, so I just—just took the only chance I thought would work. My best judgment. That's all I can say."

It was a private lunch, in the kitchen in Jordan's apartment. Paul did the serving, simple sandwiches, and neither of them did more than pick at the food.

"Damn," Jordan said. He had said very little up to that point, had let Justin get it out in order. "Damn, you should have told me what was going on. I *told* you—"

"I couldn't get to you. It'd make everything I did look like it was your doing. I didn't want to lay a trail."

"Did you? Did you lay one?"

"Pretty plain where I'm concerned, I'm afraid. But that's part of the deal. That's why I stayed here. Ari's got something on me. She's got me to use against you, the way she planned to use Grant against me. Now she doesn't need him, does she?"

"You're damn right she doesn't need him! My God, son—"

"It's not that bad." He kept his voice ever so steady. "I called her bluff. I stayed around. She said— She said that this is the way it's going to work: you get your transfer as soon as the facility is built, earnest of her good faith. Then I get Grant to go out there to you, earnest of mine. That way—"

"That way you're left here where she can do anything she damn well pleases!"

"That way," he reprised, calmly, carefully, "she knows that she can hold on to me and keep you quiet until her projects are too far advanced to stop. And the military won't let you go public. That's what she's after. She's got it. But there's a limit to what she can do—and this way all of us get out. Eventually."

Jordan said nothing, for a long, long while, then lifted his wine glass and took a drink and set it down.

And still said nothing, for minutes upon minutes.

"I should never, never have kept Grant," Jordan said finally, "when things blew up with Ari. I knew it would happen. Damn, I knew it would, all those years ago. Don't ever, *ever* take favors from your enemies."

"It was too late then, wasn't it?" Justin said. The bluntness shocked his nerves, brought him close to tears, an anger without focus. "God, what could we do?"

"Are you sure he's all right?"

"I haven't dared try to find out. I think Ari would have told me if she knew anything different. I set everything up. If the number I gave him doesn't answer, Krugers will keep him safe till it does."

"Merild's number?"

Justin nodded.

"God." Jordan raked his hair back and looked at him in despair. "Son, Merild's no match for the police."

"You always said—if anything happened— And you always said he was a friend of the Krugers. And Ari's not going to call the police. Or try anything herself. She said that. I've got all the ends of this. I really think I have."

"Then you're a damn sight more confident than you ought to be," Jordan snapped. "Grant's somewhere we're not sure, Krugers could have the police on their doorstep—Merild may or may not be available, for God's sake, he practices all over the continent."

"*Well, I couldn't damn well phone ahead, could I?*"

Jordan's face was red. He took another drink of wine, and the level in the glass measurably diminished.

"Merild's a lawyer. He's got ethics to worry about."

"He's also got friends. Hasn't he? A lot of friends."

"He's not going to like this."

"It's the same as me coming to him, isn't it?" He was suddenly on the defensive, fighting on the retreat. "Grant's no different. Merild knows that, doesn't he? Where's ethics, if it turns Grant over to the police?"

"You'd have been a hell of a lot easier to answer for. If you'd had the sense to go *with* him, for God's sake—"

"He's not ours! He belongs to the labs! My being with him couldn't make it legal."

"You're also a minor under the law and there're extenuating circumstances—you'd have been *out* of here—"

"And they'd bring it to court and God knows what they could find for charges. Isn't that so?"

Jordan let go a long breath and looked up from under his brows.

He wanted, he desperately wanted Jordan to say no, that's wrong, there is something— Then everything became possible.

But: "yes," Jordan said in a low voice, dashing his hopes.

"So it's fixed," Justin said. "Isn't it? And you don't have to do anything unless the deal comes unfixed. I can tell you if I'm getting trouble from Ari. Can't I?"

"Like this time?" Jordan returned.

"Better than this time. I promise you. I promise. All right?"

Jordan picked at his sandwich, sidestepping the question. It was not all right. Justin knew that. But it was what there was.

"You're not going to end up staying here when I transfer," Jordan said. "I'll work something out."

"Just don't give anything away."

"I'm not giving a damned thing away. Ari's not through. You'd better understand that. She doesn't keep her agreements longer than she has to. Grant's proof of that. She's damned well capable of cutting throats, hear me, son, and you'd better take that into account the next time you want to bluff. She doesn't think any more of you or me or anyone than the subjects in her labs, than the poor nine-year-old azi down there in the yards that she decides to mindwipe and ship off to some damn sweathouse because he's just not going to work out; because she needs the space, for God's sake! Or the problem cases she won't solve, she won't even run them past my staff—she's not going to use that geneset again anyway and she damned well put three healthy azi down last month, just declared them hazards, because she didn't want to take the time with them, the experiment they were in is over, and that's all she needed. I can't prove it because I didn't get the data, but I know it happened. That's who you're playing games with. She doesn't give a damn for any life, God help her lab subjects, and she's gotten beyond what public opinion might make of it—that's what she's gotten to, she's so smart they can't figure out her notes, she's answerable only to Union law, and she's got that in her pocket— she just doesn't give a damn, and we're all under her microscope—" Jordan shoved his plate away and stared at it a moment before he looked up. "Son, *don't* trust there's anything she won't do. There isn't."

He listened. He listened very hard. And heard Ari saying that accidents at Reseune were easy.

vii

His watch showed 2030 when he exited the shower and picked it up to put it on . . . in an apartment entirely too quiet and depressingly empty.

He was halfway glad not to spend the night here, with the silence and Grant's empty room, glad the way biting one's lip did something to make a smashed finger hurt less, that was about the way of it. Losing Grant hurt worse than anything else could, and Ari's harassment, he reckoned, even became a kind of anodyne to the other, sharper misery she had put him to.

Damned bitch, he thought, and his eyes stung, which was a humiliation he refused to give way to on her account. It was Grant had him unhinged, it was the whole damned mess Grant was in that had his hands shaking so badly he had trouble with the aerosol cap and popped it a ricocheting course around the mirrored sink alcove. It infuriated him. Everything conspired to irritate him out of all reason, and he set the bottle down with measured control and shaved the scant amount he had to.

Like preparing a corpse for the funeral, he thought. Everyone in Reseune had a say in his future, everyone had a mortgage on him, even his father, who had not asked his son whether he wanted to grow up with a PR on his name and know every line he was to get before he was forty, not, thank God, a bad sort of face, but not an original, either, —a face carrying all sorts of significances with his father's friends—and enemies; and Ari cornering him that first time in the lab storage room—

He had not known what to do, then; he had wished a thousand times since he had grabbed hold of her and given her what she was evidently not expecting out of a seventeen-year-old kid with a woman more than twice old enough to be his grandmother. But being seventeen, and shocked and not having thought through what his choices were before this, he had frozen and stammered something idiotic about having to go, he had a meeting he had to make, had she got the report he had turned in on a project whose number he could not even remember—

His face burned whenever he thought about it. He had gotten out that door so fast he had forgotten his clipboard and the reports and had to rewrite them rather than go back after them. He headed toward this appointment of Ari's, this damnable, no-way-out-of-it meeting, with a carefully nurtured feeling that he might, maybe, get something of his self-respect back if he played it right now.

She was old, but she was not quite beyond her rejuv. She looked—maybe late forties; and he had seen holos of her at twelve and sixteen, a face not yet settled into the hard handsomeness it had now. As women six times his age went, she was still worth looking at, what she had was the same as Julia Carnath's in the dark, he told himself with a carefully held cynicism—and better than Julia, at least Ari was up front with what she was after. Everybody in Reseune slept with everybody else reasonable at some time or another, it was not totally out of line that Ari Emory wanted to renew her youth with a replicate of a man who would have been three times too young for her when *he* was seventeen. The situation might have deserved a real laugh, if things were not so grim, and he were not the seventeen-year-old in question.

It was not sure he could do a damned thing, but, he told himself, she might at least be an experience: his was limited to Julia, who had ended up asking him for Grant—which had hurt so badly he had never gone back to her. Which was about the sum of his love affairs, and he had almost decided Jordan was right in his misogyny. Ari was a snake, she was everything reprehensible, but the key to the whole thing, he thought, was his own attitude. If he used it, if he handled it as if it were what Jordan called one of his damnfool stunts, then Ari had no weapon to use. That was the best way to take care of the problem, and that was what he had made up his mind to do—be a man, go along with the whole mess, learn from it (God *knew* a woman Ari's age had something to teach him . . . in several senses)—let Ari do what she wanted, play her little games, and either lose interest or not.

He reckoned he could take a page from Ari's notebook—that a seventeen-year-old wasn't going to be besotted with a woman her age—but a woman her age might have a real emotional need for a handsome, good-humored CIT bedmate. Let her get hooked.

Let *her* have the problem, and him have the solution.

Age and vanity might be the way to deal with her, the weakness no one else could find, because no one else was the seventeen-year-old boy she wanted.

viii

His watch showed 2105 when he walked up to the door and rang the bell of Ari's apartment—the five because he meant to make Ari wonder if he was going to show or if instead he and Jordan were going to come up with something; and no more than five because he was afraid if Ari thought that, then Ari might initiate some action even she might not be able to stop.

It was Catlin who opened the door, on an apartment he had never seen—mostly buff travertine and white furniture, very expensive, the sort of appointments Ari could afford and the rest of them only saw in places like the Hall of State, on newscasts: and blond, braid-crowned Catlin immaculate in her black uniform, very formal—but then, Catlin always was. "Good evening," Catlin said to him, one of the few times he had ever had a pleasant word from her.

"Good evening," he said, as Catlin let the door close. There was a drift of music, barely intruding on the ears . . . electronic flute, cold as the stone halls through which it moved. He felt a shiver in his bones. He had eaten nothing but that handful of salted chips at lunch and a piece of dry toast at suppertime, thinking that if there were anything in his stomach he would throw up. Now he felt weak in the knees and light-headed and regretted that mistake.

"Sera doesn't entertain in this end of the apartments," Catlin said, leading him through to another hall. "It's only for appearances. Mind your step, ser, these rugs are treacherous on the stone. I keep telling sera. —Have you heard from Grant at all?"

"No." His stomach tightened at the sudden, mildly delivered flank attack. "I don't expect to."

"I'm glad he's safe," Catlin said confidentially, as she might have said how nice the weather was, that same silky voice, so he had no idea whether Catlin was ever glad of anything or ever cared for anyone. She was cold and beautiful as the music, as the hall she led him through; and her opposite number met them at the end of the hall, in a large sunken den, paneled in glazed woolwood, all gray-blue and fabric-like under a sheen of plastic, carpeted in long white shag furnished with gray-green chairs and a large beige couch. Florian came from the hall beyond, likewise in uniform, dark and slight to Catlin's athletic fairness. He laid a companionable hand on Justin's shoulder. "Tell sera her guest is here," he said to Catlin. "Would you like a drink, ser?"

"Yes," he said. "Vodka and *pechi*, if you've got it." *Pechi* was an import, extravagant enough; and he was still in shock from the richness Ari managed inside Reseune. He looked around him at Downer statuary in the far corner beyond the bar, wide-eyed ritual images; at steel-sculpture and at a few paintings about the woolwood walls, God, he had seen in tapes as classics from the sublight ships. Stuck in this place, where only Ari and her guests saw them.

It was a monument to self-indulgence.

And he thought of the nine-year-old azi his father had mentioned.

Florian brought him the drink. "Do sit down," Florian said, but he walked the raised gallery about the rim of the room looking at the paintings, one after the other, sipping at a drink he had only had once in his life, and trying to calm his nerves.

He heard a step behind him, turned as Ari walked up on him, Ari in a geometric-print robe lapped at the waist, that glittered with the lights, decidedly no fit attire to meet business company. He stared at her, his heart hammering away in him in the panicked realization that Ari was very real, that he was in a situation he did not know the limits of, and there was no way out from here.

"Enjoying my collection?" She indicated the painting he had been looking at. "That's my uncle's. Quite an artist."

"He was good." He was off his stride for a moment. Least of all did he expect Ari to start off with reminiscences.

"He was good at a lot of things. You never knew him? Of course not. He died in '45."

"Before I was born."

"Damn, it's hard to keep up with things." She slipped her arm into his and guided him toward the next painting. "That one's a real prize. Fausberg. A naive artist, but a first view of Alpha Cent. Where no human goes now. I love that piece."

"That's something." He stared at it with a strange feeling of time and antiquity, realizing it was real, from the hand of someone who had been there, to a star humankind had lost.

"There was a time no one knew what that was worth," she said. "I did. There were a lot of primitive artists on the first ships. Sublight space gave them a lot of time to create. Fausberg worked in chart-pens and acrylics, and damn, they had to invent whole new preservation techniques up on station— *I* insisted. My uncle bought the lot, I wanted them preserved, and that's why the *Argo* paintings got saved at all. Most of them are in the museum at Novgorod. Now Sol Station wants one of the Fausberg *61 Cygni*'s really, really bad. And we may agree—for something of equal value. I have a certain Corot in mind."

"Who's Corot?"

"God, child. Trees. Green trees. Have you seen the Terran tapes?"

"A lot of them." He forgot his anxiety for a moment, recollecting a profusion of landscapes stranger than native Cyteen.

"Well, Corot painted landscapes. Among other things. I should lend you some of my tapes. I should put them on tonight— Catlin, have you got that *Origins of Human Art* series?"

"I'm sure we do, sera. I'll key it up."

"Among others. —That, young friend, is one of our own. Shevchenki. We have him on file. He died, poor fellow, of lifesupport failure, when they were setting up Pytho, up on the coast. But he really did remarkable work."

Red cliffs and the blue of woolwood. That was too familiar to interest him. *He* could do that, he thought privately. But he was too polite to say it. He sketched. He even painted, or had, when he was fresh from the inspiration of the explorer-painters. Ground-bound, he imagined stars and alien worlds. And had never in his life expected to get clear of Reseune.

Until it looked like Jordan might.

Florian came up and offered Ari a drink, a bright golden concoction in a cut-crystal glass. "Orange and vodka," she said. "Have you ever tasted orange?"

"Synthetic," he said. Everyone had.

"No, real. Here. Have a sip."

He took a little from the offered glass. It was strange, a complicated, sour-sweet-bitter taste under the alcohol. A taste of old Earth, if she was serious, and no one who had these paintings on her walls could be otherwise.

"It's nice," he said.

"Nice. It's marvelous. AG is going to make a try with the trees. We think we have a site for them—no messing about with genetics: we think the Zones can accommodate them just the way they are. It's a bright orange fruit. Just like the name. Full of good things. Go on. Take it. Florian, do me another, will you?" She locked her arm tighter, steered him toward the steps and down, toward the couch. "What did you tell Jordan?"

"Just that Grant was out of the way and everything was all right." He sat down, took a large swallow of the drink, then set it down on the brass counter behind the couch, having gotten control of his nerves as much as he figured was likely in this place, in present company. "I didn't tell him anything else. I figure it's my business."

"Is it?" Ari settled close to him, at which his stomach tightened and felt utterly queasy. She laid her hand on his leg and leaned against him, and all he could think of was the azi Jordan had talked about, the ones she had put down for no reason at all, the poor damned azi not even knowing they were dying— just some order to report for a medical. "Sit a little closer, dear. That's all right. It's just pleasant, isn't it? You really shouldn't tense up like that, all nervous." She slipped her arm about his ribs and rubbed his back. "There, relax. That feels good, doesn't it? Turn around and let me do something for those shoulders."

It was like when she had trapped him in the lab. He tried to think what to answer to something that outrageous and failed, completely. He picked up the drink and took a heavy swallow and another and did not do what she asked. Neither did her hand stop its slow movement.

"You're so tight. Look, it's a simple little bargain. And you don't have to be here. All you have to do is walk out the door."

"Sure. Why don't we just go into the bedroom, dammit?" His hands were close to shaking. The chill of the ice went right through his fingers to the bone. He finished the drink without looking at her.

I could kill her, he thought, not angrily. *Just as a solution to the insoluble. Before Florian and Catlin could stop me. I could just break her neck. What could they do then?*

Psychprobe me and find out everything she did? That'd fix her.

It might be the way. It might be the way to get out of this.

"Florian, he's out of orange juice. Get him another. —Come on, sweet. Relax. You really can't do anything like that, you know better and I know better. You want to try it yourself? Is that the problem?"

"I want the drink," he muttered. Everything seemed unreal, nightmarish. In a moment she was going to start talking to him the way she had in the interviews, and that was all part of it, a sordid, dirty business he did not know how to get through, but he wanted to be very drunk, very, very drunk, so that possibly he would get sick, turn out incapable, and she would just give up on this.

"You said you never had experimented around," Ari said. "Just the tapes. Is that the truth?"

He did not answer. He only twisted round on the couch to see how long it was going to take Florian to get him the drink, to have any distraction that might turn this in some other direction.

"Do you think you're normal?" Ari asked. He did not answer that either. He watched Florian's back as Florian poured and mixed the drink. He felt Ari's hands on his back, felt the cushion give as she shifted against him, as her hand came around his side.

Florian handed him the drink, and he leaned there with his elbow on the back of the couch sipping the orange drink and feeling the slow, light movement of Ari's hands on his back.

"Let me tell you something," Ari said softly, behind him. "You remember what I told you about family relationships? That they're a liability? I'm going to do you a real favor. Ask me what that is."

"What?" he asked because he had to.

Her arms came around him, and he took a drink, trying to ignore the nausea she made in his gut.

"You think tenderness ought to have something to do with this," Ari said. "Wrong. Tenderness hasn't got a thing to do with it. Sex is what you do for yourself, for your own reasons, sweet, just because it feels good. That's all. Now sometimes you get real close to somebody and you want to do it back and forth, that's fine, and maybe you trust them, but you shouldn't. You really shouldn't. The first thing you have to learn is that you can get it anywhere. The second thing—it ties you to people who aren't family and it mucks up your judgment unless you remember the first rule. That's how I'm going to do you a favor, sweet. You're not going to confuse what we're doing here. Does that feel good?"

It was hard to breathe. It was hard to think. His heart was hammering and her hands did quiet, disturbing things that made his skin all too sensitive, the edge of pleasure—or intense discomfort. He was no longer sure which. He drank a large gulp of the orange and vodka and tried to put his mind anywhere else, anywhere at all, in a kind of fog in which he was less and less in control of himself.

"How are you doing, dear?"

Not well, he thought, and thought that he was drunk. But at the edge of his senses he felt a dislocation, a difficulty in spatial relationships—like the feeling that Ari was a thousand miles away, her voice coming from behind him and not straight back, but aside in a strange and asymmetrical way—

It was a cataphoric. Tapestudy drug. Panic raced through his brain, chaotic, stimuli coming in on him too fast, while the body seemed to lag in an atmosphere gone to syrup. Not a high dosage. He could see. He could still feel Ari tug his shirt up, run her hands over his bare skin, even while his sense of balance deserted him and he felt his head spinning, the whole room going around. He lost the glass and felt the chill of ice and liquid spreading against his hip and under his buttocks.

"Oh, dear. Florian. Get that."

He was sinking. He was still aware. He tried to move, but confusion set in, a roaring muddle of sound and sensation. He tried to doubt. That was the hardest thing. He was quite aware that Florian had rescued the glass and that his head was back in Ari's lap, in the hollow of her crossed legs, that he was gazing up into Ari's face upside down and that she was unfastening his shirt.

She was not the only one unfastening his clothing. He heard a murmur of voices, but none of them involved him. "Justin," a voice said, and Ari turned his head between her hands. "You can blink when you need to," she whispered, the way the tapes would. "Are you comfortable?"

He did not know. He was terrified and ashamed, and in a long nightmare he felt touches go over him, felt himself lifted up and dragged off whatever he was lying on and down onto the floor.

It was Catlin and Florian who hovered over him. It was Catlin and Florian who touched him and moved him and did things to him that he was aware of in a kind of vague nowhere way, which were wrong, wrong and terrible.

Stop this, he thought. *Stop this. I don't agree with this.*

I don't want this.

But there was pleasure. There was an explosion in his senses, somewhere infinite, somewhere dark.

Help me.

I don't want this.

He was half conscious when Ari said to him: "You're awake, aren't you?

Do you understand now? There's nothing more than this. That's as good as it gets. There's nothing more than this, no matter who it's with. Just biological reactions. That's the first and the second rule. . . ."

"Watch the screen."

Tape was running. It was erotic. It blurred into what was happening to him. It felt good and he did not want it to, but he was not responsible for it, he was not responsible for anything and it was not his fault. . . .

"I think he's coming out of it. . . ."

"Just give him a little more. He'll do fine."

"There's nothing can do to you what tape can do. Can it, boy? No matter who it is. Biological reactions. Whatever does it for you. . . ."

"Don't move. . . ."

"Pain and pleasure, sweet, are so thin a line. You can cross it a dozen times a minute, and the pain becomes the pleasure. I can show you. You'll remember what I can do for you, sweet, and nothing will ever be like it. You'll think about that, you'll think about it for the rest of your life . . . and nothing will ever be the same. . . ."

He opened his eyes and found a shadow over him, himself naked, in a bed he did not know, a hand patting his shoulder, moving to brush hair from his brow. "Well, well, awake," Ari said. It was her weight that pushed down the edge of the mattress, Ari sitting there dressed and he—

His heart jumped and started hammering.

"I'm off to the office, sweet. You can sleep in, if you like. Florian will serve you breakfast."

"I'm going home," he said, and dragged the sheet over him.

"Whatever you like." Ariane got up, releasing the mattress, and walked across to take a look in the wall mirror, demonstrative unconcern that crawled over his nerves and unsettled his stomach. "Come in when you like. —Talk to Jordan if you like."

"What am I supposed to do?"

"Whatever you like."

"Am I supposed to *stay* here?" Panic sharpened his voice. He knew the danger in Ari hearing it, acting on it, working on it. It was a threat she had just made. He thought that it was. Her tone was blank, void of cues. Her voice tweaked at nerves and made him forget for a handful of seconds that he had a counter-threat in Grant, upriver. "It won't work."

"Won't it?" Ari gave her hair a pat. She was elegant, in a beige suit. She turned and smiled at him. "Come in when you like. You can go home tonight. Maybe we'll do it again, who knows? Maybe you can tell your father and get him to pass it off, hmmn? Tell him whatever you like. Of course I had a recorder on. There's plenty of evidence if he wants to go to the Bureau."

He felt cold through and through. He tried not to show it. He glared at her, jaw set, as she smiled and walked out the door. And for a long while he lay there cold as ice, sick to his stomach, darts of headache going from the top of his skull through to the nape of his neck. His skin felt hypersensitized, sore in places. There were bruises on his arm, the marks of fingers.

—Florian—

A flash came back to him, sensation and image from out of the dark, and he plunged his face into his hands and tried to shove it out. Tape-flash. Deep-tape. More and more of them would come back. He did not know *what* could come back. And they would, bits of memory floating up to the surface and showing a moment, a drift of words and feeling and vision, before they rolled over and sank again into the dark, nothing complete—just more and more of them. He could not stop it.

He threw the sheets back and got out of bed, unfocusing his eyes where it came to his own body. He staggered into the bathroom, turned on the shower and bathed, soaped himself again and again and again, scrubbed without looking at himself, trying not to feel anything, remember anything, wonder anything. He scrubbed his face and hair and even the inside of his mouth with the perfumed soap, because he did not know if there was anything else to use; and spat and spat and gagged from the sharp, soapy taste, but it did not make him clean. It was a scent he remembered as hers. Now *he* smelled like it, and tasted it in the back of his throat.

And when he had chafed himself dry in the shower-cabinet blower and he had come out into the cold air of the bathroom, Florian walked in with a folded stack of his clothes.

"There's coffee, ser, if you like."

Bland as if nothing had happened. As if none of it were real. "Where's a shaver?" he asked.

"The counter, ser." Florian motioned toward the mirrored end of the bath. "Toothbrush, comb, lotion. Is there anything you need?"

"No." He kept his voice even. He thought of going home. He thought of killing himself. Of knives in the kitchen. Of pills in the bathroom cabinet. But the investigation afterward would open everything up to politics, and politics would swallow his father up. In the same moment he thought of subliminals that might have been buried in his mind last night, urges to suicide, God knew what. Any irrational thought was suspect. He could not trust them. A series of tape-flashes ripped past him, sensations, erotic visions, landscapes and ancient artworks. . . .

Then real things, set in the future. Images of Jordan's outrage. Himself, dead, on the floor of his kitchen. He rebuilt the image and tried to make it something exotic: himself, just walking out beyond the precip towers, a body to be found like a scrap of white rag by air-search a few hours later . . . "Sorry, ser, looks like we've found him—"

But that was not a valid test of any suspected subliminal Ari might have put into his tape. When a mind drank in tapestudy, it incorporated it. Tape images faded and resident memory wove itself into the implant-structure and grew and grew in its own way. There was no reliable way to detect an embedded command; but it could not make him act when he was conscious, unless it accurately triggered some predisposition. Only when drugs had the threshold flat, then he would take in stimuli without censoring, answer what he was asked, do whatever he was told—

Anything he was asked, anything he was told, if it slipped past the sub-conscious barriers of his value-sets and his natural blocks. A psychsurgeon could, given time, get answers that revealed the sets and their configurations, then just insert an argument or two that confounded the internal logic: rear-range the set after that, create a new microstructure and link it where the surgeon chose—

All those questions, those questions in the damned psych-tests Ari had given him, calling them routine for Wing One aides . . . questions about his work, his beliefs, his sexual experiences . . . that he, being a fool, had thought were simply Ari's way of tormenting him . . .

He dressed without looking at the mirrors. He shaved and brushed his teeth and combed his hair. There was nothing wrong with his face, no mark on it, nothing to betray what had happened. It was the same ordinary face. Jordan's face.

She must have gotten a real satisfaction out of that.

He smiled at himself, testing whether he could control himself. He could. He had that back, as long as he was not facing Ari herself. Her azi he could handle.

Correction. *Florian* he could handle. He thanked God it was Florian she had left with him and not Catlin, and then a wild flutter of mental panic wanted to know why he reacted that way, why the thought of dealing with Catlin-the-icicle sent a disorganizing quiver through his nerves. Fear of women?

Are you afraid of women, sweet? You know your father is.

He combed his hair. He wanted to throw up. He smiled instead, a re-testing of his control, and carefully wiped the tension of the headache from the small muscles around his eyes, relaxed the tension from his shoulders. He walked out and gave that smile to Florian.

He'll report to her. I can't think with my head splitting. Damn, just let him tell her I was all right, that's all I have to do, keep my face on straight and get out of here.

The sitting room, the white rug, the paintings on the walls, brought back a flash of memory, of pain and erotic sensation.

But everything had happened to him. It was a kind of armor. There was nothing left to be afraid of. He took the cup from Florian and sipped at it, stopping the tremor of his hand, a shiver which hit of a sudden as internal chill and a cold draft from the air-conditioning coincided. "Cold," he said. "I think it's the hangover."

"I'm really sorry," Florian said, and met his eyes with an azi's calm, anx-ious honesty: at least it seemed to be and probably it was very real. There was not a shred of morality involved, of course, except an azi's, which was to avoid rows with citizens who might find ways to retaliate. Florian had real cause to worry in his case.

—Florian, last night: *I don't want to hurt you. Relax. Relax—*

The face had nothing to do with the mind. The face kept smiling. "Thanks."

Far, far easier to torment Florian. If it was Ari, he would fall apart. He had, last night. Seeing Florian afraid . . .

. . . pain and pleasure. Interfaces . . .

He smiled and sipped his coffee and enjoyed what he was doing with a bitter, ugly pleasure even while he was scared of what he was doing, meddling with one of Ari's azi; and twice scared of the fact that he enjoyed it. It was, he told himself, only a human impulse, revenge for his humiliation. He would have thought the same thing, done the same thing, the day before.

Only he would not have known why he enjoyed it, or even *that* he enjoyed it. He would not have thought of a dozen ways to make Florian sweat, or considered with pleasure the fact that, if he could maneuver Florian into some situation, say, down at the AG pens, far away from the House, on terms that did not involve protecting Ari, he could pay Florian in kind—Florian being azi, and vulnerable in a dozen ways he could think of . . . without Ari around.

Florian undoubtedly knew it. And because Florian was Ari's, Ari probably fed off Florian's discomfiture in leaving Florian alone with him. It fitted with everything else.

"I feel sorry for you," Justin said, and put his hand on Florian's shoulder, squeezed hard. On the edge of pain. "You don't have a real comfortable spot here, do you? You *like* her?"

—The first thing you have to learn is that you can get it anywhere. The second thing—it ties you to people who aren't family and it mucks up your judgment unless you remember the first rule. That's how I'm going to do you a favor, sweet. You're not going to confuse what we're doing here. . . .

Florian only stared at him, not moving. Even though the grip on his shoulder undoubtedly hurt, and even though Florian could break it with a shrug. And maybe his arm, into the bargain. That stoic patience was, Justin thought, what one could expect, in this place, of Ari's azi.

"What does Ari really want me to do?" Justin asked. "Have you got it figured out? Am I supposed to stay here? Am I supposed to go home?"

As if he and Florian were the same thing. Co-conspirators, azi both. He loathed the thought. But Florian was, in a way, his ally, a page he could read and a subject he could handle; and he still could not read the truth in Ari's eyes, not even when she was answering his questions in all sobriety.

"She expects you to go home, ser."

"Do I get other invitations?"

"I think so," Florian said in a quiet, quiet voice.

"Tonight?"

"I don't know," Florian said. And added: "Sera will probably sleep tonight."

As if it were all a long-familiar sequence of events.

A queasiness went through his stomach. They were all caught in this.

Attitude, Jordan would say. Everything is attitude. You can do anything if you're in control of it. You have to know what your profit is in doing it, that's all.

Life was not enough, to trade a soul for. But power . . . power to stop it happening, power to pay it back, that was worth the trade. His father's safety was. The hope someday of being in a position to do something about Ariane Emory—that was.

"I'm going to go home," he said to Florian, "take something for my headache, get my messages, and go on to the office. I don't suppose my father's called my apartment."

"I wouldn't know, ser."

"I thought you kept up with things like that," he said, soft and sharp as a paper-cut. He set down the coffee cup, remembering where the outside door was, and headed off through the halls, with Florian trailing him like an anxious shadow . . . Ari's guard, too polite to show it, and much too worried to let him walk that course through Ari's apartments unwatched.

For half a heartbeat he thought ahead to the safety of his own rooms upstairs and expected Grant would be there to confide in, the two of them would think things out—it was the habit of a lifetime, a stupid kind of reflex, that suddenly wrenched at a stomach ravaged by too little food, too much drink, too many drugs, too much shock. He went light-headed and grayed out, kept walking all the same, remembering the way from here, that it was a straight course down a hall decorated with fragile tables and more fragile pottery.

A triple archway, then, of square travertine pillars. And the reception room, the one Catlin had said was for show. He remembered the warning about the rugs and the floor, negotiated the travertine steps and crossed the room, up the slight rise to the door.

He reached to the door-lock to let himself out, except Florian interposed his hand and pushed the latch himself. "Be careful, ser," Florian said. And meant more, he was sure, than the walk home.

He remembered the nine-year-old. And the azi Ariane had killed. Remembered the vulnerability any azi had, even Grant. And saw Florian's—who had never had a chance since the day he was created and who was, excepting his dark side, gentle and honest as a saint, because he was made that way and tapes kept him that way despite all else Ari made him be.

It was that enigma that dogged him out the door and down the hall, in a confusion of graying vision and weakness, all part of the nightmare that crowded on his senses—tape-flash and physical exhaustion.

Ari had shaped Florian—in both his aspects, with all his capacities—the dark and the light. She might not have made him in the first place, but she maintained him according to the original design . . . from her own youth.

To have a victim? he wondered. Was that all it was?

Test subject—for an ongoing project?

Interface, the answer came rolling up to the surface and dived down again, nightmarish as a drowned body. *Crossing of the line.*

Truth lies at the interface of extremes.

Opposites are mutually necessary.

Pleasure and pain, sweet.

Everything oscillates . . . or there's nothing. Everything can be in another state, or it can't change at all. Ships move on that principle. The stars burn. Species evolve.

He reached the lift. He got himself inside and leaned against the wall until the door opened. He walked into a reeling hall, kept his balance as far as his own apartment and managed the key.

"No entries since the last use of this key."

Can't depend on that, he thought, in gray-out, in a sudden weakness that made the couch seem very far away, and nothing safe. *Can't depend on anything. She can get into anything, even the security systems. Probably bugged the place while I was out. She'd do a thing like that. And you can't know if the Minder can catch the kind of things she can lay hands on. State of the art. Expensive stuff. Classified stuff. She could get it.*

Maybe Jordan can.

He reached the couch and sat down, lay back and shut his eyes.

What if I'm not alone?

Ari's voice, soft and hateful:

I planned your father's actions. Every one of them. Even if I couldn't predict the microstructures. Microstructures aren't that important.

Tape-designer's aphorism: macrostructure determines microstructure. The value-framework governs everything.

I even planned you, sweet. I planted the idea. Jordan has this terrible need for companionship. Am I lying? You owe your existence to me.

He imagined for a heartbeat that Grant would walk in from the other room, Grant would ask what was the matter, Grant would help him unweave the maze in which he found himself. Grant had experienced deep-tape. God knew.

But it was only a ghost. A habit hard to break.

And Grant, certainly, I planned. I made him, after all.

He had to go to the lab. He had to get out of the isolation in which the tape-structures could fester and spread before he could deal with them. He had to get about routine, occupy his mind, let his mind rest and sort things out slowly.

If the body could only have a little sleep.

"Messages, please," he murmured, remembering he had to know, *had* to know if he had calls from Jordan. Or elsewhere.

They were generally trivia. Advisories from the wing. From Administration. A note of reprimand about the illicit entry. He drifted in the middle of it, woke with a start and a clutch at the couch, the erotic flush fading into a lightning-flash clinical recollection that he was going to have to wear long sleeves and high collars and put some Fade on the bruises: he could put Jordan off with a claim that Ari had him on extra lab duty, logical, since Ari had no reason, in what he had told Jordan, to be pleased with him. He could *not* face Jordan at close quarters until he had better control of himself.

In the next heartbeat as the Minder's half-heard report clicked off, he realized that he had lost track of the playback, and that two days ago he had defaulted the Minder's message-function to play-and-erase.

ix

Grant could see the plane long before they reached the strip—not the sleek elegance of RESEUNEAIR by any stretch of the imagination, just a cargo plane with shielded windows. The car pulled up where people were waiting. "There," the driver said, virtually the only word he had spoken the entire trip, and indicated the people he was supposed to go to.

"Thank you," Grant murmured absently, and opened his own door and got out, taking his lunchbag with him, walking with pounding heart up to total strangers.

Not all strangers, thank God, Hensen Kruger himself was there to do the talking. "This is Grant. Grant, these people will take you from here." Kruger stuck out his hand and he was supposed to shake it, which he was not used to people doing: it made him feel awkward. Everything did. One of the men introduced himself as Winfield; introduced the woman in the group, the pilot, he supposed, in coveralls and without any kind of badge or company name, as Kenney; and there were two other men, Rentz and Jeffrey, last name or first or azi-name, he was not sure. "Let's get going," Kenney said. Everything about her was nervous: the shift of her glance, the stiffness of her movements as she wiped her hands on her grease-smeared coveralls. "Come on, let's move it, huh?"

The men exchanged looks that sent little twitches through Grant's taut nerves. He looked from one to the other, trying to figure whether he was the object of contention. Arguing with strangers was difficult for him: Justin always fended problems for him. He knew his place in the world, which was to handle what his employer wanted handled. And Justin had told him to object.

"We're going to Merild?" he asked, because he had not heard that name, and he was determined to hear it before he went anywhere.

"We're going to Merild," Winfield said. "Come on, up you go. —Hensen—"

"No problem. I'll contact you later. All right?"

Grant hesitated, looking at Kruger, understanding that things were passing he did not understand. But he knew, he thought, as much as they were going to tell him; and he went ahead to the steps of the jet.

It had no company markings, just a serial number. A7998. White plane, with paint missing here and there and the spatter of red mud on its underside. Dangerous, he thought. Don't they foam it down here? Where's Decon? He climbed up into the barren interior, past the cockpit, and uncertainly looked back at Jeffrey and Rentz, who followed him, a little ahead of Winfield.

The door whined up and Winfield locked it. There were jump-seats of a kind, along the wall. Jeffrey took him by the arm, pulled a seat down and helped him belt in. "Just stay there," Jeffrey said.

He did, heart thumping as the plane took its roll and glided into the sky. He was not used to flying. He twisted about and lifted a windowshade to look out. It was the only light. He saw the precip towers and the cliffs and the docks passing under them as they came about.

"Leave that down," Winfield said.

"Sorry," he said; and drew the shade down again. It annoyed him: he very much wanted the view. But they were not people to argue with, he sensed that in the tone. He opened the bag the Krugers had fixed for him, examined what he had for breakfast, and then thought it was rude to eat when no one else had anything. He folded it closed again until he saw one of them, Rentz, get up and go aft and come back with a few canned drinks. Rentz offered one to him, the first kind gesture he had had out of them.

"Thank you," he said, "they sent one."

He thought it would be all right to eat, then. He had been so exhausted last night he had only picked at supper, and the salt fish and bread and soft drink Krugers had sent were welcome, even if he had rather have had coffee.

The jet roared away and the men drank their soft drinks and took occasional looks out under the shades, mostly on the right side of the aircraft. Sometimes the pilot talked to them, a kind of sputter from the intercom. Grant finished his fish and bread and his drink and heard that they had reached seven thousand meters; then ten.

"Ser," someone had said that morning, opening the door to his room in Kruger's House, and Grant had waked in alarm, confused by his surroundings, the stranger who had to be speaking to him, calling *him* ser. He had hardly slept; and finally drowsed, to wake muddled and not sure what time it was or whether something had gone wrong.

They had taken his card last night, when the night watch had brought him up from the dock and the warehouses, into the House itself, up the hill. Hensen Kruger himself had looked it over and gone somewhere with it, to test its validity, Grant had thought; and he had been terrified: that card was his identity. If anything happened to it, it would take tissue-typing to prove who he was after that, even if there *was* only one of him, which he had never, despite Jordan's assurances, been convinced was the case.

But the card had turned up with the stack of clothing and towels the man laid on the chair by the door. The man told him to shower, that a plane had landed and a car was coming for him.

Grant had hurried, then, rolled out of bed, still dazed and blurry-eyed, and staggered his way to the bathroom, rubbed his face with cold water and looked in the mirror, at eyes that wanted sleep and auburn hair standing up in spikes.

God. He wanted desperately to make a good impression, look sane and sensible and not, not what Reseune might well report to them—an Alpha gone schiz and possibly dangerous.

He could end up back in Reseune if they thought that. They would not even bother with the police; and Ari might have tried some such move. Justin would have answered to Ari by now—however he was going to do it Grant had no idea. He tried not to think about it, as he had tried to send the thoughts away all night long, lying there listening to the sounds of a strange House—doors opening and closing, heaters and pumps going on, cars coming and going in the dark.

He had showered in haste, dressed in the clothes they had laid out for him, a shirt that fit, trousers a bit too large or cut wrong or something—given his hair a careful combing and a second check in the mirror, then headed downstairs.

"Good morning," one of the household had said to him, a young man. "Breakfast on the table there. They're on their way. Just grab it and come on."

He was terrified for no specific cause, except he was being rushed, except that his life had been carefully ordered and he had always known who would hurt him and who would help him. Now, when Justin had told him he would be free and safe, he had no idea how to defend himself, except to do everything they told him. Azi-like. Yes, ser.

He dropped his head onto his chest while the plane droned on, and shut his eyes finally, exhausted and having nothing to look at but the barren deck, closed windows, and the sullen men who flew with him: perhaps, he thought, if he simply said nothing to them the trip would be easier, and he would wake up in Novgorod, to meet Merild, who would take care of him.

He waked when he felt the plane change pitch and heard a difference in the engines. And panicked, because he knew it was supposed to be three hours to Novgorod, and he was sure it had not been. "Are we landing?" he asked. "Is something wrong?"

"Everything's fine," Winfield said; and: "Leave that alone!" when he reached for the shade, thinking it could surely make no difference. But evidently it did.

The plane wallowed its way down, touched pavement, braked and bumped and rolled its way, he reckoned, toward the Novgorod terminal. It stopped and everyone got up, while the door unsealed and the hydraulics began to let the ladder down; he got up, taking the wadded-up paper bag with him—he was determined not to give them a chance to complain of his manners—and waited as Winfield took his arm.

There were no large buildings outside. Just cliffs and a deserted-looking cluster of hangars; and the air smelled raw and dry. A bus was moving up to the foot of the ladder.

"Where are we?" he asked, on the edge of panic. "Is this Merild's place?"

"It's all right. Come on."

He froze a moment. He could refuse to go. He could fight. And then there was nothing he could do, because he had no idea where he was or how to fly a plane if he could take it over. The bus down there—he might use to escape; but he had no idea where in the world he was, and if he ran beyond the fuel capacity in raw outback, he was dead, that was all. Outback was all around them: he could see the land beyond the buildings.

He could hope to get to a phone, if they got the idea he was compliant enough to turn their backs on. He had memorized Merild's number. He thought of all that in the second between seeing where he was and feeling Winfield take his arm.

"Yes, ser," he said meekly, and walked down the steps where they wanted him to go—which still might be to Merild. He still hoped that they were telling the truth. But he no longer believed it.

Winfield took him down to the waiting bus and opened the door to put him in, then got in after, with Jeffrey and Rentz. There were seven seats, one set by each window and across the back; Grant took the first and Winfield sat beside him as the other pair settled in behind them.

He scanned the windows and doors: elaborately airsealed. An outback vehicle.

He clasped his hands in his lap and sat quietly watching as the driver started up and the bus whipped away across the pavement, not for the buildings: for a line road, probably the one they used to get to the precip towers. In a little time they were traveling on dirt, and in a little time more they were climbing, up from the lowland and onto the heights beyond the safety the towers maintained.

Wild land.

Perhaps he was going to die, after they had stripped his mind down for what he knew. They might be Ari's; but it was a very strange way for Reseune to handle its problems, when they could easily bring him back to Reseune without Jordan or Justin knowing, just land like one of the regular transport flights and send him off in the bus to one of the outlying buildings where they could do whatever they liked till they were ready (if ever) to admit they had him.

They might, more likely, be Ari's enemies, in which case they might do almost anything, and in that case they might not want him to survive to testify.

Whatever had happened, Kruger was involved in it, beyond a doubt, and it could even be monetary . . . perhaps everything rumor had said about Kruger's humanitarian concerns was a lie. Reseune was full of lies. Perhaps it was something Ari herself maintained. Perhaps Kruger had just fooled everyone, perhaps he was engaged in a little side business, in forged Contracts whenever he got a likely prospect. Maybe he was being sold off to some mining site in the hinterlands, or, God, some place where they could try to retrain him. *Try.* Anyone who started meddling with his tape-structures on a certain level, he could handle. On others . . .

He was not so sure.

There were four of them, counting the driver, and such men might well have guns. The bus seals were life itself.

He clasped his hands together and tried desperately to think the thing through. A phone was the best hope. Maybe stealing the bus once they trusted him, once he knew where civilization was and whether the bus had the fuel to get there. It could take days to get a chance. Weeks.

"I think you know by now," Winfield said finally, "this isn't where you're supposed to be."

"Yes, ser."

"We're friends. You should believe that."

"Whose friends?"

Winfield put his hand on his arm. "Your friends."

"Yes, ser." Agree to anything. Be perfectly compliant. Yes, ser. Whatever you want, ser.

"Are you upset?"

Like a damned field supervisor, talking to some Mu-class worker. The man *thought* he knew what he was doing. That was good news and bad . . . depending what this fool thought he was qualified to do with tape and drugs. Winfield had mismanaged him thus far. He did not give way to instincts simply because he reckoned that they did not profit him in this situation, and because there was far more profit in keeping his head down . . . reckoning that his handlers were not stupid, but simply too ignorant to realize that the Alpha-rating on his card meant he could not have the kind of inhibitions born-men were used to in azi. They should have drugged him and transported him under restraint.

He was certainly not about to tell them so.

"Yes, ser," he said, with the breathless anxiousness of a Theta.

Winfield patted his arm. "It's all right. You're a free man. You will be."

He blinked. That took no acting. 'Free man' added a few more dimensions to the equation; and he did not like any of them.

"We're going up in the hills a ways. A safe place. You'll be perfectly all right. We'll give you a new card. We'll teach you how to get along in the city."

Teach you. Retraining. God, what am I into?

Is there any way this could be what Justin intended?

He was afraid, suddenly, in ways that none of the rest of this had touched . . . that he did *not* have it figured, that defying these people might foul up something Justin had arranged—

—or Jordan, finding out about it, intervening—

They *might* be what the only friends he had in the world had intended for him, they *might* be heading him for real freedom. But retraining, if that was what they had in mind, would reach into all his psychsets and disturb them. He did not have much in the world. He did not own anything, even his own person and the thoughts that ran in his brain. His loyalties were azi-loyalties, he knew that, and accepted that, and did not mind that he had had no choice in them: they were real, and they were all he was.

These people talked about freedom. And teaching. And maybe the Warricks wanted that to happen to him and he had to accept it, even if it took everything away from him and left him some cold *freedom* where home had been. Because the Warricks could not afford to have him near them anymore, because loving him was too dangerous for all of them. Life seemed over-whelmed with paradoxes.

God, now he did not know, he did not know who had him or what he was supposed to do.

Ask them to use the phone, get a message to Merild to ask whether this was all right?

But if they were not with Merild that would tip them off that he was not the compliant type they took him for. And if they were the other thing, if this was not the Warricks' doing, then they would see he had no chance at all.

So he watched the landscape pass the windows and endured Winfield's hand on his arm, with his heart beating so hard it hurt.

---------------------------------- X ----------------------------------

It was surreal, the way the day fell into its accustomed order, an inertia in the affairs of Reseune that refused to be shaken, no matter what had happened, no matter that his body was sore and the damnedest innocent things brought on tape-flashes that hour by hour assumed a more and more mundane and placid level of existence—of *course* that was what it felt like, of course people from the dawn of time had done sex with mixed partners, paid sex for safety, it was the world, that was all, and he was no kid to be devastated by it—it was more the hangover that had him fogged, and now he was on the other side of an experience he had rather not have had, he was still alive, Grant was downriver safe, Jordan was all right; and he had damned well better figure Ari Emory had more than that in mind—

Shake the kid up, play games with his mind, go on till he cracked.

You wanted Grant free, boy, you can substitute, can't you?

—leave the apartment, report to the office, smile at familiar people and hear the business go on about him that had gone on yesterday, that went on every day in Wing One—Jane Strassen cursing her aides and creating a furor because of some glitch-up in equipment repair; Yanni Schwartz trying to mol-lify her, a dull murmur of argument down the hall. Justin kept to his key-board and immersed himself in a routine, in a problem in tape-structure Ari had set him a week ago, complex enough to keep the mind busy hunting link-ages.

He was careful. There were things the AI checker might not catch. There were higher-level designers between his efforts and an azi test-subject, and there were trap-programs designed to catch accidental linkages in a particular psychset but it was no generic teaching-tape: it was deep-tape, specifically one that a psychsurgeon might use to fit certain of the KU-89 subsets for limited managerial functions.

A mistake that got by the master-designers could be expensive—could cause grief for the KU-89s and the azi they might manage; could cause termi-nations, if it went truly awry—it was every designer's nightmare, installing a glitch that would run quietly amok in a living intellect for weeks and years, till it synthesized a crazier and crazier logic-set and surfaced on some completely illogical trigger.

There was a book making the rounds, a science fiction thriller called *Error Message*, that had Giraud Nye upset: a not too well disguised Reseune marketed an entertainment tape with a worm in it, and civilization came apart. There was a copy in library, on CIT-only check-out, with a long waiting list; and he and Grant had both read it—of course. Like most every House azi except Nye's, it was a good bet.

And he and Grant had tried designing a worm, just to see where it would go. —"Hey," Grant had said, sitting on the floor at his feet, starting to draw logic-flows, "we've got an Alpha-set we can use, hell with the Rho-sets."

It had scared him. It had gone unfunny right there. "Don't even think about it," he had said, because if there was such a thing as a worm and they designed one that would work, *thinking* about it could be dangerous; and it was Grant's own set Grant meant. Grant had his own manual.

Grant had laughed, with that wicked, under the brows grin he had when he had tagged his CIT good.

"I don't think we ought to do this," Justin had said, and grabbed the notebook. "I don't think we ought to mess around with it."

"Hey, there isn't any such thing."

"I don't want to find out." It was hard to be the Authority for the moment, to pull CIT-rank on Grant and treat him like that. It hurt. It made him feel like hell. Suddenly and glumly sober, Grant had crumpled up his design-start, and the disappointment in Grant's eyes had gone right to his gut.

Till Grant had come into his room that night and waked him out of a sound sleep, saying he had thought of a worm, and it worked—whereupon Grant had laughed like a lunatic, pounced on him in the dark and scared hell out of him.

"Lights!" he had yelled at the Minder, and Grant had fallen on the floor laughing.

Which was the way Grant was, too damned resilient to let anything come between them. And damned well knowing what he deserved for his pretensions to godhood.

He sat motionless at the keyboard, staring at nothing, with a dull ache inside that was purely selfish. Grant was all right. Absolutely all right.

The intercom blipped. He summoned up the fortitude to deal with it and punched the console button. "Yes," he said, expecting Ari or Ari's office.

"Justin." It was his father's voice. "I want to talk to you. My office. Now."

He did not dare ask a question. "I'm coming," he said, shut down and went, immediately.

He was back an hour later, in the same chair, staring at a lifeless screen for a long while before he finally summoned the self-control to key the project-restore.

The comp brought the program up and found his place. He was a thousand miles away, halfway numb, the way he had made himself when Jordan told him he had gotten a call through to Merild and Merild had given a puzzled negative to a coded query.

Merild had gotten no message. Merild had gotten nothing at all that he would have recognized as the subject of Jordan's inquiry. Total zero.

Maybe it was too soon. Maybe there was some reason Krugers had held Grant there and not called Merild yet. Maybe they were afraid of Reseune. Or the police.

Maybe Grant had never gotten there.

He had been in shock as Jordan had sat down on the arm of the office chair and put his arm about him and told him not to give up yet. But there was nothing they could do. Neither of them and no one they knew could start a search, and Jordan could not involve Merild by giving him the details over the House phone. He had called Krugers and flatly asked if a shipment got through. Krugers avowed it had gone out on schedule. Someone was lying.

"I thought we could trust Merild," was all he had been able to say.

"I don't know what's going on," Jordan had said. "I didn't want to tell you. But if Ari knows something about this she's going to spring it on you. I figured I'd better let you know."

He had not broken down at all—until he had gotten up, had said he had to get back to his office, and Jordan hugged him and held him. Then he had fallen apart. But it was only what a boy would do, who had just been told his brother might be dead.

Or in Ari's hands.

He had gotten his eyes dry, his face composed. He had walked back through the security checkpoint and into Ari's wing, back past the continuing upset in Jane Strassen's staff, people trying to get a shipment out on the plane that was going after supplies, because Jane was so damned tight she refused to move with anything but a full load.

He sat now staring at the problem in front of him, sick at his stomach and hating Ari, *hating* her, more than he had ever conceived of hating anyone, even while he did not know where Grant was, or whether he himself had killed him, sending him out in that boat.

And he could not tell Jordan the full extent of what was going on. He could not tell Jordan a damned thing, without triggering all the traps set for him.

He killed the power again, walked out and down the hall to Ari's office, ignoring the to-do in the hall. He walked in and faced Florian, who had the reception desk. "I've got to talk to her," he said. "Now."

Florian lifted a brow, looked doubtful, and then called through.

"How are we?" Ari asked him; and he was shaking so badly, standing in front of Ari's desk, that he could hardly talk.

"Where's Grant?"

Ari blinked. One fast, perhaps-honest reaction. "Where's Grant? —Sit down. Let's go through this in order."

He sat down in the leather chair at the corner of her desk and clenched his hands on its arms. "Grant's gone missing. Where is he?"

Ari took in a long slow breath. Either she had prepared her act or she was not troubling to mask at all. "He got as far as Krugers. A plane came in this morning and he might have left on it. Two barges left this morning and he could have been on those."

"*Where is he, dammit? Where have you got him?*"

"Boy, I do appreciate your distress, but get a grip on it. You won't get a thing out of me by shouting, and I'd really be surprised if the hysteria is an act. So let's talk about this quietly, shall we?"

"*Please.*"

"Oh, dear boy, that's just awfully stupid. You know I'm not your friend."

"Where is he?"

"Calm down. I don't have him. Of course I've had him tracked. Where *ought* he to be?"

He said nothing. He sat there trying to get his composure back, seeing the pit in front of him.

"I can't help you at all if you won't give me anything to work on."

"You can damn well help me if you want to. You know damn well where he is!"

"Dear, you really can go to hell. Or you can answer my questions and I promise you I'll do everything I can to extricate him from whatever he's gotten into. I won't have Krugers arrested. I won't have your friend in Novgorod picked up. I don't suppose Jordan's phone call a while ago had anything to do with your leaving your office and coming in here. You two really aren't doing well this week."

He sat and stared at her a long, long moment. "What do you want?"

"The truth, as it happens. Let me tell you where I think he was supposed to go and you just confirm it. A nod of the head will do. From here to Krugers. From Krugers to a man named Merild, a friend of Corain's."

He clenched his hands the tighter on the chair. And nodded.

"All right. Possibly he was on his way on the barges. It was supposed to be air, though, wasn't it?"

"I don't know."

"Is that the truth?"

"It's the truth."

"Possibly he just hasn't left yet. But I don't like the rest of the pattern. Corain isn't the only political friend Kruger's got. Does the name de Forte mean anything to you?"

He shook his head, bewildered.

"Rocher?"

"Abolitionists?" His heart skipped a beat, hope and misery tangled up together. Rocher was a lunatic.

"You've got it, sweet. That plane this morning landed over at Big Blue, and a bus met it and headed off on the Bertille-Sanguey road. I've got people moving on it, but it takes a little organizing even for me to get people in there that can get Grant out without them cutting his throat— They *will*, boy. The Abolitionists aren't all in it for pure and holy reasons, and if they've played a hand that blows Kruger, you can damn well bet they aren't doing it for the sake of one azi, are you hearing me, boy?''

He heard. He thought he understood. But he had not done well in this, Ari had said it; and he wanted it from her. "What do you think they're after?"

"Your father. And Councillor Corain. Grant's a Reseune azi. He's a Warrick azi, damn near as good as getting their hands on Paul; and de Forte's after Corain's head, boy, because Corain sold out to *me*, Corain made a deal on the Fargone project and on the Hope project, your father's the center of it, and damned if you didn't go and throw Grant right into Kruger's lap."

"You're after him to haul him back."

"I want him back. *I want him away from Rocher*, you damned little idiot, and if you want him alive, you'd better start telling me any secrets you've got left. You *didn't* know about the Rocher connection, did you, didn't know a thing about Kruger's radical friends—"

"I didn't. I don't. I—"

"Let me tell you what they'll do to him. They'll get him out someplace, fill him full of drugs and interrogate him. Maybe they'll bother to give him tape while they're at it. They'll try to find out what he knows about the Rubin project and the Hope project and anything else he knows. They'll *try* to subvert him, God knows. But that isn't necessarily what they're after. I'll tell you what I think has happened. I think Kruger's being blackmailed by this lot, I think they had a man in his organization, and I think when they knew what you'd dropped in his lap, Merild never got a word of it: Rocher did, and Rocher's picked him up. Probably they have him sedated. When he does come around, what's he going to think? That these are friends of yours? That everything that's happening to him is your doing?''

"For God's sake—"

"It *is*, you know. Calm down and think this through. We can't go breaking in shooting Rocher's people if we aren't damned sure he's with them. We're getting a Locator into position. We missed a shot at the Bertille airport; we're not sure we're going to get any fix on them at Big Blue. We'll try. In the meanwhile we aren't a hundred percent sure he's not still at Kruger's. Now, I can get a warrant for a search there. But I'm going to take another tack. I can damn well guess how they're blackmailing Kruger: I can bet a lot of his azi contracts are real suspect; and I can arrange an audit. I've got a plane on its way over there. In the meanwhile Giraud is going to fly over to Corain at Gagaringrad and talk to him. *You're* going to explain this to Jordan, and tell Jordan I'd really appreciate it if he'd get onto this and get Merild on Kruger's case."

"We get him out," he said, "and he goes to Merild. Merild won't blow anything."

"Sweet," Ari said, "you know me better than that. We get him out and he comes right back to Reseune. He'll have been in their hands better than forty-eight hours, best we can do, if it isn't longer than that. We'll have to have him in for a check, —won't we? They could have done him all sorts of nastiness. And you wouldn't want to leave him to nurse that kind of damage all on his own, now, would you?"

"You want this blown wide open—"

"Sweet, *you* don't want it blown wide open. *You* don't want your father involved. He's going to be well aware when we pull Grant back here. If we can get him back alive. He's going to be well aware we have Grant in hospital, —isn't he? And he's going to be worried. I'll trust you keep your bargain with me, sweet."

He said nothing, finding no argument, no weapon left.

"That's supposing," she said, "that he's salvageable. It may take years of treatment—if I can straighten him out. Of course, we have to get him away alive. That's first."

"You're threatening me."

"Sweet, I can't predict what Rocher will do. Or where shots may go. I'm only warning you—"

"I told you I'd do what you want!"

"For your father's sake. Yes. I'm sure you will. And we'll talk about Grant after I've got him." She flipped the cover on the intercom and punched a button. "Jordan? Ari here."

"What is it?" Jordan's voice came back.

"I've got your son in my office. Seems we've both noticed a little problem. Would you mind calling your contact in Novgorod again and telling him he really needs to get Kruger to give me a call. . . ."

_____ **xi** _____

There was break-time, finally, in the dingy little precip station where they had pulled in an underground garage and a concrete stairs and this place, that was mostly crumbling concrete. There were only three rooms to it, excluding the bath and the kitchen. It had no windows, because windows were a liability in a place like this, just a kind of a periscope rig that would give a 360° scan of the area; but Grant had no access to it. He sat and answered questions, most of the time truthfully, often enough not, which was the only defense he could muster. There was not a phone in the place. There was a radio. He had no idea in the world how to work it, except having seen Jordan use one on the boat years ago.

He was still not sure what they were. Or whose they were. He just mumbled answers to Winfield's questions and complained, complained about the lack of coffee, complained about the uncomfortable accommodations, complained about everything, figuring to push them as far as he could, make them mad if he could, and get them to react. He played a slow relaxation, a gathering confidence in his safety, flowered into the worst bitch House-azi he could script—he built off Abban, as it happened, Giraud Nye's insufferable staffer, who was a prime pain to the janitorial and the kitchen staff, not mentioning any azi he thought he outranked.

There was a tape-machine in the bedroom. He did not like the look of that. It was not an unexpected thing to find in an out-of-the-way place: entertainment would be high among priorities for a line-keeper stationed out here, wherever *here* was. But it was not a little entertainment rig; it was new equipment, it looked like it had monitor plugs, and he was nervous about it. He figured to push them to the point where any reasonable CIT would lose his temper and see what sort they were.

"Sit down," Rentz said when he got up to follow Winfield to the kitchen.

"I thought I could help, ser. I—"

He heard a car. The others heard it too, and all at once Rentz and Jeffrey were on their feet, Winfield coming back from the kitchen, Winfield very quick to take a look with the periscope.

"Looks like Krahler."

"Who's—" Grant asked.

"Just sit down." Rentz put a hand on Grant's shoulder and shoved him into the chair, held him there while the sound of the car grew louder. The garage door went up without anyone in the room doing anything.

"That's Krahler," Winfield said. The lessening of tension was palpable, all around the room.

The car drove in, the noise vibrating through the wall that divided them from the underground garage, the garage door went down, the Decon spray hissed for a moment, then, car doors opened and slammed, and someone came up the steps.

"Who's Krahler, ser?"

"A friend," Winfield said. "Jeffrey, take him on into the bedroom."

"Ser, *where* is Merild? Why hasn't he come? Is—"

Jeffrey hauled him out of the chair and headed him for the bedroom, pushing him at the bed. "Lie down," Jeffrey said, in a tone that encouraged no argument.

"Ser, I want to know where Merild is, I want to know—"

Rentz had followed him. It was the best set he was likely to have. He whirled and took out Jeffrey with his elbow, Rentz with his other hand, and rushed the other room, where Winfield had realized his danger—

Winfield pulled a gun from his pocket, and Grant dodged. But Winfield did not panic as he might. Winfield had a steady hand and an unmissable shot; and Grant froze where he was, against the doorframe, while the door from the garage opened and a trio of men came in, two of them fast and armed.

One of the men behind him was getting up. Grant stood very still, until someone grabbed him from behind. He could have broken the man's arm. He did not. He let the man pull him back, while Winfield followed up and kept the gun on him.

"This the way it's been going here?" one of the newcomers asked.

Winfield did not laugh. "Lie down," he said to Grant, and Grant backed up to the bed and sat down. *"Down!"*

He did what Winfield wanted. Jeffrey got cord from his pocket and tied his right wrist to the bedframe, while Rentz was moaning on the floor and the several armed men stood there with their guns aimed in Grant's direction.

The other wrist, then, at an uncomfortable stretch. Grant looked at the men who had come in, two of them large, strong men; and one older, slight, the only one without a gun. It was his look Grant distrusted. It was this man that the others deferred to.

Krahler, the others had called him. More names he did not know, names that had nothing to do with Merild.

They put away the guns. They helped Rentz up. Jeffrey stayed while all the others left, and Grant stared at the ceiling, trying not to think how unprotected his gut was at the moment.

Jeffrey just pulled the drawer open under the tape machine and took out a hypospray. He put it against Grant's arm and triggered it.

Grant winced at the kick and shut his eyes, because he would not remember to do that in a few moments and he did not trust them to remind him. He gathered up the defenses he had in his psychset and thought mostly of Justin, not wasting time with the physical attack that had gone wrong: the next level of this was a fight of a very different sort. He had no more doubts. The guns had proved it. What they were about to do proved it. And he was, azi that he was, a Reseune apprentice, in Ariane Emory's wing: Ariane Emory had created him, Ari and Jordan had done his psychsets, and damned if somebody he had never heard of could crack them.

He was slipping. He felt the dissociation start. He knew that the Man was back and they were starting the tape. He was going far, far under. Heavy dose. Deep-tape with a vengeance. He had expected that.

They asked his name. They asked other things. They told him they owned his Contract. He was able to remember otherwise.

He waked finally. They let him loose to drink and relieve himself; they insisted he eat, even if it nauseated him. They gave him a little respite.

After that they did it all again, and the time blurred. There might have been more such wakings. Misery made them all one thing. His arms and back ached when he came to. He answered questions. Mostly he did not know where he was, or remember clearly why he had deserved this.

Then he heard a thumping sound. He saw blood spatter across the walls of the room. He smelled something burning.

He thought that he had died then, and men came and wrapped him in a blanket, while the burning-smell grew worse and worse.

Up and down went crazy for a while. And tilted, and the air had a heartbeat.

"He's waking up," someone said. "Give him another one."

He saw a man in blue coveralls. Saw the Infinite Man emblem of Reseune staff.

Then he was not sure of anything he had surmised. Then he was not sure where the tape had started or what was real.

"Get the damn hypo!" someone yelled in his ear. *"Dammit, hold him down!"*

"Justin!" he screamed, because he believed now he had always been home, and there was the remote chance Justin might hear him, help him, get him out of this. *"Justin—!"*

The hypo hit. He fought, and bodies lay on him until the weight of the drug became too much for him, and the world reeled and turned under him.

He waked in a bed, in a white room, with restraints across him. He was naked under the sheets. There were biosensors on a band about his chest and around his right wrist. The left was bandaged. An alarm beeped. He was doing it. His pulse rate was, a silent scream he tried to slow and hush.

But the door opened. A technician came in. It was Dr. Ivanov.

"It's all right," Dr. Ivanov said, and came and sat down on the side of his bed. "They brought you in this afternoon. It's all right. They blew those bastards to bloody hell."

"Where was I?" he asked, calmly, very calmly. "Where am I now?"

"Hospital. It's all right."

The monitor beeped again, rapidly. He tried to calm his pulse. He was disoriented. He was no longer sure where he had been, or what was real. "Where's Justin, ser?"

"Waiting to see you're coming round. How are you doing? All right?"

"Yes, ser. Please. Can you take this damn stuff off?"

Ivanov smiled and patted his shoulder. "Look, lad, you know and I know you're sane as they come, but for your own good, we're just going to leave that on a while. How's the bladder?"

"I'm all right." It was one more indignity atop the rest. He felt his face go red. "Please. Can I talk to Justin?"

"Not a long talk, I'm afraid. They really don't want you talking to much of anybody till the police have a go at you—it's all right, just formalities. You just answer two questions, they'll make out their reports, that's all there is to it. Then you'll take a few tests. Be back up at the House in no time. Is that all right?"

"Yes, ser." The damned monitor beeped and stopped as he got control of his pulse-rate. "What about Justin? Please."

Ivanov patted his shoulder again and got up and went to the door and opened it.

It was Justin who came in. The monitor fluttered and steadied and went silent again; and Grant looked at him through a shimmering film. Jordan was there too. Both of them. And he was terribly ashamed.

"Are you all right?" Justin asked.

"I'm fine," he said, and lost control of the monitor again, and of his blinking, which spilled tears down his face. "I guess I'm in a lot of trouble."

"No," Justin said, and came and gripped his hand, hard, saying different things with his face. The monitor fluttered and quieted again. "It's all right. It was a damn fool stunt. But you're coming back to the House. Hear?"

"Yes."

Justin bent over and hugged him, restraints and all. And drew back. Jordan came and did the same, held him by the shoulders and said:

"Just answer their questions. All right?"

"Yes, ser," he said. "Can you make them let me go?"

"No," Jordan said. "It's for your safety. All right?" Jordan kissed him on the forehead. He had not done that since he was a small boy. "Get some sleep. Hear? Whatever tape you get, I'll vet. Personally."

"Yes, ser," he said.

And lay there and watched Jordan and Justin go out the door.

The monitor beeped in panic.

He was lost. He had hell to go through before he got out of this place. He had looked at Justin's face past Jordan's shoulder and seen hell enough right there.

Where was I? What really happened to me? Have I ever left this place?

A nurse came in, with a hypo, and there was no way to argue with it. He tried to quiet the monitor, tried to protest.

"Just a sedative," the nurse said, and shot it off against his arm.

Or Jeffrey had. He went reeling backward and forward and saw the blood spatter the white wall, heard people yelling.

xii

"Good enough?" Ari asked Justin, in her office. Alone.

"When can he get out?"

"Oh," Ari said, "I don't know. I really don't know. Like I don't know now about the bargain we worked out—which seems rather moot, right now, doesn't it? What coin have you left to trade in?"

"My silence."

"Sweet, you have a lot to lose if you break that silence. So does Jordan. Isn't that why we're doing all this?"

He was trembling. He tried not to show it. "No, we're doing this because you don't want your precious project blown. Because *you* don't want publicity right now. Because you've got a lot to lose. Otherwise you wouldn't be this patient."

A slow smile spread on Ari's lips. "I like you, boy, I really rather like you. Loyalty's the rarest thing in Reseune. And you have so much of it. What if I gave you Grant, untouched, unaltered? What's he worth to you?"

"It's possible," Justin said, in a measured, careful tone, "you can misjudge how far you can push me."

"What's he worth?"

"You release him. You don't run tape on him."

"Sweet, he's a little confused. He's been through hell. He *needs* rest and treatment."

"I'll see he gets it. Jordan will. I'm telling you; don't push me too far. You don't know what I'd do."

"Oh, sweet, I know what you can do. A lot of it really exquisite. And I don't have to deal with you about Grant at all. I have some very different kind of tapes. Your father would die, he would outright die."

"Maybe you underestimate him."

"Oh? Have you told him? —I thought not. You have to understand the situation, you see. It's not just his son. It's not 'some woman.' You're his twin. It's *me*, Ari Emory. Not mentioning the azi." She chuckled softly. "It's a marvelously good try, it really is. I respect that. I respect it enough to give you a little latitude. Come here, boy. Come here."

She held out her hand. He hesitated in confusion and finally held out his own within her reach. She took it gently, and his nerves jumped, his pulse fluttered and a flush came over his skin, confusing all his thinking.

He did not jerk away. He did not dare. He could not formulate a sarcasm. His mind was darting too fast in a dozen directions, like something small and panicked.

"You want a favor? You want Grant back? I'll tell you what, sweet: you just go on cooperating and we'll just make that our private little deal. If you and I get along till your father goes, if you keep your mouth shut, I'll make him a present to you."

"You're using deep-tape."

"On you? Nothing to really bend your mind. What do you think, that I can take a normal, healthy mind and redesign it? You've been reading too many of those books. The tapes I used with you—are recreational. They're what the Mu-class azi get, when they're really, really good. You think you can't stand them? You think they've corrupted you? Reseune will do worse than that, sweet, and I can teach you. I told you: I *like* you. Someday you'll be a power in Reseune—here, or Fargone, or wherever. You've got the ability. I'd really like to see you survive."

"That's a lie."

"Is it? It doesn't matter." She squeezed his fingers. "I'll see you at my place. Same time. Hear?"

He drew his hand back.

"It's not like I don't give you a choice." She smiled at him. "All you have to do is keep things quiet. That's not much, for as much as you're asking. You make my life tranquil, sweet, and stand between me and Jordan, and I won't have his friends arrested, and I won't do a mindwipe on Grant. I'll even stop giving you hell in the office. You know what the cost is, for all those transfers you want."

"You sign Grant over to me."

"Next week. In case something comes up. You're such a clever lad. You understand me. Make it 2200 this evening. I'm working late."

ATTENTION OPERATOR
BATCH ML-8986: BATCH BY-9806: FINALFINALFINAL

The computers flash completion, appealing for human intervention. The chief technician alerts the appropriate personnel and begins the birth-process.

There are no surprises: the womb-tanks, gently moving and contracting, have all manner of sensors. The two ML-8986s, female, Mu-class, have reached the mandated 4.02 kilo birth-weight. There are no visible abnormalities. The two BY-9806s, Gamma-class, are likewise in good health. The techs know their charges. The BY-9806s, highly active, are favorites, already tagged with names, but the names will not stay with them: the techs will have no prolonged contact with them.

The wombs enter labor-state, and after a space, send their contents sliding down into fluid-cushioned trays and the gloved hands of waiting techs. There are no crises. There is little stress. The Mu-class females are broad-faced, placid, with colorless hair; the two Betas are longer, thin-limbed, with shocks of dark hair, not so handsome as the Mu-classes. They make faces and the techs laugh.

The cords are tied, the afterbirth voided from the bottom of the tray, and clean warm water gives the infants their first baths. The techs weigh them as a formality, and enter the data on a record which began with conception, two hundred ninety-five days ago, and which will have increasingly fewer entries as the infants pass from a state of total moment-by-moment dependency into the first unmonitored moments of their lives.

Azi attendants receive them, wrap them in soft white blankets, to be tenderly handled, held and rocked in azi arms.

In intervals between diaper changes and feeding, they lie in cribs which, like the wombs, gently rock, to the sound of human heartbeat and distant voice, the same voice that spoke to them in the womb, soft and reassuring. Sometimes it sings to them. Sometimes it merely speaks.

Someday it will give them instruction. The voice is tape. As yet it is only subliminal, a focus of confidence. Even at this point it rewards good behavior. One day it will speak with disapproval, but at this stage there are no misbehaviors, only slight restlessness from the Betas. . . .

BATCH AGCULT-789X: EMERGENCYEMERGENCY

AGCULT-789X is in trouble. The experimental geneset is not a success, and after staff consultations, a tech withdraws lifesupport and voids AGCULT-789X for autopsy.

The azi techs swab out the womb, flush it repeatedly, and the chief tech begins the process that will coat it in bioplasm.

It will receive another tenant as soon as the coating is ready. The staff waits results of the autopsy before it attempts the fix.

In the meanwhile the womb receives the male egg AGCULT-894, same species. This is not the first failure. Engineering adaptations is a complex process, and failures are frequent. But AGCULT-894 is a different individual with a similar alteration: there is the chance it will work. If it fails it will still provide valuable comparisons.

Reshaping the land and altering the atmosphere is not enough to claim a world for human occupation. The millions of years of adaptation which interlocked Terran species into complex ecosystems are not an option on Cyteen.

Reseune operates in the place of time and natural selection. Like nature, it loses individuals, but its choices are more rapid and guided by intelligence. Some argue that there are consequences to this, a culling of the ornamental and nonfunctional elements which give Terran life its variety, with an emphasis on certain traits and diminution of others.

But Reseune has lost nothing. It plans deepspace arks, simple tin cans parked around certain stars, vessels without propulsion, inexpensive to produce, storage for genetic material in more than one location, shielded and protected against radiation. They contain actual genetic samples; and digital recording of genesets; and records to enable the reading of those genesets by any intelligence advanced enough to understand the contents of the arks.

A million years was sufficient for humankind to evolve from primitive antecedents to a spacefaring sapient. A million years from now humankind will, thanks to these arks, have genetic records of its own past and the past of every species to which Reseune has access, of our own heritage and the genetic heritages of every lifebearing world we touch, preserved against chance and time. . . .

The arks preserve such fragmentary codes as have been recovered from human specimens thousands of years old, from Terran genepools predating the development of genebanks in the 20th century, from the last pre-mixing genepools of the motherworld, and from remains both animal and human preserved through centuries of natural freezing and other circumstances which have preserved some internal cellular structure.

Imagine the difference such reference would make today, if such arks had preserved the genetic information of the geologic past. Earth, thus far unique in its evidences of cataclysmic extinctions of high lifeforms, might, with such libraries, recover the richness of all its evolutionary lines, and solve the persistent enigmas of its past. . . .

Reseune has never abandoned a genetic option. It has seen to the preservation of those options to a degree unprecedented in the history of the human species, and, working as it does with a view toward evolutionary change, has preserved all the possible divergences. . . .

CHAPTER 3

Time stopped being. There was just the tape-flow, mostly placid, occasionally disturbing. There were intervals of muzzy waking, but the trank continued—until now, that Grant drifted closer to the surface.

"Come on, you've got a visitor," someone said, and a damp cloth touched his face. The washing proceeded downward, gently, neck and chest, with an astringent smell. "Wake up."

He slitted his eyes. He stared at the ceiling while the washing proceeded, and hoped they would let him loose, but it was not much hope. He wished they would give him trank again, because the fear was back, and he had been comfortable while it lasted.

He grew chill with the air moving over damp skin. He wanted the sheet back again. But he did not ask. He had stopped trying to communicate with the people that handled him and they did not hurt him anymore. That was all he asked. He remembered to blink. He saw nothing. He tried not to feel the cold. He felt a twinge when the tech jostled the needle in his arm. His back ached, and it would be the most wonderful relief if they would change the position of the bed.

"There." The sheet settled over him again. A light slap popped against his face, but he felt no pain. "Come on. Eyes open."

"Yes," he murmured. And shut them again the moment the azi tech left him alone.

He heard another voice then, at the door, young and male. He lifted his

96

head and looked and saw Justin there. He distrusted the vision at once, and jerked at the restraints.

But Justin came to him, sat down on the side of his bed and took his hand despite the restraint that gave him only a little movement. It was a warm grip. It felt very real.

"Grant?"

"Please don't do this."

"Grant, for God's sake— Grant, you're home. You understand me?"

It was very dangerous even to think about believing. It meant giving up. There was no secret sign his own mind could not manufacture. There was no illusion tape could not create. Justin was what they would use. Of course.

"Grant?"

Tape could even make him think he was awake. Or that the mattress gave, or that Justin held him by the shoulder. Only the keen pain in his back penetrated the illusion. It was not perfect.

Reality—had such little discordances.

"They won't let me take you back to the apartment yet. Ari won't. What are they doing? Are you all right? Grant?"

Questions. He could not figure how they fitted. There was usually a pattern. These had to do with credibility. That was the game.

"Grant, dammit!" Justin popped his hand against his cheek, gently. "Come on. Eyes open. Eyes open."

He resisted. That was how he knew he was doing better. He drew several breaths and his back and shoulders hurt like hell. He was in terrible danger . . . because he thought that the illusion was real. Or because he had lost the distinction.

"Come on, dammit."

He slitted his eyes cautiously. Saw Justin's face, Justin with a frightened look.

"You're home. In hospital. You understand? Ari blew them all to hell and got you out."

(Blood spattering the walls. The smell of smoke.)

It looked like hospital. It looked like Justin. There was no test that would confirm it, not even if they let him out to walk around. Only time would do that, time that went on longer than any tape-illusion.

"Come on, Grant. Tell me you're all right."

"I'm all right." He drew a breath that hurt his back and realized he could get things out of this illusion. "My back's killing me. My arms hurt. Can you move the bed?"

"I'll get them to take those off."

"I don't think they will. But I'd like the bed moved. There—" The surface under him flexed like a living thing and shifted upward, bringing his head up. The whole surface made a series of waves that flexed muscles and joints. "Oh, that's better."

Justin settled back on the edge, making a difference in the ripples. "Ari tracked you to Kruger's. Kruger was being blackmailed. He handed you over to the Abolitionists. I had to go to Ari. She got somebody—I don't know who—to go in after you. She said they'd been running tape."

He had had no structure for that time. No division between there and here. He examined the gift very carefully. "How long?"

"Two days."

Possible.

"You've been *here* two days," Justin said. "They let Jordan and me in right after they brought you in. Now they say I can visit."

It frightened him. It wanted to move in permanently, an illusion against which his defenses were very limited. He was losing. He sat there and cried, feeling the tears slip down his face.

"Grant."

"All right." He was nearly gone. "But if I tell you to leave, you leave."

"Grant, it's not tape. You're *here*, dammit." Justin squeezed his hand till the bones ground together. "Focus. Look at me. All right?"

He did. "If I tell you to leave—"

"I'll go. All right. Do you want me to?"

"Don't do that to me. For God's sake—"

"I'll get Ivanov. Damn them. Damn them."

Justin was on his way to his feet. Grant clenched his hand, holding on to him. Held on and held tight; and Justin sat down again and hugged him hard.

"Unnnh." It hurt. It felt real. Justin could pull him back. Justin knew what he was doing, knew what was the matter with him, knew why he was afraid. Was his ally. Or he was lost. "It's going to take a while."

"About a week to get you out of here. Ari says."

He remembered crises other than his own. He looked at Justin as Justin sat back. Remembered why he had gone down the river. "She give you trouble?"

"I'm all right."

Lie. More and more real. Tape was better than this. In a while Justin would go away and he would remember believing it and be afraid. But in the meanwhile it made him afraid for a different, more tangible reason. Jordan's transfer; Justin's sending him away—the fragments assumed a time-sense. *When* existed again. The real world had traps in it, traps involved Ari, Justin had tried to get him free, he was home and Justin was in trouble.

No. Careful.

Careful.

"What did she do when she found out I was gone?"

"I'll tell you later."

Dammit, he did not need worry to upset his stomach. It felt like home. Secrets, Ari, and trouble. And everything he loved. He took in a slow, long breath. "I'm holding on," he said, knowing Justin would understand. "I don't want any more tape. I don't want any more sedation. I need to stay awake. I want them to leave the lights on. All the time. I want to get this damn tube out of my arm."

"I haven't got any authority. You know that. But I'll tell Ivanov. I'll make it real strong with him. And I'll take the tube out. Here."

It stung. "That's going to drip all over the floor."

"Hell with it. There." He stopped the drip. "They're going to put a phone in here. And a vid."

His heart jumped. He remembered why a phone was important. But he was not there anymore. Or none of it had happened. Or there were possibilities he had missed.

"You know I'm not really well-hinged."

"Hell, I don't notice a difference."

He laughed, a little laugh, automatic, glad Justin was willing to joke with him; and realized that had come totally around a blind corner. Surprised him, when he had been expecting smooth, professional pity. It was not a funny laugh. Surprise-laugh.

Tape could hardly get Justin down pat enough to do something his mind had not expected, not when he was resisting it and not cooperating out of his subconscious.

He laughed again, just to test it, saw Justin look like he had glass in his gut, and hope at the same time.

"It's a worm," he told Justin. And grinned wide, wider as he saw an instant of real horror on Justin's face.

"You damn lunatic!"

He laughed outright. It hurt, but it felt good. He tried to draw his legs up. Wrong. "Oh, damn. You think they can get my legs free?"

"Soon as you know where you are."

He sighed and felt tension ebbing out of him. He melted back against the moving bed and looked at Justin with a placidity different than tape offered. It still hurt. Muscle tension. Sprain. God knew what he had done to himself, or what they had done to him. "I had you, huh?"

"If you put this on for an act—"

"I wish. I'm fogged. I think I'm going to have flashes off this. I think they'll go away. I'm really scared, if you don't come back. Dr. Ivanov's running this, isn't he?"

"He's taking care of you. You trust him, don't you?"

"Not when he takes Ari's orders. I'm scared. I'm really scared. I wish you could stay here."

"I'll stay here through supper. I'll come back for breakfast in the morning; every hour I can get free till they throw me out. I'm going to talk to Ivanov. Why don't you try to sleep while I'm here? I'll sit in the chair over there and you can rest."

His eyes were trying to close. He realized it suddenly and tried to fight it. "You won't leave. You have to wake me up."

"I'll let you sleep half an hour. It's nearly suppertime. You're going to eat something. Hear? No more of this refusing food."

"Mmnn." He let his eyes shut. He went away awhile, away from the discomfort. He felt Justin get up, heard him settle into the chair, checked after a moment to be sure Justin really was there and rested awhile more.

He felt clearer than he had been. He even felt safe, from moment to moment. He had known, if the world was halfway worth living in, that Justin or Jordan would get to him and pull him back to it. Somehow. When it came he had to believe it or he would never believe anything again, and never come back from the trip he had gone on.

---

ii

The reports came in and Giraud Nye gnawed his stylus and stared at the monitor with stomach-churning tension.

The news-services reported the kidnapping of a Reseune azi by radical elements, reported a joint police–Reseune Security raid on a remote precip station on the heights above Big Blue, with explicit and ugly interior scenes from the police cameras—the azi, spattered with the blood of his captors, being rescued and bundled aboard a police transport. It had taken something, for sharpshooters in outback gear to hike in, break into the garage via a side door, and make a flying attack up the stairs. One officer wounded. Three radical Abolitionists killed, in full view of the cameras. Good coverage and bodies accounted for, which left no way for Ianni Merino and the Abolition Centrists to raise a howl and convoke Council: publicly, Merino was distancing himself as far and as fast as he could from the incident. Rocher was deluging the Ministry of Information with demands for coverage for a press conference: he got nothing. Which meant that the police would be watching Rocher very carefully—the last time Rocher got blacked out, someone had unfurled a huge Full Abolition banner in the Novgorod subway and sabotaged the rails, snarling traffic in a jam the news-services could not easily ignore.

God knew it had not won Rocher the gratitude of commuters. But he had his sympathizers, and a little display of power meant recruits.

About time, he thought, to do something about Rocher and de Forte. Thus far they had been a convenient embarrassment to Corain and to Merino, discrediting the Centrists. Now Rocher had crossed the line and become a nuisance.

Convenient if the damage to Grant had been extreme. A before-and-after clip given to the news-services would show the Abolitionists up for the hounds they were. Honest citizens never saw a mindwipe in progress. Or botched. Convenient if they could take the azi down for extreme retraining—or take him down altogether. God knew he was Alpha, and a Warrick product, and God knew what Rocher's tapes had done: *he* had rather be safe; he had told Ari as much.

Absolutely not, Ari had said. What are you thinking of? In the first place, he's a lever. In the second, he's a witness against Rocher. Don't touch him.

Lever with whom, Giraud thought sourly. Ari was holding night-sessions with young Justin, and Ari was, between driving Jane Strassen to ulcers over the refitting of Lab One and the relocation of eight research students, so damned wrapped up in her obsession with the Rubin project that nobody got time with her *except* her azi and Justin Warrick.

Got herself a major triste. *Lost youth and all of that.*

Goes off and leaves me to mop up the mess in Novgorod. 'Don't touch Merild or Krugers. We don't want to drive the enemy underground. Cut a deal with Corain. That's not hard, is it?'

The hell.

The phone rang. It was Warrick. Senior. Demanding Grant's release to his custody.

"That's not my decision, Jordie."

"*Dammit, it doesn't seem to be anybody's, does it? I want that boy out of there.*"

"Look, Jordie—"

"*I don't care whose fault it isn't.*"

"Jordie, you're damn lucky no one's prosecuting that kid of yours. It's his damn fault this came down, don't yell at me—"

"*Petros says you're the one has to authorize a release.*"

"That's a medical matter. I don't interfere in medical decisions. If you care about that boy, I'd suggest you let Petros do his job and stay—"

"*He passed the mess to you, Gerry. So did Denys. We're not talking about a damn records problem. We're talking about a scared kid, Gerry.*"

"Another week—"

"*The hell with another week. You can start by giving me a security clearance over there, and get Petros to return my calls.*"

"Your son is over there right now. He's got absolute clearance, God knows why. He'll take care of him."

There was silence on the other end.

"Look, Jordie, they say about another week. Two at most."

"*Justin's got clearance.*"

"He's with him right now. It's all right. I'm telling you it's all right. They've stopped the sedation. Justin's got visiting privileges, I've got it right here on my sheet, all right?"

"*I want him out.*"

"That's real fine. Look, I'll *talk* to Petros. Is that all right? In the meantime your kid's with Grant, probably the best medicine he could get. Give me a few hours. I'll get you the med reports. Will that satisfy you?"

"*I'll be back to you.*"

"Fine, I'll be here."

"*Thanks,*" came the mutter from the other end.

"Sure," Giraud muttered; and when the contact broke: "Damn hothead." He went back to the draft of the points he meant to make with Corain, interrupted himself to key a query to Ivanov's office, quick request for med records on Grant to Jordan Warrick's office. And added, on a second thought, because he did not know what might be *in* those records, or what Ari had ordered: SCP, *security considerations permitting.*

<hr>

iii

The new separator was working. The rest of the equipment was scheduled for checkout. Ari made notes by hand, but mostly because she worked on a system and the Scriber got in her way: in some things only state of the art would do, but when it came to her notes, she still wrote them with a light-pen on the TranSlate, in a shorthand her Base in the House system continually dumped into her archives because it knew her handwriting: old-fashioned program, but it equally well served as a privacy barrier. The Base then went on to translate, transcribe and archive under her passwords and handprint, because she had given it the password at the top of the input.

Nothing today of a real security nature. Lab-work. Student-work. Any of the azi techs could be down here checking things, but she enjoyed this return to the old days. She had helped wear smooth the wooden seats in Lab One, hours and hours over the equipment, doing just this sort of thing, on equipment that made the rejected separator look like a technologist's dream.

That part of it she had no desire to recreate. But quite plainly, she wanted to say *I* in her write-up of this project. She wanted her stamp on it and her hand on the fine details right from the conception upward. *I was most careful, in the initiation of this project—*

I prepared the tank—

There were very few nowadays who *were* trained in all the steps. Everyone specialized. She belonged to the colonial period, to the beginnings of the science. Nowadays there were colleges turning out educated apes, so-named scientists who punched buttons and read tapes without understanding how the biology worked. She fought that push-the-button tendency, put an especially high priority on producing methodology tapes even while Reseune kept its essential secrets.

Some of those secrets would come out in her book. She had intended it that way. It would be a classic work of science—the entire evolution of Reseune's procedures, with the Rubin project hindmost in its proper perspective, as the test of theories developed over the decades of her research. *IN PRINCIPIO* was the title she had tentatively adopted. She was still searching for a better one.

The machine came up with the answer on a known sequence. The comp blinked red on an area of discrepancy.

Damn it to bloody hell. Was it contamination or was it a glitch-up in the machine? She made the note, mercilessly honest. And wondered whether to lose the time to replace the damn thing again and try with a completely different test sample, or whether to try to ferret out the cause and document it for the sake of the record. Doing the former, was a dirty solution. Being reduced to the latter and, God help her, failing to find solid evidence, which was a good bet in a mechanical glitch-up, made her look like a damn fool or forced her to have recourse to the techs more current with the equipment.

Dump the machine *and* consign it to the techs, run the suspect sample in a clean machine, and install a third machine for the project, *with* a new sample-run.

Every real-life project is bound to have its glitch-ups, or the researcher is lying . . .

The outer lab-door opened. There were distant voices. Florian and Catlin. And another one she knew. Damn.

"Jordan?" she yelled, loud enough to carry. "What's your problem?"

She heard the footsteps. She heard Florian's and Catlin's. She had confused the azi, and they trailed Jordan as far as the cold-lab door.

"I need to talk to you."

"Jordie, I've got a problem here. Can we do it in about an hour? My office?"

"Here is just fine. Now. In private."

She drew a long breath. Let it go again. *Grant*, she thought. *Or Merild and Corain*. "All right. Damn, we're going to have Jane and her clutch traipsing through the lab out there in about thirty minutes. —Florian, go over to B and tell them their damn machine won't work." She turned and ejected the sample. "I want another one. We'll go through every damn machine they've got if that's what it takes. I want the thing cleaner than it's providing. God, what kind of tolerances are they accepting these days? And you bring it over yourself. I don't trust those aides. Catlin, get up there and tell Jane she can take her damn students somewhere else. I'm shutting down this lab until I get this thing running." She drew a second long breath and used the waldo to send the offending sample back through cryogenics, then ejected the sample-chamber to a safe-cell and sent it the same route. When she turned around the azi were gone and Jordan was still standing there.

iv

It was a hike from the hospital over to the House itself, a long round-about if the weather made it necessary to go through the halls and the tunnel, a good deal shorter to walk over under open sky. Justin opted for the open air, though the shadows of the cliffs had cut off the sun and he ought to have brought a coat. He got tape-flash. He got it almost everywhere. The sensations got to him most, and his stomach stayed upset— "*You* eat the damn stuff," Grant had challenged him, since hospital staff had brought two dinners. "I'll match you."

He had gotten it down. He was not sure it was going to stay there. It had been worth everything to have Grant able to sit up and laugh—they had let him free to have his supper and Grant had sat cross-legged in bed and managed the dessert with some enthusiasm. Even if the nurses said they were going to have to put the restraints back on when he was alone for the night.

He would not have left for the night at all, and Ivanov would have let him stay; except he had an appointment with Ari, and he could not tell Grant that. Late work at the lab, he had said. But Grant had been a hundred percent better when he had left him than when he had come in, quickly exhausted, but with liveliness in his eyes, the ability to laugh—perhaps a little too much, perhaps a little too forced, but the way the eyes looked said that Grant was back again.

Just when he was leaving the mask had come down, and Grant had looked sober and miserable.

"Back in the morning," Justin had promised.

"Hey, you don't have to, it's a long walk over here."

"I want to, all right?"

And Grant had looked ineffably relieved.

That was the good in the day. It was worth everything he paid for it. He felt for the first time since that day in Ari's office, that there might be a way out of this.

If—if Ari had enough to keep her busy, if—

He thought of Grant and Ari, Grant already on the edge of his sanity—

Grant, who had the looks, the grace that every girl he had ever known had preferred to him—

He waded through tape-flash that diminished only to shameful memory, through a muddle of anguish and exhaustion. He was not going to be worth anything. He wanted to go somewhere and be sick—he could call Ari and plead that he was sick, truly he was, he was not lying, she could ask him the next time he—

O God. But then there was the agreement that let him get to Grant. There was the agreement that promised Grant would be free. She could mindwipe Grant. She could do anything. She had threatened Jordan. Everything was on him, and he could not tell Grant, not in the state Grant was in.

He took in his breath and slogged on down the path that led around the corner toward the main door—a jet was coming in. He heard it. It was ordinary. RESEUNEAIR flew at need, as well as on a weekly schedule. He saw it touch down, walking along by the gravel bed and the adapted shrubbery that led to the front doors. The bus started up from in front of the doors and passed him on its way around the drive and down toward the main road. On its way to pick up someone on the jet, he reckoned, and wondered who in the House had been downriver in all this chaos.

He walked in through the automatic doors, using his keycard in the brass slot, clipped the keycard back to his shirt and headed immediately for the lift that would take him up to his apartment.

Phone Jordan first thing he got in and tell him Grant was better. He wished he had had time to call while he was in the hospital, but Grant had not wanted him out of his sight, and he had not wanted to upset him.

"Justin Warrick."

He turned and looked at the Security guards, putting their presence together with the plane and the bus and instantly thought that some visitor must be coming in.

"Come with us, please."

He indicated the lift buttons. "I'm just going up to my room. I'll be out of here."

"Come with us, please."

"Oh, damn, just use the com, ask your Supervisor— You don't touch me!" As one of them reached for him. But they took him by the arms and leaned him up against the wall. "My God," he said, unnerved and exasperated, as they proceeded to search him thoroughly. It was a mistake. They were azi. They got their instructions upside down and they went damned well too far.

They wrenched his arms back and he felt the chill of metal at his wrists. "Hey!"

The cuffs clicked shut. They faced him about again and walked him down the hall. He balked, and they jerked him into motion, down the hall toward the Security office.

God. Ari had filed charges. On him, on Jordan, Kruger, everyone involved with Grant. That was what had happened. Somewhere she had gotten the leverage she wanted, something to silence them and bring everything down on them; and he had done it, he, thinking he could deal with her.

He walked where they wanted him to go, down the hall and into the office with the glass doors, where the Supervisor sat. "In there," the Supervisor said with a wave of her hand toward the back of the office.

"What in hell's going on?" he demanded, trying bluff in the absence of everything else. "Dammit, *call Ari Emory!*"

But they took him past steel doors, past the security lock, put him in a bare, concrete room, and shut the door.

"*Dammit, you have to read me the charges!*"

There was no answer.

V

The body was quite, quite frozen, fallen right at the vault door, mostly prone, twisted a little. Surfaces in the vault still were frost-coated and painful to the touch. "Patch of ice," the investigator said, and recorded the scene with his camera, posthumous indignity. Ari would have resented that like hell, Giraud thought, and stared at the corpse, still unable to think that Ari was not going to move, that stiff limbs and glazed eyes and half-open mouth were not going to suddenly find life. She was wearing a sweater. Researchers would, who worked in the antiquated cold-lab: nothing heavier. But no cold-suit would have saved her.

"There wouldn't have been any damn patch of ice then," Petros muttered. "No way."

"She work with the door shut?" The investigator from Moreyville, small-town and all the law there was for a thousand miles in all directions, laid his hand on the vault door. It started swinging to at that mere touch. "Damn." He stopped it with a shove, balanced it carefully and gingerly let go of it.

"There's an intercom," Petros said. "That door's swung to on most of us, sooner or later, we all know about it. It's something in the way the building's settled. You get locked in, you just call Security, you call Strassen's office, and somebody comes down and gets you out, it's no big thing."

"It was this time." The investigator—Stern, his name was—reached up and punched the button on the intercom. The casing broke like wax. "Cold. I'll want this piece," he said to his assistant, who was following him with a Scriber. "Does anyone hear?"

There was no sound out of the unit.

"Not working."

"Maybe it's the cold," Giraud said. "There wasn't any call."

"Pressure drop was the first you knew something was wrong."

"Pressure in the liquid nitrogen tank. The techs knew. I got a call a minute or so later."

"Wasn't there an on-site alarm?"

"It sounded," Giraud said, indicating the unit on the wall, "down here. No one works back here. The way the acoustics are, no one could figure out where it was coming from. We didn't know till we got the call from the techs that it was a nitrogen line. Then we knew it was the cold-lab. We came running down here and got the door open."

"Ummn. And the azi weren't here. Just Jordan Warrick. Who was back upstairs when the alarm went off. I want a report on that intercom unit."

"We can do that," Giraud said.

"Better if my office does."

"You're here for official reasons. For the record. This is not your jurisdiction, captain."

Stern looked at him—a heavy-set, dour man with the light of intelligence in his eyes. Intelligence enough to know Reseune swallowed its secrets.

And that, since Reseune had friends high in Internal Affairs, promotion or real trouble could follow a decision.

"I think," Stern said, "I'd better talk to Warrick." It was a cue to retire to private interviews. Giraud's first impulse was to follow him and cover what had to be covered. His second was a genuine panic, a sudden realization of the calamity that had overtaken Reseune, overtaken all their plans, the fact that the brain that had been so active, held so much secret—was no more than a lump of ice. The body was impossible, frozen as it was, to transport with any dignity. Even that simple necessity was a grotesque mess.

And Corain— This is going to hit the news-services before morning.
What in hell do we do? What do we do now?
Ari, dammit, what do we do?

Florian waited, sitting on a bench in the waiting room, in the west wing of the hospital. He leaned his elbows against his knees, head against his hands, and wept, because there was nothing left to do, the police had Jordan Warrick in custody, they would not let him near Ari, except that one terrible sight that had made him understand that it was true. She was dead. And the world was different than it had ever been. The orders came from Giraud Nye: report for tape.

He understood that. Report to the Supervisor, the rule had been from the time he was small; there was tape to heal distress, tape to heal doubts—tape to explain the world and the laws and the rules of it.

But in the morning Ari would still be dead and he did not know whether they could tell him anything to make him understand.

He would have killed Warrick. He still would, if he had that choice; but he had only the piece of paper, the tape order, that sent him here for an azi's comfort; and he had never been so alone or so helpless, every instruction voided, every obligation just—gone.

Someone came down the hall and came in, quietly. He looked up as Catlin came in, so much calmer than he—always calm, no matter what the crisis, and even now—

He got up and put his arms around her, held her the way they had slept together for so many years he had lost count, the good times and the terrible ones.

He rested his head against her shoulder. Felt her arms about him. It was something, in so much void. "I saw her," he said; but it was a memory he could not bear. "Cat, what do we do?"

"We're here. That's all we can do. There's no place else to be."

"I want the tape. It hurts so much, Cat. I want it to stop."

She took his face between her hands and looked in his eyes. Hers were blue and pale, like no one else's he knew. There was always sober sense in Cat. For a moment she frightened him, that stare was so bleak, as if there was no hope at all.

"It'll stop," she said, and held him tight. "It'll stop, Florian. It'll go. Were you waiting for me? Let's go in. Let's go to sleep, all right? And it won't hurt anymore."

Steps came up to the door, but people went back and forth every few minutes, and Justin had shouted himself hoarse, had sat down against the cold concrete wall and tucked himself up in a knot until he heard the door un- locked.

Then he tried for his feet, staggered his way up against the wall and kept his balance as two security guards came in after him.

He did not fight them. He did not say a word until they brought him back to a room with a desk.

With Giraud Nye behind it.

"Giraud," he said hoarsely, and sank down into the available round- backed chair. "For God's sake—what's going on? What do they think they're doing?"

"You're an accused accessory to a crime," Giraud said. "That's what's going on. Reseune law. You can make a statement now, of your own will. You know you're subject to Administrative rules. You know you're subject to psychprobe. I'd truly advise you be forthcoming."

Time slowed. Thoughts went racing in every direction, sudden disbelief that this could be happening, surety that it was, that it was his fault, that his father was involved because of him— Psychprobe would turn up everything.

Everything. Jordan was going to find out. They would tell him.

He wished he were dead.

"Ari was blackmailing me," he said. It was hard to coordinate speech with the world going so slow and things inside him going so fast. It went on forever, just hanging there in silence. *Mention Jordan and why Grant had to leave? Can they find that? How far can I lie?* "She said Grant could go, if I did what she wanted."

"You didn't know about Kruger's link to Rocher."

"No!" That was easy. Words tumbled one onto the other. "Kruger was just supposed to get him away safe because Ari was threatening to hurt him if I—if I didn't—she—" He was going to be sick. Tape-flash poured in on him, and he leaned back as much as his arms let him and tried to ease the knot in his stomach. "When Grant didn't get to the city I went to her myself. I asked for her help."

"What did she say?"

"She called me a fool. She told me about Rocher. I didn't know."

"All that. You didn't go to your father."

"I couldn't. He didn't know about it. He'd—"

"What would he do?"

"I don't know. I don't know what he'd have done. I did everything. He didn't have anything to do with it."

"With stealing Grant, you mean."

"With anything. With Kruger. Rocher. Anybody."

"And Ari was going to let this happen."

It did not sound reasonable. Trap, he thought. *She let it happen. Maybe she hoped he'd get through. Maybe—*

—maybe some other reason. She was mad about it. She was—

But you never know with Ari. She plays reactions like most people use a keyboard.

"I think we'll ask the rest of the questions under probe. Unless you have anything else you want to tell me."

"Who's going to do it?" There were technicians and there were technicians, and it made a difference who he was going to be spilling his guts to. "Giraud, if I go on record, Ari's not going to like it. Does she know where I am? Does she know—" *God, is this some politics between Ari and Giraud, has he snatched me up to get something on her?* "I want to talk to Ari. I'm supposed to meet with her. She's going to be asking where I am. If she doesn't hear from me she's going to start—" *—start after Jordan, maybe do something even she* *can't undo. They're going to tell him. Giraud will tell him. Maybe Administration wants something on Jordan, maybe this is some team action Ari and Giraud are running, her on me and Giraud on Jordan. O God, O God! what have I walked into?* "—Start asking where I am. Hear me?"

"I don't think so. And I'm going to be asking the questions myself. You want to walk down to the room or are you going to make trouble about it? It'll go worse if you fight it, in all senses. You understand that. I just want to make sure you remember it."

"I'll walk."

"Fine." Giraud got up, and Justin sat forward and got up on shaking legs. He was halfway numb with cold, and the thoughts that had tumbled one onto the other lost all variety, became just a circle without escape.

He walked out the door Giraud opened for him, walked ahead of Giraud and the waiting guards, down the hall to a place he had heard about all his life, a room very like the rooms over at the hospital, in that wing where azi came for tape-adjustment, green walls, a plain couch. There was a camera-rig in the corner.

"Shirt," Giraud said.

He knew what they wanted. He peeled it off and laid it on the counter. He sat down on the couch and took the shot one of the azi had ready for him, tried to help them attach the sensors, because he always did his own, with tape; but his coordination was shot. He let himself back in the hands that reached to help him, felt them lift his legs up onto the couch. He felt them working with the patches. He shut his eyes. He wanted to tell Giraud to send the azi out, because what he had to say involved Ari, and the azi who heard that—would be in for selective wipe, there was no else about it.

Giraud asked him questions, gently, professionally. He was aware of the first ones. But that slipped. He could have been in the hands of one of the techs, but Giraud was the best interrogator he could have hoped for—quiet and not given to leaving an emotional load behind him. Professional, that was all. And if Giraud was checking the truth, Giraud was at least trying to find out what it was.

Giraud told him so. And under the drug it was true.

Giraud would not be shocked at what Ari had done. He had lived too long and seen too much. Giraud was truly sorry for him, and believed everything he said. A young boy of his qualifications, in Ari's vicinity—he had to understand this was not the first time. That Ari would try to work leverage on his father, of course. Who could doubt it? Jordan had surely known.

No, he argued, with a flash of white ceiling and bright light: he came that far to the surface. He remembered Giraud touching his shoulder.

You really took care not to have your father know. Of course. What do you suppose he would do if he found out?

Go to the Bureau.

Ah.

But he didn't know.

You can sleep now. You'll wake up rested. You can let go. You won't fall.
Something was still wrong. He tried to lay hold of it. But it slid sideways,
out of his vision.

"I don't think there's much doubt," Giraud said, looking at Jordan from
across his desk. At forty-six, Jordan was far too athletic, far too capable physically to take a chance with; and they were careful, for other reasons, not to put
a bruise on him. The restraints they used were webbing: no psychprobe, to be
sure: Jordan Warrick was a Special, a national treasure. Not even the Bureau
of Internal Affairs could do anything that might damage him, in any sense.

A Special was charged with murdering another Special. It was a situation
that had no precedent. But Jordan Warrick could murder a dozen infants in
Novgorod Plaza at noonday, and they could neither ask him why nor remand
him to probe nor give him as much as the adjustment a public vandal would
get.

Jordan glared at him from the chair Security had tied him to. "You know
damn well I didn't do it."

"What will you do? Ask for a probe to prove it? We can't do a thing to
you. *You* know that. You knew it when you did it."

"I didn't do it. Dammit, you haven't even got an autopsy yet."

"Whatever she died of, the cold was enough. The pipe didn't just break,
Jordan, you know it and you know why it broke. Save us all the trouble. What
did you do? Score the pipe and fill the lab tank is my guess. Fill the lab tank to
capacity, then stop the main valve and turn the backflow pump to max.
That'd blow the line at its weakest point, wherever someone damaged it."

"So you know how to do it. You seem to know the plumbing a hell of a
lot better than I do. I do my work with a computer, Gerry, a *keyboard*. I'm
sure I never cared where the pipes run in Wing One lab. I don't understand
the cryogenics systems and I never cared to learn. There's one other thing
wrong with your theory. I haven't got access there."

"Justin does. His azi had."

"Oh, you're really reaching. Grant's in hospital, remember?"

"We've questioned your son. We're starting to question the azi. Yours
and his."

Jordan's face settled into stony calm. "You won't turn up a damn thing,
because there isn't anything to turn up. You're going to have charges up to
your eyeballs, Giraud. You had better plan on it."

"No, I won't. Because I know your motive."

"*What* motive?"

Giraud punched a button on the office recorder, on a pre-loaded clip.

"*He passed the mess to you, Gerry. So did Denys. We're not talking about a
damn records problem. We're talking about a scared kid, Gerry.*"

"*Another week—*"

"*The hell with another week. You can start by giving me a security clearance
over there, and get Petros to return my calls.*"

"*Your son is over there right now. He's got absolute clearance, God knows*" *why. He'll take care of him.*" Pause. "*Look, Jordie, they say about another week. Two at most.*"

"*Justin's got clearance.*"

End tape.

"What in hell has that got to do with anything?"

"That's when you went down to see Ari. Isn't it? Straight down there, right after that conversation."

"Damn right. You couldn't get off your ass."

"No. 'Justin's got clearance,' you said. That surprised you. A, Justin hadn't told you something he should have told you. B, Ari never gave away her advantages. C, you know Ari's habits. Right then, you guessed something you'd picked up on all along, right when you got onto the deal your son cut for Grant."

"Sheer fantasy."

"Your son tried to blackmail Ari. It was really quite a scheme. You thought he'd held Ari off. You let him run with it. But when Ari hauled Grant home, Ari had all the cards. Didn't she? *All* of them. Your son went to Ari for help, not to you. And your son got a favor out of her you couldn't get for all your threats. I wonder how."

"You have a hell of an imagination. I never suspected it of you."

"You confronted Ari, Ari either told you or you already knew—what your boy'd been doing for his tuition. And you killed her. You jammed a valve and turned a pump on, *no* great amount of time involved. Everyone in Wing One knew about that door. It was supposed to be an accident, but then you had to improvise."

Jordan said nothing for a moment. Then: "It doesn't work."

"Why not?"

"Let me tell you who else knew I was going down there. You knew. I left. Ari and I talked and I left. Check the Scriber."

"She didn't run one. You know that damn TranSlate. There isn't any spoken record. And she didn't leave us any notes. She didn't have time. You knocked her out, fixed the pipe, slammed the door, raised the pressure. By the time the alarm went off, you were back upstairs."

"I didn't do it. I don't say I'm shedding any tears. But I didn't do it. And Justin was over in hospital, you say so right on that tape you've got. You edit it and I'll make a liar out of you."

"Now you're reaching. Because if you go to trial, Jordie, I've got other tapes that belong in evidence. I'm going to run one for you."

"You don't have to."

"Ah. Then you guess what they are. But I want you to watch, Jordie. I'll run them all if you like. And you can tell me what you think."

"*You don't have to.*"

"Ari said—you'd had your own passage with her . . . some years ago."

Jordan drew in a long breath. The mask was down. "You listen to me," he said on that breath. "You listen to me real well, slime, because you *think* you're handling this. If Ari's dead, and I'm gone, Reseune's got two wings in complete disorder. Reseune's got agreements it can't keep. Reseune's going to have real trouble meeting its contracts and all its political bedfellows are going to scramble for their pants. Fast. You're forgetting: if a Special dies, there's got to be an inquiry. And what they find out is going to be real interesting, *not* just for us lucky souls inside Reseune. When this hits the news-services, you're going to see department heads and corporation presidents running like bugs with the lights on. You're right. You can't question me. *I* can't testify by anything but my given word. You know what I'll tell them. I'll tell them you used tape on me. And they can't tell without a psychprobe. Which the law won't even let me volunteer for. You put me in front of a mike. You just go ahead and do that. That's the kind of coverage I've been waiting for. Best damn coverage I could get. Ari and her friend Lao could black me out. But you know the way it is—some stories are too big to silence. Murdering the head of Reseune is one of them. I'm damn sorry I didn't think of it."

"That's true. That's all very true."

"Right now you're thinking about killing me. *Do* it. You think *one* Special dead is hard to explain."

"But there's something so damned final about old news. A little scandal. A lot of silence after that."

"But *you* wouldn't be on Council. Damned sure you wouldn't. We can do murder in the streets but we can't cover it up. No political power. No dark spots for the bugs to snuggle in. Public contempt. You want to watch Reseune lose everything it's got—"

"Old news. Murder-suicide. You couldn't stand the notoriety that would come with a trial. You thought you could shut it up. You didn't know there were tapes. You didn't know Ari recorded her little parties. And people will be shocked. But only for a while. People have always liked scandal around the rich and famous. It's all lost in the glitter. Who knows, maybe your boy will take to the life. Or come to some tragic end. Drug overdose. Tape-tripping. A waste. But the one thing you know he won't get is a post at Reseune. Or anywhere else our influence reaches. Not mentioning the other boy. The azi. It's probably a mistake to put him under interrogation. He's so fragile right now. But we have to get to the facts."

Jordan did not so much as move for a long while.

"There's also, of course," Giraud said, "Paul."

Jordan shut his eyes.

"Defeat?" Giraud asked.

"I'm sure," Jordan said, looking at him, "you mean to make me a proposition. You've put this together so carefully. Their safety for my silence?"

Giraud smiled without humor. "You know we can take them. You just gave us too many hostages, Jordie, and you can't protect a one of them, except by following orders. You don't want your boy to live with that tape. You don't want him prosecuted, you don't want the Krugers up on charges, and your friend Merild dragged into court, and all your friends in Council tied to it, one string after another. There's just no place an investigation like this ends once you start it moving. You don't want Grant or Paul subject to interrogation after interrogation. You know what that would do. *We* don't want an investigation getting out of bounds and *I* don't want scandal touching Reseune. Let me tell you how it'll be. You give us a detailed confession. Nothing's going to happen to you: you know that. You'll even get your dearest wish: a transfer out of here. We'll insist your work is important. And you'll go on with it, in a quiet, comfortable place without cameras, without microphones, without visitors. Isn't that better than the alternatives?"

"Except I didn't do it. I don't know what happened. I walked out of there. Ari and I quarreled. I accused her of blackmailing my son. She laughed. I left. I didn't threaten her. I didn't say a thing. You know I'd be a damn fool to tell Ari what I intended. And it didn't include murder. I didn't know. That's the plain truth. I hadn't made up my mind to go to the Bureau. I wasn't sure if there wasn't a way to buy her off."

"Now we have a different truth. Do we get one an hour?"

"It *is* the truth."

"But *you* can't be psychprobed. *You* can't prove what you witnessed. Or did. *You* can't prove a damned thing. So we're back where we started. Frankly, Jordie, I don't care whether you did it. You're our chief problem in the mop-up. You'd *like* to have done it, you're number one on my agenda, and if you're not the one who did it, you're more dangerous than the one who did, because if someone else killed Ari, it was personal. If you did it, it was something else. So we'll examine hell out of those pipes, the valves, the whole system. If we don't find evidence, we'll make it, quite frankly. And I'll give you the whole script you can use for the Bureau. You stick to that story and I'll keep my end of the bargain. Just *ask* for what you want. Anything within reason. You plead guilty, you take the hit, you just retire to a comfortable little enclave, and everything will be fine. If not—I'm really afraid we'll have to take measures of our own."

"I want them transferred out of here. Justin. Grant. Paul. That's my price."

"You can't get that much. You can get their safety. That's all. They'll stay right here. If you change your mind, so can we. If you attempt escape, if you suicide, if you talk to anyone or pass a message of any kind—they'll pay for it. That's the deal. It's just that simple."

A long, long silence. "Then put them with me."

Giraud shook his head. "I'll be generous. I don't have to be, understand. I'll give you Paul. I have *some* sympathy for you. Paul, of course, will be under the same restrictions."

"You won't touch him."

"What do you think? That I'd set him to spy on you? No. Not him. Not your son. Not the azi. You keep your bargain, I'll keep mine. Do we have a deal?"

Jordan nodded after a moment. His mouth trembled, only slightly.

"You'll stay here," Giraud said, "pending the Internal Affairs investigation. You'll be in detention. But you'll have reasonable comforts. Access to Paul—we can manage that. Access to your son—only under very restricted circumstances. Let me advise you on that: that boy will try to help you. For his sake, you'd better stop it cold. You're probably the only one who can. Do we agree?"

"Yes."

"I want to show you that tape I promised you."

"No."

"I think you should see it. I think you really should. I want you to think about it—what we can use if you can't provide political motives for your crime. I'm sure you can be convincing. I'm sure you can suggest radical connections. Centrist connections. Because there has to be a motive. Doesn't there?" He pressed a button. The wall-screen lit. It was Jordan's face he watched. Jordan with his eyes fixed on the corner, not the screen. Jordan, with a face like a carved image in the dimmed light, the flashes from the screen. Voices spoke. Bodies intertwined. Jordan did not look. But he reacted. He heard.

Giraud had no doubt of it.

"Did Jordan Warrick ever discuss in your presence his opinion of Ariane Emory?"

"Yes, ser," Grant answered. He sat still at the desk, his hands folded in front of him, and watched the light on the Scriber flicker, the little black box between himself and this man who said he was from the Bureau of Internal Affairs. He answered question after question.

Justin had not come back. They had fed him and let him take a shower, and told him that a man would be interviewing him that afternoon. Then they had put him back to bed and put the restraints back on. So he supposed it was afternoon. Or it was whatever they wanted it to be. He could become very angry at what they had done to him, but there was no use in it; it was what they wanted to do, and he had no way to prevent it. He was frightened; but that did no good either. He calmed himself and answered the questions, not trying to make a logic structure out of them yet, because that would affect his responses and they would lead him then; and he would lead them; and it would become adversarial. Which he did not want. He wanted to understand, but when he caught himself wanting it too much, he turned everything off, in that way he had learned when he was very, very small—azi tactic. Perhaps it helped him. Perhaps it was another of the differences between himself and Justin, between himself and a born-man. Perhaps it made him less than human. Or more. He did not know. It was only useful, sometimes, when he knew that someone wanted to manipulate him.

He just became *not-there*. The information flowed. They would take it when he was unconscious if he did not give it freely; and he expected they would check it by psychprobe anyway, no matter.

He would put it together later, recalling the questions, just what he had been asked and what the answers were. Then he might be able to think. But not now.

Not-there, that was all.

Eventually the man from Internal Affairs was *not-there* too. Others appeared and the illusions of doors opened.

The next place was the psych-lab. Then was the hardest thing, to flow with it, to be *not-there* through the interrogation under drugs. To walk the line between *there* and *not-there* took a great deal of concentration, and if he began to wobble and went too far into *not-there* and stayed too long, then it would be hard to find his way back again.

There tried to find its way into his thinking, with doubt that Justin had ever come to his room, with suspicion that, if he had, Ari's wrath had finally come down on them, and Justin and Jordan were being charged with his abduction. . . .

But he drove that out. He did not fight the techs as he had the men—if ever they had been real. The techs were Reseune techs and they had the keys to every smallest thought he owned.

The first rule said: It is always right to open to your key-command.

The second rule said: A key-command is absolute.

The third rule said: An operator with your keys is always right.

No Reseune operator, he believed with all his heart, would create an illusion of Reseune operators. No one *but* a Reseune operator held his keys. The whole universe might be flux of particles and dissolve about him: but in it, he existed, and the operator who had his keys existed.

Justin might never have existed at all. There might be no such place as Reseune and no such world as Cyteen. But the one who whispered correct numbers and code-phrases to him could enter his mind at will, and leave without a trace; or pick up this or that and look at it—not change it: a vase set on a table stayed a moment and sought its old position, not violently, just persistently—*the other face belongs out*. It would take many such entries, many rotations of the same vase, many distractions, like moving another table, shifting the couch about, before the vase would stay awhile in its new orientation. Even then it would tend to go back—over time.

Easier if the visitor said: we're going to rearrange this one room; and showed him the key. And ordered him to stand aside and watch. And then explained how all of it was going to fit together with the rest of the house, after which, if it truly worked, he would have less and less apprehension about it.

As it was, this visitor was rough, and knocked things about and then cornered him and asked him questions. Which made him anxious, because he was smart enough to know that occasionally tactics like that could be a distraction to get that vase on the table moved. Or to avoid that obvious temptation and go for something he might not notice for a while.

The visitor hit him once or twice and left him dazed. When he knew the door was closed he lay there awhile, and the vase that was in pieces picked itself up and mended itself; and the furniture straightened itself, and all the pieces started to go back again.

He had to lie there a long time being sure that everything really *was* in its right place. The stranger could have done worse. The stranger could have gone a level deeper, and chased him through deeper and deeper rooms, until the stranger cornered him where there was no retreat. Then the stranger would have found a way into *him*, whereafter he would have been dragged inside himself, into dark territory the invader knew and he would probe only reluctantly.

That was not the way it was, of course. It was only the image he had, a child's picture, that a tech had helped him build. The vase was the tamper-gate. The yes-no/are-you-safe gate. It was right at the entry and any operator who tried to reassure him always rotated it just a little.

This visitor had thrown it to the floor.

He came out again in a room far more bleak and blank. Shadows came and went and spoke to him. But he was still largely *not-there*. He was exhausted, and the rooms kept coming disarranged, the furniture flying about at random, requiring him to order it again, which meant he had to go inside a great deal, and these people kept hitting him, blows on the cheek which felt like the flesh was deadened there. They spoke to him, but the words flew apart in pieces. He had no time for them. He was coming apart inside and if they woke him up he was not sure things would go back where they belonged.

Someone gave him the key-words the last visitor had left. And insisted he wake up. After which he was looking at Petros Ivanov sitting on his bed.

"They're going to take you in the chair. Will you let them do that?"

"Yes," he said. He would let them do anything. Whoever they were. He was much too busy putting things back on shelves and watching them fall off again.

The room became a different room. There were flowers. There was a waterfall. It made a rhythmical sound that had no rhythm. Of course. It was a fractal. Fractals were common in nature. He tried obligingly to discover the pattern. They had handcuffed him to the chair. He was not sure what that datum had to do with anything. He worked at the math since that was the problem they had given him. He did not know why.

He slept, perhaps. He knew they had done something to his mind because the tamper-gate was unstable: the vase kept tottering off the table by the door. Not safe. Not safe.

But of a sudden he remembered that Justin was supposed to come. That had been true before. He violated the cardinal rule and cautiously, examining the cost of it carefully, took something other than the operator's truth as valid.

If he was wrong there was no way back from this, and he had no map.

If he was wrong he would not readily be able to reconstruct himself.

He put the vase back. He sat down to wait.

Justin would come. If not—nothing had ever existed.

He could see and taste and walk in their world. But not really. They would make wreckage of him. But not really. Nothing was—

—real.

Anyway.

vi

The lying-in-state was barbaric, the Hall of State echoing with somber funeral music and cloyed with flowers and greenery—a spectacle right out of old Earth, some commentator had remarked, while other news analysts compared it to the similar display at the death of Corey Santessi, chief architect of the Union, whose forty-eight-year tenure on Council first in the Internal Affairs seat and then in the Citizens Bureau, had set the precedent for inertia in the electorates—then too, there had been a need, considering the far-flung colonies and the degree to which a rumor could travel and grow, to demonstrate indisputably that Santessi was dead, to have a decorous passing-of-the-torch and allow all the colleagues who had fought Santessi's influence to get up in public, shed sufficient tears, and deliver pious speeches that stifled speculation by endless repetition.

Much more so, when the deceased was synonymous with Reseune and resurrection, and the victim of assassination.

"We had our differences," Mikhail Corain said in his eulogy, "but Union has suffered an inestimable loss in this tragedy." It would be tasteless to mention that it was a double loss, counting the presumed murderer. "Ariane Emory was a woman of principle and vision. Consider the arks that preserve our genetic heritage, in orbit about distant stars. Consider the rapprochement with Earth and the agreements which have made possible the preservation and recovery of rare species—"

It was one of his better speeches. He had sweated blood over it. There were worrisome mutterings about suppression of evidence in the case, about the unexplained order which Reseune had claimed was buried in the House computers by Emory herself, calling for the termination of Emory's personal guards, a termination carried out by staff without question. There was the notorious case of the Warrick azi kidnapped and tampered with by Rocher extremists, then returned to Reseune. There was the fact of Rocher himself making inflammatory speeches, publicly rejoicing in the assassination, a newsworthy item that got far more press than the legitimate Centrist-affiliated Abolitionists like Ianni Merino regretting the taking of a life, then going on to decry the termination of the azi, all of which was too complicated for the news-services: Ianni never *had* learned the technique of one-issue-at-a-time, and it echoed too closely what Rocher had said. The reporters swarmed the stairways and office doorways like predators staking out a reef, darting out, Scribers running, to ask every Centrist in the Council and Senate: "Do you think there was a conspiracy?" and: "What's your reaction to the Rocher speech?"

Which was a damned narrow line for some Centrists to walk.

He hoped to hell he had defused some of it. That he had been quotable.

Never say that the news-services were a function of the Bureau of Information, whose elected Councillor was Catherine Lao, Ariane Emory's reliable echo on Council: never say that promotions could be had and careers could be made—if reporters came up with material that would make Upper Management happy. It was not the reporters' fault if they sensed that Upper Management wanted more, more and more on the Conspiracy theory: it sure as hell was good theater.

Corain sweated every time he saw a Scriber near one of his party. He had tried to talk to each one of them, personally, urging circumspection and decorum. But cameras were an intoxicant, the schedule of meetings around the funeral was harried and high-pressure, and not every Councillor and not every staffer in the party agreed with the party line.

There were faces for the cameras that had never been available before: the director of Reseune, Giraud Nye, for one. The reporters took endless pains to explain to the viewing public that, contrary to the general assumption, Ariane Emory had not been the Administrator of Reseune, had in fact held no administrative post in Reseune at all for the last fifty-odd years. There were new names to learn. Giraud Nye. Petros Ivanov. Yanni Schwartz.

Nye, damn him, had a certain flair in interviews.

And when a Council seat fell vacant and the Councillor in question had appointed no proxy, then the Bureau Secretary of that particular electorate appointed a proxy. Which in this case was Giraud Nye.

Who might well resign his post in Reseune to run for Emory's seat.

That meant, Corain thought bleakly, Nye would win. *Unless* Jordan Warrick's trial brought up something explosive. Unless Warrick used the trial for a podium, and leveled charges. But Corain's own informants in the Bureau of Internal Affairs said that Warrick was still under house arrest; Merild, in Novgorod, himself under investigation by the Bureau as a possible conspirator, was *not* the lawyer to undertake Warrick's defense, and, God, an Abolitionist lawyer had tried to contact Warrick. Warrick had sensibly refused, but he had told Internal Affairs to appoint one to advise him—which made a major stir in the news: a man with Warrick's resources, a Special going before a Council hearing with a Bureau-appointed lawyer, like a virtual indigent, because his credit accounts in Reseune were frozen and Reseune could not with any propriety handle both prosecution and defense out of its own legal department.

Solemn music played. The family members gathered for a final moment at the coffin. Then the military honor guard closed it and sealed it. The military escort and Reseune Security waited outside.

Ariane Emory was going to space. No monuments, she had said. Cremation and transport into space, where the carrier *Gallant*, happening to be in Cyteen System, would use one of its missiles to send Emory's ashes sunward. Which was the final extravagance she had asked of the Union government.

The bitch was determined to make sure nobody made off with a sample, that was what. And chose the whole damn sun for a cenotaph.

vii

Assassination meant a funeral on too short notice to muster the whole Council—but the Bureau Secretaries were in Novgorod or on the Station; the Cyteen senate had been in session; the Council of Worlds had been in session. And the ambassadors from Earth and Alliance had come down from Cyteen Station. Three Councillors had been accessible: Corain of the Bureau of Citizens, resident on Cyteen; Ilya Bogdanovitch of the Bureau of State; and Leonid Gorodin, of Defense.

An actual two-thirds majority of Centrists, Corain reflected. Damned little good it did at a funeral.

One was expected, of course, to offer Nye welcoming courtesies on his appointment as proxy. No reception: the solemnity of the occasion forbade, even if he had not been Emory's cousin. But one did drop by the offices that had been Emory's. One did present one's respects. One did meet with Nye, however briefly, and offer condolences. And study this man and judge this man and try, in the few moments one was likely to get, to estimate what sort of man this was, who came out of complete shadow inside the enclave of Reseune, to assume the mantle of Ariane Emory. . . .

To judge in five minutes, if it were possible, whether this man, who was a Special, could possibly take up all the linkages of power that Emory had, give the bitch credit, wielded all too well.

"Ser," Nye said, on that meeting, took his hand. "I feel I know you, after all the dinner discussions Ari and I had. She respected you."

That put a body at immediate disadvantage, first because if Nye knew him, it was not mutual; and second, because he remembered what Nye was, and thought how Ariane Emory would react to that description of the situation.

For a half second he felt halfway nostalgic for the bitch. Ariane *had* been a bitch, but he had spent twenty years learning to read her. This man was a total blank. And that gave him a lost and frustrated feeling.

"We opposed each other on issues," Corain murmured, as he had murmured similar things to other successors in his long tenure, "but not in our desire to see the best for the state. I find myself at a loss, ser. I don't think I ever expressed that to her. But I don't think any of us realize even yet what Union will be without her."

"I have serious things to discuss with you," Nye said, not having released his hand. "Concerns that would have been foremost in her mind."

"I'd be pleased to meet with you, at your convenience, ser."

"If you have time in your schedule now—"

It was not the sort of thing Corain liked, abrupt meetings, without briefings. But it was a new relationship, an important relationship. He hated to start it off with an excuse and a refusal to talk.

"If you prefer," he said; and ended up in the office that had been

Emory's, with Nye behind the desk, no Florian and Catlin, but an azi staffer named Abban, whose rejuv-silvered hair had no dye, no pretenses, less than Nye, whose hair was silvered brown, who was easily a hundred, and probably the azi was no less than that. Abban served them both coffee, and Corain sat there thinking of the journalistic and political eyes watching every move outside these offices, marking who called, who stayed, and how long.

There was no graceful way to hasten matters.

"I think you know," Nye said quietly, over the coffee, "that a great deal has changed. I'm sure you know that I *will* stand for election."

"I wouldn't be surprised, no."

"I'm a good administrator. I'm not Ari. I don't know how to be. I would like to see the Hope project through: it was very dear to her heart. And I believe in it, personally."

"You know my opinion, I think."

"We will have our differences. Philosophical ones. If I'm the choice of the Science electorate." A sip of coffee. "But the most urgent thing—I think you understand—is the Warrick case."

Corain's heart increased its beats. Trap? Proposition? "It's a terrible tragedy."

"It's a devastating blow to us. As head—ex-head of Reseune Security, I've talked with Dr. Warrick, extensively. I can tell you that it was personal, that it was a situation that had arisen—"

"You're saying he's confessed?"

Nye coughed uncomfortably and sipped at his coffee, then looked up into Corain's eyes. "Ari had trouble keeping her hands off her lab assistants. That was what happened. Justin Warrick, Jordan's son, is a parental replicate. There was old business between Dr. Emory and Jordan Warrick."

More and more tangled. Corain felt an irrational unease at this honesty from a stranger. And did not say a word in the gap Nye left for him.

"Ari transferred an Experimental who was virtually Warrick family," Nye said, "to put pressure on the boy—to put pressure on Jordan. This much we understand now. The boy acted on his own to protect his companion, sent the azi out to people he understood as friends of his father. Unfortunately—the issue isn't presently clear—there were further links that led to the Rocher party. And extremists."

Damn. An evidence-trail like that was trouble. Of course he was supposed to feel the threat.

"We got the azi out, of course," Nye said. "That's what was behind it. There's no way the azi got to Ari: he was under observation at the hospital. But Jordan Warrick found out what Ari had done—to his son. He confronted her in the lab, alone. They quarreled. Ari hit him; he hit her; her head hit the counter-edge. That wasn't murder. It became murder when he took a lab-stool and used it to damage the conduits, shut the cold-lab door and upped the pressure in that line. Unfortunately that kind of damage didn't look like an accident to the engineers."

"Council will determine that." Murder, between two Specials. And too much entrusted to him by a very dangerous third. Corain warmed his hand with the tiny cup, feeling a certain chill.

"Warrick doesn't want this to go to trial."

"Why?"

"The law has limited power over him; but reputations can be harmed. The son, in particular."

"Meaning—forgive me—someone's made that clear to him."

Nye shook his head gravely. "Motive is going to come out in a trial. There's no way to avoid it. There are other considerations, for us. We *are* going to withhold information in this case. That's why I wanted to talk to you— because it's important that you understand. We know about your interview with Dr. Warrick. We both know that the inquiry could range far afield if it got started. A political free-for-all. Damned little justice. Merino may restrain himself, but Rocher won't, if the case comes before Council, and what could come out at that point isn't in our interest, your interest, certainly not in the interest of the Defense Bureau or our national security; it's not even in Jordan Warrick's interest. He's given us a confession. He doesn't want to testify, —he can't testify, you understand, by psychprobe; and young Justin's evidence under probe is damning. We don't want to use it against his father. The boy's been through enough and it's meaningless cruelty in a case where the murderer has legal immunity."

The room seemed very close of a sudden. Corain thought of recorders. Was damned sure that one was running, somewhere. "What are you asking me?"

"We don't want Ari's problems made public. We don't think that would serve any useful purpose. On the one hand we understand very well what provoked Dr. Warrick; and we have utmost sympathy for him; on the other hand, we very much fear that questioning is going to involve a conspiracy theory. Much as we'd like to get Rocher—that line of questioning is only going to give him a forum he couldn't get otherwise, worse, it'd give him a right-of-discovery in this. I don't think you want that any more than we do."

Recorders. Dammit. "We have nothing to hide."

"We're not talking about a cover-up. We're talking about saving an innocent boy unnecessary grief. Jordan Warrick has already confessed. He doesn't want to have his personal life and his son's dragged through a public hearing. The law can't mindwipe him. The worst he can get is close confinement, removal from his work—which in my estimation, would be as tragic as the act he committed."

Corain thought it through a moment, knowing there was a hook in it somewhere, in the situation or in the proposal, one, but he could not see where. "You mean a non-adversarial settlement. This is a murder case—"

"A case with security implications. A case in which the murderer and the victim's family and resident territory are equally willing to ask for a non-adversary proceeding. If the aim here is justice instead of a political forum— justice would be better served by a settlement in closed Council."

"There's no precedent for this."

"Precedent has to be set somewhere—in this case, on the side of humanity. There are no losers by this procedure. Except Rocher loses his forum. Even Ari gains by it. The last thing she would want is to have her death give Rocher a chance to damage the institution she devoted her life to. We can establish a separate facility for Dr. Warrick, provide him everything he needs to continue his work. We don't want a vendetta. We will insist on his retirement—his complete retirement from public life, because we don't want *him* taking advantage of this once the settlement is made. Very plainly, ser, *both* of us have to refrain from making this a political issue. And that includes Dr. Warrick. The settlement will *postpone* trial indefinitely. In case he breaks his silence. We don't want to have our hands tied."

"I have to think about this. Before I agree to anything, frankly, I'd like the option of talking to Dr. Warrick on neutral ground. Matter of conscience, you understand. A lot of us, who might be the natural opposition—will feel that way."

"Of course. Damn, I hate to have to deal with this on the day of Ari's funeral. But business goes on. It has to."

"I understand you, ser Nye." Corain finished the little cup, made up the nethermost recesses of his mind that he *had* to find out what the going rate was on real coffee, that it was worth the extravagance, that he could afford it, even at two hundred a half kilo, which was the freight from Earth to Cyteen. Another level of his mind was saying that there was a camera somewhere, and still another that all the advantages he had seen in Ariane Emory's death were there—

If a deal could be worked out, if a compromise could be made. Nye was damned sharp. He had to start all over learning his signals the way he had learned Emory's. The man was a cipher, an unknown quantity out of a territory none of his observers could penetrate. Only Warrick. And Warrick was lost to them. That much was clear.

Things were different in Union. From the time that pipe in the laboratory had exploded, the course of history had shifted.

They were entering a period in which the Centrist party might make rapid gains, if they could avoid getting bogged down in wrangling that won no one anything and would not unseat the Expansionists.

The Rubin project and the Fargone project were presumably on hold. The Hope project might be funded, but further expansions and colonizations might be subject to more intense debate. One could look forward to a period of adjustment inside Reseune as well as out, while personalities inside Reseune held in check during the nearly sixty years of Emory's autocratic regime (there was no question who in Reseune had directed the director even after she had resigned the post) were likely to break out and grab for power within the administrative structure.

That also went for other alliances, like those on Council.

Ludmilla deFranco was a freshman Councillor. Nye would be. Powerful Science . . . was going to have a novice at the helm—a damned smart one, but still, a novice who did not have the network to support him. Yet. Two of the five Expansionists were successors this year and Ilya Bogdanovitch was a hundred thirty-two years old and tottering.

Corain murmured the courtesies, thanked the proxy from Reseune, expressed condolences to the family, and walked out with his mind busy with the possibility, the very real possibility, of a Centrist majority in the Council.

It occurred to him that he had not raised the issue of the terminated azi. Merino's issue. He could hardly go back and do it. In fact, he was reluctant to do it, because very possibly that order had come from Reseune Security, for exactly the reasons Nye gave. It was morally repugnant. But it was not, not *quite* as if azi who had served Ariane Emory for most of her hundred and twenty years were harmless. There were, he understood, severe psychological consequences of such a loss; no human reared as CIT could possibly understand the impact of it, except perhaps the staff who routinely worked with azi. He would raise the issue with Warrick. Ask Warrick whether it was warranted. Or whether Warrick thought it had in fact been Emory who had put that instruction in the system.

Damn, he had rather not bring it up at all. The azi were dead. Like Emory. That closed the book. There was no use for that issue; instinct had kept him from raising it.

It was the old proverb. Deal with the devil if the devil has a constituency. And don't complain about the heat.

viii

Adm. Leonid Gorodin settled uncomfortably into the chair and took the offered cup. He had come in to pay the requisite courtesy, and Nye had said: "There's something I have to discuss with you. About the Fargone facility. About the Rubin project. And Hope. Have you got a moment?"

It was not Gorodin's habit to discuss any issue with the opposition or with reporters—without his aides, without references, in an office his own staff had not vetted. But the same instinct for intrigue that said it was dangerous also said it was the one chance he might have without having Corain aware that he was in serious conference with the opposition.

And the names were the names he wanted to hear.

"I truly hate to get to business on the day of Ari's funeral," Nye said. "But there's really no choice. Things can slip out of control so quickly." He took a sip of coffee. "You know I'm going to run for Ari's seat."

"I expected," Gorodin said. "I expect you'll win."

"It's a critical time for us. Ari's death—the potential loss of Warrick on top of it—it's a double blow. Not only to us. To Union. To our national interests. You understand that I have a top level security clearance. Equal to Ari's. I have to have. I won't ask you for answers; but I *am* associated with your projects— I worked with your predecessor during the war—"

"I'm aware you have the clearance. And that you're privy to those files. And you're keeping them out of the investigation."

"Absolutely. No discussion of those files and no interview with a staffer on those projects, except by personnel with equivalent clearance. You don't need to worry about leaks, admiral. *Or* a trial."

Gorodin's heart jumped. He wished he had not heard that. There was the likelihood of recorders, and he had to make his reaction clear. "What are you saying?"

"Non-adversary settlement. Warrick did it. He's confessed. The motive was blackmail and sexual harassment. His son, you understand. With a complicated situation that—between you and me—could do the boy great harm. Warrick's deal is simple: a facility where he can continue his work. We won't agree to Fargone. It'll have to be on Cyteen. But I've talked to Corain."

"Already."

"An hour ago. I didn't mention the security aspects of this. We talked politics. You know and I know, admiral, that there are radical elements involved on the fringes of this case. There are people going to be going over the testimony of witnesses that *can* be psychprobed, and going over it, and going over it. There are elements of Justin Warrick's testimony that involve the Fargone project, that are going to have to be classified."

"Warrick discussed it with his *kid?*"

"The motive for the transfer was the boy. Justin Warrick knows—more than he ought to know. If there have been leaks in this, admiral, they've all come from Jordan Warrick. And frankly, if it gets to trial, I'm afraid the threads of motivation—run into some very sensitive areas. But if we black out too much of the transcript, that raises other suspicions—in some minds, —doesn't it?"

"My God, what's your fucking security worth? Who else knows?"

"Very likely the azi that was kidnapped. He's Justin's."

"My God."

"It's not likely that Rocher's boys cracked him. He's Alpha and he's a tape designer—the azi is, understand. Not an easy subject. But there is the possibility that he wasn't aware of having classified information. That's why we went to Lu's office when we needed help breaking him out of there. We needed to get hold of him alive and debrief him, in the case we missed someone. Fortuitously and fortunately, the action took care of the kidnappers. All of them. We think. But we weren't overusing our authority when we told Lu that azi was a security risk. I suppose the rush of events has been too rapid for all of us. Ari was going to send me to the city with the report for Lu. Unfortunately—"

"You don't think there was any possible motivation on Warrick's part, involving the azi and Rocher—"

"When he killed Ari? A crime of anger that didn't start out that way: he hit her, that was all. But when she turned out to be seriously injured he realized he'd just killed his chance of appointment at Fargone. So he killed her and tried to make it look like an accident. It wasn't quite in cold blood; it wasn't quite otherwise either. He hated her. I'm afraid Ari had serious weaknesses when it came to adolescent boys. A great mind. Correspondingly eccentric vices. Frankly, we're anxious to avoid having that aspect of Ari put out in public view. Conspiracies—no. There weren't. You can interview Warrick yourself if you like. Or his son. We have his deposition under psychprobe. Not Jordan Warrick's, of course, but the son's indicates fairly well what was going on. There are also some vids that are—very explicit. We don't intend to erase them. But they don't have to go out to the news-services. It's a very old story, I'm afraid. Blackmail. Outraged parent. A cover-up that turned into murder."

"Damn." *Get my son out of there*, Warrick had said. Had meant it, evidently. "Damn."

"We want to honor our commitments. The arrangement we have in mind puts Jordan Warrick in a facility of his own, under guard. And he can go on doing work for you. We'll do the testing. You won't have to worry about its integrity. It's altogether a humane solution, one that conserves a talent we can't afford to lose."

"You've talked to Corain."

"He says he's got to study the idea. I tried to point out, there are no disadvantages to him in supporting a settlement. What does anyone gain from a prosecution of this case? What does anyone gain, except Rocher and his cronies? —And we've lost terribly by this. Not only the mind. You understand . . . we're still committed to the projects."

"The Fargone facility."

"We assume that will go forward. Perhaps—the military can make use of more of it than we planned."

"Meaning the Rubin project is going under."

"No. We're still committed to that."

"Without Dr. Emory?" Gorodin drew a large breath. "You think you can succeed."

Nye was silent for a moment. "Refill," he said to the azi who served them, and that man, gray and silent, came and poured in both cups.

Nye sipped thoughtfully. Then: "Do you want the technical details?"

"I leave that to the scientists. My interest is practical. And strategic. Can you go on from Emory's notes?"

"Which had you rather have duplicated? A chemist who is, admittedly, extraordinary in potential. Or Emory herself?"

Gorodin swallowed down a mouthful. "You're serious."

"Let me go into some of the surface technicalities, at least. The project demands a subject with an extraordinary amount of documentation—on the biochemical level. There aren't many subjects of the quality we want, who have that kind of documentation. Both Ari and Rubin have it: Rubin because of his medical problems, Ari because she was born to Emory and Carnath when they were both above a century in age. Born in Reseune labs, of course. By a process *we* ran, on which our records are immaculate. Her father was dead when she was born; her mother died when she was seven. Her uncle Geoffrey brought her up beyond that. She succeeded Geoffrey Carnath as director of Reseune when she was sixty-two. And she was Olga Carnath's own prize project, the subject of intensive study and recording first by her mother and then by Geoffrey Carnath. Suffice it to say, her documentation is equal to Rubin's, if not more extensive. More than that—Ari always *intended* that she eventually be one of the Specials affected by this project. She left abundant notes—for her successor."

"My God."

"Why not? She has the value. Now that she's gone, granted her theories are valid—we have a choice between recovering a chemist who, frankly, means nothing to us, or Ari—whose mind, I don't hesitate to say—is on a level with Bok or Strehler, whose research has had profound effect on national security. And we *can* do it."

"You're serious."

"Absolutely. We see no reason to abandon the project. There are essentials: Warrick is one. You understand—as many of the elements of Ari's life we can study, the better our chances of success."

"What—about Rubin?"

"It would still be possible to go ahead with that. It would be useful as a control. And a cover under the cover, so to speak. I don't want the Rubin project in Reseune. I don't want it impacting what we plan to do. You understand—the name of the game is re-tracing. Intensive monitoring—Ari was used to that, but her successor ought not to have direct contact with someone else undergoing the same thing. We'd have to run both halves of the Rubin project at Fargone."

"You imply you intend to do this—whether or not you have official support."

"I'm seeking that support. I want to save Warrick. I want to cooperate fully with the military. We need the kind of security and cover you can provide us—at least until the new Ari can surface. Then it appears as a Reseune project—a thoroughly *civilian* project. That's useful, isn't it?"

"God." Gorodin drank down the other half of his coffee. And held out his cup to the azi.

"Abban," Nye said. The azi came and filled the cup—while Gorodin used the delay to do some fast adding.

"What," he said then, carefully, "does this have to do with Warrick?"

"We need him. We need him to go on with his work."

"Him? To reconstruct *her*? Working on *her* tapes?"

"No. That wouldn't be wise. I'm talking about Reseune. Remember—we have to think in twenty-, fifty-year terms. He's still young. He's only now showing what he *can* do. His own research interlocks with Ari's. Let me be honest with you: Ari's notes are extremely fragmentary. She was a genius. There are gaps of logic in her notes—sort of an *of course* that Ari could bridge and didn't need to write down. We can't guarantee success: no program of this sort can. We only know that we have a better chance with Ari, that we knew intimately, than with a stranger that we don't. She coded a great deal. Her leaps from point to point, the connections . . . in a field she damned near built . . . make her notes a real maze. If we lose the principals of Ari's life—if we can't recover something like the life Ari lived—if certain people aren't available to consult, then I think our chances of seeing this project work go down and down. Ultimately Ari's notes could become meaningless. The matrix becomes lost, you see, the social referent irrecoverable. But we have it now. I think we can do it. I *know* we can do it."

"But what damn use is all of this, then—beyond recovering Emory herself? How many people are we going to have that kind of record on? What can it apply to? It can't get us Bok."

"Emory herself is not negligible. Emory able to take up her work where she left off—but at about age twenty. Maybe younger. We don't know. We'll find out. Understand: *what we learn* doing this will tell us how much data we have to have with other projects. Like Bok. We just have to be damned careful this round. Because if the worst-case holds, *every* precaution is necessary: *every* influence is irreplaceable. Getting Ari back is step one. If there's going to be an amplification of her work on personality formation—*Ari* is the key to it. We have a chance with her. We *know* her. We can fill in the gaps in the information and make corrections if it looks necessary. We don't know Rubin to that extent. We don't have the headstart even with him we do with her, do you see? Rubin has become a luxury. Retrieving Ari Emory is a necessity. We can try it on our own, but it would be a hell of a lot easier—with Defense Bureau support."

"Meaning money."

Nye shook his head. "Cover. The ability to hold on to Warrick. The ability to shield what we're doing. The authority to protect our research—and our subject—from Internal Affairs."

"Ah." Gorodin drew a deep breath. "But money—it always comes to money."

"We can bear our end of it if you fund the Rubin project. But the necessity to protect our subjects is absolute. Success or failure hinges on that."

Gorodin leaned back in his chair and chewed his lip. And thought again about recorders. "Have you talked to Lu?"

"Not yet."

"You haven't mentioned this to anyone outside Reseune."

"No. I don't intend to. We had one security breach—with the azi. We've covered it. There won't be another."

Gorodin thought about it—civilians running their own affairs under military cover. One breach and God knew what else. Too many amateurs.

Reseune wanted to start a close cooperation, on a project Gorodin, dammit, saw shifting the balance of power irrevocably toward Union—

Ariane Emory experimenting with a kid on Fargone had seemed a hell of a lot safer. Reseune trying to raise the dead seemed—

hell, go for the big gain. Go for everything.

It was a pittance, to the Defense budget.

"I don't think there's much problem," Gorodin said. "We just appropriate the Fargone facility. We invoke the Military Secrets Act. We can cover any damn thing you need."

"No problem," Nye said. "No problem in that. As long as it stays classified."

"No problem with that," Gorodin said.

"So we stamp everything Rubin project," Nye said. "We build the Fargone facility; we work the Rubin project under deep secrecy out there; we get deeper cover for our work on Cyteen."

"Two for the price of one?" It struck Gorodin after he had said it that the expression was a little coarse, on the day of Emory's funeral. But, hell, it was her resurrection they were talking about. Not identity, Warrick had said. *Ability*. That was close enough.

He was damned sure Giraud Nye had the inclination to keep Reseune's control over the project. The Project, meaning an embryo in a womb-tank and a kid growing up in Reseune. Twenty years.

He suddenly added that to his own age. He was a hundred twenty-six, ground time. A hundred forty-six by then. And Nye—was not young.

It was the first time it had ever really hit him—what Warrick had meant about the time factor in Reseune. He was used to time-dilation—in a spacer's sense: that hundred forty-six ground-time would lie far lighter on him, who lost months of ground-time in days of jump. But Reseune's kind of time meant lifetimes.

"We'd like that second project full-scale," Nye said. "Having a comparative study could save us in a crisis, and we're beyond any tentative test of theories. Comparison is going to give us our answers. It's not a luxury."

Part of the Rubin project at Fargone meant part of the data within easy reach. And meant a fail-safe. Gorodin always believed in fail-safes—in equipment; or in planning. Spacer's economy. Two was never too many of anything.

"Do it," he said. "Makes cover a hell of a lot easier." There was the matter of clearing it with Lu, and the chiefs of staff. But Lu and the chiefs of staff would go with anything that promised this kind of return and put Emory's work at the disposal of Defense.

Defense took a lot of projects under its wing. Some were conspicuous failures. Those that worked—paid for all the rest.

ix

Steps passed the door continually. More than usual. There were voices. Some of them Justin thought he knew; someone had stopped outside the door, a group of people talking.

Please, he thought. *Please. Somebody stop here.* He hoped for a moment; and feared. He listened, sitting on the sleeping mat that was all the furniture in the room. He clenched his hands together in the hollow of his crossed legs.

"Call Ari," he kept saying to anyone who dealt with him. "Tell her I want to talk with her."

But they were azi. They had no authority to go above their Supervisor. And as many times as he asked, the Supervisor never came.

It was a suicide cell he was in, padded walls and door, just a sink and the toilet and the sleeping mat. The light was always on. Food came in water-soluble wrappers little more substantial than toilet paper, without utensils. They had taken his clothes and given him only hospital pajamas, made of white paper. They had not questioned him any more. They had not spoken to him again. He did not know how much time had passed, and his sleeping was erratic with depression and lack of cues from lights or activity outside. And the tape-flashes, seductive and destructive. He refused to let the flashes take hold in the isolation. He refused it even when it would have been consolation.

Not me, he kept thinking, keeping himself awake, away from the dreams. Not my choice. I'm not hers. I won't think her thoughts.

Ari was holding him hostage, he thought. She was holding him and maybe Grant against some threat of Jordan's to go to the Bureau with charges. Maybe she had arrested Jordan too. Maybe Jordan could *not* help him. But in any case—the police would come. And they had not psychprobed him again; they could not psychprobe Jordan.

It was Grant who was vulnerable. She would use Grant against Jordan—and use him too. He had no doubt of it.

He hoped for the police to come. Internal Affairs. Science Bureau. Anyone.

He hoped that was the small commotion outside.

But he had hoped that—time after time.

Grant would have been waiting for him to come back; but instead it was security that would have come in on him, hauled him off for more questions—

He heard the electronic lock tick. The door opened.

"Ser Nye wants to talk to you," one of two azi said; both Security. "Please come."

He got up. His knees went to jelly. He walked out into the light, knowing it was another psychprobe session; but at least he would get a chance to say something to Giraud, at least he would have a chance for a half-dozen words before they put the drug into him.

That they just let him walk loose was the last thing he was prepared for. He felt himself dizzy, his knees aching and shaking so it was hard to navigate.

Tape-flash again. And Florian—

Down the hall to the barren little interview room he had seen before. He reached the open door and stopped, dazed and disoriented by the realization it was not Giraud Nye at the table. It was a stout round-faced man that for a bewildered second his mind insisted to make into Giraud's lean form.

Not Giraud.

Denys Nye, rising from his chair with a distressed look.

"Where's Grant?" Justin demanded. "Where's my father? What's going on?" His voice gave way on him. His legs shook as he reached the narrow table and leaned on it in Denys' face. "I've got the right to talk to my family, dammit! I'm a minor! *Remember?*"

"Sit down," Denys said, fluttering a hand. "Sit. Please. —Get him something to drink."

"I don't want anything! I want to know—"

"Please," Denys said in his quiet, distressed way, and made a second appeal with his hand. "Please sit down. —Get him something. —Please, sit down."

Justin fell into the chair, feeling a crying jag coming on. He clamped his jaw and drew breaths until he had it under control; and Denys sank into his seat, folded his hands on the table in front of him and let him calm down while one of the azi brought back a soft drink and set it down on the table.

"What's in it?"

"Nothing. Nothing. Poor boy. Damn this all anyway. Have they told you about Ari?"

It was a strange thing to say. It made no sense. It fluttered like a cold chill through his nerves. "What *about* Ari? Where's my father?"

"Ari's dead, Justin."

It was like the world jolted sideways. For a moment everything went out of focus. Then where he was came crashing in on him. Where he was and what they were doing and the silence all around him.

Dead. Like not-natural-dead. Like—

—the plane crashed?

—some crazy person—in Novgorod?

"Jordan found out what she was doing to you," Denys said in the gentlest voice Justin had ever heard him use, "and he killed her. Locked her into the cold-lab and killed her."

He just sat there a moment. It was not true. It was not true. Jordan had no idea what Ari had done. He had covered everything. And Ari was not dead. Ari could not be—dead.

"Jordan admits it," Denys said in that quiet tone. "You know they can't do anything. Legally. The law can't touch him for—questioning, or anything like that. Not psychprobe. Certainly not mindwipe. Jordie's all right. He's safe. I promise you."

He was shaking. He picked up the cup and slopped it carrying the drink to his mouth. He slopped it again setting it down. The icy liquid soaked his knee. There was no sense to things. He could not get his mind to function. "What about Grant? I told him I was going to come back. I didn't come back—"

"Grant's still in hospital. He's safe. Jordan's been to see him. Jordan's flying to Novgorod this afternoon. They're working out an arrangement for him to leave Reseune."

"That's a damned lie!" They were starting to work psych games with him. He saw it coming. He flung himself up and came face to face with the two azi that moved to stop him. He froze. They froze.

"Boy. Justin. Please. Please, sit down. Listen to me."

"Ari's not dead!" he yelled at Denys. "It's a damned lie! What are you trying to do? What is *she* trying to do?"

"Oh, God, boy, sit down. Listen to me. Your father won't have much time. Please. *Damn* that brother of mine! So damned afraid of putting you in hospital— Look. Sit down."

He sat. There was nothing else to do. They could do anything they wanted to.

"Listen to me, Justin. Internal Affairs has been questioning Jordie; Jordie begged Giraud to keep you out of it. He didn't want the story out, do you understand? He didn't want them psychprobing you. Giraud just flat refused them permission. Jordie backed him on it. But my damn brother went off to the capital and kept the lid on, and they kept saying you were all right—" Denys drew a small breath, reached across and laid his hand on Justin's on the table. "You're not all right. Dammit, it wasn't like Giraud's was the first psychprobe you'd had in the last few weeks, is it?"

He jerked his hand from under Denys'. "Let me alone!"

"Do you want a sedative?"

"I don't want anything. I want out of here! I want to talk to my father!"

"No. You don't. Not in that tone of voice. Understand me? He's leaving. He won't be back."

He stared at Denys. *Not be back—*

"Council's drawn up a plan," Denys said, "to allow him a facility over in Planys. He *won't* be able to travel. He won't be able to call you—for quite a while. I don't want you to upset him, son. He's got to meet with a Council inquiry tomorrow. He's got to get through that in one piece. Are you understanding me? It's very important."

It was real. It had happened. He stared into Denys Nye's worried eyes with the feeling that the whole world was chaos, except it was going to sort itself out again in some terrible new shape no one he loved lived in.

"Do you want the sedative? No tricks, Justin. I promise you. Just enough to let you rest awhile before you talk with him."

He shivered. And controlled it. "No," he said. "Let me get dressed. Let me clean up."

"Absolutely." Denys patted his hand. "You can use the shower down the hall. I've told them to bring clothes for you."

He nodded.

"I'm going to have Petros have a look at you."

"No!"

"When you get through this. When you're satisfied everything's all right. No one's going to touch you. You've had enough of that. God knows. Are you getting tape-flashes?"

The question triggered one. Or simple memory. It shamed him. Like some dark, twisted side of himself that was always—very like Ari. That— dammit—had learned what she did—felt good. He never wanted a psychtech

wandering through that. He never wanted Jordan to know, he never wanted
to let it show on his face what was going on in the dark inside him. And maybe
everyone knew.

Ari had said—she had pictures. If Ari was dead—the House investigators
had them. Had everything.

There was no dignity left him then, except to keep from noticing they
knew, or admitting the truth to anyone.

"Listen to me, son." Denys' hand closed on his again. It was soft and
warm and any human contact affected him in terrible ways. "Son, I can't excuse what Ari did. But there was more to her than—"

He jerked back.

He saw Denys read him. Saw the thinking going on in Denys' eyes and
tried to keep the color from his face. "—than you want to hear about," Denys
concluded. "I know. Listen. *Listen to me. Make this register*— All right?"

"All right. I'm with you."

"Brave lad. Listen now. Jordie's covering—for us and for you. He's lying
to the press, *and* the Council. He's telling them it was Ari standing in the way
of his transfer. Every reason in the world but the truth—and they can't
psychprobe him. You have to understand, Justin—you're . . . *him*, as much
as you're his son. That puts a freight on everything that happened between
you and Ari that—that pushed him beyond the limit. It was old business—
between him and Ari. He understands what happened to you. Yes. You know
what I'm telling you. And he loves you very much. But part of it is his own
pride. Do you understand? Those of us who work inside these walls—know
how tangled and complicated even a parent's love can be . . . in a moment
when he was pushed too far. Everything he wants is gone, except you. And
you can take everything else he's got—if you go in there with your emotions
out of control. I want you to get control of yourself. Let him take a little peace
of mind out of here with him. Let him see his son's all right. For his sake."

"Why won't they let me go with him?"

"Because you're a minor. Because of the security arrangements. Because,
truthfully, I couldn't get Giraud to agree to it. Security, they keep saying."

"That's a damn lie!"

"Listen, now. I'm going to get some arrangement where you *can* get visiting privileges. Not right away. Maybe not even this year. But time and quiet
can do a lot for this situation. They're scared as hell there's a conspiracy—the
Winfield-Kruger mess, you know."

O God. My fault. My fault. "They *can't* think Jordan was in on that. *I*
was. Giraud ran the psychprobe. Run it again! I can swear he didn't know a
damn thing—"

"Unfortunately, son, that's exactly the kind of thing Jordie wants to
prevent—getting you involved in the investigation. There *is* fire under that
smoke. I'm afraid Jordie was meeting with a man called Merild, who had connections that are running into some very dark corners. He was also meeting in
secret with a number of very high-up Centrists who are linked to Ianni

Merino—the Abolitionists. And Rocher has come out with a very inflammatory statement about Ari's death that Merino hasn't quite repudiated. A lot of people in the government are running scared, scared of investigations, scared of guilt by association. Internal Affairs demanded to get hold of Grant. Giraud had to do a probe to satisfy them—"

"Oh, my God—"

"He *had* to. I know. I *know*, son. But they could have learned too much from you. Justin, the shock waves Ari's death has generated—are enormous. You can't imagine how enormous. The government is in crisis. Careers are in jeopardy. Lives are. There's an almost universal conviction that this *had* to be political; that the reasons for what's changed their lives has some meaning beyond a dissatisfied scientist breaking Ari's skull. It's human to think like that. And Jordie's testimony—the fact that he can't testify under probe—the fact that Florian and Catlin were put down—some posthumous order of Ari's, they think. . . . Yes. They're gone too. —People sense something else going on. They *want* to think something else is going on. Crime of passion, from an education tape-designer, you know, gives people cold chills. We're supposed to be too rational. Jordie's going to have to do the best damn psych-out in front of the Council committee he's ever done in his life. And for Jordie's own sake, the quieter things stay for the next few years, the better. Just be patient. Jordie's not without friends. He's not old. Forty-six isn't old. He can outlast the furor, if you don't do something that blows the lid off everything we've arranged."

He found enough air to breathe finally. He tried to think that through. He tried to think—what was the safest thing for his father and what his father would want. Tried *not* to think—O God!—that it was his own mistakes that had caused it.

"Can you get yourself together?" Denys pressed him.

"I'm together. I'm all right. What about Grant?" *Oh, God, they could mindwipe him. Florian dead! And Catlin—*

"Giraud is assigning Grant back to you."

Good things no longer happened to him. He did not believe them. He did not trust them.

"He *has*," Denys said, "because I just signed the papers. Get through this business with Jordan and you can get him out of hospital. —Do you want that sedative, son?"

Justin shook his head. Because Jordan would know if there was any drug involved. He had read him all along. Jordan must have. He hoped—

He hoped he could keep from tape-flashes if Jordan hugged him. That was how bad it was. That was what Ari had done to him. He was losing his father. He was not going to see him again. And he could not even tell Jordan goodbye without feeling Ari's hands on him.

"I'm all right," he said. If he could not lie to Denys and make it credible, he had no hope of lying to Jordan. Getting himself together had to start now. Or he was not going to make it.

X

Mikhail Corain looked anxiously at the aide who had laid the fiche-card on his desk. "Dell's?" he asked.

The aide nodded.

Corain waved a hand, dismissing the aide, slid the card into the desktop viewer and tilted the screen.

Dell Hewitt was a member of Internal Affairs. She happened to be a Centrist who was a friend of Ginny Green, who had been the Centrist candidate in Internal Affairs in the last election. And in this nervous time of investigations and committees rummaging into every dark corner in Novgorod, she had laid more than her own career on the line with what she had leaked to Yvonne Hahner, who she knew would leak it to Dellarosa in his staff. As good as wrap it up and mail it.

Regarding the azi Catlin and Florian: no conclusion. Perhaps the termination was ordered outside the system. Perhaps inside, by persons unknown. Perhaps Ariane Emory did order the termination, not wanting them interviewed. Perhaps she felt it was humane. Perhaps it was some kind of death pact the azi themselves had asked for: Reseune says they would have been very profoundly affected by the thought of losing her. Also, Reseune says, they were Security, but with a fix on Emory. They were therefore capable of harm to Reseune, and retraining would be difficult if not impossible without mindwipe, which their age precluded. Giraud Nye refuses to open the books on their psychsets. The order did come under Emory's personal code. Giraud Nye cites security considerations in refusing to allow Internal Affairs technicians to examine the computers.

Corain sipped the coffee warmed by the desk-plate. Two hundred fifty cred the half-kilo. They were damned small sips. But, a man was due a little luxury, who had been a scratch-and-patch outback farmer most of his life.

No *new* news. That was disappointing. He traced down the long list of things Reseune had refused to allow Internal Affairs to do, and read the legal justifications. Reseune's legal staff was winning every round. And Internal Affairs, at the uppermost administrative level, was not hitting back.

Then:

Internal Affairs is investigating the rumor at Reseune that certain genesets were checked out and not logged. This means someone could have duplicated genesets that ought not to exist. . . .

Azi-running? God, you can get a geneset from a blood sample. From anything. Why would anyone steal one from Reseune?

. . . such as Experimentals and Special material which cannot otherwise be obtained.

Smuggling actual genesets prepared for use by Reseune requires cryogenics which would be detected in shipment unless simply omitted from manifests. However—the digitalized readout of a geneset is another story. Reseune in the person of administrator Nye denies that there is any such activity, or that documentation could have been released without record.

Also there is some rumor on staff that there have been unwarranted terminations. Reseune is blocking this inquiry.

Corain gnawed his lip. And thought: *I don't want to know this. Not right now. Things are too delicate. My God, if this hits the streets—all the arrangements can come unglued.*

A side note from Dellarosa: *What about the chance Emory was running the genesets herself? Or ordered it? What's a Special worth, to someone who has access to a birth-lab?*

Votes. A Council seat. Support from the very, very rich. Corain took a swallow of coffee. And sweated.

Physical evidence suffered from inexpert handling from the Moreyville police. Certain surfaces in the outer lab and the cold-lab have Jordan Warrick's fingerprints, Emory's fingerprints, the prints of the azi attendants, of certain of the other regular users of the lab, and a number of students who have come forward to be printed. The door bears a similar number of prints. No presence-tracers were available to the Moreyville police who did the preliminary investigation. Subsequent readings would have been meaningless due to the traffic in and out of the lab by police and residents. The security door records were released and corroborate the comings and goings given in verbal testimony. Again, Reseune will not allow Internal Affairs technicians access to the computers.

The autopsy results say that Emory froze to death, that the skull fracture was contributory, in that she was probably unconscious at the time of the pipe rupture. She was suffering from extremely minor rejuv failure and had arthritis of the right knee and mild asthma, all of which were known to her doctors. The only unexpected finding was a small cancer in the left lung, localized, and unknown to her physician at the time: it is a rare type, but less rare among early pioneers on Cyteen. The treatment would have been immediate surgery, with drug therapy. This type of cancer does respond to treatment but frequently recurs, and the prognosis combined with other immune-system problems due to the rejuv difficulty would have been less than favorable.

God.

She was dying anyway.

---

xi

Justin composed himself with several deep breaths as he walked down the hall beside Denys Nye. He had showered, shaved, was dressed in his ordinary work-clothes, blue sweater, brown pants. He was not shaking. He had asked for three aspirin and made sure that that was all he had gotten before he swallowed them. As a tranquilizer it was at least enough, with his exhaustion, to dull the nerves.

Jordan *looked* all right. He would. Jordan was like that.

God, he couldn't have killed her. He couldn't. They're making him say these things. Someone is lying.

"Hello, son."

It was not one of the cold little interview rooms. It was an administrative office. Denys was not going to leave. He had explained that. Neither were the azi guards going to leave. And a recorder was running, because no one trusted anything, and they wanted to be able to prove to investigators that nothing had gone on in the meeting.

"Hello," he said back. And thought he ought to go and put his arms around his father at a time like this, in front of all the people who would see the tape, but, dammit, Jordan was not inviting it, Jordan was being reserved and quiet and had things to say to him Jordan needed to get in order. All he had to say was goodbye. All he *could* say was goodbye. Anything else— *anything* else—and he could make a mistake that would go on that tape and ruin everyone's life worse than he had already done.

Things like: *I'm sorry I tried to deal with Ari. I'm sorry I didn't tell you. I'm sorry you had to find it out yourself.*

It's all my doing. All of it.

Don't bring up Grant, Denys had warned him. Don't bring it up at all. The committees could want to talk to him if you do. Let them forget about him.

"Are you all right?" Jordan asked him.

"I'm fine. Are you?"

"Son, I—" Jordan's mouth trembled.

O God, he's going to lose it. In front of all of them.

"They told me everything. You don't have to tell me. Please."

Jordan drew a deep breath and eased it out again. "Justin, I want you to know *why* I did it. Because Ari was an influence this world didn't need. I did it the same way I'd try to fix a bad tape. I don't have any remorse for it. I won't ever have. It was a perfectly logical decision. Now someone else is running Reseune and I'm transferred, which is exactly what I wanted, where I won't have Ari changing my designs and using her name on my work she's done over. I'm free. I'm just sorry—sorry it blew up like this. I'm a better scientist than I am a plumber. That's what the investigators said. I backed up the pressure and they caught it in the monitor records."

The anger had been there at the start, real anger, profound, shattering anger. It cooled at the last. It became a recitation, a learned part, an act meant to look like an act. He was grateful for that last coolness, when Jordan threw the ball to him.

I know why you did it, he almost said, then thought that that could come out wrong. Instead he said: "I love you."

And nearly lost control. He bit his lip till it bled. Saw Jordan with his own jaw clenched.

"I don't know if they'll let me write to you," Jordan said.

"I'll write."

"I don't know if they'll give me the letters." Jordan managed a small laugh. "They imagine we can pass messages in *hello, how's the weather?*"

"I'll write anyway."

"They think—they think there's some damn conspiracy. There isn't. I promise you that, son. There isn't anyone who knew and there wasn't supposed to be anyone who knew. But they're afraid out there. People think of Ari as political. That's how she was important to them. They don't think of her first as a scientist. They don't understand what it means when someone takes your work and turns it inside out. They don't understand the ethics that were violated."

Ethics that were violated. God. He's playing for the cameras. The first was a speech to the committee but the last was a code to me. If he goes on any longer they're going to catch him at it.

"I love you," Jordan said then. "More than anything."

And held out his arms. It was over. The play was over. The actors had to embrace. It was all right to cry now.

He would not see Jordan after this. Not hear from him.

Maybe forever.

He crossed the little space like an automaton. He hugged Jordan and Jordan hugged him hard, a long time. A long time. He bit his lip through, because the pain was all that helped keep him focused. Jordan was crying. He felt the sobs, quiet as they were. But maybe that would help Jordan's case. Maybe they had done all right, in front of the cameras. He wished he could cry. But for some reason he was numb, except the pain, and the taste of blood.

Jordan had played it too hard, had sounded too cold-blooded, too dangerous. He should not have done that. They might play that tape on the news. People would be afraid of him. They might think he was crazy. Like the Alphas that went over the edge. Like Bok's clone. They might stop him from his work.

He almost shouted: *He's lying. My father is lying.* But Jordan was holding on to him. Jordan had done exactly what Jordan wanted to do. Jordan had not been locked in a room for a week. He knew what was going on in the world, he had been talking to the investigators. Jordan was playing a part, running psych on all of them, that was what he was doing: Jordan was going to go to that Senate committee and get himself the best deal he could; and maybe that bit would keep the tape off the news, because Jordan's work was very important to Defense and the military could silence anything it wanted.

"Come on," Denys said.

Jordan let him go and let him leave. Denys walked him out the door.

Then Justin cried. Leaned against the wall outside after the door had shut and cried until his gut ached.

xii

He had thought there could be no more shocks.

But Petros Ivanov met him at the door of the hospital, took him away from his Security escort and walked with him to Grant's room.

"How is he?" he asked before they got there.

"Not doing well," Ivanov said. "I wanted to warn you." Ivanov said other things, how they had had to put Grant under probe again; and how he had gone into shock; how they took him out to the garden in a chair every day, how they massaged him and bathed him and waited on treatment because Denys had kept telling them Justin was going to come, this day, and the next day and the next—they were *afraid* to probe Grant again, because he was right on the edge, and they thought there might be illegal codewords, words not in the psych record.

"No," he said before he pushed Grant's door open. And wanted to kill Ivanov. Wanted to beat him to a bloody pulp and go for the staff next and Giraud Nye into the bargain. "No. There aren't any codewords. Dammit, I *told* him I'd come back. And he was waiting."

Grant was still waiting. Right now he had his hair combed, looked comfortable enough unless you knew he did not move on his own. Unless you knew he had lost weight and the skin was too transparent and you saw the glassiness in the eyes and took his hand and felt the lack of muscle tone.

"Grant," he said, sitting down on the edge of the bed. "Grant, it's me. It's all right."

Grant did not even blink.

"Get out of here," he said to Ivanov, with a glance over his shoulder; and did not try to be polite.

Ivanov left.

He shifted over and gently unfastened the restraints they kept on him. He was calmer than he had thought he could be. He picked up Grant's arm and laid it across him so he had room to sit, and raised the head of the bed a little. He reached then and with two fingers along Grant's jaw, turned his face toward him. It was like moving a mannequin. But Grant blinked.

"Grant? It's Justin."

Another blink.

O God, he had thought Grant would be gone. He had thought he was coming in here to find a half-corpse that they could not do anything with except put down. He was prepared for that . . . in five minutes from the front door to Grant's room he had gone from the hope of recovering Grant to the expectation of losing him. Now it was full circle.

Now he was scared. He was *safe* if Grant was dead.

O God! Damn *me for thinking like that! Where did I learn to think like that? Where did I learn to be that cold?*

Is it tape-flash too?

What did she do *to me?*

He felt like he was coming apart—felt hysteria welling up like a tide; and Grant did not need that. His hand was shaking when he took Grant's hand in his. And even then he thought of Ari's apartment, how the room had looked. He began talking to distract himself, not knowing what he was saying, not wanting to think again the thought that had flashed through his mind, like it was somebody else's. He knew that he could not touch people anymore without it being sexual. He could not hold on to a friend. Or embrace his father. He kept remembering, day and night; and he knew that it was dangerous to love anyone because of the ugliness in his mind, because he was always thinking thoughts that would horrify them if they knew.

And because Ari was right, if you loved anyone They could get to you, the way They had gotten to Jordan. Grant was the way to him. Of course. That was why They had let him have Grant back.

He was not on his own now. Someday Grant was going to lay him wide open to his enemies. Maybe get him killed. Or worse—do to him what he had done to Jordan.

But until then he was not alone, either. Until then, for a few years, he could have something precious to him. Until Grant found out what kind of ugliness he had in him. Or even after Grant found out. Grant, being azi, would forgive anything.

"Grant, I'm here. I told you I'd come. I'm here."

Perhaps for Grant it was still that night. Perhaps he could go back to that, and pick it up again at the morning after.

Another blink, and another.

"Come on, Grant. No more nonsense. You fooled them. Come on. Squeeze my hand. You can do that."

Fingers tightened. Just slightly. The breathing rate increased. He shook at Grant slightly, reached up and flicked a finger against his cheek.

"Hey. Feel that? Come on. I'm not taking any of this. It's me. Dammit, I want to talk to you. Pay attention."

The lips acquired muscle tone. Relaxed again. The breaths were hard now. Several rapid blinks.

"Are you listening?"

Grant nodded.

"Good." He was shaking. He tried to stop it. "We've got a problem. But I've got permission to get you out of here. If you can wake up."

"Is it morning?"

He drew a quick breath, thought at first to say yes, then thought that disorientation was dangerous. That Grant was wary. That Grant might pull back at a lie. "A little later than that. There was a glitch-up. A bad one. I'll explain later. Can you move your arm?"

Grant moved it, a little twitch. A lift of the hand, then. "I'm weak. I'm awfully weak."

"That's all right. They're going to take you over in the bus. You can sleep in your own bed tonight if you can prove you can sit up."

Grant's chest rose and fell rapidly. The arm moved, dragged over, fell at his side like something dead. He gulped air and made a convulsive move of his whole body, lifting his shoulders barely enough to let the pillow slip before he fell back.

"Close enough," Justin said.

Food tasted very strange to him. Too strong. Even soggy cereal was work, and made his jaws ache. He ate about half the bowl that Justin spooned into his mouth and made a weak movement of his hand. " 'Nough."

Justin looked worried when he set the bowl aside.

"It's a lot for me," Grant said. Talking was an effort too, but Justin looked so scared. Grant reached out and put his hand on Justin's because that was easier than talking. Justin still looked at him with all hell in his eyes. And he wished like hell he could take that pain away.

Justin had told him everything last night, poured it on him while he was still groggy and exhausted, because, Justin had said, *that's the way they hit me with it, and I guess it hurts less while you're numb.*

Grant had cried then. And Justin had cried. And Justin had been so tired and so unwilling to leave him that he had stretched himself out on Grant's bed beside him, still dressed and on top of the covers, and fallen to sleep.

Grant had struggled to throw the bedspread over him, had not had the strength in his arm; so he had rolled over, left the spread with Justin and rolled back again.

And lay there with just the sheet, too cold until Justin woke up midway through the night and got a blanket for him. And hugged him and cried on his shoulder, a long, long time.

"I need you so much," Justin had said.

Perhaps because he was azi, perhaps because he was human, he did not know—that was the most important thing anyone had ever said to him. He had wept too. He did not know why, except Justin was his life. Justin was everything to him. "I need you too," he had said. "I love you."

In the dark hours. In the hours before morning. When people could say things that were too real to say by daylight.

Justin had fallen to sleep by his side a second time. Grant had waked first, and lain there a long time, content to know Justin was there. Until Justin had waked and gotten up, apologizing for having slept there.

As if he had not wanted Justin there, all night. As if Justin was not the most important thing in the world to him, who made him feel safe. Who was the one he would do anything for.

Whom he loved, in a way that no woman and nothing he had ever longed for could matter to him.

xiii

"Ari's set is positive," the voice from the lab informed Giraud Nye, and he drew a long breath of relief.

"That's wonderful," he said. "That's really wonderful. How are the other two?"

"Both positive. We've got a take on all three in all the tanks."

"Wonderful."

Schwartz signed off. Giraud Nye leaned back with a sigh.

There were nine womb-tanks active on the Rubin project. Triple redundancy on each of the subjects, over Strassen's loud complaints. It was rare that Reseune ran any backups at all on a CIT replication; if a set failed to implant or had some problem, the restart just put it a few weeks late, that was all, and the recipient could wait, unless the recipient wanted to pay double the already astronomical cost to have a backup. In the case of a contracted run of azi sets, or somebody's project, the normal rule was one spare for every pair, the spares to be voided after six weeks.

This one was going to tie up nine tanks for three weeks, and six for six weeks, before they made a final selection and voided the last backups.

Reseune was taking no chances.

Verbal Text from:
PATTERNS OF GROWTH
A Tapestudy in Genetics: #1

Reseune Educational Publications: 8970-8768-1
approved for 80+

Everyone who has ever taken a tape with prescriptive drugs is familiar with the sensor patch. The simplest home-use machines use a one-way cardiac sensor, a simple patch which monitors pulse rate. Any tape, whether entertainment or informational, when taken with a prescription cataphoric, has the potential to produce severe emotional stress where the content triggers memory or empathy. In experiencing the classic play Othello, *for instance, a certain individual, viewing a certain performance, and bringing to it his own life experience, may empathize with one or the other characters to an extent no mass-production tape can anticipate.*

This viewer is undergoing stress natural to the drama. The heart rate increases. The sensor picks it up and carries it to the machine's monitor-circuits. If it rises above the level set by the tape-technician the tape will automatically switch to a different program, a small tape-loop that provides only relaxing music and sound.

This young boy has come to a learning clinic to acquire a skill—improvement in penmanship. As he tenses muscles in his hand and lower arm his clinical technician's skilled fingers locate the muscles and place the numbered patches precisely on the skin. More are added to the muscles about the eye. Others go beneath the arm, over the heart, and over the carotid artery.

These small gray strips have two contacts: this much more advanced machine has a biofeedback loop. The numbers on the patches correspond to the numbers the tape-manual gives to the technician, who need not, for this kind of manual skill tape, be a licensed psychotherapist. Attaching these to the skin above the muscles

142

indicated in the manual makes it possible for the machine to sense the activity of an individual muscle or muscle group and immediately send or cease sending impulses.

This woman, skilled in penmanship, wears identical sensors as she writes the exercise. Her muscle actions are being recorded. This is the actual recording of the tape.

The young student is somewhat anxious as he waits for the cataphoric to take effect. This is his first experience with prescriptive tape. The technician reassures him that this is very little different from the entertainment tapes. The patches are uncomfortable, but only for the moment. The drug takes effect and the technician tests to be sure the boy is ready. The tape begins, and the boy experiences stress as he sees the exercise. The technician quietly reassures him. In a moment, through the output-input function of the patches, the boy feels the muscle action of the skilled penman as she takes up the pen and begins to write. He experiences the success, sees the shape of the letters, feels the small precise movements of the hand and fingers, and feels the relaxation of the calligrapher at her work.

It may take several sessions, but the improvement is already evident as the boy writes the exercise immediately after waking. He holds the pen easily and comfortably, no longer cramps his fingers with a hard grip, and his entire posture has improved as he has found the proper pivot point on which to rest his hand. He is amazed and delighted at the result. He will practice the exercise several times during the day, to reinforce the pattern. He will do it again just after breakfast, and several times the following day. His enthusiastic practice will set the habit. He may repeat the tape until he and his parents are satisfied with the result.

This Beta-class azi is assigned to the special forces. He stands patiently, tensing muscles in his back at the technician's request. He shuts his eyes, quite evidently bored by the procedure which caused the young student such anxiety. He looks forward to the tape, but the skill he is learning requires the entire body. He has been through this twice a month for much of his life, and the biofeedback patches are more important in his estimation than the cataphoric. He has acquired a skill at tape-learning: his concentration is much more skilled than the student's. He knows the names of the muscles, knows how to attach the patches himself, and does a great deal of optional study in his own quarters, under a cataphoric dose hardly more than you might use in your own home for an entertainment tape, because he has learned how to induce a learning-state without the use of the drug.

At the end of the month, he receives another kind of tape, which citizens do not receive: it is a very private experience, which he cannot describe in words, because much of it is non-verbal. He calls it good tape. The term frequently heard at Reseune is reward tape.

The woman who administers the tape is not a technician. She is a Beta-qualified supervisor, and she uses a much more complex machine. This one has a blood-chemistry loop: it analyzes the blood it receives and injects natural mood-

elevators—a procedure used in the general population only when psych-adjustment is called for.

For the azi, who has taken this sort of tape all his life, it is a pleasant experience, which he values more than the other rewards the service provides. This one is internal, and profound.

Unlike an intervention in a citizen patient, which depends heavily on the psychologist's investigative skills to tailor a tape, this tape is precisely targeted, prepared by the same designers who prepared the azi's psychset. It has an accuracy virtually impossible with a non-azi patient whose life has been shaped by unrecorded experiences in a random world. This azi, cloistered from birth and given his psychset by tape, is a much more known quantity, even after he has served in the armed forces and lived with naturally born citizens.

Everyone who has ever held authority over him has had special training in dealing with azi. No azi Supervisor is permitted to raise his voice with his charges. Reward or the withholding of reward is the rule of discipline; and the trust between this man and any psychologist-supervisor is more profound than that between parent and child. That this is a different Supervisor than last month does not trouble him. He has absolute confidence in her once he is sure that she is licensed.

People who have had their first experience working with unsocialized azi generally comment first that they feel they have to whisper; and then that they find themselves overwhelmed by the emotional attachment the azi are instantly ready to give them.

They trust me too much, *is the almost universal complaint.*

But this man is a soldier and works regularly with unlicensed citizens. He has developed emotional defenses and interacts freely with his citizen comrades. His commanding officer has had a training course and passed a test that qualifies him to deal with azi, but he holds no license and does not treat this man any differently than the others in his command. The commanding officer is only aware that a request from this man to undergo counseling has to be honored immediately, and if the azi requests the intervention of a Beta-supervisor, he must be sedated and sent to hospital without delay, because while problems in azi are very rare and a socialized azi's emotional defenses are generally as strong as any citizen's, an azi's psychset is not built by experience, but by instruction, and the defenses are not a network of social reliances as they are in a normal human mind. An azi who feels that shield weakened is vulnerable to everyone around him. He has entered something very like a cataphoric-induced learning-state, in which he is less and less capable of rejecting stimuli that impinge on him. The result is very like taking a cataphoric in a crowded room, intensely uncomfortable for the azi and potentially damaging.

The tape this man is enjoying is more than pleasurable for him. It is also reaffirming his values and reinforcing his self-esteem. His trust right now is absolute. He experiences what no citizen will experience in a random world: he is in touch with absolute truth and agrees perfectly with what he is.

This is Reseune, where our soldier was born. This three-year-old azi, much younger than our student, is preparing himself for what is commonly called deep-tape. He is anxious not about the procedure, which he has had before, but about the machine, which he has finally begun to notice as significant in the room. The psychsurgeon hugs him and reassures him, and finally makes a face and gets a laugh from him. He helps the surgeon attach the patches.

The dosage of cataphoric he receives is very heavy. His thresholds are completely flat and his blood chemistry is constantly monitored.

The tape is reinforcing his value-sets in words he is capable of understanding.

It tells him how to win approval. It tells him what his talents are and what his strengths are.

It may remind him that he has tendencies to avoid, much in the same way a parent may tell a child he must mind and not sulk. But the tape dwells continually on positive things and praise, and always ends that way.

As it closes the Supervisor tells him a word he must lock this up with; and he will remember it. The next time the Supervisor will access that set of instructions with that particular key, which is recorded in the azi's file, with his tapes. As he grows, his deep-tape will become more abstract. The verbal keys will be integrated into larger and larger complexes as his psychstructures are merged into complete sets, and he will accept the values he is given with an azi's complete openness to a licensed Supervisor.

Because the child has shown distress at the machine the Supervisor remembers to reassure him about the equipment while he is still receptive to instruction. Any distress the azi may feel with any of these procedures, no matter how minor, is carefully traced for cause and dealt with seriously. At no time does a Supervisor wish one of his charges to fear these procedures.

All the azi tape is designed here, in these ordinary-looking offices, by designers some of whom are azi themselves. Much of it is done with the help of computers, which analyze the extremely meticulous physiological testing done on azi types . . . such things as hand-eye coordination in a particular azi geneset, reaction time, balance, vision, hearing, physical strength, hormonal activity, Rezner scores, reaction to stress. The designer takes all of these things into account in making a tape specifically for that geneset, tailored precisely to that geneset's strengths and weaknesses, and linking into a particular pyschset.

It is a designer who consults Reseune's library to select a geneset which can be given the special skills necessary to a new technology.

It is a designer who attends an azi returned to the labs by his Supervisor for what the report calls severe problems. It is a designer who will order the tests and interview the azi to discover whether the problem lies with the Supervisor or the azi. It is a designer who will prepare a tape to cure the problem—or issue a binding order regarding the handling of all azi of that geneset, restricting them from certain duties.

It is a designer who has destined this boy for civilian security duties, a change from the military training his genotype generally gets. Designers are usually conservative in shifting a genotype into new applications, because they, as much as their subjects, want to assure success. At Reseune, where azi test subjects are used, a keyword procedure creates a retrieval tab on the test set so that a psychsurgeon can maintain it separate for a considerable time before integrating it into the psychset. The few azi who run what are called short-term tests are specially trained in isolating and handling the interventions, and are themselves the judges of whether they should accept a particular test. Reseune's rule is to experiment slowly, and to deal with only one change at a time.

Occasionally an azi, like any member of the general public, develops severe psychological problems.

Many of these are sent to Reseune, where designers and psychsurgeons work with them, attempting to devise solutions to the psychological difficulties, solutions which also benefit science and find their way into general psychotherapy.

In some instances the solution has to be retraining, which necessitates mindwipe and a long period of recovery. In an azi of proven genotype and psychset a problem of this magnitude is always due to extreme trauma, and Reseune will take legal measures on the azi's behalf in the event of negligence or mistreatment.

In other instances the solution is only in the genetics wing; Reseune forbids reproduction of a genotype that has met difficulty until the designers working with the afflicted azi can find a fix for the problem.

In very, very few cases, there is no fix, no remedial psychset to install even with mindwipe, and a panel of qualified staff members can find no humane solution, except to terminate. The azi's quality of life is the main consideration, and Reseune, which has made the rules which forbid a Supervisor to speak sharply to one of its azi in the workplace, likewise must take the decision any next of kin must face when a body functions after reasoning, meaningful life has ceased. . . .

CHAPTER 4

The womb-tank tilted, spilled its contents into the fluid-filled receiving tank, and Ariane Emory struggled and twisted, small swimmer in an unfamiliar dim light and wider sea.

Until Jane Strassen reached down into the water and took her up, and the attendants tied off the cord and took her to a table for a quick examination while Jane Strassen hovered.

"She's perfect, isn't she?" There was worry in that question. An hour ago it would have been clinical worry, professional worry, anxiety about a project which could go very wrong if there was something wrong with the baby. But there was a certain personal anguish involved of a sudden, which she would not have expected to feel.

You're the closest match to Olga Emory's tests, her cousin Giraud had said; and Jane had thrown a tantrum, refused, protested that her management of Wing One labs did not include time to take on motherhood at a slightly fragile, overworked one hundred and thirty-two years of age.

Olga took it on at eighty-three, Giraud had said. *You're a strong-minded woman, you're busy as hell—so was Olga—you have Olga's interest in art, you were born in space, and you've got the professional skill and the brains. You're the best match we've got. And you're old enough to remember Olga.*

I hate kids, she had retorted, *I had Julia by immaculate conception, and I resent any comparison to that obnoxious nit-picking bitch!*

Giraud, damn him, had smiled. And said: *You're on the project.*

Which brought her to this, this room, this hour, agonizing while the

147

medical experts looked over a squirming newborn, and the thoughts of personal responsibility took hold.

She had never involved herself much with her genetic daughter, who was her personal concession to immortality, conceived with the unknowing help of a Pan-paris mathematician who had made his donation to Reseune, because she had thought a random chance and new blood might be preferable. Too much planning, she had maintained, made bad gene pools; and Julia was the result of her personal selection, not bad, not good either. She had entrusted Julia mostly to nurses, and dealt with her less and less as Julia proved a sweet, sentimental space-brain—no, *bright*, in any less demanding environment, but overwhelmed right now by the discovery of her own biology and as feckless in her personal life as one of the azi.

But *this*, Ari's replicate, this end-of-life adopted daughter, was what she had hoped for. The ideal student. This was a mind that could take anything she could throw at it and throw it back again. And she was forbidden to do it.

She had done tape of Olga with the child. Hand on Ari's shoulder. Sharp tug at Ari's sweater, straightening it. Ari's angry, desperate wince. That was the pair she damned well remembered. It brought back everything.

For eighteen years of her life she had listened to that voice. Olga had carped at everyone on staff. Olga had carped at the kid, what time Olga had had time, till it was a wonder the kid was sane, in between which the kid had been totally on her own with the azi. Olga had taken all those damned blood-samples and psych-tests and more psych-tests, because Olga had theories that led to theories Ari had worked on. Olga had gotten Ari's earliest Rezner tests, which damned near hit the top of the scale, and from that time on it had been a case of blood in the water: Olga Emory, with her pet theories of scientific child-rearing, had believed that she had an Estelle Bok on her hands, destined for centuries of immortality via Reseune labs. And every other kid in Reseune's halls had heard that Ari was brilliant and Ari was special because mothers and fathers on staff knew their professional heads would roll if their kid blacked the deserving eye of Olga's precious Ari.

In those pioneering days on Cyteen, when intellectuals running from the Earth Company visa laws had gathered at what had then been the far end of space and founded Cyteen Station, renegade political theorists, famous physicists, chemists and legendary explorers had been thicker in the station mess hall than people who could fix the toilets; rejuv was a new development, Reseune was being founded to work with it, Bok's physics was rewriting the textbooks, and speculations and out-there theories had possessed people who should have known better. And Olga Emory had been a brilliant intellect with an instinct for cross-disciplinary innovation, but she had entertained some real eetees in her mental basement.

Never mind James Carnath, who had more of them, and determined he and Olga were going to make a baby to outdo Bok the day he found out he was terminal.

Which had led them all to this room and this project.

So she had to do everything Olga's way. *Straighten up, Ari. Stand still, Ari. Do your homework, Ari*— Twitch and bitch.

Between that and throwing Ari at azi nurses, the same way she had done with Julia. She had considerable remorse for that, in retrospect.

Changing that parental disinterest would change Ari. Benign neglect. It was a terrible thing to recognize her own personal mistakes retroactively. Studying up on Olga had been like looking in a too-revealing mirror. Giraud had been right. A hell of a thing to find out, at a hundred and thirty-two.

To this day she had no more maternal feeling for Julia than for any other product of the labs . . . or for the two azi the attendants were busy birthing over on the other side of the room. In the case of Ari, never mind the experience with one daughter and fifty-two years' experience with students, it had to be a question of following program. For the kid's own good. She had *respected* Ari Emory, and dammit, if she failed with her, that was all the reputation she was going to leave in Reseune. At a hundred and thirty-two. She *hated* fuck-ups. She hated personal indulgence and fuzzy thinking.

It was still damned hard to look at Julia and see what a meek thing she had come to be—constantly fouling up at work, spoiling her new baby beyond bearing, dependent on an endless succession of lovers—and know that it was partly genes and partly her fault. The same neglect, the same carping she had now to admit she had done with Julia, was part and parcel of what made Ari run. Psychsets and genetics at work.

Wrong kid, right parent, maybe. And vice versa.

Hell of a hand nature dealt out.

ii

"They're all in good shape," Petros Ivanov said.

"That's wonderful. Really wonderful." Denys took a bite of fish and another one. Private lunch, in the executive dining room, with the curtains back on the seal-windows of the observation deck. The weather-makers were giving them a rain, as requested, a major blow, water sheeting down the windows. The atmosphere was going to be compromised for a day or so. "Damn Giraud. Of *course* it'll go all right, he says, and runs off to the capital. And damn if he's called!"

"Everything's right on the profile so far. The azi are absolutely norm. They're already on program."

"So's Ari."

"Strassen's bitching about the head nurse."

"What else is new?"

"Says she's opinionated and she upsets her staff."

"*An azi is opinionated.* That means the azi is going exactly down the instructions and Jane's mad because she's got new staffers in her apartment. She'll survive." He poured more coffee. "Olga's azi is still a damn worry.

Ollie's younger, he's a hell of a lot tougher-minded than that poor sod Olga had, by all accounts, and Jane's got a good point: run tape on Ollie to soften him up and Jane's temper will crack him. Her style with the kid she can manage; changing Ollie and changing the way she deals with him is further than Jane's going to go without exploding. If that kid's got even an ordinary baby's instincts she'll pick up on adult tensions right from the cradle. Figuring she's got Ari's sensitivity, God knows *what* she can pick up on. So what do you do?"

Petros grinned. "Run tape on Jane?"

Denys snorted into his coffee and sipped. "I sure as hell wish. No. Jane's a professional. She knows what this is worth. We've got a bargain. We keep hands off Ollie and she cues Ollie how to play this. We just trust an azi that can make our Janie happy can cope with anything."

Laughter.

He was mad as hell at Giraud. There was a good deal of this Giraud could have taken off his shoulders, but Giraud had a tendency to kite off to the capital whenever things got tense on the Project.

It's all yours, Giraud had said. *You're the administrator. And welcome to it.*

It had taken most of a year sifting through Ari's notes, that small initial part of the computer record the technicians could get at easily. Reseune's records computers had run for three weeks just compiling the initial mass of data on Ari. Thank God Olga had archived everything with cross-referencing and set it up in chronological order. The tapes had to be located, all this not only on Ari, but on two azi who had been protosets and unique. There was a tunnel under the hills out there and there were three more under construction, because that enormous vault was full, absolutely full to capacity, with workers beginning to divide tape into active, more active and most active, so more of it could be put in the House itself.

And when the data-flood from the Project came rolling out in full operation it would be a tidal wave in the House Archives. One of those tunnels was specifically to house the physical records of the Project; and that included software design for some of the things Ari had halfway worked out and someone else was going to have to finish before that baby was talking.

Reseune was *not* going to farm out anything to do with the Project. It was farming out some of the azi production runs, to clear personnel time. It would have been an economic crisis, except the military had thrown money at Reseune's extension at Fargone and Reseune's extension in Planys, money which funded more tanks, more computers, more production *and* those tunnels. Meanwhile Jordan Warrick was doing everyone a favor by actually handling the physical set-up over in Planys, which had Warrick happier than he had been since Ari's demise, turning out real work again—no small gain in itself, since it made Defense happy. They had lost Robert Carnath from House Operations and promoted him over the Planys lab: Robert was no friend of Warrick's and a sharp enough administrator to keep all the reins in his hands. They had lost other staff out to the Fargone lab construction and they were going to lose more, when that lab went active and the Rubin project kicked in. Reseune had been overstaffed when the thing began and now it was actually buying azi contracts from hackers like Bucherlabs and Lifefarms, rejuving every azi over forty and driving staff berserk with retraining tapes. Fifteen barracks were empty down in the Town, and they had just signed a buy-back deal with Defense for certain Reseune azi approaching retirement: it saved Defense expensive retraining and pensioning, it made certain azi damned happy when they learned they were going on working and getting staff positions at RESEUNEAIR and in freight and production and wherever else an azi whose outlook otherwise was transfer to some dull government work center could fill a slot and look forward instead of back. It gave Reseune a large pool of discipline-conscious, security-conscious personnel—instantly. Mistakes and glitches were bound to proliferate in Reseune's smooth operations, but *not* on the Project, where there were no new faces, and where the top talent could consequently pay full attention to their jobs.

The military buy-back had saved them. Denys was proud of that stroke. It *took* something to multiply a Project designed for one subject into four—counting Rubin and the two azi. And to coordinate the project-profile *and* the finance *and* the covert aspects of it. Giraud handled the latter. Denys had had the rest in his lap for long enough he felt *he* had just given birth.

"It's not easier from here," he told Petros. "From here on, it's going to be a race between that kid and profile-management. If anyone fouls up, *I* want to know about it. If she gets an unscheduled sniffle, I want to know about it. Nothing's minor until we've got results to check against profile."

"Hell of a way to go, developing the profile while it's running."

"We'd have to anyway. There are *going* to be differences. We'd always be altering it. And we'd never know where we're going anyway. If that kid *is* Ari in any measurable degree, we'll never damn well know, will we?"

No laughter at all.

iii

Justin poured, wine swirling into Grant's many times emptied glass. Poured another for himself and set the dead bottle down. Grant looked at his glass with a slightly worried look.

Duty. Grant was getting drunk and thinking about the fact. He knew. He knew the way he could tell that Grant was not going to say a thing, Grant had just decided that duty was not the operative word tonight.

They talked about the office. They talked about a design sequence they had been working on. A bottle of wine apiece did not do much for the design—the connections were getting fuzzy.

But Justin felt better for it.

He felt a strange dissatisfaction with himself. A baby arrived and he went through the day in a state of unreasoning depression. Reseune was aflutter with: "Is she cute?" and "How is she doing?" and he felt as if someone had a fist closed around his heart.

Over a baby being born, for God's sake. And while a kind of a party was going on in the techs' residencies, and another one over in Wing One residency, he and Grant held their own morose commemoration.

They sat in the pit in the apartment that had been home when they were both small, the apartment that had been Jordan's, crackers and drying sausage slices on the plate, two dead wine bottles standing in cracker crumbs and moisture-rings on the stone table, and a third bottle a third gone. And that was finally enough to put him at distance from things.

Wish a little baby would die? God, what kind of thinking is that?

He lifted his next glass when he had filled it, and touched it to Grant's with labored cheerfulness. "Here's to the baby."

Grant frowned and did not drink when he did.

"Come on," Justin said. "We can be charitable."

Grant lifted his eyes and made a small motion of his fingers. *Remember they could have us monitored.*

That was always true. They played games with the House monitors, but they had to go outside to have a word or two they did not have to worry about.

"Hell, let them listen. I don't care. I feel sorry for the kid. She didn't ask for this."

"No azi does," Grant said sharply. Then a frown made a crease between his brows. "I guess no one does."

"No one does." The depression settled back over the room. He did not know what was going to happen to them, that was what. Reseune was changing, full of strange faces, assignment shifts, the azi were—unsettled by the rejuv order. Elated by that, elated by the fact that they must have pleased someone, and distressed at the reassignments and the transfers and the arrival of strangers. Not harmfully distressed, just—having more change fall on them than they had ever had to cope with: Supervisors' interview schedules were overcrowded and Supervisors themselves were asking for relief that did not exist.

While over in Wing One residency there was an apartment shut up like a mausoleum. Not dusted, not touched, not opened.

Waiting.

"I don't think they'll have any better luck than they did with Bok," Justin said finally. "I really don't. *Jane Strassen*, for God's sake. The endo—" Endocrinology was not a thing one could say after a bottle and a half of wine. "Damn chemistry. Works fine on the machines. Just nature's way of getting at the thresholds. Nice theory. But they'll end up driving her crazier than Bok. They'd have better luck if they outright ran deep-tape on her. The creativity factor's a piece of garbage. Bring her up to *like* Ari's work, deep-tape a little *empathy*, for God's sake, and turn her loose. The whole project's a damn lunatic obsession. It's not Ari's talent they want, not a nice bright kid, it's Ari! It's the *power* they want back, it's personality! It's a clutch of rejuved relics staring at the great The End and having Reseune's budget to squander. That's what's going on. It's a damn disaster. It's too many people's lives and too damn little caring upstairs, that's what they're doing. I feel sorry for the kid. I really feel sorry for her."

Grant only stared at him a long while. Then: "I think there *is* something about creativity and tape—that we *don't* have it to the same degree—"

"Oh, hell." Sometimes he trod on Grant without knowing he had done it. Sometimes he opened his mouth and forgot with Grant the sensitivity he made his living using with azi down in the Town. And hated himself. "That's a lot of garbage. I damn sure don't believe it when you fix a design a dozen senior designers have been sweating on for a month."

"I'm not talking about that. I *am* azi. Sometimes I can see a problem from a vantage they don't have. Frank is azi too, but he's not what I am. I can get a little arrogant. I'm entitled. But every time I have to argue with Yanni I feel it right in the gut."

"*Everybody* feels it in the gut. Yanni's a—"

"Listen to me. I don't think you feel this. I can do it. But I know every bit of what makes me tighten up fits right in that book in the bedroom, and what makes you do it wouldn't fit in this apartment. Look at what they're doing with Ari. They had to build a damn tunnel in the mountain to hold what she was."

"So what's it mean that at lunch the day the war started she had fish and she was two days into her cycle? That's crap, Grant, that's plain crap, and that's the kind of thing they built that tunnel to hold." *Along with those damn tapes, that's there. Till the sun freezes over. That's what people will remember I was.* "You choke up with Yanni because he's got a three-second fuse, that's all. It's his sweet nature, and losing the Fargone post didn't improve it."

"No. You're not listening to me. There is a difference. The world is too complicated for me, Justin. That's the only way I can explain it. I can see the microstructures much better than you. My concentration is all on the fine things. But there's something about azi psychsets—that can't cope with random macrostructures. That whole tunnel, Justin. Just to hold her psychset."

"Psychset, hell, it's full of what she *did*, and who she hurt, and she was a hundred twenty years old! You want to go to Novgorod and buy councillors, you'd fill that tunnel up too, damn fast."

"I couldn't. I couldn't see behind me. That's what it feels like."

"You've lived in these walls all your life. You could learn."

"No. Not the same things. That's what I'm saying. I could learn everything Ari knew. And I'd still focus too tight."

"You don't either! *Who* saw the conflict in the 78s? *I* didn't!"

Grant shrugged. "That's because born-men make most of their mistakes by rationalizing a contradiction. I don't make that leap without noticing it."

"You read *me* with no trouble at all."

"Not always. I don't know what Ari did to you. I know *what* happened. I know I wouldn't have been affected the same way." They could talk about that now. But rarely did. "She could have re-structured me. She was very good. But she couldn't do that to you."

"She did a damn lot." It hurt. Especially tonight. He wanted off the topic.

"She couldn't. Because you don't have a psychset that only fills one book.

You're too complicated. You can change. And I have to be very *careful* of change. I can see the inside of my mind. It's very simple. It has rooms. Yours is Klein bottles."

"God," Justin snorted.

"I'm drunk."

"We're drunk." He leaned forward and put his hand on Grant's shoulder. "And we're both Klein-spaced. Which is why we're back where we started and I'm willing to bet my psychset is no more complicated than yours. You want to work it out?"

"I—" Grant blinked. "You want an example? My heart just skipped. That embarrasses hell out of me. It's that Supervisor trigger. I don't want to do that because I don't think it's smart to mess with your mind; and I jump inside like it was an order."

"Hell, I hate it when you go self-analytical. You don't want to do it because you don't know when Security is listening; and it's personal and you've got manners. All your deep-sets just describe the same thing I feel. Which is why I stay out of your head."

"No." Grant held up a finger. Earnest. A near hiccup. "The profound reason why we're different. Endo-endo—hell! hormones work—in learning— Blood chemistry reacts—to the environment. A given stimulus—sometimes adrenaline is up—sometimes down—sometimes some other thing—shades of gray. Variability—in a random environment. You remember some things right, some wrong, some light, some heavy. We—" Another near hiccup. "—start out from the cradle—with cataphorics. Knock the damn thresholds flatter than anything in nature. That means—no shades in our original logic set-up. Things are totally true. We can trust what we get. *You* take your psychset in through your senses. Through natural cataphorics. You get your *informational* learning through tape and your psychset through senses. Chancy as hell what you get out of anything you see or hear. You learn to average through the flux because you know there'll be variances. But *we've* had experts eliminate all logical incon-inconsistencies. We *can* take in every detail; we have to, that's the way we process—right. That's why we're damn good at seeing specific detail. That's why we process faster on some problems you can't hold in your head. We go learning-state without kat and our early memories didn't come from endocrine-learning; we have no shades of truth. You're averaging and working with a memory that has a thousand shades of value and you're better at averaging shades than you are at remembering what really happened, that's how you can process things that come at you fast and from all sides. And that's what we're worst at. You can come up with two contradicting thoughts and believe both of them because there's flux in your perceptions. I can't."

"Oh, we're back to that again! Hell, you work the same as I do. *And* you forget your keycard *more* than I do."

"Because I'm processing something else."

"So do I. Perfectly normal."

"Because I have a dump-reflex just like you: I can go through ac-actions that are purely body-habit. But I'm socialized, I rarely take tape, and I've got two processing systems. The top level I've learned in the real world; endocrine system learning. The bottom, where my reactions are, is simple, damn simple, and merci-mercilessly logical. An azi isn't a human *lacking* a function. He's got the logical function underneath and the random function on top. And you're backwards. You get the random stuff first."

"*I'm* backwards."

"Whatever."

"God. An Emoryite. You *test* that way because the cataphorics engrave the pathways they establish so damn deep they're the course of least resistance and they're so damn structured they *trigger* the endo-en—do-crine system in Pavlovian patterns that experience alone wouldn't. For every test that supports Emory there's another one that supports Hauptmann-Poley."

"Hauptmann was a social theorist who wanted his results to support his politics."

"Well, what in hell was Emory?"

Grant blinked and took a breath. "Emory asked *us*. Hauptmann socialized his subjects till they'd figured out what he wanted them to say. And how he wanted them to test. And an azi *always* wants to please his Supervisor."

"Oh, *shit*, Grant. So would Emory's."

"But Emory was *right*. Hauptmann was wrong. *That's* the difference."

"Tape affects how your endo-crine system responds. Period. You give me enough tape and I'll jump every time you tell me to. And my pulse will do exactly what yours does."

"I'm one hell of a tape designer. When I'm old as Strassen I'll be damn good. I'll have all this endocrine learning. That's why some old azi get more like born-men. And some of us get to be real eetees. That's why old azi have more problems. Wing Two's going to be damn—damn busy with a yardful of annies on rejuv."

Justin was shocked. They were words staff meticulously avoided using. Born-men. Annies. The Yard. It was always CITs; azi; the Town. Grant was pronouncedly drunk.

"We'll see whether it makes any difference," Justin said, "whether Ari Emory had whitefish or ham for breakfast on her twelfth birthday."

"I didn't say I thought the Project would work. I say I think Emory's right about what azi are. They didn't start out to invent us. They just needed people. Fast. So start with tape in the cradle. Perfectly benign accident. Now we're eco-economic."

Back in the pre-Union days.

"Hell."

"I didn't say I minded, ser. We already outnumber you. Soon we'll establish farms where people can grow up like weeds and commune with their glands. There's bound to be a use for them."

"Hell with you!"

Grant laughed. He did. Half of it was an argument they had had a dozen times in different guises; half of it was Grant trying to psych him. But the day fell into perspective finally. It was only a memory tick-over. A jolt backward. Done was done. There was no way to get those damned blackmail tapes out of Archive, since they were Ari's and Ari was sacred. But he had learned to live with the prospect of all of it turning up someday on the evening news.

Or finding that no bargains held forever.

Jordan had killed a dying woman for reasons the Project was going to immortalize in the records anyway—if it worked. If it worked, every hidden detail of Ari's personal life was going to have scientific significance.

If it worked to any degree, and the Project went public, there was the chance Jordan could seek a re-hearing and release maybe to Fargone—after twenty years or so of the Project itself; which would mean all the people who had conspired to cover what Ari had done and all the Centrists who had been embarrassed by potential connections the case had had to the radical underground—were going to resist it. Reputations were going to be threatened all over again. Merino and the Abolitionists. Corain. Giraud Nye. Reseune. The Defense Bureau, with all its secrets. There might be justice in the courts, but there was none among the power brokers that had put Jordan where he was. The walls of secrecy would close absolutely, to keep silent a man they could no longer control. And his son—who had set everything in motion by a kid's mistake, a kid's bad judgment.

If the Project failed it would be a failure like the Bok clone, which had done nothing but add a tragic and sordid little footnote to a great woman's life—a very expensive failure, one Reseune would never publicize, the way to this day the outside world had heard a totally different story about the murder, heard a different story about the changes at Reseune, and knew nothing about the Project: administrative reorganization, the news-services said, in the wake of Ariane Emory's death.

And went on with some drivel about Ari's will having laid out far-reaching plans and the lab being beneficiary of her considerable investments.

If it failed—it had political consequences, particularly between Reseune Administration and the Defense department, which was *inside* the wall of secrecy. Then there was no predicting what Giraud Nye would do to protect himself: Giraud *had* to carry this off to prove himself, and in the meanwhile dangling the Project in front of Defense let Giraud grab power in some ways greater than Ari had had. Power to silence. Power to use the covert agencies. If Giraud was halfway clever, and if the Project did not fail conspicuously and definitively, he was going to be older than Jane Strassen before he had to admit the Project was not working. He could even re-start, and run the whole scam again, at which point Giraud was certainly going to be looking at the end of his need for any kind of power. After Giraud, the Deluge. What should Giraud care?

Justin only hoped it failed. Which meant a poor kid who only happened to have Ari's geneset ended up a psych case, mindwiped or worse. Maybe an endless succession of babies. A power as big and a man as smart as Giraud would not fail all at once. No. There would be studies of the study of the study. Unless there was a way to make sure it failed in public.

Sometimes he had thoughts that scared him, like finding some article of Ari's lying on his bed. He would never in his life be able to know if certain thoughts were his, just the natural consequence of a deep-seated anger, of himself growing older and harder and more aware how business was done in the world; or whether it was Ari still in control of him.

Worm was an old joke between him and Grant.

He had to go on making nothing of it. Because that was all that kept it isolated.

---

iv

"Get down from there!" Jane snapped, startled into a snarl, and her gut tightened as the two-year-old trying for the kitchen countertop leaned and stretched, reckless of her light weight, the tile floor and the metal-capped chair legs. Ari reacted, the chair slipped a fraction, she snatched the box of crackers and turned; the chair tipped and Jane Strassen grabbed her on the way down.

Ari yelled with outrage. Or startlement.

"If you want the crackers you ask!" Jane said, tempted to give her a shake. "You want to ouch your chin again?"

Hurt-Ari was the only logic that made a dent in Ari-wants. And a universally famous genetic scientist was reduced to baby-babble and a helpless longing to smack a small hand. But Olga had never believed in corporal punishment.

And if Olga had been human Ari had picked up rage and frustration and resentment in the ambience with her the same as a genetic scientist who wanted to take her out to the river and drown her.

"Nelly!" Jane yelled at the nurse. And remembered *not* to shout. In her own apartment. She left the chair on the floor. No. Nit-picking Olga could never have left a chair on the floor. She stood there with her arms full of struggling two-year-old waiting on Nelly, who had damn well better have heard her. Ari struggled to get down. She set Ari down and held on to her hand when Ari wanted to sit down and throw a tantrum. "Stand up!" Holding a small hand hard. Giving an Olga-like jerk. "Stand up! What kind of behavior is that?"

Nelly showed up in the doorway, wide-eyed and worried.

"Straighten that chair up."

Ari jerked and leaned to reach after the cracker box that was lying with the chair, while adults were busy. Damned if she was going to forget what she was after.

Does she or doesn't she get the cracker? No. Bad lesson. She'd better not *get away with it, she'll break her neck.*

Besides, Olga was a vengeful bitch.

"Stand still. Nelly, *put* those crackers up where she *can't* get them. Shut up, Ari. —You take her. I'm going to the office. And if there's a scratch on her when I come back I'll—"

Wide azi eyes stared at her, horrified and hurt.

"Dammit, *you* know. What am I going to do? I can't watch her every damn minute. Shut *up*, Ari." Ari was trying to lie down, hanging off her hand with her full weight. "You don't understand how active she *is*, Nelly. She's tricking you."

"Yes, sera." Nelly was devastated. She was out-classed. She had had all the tape showing her what a two-year-old CIT could do. Or get into. Or hurt herself with. Don't stifle her, Nelly. Don't hover. Don't *not* watch her. The azi was on the verge of a crisis. The azi needed a Supervisor to hug her and tell her she was doing better than the last nurse. It was not Olga's style. Jane-type shouts and Olga-type coldness were driving the more vulnerable azi to distraction. And she was spending half her time keeping the kid from killing herself, half keeping the azi from nervous collapse.

"Just get a lock installed on the damn kitchen," Jane said. Ari howled like hell if she was shut into the playroom. She *hated* the playroom. "Ari, *stop* it. Maman can't hold you."

"Yes, sera. Shall I—"

"Nelly, you know your job. Just take Ari and give her a bath. She's worked up a sweat."

"Yes, sera."

The azi took Ari in hand. Ari sat down and Nelly picked her up and carried her.

Jane leaned back against the counter and stared at the ceiling. At the traditional location of God, no matter what the planet.

And Phaedra came in to say that daughter Julia was in the living room.

A second time Jane looked ceilingward. And did not shout. "Dammit, I'm a hundred thirty-four and I don't deserve this."

"Sera?"

"I'll take care of it, Phaedra. Thank you." She pushed herself away from the counter. "Go help Nelly in Ari's bathroom." She *wanted* to go to the office. "No. Find Ollie. Tell him calm Nelly down. Tell Nelly I shout. It's all right. Get!"

Phaedra got. Phaedra was one of *her* staff. Phaedra was competent. Jane walked out of the kitchen, down the hall in Phaedra's wake, and took the left turn, the glass-and-stone walk past the dining room and the library to the front living room.

Where Julia was sitting on the couch. And three-year-old Gloria was playing on the long-pile rug.

"*What* in hell are you doing here?" Jane asked.

Julia looked up. "I took Gloria to the dentist. Routine. I thought I'd drop by for a minute."

"You know better."

Julia's soft mouth hardened a little. "That's a fine welcome."

Jane took a deep breath and went over and sat down with her hands locked between her knees. Gloria sat up. Another baby. Meditating destruction of something. The apartment was safed for a two-year-old's reach. Gloria was a tall three. "Look, Julia. You know the situation. You're *not* supposed to bring Gloria in here."

"It's not like the baby was going to catch something. I was just passing by. I thought we could go out for lunch."

"That's not the *point*, Julia. We're being taped. You know that. I don't want any question of compromise. You understand me. You're not a child. You're twenty-two years old, and it's about time—"

"I said we could go out for lunch."

With Gloria. God. Her nerves were at the breaking point. "We'll go out for lunch—" Gloria was over at the bookcase. Gloria was after a piece of pottery. "*Gloria, dammit!*" No platythere and no three-year-old ever turned from an objective. She got up and snatched the kid back, dragged her toward the couch and Gloria started to scream. Which could carry all the way down the damn hall where another little girl was trying to drown her nurse. Jane shifted her grip and clamped her hand over Gloria's mouth. "Shut that up! *Julia, dammit, get this kid out of here!*"

"*She's your granddaughter!*"

"*I don't care* what *she is, get her out of here!*" Gloria was struggling hysterically and kicking her shin. "*Out, dammit!*"

Julia got that desperate, offended, out-of-breath look; came and snatched Gloria away, and Gloria, uncorked, screamed as if she was being skinned.

"*Get out!*" Jane shouted. "Dammit, shut her up!"

"You don't care about your own granddaughter!"

"We'll go to lunch tomorrow! *Bring* her! Just shut her up!"

"*She's not one of the damn azi!*"

"Watch your mouth! What kind of language is that?"

"You've got a granddaughter! You've got *me*, for God's sake, and you don't bloody care!"

Hysterical howls from Gloria.

"I'm not going to talk about it now! *Out!*"

"*Damn you then!*" Julia started crying. Gloria was still screaming. Julia grabbed Gloria up and hauled her to the door and out it.

Jane stood in the quiet and felt her stomach profoundly upset. Julia had finally got some guts. And damn near sabotaged the Project. There was not *supposed* to be another little girl. They were still feeling their way. Little changes in self-percept while it was forming at incremental rates could have big effects down the line. If the start was true, Ari would *handle* course deviations at the far end just fine.

Ari did not need to be wondering, Maman, who was that?

Ari had been an only child.

So now the damn Project had Julia's nose out of joint. Because *mother* was one of Julia's triggers, *mother* was the root of all Julia's problems, *mother* was what Julia was determined to succeed in being, because Julia knew that that was the one place where the great and famous Jane Strassen had messed up and Julia was sure she could do it right. Julia felt deprived in her childhood so she was going to the other extreme, ruining her own kid with smothering: *that* little brat knew exactly how to get everything from mama but consistency, and she needed a firm hand and a month away from mama before it was too late.

Amazing how accurate hindsight could be.

v

It was patches again. Florian felt himself a little fluttery, fluttery like when things got confused. The big building and sitting on the edge of the table always made him feel that way, but he could answer when the Super asked him where the One patch went. Right over his heart. He knew that. He had a doll he could patch. But it didn't have so many.

"That's right," the Super said, and patted him. "You're an awfully good boy, Florian. You're very smart and you're very quick to do things. Can you tell me how old you are?"

Old meant big and as he got bigger and smarter the right answer meant more fingers. Right now he got to hold up the first and the next and the next, and stop. Which was hard to do without letting them all come up. When he did it right he felt good all over. The Super gave him a hug.

When he got through there was always a sweet. And he knew all the answers to everything the Super asked. He felt fluttery but it was a good fluttery.

He just wished they would give him the sweet now and forget about the patches.

vi

Ari was tremendously excited. She had a new suit—red, with a glittery pattern on the front and on one sleeve. Nelly had brushed her hair till it crackled and flew, all black and shiny, and then Ari, all dressed, had had to dither about the living room till maman and Ollie were ready. Maman looked very tall and very beautiful, glittery with silver, and the silver in her hair was pretty. Ollie went too, handsome in the black the azi wore. Ollie was a special azi. He was always with maman, and if Ollie said something Ari had to do it. She did, or at least she did today, because maman and Ollie were going to take her to a Party.

There were going to be a lot of big people there. She would go there and then Ollie would take her to Valery's to a children's party.

Valery was a boy. He was sera Schwartz's. Azi would watch them and they would play games and there would be ices, on a table their size. And other children. But mostly she liked Valery. Valery had a spaceship that had red lights. He had a glass thing you could look through and it made patterns.

Most of all she hoped there would be presents. Sometimes there were. Since everyone was dressed up, there might be.

But it was special, to go where the big people were. To walk down the hall holding maman's hand, dressed up and acting nice, because you were supposed to, and not make trouble. Especially when there could be presents.

They rode the lift downstairs. She saw a lot of tall azi in the hall: azi wore black more than they wore other colors; and even if they didn't, she could always tell them. They were not like maman or uncle Denys, they looked like azi. Sometimes she pretended to be them. She walked very quiet and stood straight and looked very straight like Ollie and said yes, sera to maman. (Not to Nelly. To Nelly you said, yes.) Sometimes she pretended to be maman and she told Nelly, make my bed, Nelly, please. (And to Ollie, once: Ollie, dammit, I want a drink. But that had not been a good idea. Ollie had brought her the drink and told maman. And maman had said it was not nice and Ollie was not going to do things for her when she was rude. So she said dammit to Nelly instead.)

Maman led her down the hall through the azi and through a doorway where there were a lot of people in the doorway. One woman said: "Happy new year, Ari." And bent over in her face. She had a pretty necklace and you could see way down her blouse. It was interesting. But Ollie picked her up. That was better. She could see people's faces.

The woman talked to maman, and people crowded in, all talking at once, and everything smelled like perfume and food and powder.

Someone patted her on the shoulder as Ollie held her. It was uncle Denys. Denys was fat. He made a lot of room around him. She wondered whether he was solid all the way through or sort of held his breath more than regular people to keep him so round.

"How are you, Ari?" uncle Denys yelled at her in all the racket, and all of a sudden the people stopped talking and looked at them. "Happy new year."

She was puzzled then, but interested. If it was her new year it was a birthday, and if it was a birthday party people were supposed to come to her apartment and bring her presents. She didn't see any.

"Happy new year," people said. She looked at them hopefully. But there were no presents. She sighed, and then as Ollie brought her through the crowd, she caught sight of the punch and the cake.

Ollie knew. "Do you want some punch?" he asked.

She nodded. There was a lot of noise. She was not sure she liked this many big people. The party did not make sense. But punch and cake was looking better. She clung to Ollie's strong shoulder and felt a good deal more cheerful, because Ollie could carry her right through to the table with the punch bowl and Ollie understood very well what was important. Punch, especially in a pretty bowl and with a big cake, was almost as good as presents.

"I've got to set you down," Ollie said. "All right? You stand right there and I'll get your punch."

That was not all right. Everyone was tall, the music was awfully loud, and when she was standing on the floor she could not see anything but people's legs. Somebody might step on her. But Ollie set her down, and maman was coming, with uncle Denys. And the crowd did not step on her. A lot of people looked at her. Some smiled. So she felt safe.

"Ari." Ollie gave her the cup. "Don't spill."

The punch was green. She was not altogether sure of it, but it smelled good and it tasted better.

"You're getting too big to carry," uncle Denys said. She looked up and wrinkled her nose at him. She was not sure she liked that idea. Maman said the same thing. But Ollie didn't. Ollie was big and he was very strong. He felt different than anyone. She liked him to carry her: she liked to put her arms around his neck and lean on him, because he was like a chair you could climb on, and you couldn't feel his bones, just a kind of solid. He was warm, too. And smelled good. But Ollie was getting punch for maman and uncle Denys from another bowl, and she just kept close to him and drank her punch while Denys and maman talked and loud music played.

Ollie looked down at her when maman and Denys had their punch. "Do you want some cake?" Ollie asked, talking loud. "They're going to have cake at the children's party."

That promised better. "I want some more punch," she said, and gave Ollie her cup. "And cake, please." She stood there in a little open space to wait. She put her hands behind her, and remembered maman said not to rock back and forth, it was stupid-looking. People she did not know came up and said she was pretty, and wished her happy new year, but she was ready to leave, except for the punch and cake Ollie was getting. She was going to stay for that.

Children's party sounded a lot better.

Maybe there would be presents *there*.

"Come on over and sit down," Ollie said, not giving her the cake or the punch. He carried it for her. There were chairs along the wall. She was relieved. If she got punch on her new suit she would look bad and maman would scold her. She climbed up onto a chair and Ollie set the dish in her lap and set the cup on the seat beside her. She had the whole row to herself.

"I'm going to get mine," Ollie said. "Stay there. I'll be back."

She nodded, with cake in her mouth. White cake. The nice kind. With good icing. She was much happier. She swung her feet and ate cake and licked her fingers while Ollie waited at the punch bowl and maman talked with Denys and Giraud.

Maybe they waited about the presents. Maybe something interesting was going to happen. They all glittered. Some of them she had seen at home. But a lot were strange. She finished her cake and licked her fingers and slid off the chair to stand, because most of the people were around the tables and the floor was mostly clear.

She walked out to see how far Ollie had got in the line. But someone had distracted Ollie. That was a chance to walk around.

So she walked. Not far. She did not want maman and Ollie to leave and lose her. She looked back to see if she could still see maman. Yes. But maman was still busy talking. Good. If maman scolded her she could say, I was right here, maman. Maman could not be too mad.

A lot of the clothes were pretty. She liked the green blouse you could see through. And the black one a man was wearing, all shimmery. But maman's jewelry was still the best.

There was a man with bright red hair.

In black. Azi. She watched him. She said hello when somebody said hello to her, but she was not interested in that. She had always thought her hair was pretty. Prettier than anybody's. But his was *pretty. He* was. It was not fair. If there was hair like that *she* wanted it. She was suddenly dissatisfied with her own.

He looked at her. He was not azi. No. Yes. His face went all straight and he turned his chin, so, and pretended he did not see her looking at him. He was with a dark-haired man. That man looked at her, but the azi did not want him to.

He looked at her anyway. He was handsome like Ollie. He looked at her different than grown-ups and she thought he was not supposed to do that, but she did not want to look anywhere else, because he was different than everyone. The azi with red hair was by him, but he was not the important one. The man was. The man was looking at her, and she had never even seen him. He had never come to visit. He had never brought presents.

She went closer. The azi didn't want her to be close to his friend. He had his hand on the man's shoulder. Like she was going to get him. But the man watched her like she was maman. Like he had done something bad and she was maman.

He was being her. And she was being maman. And the azi was being Ollie, when maman was yelling.

Then the azi saw something dangerous behind her. She looked.

Maman was coming. But maman stopped when she looked.

Everyone was stopped. Everyone was watching. They had stopped talking. There was just the music. Everyone was afraid.

She started toward maman.

Everyone twitched.

She stopped. And everyone twitched again. Even maman.

She had done that.

She looked back at maman. Twitch.

She looked back at the man.

Twitch. Everybody.

She didn't know she could do that.

Maman was going to be mad, later. Ollie was.

If maman was going to shout she might as well *do* something first.

The azi and the man looked at her when she walked up to them. The man looked like she was going to get him. The azi thought so too.

The man had pretty hands like Ollie. He was a lot like Ollie. People all thought he was dangerous. That was wrong. She knew it was. She could scare them good.

She came up and took his hand. Everyone was doing what she wanted. Even he was. She had maman good. The way she could do Nelly.

She *liked* that.

"My name's Ari," Ari said.

"Mine's Justin," Justin said quietly. In all that quiet.

"I'm going to a party," she said. "At Valery's."

Jane Strassen came to collect the child. Firmly. Grant got between them, and put his hand on Justin's shoulder, and turned him away.

They left. That was all there was to do.

"Damn," Grant said, when they were back in the apartment, "if no one had moved it would have been nothing. Nothing at all. She picked up on it. She picked up on it like it was broadcast."

"I had to see her," Justin said.

He could not say why. Except they said she *was* Ari. And he had not believed it until then.

<hr />

vii

"Night, sweet," maman said; and kissed her. Ari put her arms up and hugged maman and kissed her too. Smack.

Maman went out and it was dark then. Ari snuggled down in bed with Poo-thing. She was full of cake and punch. She shut her eyes and all the people were glittery. Ollie got her cake. And all the people looked at her. Valery's party was nice. They played music-chairs and had favors. Hers was a glittery star. Valery's was a ball. They were real sorry about sera Schwartz's lamp.

New year was fun.

"Is she all right?" Ollie asked in the bedroom. And Jane nodded, while he unhooked her blouse. "Sera, I am sorry—"

"Don't talk about it. Don't fret about it. It's all right." He finished; she slid the silver blouse down her arms and threw it on the chair back. Ollie was still shaken.

So, in fact, was she. Not mentioning it was Denys' and Giraud's damn idea.

Olga had had the kid up in front of visitors, hauled her around like a little mannequin—subjected her to the high-pressure social circuit in which Ari's sensitive nerves must have been raw.

They could not take the curtain of secrecy off. There was only one part of that high-tension atmosphere they could access, that inside Reseune itself.

The Family. In all its multifarious, *ne*farious glory.

Enough sugar in her often-tested metabolism, enough no-don't and behave-Ari and promised rewards to be sure a four-year-old was going to be hyper as hell.

She felt, somehow, sick at her stomach.

viii

Justin hugged his coat about him as he and Grant took the outside walk between Residency and the office, and jammed his hands into his pockets. Not a fast walk, despite the morning chill, on a New Year's morning where everyone was slow getting started.

He stopped at the fishpond, bent and fed the fish. The koi knew him. They expected him and came swimming up under the brown-edged lotus. They ruled their little pool between the buildings, they entertained the children of the House and begat their generations completely oblivious to the fact that they were not on the world of their origin.

Here was here. The white old fellow with the orange patches had been taking food from his hand since he was a young boy, and daily, now, since Jordan had gone and he and Grant had sought the outside whenever they could. Every morning.

Spy-dishes could pick up their voices from the House, could pick them up anywhere. But surely, surely, Security just did the easy thing, and caught the temperature of things from time to time by flipping a monitor switch on the apartment, not wasting overmuch time on a quiet pair of tape-designers who had not made the House trouble in years. Security could bring them in for psychprobe anytime it wanted. That they had not—meant Security was not interested. Yet.

Still, they were careful.

"He's hungry," Justin said of the white koi. "Winter; and children don't remember."

"One of the differences," Grant said, sitting on the rock near him. "Azi children would."

Justin laughed in spite of the distress that hovered over them. "You're so damn superior."

Grant shrugged cheerfully. "Born-men are so blind to other norms. We aren't." Another piece of wafer hit the water, and a koi took it, sending out ripples that disturbed the lotus. "I tell you, all the trouble with alien contacts is preconceptions. They should send us."

"This is the man who says Novgorod would be too foreign."

"Us. You and me. I wouldn't worry then."

A long pause. Justin held the napkin of wafers still in his hands. "I wish to hell there was a place."

"Don't worry about it." It was not Novgorod Grant meant. Of a sudden the shadow was back. The cold was back in the wind. "Don't. It's all right."

Justin nodded, mute. They were so close. He had had letters from Jordan. They looked like lace, with sentences physically cut from the paper. But they said, in one salutation: *Hello, son. I hear you and Grant are well. I read and re-read all your letters. The old ones are wearing out. Please send more.*

His sense of humor is intact, he had commented to Grant. And he and Grant had read and re-read that letter too, for all the little cues it had given him about Jordan's state of mind. Read and re-read the others that got through. Page after page of how the weather was. Talk about Paul—constantly, *Paul and I*. That had reassured him too.

Things are moving, Denys had said, when he brought up the subject of sending voice tapes. Or making phone calls, carefully monitored.

And they had been so close to getting that permission.

"I can't help but worry," Justin said. "Grant, we've got to be so damn clean for the next little while. And it won't finish it. It won't be the last time. You or I don't have to have done anything."

"They brought the girl there. They didn't stop us from coming. Maybe they didn't expect what happened, but it wasn't our doing. A roomful of psychologists—and they froze. They cued the girl. She was reading *them*, not us. It's that flux-thinking again. Born-men. They didn't want what happened; and they *did* want it, they set up the whole thing to show Ari off, and she was *doing* it—she was proving what they've worked to prove. And proving nothing. Maybe we cued her. We were watching her. I got caught at it. Maybe that made her curious. She's four years old, Justin. And the whole room jumped. What's any four-year-old going to do?"

"Run to her mother, dammit. She started to. Then everybody relaxed and she picked that up too. And got this look—" He twitched his shoulders as a sudden chill got down his neck. Then shoved his imagination back down again and tried to think. The way no one had, last night.

"Does it occur to you," Grant said, "the fallibility of CIT memory? Flux-thinking. You have prophetic dreams, remember? *You* can dream about a man drinking a glass of milk. A week later you can see Yanni drinking tea at lunch and if seeing him do that has a high shock-value, you'll super the dream-state right over him, you'll swear you dreamed about him doing that, exactly at that table, and even psychprobe can't sort it out after that. It's happened to me twice in my life. And when it does, I take my tape out of the vault and betake myself to the couch for a session until I feel better. Listen to me: I'll concede the child's behavior may have been significant. I'll wait to see how it integrates with other behavior. But if you want my analysis of the situation, every CIT in that room went dream-state. Including you. Mass hallucination. The only sane people in that room for thirty seconds were the azi and that kid, and most of us were keyed on our CITs and bewildered as hell."

"Except you?"

"I was watching you *and* her."

Justin gave a heavy sigh and some of the tension went out of him. It was nothing, God knew, he did not *know*. It was what Grant said, a roomful of psychologists forgot their science. Flux-thinking. Shades of values. "Hell with Hauptmann," he muttered. "I'm becoming an Emoryite." Two more quiet breaths. He could remember it with less emotional charge now and see the child—instead of the woman. *I'm going to a party at Valery's.*

Not a touch of maliciousness in that. She had not been playing her game then. She had looked up with a face as innocent as any child's and offered a let's-be-friends opening. Them and Us. Peace-making, maybe. He was not in touch with his own four-year-old memories. Jacobs, who worked that level in citizen psych, could tell him what a four-year-old CIT was like. But he could haul up a few things out of that dark water: Jordan's face when he was in his thirties.

Himself and Grant feeding the pond-fish. Four or five or six. He was not sure. It was one of his oldest memories and he could not pin it down.

And he sweated, suddenly, shying off.

Why? Why do I do that?

What's wrong with me?

Walls.

Children—had not been an interest of his. Emphatically—not an interest of his. He had mentally shied off every chance to learn, fled his own childhood like a territory he was not going back to; and the preoccupation of Rescue with the Project had disgusted him.

Twenty-three years old and a fool, doing routine work, wasting himself, not thinking to left and right. Just straight down a track. Not checking out much tape because tape meant helplessness; because tape opened up areas he did not want opened.

Throwing down those walls to *then*, to Jordan, to anything that had been—brought the anger up, made his palms sweat. Getting involved—

But they had *become* involved.

"It's a trap, isn't it?" he said to Grant. "Your psychset won't let you see what I saw. But is it valid for *her*, Grant? She has that flux-dimension, and so do all us CITs."

Grant gave a humorless laugh. "You're conceding I'm right."

"It was a roomful of CITs being fools. But maybe we saw something you didn't."

"Flux. Flux. Klein bottles. True and not-true. I'm *glad* I know what planet I'm standing on, all the time. And I saw what I saw without supering the past *or* the future."

"Damn. Sometimes I wish I could borrow your tape."

Grant shook his head. "You're right too. About seeing things I don't. I know you do. I'm worried. I'm worried because I know I can't see the situation the way a CIT does. I can logic my way through what you'll do, but damned if I can understand the flux."

"You mean your pathways are so down azi-tracks you don't see it." He could not let the Hauptmann-Emory debate pass; Grant nattered at him with it all the time, and Grant was trying him with it now. Under the other things, a little touch of clinical perspective: *get out of it, Justin. Don't react. Think.*

"I mean," Grant said, "if we were all azi we wouldn't *have* this problem. And *she* wouldn't: they could install the damn psychset and she'd be exactly what they wanted. But she isn't. They aren't. Rationality isn't what they're after, it's not what they're practicing. From where I stand, you're as upside down as they are, and I wish to hell you'd listen to me and keep your head down, throw out the hallucinations, and don't react. Any possible trouble is years away. There's time to prepare for it."

"You're absolutely right: we're not dealing with azi mindset here. They're not a hell of a lot careful. If anything goes wrong with their precious project next week they'll know it was my fault. Anytime that kid crosses my path—there's no way I can be innocent. Facts have nothing to do with it. She's just damn well killed any chance of getting any give in Jordan's situation; hell, they may not even let the letters through—"

"Don't *look* for blame. Don't act as if you have it. Mark me: if you go around reacting, they'll react."

Ari's voice. Out of the past. *Sweet, get control of yourself.*

Boy, I do appreciate your distress, but get a grip on it.

Are you afraid of women, sweet? Your father is.

Family is such a liability.

He rested his head in his hands and knew even when he did it that he had lost his edge, lost everything, scattered it as thoroughly as he could manage it—all the fine-edged logic, all the control, all the defensive mechanisms. He walked Reseune's corridors like a ghost, laid himself open to everyone, shielded no reactions. *See, I'm harmless.*

No one had to worry about him. He was all nerves and reactions. He detected everyone's vague distaste and their caution around him. Jordan's calamity and his own guilt over precipitating it had taken the fight out of him, maybe made him half crazy, that was what they had to think.

Except the handful who had seen the tapes. Who had seen those damnable tapes and knew what Ari had done, knew why he waked in cold sweats and why he shied off from people touching him or being near him. Especially Petros Ivanov knew, having probed his mind after Giraud and everyone had done with him. *I'm going to do a little intervention,* Petros had said, patting his shoulder while he was going under; it had taken three large Security men to get him over there to hospital and several interns to get the drug into him. Giraud's orders. *I'm just going to tell you it's all right. That you're safe. You've been through trauma. I'm going to close off that time. All right? Relax. You know me, Justin. You know I'm on your side. . . .*

O God, what did they do to me? Ari, Giraud, Petros—

He wept. Grant put a hand on his arm. Grant was the only one, the only one who could. The child had touched his hand. And he had flashed-back. It was like touching a corpse.

He sat like that for a long time. Until he heard voices, and knew other people were on the walk, far across the quadrangle. There was a hedge to hide them. But he made the effort to pull himself together.

"Justin?" Grant said.

"I'm all right. Dammit." And, which he had never said to Grant: "Petros did something to me. Or Giraud did. Or Ari. Don't you see it? Don't you see a difference?"

"No."

"Tell me the truth, dammit!"

Grant flinched. A strange, distant kind of flinching. And pain, after that. Profound pain.

"Grant? Do *you* think they did something to me?"

"I don't understand born-men," Grant said.

"Don't give me that shit!"

"—I was about to say—" Grant's face was white, his lips all but trembling. "Justin, you people—I don't understand."

"Don't lie to me. What were you going to say?"

"I don't know the answer. God, you'd been shocked over and over; if you were azi you'd have gone like I did. Better if you could have. I don't know what's going on inside you. I see—I see you—"

"Spit it out, Grant!"

"—You're not—not like you would have been if it hadn't happened. Who could be? You learn. You adjust."

"That's not what I'm asking. *Did they do anything?*"

"I don't know," Grant said. All but stammered. "I don't know. I can't judge CIT psychsets."

"You can judge *mine*."

"Don't back me into a corner, Justin. I *don't know*. I don't know and I don't know how to know."

"I'm psyched. Is that what you see? Come on. Give me some *help*, Grant."

"I think you've got scars. I don't know whether Petros helped or hurt."

"Or knocked me the rest of the way down and did it to me like Ari did. The kid—" It had been a jolt. A severe jolt. Time-trip. *I'm afraid of the tape-flashes. I shut them out. I warp myself away from that time. That in itself is a decision, isn't it?*

Petros: *"I'm going to close it down."*

Wall it off.

God. It's a psychblock. It could *be.*

They weren't my friends. Or Jordan's. I know that.

He drew a deep, sudden gulp of air. *I'm blocking off everything I learned from her. I'm scared stiff of it.*

"Justin?"

The kid's shaken it loose. The kid's thrown me back before Petros. Before Giraud. Back when there was just Ari.

Back when I didn't believe anything could get to me. I walked in her door that night thinking I was in control.

Two seconds later I knew I wasn't.

Family is a liability, sweet.

What was she telling me?

"Justin?"

Would she want *what Reseune is becoming? Would she* want *that kid in Giraud's hands? Damn, he was in Ari's pocket while she was alive. But after she died—*

"Justin!"

He became aware of Grant shaking at him. Of real fear. "I'm all right," he mumbled. "I'm all right."

He felt Grant's hand close on his. Grant's hand was warm. The wind had gone through him. What he was looking at, he did not know. The garden. The pond. "Grant, —whether or not that kid's Ari reincarnate, she's smart. She's figured out how to psych *them*. Isn't that what it's all about? She's figured out what they want, isn't that what you say about Hauptmann's subjects? She's got them believing all of it. Denys and Jane and Giraud and all of them. *I* don't have to believe in it to believe what can happen to us if Giraud thinks we're a threat."

"Justin. Let it alone. Let's go. It's cold out here."

"*Do* you think they ran a psychblock on me?" He dragged himself back from out-there; looked at Grant's pale, cold-stung face. "Give me the truth, Grant."

A long silence. Grant was breathing hard. Holding back. It took no skill to see that.

"I think they could have," Grant said finally. The grip on his hand hurt. There was a tremor in Grant's voice. "I've done whatever I could. I've tried. Ever since. Don't slip on me. Don't let them get their hands on you again. And they can—if you give them any excuse. You know they can."

"I'm not going under. I'm not. I *know* what they did." He took a deep breath and drew Grant closer, hugged him, leaned against him, exhausted. "I'm doing all right. Maybe I'm doing better than I have been in the last six years."

Grant looked at him, pale and panicked.

"I swear," Justin said. He was beyond cold. Frozen through. Numb. "Damn," he said. "We've got time, don't we?"

"We've got time," Grant said. And pulled at him. "Come on. You're freezing. So am I. Let's get inside."

He got up. He threw the rest of the food to the fish, stuffed the napkin into his pocket with numb fingers, and walked. He was not thoroughly conscious of the route, of all the automatic things. Grant had no more to say until they got to the office in Wing Two.

Then Grant lingered at the door of his office. Just looked at him, as if to ask if he was all right. "I've got to run to library."

He gave Grant a silent lift of the chin. I'm all right. "Go on, then."

Grant bit his lip. "See you at lunch."

"Right."

Grant left. He sat down in the disordered little office, logged on to the House system, and prepared to get to work. But a message-dot was blinking on the corner of his screen. He windowed it up.

See me first thing, my office, it said. *Giraud Nye.*

He sat there staring at the thing. He found his hand shaking when he reached to punch the off switch.

He was not ready for this. Psychprobe flashed into his mind; all the old nightmares. He needed all his self-control.

All the old reflexes were gone. Everything. *He* was vulnerable. Grant was.

He had whatever time it took to walk over there to pull himself together. He did not know what to do, whether to route himself past the library and try to warn Grant—but that looked guilty. Every move he could make could damn him.

No, he thought then, and bit his lip till it bled. It flashed back to another meeting. A taste of blood in his mouth. Hysteria jammed behind his teeth.

It's started, he thought. *It's happened.*

He turned the machine on, sent a message over to Grant's office: *Giraud wants to see me. I may be held up on the lunch. —J.* It was warning enough. What Grant could do about it, he had no idea.

Worry. That was what.

He shut down again, got up, locked the office, and walked down the corridor, still tasting the blood. He kept looking at things and people with the thought that he might not be back. That the next thing he and Grant might see might be an interview room in the hospital.

ix

Giraud's office was the same he had always had, in the Administrative Wing, the same paneled and unobtrusive entry with the outside lock—more security than Ari had ever used. Giraud was no longer official head of Security. He was *Councillor* Nye these days—for outsiders' information. But everyone in the House knew who was running Security—still.

Justin slid his card into the lock, heard it click, set for his CIT-number. He walked into the short paneled hall and opened the inside door, on the office where Giraud's azi Abban was at his accustomed desk.

That was the first thing he saw. In the next split-second he saw the two Security officers and Abban was rising casually from his chair.

He stopped cold. And looked at the nearer of the azi officers, eye to eye, calmly: *Let's be civilized.* He took the next quiet step inside and let the door shut at his back.

They had a body-scanner. "Arms out, ser," the one on the left said. He obliged them, let them pass the wand over him. It found something in his coat pocket. The officer pulled out the paper napkin. Justin gave him a disparaging look in spite of the fact that his heart was going like a hammer and the air in the room seemed too thin.

They satisfied themselves he was not armed. Abban opened the door and they took him through it.

Giraud was not the only one there. Denys was. And Petros Ivanov. He felt his heart trying to come up his throat. One of the officers held him lightly by the arm and guided him to the remaining chair, in front of Giraud's desk. Denys sat in a chair to the left of the desk, Petros to the right.

Like a tribunal.

And the Security men stayed, one with his hand on the back of Justin's chair, until Giraud lifted a hand and told them to leave. But Justin's ears told him someone had stayed when the door had shut.

Abban, he thought.

"You understand why you're here," Giraud said. "I don't have to tell you."

Giraud wanted an answer. "Yes, ser," he said in a muted voice.

They'll do what they damned well please.

Why have they got Petros here? Unless they're going to run a probe.

"Have you got anything to say?" Giraud asked.

"I don't think I should have to." He found a tenuous control of his voice. *Dammit, get a grip on things.*

And like a wind out of the dark: *Steady, sweet. Don't give everything away.*

"I didn't provoke that. God *knows* I didn't want it."

"You could have damn well left."

"I left."

"*After.*" Giraud's face was thin-lipped with anger. He picked up a stylus and posed it between his fingers. "What's your intention? To sabotage the project?"

"No. I was there like everyone else. No different. I was minding my own business. What did you do, prime her for that show? Is *that* it? A little show? Impress the Family? Con the press? I'll *bet* you've got tape."

Giraud had not expected that. He gave away very little. Denys and Petros looked distressed.

"The child wasn't prompted," Denys said quietly. "You have my word, Justin, it wasn't prompted."

"The hell it wasn't. It's a damn good show for the news, isn't it—just the sort of thing that makes great fodder for the eetees out there. The kid singles out the killer's replicate. God! what a piece of science!"

"Don't bother to play for a camera," Giraud said. "We're not being taped."

"I didn't expect." He was shaking. He shifted his foot to relax his leg, to keep it from trembling. But, God, the brain was working. They were going to haul him off for another session, that was what they were working up to; and somehow that shook the fog out of his mind. "I imagine you'll work me over good before I get to the cameras. But it'd be sloppy as hell to have me on the tape in that party and dropping right out again. Or turning up dead. Makes a problem for you, doesn't it?"

"Justin," Petros said, a tone of appeal. "No one's going to 'work you over.' That's not what we're about here."

"Sure."

"What we're about," Giraud said in a hard, clipped voice, "is one clear question. Did *you* cue her?"

"You find your own answers. Write down whatever you want. Look at the damn tape."

"We have," Giraud said. "Grant had eye contact with her. So did you, right before she moved."

Attack on a new target. Of course they got around to Grant. "What else were people looking at? What else were we *there* to look at? I looked at her. Did you think I'd come there and *not*? You saw me there. You could have told me to leave. But of course you didn't. You set me up. You set up the whole thing. How many people in there knew it? Just you?"

"You maintain you didn't cue her."

"Dammit, no. Neither of us did. I asked Grant. He wouldn't lie to me. He admits the eye contact. He was looking at her. 'I got caught at it,' was the way he put it. It wasn't his fault. It wasn't mine."

Petros stirred in his chair. Leaned toward Giraud. "Gerry, I think you have to take into account what I said."

Giraud touched the desk control. The screen tilted up out of the surface; he typed something with his right hand, likely a file-scan. Dataflow reflected off the metal on his collar, a flicker of green.

Manipulation of more than data. Orchestrated, Justin told himself. The whole play. A little moment of suspense now. Secrets.

And he still could not keep himself from reacting.

Giraud read or mimed reading. His breathing grew larger. His face was no friendlier when he looked up. "You don't like tapestudy. Odd, in a designer."

"I don't damn well trust it. Can you blame me?"

"You don't even do entertainment tapes."

"I work hard."

"Let's not have that kind of answer. You skipped out on your follow-ups with Petros. You don't take tape more than once every month or so. That's a damned strange attitude in a designer."

He said nothing. He had used all the glib answers.

"Even Grant," Giraud said, "doesn't go into the lab for his. He uses a home unit. Not at all regulation."

"There's no rule about that. If that satisfies him, it satisfies him. Grant's bright, he's got good absorption—"

"It's not your instruction to do that."

"No, it's not my instruction."

"You know," Petros said, "Grant's self-sufficient, completely social. He doesn't need that kind of reinforcement as often as some. But considering what he's been through, it would be better if he took it deep. Just as a checkup."

"Considering what you put him through? No!"

"So it is your instruction," Giraud said.

"No. It's his choice. It's his choice, he's entitled, the same as I am, the last I heard."

"I'm not sure we *need* a designer-team that's phobic about tape."

"Go to hell."

"Easy," Denys said. "Take it easy. Giraud, there's nothing wrong with his output. Or Grant's. That's not at issue."

"There was more than one victim in Ari's murder," Petros said. "Justin was. Grant was. I don't think you can ignore that fact. You're dealing with someone who was a boy when the incident happened, who was, in fact, the victim of Ari's own criminal act, among others. I haven't wanted to press the issue. I've been keeping an eye on him. I've sent him requests to come in to talk. Is that true, Justin?"

"It's true."

"You haven't answered, have you?"

"No." Panic pressed on him. He felt sick inside.

"The whole situation with the Project," Petros said, "has bothered you quite a bit, hasn't it?"

"Live and let live. I'm sorry for the kid. I'm sure you've got all the benefit of Security's eavesdropping in my apartment. I hope you get a lot of entertainment out of the intimate bits."

"Justin."

"You can go to hell too, Petros."

"Justin. Tell me the truth. *Are* you still getting tape-flashes?"

"No."

"You're sure."

"Yes, I'm sure."

"You felt a lot of stress when you walked into the party, didn't you?"

"Hell, no. Why should I?"

"I think that's your answer," Petros said to Giraud. "He came in there stressed. Both of them did. Ari had no trouble picking up on it. That's all there is to it. I don't think it was intended. I'm more disturbed about Justin's state of mind. I think it's just best he go back to his wing, and show up at family functions, and carry on as normally as he can. I don't think anything useful is served by a probe. He's carrying enough stress as it is. I do want him to come in for counseling."

"Giraud," Denys said, "if you *believe* young Ari's sensitivities, bear in mind she wasn't afraid of Justin. Stressed as he was, she wasn't afraid of him. Quite the opposite."

"I don't like that either." Giraud drew a breath and leaned back, looking at Justin from under his brows. "You'll take Petros' prescription. If he tells me you're not cooperating, you'll be tending a precip station before sundown. Hear me?"

"Yes, ser."

"You'll go on working. If something takes you across Ari's path, you speak to her or not according to your judgment, whichever will provoke the least curiosity. You'll show up at Family functions. If she speaks to you, be pleasant. No more than that. You stray off that line, you'll be in here again and I won't be in a good mood. And that goes for Grant, just the same. You make it clear to him. Do you understand me?"

"Yes, ser." Like any azi. Quiet. Respectful. *It's a trap. It'll still close. There's something more to this.*

"You can go. Open the door, Abban."

The door did open. He shoved himself out of his chair. Denys did the same. He made it as far as the door and Denys went out it with him, caught his arm, steered him past Security out into the small box of the entry hall and out again into the main corridor.

Then Denys tugged him to a stop. "Justin."

He stayed stopped. He was shaking, still. But defiance did not serve anything.

"Justin, you're under a lot of pressure. But you know and I know—there's no memory transfer. It's *not* the old Ari. We don't want, frankly, another case of animosity with the Warricks. We don't *want* you taking Jordan's part in this. You know what's at stake."

He nodded.

"Justin, listen to me. Giraud did the probe on you. He knows damned well you're honest. He's just—"

"A bastard."

"Justin. Don't make things hard. Do what Giraud says. Don't make a mistake. You don't want to hurt the little girl. I know you don't. What Ari did to you—has nothing to do with her. And you wouldn't hurt her."

"No. I never did anything to *Ari*, for God's sake. You think I'd hurt a kid?"

"I know. I know that's true. Just think about that. Think about it the next time you have to deal with her. Ari tore you up. You can do the same thing to that child. You can hurt her. I want you to think seriously about that."

"I didn't do anything to her!"

"You didn't do anything. Calm down. Calm down and take a breath. Listen to me. If you can handle this right, it could help you."

"Sure."

Denys took his arm again, faced him closer to the wall as Security left the office. Held on to him. "Justin. I wanted to tell you—the request that's on my desk, the phone link: I'm going to give it a few weeks and then allow it. You'll be on some kind of delay—Jordan's clever, and Security has to have time to think. That's the best I can do. Does that make you feel better?"

"What's it cost me?"

"Nothing. Nothing. Just don't foul it up. Stay out of trouble. All right?"

He stared at the wall, at travertine patterns that blurred in front of his eyes. He felt Denys pat his shoulder.

"I'm damn sorry. I'm damn sorry. I know. You haven't had a day of peace. But I want you *on* the Project. That's why I fought Giraud to keep you here. Ari liked you—no. Listen to me. Ari *liked* you. Never mind what she did. I know her—posthumously—as well as I know myself. Ari's feud with Jordan was old and it was bitter. But she got your test scores and made up her mind she wanted you."

"They were faked!"

"No, they weren't. Not outstandingly high, *you* know that. But scattered through half a dozen fields. You had the qualities *she* had. Not her match, but then, you hadn't had Olga Emory pushing you. She told me—personally— and this is no lie, son, that she *wanted* you in her wing, that you were better than the tests showed, a damned lot better, she said, than Jordan. Her words, not mine."

"Science wasn't what she had in mind, you know that."

"You're wrong. It's not what you want to hear, God knows. But if you want to understand why she did what she did—that's something you *should* know. I have one interest in this. Ari. Understand—she had cancer. Rejuv breakdown. The doctors argue whether the cancer kicked the rejuv or whether the rejuv was failing naturally and let the cancer develop. Whatever was going on, she *knew* she was in trouble and the timing couldn't have been worse. Surgery would have delayed the project, so she put Petros and Irina under orders and covered it up. She set the whole project up, so that when she had to go for surgery—I'm sure she didn't rule that out: she wasn't a fool; but so when she did, it wouldn't leave the subject without support, you understand, and it could run a few months with a light hand. Understand: I knew, because I was her friend, Justin. I was the one she allowed access to her notes. Giraud's damn good at the money end of this. But my concern is her concern: the Project. I think you have your sincere doubts about it. No controls, no duplicatable result— But it's founded on two centuries of duplicatable results with the azi. And of course it's not the kind of thing that we can quantify: we're dealing with a human life, an emotional dimension, a subjective dimension. We may disagree like hell, Justin, in there, in private, and I respect you for your professional honesty. But if you try to sabotage us, you'll have me for an enemy. Do you understand me?"

"Yes, ser."

"I'll tell you another thing: Ari did some very wrong things. But she was a great woman. She *was* Reseune. And she was my friend. I've protected you; and I've protected her reputation by the same stroke; and *damned* if I'll see some sordid little incident destroy that reputation. I'll keep you from that. You understand me?"

"You've got the tapes in the archives! If this poor kid halfway follows in Ari's track, researchers are going to want every last detail—and that's no small one."

"No. That won't matter. That's from the *end* of her life, beyond the scope of their legitimate interest. And even so, that's why we're working with Rubin. Rubin's the one the military can paw over. Ari is *our* project. *We* keep title on the techniques. Did Reseune ever release anything—it has a financial interest in?"

"My God, you can run that scam on the military for years. Admit it. It's Giraud's damn fund-raiser. His bottomless source of military projects."

Denys smiled and shook his head. "It's going to *work*, Justin. We didn't prompt her."

"Then tell me this: are you sure *Giraud* didn't?"

Denys' eyes reacted minutely. The face did not. It went on smiling. "Time will prove it, won't it? In your position, rather than be made a public fool, I'd keep my mouth shut, Justin Warrick. I've helped you. I've spoken for you and Jordan and Grant when no one else did. I've been your patron. But remember I was Ari's friend. And I *won't* see this project sabotaged."

The threat was there. It was real. He had no doubt of it. "Yes, ser," he said in half a voice.

Denys patted his shoulder again. "That's the only time I'm going to say that. I don't want ever to say it again. I want you to take the favor I'm doing you and remember what I told you. All right?"

"Yes, ser."

"Are *you* all right?"

He drew a breath. "That depends on what Petros is going to do, doesn't it?"

"He's just going to talk to you. That's all." Denys shook at him gently. "Justin, —are you getting tape-flashes?"

"No," he said. "No." His mouth trembled. He let it. It made the point with Denys. "I've just had enough hell. The hospital panics me, all right? Do you blame me? I don't trust Petros. Or anyone on his staff. I'll answer his questions. If you want my cooperation, keep him away from me and Grant."

"Is that blackmail?"

"God, I couldn't have learned anything about that, could I? No. I'm asking you. I'll do anything you want me to. I've got no percentage in hurting the kid. I don't want that. I just want my job, I want the phone-link, I want to—"

He lost his composure, turned and leaned against the wall until he had gotten his breath.

Hand them all the keys, sweet, that's right.

Damn stupid.

"You've got all that," Denys said. "Look. You answer Petros' questions. You try to work this thing out. You were a scared kid yourself. You're still scared, and I'm terribly afraid all this did you more damage than you're willing to have known—"

"I can do my job. You said that."

"That's not in question. I assure you it's not. You don't know who to trust. You think you're all alone. You're not. Petros does care. I do. I know, that's not what you want to hear. But you can come to me if you feel you need help. I've told you my conditions. I want your help. I *don't* want any accusations against Ari, the project, or the staff."

"Then keep Petros' hands off me and Grant. Tell Security to take their damn equipment out. Let me live my life and do my work, that's all."

"I want to help you."

"Then help me! Do what I asked. You'll get my cooperation. I'm not carrying on a feud. I just want a little peace, Denys. I just want a little peace, after all these years. Have I—ever—done anyone any harm?"

"No." A pat on his shoulder, on his back. "No. You haven't. Never anything. The harm was all against you."

He turned, leaning against the wall. "Then leave me *alone*, for God's sake, let me talk to my father, let me do my work, I'll be all right, just let me alone and *get Security out of my bedroom!*"

Denys looked at him a long time. "All right," he said. "We'll try that awhile. We'll try it, at least on the home front. I don't say we won't notice who comes and goes through your door. If something looks suspicious they'll be on you. Not otherwise. I'll give that order. Just don't give me any cause to regret it."

"No, ser," he said, because it was all he could get out.

Denys left him then.

When he got back to the office Grant met him in the doorway—Grant, scared and silent, asking questions just by being there.

"It's all right," he said. "They asked if we meant to do it. I said no. I said some other things. Denys said they were going to get Security off our tails."

Grant gave him a look that wondered who was listening and who he was playing for.

"No, it's what he said," he answered Grant. And shut the door for what privacy they had. He remembered the other thing, the important thing, then, the back and forth of promises and threats like so many hammer-blows, and he leaned on the back of the work-station chair, finding himself short of breath. "He said they were going to let us talk to Jordan."

"Is that true?" Grant wondered.

That was the thing that threw him off his balance, that they suddenly promised him favors when they had least reason. When they could haul him off to hospital by force and they had just demonstrated that.

Something was going on.

<hr>

X

"Music," he told the Minder that night, when they walked in the door. It started the tape at the cutoff point. It reported on calls. There were none. "We're not popular," he said to Grant. There was usually at least one, something from the lab, somebody asking about business, who had failed to catch them at the office.

"Ah, human inconstancy." Grant laid his briefcase on the accustomed table, shed his coat into the closet, and walked over to the sideboard and the liquor cabinet while Justin hung his up. He mixed two drinks and brought them back. "Double for you. Shoes off, feet up, sit. You can use it."

He sat down, kicked the shoes off, leaned back in the cushions and drank. Whiskey and water, a taste that promised present relief for frayed nerves. He saw Grant with the little plastic slate they used—writing things they dared not say aloud; and Grant wrote:

Do we believe them about dropping the bugging?

Justin shook his head. Set the glass down on the stone rim of the cushioned pit-group and reached for the tablet. *We feed them a little disinformation and see if we can catch them.*

Back to Grant; a nod. *Idea?*

To him. *Not yet. Thinking.*

Grant: *I suppose I have to wait till fishfeed to find out what happened.*

Himself: *Complicated. Dangerous. Petros is going to do interviews with me.*

Grant: a disturbed look. Unspoken question.

Himself: *They suspect about the flashes.*

Grant: underline of word *interviews*. Question mark.

Himself: *Denys said. No probe.* Then he added: *They've realized I have a problem with tape. I'm scared. I'm afraid they were doing a voice-stress. If so, I flunked. Will flunk Petros' test worse. Long time—I tried to think the flashes were trauma. Now I think maybe a botched-up block: deliberate. Maybe they want me like this.*

Grant read it with a frown growing on his face. He wrote with some deliberation. Cleared the slate and tried again. And again. Finally a brief: *I think not deliberate block. I think too many probes.*

Himself: *Then why in hell are we writing notes in our own living room?* Triple underlined.

Grant reacted with a little lift of the brows. And wrote: *Because anything is possible. But I don't think deliberate block. Damage. Giraud came in asking questions on top of an intervention Ari was running and hadn't finished. If that isn't enough, what is? Whatever Ari did would have been extensive and subtle. She could run an intervention with a single sentence. We know that. Giraud came breaking in and messed something up.*

Justin read that and felt the cold go a little deeper. He chewed the stylus a moment and wrote: *Giraud had seen the tapes. Giraud knew what she did. Giraud may work more with military psychsets, and that doesn't reassure me either. They got him that damn Special rating. Politics. Not talent. God knows what he did to me. Or what Petros did.*

Grant read and a frown came onto his face. He wrote: *I can't believe it of Petros. Giraud, yes. But Petros is independent.*

Himself: *I don't trust him. And I've got to face those interviews. They can take me off job. Call me unstable, suspend Alpha license. Transfer you. Whole damn thing over again.*

Grant grabbed the slate and wrote, frowning: *You're Jordan's replicate. If you show talent matching his without psychogenics program at same time they're running Rubin Project you could call their results into question. Also me. Remember Ari created me from a Special. You and I: possible controls on Project. Is that why Ari wanted us? Is that why Giraud doesn't?*

The thought upset his stomach. *I don't know*, he wrote.

Grant: *Giraud and Denys run the Project without controls except Rubin himself, and there's no knowing how honest those results will be. We are inconvenient. Ari wouldn't ever have worked the way they're working. Ari used controls, far as you can with human psych. I think she wanted us both.*

Himself: *Denys swears the Project is valid. But it's compromised every step of the way.*

Grant: *It's valid if it works. Like you've always said: They don't plan to release data if it does work. Reseune never releases data. Reseune makes money off its discoveries. If Reseune gets Ari back, an Ari to direct further research, will they release notes to general publication? No. Reseune will get big Defense contracts. Lot of power, power of secrecy, lot of money, but Reseune will run whole deal and get more and more power. Reseune will never release the findings. Reseune will work on contract for Defense, and get anything Reseune wants as long as Defense gets promises of recovering individuals—which even Reseune won't be able to do without the kind of documentation under that mountain out there. That takes years. Takes lifetimes. In the meantime, Reseune does some things for Defense, lot of things for itself. Do I read born-men right?*

He read and nodded, with a worse and worse feeling in his gut.

Grant: *You're very strange, you CITs. Perhaps it goes with devising your own psychsets—and having your logic on top. We know our bottom strata are sound. Who am I to judge my makers?*

---

xi

Jane sat down on the edge of the bed and pulled her hair out of the way as Ollie sat down by her and brushed his lips across her nape.

The Child, thank God, was asleep, and Nelly had won the battle of wills for the night.

Ari was hyper—*had* been hyper, all day, wanting to go back to Valery's place and play.

Time for *that* to change. Valery had become a problem, as she had predicted. Time for Ari to have another playmate. There had never been only one.

Damn. Hell of a thing to do to the kid.

Ollie's arms came around her, hugged her against him. "Is something the matter?" Ollie asked.

"Do something distracting, Ollie dear. I don't want to think tonight."

Damn. I'm even beginning to talk like Olga.

Ollie slid a hand lower and kissed her shoulder.

"Come on, Ollie, dammit, let's get rough. I'm in a mood to kill something."

Ollie understood then. Ollie pushed her down on the bed and made himself a major distraction, holding her hands because Ollie had no particular desire to end up with scratch marks.

Ollie was damned good. Like most azi who took the training, he was very, very good, and trying to keep him at bay was a game he won only slowly and with deliberation, a game precisely timed to what would work with her.

Work, it did. Jane sighed, and gave herself up after a while to Ollie's gentler tactics. Nice thing about an azi lover—he was always in the mood. Always more worried about her than about himself. She had had a dozen CIT lovers. But funny thing . . . she cared more about Ollie. And he would never expect that.

"I love you," she said into his ear, when he was almost asleep, his head on her shoulder. She ran her fingers through his sweat-damp hair and he looked at her with a puzzled, pleased expression. "I really do, Ollie."

"Sera," he said. And stayed very still, as if she had lost her mind after all these years. He was exhausted. She was still insomniac. But he was going to stay awake if his eyes crossed, if she wanted to talk, she knew that. She had his attention.

"That's all," she said. "I just decided to tell you that."

"Thank you," he said, not moving. Looking as if he still thought there was more to this.

"Nothing else." She rubbed his shoulder. "You ever wanted to be a CIT? Take the final tape? Go out of here?"

"No," he said. Sleep seemed to leave him. His breathing quickened. "I really don't. I don't want to. I couldn't leave you."

"You could. The tape would fix that."

"I don't want it. I truly don't want it. It couldn't make me not want to be here. Nothing could do that. Don't tell me to take it."

"I won't. No one will. I only wondered, Ollie. So you don't want to leave here. But what if I have to?"

"I'll go with you!"

"Will you?"

"Where will we go?"

"Fargone. Not for a while yet. But I really want to be sure you're all right. Because I do love you. I love you more than I do anyone. Enough to leave you here if that's what you want, or to take you with me, or to do anything you want me to. You deserve that, after all these years. I want you to be happy."

He started to answer, hitching up on one elbow. Facile and quick, an azi's ready and sincere protest of loyalty. She stopped him with a hand on his lips.

"No. Listen to me. I'm getting older, Ollie. I'm not immortal. And they're so damn scared I won't turn Ari loose when I have to— That's coming, Ollie. Two more years. God, how fast it's gone! Sometimes I could kill her; and sometimes—sometimes I feel so damn sorry for her. Which is what they don't want. They're afraid I'll break the rules, that's at the center of it. They—Giraud and Denys, damn their hearts, have decided she's too attached to you. They want that to stop. No more contact with her. Cold and critical. That's the prescription. Sometimes I think they earnestly hope I'll drop dead on cue, just like the damn script. I had a talk with Giraud today—" She drew a deep breath and something hurt behind her eyes and around her heart. "They offered me the directorship at RESEUNESPACE. Fargone. The Rubin Project, with bows and ribbons on it."

"Did you take it?" he asked, finally, when breath was too choked in her to go on.

She nodded, bit her lip and got it under control. "I did. Sweet Giraud. *Oh, you just withdraw to Wing One when she's seven*, that was what they told me when I took this on. Now they've got the nervies about it and they want me the hell out of reach. *It's not enough*, Giraud says. *Olga died when Ari was seven. Being over in Wing One, just walking out of her life, that's too much rejection, too attainable an object.* Dammit. So they offer me the directorship. Morley's out, I'm in, dammit."

"You always said you wanted to go back to space."

Another several breaths. "Ollie, I wanted to. I've wanted to for years and years. Until—somewhere I just got old. And they offered me this, and I realized I don't want to go anymore. That's a terrible thing to realize, for an old spacer brat. I've gotten old on the ground, and all the things I know are here, everything that's familiar, and I want it around me, that's all—" Another breath. "Not the way I'm going to have it, though. They can promote me. Or they can retire me. Damned if I'll take retirement. That's the trouble of doing your job and never bothering to power-grab. That upstart Giraud can fire me. That's what it comes down to. Damn his guts. So I go to Fargone. And start the whole thing over with another damn brat, this one with medical problems. Shit, Ollie. Do somebody a favor and look at what they do to you."

Ollie brushed at her hair. Stroked her shoulder. Ached his heart out for her, that was what Ollie would do, because she was his Supervisor, and god was in trouble.

"Well, hell if I want to drag you into the same mess. Think what it'll be, if you go out there. I'll die on you in not so many years—add it up, Ollie; and there you are, twenty lightyears from civilization. What kind of thing is that to do to somebody who's got less choice than I do? Huh? I don't want to put you in that kind of position. If you like it here at Reseune, I can get you that CIT tape and you can stay here where it's civilized, no take-hold drills and no Keis and fishcakes and no corridors where people walk off the ceiling . . ."

"Jane, if I tell you I want to go, what will you tell me? That I'm a stupid azi who doesn't know what he wants? I know. Am I going to let you go off with some damn azi out of the Town?"

"I'm a hundred and—"

"—I don't care. I don't care. Don't make us both miserable. Don't playact with me. You want me to tell you I want to be with you, I'm telling you. But it's not fair to hold this over me. I can hear it. *Dammit, Ollie, I'll leave you behind, I will*— I don't want to listen to that for two years. I don't even want to think about it."

Ollie was not one to get upset. He was. She saw that finally and reached up and brushed his cheek with her fingertips. "I won't do that. I won't do it.

Damn, this is too much seriousness. Damn Giraud. Damn the project. Ollie, they don't want you to touch Ari after this."

His brow furrowed in distress. "They blame me."

"It's not a question of blame. They see she likes you. It's the damn program. They wanted to take you out of here right away and I told them go to hell. I told them I'd blow it, right then. Tell the kid everything. And *they'll* walk a narrow line, damn right they will. So they had a counteroffer ready. One they thought I'd jump at. And a threat. Retirement. So what could I do? I took the directorship. I get myself and you—you—out of here. I should be glad of that."

"I'm sorry if I did this."

"Dammit, no, you didn't. I didn't. No one did it. Olga never beat the kid. Thank God. But I can't stand it, Ollie. I can't stand it anymore."

"Don't cry. I can't stand that."

"I'm not about to. Shut up. Roll over. It's my turn. Do you mind?"

xii

"Of course not," he said to Petros, across the desk from him, while the Scriber ran, and he knew well enough they had a voice-stress running, that was probably reading-out to Petros on that little screen. Petros glanced from it often and sometimes smiled at him in his best bedside manner.

"You're involved in an intimate relationship with your companion," Petros said. "Don't you have any misgivings about that? You know an azi really can't defend himself against that kind of thing."

"I've really thought about that. I've talked with Grant about it. But it's the pattern we were brought up with, isn't it? And for various reasons, you know what I'm talking about, we both have problems that cut us off from the rest of the House, and we were both—let's call it—in need of support."

"Describe these problems."

"Oh, come on, Petros, you know and I know we're not on top of the social set. Political contagion. I don't have to describe it for you."

"You feel isolated."

He laughed. "My God, were you at the party? I thought you were."

"Well, yes." A glance at the monitor. "I was. She's a nice little kid. What do you think?"

He looked at Petros, raised an eyebrow at Petros' dour drollery, and gave a bitter laugh. "I think she's a bit of a brat, and what kid isn't?" He made it a quiet smile, catching Petros' eye. "Thank God *I* couldn't get pregnant. You might have a kid of mine to play with. Put that in your tapes and file it. How am I doing on voice-stress?"

"Well, that was tolerably stressed."

"I thought it was. You're trying to get me to react, but do we have to be grotesque?"

"You consider the child grotesque."

"I consider the kid charming. I think her situation is grotesque. But evidently your ethics can compass it. They're holding my father at gunpoint as far as I'm concerned, so I'm damn well not going to make a move. Those are my ethics. Am I lying?"

Petros was not smiling. He was watching the monitor. "Nice. Nice reaction."

"I'm sure."

"Annoyed as hell, are you? What do you think of Giraud?"

"I love him like my own father. How's that for comparisons? True or false?"

"Don't play games with this. You can do yourself harm."

"Register a threat to the patient."

"I'm sure that's not what I intended. I am going to insist you undergo some therapy. Mmmmn, got a little heartbeat there."

"Of course you did. I'll do your therapy, in your facility. As long as my azi sits through it with me."

"Irregular."

"Look, Petros, I've been through hell in this place. Are you trying to drive me crazy or are you going to give me a reasonable safeguard? Even a non-professional has a right to audit a psych procedure if the patient requests it. And I'm requesting a second opinion. That's all. Do it right and you won't even need Security to bring me in. Do it wrong and I'll consider other options. I'm not a panicked kid anymore. I know where I can file a protest, unless you plan to lock me up and have me disappear—damned bad for your tape record, isn't it?"

"I'll do better than that." Petros flipped switches and the monitor swung aside, dead. "I'll give you the tape and you can take it home. I just want your word you're going to use it."

"Now you've got real surprise. Pity you cut the monitor."

"You're scared out of good sense," Petros said. "I don't blame you. Good voice control, but your pulse rate is way up. Psyched yourself for this, have you? I could order a blood test. Verbal intervention? Grant try to prep you?"

"I have to sign a consent."

Petros let out a slow breath, arms on the desk. "Keep yourself out of trouble, Justin. This is off the record. Keep yourself out of trouble. Take the orders. They *are* going to put off the phone calls."

"Sure." The disappointment made a lump in his chest. "I figured. It's all a game, anyway. And I believed Denys. I knew better."

"It's not Denys. Military security nixed it. Denys is going to put together a file that may convince them. Just cooperate for a while. You can't improve things by the show you just put on. You understand me. Keep out of trouble. You will go on getting the letters." Another sigh, an intensely unhappy look. "I'm going to see Jordan. Is there anything you want to tell him?"

"What are they doing with him?"

"Nothing. Nothing. Calm down. I'm just going over there to check out some equipment. Supering my techs. I just thought I'd offer. I thought it might make you feel better. I'm going to take him a photo of you. I thought he'd like that. I'm going to bring one back—or try."

"Sure."

"I'm going to. For his sake, as much as yours. I was his friend."

"The number of my father's friends amazes me."

"I won't argue with you. Any message?"

"Tell him I love him. What else won't be censored?"

"I'll tell him as much as I can. This is still off the record. I have a job here. Someone else would do it worse. Think about that for yourself. Go home. Go to your office. Don't forget to pick up the tape at the counter."

He was not sure, when he had left, when he was walking back across the quadrangle toward the House with the tape and a prescription, whether he had won or lost the encounter. Or what faction in the House had won or lost.

But he had not known that for years.

Verbal Text from:
PATTERNS OF GROWTH
A Tapestudy in Genetics: #1
"An Interview with
Ariane Emory": pt. 1

Reseune Educational Publications: 8970-8768-1
approved for 80+

Q: Dr. Emory, thank you for giving us the chance for a few direct questions about your work.

A: I'm glad to have the opportunity. Thank you. Go on.

Q: Your parents founded Reseune. Everyone knows that. Are you aware some biographers have called you the chief architect of Union?

A: I've heard the charge. [mild laughter] I wish they'd wait till I'm dead.

Q: You deny your effect—politically as well as scientifically?

A: I'm no more the architect than Bok was. Science is not politics. It may affect it. We have so little time. Could I interject an observation of my own—which may answer some of your questions in one?

Q: By all means.

A: When we came out from Earth we were a selected genepool. We were sifted by politics, by economics, by the very fact that we were fit for space. Most of the wave that reached the Hinder Stars were colonists and crews very carefully vetted by Sol Station, the allegedly unfit turned down, the brightest and the best, I think the phrase was then, sent out to the stars. By the time the wave reached Pell, the genepool had widened a bit, but not at all representative of Sol Station, let alone Earth—we did get one large influx when politics on Earth took a hand, and the wave that founded Union ended up mostly Eastern bloc, as they used to call it. A lot of chance entered the genepool in that final push—before Earth slammed the embargo down and stopped genetic export for a long time.

Cyteen was the sifting of the sifting of the sifting . . . meaning that if there was one population artificially selected to the extreme, it was Cyteen—which was mostly Eastern bloc, mostly scientists, and very, very small, and very far, at that time, from trade and the—call it . . . pollination . . . performed by the merchanters. That was a dangerous situation. Hence Reseune. That's where we began. That's what we're really for. People think of Reseune and azi. Azi were only a means to an end, and one day, when the population has reached what they call tech-growth positive, meaning that consumption will sustain mass production—azi will no longer be produced in those areas.

But meanwhile azi serve another function. Azi are the reservoir of every genetic trait we've been able to identify. We have tended to cull the evidently deleterious genes, of course. But there's a downside to small genepools, no matter how carefully selected, there's a downside in lack of resiliency, lack of available responses to the environment. Expansion is absolutely necessary, to avoid concentration of an originally limited genepool in the central locus of Union. We are not speaking of eugenics. We are speaking of diaspora. We are speaking of the necessary dispersion of genetic information in essentially the same ratios as that present on ancestral Earth. And we have so little time.

Q: Why—so little time?

A: Because population increases exponentially and fills an ecosystem, be it planet or station, in a relatively short time. If that population contains insufficient genetic information, that population, especially a population at greater density than the peripheries of the system—we are of course speaking of Cyteen—and sitting at the cultural center of Union, which is another dimension not available to lower lifeforms, but very significant in terms of a creature able to engineer its own systems in all senses—if that population, I say, in such power, contains inadequate genetic information, it will run into trouble and confront itself with emergency choices which may be culturally or genetically radical. In spreading into space at much lesser density and with such preselection at work, humankind faces potential evolutionary catastrophe in a relatively small number of generations—either divergence too extreme to survive severe challenge or divergence into a genetic crisis of a different and unpredictable outcome—certainly the creation of new species of genus homo and very probably the creation of genetic dead ends and political tragedy. Never forget that we are more than a social animal, we are a political animal; and we are capable of becoming our own competitor.

Q: You mean war.

A: Or predation. Or predation. Never forget that. Dispersion is absolutely essential, but so are adequately diverse genepools in the scattered pockets that result. That is the reason azi were created and continue to be created. They are the vectors of that diversity, and that some economic interests have found them—profitable—is understandable but overall repugnant to me personally and to everything Reseune stands for. History may accuse me of many things, ser, but I care profoundly what becomes of the azi, and I have exerted every influence to assure their legal protection. We do not create Thetas because we want cheap labor. We create Thetas because they are an essential and important part of human alternatives. The ThR-23 hand-eye coordination, for instance, is exceptional. Their psychset lets them operate very well in environments in which CIT geniuses would assuredly fail. They are tough, ser, in ways I find thoroughly admirable, and I recommend you, if you ever find yourself in a difficult situation in Cyteen's wilderness, hope your companion is a ThR azi, who will survive, ser, to perpetuate his type, even if you do not. That is genetic alternative at work.

Someday there will be no more azi. They will have fulfilled their purpose, which is to increase, and multiply, and fill the gaps in the human record as the original genepool disperses to a mathematically determined population density—as it must disperse, for its own future well-being, its own genetic health.

I say again: azi are genetic alternative. They are the vector for change and adaptation in the greatest challenge the human species has yet faced. They are as they are precisely because the time within which this can be accomplished is so very brief. Reseune has not opposed the creation of additional labs, simply because its interests are primarily scientific and because the task of maintaining the impetus to expansion requires vast production and education facilities. But Reseune has never relinquished its role in the creation and selection of new genesets: no other laboratory has the right to originate genetic material.

While you're being patient, let me make two most essential points: one—Reseune insists on the full integration of all azi genesets into the citizen population in any area of Union that has achieved class one status: in practical terms—azi are ideally a one-generation proposition: their primary purpose is not labor, but to open a colonial area, bring it up to productivity, and produce offspring who will enter the citizen genepool in sufficient numbers to guarantee genetic variety. The only azi who should be produced for any other purpose are those generated as a stopgap measure for defense and other emergencies in the national interest; those engaged in certain critical job classifications; and those generated for appropriate research in licensed facilities.

Two—Reseune will oppose any interest which seeks to institutionalize azi as an economic necessity. In no wise should the birthlabs be perpetuated as a purely profit-making operation. That was never their purpose.

Q: Are you saying you have interests in common with the Abolitionists?

A: Absolutely. We always have had.

CHAPTER 5

Florian ran along the sidewalk that crossed the face of Barracks 3, remembered politeness when he met a handful of adults coming the other way, stopped, stood aside, panting, and gave a little bow that the adults returned with the slightest nods of their heads. Because they were older. Because Florian was six and because it was natural for a boy to want to run but it was also natural for adults to have serious business on their minds.

So, this time, did Florian have business. He was fresh from tapestudy. He had an Assignment, a real, every-morning Assignment. It was the most important thing that had ever happened to him, he loved everything about it, and he had been so excited he had begged the Super twice to let him go there and not to the Rec Hall where he was supposed to go after tape.

"What," the Super had said, with a smile and a little twinkle in her eye that he was sure meant she was going to let him, "no Rec? Work and Rec are both important, Florian."

"I've had Rec before," he had said. *"Please."*

She had given him the chit then, *and* the Rec chit, for later, she had said, as long as he showed it to the Work Super first. And held out her arms. Hug the Super, the very *nice* Super, and *don't* run in the hall, walk, walk, and walk, as far as the door, walk down the sidewalk until he hit the downhill road, and then *run*, fast as he could.

Which was fast, because he was not only Alpha-smart, he was good at running.

Down the shortcut between Barracks 4 and 5, zip across the road, and shortcut again to the path that led to the AG building. He slowed down finally because his side was hurting, and he hoped in the way of things that moved everybody around all the time, Olders with younger boys, they were going to check him into a bunk a little closer to AG next month: it was *far* from Barracks 104.

Olders with jobs had priority on the bunks nearest. That was what he had heard from an Older, who was Kappa, who said he was always in the same barracks-group.

He caught his breath as he walked up to AG-100. He had been near here before. He had seen the pens. He liked the smell. It was—it was the way AG smelled, that was all, and there was nothing like it.

It was a kind of an Ad place in front. All white, with a seal-door, of course. You were supposed to go to Ad. He knew that the way tape showed you things. He pulled down the door-latch and it let him into a busy office, where there was a counter he was supposed to go to.

He could lean on counters lately. Just barely. He was not as tall as other sixes. Taller than some, though. He waited till a Worker turned around and came to see what he wanted.

"I'm Florian AF-9979," he said, and held up the red chit. "I'm Assigned here."

She gave him a polite nod and took the chit. He waited, licking dry lips, not fidgeting while she put it in the machine.

"You certainly are," she said. "Do you know how to follow the colors?"

"Yes," he said with no doubt at all.

And didn't ask questions because she was a Worker doing her Job and she would probably say. If you didn't get everything you needed when she was finished then you asked. That way you didn't make people make mistakes. Which was a Fault on your side. He knew.

She sat down at a keyboard, she typed, and the machine put out a card she took and added a clip to. He watched, excited because he knew it was a keycard, and it was probably his because she was working on his Business.

She brought it to him and leaned over the counter to show him things about it; he stood on tiptoe and twisted around so they could both see.

"There's your name, there are your colors. This is a keycard. You clip it to your pocket. Whenever you change clothes you clip it to your pocket. That's very serious. If you lose it come to this office immediately."

"Yes," he said. It all clicked with things tape said.

"Have you any questions?"

"No. Thank you."

"Thank you, Florian."

Little bow. *Walk*, then, back out the door and onto the walk and look up at the corner of the building where the color-codes started, but he could read all the words on the card anyway: and on the building.

Walk. No running now. This was Business and he was important. Blue was his color and white inside that and green inside the white, so he went the blue direction until he was inside blue and then inside blue's white zone. The squares told him. More and more exciting. It was the pens. He saw green finally on a sign at the intersection of the gravel walks and followed that way until he saw the green building, which also said AG 899. That was right.

It was a barn of sorts on one side. He asked an azi for the Super, the azi pointed to a big bald man talking to someone over in the big doorway, and he went there and stood until the Super was clear.

"Florian," the Super said when he had seen the card. "Well." Looking him up and down. And called an azi named Andy to take him and show him his work.

But he knew that, from tape. He was supposed to feed the chickens, make sure all the water was clean, and check the temperature on the brooders and the pig nursery. He knew how important that was. "You're awfully young," Andy said of him, "but you sound like you understand."

"Yes," he said. He was sure he did. So Andy let him show him how much he was to feed, and how he was to mark the chart every time he did, and every time he checked the water; and how you had to be careful not to frighten the chicks because they would hurt each other. He loved how they all bunched up like a fluffy tide, and all went this way or that way; and the piglets squealed and would knock you down if you let them get to swarming round you, which was why you carried a little stick.

He did everything the best he could, and Andy was happy with him, which made him the happiest he had ever been in his life.

He carried buckets and he emptied water pans and Andy said he could try to hold a piglet as long as he was there to watch. It wiggled and squealed and tramped him with its sharp little feet and it got away while he was laughing and trying to protect himself; Andy laughed and said there was a way to do it, but he would show him later.

It was a nice feeling, though. It had been warm and alive in his arms, except he knew pigs were for eating, and for making other pigs, and you had to keep that in mind and not think of them like people.

He dusted himself off and he went out to catch his breath a minute, leaning on the fence rail by the side of the barn.

He saw an animal in that pen that he had never seen, so beautiful that he just stood there with his mouth open and never wanted to blink, it was like that. Red like the cattle, but shiny-pelted, and strong, with long legs and a way of moving that was different than any animal he had ever seen. This one—didn't walk; it—went. It moved like it was playing a game all by itself.

"What's that?" he asked, hearing Andy come up by him. "What kind is that?"

"AGCULT-894X," Andy said. "That's a horse. He's the first ever lived, the first ever in the world."

ii

Ari *liked* the playschool. They got to go out in the open air and play in the sandbox every afternoon. She liked to sit barefoot and make roads with the graders and Tommy or Amy or Sam or Rene would run the trucks and dump them. Sometimes they pretended there were storms and all the toy workers would run and get in the trucks. Sometimes there was a platythere and it tore up the roads and they had to rebuild them. That was what Sam said. Sam's mother was in engineering and Sam told them about platytheres. She asked maman was that so and maman said yes. Maman had seen them big as the living room couch. There were really big ones way out west. Big as a truck. The one they had was only a middle-sized one, and it was ugly. Ari liked being it. You got to tear up the roads and the walls, just push it right through under the sand and there it all went.

She took it and shoved it along with the sand going over her hand. "Look out," she said to Sam and Amy. "Here it comes." She was tired of Amy building her House. Amy had a big one going, sand all piled up, and Amy made doors and windows in the House, and fussed and fussed with it. Which was no fun, because Sam put a tower on Amy's house and Amy knocked it off and told him go make a road up to her door, *she* was making a house and *her* house didn't have towers. Amy got a spoon and hollowed out behind the windows and put plastic in so you couldn't see inside anyway. She made a wall in front and hollowed out an arch for the road. And they both had had to sit and wait while Amy built. So Ari looked at that arch where the road was supposed to come and thought it would be just the place, and the sand would all come down. "Look out!"

"No!" Amy yelled.

Ari plowed right through it. Bang. Down came the wall. The sand came down on her arm and she just kept going, because platytheres did, no matter what. Even if Amy grabbed her arm and tried to stop her.

Sam helped her knock it down.

Amy yelled and shoved her. She shoved Amy. Phaedra got there and told them they mustn't fight and they were all going inside.

Early.

So that was nasty Amy Carnath's fault.

Amy was not back the next day. That was the way with people she fought with. She was sorry about that. You fought with them and they took them away and you only saw them at parties after. There had been Tommy and Angel and Gerry and Kate, and they were gone and couldn't play with her anymore. So when Amy was gone the next day she moped and sulked and told Phaedra she wanted Amy back.

"If you don't fight with her," Phaedra said. "We'll ask sera."

So Amy did come back. But Amy was funny after that. Even Sam was. Every time she did something they let her.

That was no fun, she thought. So she teased them. She stole Sam's trucks and turned them over. And Sam let her do that. He just sat there and frowned, all unhappy. She knocked Amy's house down before she was through with it. Amy just pouted.

So she did.

Sam turned his trucks back over and decided they had had a wreck. That was an all-right game. She played too, and set the trucks up. But Amy was still pouting, so she ran a truck at her. "Don't," Amy snapped at her. "Don't!"

So she hit her with it. Amy scrambled back and Ari got up and Amy got up. And Amy shoved her.

So she shoved her harder, and kicked her good. Amy hit her. So she hit. And they were hitting each other when Phaedra grabbed her. Amy was crying, and Ari kicked her good before Phaedra snatched her out of reach.

Sam just stood there.

"Amy was a baby," Ari said that night when maman asked her why she had hit Amy.

"Amy can't come back," maman said. "Not if you're going to fight."

So she promised they wouldn't. But she didn't think so.

Amy was out for a couple of days and she came back. She was all pouty and she kept over to herself and she wasn't any fun. She wouldn't even speak when Sam was nice to her.

So Ari walked over and kicked her good, several times. Sam tried to stop her. Phaedra grabbed her by the arm and said she was wrong and she had to sit down and play by herself.

So she did. She took the grader and made sad, angry roads. Sam came over finally and ran a truck on them, but she still hurt. Amy just sat over in the other corner and sniveled. That was what maman called it. Amy wouldn't even play anymore. Ari felt a knot in her throat that made it hard to swallow, but she was not baby enough to cry, and she hated Amy's sniveling, that hurt her and made nothing any fun anymore. Sam was sad too.

After that Amy wasn't there very often. When she was she just sat to herself and Ari hit her once, good, in the back.

Phaedra took Amy by the hand and took her to the door and inside.

Ari went back to Sam and sat down. Valery wasn't there much at all. Pete wasn't. She liked them most. That left just Sam, and Sam was just Sam, a kid with a wide face and not much expression on it. Sam was all right, but Sam hardly ever talked, except he knew about platytheres and fixing trucks. She liked him all right. But she lost everything else. If you liked it most, it went away.

It was not Amy she missed, it was Valery. Sera Schwartz had gotten transferred, so that meant Valery was. She had asked him if he would come back and see her. He had said yes. Maman had said it was too far. So she understood that he was really gone and he would not come back at all. She was mad at him for going. But it was not his fault. He gave her his spaceship with the red light. That was how sorry he was. Maman had said that she had to give it back, so she had to, before she left the Schwartzes' place and said goodbye.

She did not understand why it was wrong, but Valery had cried and she had. Sera Schwartz had been mad at her. She could tell, even if sera Schwartz was being nice and said she would miss her.

Maman had taken her home and she had cried herself to sleep. Even if maman was mad at something and told her stop crying. She did for a while. But for days after she would snivel. And maman would say stop it, so she did, because maman was getting upset and things were getting tight around the apartment—tight was all she could call it. That made everything awful. So she knew she was upsetting maman.

She was scared sometimes. She could not say why.

She was unhappy about Amy, and she tried to be good to Sam and Tommy, when he came, but she thought if she got Amy back she would hit her again.

She would hit Sam and Tommy too, but if she did she would not have anybody at all. Phaedra said she had to be good, they were running out of kids.

iii

"This is the Room," the Instructor said.

"Yes, ser," Catlin said. She was nervous and anxious at the same time. She had heard about the Room from Olders. She heard about the things they did to you, like turning the lights on and off and sometimes water on the floor. But her Instructor always had the Real Word. Her Instructor told her she had to get through a tunnel and do it fast.

"Are you ready?"

"Yes, ser."

He opened the door. It was a tiny place with another door. The one behind her shut and the lights went out.

The one in front of her opened and cold wet air hit her in the face. The place had echoes.

She moved, not even sure where the tunnel was or whether she was in it.

"Stop!" a voice yelled. And a red dot lit the wall and popped.

It was a shot. She knew that. Her body knew what to do; she was tumbling and meaning to roll and find cover, but the whole floor dropped, and she kept rolling, down a tube and splash! into cold water.

She flailed and got up in knee-deep water. You never believed a Safe. Someone had shot. You ran and got to cover.

But: *Get through*, the Instructor had said. *Fast as you can.*

So she got, fast as she could, till she ran into a wall and followed it, up again, onto the dry. In a place that rang under her boots. Noise was bad. It was dark and she was easy to see in the dark because of her pale skin and hair. She did not know whether she ought to sneak or run, but *fast* was *fast*, that was what the Instructor said.

She ran easy and quick, fingers of one hand trailing on the wall to keep her sense of place in the dark and one hand out ahead of her so she wouldn't run into something.

The tunnel did turn. She headed up a climb and down again onto concrete, and it was still dark.

Something—! she thought, just before she got to it and the Ambush grabbed her.

She elbowed it and twisted and knew it was an Enemy when she felt it grab her, but it only got cloth and twisting got her away, fast, fast, hard as she could run, heart hammering.

She hit the wall where it turned, bang! and nearly knocked herself cold, but she scrambled up and kept going, kept going—

The door opened, white and blinding.

Something made her duck and roll through it, and she landed on the floor in the tiny room, with the taste of blood in her mouth and her lip cut and her nose bleeding.

One door shut and the other opened, and the man there was not the Instructor. He had the brown of the Enemy and he had a gun.

She tried to kick him, but he Got her, she heard the buzz.

The door shut again and opened and she was getting up, mad and ashamed.

But this time it was her Instructor. "The Enemy is never fair," he said. "Let's go find out what you did right and wrong."

Catlin wiped her nose. She hurt. She was still mad and ashamed. She had gotten through. She wished she had got the man at the end. But he was an Older. That was not fair either. And her nose would not stop bleeding.

The Instructor got a cold cloth and had her put it on her neck. He said the med would look at her nose and her mouth. Meanwhile he turned on the Scriber and had her tell what she did and he told her most Sixes got stopped in the tunnel.

"You're exceptionally good," he said.

At which she felt much, much better. But she was not going to forget the Enemy at the end. They Got you here even when the lesson was over. That was the Rule. She hated being Got. She hated it. She knew when you grew up you went where Got was dead. She knew what dead was. They took the Sixes down to the slaughterhouse and they saw them kill a pig. It was fast and it stopped being a pig right there. They hauled it up and cut it and they got to see what dead meant: you just stopped, and after that you were just meat. No next time when you were dead, and you had to Get the Enemy first and make the Enemy dead fast.

She was good. But the Enemy was not fair. That was a scary thing to learn. She started shaking. She tried to stop, but the Instructor saw anyhow and said the med had better have a look at her.

"Yes, ser," she said. Her nose still bubbled and the cloth was red. She blotted at it and felt her knees wobble as she walked, but she walked all right.

The med said her nose was not broken. A tooth was loose, but that was all right, it would fix itself.

The Instructor said she was going to start marksmanship. He said she would be good in that, because her genotype was rated that way. She was expected to do well in the Room. All her genotype did. He said genotypes could sometimes get better. He said that was who she had to beat. That was who every azi had to beat. Even if she had never seen any other AC-7892.

She got a good mark for the day. She could not tell anyone. You were never supposed to. She could not talk about the tunnel. The Instructor told her so. It was a Rule.

It was only the last Enemy that worried her. The Instructor said a gun would have helped and size would have helped, but otherwise there was not much she could have done. It had not been wrong to roll at the last. Even if it put her on the floor when the door opened.

"I could have run past him," she said.

"He would have shot you in the back," the Instructor said. "Even in the hall."

She thought and thought about that.

iv

"Vid off," Justin said, and the Minder cut it. He sat in his bathrobe on the couch. Grant wandered in, likewise in his bathrobe, toweling his hair.

"What's the news tonight?" Grant asked, and Justin said, with a little unease at his stomach:

"There's some kind of flap in Novgorod. Something about a star named Gehenna."

"Where's that?" There *was* no star named Gehenna in anybody's reckoning. Or there had not been, until tonight. Grant looked suddenly sober as he sat down on the other side of the pit.

"Over toward Alliance. Past Viking." The news report had not been entirely specific. "Seems there's a planet there. With humans on it. Seems Union colonized it without telling anybody. Sixty years ago."

"My God," Grant murmured.

"Alliance ambassador's arrived at station with an official protest. They're having an emergency session of the Council. Seems we're in violation of the Treaty. About a dozen clauses of it."

"How *big* a colony?" Grant asked, right to the center of it.

"They don't know. They don't say."

"And nobody *knew* about it. Some kind of Defense base?"

"Might be. Might well be. But it isn't now. Apparently it's gone primitive."

Grant hissed softly. "Survivable world."

"Has to be, doesn't it? We're not talking about any ball of rock. The news-service is talking about the chance of some secret stuff from back in the war years."

Grant was quiet a moment, elbows on knees.

The war was the generation before them. The war was something no one wanted to repeat; but the threat was always there. Alliance merchanters came and went. Sol had explored the other side of space and got its fingers burned—dangerously. Eetees with a complex culture and an isolationist sentiment. Now Sol played desperate politics between Alliance and Union, trying to keep from falling under Alliance rule and trying to walk the narrow line that might leave it independent of Alliance ships without pushing Alliance into defending its treaty prerogatives or bringing Alliance interests and Union into conflict. Things were so damned delicate. And they had gotten gradually better.

A generation had grown up thinking it was solving the problems.

But old missiles the warships had launched a hundred years ago were still a shipping hazard. Sometimes the past came back into the daily news with a vengeance.

And old animosities surfaced like ghosts, troubling a present in which humans knew they were not alone.

"It doesn't sound like it was any case of finding three or four survivors," he said to Grant. "They're saying 'illegal colony' and they admit it's ours."

"Still going? Organized?"

"It's not real clear."

Another moment of silence. Grant sat up then and remembered to dry his hair before it dried the way it was. "Damn crazy mess," Grant said. "Did they say they got them off, or are they going to? Or what are they going to do about it?"

"Don't know yet."

"Well, we can guess where Giraud's going to be for the next week or so, can't we?"

V

Ari was bored with the offices. She watched the people come in and out. She sat at a desk in back of the office and cut out folded paper in patterns that she unfolded. She got paper and drew a fish with a long tail.

Finally she got up and slipped out while Kyle wasn't looking, while maman was doing something long and boring in the office inside; and it looked like maman was going to be talking a long time.

Which meant maman would not mind much if she walked up and down the hall. It was only offices. That meant no stores, no toys, nothing to look at and no vid. She liked sitting and coloring all right. But maman's own offices were best, because there was a window to look out.

There was nothing but doors up and down. The floor had metal stripes and she walked one, while she looked in the doors that were open. Most were.

That was how she saw Justin.

He was at a desk, working at a keyboard, very serious.

She stood in the doorway and saw him there. And waited, just watching him, for the little bit until he would see her.

He was always different from all the rest of the people. She remembered him from a glittery place, and Grant with him. She saw him only sometimes, and when she asked maman why people got upset about Justin, maman said she was imagining things.

She knew she was not. It was a danger-feeling. It was a worried feeling.

She knew she ought not to bother him. But it was all right here in the hall, where there were people going by. And she just wanted to look at him, but she did not want to go inside.

She shifted to her other foot and he saw her then.

"Hello," she said.

And got that fear-feeling again. His, as he looked up. And hers, as she thought she could get in trouble with maman.

"Hello," he said, nervous-like.

It was always like that when she was around Justin. The nervous-feeling went wherever he did, and got worse when she got close to him. From everybody. It was a puzzle she could not work out, and she sensed by the way maman shut down on questions about Justin that he was a puzzle maman did not approve of. Ollie too. Justin came to parties and she saw him from across the room, but maman always came and got her if she went to say hello. So she thought that Justin was somebody in a lot of trouble for something, and maybe there was something Wrong with him, so they were not sure he was going to behave right. Sometimes azi got like that. Sometime CITs did. Maman said. And it was harder to straighten CITs out, but easier to make azi upset. So she mustn't tease them. Except Ollie could take it all right.

There was a lot about Justin that said azi, but she knew that he wasn't. He was just Justin. And he was a puzzle that came and went and no one ever wanted kids around.

"Maman's down there with ser Peterson," she said conversationally, also because she wanted him to know she was not running around where she had no business to be. So this was Justin's office. It was awfully small. Papers were everywhere. She leaned too far and caught her balance on the door. Fool, maman would say. Stand up. Stand straight. Don't wobble around. But Justin never said much. He left everything for her to say. "Where's Grant?"

"Grant's down at the library," Justin said.

"I'm six now."

"I know."

"How do you know that?"

Justin looked uncomfortable. "Isn't your maman going to be wanting you pretty soon?"

"Maman's having a meeting. I'm tired of being down there." He was going to ignore her, going back to his work. She was not going to have him turn his shoulder to her. She walked in and up to the chair by his desk. She leaned on the arm and looked up at him. "Ollie's always working."

"So am I. I'm busy, Ari. You go along."

"What are you doing?"

"Work."

She knew a go-away when she heard one. But she did not have to mind Justin. So she leaned on her arms and frowned and tried a new approach. "I go to tapestudy. I can read that. It says *Sub—*" She twisted around, because it was a long word on the screen. "*Sub-li-min-al mat—ma-trix.*"

He turned the screen off and turned around and frowned at her.

She thought maybe she had gone too far, and oughtn't to be leaning on her elbows quite so close to him. But backing up was something she didn't like at all. She stuck out her lip at him.

"Go back to maman, Ari. She's going to be looking for you."

"I don't want to. What's a sub-liminal matrix?"

"A set of things. A special arrangement of a set." He shoved his chair back and stood up, so she stood up and got back. "I've got an appointment. I've got to lock up the office. You'd better get on back to your mother."

"I don't want to." He was awfully tall. Like Ollie. Not safe like Ollie. He was pushing her out, that was what. She stood her ground.

"Out," he said, at the door, pointing to the hall.

She went out. He walked out and locked the door. She waited for him. She had that figured out. When he walked on down the hall she went with him.

"Back," he said, stopping, pointing back toward where maman was.

She gave him a nasty smile. "I don't have to."

He looked upset then. And he got very quiet, looking down at her. "Ari, that's not nice, is it?"

"I don't have to be nice."

"I'd like you better."

That hurt. She stared up at him to see if he was being nasty, but he did not look like it. He looked as if he was the hurt one.

She could not figure him. Everybody, but not him. She just stared.

"Can I go with you?" she asked.

"Your maman wouldn't like it." He had a kind face when he talked like that. "Go on back."

"I don't want to. They just talk. I'm tired of them talking."

"Well, I've got to go meet my people, Ari. I'm sorry."

"There aren't any people," she said, calling his bluff, because he had not been going anywhere until she bothered him.

"Well, I still have to. You go on back."

She did not. But he walked away down the hall like he was really going somewhere.

She wished she could. She wished he would be nice. She was bored and she was unhappy and when she saw him she remembered the glittery people and everybody being happy, but she could not remember when that was.

Only then Ollie had been there all the time and maman had been so pretty and she had played with Valery and gotten the star that hung in her bedroom.

She walked back to ser Peterson's office very slow. Kyle didn't even notice. She sat down and she drew a star. And thought about Valery. And the red-haired man, who was Grant. Who was Justin's.

She wished Ollie and maman had more time for her.

She wished maman would come out. And they would go to lunch. Maybe Ollie could come.

But maman did not come anytime soon, so she drew lines all over the star and made it ugly.

Like everything.

---

vi

The documents show, the report came to Mikhail Corain's desk, *the operation involved a clandestine military operation and the landing of 40,000 Union personnel, the majority of them azi. The mission was launched in 2355, as a Defense operation.*

There was no further support given the colony. The operation was not sustained.

The best intelligence Alliance has mustered says that there are thousands of survivors who have devolved to a primitive lifestyle. Beyond question they are descended of azi and citizens. The assumption is that they had no rejuv and that after sixty years the survivors must be at least second and third generation. There are ruins of bubble-construction and a solar power installation. The world is extremely hospitable to human life and the survivors are in remarkably good health considering the conditions, practicing basic agriculture and hunting. The Alliance reports express doubt that the colonists can be removed from the world. The ecological damage is as yet undetermined, but there is apparently deep penetration of the colony into the ecosystem, and certain of the inhabitants have retreated into areas not easily accessible. It is the estimate of Alliance that the inhabitants would not welcome removal from the world and Alliance does not intend to remove the colony, for whatever reason.

The estimation within the Defense Bureau is that Alliance is interested in interviewing the survivors. Defense however will oppose any proposal to retrieve these Union nationals as an operation which Alliance will surely reject and which would be in any case counter-productive.

The azi were primarily but not exclusively from Reseune military contracts.
See attached reports.

The majority of citizens were military personnel.

Nye will offer a bill expressing official regret and an offer of cooperation to the Alliance in dealing with the colonists.

The Expansionist coalition will be unanimous in that vote.

Corain flipped through the reports. Pages of them. There was a sub-sapient on the world the colonists called Gehenna. There were a great many things that said Defense Bureau, and Information Unavailable.

There was no way in hell Alliance or Union was going to be able to retrieve the survivors, for one thing because they were scattered into the bush and mostly because (according to Alliance) they were illiterate primitives and Alliance was going to resist any attempt to remove them, that much was clear in the position the Alliance ambassador was taking.

Alliance was damned mad about the affair, because it had been confronted with a major and expensive problem: an Earth-class planet in its own sphere of influence with an ecological disaster and an entrenched, potentially hostile colony.

So was Corain angry about it, for reasons partly ethical and partly political outrage: Defense had overstepped itself, Defense had covered this mess up back in the war years, when (as now) Defense was in bed with Reseune and gifted with a blank credit slip.

And if Corain could manage it, there was going to be a light thrown on the whole Expansionist lunacy.

vii

Gorodin—was not accessible. That was not entirely a disaster, in Giraud Nye's estimation. Secretary of Defense Lu had sat proxy so often in the last thirty years he had far more respect on Council and far more latitude in voting his own opinion than a proxy was supposed to have, the same way the Undersecretary of Defense virtually merged his own staff with Lu's and Gorodin's on-planet office: it was in effect a troika at the top of Defense and had been, *de facto*, since the war years.

And in Giraud's unvoiced opinion it was better that the proxy was in and Gorodin was somewhere classified and inaccessible at the other end of Union space: Lu, his face a map of wise secrets as rejuv declined, his dark eyes difficult even for a veteran of Reseune to cipher, was playing his usual game of *no authority to answer that* and *I don't feel I should comment*, while reporters clamored for information and Corain called for full disclosure.

Full disclosure it had to be, at least among political allies.

And Giraud had heard enough to upset his stomach all the way from Reseune to this sound-secure office, the sound-screening working at his nerves and setting his teeth off.

"It is absolutely true," Lu said, without reference to the folio that lay under his hands. "The mission was launched in 2355; it reached the star in question and dropped the colonists and the equipment. There was never any intention to return. At the time, we knew that the world was there. We knew that Alliance knew, that it was within their reach, or Earth's, and by the accident of its position and its potential—it would be of major importance." Lu cleared his throat. "We knew we couldn't hold it in practicality, we couldn't defend it, we couldn't supply it. We did in fact purpose to remove it from profitability."

Remove it from profitability. Alliance had sent a long-prepared and careful survey to the most precious find yet in near space—and found it, to its consternation, inhabited, inhabited by humans not their own and not plausibly Earth's—leaving the absolutely undeniable conclusion, even without the ruined architecture and the fact that the survivors were azi-descended—

Union had sabotaged a living planet.

"Forty thousand people," Giraud said, feeling an emptiness at the pit of his stomach. "Dropped onto an untested planet. Just like that."

Lu blinked. Otherwise he might have been a statue. "They were military; they were expendables. It was not, you understand, my administration. Nor was there, in those days, the—sensitivity to ecological concerns. So far as anyone then was reckoning, we were in a difficult military position, we had to reckon that a Mazianni strike at Cyteen was a possibility. There were two possibilities in such a move: first, the colony would survive and maintain Union principles should we meet with disaster, should Earth have launched some suicide mission at Cyteen itself. The secrecy of the colony was important in that consideration."

"It was launched in *2355*," Giraud said. "A year after the war ended."

Lu folded his hands. "It was planned in the closing years of the war, when things were uncertain. It was executed after we had been confronted with general calamity, and that disastrous treaty. It was a hole card, if you like. To let either Earth or Alliance have a world potentially more productive than Cyteen—would have been disastrous. That was the second part of the plan: if the colony should perish, it would still contribute its microorganisms to the ecology. And in less than a century—present Alliance or whatever new owner—with a difficult problem, which our science could handle and theirs couldn't. I might say—some native microorganisms were even—engineered to accept our own engineered contributions. At your own facility. As I'm sure your records will say. Not mentioning the azi and the tape-tailoring."

"You're damn right the records show it." Giraud found his breath difficult. "My God, we never knew the thing was actually *launched*! You know what kind of a security problem we've got? This isn't the 2350s. We're not at war. Your damn little timebomb's gone off in a century when we've got aliens stirred up on Sol's far side, we've got ecological treaties—we've got our own *position*, for God's sake, on ecological responsibility, the genebanks, the arks, the—"

"It was, of course, the architect of the genebanks and the treaty and the arks who actually administered Reseune during the development of the Gehenna colony. Councillor Emory was signatory to all contracts with Defense."

"—the Abolitionists, my *God*, we've handed them the best damn *issue* they could have dreamed of! It was a study project. God, Jordan Warrick's *father* worked on those Gehenna tapes."

"We trust Reseune security procedures didn't tell the project members what they were working on."

"Trust, hell! It's on the *news*, general. The news gets to Planys, eventually. You want to gamble Jordan Warrick won't know who in what department might have been working on those tapes, and what names and what specifics to hand to investigators if they get to him?"

"Damage his own father's reputation?"

"To *protect* his father's reputation, dammit; and blast Reseune's. You spent forty thousand azi to sabotage a *planet*, for God's sake, you linked the research to the Science Bureau, and it couldn't have picked a worse time to surface."

"Oh," Lu said quietly, "I can imagine worse times than this. This is a quiet time, a time when humanity—especially Alliance—has many other worries. In fact Gehenna's done exactly what it was designed to do: there *is* ecological calamity, Alliance *is* holding off development. The course of development of the Alliance has been irrevocably altered: if they absorb that population they will absorb an ethnically unique community with Union values, if you believe in the validity of your own taped instructions. In any case, we forestalled either Alliance or Earth getting a very valuable resource—and a stepping-stone to further stars. Now Alliance will either track down a scattered lot of primitives and remove them by force—a logistic nightmare—or Alliance will have to take them into account in its own settlement of the world. If they choose to settle. Intelligence informs us they're having second thoughts. They perceive a possible difficulty if they entangle themselves with this—ground-bound culture. There was always a vocal opposition to their colonization effort. The spacers who are far and away the majority in Alliance are quite doubtful about any move that puts power in the hands of the ground-bound—blue-skyers, as spacers call them, and a pre-industrial constituency—or another, much more problematical protectorate—is more than the Council of Captains wants to take on . . . not mentioning of course, *their* science bureau, which bids fair to study it to death, while the construction companies scheduled to build a station there are holding off their creditors. The Alliance ambassador demands information for their Science people and an apology; cheap at the price. There'll be a little coolness—ultimately cooperation. I assure you, they're much more scared at what Sol has poked into than *we* are—only natural considering they're much closer to the problem. All in all, it's an excellent time for it to surface: we watched their preparations, we weren't taken by surprise—that's why Adm. Gorodin is inaccessible, as it happens. We knew this was coming."

"And kept it from us!"

Lu maintained an icy little silence. Then: "Us—meaning Science; or us, meaning Reseune?"

"Us, Reseune, dammit! Reseune has an interest in this!"

"A past interest," Lu said. "The child is far from adult. She can ride out this storm. Emory is beyond reach of any law, unless you are religious. Let them subpoena a few documents. Warrick is in quarantine, thoroughly discredited as far as testimony before the Council might go. If his father was working on the project, it can only harm the Warrick name. What is there to concern Reseune?"

Giraud shut his mouth. He was sweating. Bogdanovitch was dead four years ago, Harad of Fargone was in the seat of State and making common cause with Gorodin of Defense and deFranco of Trade, and Lao of Information. Damn them. The Expansionist coalition held firm, the Abolitionists were in retreat and Corain and the Centrists had lost ground, losing Gorodin to the Expansionist camp where he had always belonged, but Nasir Harad, damn him, snuggled close to Gorodin, the source of the fat Defense contracts for his station, and State and Defense and Information were the coalition within the Expansionist coalition—the secret bedfellows.

Reseune did not have the influence it had had. That was the bitter truth Giraud had to live with. It gave him stomach upsets and kept him awake at night. But Ari had been—so far as they understood—unique.

"Let me tell you," Giraud said, "there are things within our files which are very sensitive. We do not want them released. More, we don't want any chance of Warrick being called out of Planys to testify. You don't understand how volatile that situation is. He has to be kept quiet. His recall of small detail, things he might have heard, things he might have discussed with his father down the years—will be far better than you or I want. His memory is extremely exact. If you don't want Alliance to be able to unravel what you've done in specific detail, *keep Warrick quiet*, can I be more clear?"

"Are you saying present administration can be compromised?"

Dangerous question. Dangerous interest. Giraud took another breath. "I'm only asking you to listen to me. Before you discover that the threads of this lead, yes, under closed doors. You want the Rubin project blown to hell— you let Warrick get loose, and there won't *be* a Rubin project."

"Sometimes we're not sure there *is* a Rubin project," Lu said acidly, "since RESEUNESPACE has yet to do more than minor work. Tests, you say. Data collation. *Is* there a director?"

"There is a director. We're about to transfer the bank. It's not a small operation. This inquiry is not going to help us. We're strained as it is. There's an enormous amount of data involved. That's the nature of the process. We are in operation. We have been in operation for six years. We do not intend to waste resources in a half-hearted effort, general." Damn. It's a tactic. Distract and divert. "The point is Warrick. The point is that the Planys facility is under your security and we have to rely on it. We hope we *can* rely on it."

"Absolutely. As we hope to rely on your cooperation on the Gehenna matter, Councillor Nye."

Blackmail. Plain and simple. He saw Harad's hand in this. "To what extent?"

"Agreement to cooperate with Alliance scientists. We'll swear it was a lost operation, one concealed behind the secrecies of war. Something no one knew had been done. No one in office now. That a communications screw-up saw it launched."

"Ariane Emory's name has to be kept out of it."

"I don't think that's possible. Let the dead bear the onus of responsibility. The living have far more at stake. I assure you—far more at stake. We want to keep an active channel into this situation on Gehenna. Descendants of Union citizens are still legally our citizens. *If* we choose to take that view. We may not. In any case—Science should be interested in the impact on the ecology; and the social system. We stand to gain nothing by withholding an apparent cooperation. *Not* the actual content of the tapes, to be sure. But at least the composition of the colony, the ratio of military personnel to azi. The personal histories of some of the military. Conn, for instance. Distinguished service. They should have some recognition, after all these years."

Sentiment. Good God.

"Reseune," Giraud said, "equally values Emory's distinguished record."

"I'm afraid that part will get out. The azi, you know. Once the public knows that, there's hardly any way you can hide it. But damage control is already in operation. State is onto it."

"Harad *knew* about this operation?"

"It does fall within State's area of responsibility. Science doesn't make foreign policy. *Our* obligation in that consideration is quite different. I do urge you to think—what your contracts are worth. We do *not* contract primarily with Bucherlabs. We continue to work with you. We continue to support RESEUNESPACE—even at a cost disadvantage. We expect that relationship to be a mutually satisfactory one—one we hope we can continue."

"I see," Giraud said bitterly. "I see." And after a breath or two: "Ser Secretary, we need that data protected—for more than a dead woman's reputation. To keep Council from blowing this wide open—and destroying any chance of success."

"Now you want our help. You want me to throw myself and my Bureau on the grenade. Is that it? —Let me explain to you, ser, we *have* other considerations right now, primarily among them a rampant anti-militarism that's feeding on this scandal as it is—which is a critical danger to our national defense, at a time when we're already under budget constraints, at a time when we can't get the ships we need and we can't get the problem of expanded perimeters through the heads of the public or the opposition of Finance in Council. We have a major problem, ser, your project has become a sink into which money goes and nothing emerges, and, dammit, you want us to stand and shield you from inquiry while you refuse our requests for records. I suggest you defend *yourself*, ser—with Reseune's well-known resources. Maybe it's time to bring this project of yours out. Make a choice. Give me a *reason* I can *use* to maintain that data as Classified—or give me the records I need."

"She's not ready, my God, not *now*, in the middle of scandal that touches her predecessor. She's a six-year-old kid, she can't handle that kind of attack—"

"It's your problem," Lu said, folding his hands, settling into that implacable, bland stare. "We don't know, frankly, ser, if we *have* anything to protect. For all you've been willing to demonstrate to us, it *is* another Bok clone."

"I'll show you records."

"Bok's clone was quite good as a child. It was later the problems manifested. Wasn't it? And unless you're willing to go public with the child and give me a reason to clamp down on the records—I can't extend that protection any further than I have."

"Dammit, you leave us vulnerable and they'll find us the door that leads to your own territory."

"Through *yours*, I think. You were very active in Reseune administration in those years. Can it be—those records you defend—lay the blame to you, ser?"

"That's your guess. It may shine light where a good many people don't want it."

"So we direct the strike, don't we? It's always useful to know what you've left open for attack. I'm sorry it has to be in your territory. But I certainly won't leave it in mine."

"If you'll apply a little patience—"

"I prefer the word *progress*, which, quite truthfully, I find lacking in Reseune lately. We can discuss this. I am prepared to discuss it. But I think you'll understand I am inflexible on certain points. Cooperation is very essential just now. If we do not have a reason to withhold those records, we must provide those records. You must understand—we have to provide something to the inquiry. And soon."

One did. One sat and one listened while the Defense *proxy*, damn him to hell, laid out Gorodin's program for, as he called it, damage control.

A proposal for scientific and cultural cooperation with Alliance. Coming from Defense via the Science Bureau.

An official expression of regret from the Council in joint resolution, made possible by the release of selected documents by the present administration of Reseune, indicating Bogdanovitch, Emory, and Azov of Defense, all safely deceased, collaborated in the planning of the Gehenna operation.

Damn him.

"We'll see to Warrick," Lu said. "Actually—allowing him conference with his son might have some benefit right now. Monitored, of course."

viii

"Justin?" The voice came from the other end, Jordan's voice, his father's voice, after eight years; and Justin, who had steeled himself not to break down, *not* to break down in front of Denys, on whose desk-phone the call came, bit his lip till it bled and watched the image come out of the break-up on the screen—a Jordan older, thinner. His hair was white. Justin stared in shock, in the consciousness of lost years, and mumbled: "Jordan—God, it's good to see you. We're fine, we're all fine. Grant's not here for this one, but they'll let him next time. . . ."

". . . You're looking fine," Jordan's voice overrode him, and there was pain in his eyes. *"God, you've grown a bit, haven't you? It's good to see you, son. Where's Grant?"*

Time-delay. They were fifteen seconds lagged, by security at either end.

"You're looking good yourself." O *God*, the banalities they had to use, when there was so little time. When there was everything in the world to say, and they could not, with security waiting to break the connection at the first hint of a breach of the rules. "How's Paul? Grant and I are living in your apartment, doing real well. I'm still in design—"

A lift from Denys' hand warned him. No work discussions. He stopped himself.

". . . A little grayer. I know. I'm not doing badly at all. Good health and all that. Paul too. Damn, it's good to see your face. . . ."

"You can do that in a mirror, can't you?" He forced a little laugh. "I hope I do look that good at the same age. Got a good chance, right? —I can't report much—" They won't let me. "—I've been keeping busy. I get your letters." Cut to hell. "I really look forward to them. So does—"

His father grinned as the joke got through. *"You're my time machine. You've got a good chance. . . . I get your letters too. I keep all of them."*

"So does Grant. He's grown too. Tall. You could figure. We're sort of left hand and right. We look out for each other. We're doing fine."

"You weren't going to catch him. Not the way he was growing. Paul's gone gray too. Rejuv, of course. I'm sorry. I was absolutely certain I'd told you in the letters. I forget about it. I'm too damn lazy to dye it."

Meaning the censors had cut the part it was in, damn them.

"I think it looks pretty good. Really. You know everything looks pretty much the same at home—" Not elsewhere. "Except I miss you. Both of you."

"I miss you too, son. I really do. They're signing me I've got to close down now. Damn, there's so much to say. Be good. Stay out of trouble."

"You be good. We're all right. I love you."

The image broke up and went to snow. The vid cut itself off. He bit his lips and tried to look at Denys with dignity. The way Jordan would have. "Thanks," he said.

Denys' mouth made a little tremor of its own. "That's all right. That went fine. You want a tape? I ran one."

"Yes, ser, I would like it. For Grant."

Denys ejected it from the desk recorder and gave it to him. And nodded to him. Emphatically. "I'll tell you: they're watching you very closely. It's this Gehenna thing."

"So they want a good grip on Jordan, is that it?"

"You understand very well. Yes. That's exactly what they want. That's exactly why Defense suddenly changed its mind about priorities. There's even a chance—a chance, understand—you may get an escorted trip to Planys. But they'll be watching you every time you breathe."

That shook him. Perhaps it was meant to. "Is that in the works?"

"I'm talking with them about it. I shouldn't tell you. But, God, son, don't make any mistakes. Don't do anything. You've done spectacularly well, since you—got your personal problem worked out. Your work's quite, quite fine. You're going to be taking on more responsible things—you know what I mean. More assignments. I want you and Grant to work together on some designs. Really, I want you to work into a staff position here. Both of you."

"Why? So you've got something to take away?"

"Son,—" Denys gave a deep sigh and looked worried. "No. Precisely the opposite. I want you to be necessary here. Very necessary. They're setting up the Fargone facility. And that's a hell of a long way from Planys."

A cold feeling crept about his heart, old and familiar.

"For God's sake," Denys said, *"don't* give them a chance. That's what I'm telling you. We're not totally in control of what's happening. Defense has gotten its hands on your father. It's not going to let go. You understand, it's

Gehenna that got you what you've gotten this far: it's Gehenna and the fallout from that, that's made them think they have to give your father something to lose. But we haven't released you to them. We've kept you very quiet. The fact that you were a minor protected you and Grant from some things: but without their noticing—you've gotten old enough to mess with. And the RESEUNESPACE facility at Fargone has a military wing, where you'd make a hell of a hostage."

"Is that a threat?"

"Justin, —give me at least a little respite. Give me as much credit as I give you. And your father. I'm trying to warn you about a trap. *Think* about it, if nothing else. I truly don't trust this sudden beneficence on the part of Defense. You're right not to. And I'm trying to warn you of a possible problem. If you're essential personnel we have a hold on you, and whatever you think, you're a hell of a lot safer if we have that hold, now. Draw your own conclusions. You know damn well what an advantage it would be for them if they could have you under their hand out at Fargone and Jordan in their keeping at Planys. That's what I'm trying to tell you. Use that information any way you see fit. But I'll give you what chance I can."

He took the tape. He thought about it. "Yes, ser," he said finally. Because Denys was right. Fargone was not where he wanted to be sent, not now, not any longer. No matter what Jordan might have wanted.

ix

I thought this might handle some of your objections on MR-1959, Justin typed at the top of his explanation of the attachment to the EO-6823 work, —*JW*. And pulled the project files up and sent them over to Yanni Schwartz's office.

With trepidations.

He was working again. Working overtime and very hard, and earnestly trying, because he saw where he had gotten to. He took the tapes. He assimilated things. He tried the kind of designs he had been working on in his spare time eight years ago and tried to explain to Yanni that they were only experimental alternates to the regular assignments.

Which for some reason made Yanni madder than hell.

But then, a lot of things did.

"Look," Justin had said when Yanni blew up about the MR-1959 alternate, "Yanni, I'm doing this on my own time. I did the other thing. I just thought maybe you could give me a little help on this."

"No damn way you can *do* a thing like this," Yanni had said. "That's all there is to it."

"Explain."

"You can't link a skill tape into deep-sets. You'll turn out rats on a treadmill. That's what you're doing."

"Can we talk about this? Can we do this at lunch? I really want to talk about this, Yanni. I think I've got a way to avoid that. I think it's in there."

"I don't see any reason to waste my time on it. I'm busy, son, I'm *busy!* Go ask Strassen if you can find her. If anybody can find her. Let her play instructor. For that matter, ask Peterson. He's got patience. I don't. Just do your job and turn in your work and don't give me problems, for God's sake, I don't need any more problems!"

Peterson handled the beginners.

That was what Yanni meant.

He did not object with the fact that Denys Nye had urged him to take up his active studies. He did not object with the fact Ariane Emory had had time to look at his prototype designs. He swallowed it and told himself that Yanni always hit below the belt when he was bothered, Yanni was a psych designer, Yanni was right up there with the best they had, and Yanni working with an azi was patience itself; but Yanni arguing with a CIT cut loose with every gun he had, including the psych-tactics. Of course it stung. That was because Yanni was damned good and he was firing away at a psychological cripple who was trapped and frustrated at every turn.

So he got out of there with a quiet Yes, ser, I understand. And ached all night before he got his mental balance again, gathered up his shattered nerves, and decided: *All right, that's Yanni, isn't it? He's still the best I've got. I can wear him down. What can he do to me? What can words do?*

A hell of a lot, from a psychmaster, but living in Reseune and aiming to *be* what Yanni was, meant taking it and gathering himself up and going on.

"Don't take him so seriously," was Grant's word on the fracas—Grant, who went totally business and very shielded when he was within ten feet of Yanni Schwartz, because Yanni scared him out of good sense.

"I don't," Justin said. "I won't. He's the only one who *can* teach me any- thing, except Jane Strassen and Giraud and Denys, and hell if I'll go to the Nyes. Let's don't even think about hanging around Strassen."

"No," Grant said fervently. "I don't think you'd better do that."

Considering what else hung around Strassen's office, to be sure.

He did not consciously set up war with Yanni. Only he hurt inside, he was unsure of himself, he tried to do his best work and Yanni wanted him to design with tabs so a surgeon could pull it out again, because, as Yanni had said on a quieter day, when pressed a second time to be specific on the MR-1959 problem: "You're not that good, dammit, and a skill tape isn't a master-tape. Quit putting feathers on a pig. Stay out of the deep-sets, or haven't you got brains enough to see where that link's going? I haven't got time for this damn messing around. You're wasting your time and you're wasting mine. You might be a damn fine designer if you got a handle on your own problems and quit fucking around with things they learned eighty years ago wouldn't fucking *work!* You haven't invented the wheel, son, you've just gone down an old dead end."

"Ari never said that," he offered finally, which was like pulling his guts up. It came out in a half-breath and much too emotional.

"What did she say about it?"

"She just critiqued the design and said there were sociological ramifications I didn't have—"

"Damn right."

"She said she was going to think about it. Ari—was going to *think* about it. She didn't say she could answer me right then. She didn't say *I* should think about it. So I don't think you can toss me off like that. I can show you the one I was working on, if that makes a difference."

"Son, you'd better wake up to it, Ari was after one thing with you, and you damn well know what that was. Don't go off on some damn mental tangent and fuck yourself up six, eight years later because you're so damn sure you were better at seventeen than you are now. That's crap. Recognize it. You got fucked up in several senses, it's natural you want to try to pick up where you left off, but you'd do yourself a better service if you picked up where you *are*, son, and realized that it wasn't your *ideas* that made Ari invite you into her office and spend all that time with you. All right?"

For a moment he could hardly get his breath. They were private, in Yanni's office. No one could hear but them. But no one, *no one*, in all these years, had ever said to him as bluntly what Yanni said, not even Denys, not even Petros, and he got a fight-flight flash that shoved enough adrenaline into his system that he reacted, he knew he was reacting: he wanted to be anywhere else but trapped in this, with a man he dared not hit—God, they would have him on the table inside the hour, then—

"Fuck *you*, Yanni, what are you trying to do to me?"

"I'm trying to help you."

"Is that your best? Is that the way you deal with your patients? God help them."

He was close to breaking down. He clenched his jaw and held it. *You know I've been in therapy, you unprincipled bastard. Get off me.*

And Yanni took a long time about answering him, much more quietly. "I'm trying to tell you the truth, son. No one else is. Don't corner him, Petros says. What do you want? Petros to put a fresh coat of plaster on it? He can't lay a hand on you. *Denys* won't let him do an intervention. And that's what you fucking *need*, son, you need somebody to cut deep and grab hold of what's eating at you and show it to you in the daylight, I don't care how you hate it. I'm not your enemy. They're all so damn scared how it'll look if they bring you in for major psych. They *don't* want that for fear it'll leak and Jordan will blow. But I care about *you*, son, I care so damn much I'll rip your guts out and give them to you on a plate, and trust the old adage doesn't hold and that you *can* put yourself back together. Ari's in the news right now and it's not good; and there's too damn much media attention hovering around the edges of our security. We *can't* arrest you and haul you in for the treatment you need. You listen to me. You listen. Everybody else is saving their ass. And you're bleeding, while Petros does half-hearted patches on a situation all of us can see: Denys tried to talk to you. You won't cooperate. Thank God you *are* trying to wake up and get to work. If I did what I wanted, son, I'd have shot you full of juice before I had this little talk with you and maybe it'd sink in. But I want you to look real hard at what you're doing. You're trying to go back to where you were. You're wasting time. I want you to accept what happened, figure the past is the past, and turn me in the kind of work you're capable of. *Fast* work. You're slow. You're damned slow. You muddle along with checks and rechecks like you're scared shitless you're going to fuck up, and you don't need to do that. You're not the final checker, you don't have to work like you are, because I'm sure as hell not going to let you do that for a long while yet. So just relax, *put the work out*, and do the best you can on your own level. Not—" He made a careless flip at the pages. "Not this stuff."

He sat there in silence a while. Bleeding, like Yanni said. And because he was stubborn, because there was only one thing he wanted, he said: "Prove to me I'm wrong. Do me a critique. Run it past Sociology. Show me what the second and third generation would do. Show me how it integrates. Or doesn't."

"Have you looked around you? Have you seen the kind of schedules we've been running? Where do you think I've got the time to mess with this? Where do you think I'm going to budget Sociology to solve a problem that's been solved for eighty years?"

"I'm saying it's solved here. I'm saying I've got it. *You* critique my designs, then. You want to tell me I'm crazy, *show* me where I'm wrong."

"*Dammit*, I won't help you wallow in the very thing that's the matter with you!"

"I'm Jordan's son. I was good enough—"

"Was, was, *was*, dammit! Stop looking at the past! Six years ago wasn't worth shit, son!"

"Prove it to me. *Prove* it, Yanni, or admit you can't."

"Go to Peterson!"

"Peterson can't prove anything to me. I'm better than he is. I started that way."

"You arrogant little bastard! You're *not* better than Peterson. Peterson pays his way around here. If you weren't Jordan's son, you'd be living in a one-bedroom efficiency with an allotment your work entitles you to, which won't pay for your fancy tastes, son. Grant and you together don't earn that place you're living in."

"What does my father's work pay for, and what does he get? Send my designs to him. He'd find the time."

Yanni took in a breath. Let it out again. "Damn. What do I do with you?"

"Whatever you want. Everyone else does. Fire me. You're going to get these designs about once a week. And if you don't answer me I'll ask. Once a week. I want my education, Yanni. I'm due that. And you're the instructor I want. Do whatever you like. Say whatever you like. I won't give up."

"Dammit—"

He stared at Yanni, not even putting it beyond Yanni to get up, come around the desk and hit him. "I'd ask Strassen," he said, "but I don't think they want me near her. And I don't think she's got the time. So that leaves you, Yanni. You can fire me or you can prove I'm wrong and teach me why. But do it with logic. Psyching me doesn't do it."

"I haven't got the time!"

"No one does. So make it. It doesn't take much, if you can see so clearly where I'm wrong. Two sentences are all I need. Tell me where it'll impact the next generation."

"Get the hell out of here."

"Am I fired?"

"No," Yanni snarled. Which was the friendliest thing staff had said to him in years.

So he did two tapes. One for Yanni. One the one he wished they would let him use. Because it taught him things. Because it let him see the whole set.

Because, as Grant said, a skill was damned important to an azi.

And he still could not work out the ethics of it—whether it was right to make a Theta get real pleasure out of the work instead of the approval. There was something moral involved. And there were basic structural problems in linking that way into an azi psychset, that was the trouble with it, and Yanni was right. An artificial psychset needed simple foundations, not complicated ones, or it got into very dangerous complexities. Deep-set linkages could become neuroses and obsessive behavior that could destroy an azi and be far more cruel than any simple boredom.

But he kept turning in the study designs for Yanni to see, when Yanni was in a mellow mood; and Yanni had been, now and again.

"You're a fool," was the best he got. And sometimes a paragraph on paper, outlining repercussions. Suggesting a study-tape out of Sociology.

He cherished those notes. He got the tapes. He ran them. He found mistakes. He built around them.

"You're still a fool," Yanni said. "What you're doing, son, is making your damage slower and probably deeper. But keep working. If you've got all this spare time I can suggest some useful things to do with it. We've got a glitch-up in a Beta set. We've got everything we can handle. The set is ten years old and it's glitching off one of three manual skills tapes. We think. The instructor thinks. You've got the case histories in this fiche. Apply your talents to that and see if you and Grant can come up with some answers."

He went away with the fiche and the folder, with a trouble-shoot to run, which was hell and away more real work than Yanni had yet trusted him with.

Which was, when he got it on the screen, a real bitch. The three azi had had enough tape run on them over the years to fill a page, and each one had been in a different application. But the glitch was a bad one. The azi were all under patch-tape, a generic calm-down-it's-not-your-fault, meaning three azi were waiting real-time in some anguish for some designer to come up with something to take their nameless distress and deal with it in a sensible way.

God, it was months old. They were not on Cyteen. Local Master Supervisors had all had a hand in the analysis, run two fixes on one, and they had gone badly sour.

Which meant it was beyond ordinary distress. It was not a theoretical problem.

He made two calls, one to Grant. "I need an opinion."

One to Yanni. "Tell me someone else is working on this. Yanni, this is a probable wipe, for God's sake, give it to someone who knows what he's doing."

"You claim you do," Yanni said, and hung up on him.

"Damn you!" he yelled at Yanni after the fact.

And when Grant got there, they threw out everything they were both working on and got on it.

For three damnable sleep-deprived weeks before they comped a deep-set intersect in a skills tape. In all three.

"Dammit," he yelled at Yanni when he turned it in, "this is a mess, Yanni! You could have found this thing in a week. These are human beings, for God's sake, one of them's running with a botch-up on top of the other damage—"

"Well, you manage, don't you? I thought you'd empathize. Go do a fix."

"What do you mean, 'do a fix'? Run me a check!"

"This one's all yours. Do me a fix. You don't need a check."

He drew a long, a desperate breath. And stared at Yanni with the thought of breaking his neck. "*Is* this a real-time problem? Or is this some damn trick? Some damn exercise you've cooked up?"

"Yes, it's real-time. And while you're standing here arguing, they're still waiting. So get on it. You did that fairly fast. Let's see what else you can do."

"I know what you're doing to me, dammit! Don't take it out on the azi!"

"Don't you," Yanni said. And walked off into his inner office and shut the door.

He stood there. He looked desperately at Marge, Yanni's aide.

Marge gave him a sympathetic look and shook her head.

So he went back and broke the news to Grant.

And turned in the fix in three days.

"Fine," Yanni said. "I hope it works. I've got another case for you."

X

"This is part of my work," maman said, and Ari, walking with her hand in maman's, not because she was a baby, but because the machinery was huge and things moved and everything was dangerous, looked around at the shiny steel things they called womb-tanks, each one as big as a bus, and asked, loudly:

"Where are the babies?"

"Inside the tanks," maman said. An azi came up and maman said: "This is my daughter Ari. She's going to take a look at a few of the screens."

"Yes, Dr. Strassen," the azi said. Everyone talked loud. "Hello, Ari."

"Hello," she yelled up at the azi, who was a woman. And held on to maman's hand, because maman was following the azi down the long row.

It was only another desk, after all, and a monitor screen. But maman said: "What's the earliest here?"

"Number ten's a week down."

"Ari, can you count ten tanks down? That's nearly to the wall."

Ari looked. And counted. She nodded.

"All right," maman said. "Mary, let's have a look. —Ari, Mary here is going to show you the baby inside number ten, right here on the screen."

"Can't we look inside?"

"The light would bother the baby," maman said. "They're like birthday presents. You can't open them till it's the baby's birthday. All right?"

That was funny. Ari laughed and plumped herself down on the seat. And what came on the screen was a red little something.

"That's the baby," maman said, and pointed. "Right there."

"Ugh." It clicked with something she had seen somewhere. Which was probably tape. It was a kind of a baby.

"Oh, yes. Ugh. All babies look that way when they're a week old. It takes them how many weeks to be born?"

"Forty and some," Ari said. She remembered that from down deep too. "Are they all like this?"

"What's closest to eight weeks, Mary?"

"Four and five are nine," Mary said.

"That's tanks four and five, Ari. Look where they are, and we'll show you—which one, Mary?"

"Number four, sera. Here we are."

"It's still ugly," Ari said. "Can we see a pretty one?"

"Well, let's just keep hunting."

The next was better. The next was better still. Finally the babies got so big they were too big to see all of. And they moved around. Ari was excited, really excited, because maman said they were going to birth one.

There were a lot of techs when they got around to that. Maman took firm hold of Ari's shoulders and made her stand right in front of her so she would be able to see; and told her where to look, right there, right in that tank.

"Won't it drown?" Ari asked.

"No, no, babies live in liquid, don't they? Now, right now, the inside of the tank is doing just what the inside of a person does when birth happens. It's going to push the baby right out. Like muscles, only this is all pumps. It's really going to bleed, because there's a lot of blood going in and out of the pumps and it's going to break some of the vessels in the bioplasm when it pushes like that."

"Does the baby have a cord and everything?"

"Oh, yes, babies have to have. It's a real one. Everything is real right up to the bioplasm: that's the most complicated thing—it can really grow a blood system. Watch out now, see the light blink. That means the techs should get ready. Here it comes. There's its head. That's the direction babies are supposed to face."

"Sploosh!" Ari cried, and clapped her hands when it hit the tank. And stood still as it started swimming and the nasty stuff went through the water. "Ugh."

But the azi techs got it out of there, and got the cord, and it did go on moving. Ari stood up on her toes trying to see as they took it over to the counter, but Mary the azi made them stop to show her the baby making faces. It was a boy baby.

Then they washed it and powdered it and wrapped it up, and Mary held it and rocked it.

"This is GY-7688," maman said. "His name is August. He's going to be one of our security guards when he grows up. But he'll be a baby for a long time yet. When you're twelve, he'll be as old as you are now."

Ari was fascinated. They let her wash her hands and touch the baby. It waved a fist at her and kicked and she laughed out loud, it was so funny.

"Say goodbye," maman said then. "Thank Mary."

"Thank you," Ari said, and meant it. It was fun. She hoped they could come back again.

"Did you like the lab?" maman asked.

"I liked it when the baby was born."

"Ollie was born like that. He was born right in this lab."

She could not imagine Ollie tiny and funny like that. She did not want to think of Ollie like that. She wrinkled her nose and made Ollie all right in her mind again.

Grown up and handsome in his black uniform.

"Sometimes CITs are born out of the tanks," maman said. "If for some reason their mamans can't carry them. The tanks can do that. Do you know the difference between an azi and a CIT, when they're born the same way?"

That was a hard question. There were a lot of differences. Some were rules and some were the way azi were.

"What's that?" she asked maman.

"How old were you when you had tape the first time?"

"I'm six."

"That's right. And you had your first tape the day after your birthday. Didn't scare you, did it?"

"No," she said; and shook her head so her hair flew. Because she liked to do that. Maman was slow with her questions and she got bored in between.

"You know when August will have his first tape?"

"When?"

"Today. Right now. They put him in a cradle and it has a kind of a tape going, so he can hear it."

She was impressed. Jealous, even. August was a threat if he was going to be that smart.

"Why didn't I do that?"

"Because you were going to be a CIT. Because you have to learn a lot of things the old-fashioned way. Because tapes are good, but if you've got a maman or a papa to take care of you, you learn all kinds of things August won't learn until he's older. CITs get a head start in a way. Azi learn a lot about how to be good and how to do their jobs, but they're not very good at figuring out what to do with things they've never met before. CITs are good at taking care of emergencies. CITs can make up what to do. They learn that from their mamans. Tape-learning is good, but it isn't everything. That's why maman tells you to pay attention to what you see and hear. That's why you're supposed to learn from that first, so you know tape isn't as important as your own eyes and ears. If August had a maman to take him home today he'd be a CIT."

"Why can't Mary be his maman?"

"Because Mary has too many kids to take care of. She has five hundred every year. Sometimes more than that. She couldn't do all that work. So the tape has to do it. That's why azi can't have mamans. There just aren't enough to go around."

"*I* could take August."

"No, you couldn't. Mamans have to be grown up. *I'd* have to take him home, and he'd have to sleep in your bed and share your toys and have dirty diapers and cry a lot. And you'd have to share maman with him forever and ever. You can't send a baby back just because you get tired of him. Would you like to have him take half your room and maman and Nelly and Ollie have to take care of him all the time? —because he'd be the baby then and he'd have to have all maman's time."

"No!" That was not a good idea. She grabbed onto maman's hand and made up her mind no baby was going to sneak in and take half of everything. Sharing with nasty friends was bad enough.

"Come on," maman said, and took her outside, in the sun, and into the garden where the fish were. Ari looked in her pants-pockets, but there was no crumb of bread or anything. Nelly had made her put on clean.

"Have you got fish-food?"

"No," maman said, and patted the rock she sat on. "Come sit by maman, Ari. Tell me what you think about the babies."

Lessons. Ari sighed and left the fish that swam up under the lilies; she squatted down on a smaller rock where she could see maman's face and leaned her elbows on her knees.

"What do you think about them?"

"They're all right."

"You know Ollie was born there."

"Is that baby going to be another Ollie?"

"You know he can't. Why?"

She screwed up her face and thought. "He's GY something and Ollie's AO. He's not even an Alpha."

"That's right. That's exactly right. You're very smart."

She liked to hear that. She fidgeted.

"You know, you were born in that room, Ari."

She heard that again in her head. And was not sure maman was not teasing her. She looked at maman, trying to figure out if it was a game. It didn't *look* like a game.

"Maman couldn't carry you. Maman's much too old. Maman's been on rejuv for years and years and she can't have babies anymore. But the tanks can. So she told Mary to make a special baby. And maman was there at the tank when it was birthed, and maman picked it up out of the water, and that was you, Ari."

She stared at maman. And tried to put herself in that room and in that tank, and be that baby Mary had picked up. She felt all different. She felt like she was different from herself. She did not know what to do about it.

Maman held her hands out. "Do you want maman to hold you, sweet? I will."

Yes, she wanted that. She wanted to be little and fit on maman's lap, and she tried, but she hurt maman, she was so big, so she just tucked up beside maman on the rock and felt big and clumsy while maman hugged her and rocked her. But it felt safer.

"Maman loves you, sweet. Maman truly does. There's nothing wrong at all in being born out of that room. You're the best little girl maman could have. I wouldn't trade you for anybody."

"I'm still yours."

Maman was not going to answer/maman was, so fast a change it scared her till maman said: "You're still mine, sweet."

She did not know why her heart was beating so hard. She did not know why it felt like maman was not going to say that at first. That scared her more than anything. She was glad maman had her arms around her. She was cold.

"I told you not everybody has a papa. But you did, Ari. His name was James Carnath. That's why Amy's your cousin."

"Amy's my cousin?" She was disgusted. People had cousins. It meant they were related. Nasty old Amelie Carnath was not anybody she wanted to be related to.

"Where *is* my papa?"

"Dead, sweet. He died before you were born."

"Couldn't Ollie be my father?"

"Ollie can't, sweet. He's on rejuv too."

"He doesn't have white hair."

"He dyes it, the same as I do."

That was an awful shock. She couldn't think of Ollie being old like maman. Ollie was young and handsome.

"I want Ollie to be my papa."

Maman made that upset-feeling again. She felt it in maman's arms. In the way maman breathed. "Well, it was James Carnath. He was a scientist like maman. He was very smart. That's where you get half your smart, you know. You know when you're going on rejuv and you know you might want a baby later you have to put your geneset in the bank so it's there after you can't make a baby anymore. Well, that was how you could be started even if your papa died a long time ago. And there you waited, in the genebank, all the years until maman was ready to take care of a baby."

"I wish you'd done it sooner," Ari said. "Then you wouldn't be so old."

Maman cried.

And she did, because maman was unhappy. But maman kissed her and called her sweet, and said she loved her, so she guessed it was as all right as it was going to get.

She thought about it a lot. She had always thought she came out of maman. It was all right if maman wanted her to be born from the tanks. It didn't make her an azi. Maman saw to that.

It was nice to be born where Ollie was born. She liked that idea. She didn't care about whoever James Carnath was. He was *Carnath*. Ugh. Like Amy.

She thought when Ollie was a baby he would have had black hair and he would be prettier than August was.

She thought when she grew up to be as old as maman she would have her own Ollie. And she would have a Nelly.

But not a Phaedra. Phaedra bossed too much.

You didn't have to have azi if you didn't want them. You had to order them or they didn't get born.

That, for Phaedra, who tattled on her. She would get August instead when he grew up, and he would be Security in their hall, and say *good morning, sera* to her just like Security did to maman.

She would have a Grant too. With red hair. She would dress him in black the way a lot of azi did and he would be very handsome. She did not know what he would do, but she would like to have an azi with red hair all the same.

She would be rich like maman.

She would be beautiful.

She would fly in the plane and go to the city and she would buy lots and lots of pretty clothes and jewels like maman's, so when they went to New Year they would make everybody say how beautiful they all were.

She would find Valery and tell him come back. And sera Schwartz too.

They would all be happy.

Verbal Text from:
PATTERNS OF GROWTH
A Tapestudy in Genetics: #1
"An Interview with
Ariane Emory": pt. 2

**Reseune Educational Publications: 8970-8768-1
approved for 80+**

Q: Dr. Emory, we have time perhaps for a few more questions, if you wouldn't mind.

A: Go ahead.

Q: You're one of the Specials. Some people say that you may be one of the greatest minds that's ever lived, in the class of da Vinci, Einstein, and Bok. How do you feel about that comparison?

A: I would like to have known any one of them. I think it would be interesting. I think I can guess your next question, by the way.

Q: Oh?

A: Ask it.

Q: How do you compare yourself to other people?

A: Mmmn. That's not the one. Other people. I'm not sure I know. I live a very cloistered life. I have great respect for anyone who can drive a truck in the outback or pilot a starship. Or negotiate the Novgorod subway. [laughter] I suppose that I could. I've never tried. But life is always complex. I'm not sure whether it takes more for me to plot a genotype than for someone of requisite ability to do any of those things I find quite daunting.

Q: That's an interesting point. But do you think driving a truck is equally valuable? Should we appoint Specials for that ability? What makes you important?

A: Because I have a unique set *of abilities. No one else can do what I do. That's what a Special is.*

Q: How does it *feel* to be a Special?

A: That's very close to the question I thought you'd ask. I can tell you being a Special is a lot like being a Councillor or holding any office: very little privacy, very high security, more attention than seems to make sense.

Q: Can you explain that last—than seems to make sense?

A: [laughter] A certain publication asked me to detail a menu of my favorite foods. A reporter once asked me whether I believed in reincarnation. Do these things make sense? I'm a psychsurgeon and a geneticist and occasionally a philosopher, in which consideration the latter question actually makes more sense to me than the first, but what in hell does either one matter to the general public? More than my science, you say? No. What the reporters are looking for is an equation that finds some balance between my psyche and their demographically ideal viewer—who is a myth and a reality: what they ask may bore everyone equally by pleasing no one exactly, but never mind: which brings us finally to the question I expect you're going to ask.

Q: That's very disconcerting.

A: Ask it. I'll tell you if we've found it yet.

Q: All right. I think we've gotten there. Is this it? What do you know that no one else does?

A: Oh, I like that better. What do I know? That's interesting. No one's ever put it that way before. Shall I tell you the question they always ask? What it feels like to have a Special's ability. What do I know is a much wiser question. What I feel, I'll answer that quite briefly: the same as anyone—who is isolate, different, and capable of understanding the reason for the isolation and the difference.

What do I know? I know that I am relatively unimportant and my work is vastly important. That's the thing the interviewer missed, who asked me what I eat. My preference in wines is utter trivia, unless you're interested in my personal bio-chemistry, which does interest me, and does matter, but certainly that has very little to do with an article on famous people and food, whatever that means. If that writer discovered a true connection between genius and cheeses, I am interested, and I want to interview him.

Fortunately my staff protects me against the idly curious. The state set me apart because in the aggregate the state, the people, if you will, know that given the freedom to work, I will work, and work for the sake of my work, because I am a monomaniac. Because I do have that emotional dimension the other reporters were trying to reach, I do have an aesthetic sense about what I do, and it applies to what one very ancient Special called the pursuit of Beauty— I think everyone can understand that, on some level. On whatever level. That ancient equated it with Truth. I call it Balance. I equate it with Symmetry. That's the nature of a Special, that's what you're really looking for: a Special's mind works in abstracts that transcend the limitations of any existing language. A Special has the Long View, and equally well the Wide View, that embraces more than any single human word will embrace, simply because communicative language is the property of the masses. And the Word, the Word with a capital W, that the Special sees, understands, comprehends in the root sense of the term, is a Word outside the experience of anyone previous. So he calls it Beauty. Or Truth. Or Balance or Symmetry. Frequently he expresses himself through the highly flexible language of mathematics; or if his discipline does not express itself readily in that mode, he has to create a special meaning for certain words within the context of his work and attempt to communicate in the semantic freight his language has accumulated for centuries. My language is partly mathematical, partly biochemical, partly semantics: I study biochemical systems—human beings—which react predictably on a biochemical level to stimuli passing through a system of receptors—hardware—of biochemically determined sensitivity; through a biochemical processor of biochemically determined efficiency—hardware again— dependent on a self-programming system which is also biochemical, which produces a uniquely tailored software capable of receiving information from another human being with a degree of specificity limited principally by its own hardware, its own software, and semantics. We haven't begun to speak of the hardware and software of the second human being. Nor have we addressed the complex dimension of culture or the possibility of devising a mathematics for social systems, the games statisticians and demographers play on their level and I play on mine. I will tell you that I leave much of the work with microstructures to researchers under my direction and I have spent more of my time in thinking than I have in the laboratory. I am approaching a degree of order in that thought that I can only describe as a state of simplicity. A very wide simplicity. Things which did not seem to be related, are related. The settling of these things into order is a pleasurable sensation that increasingly lures the thinker into dimensions that have nothing to do with the senses. Attaching myself to daily life is increasingly difficult and I sometimes find myself needing that, the flesh needs affirmation, needs sensation—because otherwise I do not, personally, exist. And I exist everywhere.

At the end I will speak one Word, and it will concern humanity. I don't know if anyone will understand it. I have a very specific hope that someone will. This is the emotional dimension. But if I succeed, my successor will do something I can only see in the distance: in a sense, I am doing it, because getting this far is part of it. But the flesh needs rest from visions. Lives are short-term, even one extended by rejuv. I give you Truth. Someone, someday, will understand my notes.

That is myself, speaking the language not even another Special can understand, because his Beauty is different, and proceeds along another course. If you're religious you may think we have seen the same thing. Or that we must lead to the same thing. I am not, myself, certain. We are God's dice. To answer still another Special.

Now I've given you more than I've given any other interviewer, because you asked the best question. I'm sorry I can't answer in plain words. By now, the average citizen is capable of understanding Plato and some may know Einstein. The majority of scientists have yet to grasp Bok. You will know, in a few centuries, what I know right now. But humanity in the macrocosm is quite wise: because in the mass you are as visionary as any Special, you give me my freedom, and I prove the validity of your judgment.

Q: You can't interpret this thing you see.

A: If I could, I would. If words existed to describe it, I would not be what I am.

Q: You've served for decades in the legislature. Isn't that a waste? Isn't that a job someone else could do?

A: Good question. No. Not in this time. Not in this place. The decisions we make are very important. The events of the last five decades prove that. And I need contact with reality. I benefit in—a spiritual way, if you like. In a way that affects my personal biochemical systems and keeps them in healthy balance. It's not good for the organism, to let the abstract grow without checking the perceptions. In simpler terms, it's a remedy against intellectual isolation and a service I do my neighbors. An abstract mathematician probably doesn't have anywhere near our most junior councillor's understanding of the interstellar futures market or the pros and cons of a medical care system for merchanters on Union stations. By the very nature of my work, I do have that understanding; and I have a concern for human society. I know people criticize the Council system as wasting the time of experts. If providing expert opinion to the society in which we all live is a waste of time, then what good are we? Of course certain theorists can't communicate out-field. But certain ones can, and should. You've seen the experts disagree. Sometimes it's because one of us fails to understand something in another field. Very often it's because the best thinking in two fields fails to reconcile a question of practical effects, and that is precisely the point in which the people doing the arguing had better be experts: some very useful interdisciplinary understandings are hammered out in Council and in the private meetings, a fusion of separate bodies of knowledge that actually sustains this unique social experiment we call Union.

That's one aspect of the simplicity I can explain simply: the interests of all humans are interlocked, my own included, and politics is no more than a temporal expression of social mathematics.

CHAPTER 6

"This bell has to ring once when you push the left-hand button and twice when you push the right-hand button," the Super said, and Florian listened as the problem clicked off against the things he knew. So far it was easy to wire. "But—" Here came the real problem, Florian knew. "But you have to fix it so that if you push the left-hand button first it won't work at all and if you push the right-hand button twice it won't work until you push the left-hand button. Speed does matter. So does neatness. Go."

Parts and tools were all over the table. Florian collected what he needed. It was not particularly hard.

The next job was somebody else's project. And you had to look at the board and tell the instructor what it would do.

His fingers were very fast. He could beat the clock. Easy. The next thing was harder. The third thing was always to make up one for somebody else. He had fifteen minutes to do that.

He told the Instructor what it was.

"Show me how you'd build that," the Instructor said. So he did.

And the Instructor looked very serious and nodded finally and said: "Florian, you're going to double up on tape."

He was disappointed. "I'm sorry. It won't work?"

"Of course it'll work," the Instructor said, and smiled at him. "But I can't give that to anybody on this level. You'll do double-study on the basics and we'll see how you do with the next. All right?"

"Yes," he said. Of course it was yes. But he was worried. He was working with Olders a lot. It was hard, and took a lot of time, and they kept insisting he take his Rec time, when he had rather be at his job.

He was already late a lot, and Andy frowned at him, and helped him more than he wanted.

He thought he ought to talk to the Super about all of it. But he made them happy when he worked hard. He could still do it, even if he was tired, even if he fell into his bunk at night and couldn't even remember doing it.

The Instructor said he could go and he was late again. Andy told him the pigs didn't understand his schedule and Andy had had to feed them.

"I'll do the water," he said, and did it for Andy's too. That was fair. It made Andy happy.

It made Andy so happy Andy let him curry the Horse with him, and go with him to the special barn where they had the baby, which was a she, protected against everything and fed with a bucket you had to hold. He wasn't big enough to do that yet. You had to shower and change your clothes and be very careful, because they were giving the baby treatments they got from the Horse. But she wasn't sick. She played dodge with them and then she would smell of their fingers and play dodge again.

He had been terribly relieved when Andy told him that the horses were not for food. "What *are* they for?" he had asked then, afraid that there might be other bad answers.

"They're Experimentals," Andy had said. "I'm not sure. But they say they're working animals."

Pigs were sometimes working animals. Pigs were so good at smelling out native weeds that drifted in and rooted and they were so smart at not eating the stuff that there were azi who did nothing but walk them around, every day going over the pens and the fields with the pigs that nobody would ever make into bacon, and zapping whatever had sneaked inside the fences. The machine-sniffers were good, but Andy said the pigs were better in some ways.

That was what they meant in the tapes, Florian thought, when they said one of the first Rules of all Rules was to find ways to be useful.

---

ii

Ari read the problem, thought into her tape-knowing, and asked maman: "Does it matter how many are boys and how many are girls?"

Maman thought a moment. "Actually it does. But you can work it as if it doesn't."

"Why?"

"Because, and this is important to know, certain things are less important in certain problems; and when you're just learning how to work the problem, leaving out the things that don't matter as much helps you to remember what things are the most important in figuring it. Everything in the world is important in that problem—boys and girls, the weather, whether or not they can get enough food, whether there are things that eat them—but right now just the genes are going to matter. When you can work all those problems, then they'll tell you how to work in all the other things. One other thing. They'd hate to tell you you knew everything. There might be something else no one thought of. And if you *thought* they'd told you everything, that could trick you. So they start out simple and then start adding in whether they're boys and girls. All right?"

"It *does* matter," Ari said doggedly, "because the boy fish fight each other. But there's going to be twenty-four blue ones if nobody gets eaten. But they will, because blue ones are easy to see, and they can't hide. And if you put them with big fish there won't be any blue fish at all."

"Do you know whether a fish sees colors?"

"Do they?"

"Let's leave that for a moment. What if the females like blue males better?"

"Why should they?"

"Just figure it. Carry it another generation."

"How much better?"

"Twenty-five percent."

"All those blue ones are just going to make the big fish fatter and *they'll* have lots of babies. This is getting complicated."

Maman got this funny look like she was going to sneeze or laugh or get mad. And then she got a very funny look that was not funny at all. And gathered her up against her and hugged her.

Maman did that a lot lately. Ari thought that she ought to feel happier than she was. She had never had maman spend so much time with her. Ollie too.

But there was a danger-feeling. Maman wasn't happy. Ollie wasn't. Ollie was being azi as hard as he could, and maman and Ollie didn't shout at each other anymore. Maman didn't shout at anybody. Nelly just looked confused a lot of the time. Phaedra went around being azi too.

Ari was scared and she wanted to ask maman why, but she was afraid maman would cry. Maman always had that look lately. And it hurt when maman cried.

She just held on to maman.

Next morning she went to playschool. She was big enough to go by herself now. Maman hugged her at the door. Ollie came and hugged her too. He had not done that in a long time.

She looked back and the door was shut. She thought that was funny. But she went on to school.

iii

RESEUNE ONE left the runway and Jane clenched her hands on the leather arms of the seat. And did not look out the window. She did not want to see Reseune dwindle away. She bit her lips and shut her eyes and felt the leakage down her face while the gentle acceleration pressed her into the seat.

She turned her face toward Ollie when they reached cruising altitude. "Ollie, get me a drink. A double."

"Yes, sera," Ollie said, and unbelted and went to see to it.

Phaedra, sitting in front of them, had turned her chair around to face her across the little table. "Can I do something for you, sera?"

God, she needs to, doesn't she? Phaedra's scared. "I want you to make out a shopping list. Things you think we'll need on-ship. You'll have to place some orders when we make station. There's an orientation booklet in the outside pocket. It'll review you on procedures."

"Yes, sera."

That put a patch on Phaedra's problems. Ollie was walking wounded. He had asked her for tape. He—had asked her for tape, azi to Supervisor; and she had refused him.

"Ollie," she had said. "You're too much a CIT. I need you to be. Do you understand what I'm saying?"

"Yes," he had said. And held up better than she had.

"One for yourself too," she yelled at him, over the engine noise; and he looked around and nodded understanding. "And Phaedra!"

Peggy came up to Ollie's side at the bar, wobbled as the plane hit a little chop and then ducked down and took out a pair of glasses.

For Julia. Back in the back. Julia and Gloria.

"You've ruined my life!" Julia had screamed at her in the terminal. Right in front of Denys, the azi, and the Family that had come to see them off. While poor Gloria stood there with her chin quivering and her eyes running over. Not a bad kid. A kid who had had too much of most things, too little of what mattered, and who stared at the grandmother she had hardly ever seen and probably looked for signs of ultimate evil about her person. Gloria had no idea in the world what she was going to. No idea in the world what ship discipline meant, or the closed steel world of a working station.

"Hello, Gloria," she had said, nerving herself, trying not—God, not ever—to compare the kid against Ari—against Ari, who might hear a plane take off and might look up and realize it was *RESEUNE ONE*. Nothing more than that.

Gloria had run over to her mother. Who was about to hyperventilate. Who managed, atop it all, to impart a sense of the ridiculous to their departure. It was probably just as well they were traveling with Reseune Security. There was no trusting Julia not to bolt and run in Novgorod.

Irrationally afraid of the shuttle, the void, the jumps, all the things that involved a physics Julia had never troubled herself to learn and now decided she could not personally rely on.

Too bad, kid. I wish I could make a bubble for you where things work the way you want. I'm sorry it all overwhelms you.

It did from the moment you were born. Sorry, daughter. I'm really sorry about that.

Sorry you're going with me.

Ollie brought back the drinks. He was pale, but he was doing quite well, considering. She managed to smile at him when he handed her hers, and he looked at her again when he sat down with his own drink in hand.

She had taken half of hers down without noticing it. "I'll be all right," she said, and lifted the glass. "Skoal, Ollie. Back where I came from. Going home, finally."

And on her second double: "It feels like I was twenty again, Ollie, like nothing of Reseune ever happened."

Or she had gotten that part of her numb for a while.

----------------------- iv -----------------------

Phaedra was not at the playschool. Nelly was. Nelly was easy to get around. Sam could push her in the swing really high. Nelly worried, but Nelly wasn't going to stop them, because she would be mad at Nelly and Nelly didn't like that.

So Sam pushed her and she pushed Sam. And they climbed on the puzzle-bars.

Finally Jan came after Sam and Nelly was walking her home when uncle Denys met them in the hall.

"Nelly," Denys said, "Security wants to talk to you."

"Why?" Ari asked. Of a sudden she was afraid again. Security and Nelly were as far apart as you could think of. It was like everything else recently. It was a thing that didn't belong.

"Nelly," Denys said. "Do what I say."

"Yes, ser," Nelly said.

And Denys, big as he was, got down on one knee and took Ari's hands while Nelly was going. "Ari," he said, "something serious has happened. Your maman has to go take care of it. She's had to leave."

"Where's she going?"

"Very far away, Ari. I don't know that she *can* come back. You're going to come home with me. You and Nelly. Nelly's going to stay with you, but she's got to go take some tape that will make her feel better about it."

"Maman can too come back!"

"I don't think so, Ari. Your maman is an important woman. She has something to do. She's going—well, far as a ship can take her. She knew you'd be upset. She didn't want to worry you. So she said I should tell you goodbye for her. She said you should come home with me now and live in my apartment."

"No!" *Goodbye.* Goodbye was nothing maman would ever say. Everything was wrong. She pulled away from Denys' hands and ran, ran as hard as she could, down the halls, through the doors, into their own hall. Denys couldn't catch her. No one could. She ran until she got to her door, her place; and she unclipped her keycard from her blouse and she put it in the slot.

The door opened.

"Maman! Ollie!"

She ran through the rooms. She hunted everywhere, but she knew maman and Ollie would never hide from her.

Maman and Ollie would never leave her either. Something bad had happened to them. Something terrible had happened to them and uncle Denys was lying to her.

Maman's and Ollie's things were all off the dresser and the clothes from the closet.

Her toys were all gone. Even Poo-thing and Valery's star.

She was breathing hard. She felt like there was not enough air. She heard the door open again and ran for the living room.

"Maman! Ollie!"

But it was a Security woman who had come in; she was tall and she wore black and she had got in and she shouldn't have.

Ari just stood there and stared at her. The woman stared back. The uniformed woman, in her living room, who wasn't going to leave.

"Minder," Ari said, trying to be brave and grown-up, "call maman's office."

The Minder did not answer.

"Minder? It's Ari. Call maman's office!"

"The Minder is disconnected," the Security woman said. And it was true. The Minder hadn't said a thing when she had come in. Everything was wrong.

"Where's my mother?" she asked.

"Dr. Strassen has left. Your guardian is Dr. Nye. Please be calm, young sera. Dr. Nye is on his way."

"I don't want him!"

But the door opened and uncle Denys was there, out of breath and white-faced. In maman's apartment.

"It's all right," Denys panted. "Ari. Please."

"Get out!" she yelled at uncle Denys. "Get out, get out, get out!"

"Ari. Ari, I'm sorry. I'm terribly sorry. Listen to me."

"No, you're not sorry! I want maman! I want Ollie! Where are they?"

Denys came and tried to take hold of her. She ran for the kitchen. There were knives there. But the Security woman dived around the couch and caught her, and picked her up while she kicked and screamed.

"Careful with her!" Denys said. "Be careful. Put her down."

The woman set her feet back on the floor. Denys came and took her from the woman and held her against his shoulder.

"Cry, Ari. It's all right. Get your breath and cry."

She gasped and gasped and finally she could breathe.

"I'm going to take you home now," Denys said gently, and patted her face and her shoulders. "Are you all right, Ari? I can't carry you. Do you want the officer to? She won't hurt you. No one's going to hurt you. Or I can call the meds. Do you feel like you want me to do that?"

Take you home was not her home anymore. Something had happened to everyone.

Denys took her hand and she walked. She was too tired to do anything else. She was hardly able to do that.

Uncle Denys took her all the way to his apartment, and he set her down on his couch and he had his azi Seely get her a soft drink.

She drank it and she could hardly hold the glass without spilling it, she was shaking so.

"Nelly is staying here," uncle Denys said to her, sitting down on the other side of the table. "Nelly will be your very own."

"Where's Ollie?" she asked, clenching the glass in her lap.

"With your maman. She needed him."

Ari gulped air. It was a good thing, she thought, if maman had to go somewhere, maman and Ollie ought to be together.

"Phaedra's gone with them," Denys said.

"I don't care about Phaedra!"

"You want Nelly, don't you? Maman left you Nelly. She wanted Nelly to go on taking care of you."

She nodded. There was a large knot in her throat. Her heart was ten times too big for her chest. Her eyes stung.

"Ari, I don't know much about taking care of a little girl. Neither does Seely. But your maman sent all your things here. You'll have your very own suite, you and Nelly, right in there, do you want to go see where your room is?"

She shook her head; and tried not to cry. She tried to get a good mad. Like maman.

"We won't talk about it now. Nelly's going to be here tonight. She'll be a little upset. You know she can't take much upset. Promise me you'll be good to her, Ari. She's your azi and you have to be kind to her, because she really ought to stay in the hospital, but she's so worried about you, and I know you need her. Nelly's going to come home every night between her sessions—they're going to give her tape, you know, they have to, because she's terribly upset; but she loves you and she wants to come take care of you. I'm afraid it's you who'll have to take care of her. You understand me? You can hurt her very, very badly."

"I know," Ari said, because she did.

"There you are. You're a brave little girl. You aren't a baby at all. It's very hard, very hard. —Thank you, Seely."

Seely had brought her a glass of water and a pill, and expected her to take it. Seely was a nobody. He wasn't like Ollie. He wasn't nice, he wasn't mean, he wasn't anything but azi all the time. And he took her glass and put it on his tray and offered her the water.

"I don't want any tape!" she said.

"It's not that kind of pill," uncle Denys said. "It'll make your head stop hurting. It'll make you feel better."

She didn't remember telling him her head hurt. Maman always said don't take other people's pills. Never, never take azi-pills. But maman was not here to tell her what this one was.

Like Valery. Like sera Schwartz. Like all the Disappeareds. Maman and Ollie had gotten caught too.

Maybe I can Disappear next. And find them.

"Sera," Seely said. "Please."

She took the pill off the tray. She put it in her mouth and drank it down with the water.

"Thank you," Seely said. He was so smooth he wasn't there. He took the glass away. You would never notice Seely.

Uncle Denys sat there so fat he made the whole chair go down, with his arms on his knees and his round face upset and worried. "You won't have to go to playschool for a few days. Until you want to. You don't think you can feel better. I know. But you will. You'll feel better even tomorrow. You'll miss your maman. Of course you will. But you won't hurt as much. Every day will be a little better."

She didn't want it to be better. She didn't know who made people Disappear. But it wasn't maman. They could offer her whatever they wanted. It wouldn't make her believe what they said.

Maman and Ollie had known there was trouble. They had been terribly upset and kept hiding it from her. Maybe they thought they could take care of it and they couldn't. *She* had felt it coming and hadn't understood.

Perhaps there was a place people went to. Perhaps it was like being dead. You got in trouble and you got Disappeared somewhere in some way even maman couldn't stop it happening.

So she knew she couldn't either. She had to push and push, that was what, and get in trouble until there wasn't anybody. Maybe it was her fault. She had always thought so. But when they ran out of people to Disappear she had to find out what was going on.

Then maybe she could go.

She was Wrong, of a sudden. She couldn't feel her hands or her feet, and she felt a burning in her stomach.

She was having trouble. But Seely picked her up in his arms and the whole room swung and became the hall and became the bedroom. Seely laid her gently on the bed and took her shoes off, and put a blanket over her.

Poo-thing was beside her on the bedspread. She put out her hand and touched him. She could not remember where she had gotten Poo-thing. He had always been there. Now he was here. That was all. Now Poo-thing was all there was.

---

v

"Poor kid," Justin said, and poured more wine into the glass. "Poor little kid, dammit to *hell*, couldn't they let her come down to the airport?"

Grant just shook his head. And drank his own wine. He made a tiny handsign that warned of eavesdroppers.

Justin wiped his eyes. He never forgot that. Sometimes he found it hard to care.

"Not our problem," Grant said. "Not yours."

"I know it."

That for the listeners. That they never knew, one way or the other, whether they were there. They thought of ways to confound Security, even thought of devising a language without cognates, with erratic grammar, and using tape to memorize it. But they were afraid of the suspicion their using it might raise. So they went the simplest route: the tablet. He reached for it and scrawled: *Sometimes I'd like to run off to Novgorod and get a job in a factory. We design tape to make normal people. We build in trust and confidence and make them love each other. But the designers are all crazy.*

Grant wrote: *I have profound faith in my creators and my Supervisor. I find comfort in that.*

"You're sick," Justin said aloud.

Grant laughed. And Grant went serious again, and leaned over and took hold of Justin's knee, the two of them sitting cross-legged on the couch. "I don't understand good and evil. I've decided that. An azi has no business tossing words like that around, in the cosmic sense. But to me you're everything good."

He was touched by that. And the damned tape-flashes still bothered him. Even after this many years, like an old, old pain. With Grant it never mattered. That, as much as anything, gave him a sense of comfort. He laid his hand on Grant's, pressed it slightly, because he could not say anything.

"I mean it," Grant said. "You hold a difficult place. You do as much good as you can. Sometimes too much. Even I can rest. You should."

"What can I do when Yanni loads me down with—"

"No." Grant shook at his knee. "You can say no. You can quit working these hours. You can work on the things you want to work on. You've said yourself—you know what he's doing. Don't let them give you this other thing. Refuse it. You don't need it."

There was a baby in process on Fargone, replicate of one Benjamin Rubin, who lived in the enclave on the other side of an uncrossable wall, and worked in a lab Reseune had provided.

It provided something visible for Defense to hover over. And Jane Strassen, when she arrived, would find herself mother to another of the project's children.

He knew. They gave him Rubin's interviews. They let him do the tape-structures. He had no illusions they would run them without checks.

Not, at least, these. And that was a relief, after running without them for a year.

"It's a degree of trust, isn't it?" His voice came out hoarse, showing the strain he had not wanted to show.

"It puts another kind of load on you, a load you don't need."

"Maybe it's my chance to do something worthwhile. It's a major project.

Isn't it? It's the best thing that's happened in a long time. Maybe I can make Rubin's life—better or something." He leaned forward to pour more wine. Grant moved and did it for him. "At least Rubin had some compassion in his life. His mother lives on-station, he sees her, he's got something to hold on to."

Give or take the guards that attended a Special. Justin knew all these things. A confused, remote intellectual whose early health problems had been extreme, whose attachment to his mother was excessive and desperate; whose frail body had made health a preoccupation for him; whose various preoccupations had excluded adolescent passions, except for his work. But nothing— nothing of what had shaped Ari Emory.

Thank God.

"I can do something with it," he said. "I'm going to take some work in citizen psych. Do me some good. It's a different methodology."

Grant frowned at him. They could talk work at home, without worrying about monitors. But their line of conversation had gotten dangerous, maybe already gone over the line. He was not sure anymore. He was exhausted. Study, he thought, would take him off real-time work. Study was all he wanted. Grant was right, he was never cut out for trouble-shooting real-time situations. He cared too damn much.

Yanni had yelled at him: "Empathy is fine in an interview. It's got no place in the solution! Get it straight in your head who you're treating!"

Which made sense to him. He was not cut out for clinical psych. Because he never could get it straight, when he felt the pain himself.

By Yanni's lights, even, he thought, by Denys'—because there was no way this could have come to him without Denys working at Giraud—it was the most generous thing they could have done for him, putting him back in work that took a security clearance, re-establish his career in a slightly different field, in work very like Jordan's, let him work on a project where he could gain some reputation—CIT work was something the military would notice without actually giving the military an excuse to move on him, and it might clear him and do some good for Jordan. That was at least a possibility.

It was a kind of ultimatum, he thought, a kindness that could go entirely the other way if he tried to avoid the honor. That was always what he had to think about. Even when they were doing him favors.

vi

Ari woke with someone close to her, and remembered waking halfway through the night when someone got into bed with her, and took her in her arms and said in Nelly's voice, "I'm here, young sera. Nelly's here."

Nelly was by her in the morning, and maman was not, the bedroom was strange, it was uncle Denys' place, and Ari wanted to scream or to cry or to run again, run and run, until no one could find her.

But she lay still, because she knew maman was truly gone. And uncle

Denys was right, she was better than she was, she was thinking about breakfast in between thinking how much she hurt and how she wished Nelly was
somewhere else and maman was there instead.

It was still something, to have Nelly. She patted Nelly's face hard, until
Nelly woke up, and Nelly hugged her and stroked her hair and said:

"Nelly's here. Nelly's here." And burst into tears.

Ari held her. And felt cheated because she wanted to cry, but Nelly was
azi and crying upset her. So she was sensible like maman said, and told Nelly
to behave.

Nelly did. Nelly stopped snuffling and sniveling and got up and got
dressed; and gave Ari her bath and washed her hair and dressed her in her
clean blue pants and a sweater. And combed and combed her hair till it
crackled.

"We're supposed to go to breakfast with ser Nye," Nelly said.

That was all right. And it was a good breakfast, at uncle Denys' table, with
everything in the world to eat. Ari did eat. Uncle Denys had seconds of everything and told her she and Nelly could spend the day in the apartment, until
Nelly had to go to hospital, and then Seely would come and take care of her.

"Yes, ser," Ari said. Anything was all right. Nothing was. After yesterday she didn't care who was here. She wanted to ask Denys where maman
was, and where maman was going. But she didn't, because everything was all
right for a while and she was so tired.

And if Denys told her she wouldn't know the name of that place. She
only knew Reseune.

So she sat and let Nelly read her stories. Sometimes she cried for no reason. Sometimes she slept. When she woke up it was Nelly telling her it would
be Seely with her.

Seely would get her as many soft drinks as she wanted. And put on the
vid for her. And do anything she asked.

She asked Seely could they go for a walk and feed the fish. They did that.
They came back and Seely got her more soft drinks, and she wished she could
hear maman telling her they weren't good for her. So she stopped on her own,
and asked Seely for paper and sat and drew things.

Till uncle Denys came back and it was time for supper, and uncle Denys
talked to her about what she would do tomorrow and how he would buy her
anything she wanted.

She thought of several things. She wanted a spaceship with lights. She
wanted a new coat. If uncle Denys was going to offer, she could think of
things. She could think of really expensive things that maman never would get
her.

But none of them could make her happy. Not even Nelly. Just when they
were going to give you things, you took them, that was all, and you asked
them for lots and lots to make it hard for them, and make them think that was
important to you and you were happier with them, —but you didn't forget
your mad. Ever.

Grant sweated, waiting in Yanni Schwartz's outer office, with no appointment and only Marge's good offices to get him through the door. He heard Yanni shouting at Marge. He could not hear what he said. He imagined it had to do with interruptions and Justin Warrick.

And for a very little he would have gotten up and left, then, fast, because from moment to moment he knew he could bring trouble down on Justin by coming here. He was not sure that Yanni would not shake him badly enough to make him say something he ought not. Yanni was the kind of born-man he did not like to deal with, emotional and loud and radiating threat in every move he made. The men who had taken him to the shack in the hills had been like that. Giraud had been like that when he had questioned him. Grant sat there waiting and not panicking only by blanking himself and not thinking it through again until Marge came back and said:

"He'll see you."

He got up and made a little bow. "Thank you, Marge."

And walked into the inner office and up to the big desk and said: "Ser, I want to talk to you about my CIT."

Azi-like. Justin said Yanni could be decent enough to his patients. So he took the manner and stood very quietly.

"I'm not in consultation," Yanni said.

Yanni gave him no favors, then. Grant dropped the dumb-annie pose, pulled up the available chair and sat down. "I still want to talk to you, ser. Justin's taking the favor you're doing him and I think it's a bad mistake."

"A mistake."

"You're not going to let him have anything but the first-draft work, are you? And where does that leave him after twenty years? Nowhere. With no more than he had before."

"Training. Which he badly needs. Which you should know. Do we have to discuss your partner? You know his problems. I don't have to haul them out for you."

"Tell me what you think they are."

Yanni had been relaxed, mostly. The jaw clamped, the chin jutted, the whole pose shifted to aggression as he leaned on his desk. "Maybe you'd better have your CIT come talk to me. Did he send you? Or is this your own idea?"

"My own, ser." He was reacting, dammit. His palms were sweating. He hated that. The trick was to make the CIT calm down instead. "I'm scared of you. I don't want to do this. But Justin won't talk to you, at least he won't tell you the truth."

"Why not?"

The man *had* no quiet-mode. "Because, ser, —" Grant took a breath and tried not to pay attention to what was going on in his gut. "You're the only teacher he has. If you discard him, there's no one else good enough to teach him. You're like his Super. He has to rely on you and you're abusing him. That's very hard for me to watch."

"We're not talking azi psych, Grant. You *don't* understand what's going on, not on an operational level, and you're on dangerous personal ground— it's your own mindset I'm talking about. Don't identify. You know better. If you don't, —"

"Yes, ser, you can recommend I take tape. I know what you can do. But I want you to listen to me. *Listen!* I don't know what kind of man you are. But I've seen what you've done. I think you may be trying to help Justin. In some ways I think it has helped. But he can't go on working the way he is."

Yanni gave a growl like an engine dying and slowly leaned back on the arm of his chair, looking at him from under his brows. "Because he's not suited to real-time work. I know it. You know it. Justin knows it. I thought maybe he'd calm down, but he hasn't got the temperament for it, he can't get the perspective. He hasn't got the patience for standard design work, repetition drives him crazy. He's creative, so we put him in on the Rubin project. Denys got him that. I seconded it. It's the best damn thing we can do for him—put him where he can do theoretical work, *but not that damn out-there project of his*, and he won't concentrate on anything else, I know damn well he won't! He's worse than Jordan with an idea in his head, he won't turn it loose till it stinks. Have you got an answer? Because it's either the Rubin project or it's rot away in standard design, and I haven't got time on my staff to let one of my people take three weeks doing a project that should have been booted out the door in three days, you understand me?"

He had thought down till then that Yanni was the Enemy. But of a sudden he felt easier with Yanni. He saw a decent man who was not good at listening. Who was listening for the moment.

"Ser. Please. Justin's not Jordan. He doesn't work like Jordan. But if you give him a chance he *is* working. Listen to me. Please. You don't agree with him, but he's learning from you. You know that an azi designer has an edge in Applications. I'm an Alpha. I can take a design and internalize it and tell a hell of a lot about it. I've worked with him on his own designs, and I can tell you—I can tell you I believe in what he's trying to do."

"God, that's all I need."

"Ser, I know what his designs *feel* like, in a way no CIT can. I have the logic system."

"I'm not talking about his ability. He's fixed his rat-on-a-treadmill problems. He's got that covered. I'm talking about what happens when his sets integrate into CIT psych. Second and third and fourth generation. We don't want a work-crazy population. We don't want gray little people that go crazy when they're not on the assembly line. We don't want a suicide rate through the overhead when there's job failure or a dip in the economy. We're talking CIT psych, and that's exactly the field he's weakest in and exactly what I think he ought to go study for ten or twenty years before he does some real harm. You know what it *feels* like. Let me tell you I know something about CIT psych from the inside, plus sixty years in this field, and I trust a junior designer can appreciate that fact."

"I respect that, ser. I earnestly assure you. So does he. But his designs put—put *joy* into a psychset. Not just efficiency. The designs you say will cause trouble are their own reward tape. Isn't it true, ser, that when an azi has a CIT child, and he teaches that child as a CIT, he teaches *interpretively* what he understands out of his pyschset. And an azi with one of Justin's small routines somewhere in his sets, even if he was never as lucky as I am, to be socialized as I am, to be Alpha and have one lifelong partner, would get so much sense of purpose out of that, so much sense of purpose, he would think about his job and get better at it. And have pride in that, ser. Maybe there are still problems in it. But it's the emotional level he reaches. It's the key to the logic sets themselves. It's a self-programming interaction. That's what no one is taking into account."

"Which create a whole complex of basic structural problems in synthetic psychsets. Let's talk theory here. You're a competent designer. Let's be real blunt. They tried this eighty years ago."

"I'm familiar with that."

"And they hung a few embellishments onto the psychsets and they ended up with neuroses. Obsessive behaviors."

"You say yourself he's avoided that."

"*And it's self-programming*, do you hear yourself talking?"

"Worm," Grant said. "But a benign one."

"That's just about where that kind of theory belongs. Worm. God! If it is self-programming, you *have* created a worm of sorts, and you're playing with people's lives. If it isn't, you've got a delayed-action problem that's going to crop up in the second or third generation. Another kind of worm, if you want to put it that way. Hell if I want to give research time to it. I've got a budget. You two are on my departmental budget and you're a hell of an expense with no damned return that justifies it."

"We have justified it this last year."

"Which is killing Warrick. Isn't that your complaint? He can't go on outputting at that level. He can't take it. Psychologically he can't take it. So what are you going to do? Carry it by yourself, while Justin lives in the clouds somewhere designing sets that won't work, that I'm damned well not going to let him install in some poor sod of a Tester. No!"

"I'll do the work. Give him the freedom. Lighten the load. A little. Ser, give him the chance. He has to rely on you. No one else can help him. He is good. You know he is."

"And he's damned well wasting himself."

"What were you doing at the start? Teaching him, while you took his designs apart. Do that for him. Lighten the load a little. The work will get done. You just can't pressure him like that, because he'll do it if he thinks someone is suffering, he just won't stop, he's like that. Give us things we can handle and we'll handle them. Justin has a talent at integration that can get more out of a genotype than anyone ever did, because he does get into the emotional level. Maybe his ideas won't work, but, for God's sake, he's still studying. You don't know what he can be. Give him a chance."

Yanni looked at him a long time, upset, unhappy, with his face red and his teeth working at his lip. "You're quite a salesman, son. You know what's the matter with him on this? Ari got hold of a vulnerable kid with an idea that was real advanced for a seventeen-year-old, she flattered hell out of him, she fed him full of this crap, and psyched him right into her bed. You're aware of that?"

"Yes, ser. I'm well aware of it."

"She did a real job on him. He thinks he was brilliant. He thinks there was more there than there was, and you don't do him any service by feeding that. He's bright, he's not brilliant. He'd be damn good on the Rubin project. I've seen what he can do, and there *is* a lot in him. I respect hell out of that. I don't like to feed a delusion. I spend my life trying to make normal people and you're asking me to humor him in the biggest delusion of his poor fucked-up life. I hate that like hell, Grant. I can't tell you how much I hate it."

"*I'm* talking to a man who's the nearest thing to a Supervisor Justin's got; the man Justin fought to get to help him; who's going to take a talent that's been fucked-up and kill it because it's a drain on the teacher. What kind of man is that?"

"Dammit."

"Yes, ser. Damn *me* all you like. It's Justin I'm talking about. He trusts you and he doesn't trust many people. Are you going to damn *him* because he's trying to do something you think will fail?"

Yanni chewed on his lip. "You're one of Ari's, aren't you?"

"You know I am, ser."

"Damn, she did good work. You remind me what she was. After all that's happened."

"Yes, ser." It stung. He thought that it was meant to.

But Yanni gave a great sigh and shook his head. "I'll do this. I'll put him on the project. I'll keep the work light. *Which means, dammit, that you're going to carry some of it.*"

"Yes, ser."

"And if he does his damn designs I'll rip them apart. And teach him what I can. Everything I can. Has he got his problem with tape solved?"

"He has no problem with tape, ser."

"If you're in the room with him. That's what Petros says."

"That's so, ser. Can you blame him?"

"No. No, I can't. —I'll tell you, Grant, I *respect* what you're doing. I'd like to have a dozen of you. Unfortunately—you're not a production item."

"No, ser. Justin as much as Ari and Jordan—had a hand in my psychsets. But you're welcome to analyze them."

"Stable as hell. Good. Good for you." Yanni got up and came around the desk as Grant got up in confusion. And Yanni put his hand on his shoulder and took his hand. "Grant, come back to me if you think he can't handle things."

That affected him, when before, he doubted everything about this man's goodwill. "Yes, ser," he said, thinking that if Yanni was telling the truth, and if there was anything of himself he could give that Yanni could not have out of library and lab, he would give it. Freely.

"Out," Yanni said brusquely. "Go."

Azi-like, simple, equal to equal. When he knew that Yanni was upset about Strassen, and about everything that was going on, and it had been the worst of times to go to him.

He went, with a simplicity of courtesies he had not felt with anyone but Justin and Jordan, since he was very young.

And with an anguish over what he might have done in his presumption, adding stress to what he knew was a delicate tolerance for Justin in the House, at a delicate time and a delicate balance in Justin's own mind. He had not known, from the time he determined to go to Yanni, whether Justin would forgive him—or whether he would deserve forgiveness.

So that was where he had to go first.

"You did *what?*" Justin cried, from the gut; and felt a double blow, because Grant reacted as if he had hit him, flinched and turned his face and turned it back again, to look at him helplessly, without any of Grant's accustomed defenses.

That took the wind out of him. There was no way to shout at Grant. Grant had acted because Grant had been forced into a caretaker role by his behavior, that was what his knowledge of azi told him; and he had misread that, an Alpha Supervisor's worst mistake, and leaned on Grant for years in ways that, God help him, he had needed.

Grant going azi on him—was his fault. No one else's.

He reached out and patted Grant's shoulder and calmed himself down as much as he could, while he was shocked full of adrenaline and he could hardly breathe, as much from what he had done to Grant as from the fact that Grant might well have damned him.

So. That was not Grant's fault. Everything would be all right, if Grant had not exposed himself to Giraud's attention again. Just go back to Yanni and try to recover things without the emotionalism that would finish the job in Yanni's eyes.

He just wanted to sit down a moment. But he could not even do that without letting Grant know how badly he was upset.

"Yanni wasn't mad," Grant pleaded with him. "Justin, he wasn't mad. It wasn't like that. He just said he would lighten up."

He gave Grant a second pat on the arm. "Look, I'm sure it's all right. If it isn't, I'll fix it. Don't worry about it."

"Justin?"

There was pain in Grant's voice. His making. Just like the crisis.

"Yanni's going to have my guts for shoving you in there," Justin said. "He ought to. Grant, you don't have to go around me. I'm all right. Don't worry."

"Stop it, dammit." Grant grabbed him and spun him around, hard, face to face with him. "Don't go Supervisor on me. I knew what I was doing."

He just stared in shock.

"I'm not some dumb-annie, Justin. You can hit me, if you like. Just don't pull that calm-down routine on me." Anger. Outright anger. It shocked hell out of him. It was rescue when he thought there was none. He was shaking when Grant let go his arm and put his hand on the side of his face. "God, Justin, what do you think?"

"I put too much on you."

"No. They put too much on *you*. And I told Yanni that. I'm not plastic. I know what I'm doing. What have *you* been doing all these years? I used to be your partner. What do you think I've gotten to be? One of the psych-cases you deal with? Or what do you think I am?"

Azi, was the obvious answer. Grant challenged him to it. And he froze up inside.

"Dumb-annie, huh?"

"Cut it, Grant."

"Well?"

"Maybe—" He got his breath and turned away. "Maybe it's pride. Maybe I've been taught all my life to think I'm the stronger one. And I know I've been fractured for years. And leaning on you. Hell if I don't feel guilty about that."

"Different kind of pressure," Grant said. "Mine can't come from anywhere but you. Don't you know that, born-man?"

"Well, I sure as hell pushed you into Yanni's office."

"Give me a *chance*, friend. I'm not a damn robot. Maybe my feelings are plastic, but they're sure as hell real. You want to yell at me, yell. *Don't* pull that Supervisor crap."

"Then don't act like a damn azi!"

He could not believe he had said that. He stood there in shock. So did Grant for a moment. With that hanging in the air between them.

"Well, I am," Grant said then, with a little shrug. "But I'm not guilty about it. How about you?"

"I'm sorry."

"No, go ahead. Damn-azi all you like. I'd rather that than watch you bottle it up. You work till you're dropping, you're eating your gut out, and one more aberrant azi psychset is going to push you over the edge. So damn-azi all you like. I'm glad you've gotten self-protective. It's about time."

"God, don't psychoanalyze me."

"Sorry, can't help that. Thank God *I* only have one born-man to worry about. Two would drive me into the wards. So damn born-men too. They cause a hell of a lot of trouble. You were right about Yanni. He's quite reasonable with azi. It's other born-men he pours it out on, everything he stores up. Question is whether he was telling me the truth. But if you'll calm down and listen to me, nothing about the fact you can't handle real-time is news to him. I only pointed out you were wasted in the Rubin project, and that if he wanted motivated work, he'd do well to put up with your doing design in your spare time. Which you're damn well due. I don't think I was at all unreasonable."

Eavesdroppers, Justin thought with a jolt, and sorted back wildly to remember what they had said. He signed Grant to be careful, and Grant nodded.

"I'm sorry," Justin said then, calmer. And wishing he could find a dark place to hide him. But Grant was doing all right. Grant was holding up fine, with a dignity he could not manage. "Grant, I—just react to things. Flux-thinking. You've got to understand."

"Hey," Grant said. "I *don't* understand. I marvel at it. The number of levels you can react on is really amazing. The number of things you can believe at one time is incredible. I don't understand it. I'm going to spend days figuring that reaction and I'll probably still miss nuances."

"Real simple. I'm scared as hell. I thought I knew where things were and all of a sudden even you went sideways on me. So everything shifted to polar-opposite values. Born-men are real logical."

"God. Life would be so dull if there weren't born-men. Now I wonder which pole Yanni was at while I was talking to him. That's enough to worry hell out of you."

"Was he calm?"

"Very."

"Then you got the main set, didn't you?"

"We just have to learn not to agitate you people. I think they ought to put that in the beginning tape-sets. 'Excited born-men go to alternate programming sets. Every born-man is schiz. And he hates his alter ego.' That's the whole key to CIT behavior."

"You're not far wrong."

"Hell. I've been endocrine-learning for years. I'm really amazed. I went right over to it. Dual and triple opinions, the whole thing. I must say I prefer my natural psychset. My *natural* psychset, thank you. A lot easier on the stomach. Do you want to go to lunch?"

He looked at Grant, at Grant with the shields up again, with that slight, mocking smile that was Grant's way of defying fate, the universe, and Reseune Administration. For a moment he felt both fortunate and terrified.

As if for the first time everything that had been going away from him had stopped and trembled on the edge of reversing itself.

"Sure," he said. "Sure." He caught Grant's arm and steered him out the door. "If you could make headway with Yanni Schwartz you could hire out by the hour. Probably everybody in the Wing could use your services."

"Un-unh. No. I'm in regular employment, thanks."

People were staring. He dropped Grant's arm. And realized half the Wing must have heard him shouting at Grant. And was looking for signs of damage.

They were a source of gossip for a whole host of reasons. And now there was a new one.

That would get back to Yanni too.

viii

There were new things all the time. Nelly took Ari to the store in the North Wing, and they came back with packages. That was fun. She bought Nelly things too, and Nelly was so happy it made her feel good, to see Nelly with a new suit and looking pretty and so proud.

But Nelly was not maman. She liked it at first when Nelly put her arms around her, but Nelly always was Nelly, that was all, and all at once one night she felt so empty when Nelly did that. She didn't tell Nelly, because Nelly was telling her a story. But after that it was harder and harder to put up with Nelly holding her, when maman was gone. So she fidgeted down and sat on the floor for her stories, which Nelly seemed to think was all right.

Seely was just nobody. She teased Seely sometimes, but Seely never laughed. And that felt awful. So she left Seely alone, except when she asked him for a soft drink or a cookie. Which she got more of than maman would like. So she tried to be good and not to ask, and to eat vegetables and not have so much sugar. It's not good for you, maman would say. And anything maman said was something she tried to remember and keep doing, because everything of maman's she forgot was like forgetting maman. So she ate the damn vegetables and got a lump in her throat because some of them tasted awful, all messed up with white creamy stuff. Ugh. They made her want to throw up. But she did it because of maman and it made her so sad and so mad at the same time she felt like crying.

But if she did cry she went to her room and shut the door, and wiped her eyes and washed her face before she came out again, because she was not going to snivel.

She wanted somebody to play with but she didn't want it to be Sam. Sam knew her too well. Sam would know about her maman. And she would beat his face in, because she couldn't stand him looking at her with his face that never showed anything.

So when Nelly asked did she want to go back to playschool she said all right if Sam wasn't there.

"I don't know who there is, then," Nelly said.

"Then I'll go by myself," she said. "Let's go do the gym. All right?"

So Nelly took her. And they fed the fish and she played in the sandbox, but the sandbox was no fun by herself; and Nelly was not good at making buildings. So they just fed the fish and took walks and played on the playground and in the gym.

There was tapestudy. And a lot of the grown-ups did lessons with her. She learned a lot of things. She lay there in her bed at night with her head so full of new things she had trouble thinking of maman and Ollie.

Uncle Denys was right. It hurt less, day by day. That was the thing that scared her. Because if it didn't hurt the mad was harder to keep. So she bit her lip till it hurt and tried to keep it that way.

There was a children's party. She saw Amy there. Amy ran and got behind sera Peterson and acted like a baby. She remembered why she had wanted to hit Amy. The rest of the kids just stared at her a lot and sera Peterson told them they had to play with her.

They weren't happy about it. She could tell. There was Kate and Tommy and a kid named Pat, and Amy, who cried and snuffled over in the corner. Sam was there too. Sam came out from the others and said Hello, Ari. Sam was the only friendly one. So she said Hello, Sam. And wished she could go home, but Nelly had gone in the kitchen to have tea with sera Peterson's azi, and Nelly was having a good time.

So she went over and sat down and played their game, which was a dice game, and you moved around a board, which was Union space. You got money. All right. She played it, and everybody got to arguing and laughing and teasing each other again. Except Amy. Except they teased each other and not her. But that was all right. She learned their game. She started getting money. Sam was the luckiest one with the dice, but Sam was too careful with his money and Tommy was too reckless. "I'll sell you a station," she said. And Amy bought it for most of what Amy had. So Amy charged a lot and Ari just charged less. And what Amy had bought was off at the edge anyway. So Ari got more money and Amy got mad. And nobody wanted to trade for Amy's station, but Ari offered to buy it back, not for what Amy wanted for it.

So Amy took it and bought ships. And Ari raised her prices a little.

Amy sniveled. And pretty soon she was in trouble again, because Ari kept beating her by using her money to buy up cargoes and keeping a surplus of the only things Amy could get because stupid Amy kept coming to *her* stations instead of sticking to Tommy's. Amy wanted a fight. Amy got a fight. But she didn't want Amy to lose real soon and ruin the game, so she told Amy what she ought to do.

Amy got real mad then. And sniveled some more.

She didn't take the advice either.

So Ari got her in trouble and took all but one of her ships. Then the last one. By that time she had a way to win. But everybody else was looking unhappy and nobody was teasing anybody, except Amy left the table crying.

Nobody said anything. They all looked at Amy. They all looked at her like they wanted not to be there.

She was going to win. Except Sam didn't know it. So she said, "Sam, you can have my pieces."

And she went and got Nelly in the kitchen and said she wanted to go home. Nelly looked worried, then, and stopped having fun with Corrie, and they went home.

She moped around the rest of the day, being lonely. And mad. Which was fine. She thought of maman then. And missed Ollie. Even Phaedra.

And thought if Valery had been there he would not have been so stupid.

"What's the matter?" uncle Denys asked that evening. He was very kind about it. "Ari, dear, what happened at the party? What did they do?"

She could Disappear them all if she said they had a fight. Maybe they would anyway. She wasn't sure. At least Amy and Kate were still around, even if they were stupid.

"Uncle Denys, where did Valery go?"

"Valery Schwartz? His maman got transferred. They moved, that's all. You still remember Valery?"

"Can he come back?"

"I don't know, dear. I don't think so. His maman has a job to do. What happened at the party?"

"I just got bored. They're not much fun. Where did maman and Ollie go? What station?"

"To Fargone."

"I'm going to send maman and Ollie a letter." She had seen mail in maman's office. She had never thought of doing that. But she thought that would get to maman's office at the other place. At Fargone.

"All right. I'm sure they'd like that."

Sometimes she thought maman and Ollie weren't really anywhere. But uncle Denys talked like they were, and they were all right. That made her feel better, but it made her wonder why maman never even called on the phone.

"Can you call Fargone?"

"No," uncle Denys said. "It's faster for a ship to go. A letter gets there much faster than a phone call. In months, not years."

"Why?"

"You say hello, and it takes twenty years to get there; and they say hello and it takes twenty years to get here. And then you say your first sentence and they don't hear it for years. You could take hundreds of years having a conversation. That's why letters are faster and a whole lot cheaper, and they don't use phones and radios between any two stars. Ships carry everything, because ships go faster than light. There are more complications to the question, but that's more than you really want to know to get a message to your maman. It's just a long way. And a letter is the way you do things."

She had never understood how far far could be. Not when they were jumping ships around the board. She felt cold and lonely then. And she went to her room and wrote the letter.

She kept tearing it up because she didn't want to make maman worry about her being miserable. She didn't want to say: *maman, the kids don't like me and I'm lonely all the time.*

She said: *I miss you a lot. I miss Ollie. I'm not mad at Phaedra anymore. I want you and Ollie to come back. Phaedra too. I'll be good. Uncle Denys gives me too many cookies, but I remember what you said and I don't eat too much. I don't want to be fat. I don't want to be hyper, either. Nelly is very good to me. Uncle Denys gives me his credit card and I buy Nelly lots of things. I bought a spaceship and a car and puzzles and story tapes. And a red and white blouse and red boots. I wanted a black one but Nelly says that's for azi until I'm older. Little girls don't wear black, Nelly says. I could too, but sometimes I do what Nelly says. I mind everybody. I saw Amy Carnath today and I didn't hit her. She still snivels. I study a lot of tapes. I can do math and I can do chemistry. I can do geography and astrography and I'm going to study about Fargone because you're there. I want to go to Fargone if you can't come here. Are there any kids there? Have you got a nice place?*

Tell uncle Denys I can come. Or you come home. I'll be very good. I love you. I love Ollie. I am going to give this to uncle Denys to send to you. He says it takes a long time to get there and your letter will take a long time to get to me so please write to me as soon as you can. I think it will be almost a year. By then I will be eight. If you tell Denys to let me come real soon I guess I will be almost nine. Tell him I can bring Nelly too. She'll be scared but I'll tell her it's all right. I'm not afraid of jumps. I'm not afraid to come by myself. I do a lot of things by myself now. Uncle Denys doesn't care. I know he would let me come if you said yes. I love you.

<hr>

ix

Florian was late again. There was a shortcut along between 240 and 241 and he took it, dodging out between two groups of Olders and skipping backward to nod a courtesy and murmur: "Excuse me, please," before he turned and sprinted across the road and up to Security.

"I'm very sorry," he said, arriving at the desk inside Square One. He was trying not to pant as he handed his chit to the azi at the desk. The man looked at the chit and put it in his machine.

"Blue to white to brown," the man said. "Change in brown. Instructions there."

"Yes," he said, and looked where the man pointed. Blue started with that door and he went, not running, but going in a great hurry.

He knew he was still late when he got to brown. The azi in charge was waiting for him. "I'm sorry," he said. "I'm Florian AF-9979."

The man looked him over and said: "Size 6M, cabinets on the wall, go change. Hurry."

"Yes," he said, and went into the changing room, hunted quickly for 6M, pulled out the plastic packet and threw it onto the bench while he peeled out of his clothes. He put the black uniform on, sat down quick to pull on the socks and put on the slippers, then hung his AG uniform on the pegs beside uniforms of all sizes and colors. He was so nervous he almost forgot his new keycard, but he got it off his other coveralls and clipped it to the black ones, then raked a hand through his hair and hurried outside again.

"Down the hall," the azi with the clipboard said. "Brown to green. Run!"

He ran. And followed the halls till he found a door marked with green-in-brown. Inside, then, into a gym. He came bursting in where there was a man with a clipboard, and another Younger, who was dressed like him, in black coveralls. Who was a *girl*. He felt a shock, but gut-level, reacted to the Super and made a little bow. "Sorry I'm late, ser."

The Super looked at him just long enough to keep him worried, and he did not dare look back at the girl who was, he was sure now, here just like he was, to find her partner for this Assignment.

Then the Super made a mark on his board and said: "Florian, this is Catlin. Catlin is your partner."

Florian looked at the girl again, his heart beating hard. It was a mistake. It must be. He was late. He got a girl partner. He was supposed to change bunks and he had thought he was supposed to bunk with his partner. Wrong, then. He did not know where he was going to sleep.

He wanted his classes back. He had been upset about the new Assignment even if his old Super told him he could still have AG on his Rec hours. He wanted—

But the girl bothered him. She looked—

She was blonde, blue-eyed, a scab on her chin. She was taller than he was, but that was nothing unusual. She had a thin, very serious face. He thought he had seen her before. She stared at him, the way you weren't supposed to stare. Then he realized he was doing it too.

"Catlin," the Super said, "you know the way from here. Take Florian over to Staging, talk to the Super there."

"Yes, ser," she said, and Florian almost asked the Super to look and check if there was some mistake, but he was late, he had gotten a bad start with this man, and he did not know why he was as upset as he was, but he was panicked. Catlin was already going. He caught up with her as she walked toward another door behind the hanging buffer-mats at the end of the gym. She used her keycard, held the door for him, and led the way into another long cement hallway.

Down stairs then. And another cement hall.

"I'm supposed to have a bunk assignment?" he said finally, behind her.

She looked back on the stairs and he caught up with her in the long concrete hall at the bottom.

"22. Like me," she said. "We're going in with Olders. Partners room together, two and two."

He was shocked. But she seemed to know what was right, and *she* was not upset. So he just walked behind her, wondering if somehow the Computers had glitched up and he was supposed to have gotten tape to explain all this and help him not make mistakes. He had, he thought, to talk to the Super where they were going.

They got to the other place. Catlin keyed in, and there was a Super sitting at a desk. "Ser," Catlin said. "Catlin and Florian, ser."

"Late," the Super said.

"Yes, ser," Catlin said.

"My fault," Florian said. "Ser, —"

"Excuses don't matter. You're Assigned to Security. You go into Staging, you pick out what you think you might need. And both of you will be right. All right. Fifteen minutes to get your equipment. You do mess, you've got this evening to plan it out, you'll do a Room tomorrow morning. It's a one-hour course, you can talk about it. You're supposed to. Go."

"I—" he said. "Ser, I have to feed the pigs. I— Am I supposed to have gotten tape about this? I haven't."

The Super looked straight at him. "Florian, you'll do AG when you aren't doing Security. This is your Assignment. You can go to AG in your Rec time. Four hours Rec time for every good pass through the Room. There isn't any tape for this. It's up at 0500, drill at 0530, breakfast at 0630, then tape, Room, or Rec, whatever the schedule calls for; noon mess as you can catch it, follow your schedule; evening mess at 2000, follow your schedule, in bunks at 2300 most nights. If you've got any problems you talk to your Instructor. Catlin knows. Ask her."

"Yes, ser," Florian breathed, thinking: *What about Andy? What about the pigs? They said I could go to AG.* And because the Super had answered and he was terribly afraid this *was* the right Assignment, he caught up with Catlin.

It was a Staging-room, like in the Game he knew. His old Super had said it was an Assignment, there would be Rooms, all of this he knew: it would be like Rooms he had done before and he would be more out of Security than AG after this.

But it was not right. He was supposed to bunk with a girl. He was put into a place she knew and he didn't. He was going to make more mistakes. They always said a Super would never refuse to talk to you, but the one back there made him afraid he was already making mistakes.

Like being late to start with.

He came into the Staging-room behind Catlin; he knew it was going to be a Security kind of Room, and he was not terribly shocked to find guns and knives on the table with the tools, but he didn't even want to touch them, and there was a queasy feeling in his stomach when Catlin picked up a gun. He grabbed pliers and a circuit-tester; Catlin took a length of fine cord and he started through the components tray, grabbing things and stuffing them into his pockets by categories.

"Electronics?" she asked.

"Yes. Military?"

"Security. You know weapons?"

"No."

"Better not have one, then. What kind are your Rooms?"

"Traps. Alarms."

Catlin's pale brows went up. She nodded, looking more friendly. "Ambushes. There's usually an Enemy. He'll kill you."

"So will traps."

"Are you good?"

He nodded. "I think so."

And he was staring again. Her face had been bothering him all along. It was like he knew her. He knew her the way you knew things from tape. Maybe she was remembering him too just then, the way she was staring. He was not completely surprised, except that it had happened at all: tape never surprised him. He knew it was not a mistake if he knew her from tape. She was supposed to be important to him, if that was the case, the way his studies were important, and he had never thought that was supposed to happen until he was Contracted to somebody.

But she was azi. Like him.

And she knew all about her Assignment and he was new and full of mistakes.

"I think I'm supposed to know you," he said, worried.

"Same," she said.

No one had ever *paid* that much attention to him. Not even Andy. And he felt shaky, to know he had run into someone tape meant for him.

"Why are we partners?" he asked.

"I don't know," she said. Then: "But electronics is useful. And you know a different Room. Come on. Tell me what you know."

"You go in," he said, trying to pull up everything, fast and all of it, the way he would do for a Super. "There's a door. There can be all kinds of traps. If you make one go off you lose. Sometimes there's noise. Sometimes the lights go out. Sometimes there's someone after you and you have to get through and rig traps. Sometimes there's an AI lock. Sometimes there's water and that's real dangerous if there's a line loose. But it's pretend, you don't really get electrocuted."

"Dead is dead," she said. "They shoot at you and they trap the doors and if you don't blow them up they'll blow you up; and sometimes all the things you said. Sometimes gas. Sometimes Ambushes. Sometimes it's outside and sometimes it's a building. Some people get killed for real. I saw one. He broke his neck."

He was shocked. And then he thought it could be him. And he thought about door traps. He took a battery and a coil of wire and a penlight, and Catlin gave him a black scarf—for your face, she said. She took a lot of other things, like face-black and cord and some things that might be weapons, but he didn't know.

"If they have gas masks in Staging it's a good idea to have one," Catlin said, "but there aren't. So they probably won't do gas, but you don't know. They aren't fair."

A bell rang.

Time was up.

"Come on," Catlin said, and the door opened and let them out with what they had.

Down a hall and through more doors. And upstairs again, until they came out in another concrete hall.

With a lot of doors.

"We're looking for 22," Catlin said.

That was two more. Catlin opened the door and let them into a plain little room with a double bunk.

"Top or bottom?" Catlin asked.

"I don't care," he said. He had never thought about a room all his own. Or even half his. There was a table and two chairs. There was a door.

"Where does that go?"

"Bathroom," Catlin said. "We share with the room next door. They're Olders. You knock before you go in. That's their Rule. If they're Olders you take their Rules."

"I'm lost," he said.

"That's all right," Catlin said, emptying her pockets onto the table. "I've been here five days. I know a lot of the Rules. The Olders are pretty patient. They tell you. But you better remember or they'll tell the Instructor and you're in trouble."

"I'll remember." He looked at her emptying her pockets and thought how his stuff was right where he wanted it. "Do we have to change clothes for the Room?"

"In the morning, always."

He emptied his pockets, but he put everything together the way he wanted it. Catlin looked at what he was doing.

"That's smart," she said. "You always know where all that stuff is."

He looked at her. She was serious. "Of course," he said.

"You're all right," she said.

"I think you must be pretty good," he said.

"They don't Get me often," she said. And pulled back the chair and sat down with her arms on the table while he was emptying his pockets. "Do they you?"

"No," he said.

She looked quite happy in her sober way. And picked up the gun and flipped up the panel on the grip and snapped it shut again. "The gun's real," she said. "But the charges aren't. You still have to check, though. Rounds can get mixed up. Once somebody's did. You always think about that. The Enemy could have mixed-up rounds. And blow you to bits. The practice rounds have a big black band. The real ones don't. But these can still kill you if you get hit close up. You have to be careful when you're working partners. More people get killed with practice rounds than anything else in training."

Catlin knew more stories about how people got killed than he had ever heard in his life. He felt his stomach upset.

But Catlin wanted to know all about the traps, all about the things he had seen. She was full of questions and with everything he said he saw her strange eyes concentrate in the way people would if they were smart and they were going to remember. So he asked about Ambushes, and she told him a lot of things she had seen.

She *was* smart, he thought. She sounded like she could do the things she said. He had never planned to be in Security. He had never planned to have a girl for a partner and he never imagined anyone like Catlin. She did sort of smile. It lit up her eyes, but her mouth hardly moved. She made him so nervous he was gladder when she did that than when most people smiled wide open. A smile out of Catlin was hard to get. You had to really tell her something that impressed her. And when you got one you wanted another one because in between there was just nothing.

They went to mess, which was what they called the dining hall here. They all had to stand and wait till they could sit, and they were years younger than anyone. Most were boys, very tall, a few were girls, all of them were in their teens and everybody was on strict manners. He would have been terribly nervous if Catlin had not known when to stand and when to sit and tugged at his sleeve to cue him. But it was very good food, and as much as you wanted, and when the near-grown boys around them talked they were polite and didn't act annoyed that they were there. Who's your partner? one asked Catlin, and she said: Florian AF, ser. Like talking to a Super.

Welcome in, that boy said. And they made him stand up so people could see him. He was nervous. But the boy stood up beside him and introduced him as Florian AF, Catlin's partner, a tech. He wasn't sure he was, but it was something like; and they all looked at him a moment, then they gave a kind of Welcome In and he could sit down. It was not too different from a dorm, except there they never made you stand up at table, because your dining hall was a whole lot of dorms. Green Barracks had its own kitchen, and there were seconds and thirds if you wanted them, you didn't have to have a med's order.

The Instructor said they had two hours for Rec then and then they had to have lights out by 2300.

But Catlin thought they ought to go back to their quarters—that was what they called it in Green Barracks—and figure out about the Room, because the Instructor said they could do that; and they asked each other questions about the Room until just before their lights-out.

He was anxious about undressing. He had never undressed around girls, just the meds and the techs, and they had always been careful to give him something to put on and to turn their backs or leave the room till he had. Catlin said it was all right if they were roommates, everybody else did; so she took off her shirt and pants, he took off his, and she went to take a shower first. She came back in her clean underwear and threw the dirty clothes in the hamper.

She was like he thought she would be under her clothes, all bones and skinny muscle that would have made him think they didn't feed you much in Security, except he had just had one of their meals. She was shaped different, all right, thinner around the chest—her ribs showed—and flat where boys weren't. He had never seen a girl in her underwear. It was thin and didn't hide much, and he tried not to stare or to think about her staring at him. He wasn't sure *why* it was bad, it still didn't feel right. But that was the way it had to be, because sleeping in their clothes would make them a mess.

So they had to be polite with each other and get along with the situation.

He took his shower fast, like Catlin said, because the Olders would want it soon; and he put on his clean underwear and came and got in the bottom bunk, because Catlin had the top. He got in fast, because she was under her covers and he was out there all alone in his underwear.

"Last one," Catlin said from up above, "has to turn the lights out. It's *my* Rule. All right?"

He looked for the switch from where he was lying. He had never been in a place where the lights didn't just go out at the right time. He had never slept anywhere but a barracks with fifty or so boys in the same room. He slithered out of the covers again and dived over and hit the switch and dived back again, remembering the straight line to the bunk, so hard it made the bed shake.

He realized he had shaken up Catlin too. "Sorry," he said, and tried to be quieter getting under the covers again. He was very conscious he was with a stranger, who might be a seven, but they were different from each other, she was Security and Security was very stiff and cold. He didn't want to do wrong or make her annoyed with him. He lay there in the dark in a place with only one person in it, worse than being in a new dorm, very much worse. He felt cold and it was only partly because the sheets were. All the sounds were gone, except one of the Olders starting up the shower.

He wondered where Catlin had lived before this. She didn't seem nervous. Somebody had told her everything that would happen. Or she was just able to *do* everything. Having a boy for a partner didn't bother *her*. She was glad about him being good at traps. He hoped he was as good as she expected. He would be terribly embarrassed if he got them Blown Up in the first doorway.

And he was terribly afraid he was going to have to do Traps in the dark, which was the hardest, and that meant he was going to need the penlight. Catlin said he could hide that with his coat, they usually let you have one. Because working against the light he was a target for sure.

Don't make noise, she had said. I'll watch your back; you just work; but noise is going to help the Enemy. We can try to Get one that way, but that depends on how much time we have. Or whether it's a speed run or a kill run. They'll tell us that.

What's a kill run? he had asked.

Where you get most of your points for Getting the Enemy.

Like where you have to *set* the Traps, he had said, relieved he understood. Sometimes we do it both ways—you have to take one apart and leave one for the Enemy following you. You get extra points if he misses it. Sometimes they make you go back through right away, and you don't know whether it's your Trap or his or whether he got stopped. The blow-ups show, but you can't trust those either, because he could touch it off and set another one.

That's sneaky, she had said, her eyes lighting the way they could. That's *good*.

He wanted to go blank so that he could go to sleep: there was a Room to do in the morning; and he knew he had to rest, but that was hard to do, his mind was so full of things without answers.

The Room did not make him half so anxious as this place did.

Why are they doing this? he wondered. And thinking of the gun on the table and about the too-quiet mess hall and all of Catlin's stories about people shooting each other in the Game: *Are they sure I belong here?*

It's not a Game, Catlin had said sternly when he had called it that. A game is what you do on the computers in Rec. This is real, and they cheat.

He really wanted to go back to AG. He wanted to see the Horse. He wanted to feed the baby in the morning.

But you had to survive the Room to do that for just four hours.

From now on.

He really tried to go blank. He tried hard.
Why don't they give me tape? Why don't they make it so I know what to do?
Why don't they make it so I feel better about this?
Has the Computer forgotten about me?

X

Ari thought every night how her letter was on its way now and she figured out where it had to be if it took so many months. Maman and Ollie would be at Fargone now. She felt a lot better to know where they were. She looked at pictures of Fargone and she could imagine them being there. Uncle Denys brought her a publicity booklet for RESEUNESPACE that had maman's name in it. And pictures of where maman would be working. She kept it in her desk drawer and she liked to look at it and imagine herself going there. She wrote another letter every few days, and she told maman how she was doing. Uncle Denys said he would have to save up a packet of her letters and send them in a bundle because it was awfully expensive and maman wouldn't care if she got them all at once, all in one envelope. She wanted to address it to maman and Ollie, but uncle Denys said that would confuse the postal people, and if she was going to write to Ollie, maman would give it to him: the law said an azi couldn't receive any mail except through his Supervisor, which was silly for Ollie, nothing could upset him; but it was the law.

So the address had to be:
Dr. Jane Strassen
Director
RESEUNESPACE
Fargone Station
And her return address was:
Dr. Denys Nye
Administrator
Reseune Administrative Territory
Postal District 3
Cyteen Station
She wanted to put her own name on the letter, but uncle Denys said she would have to wait until she was grown up and had her own address. Besides, he said, if it was from the Administrator of Reseune to the Director of RESEUNESPACE it looked like business and it would get right to maman's desk without anybody waiting.

She was in favor of that.

She asked why their address was Cyteen Station when they lived on Cyteen, and he said mail didn't go to planets without going through stations; and if you wanted to write to somebody on Earth the address was always Sol Station, but because there was Mars and the Moon you had to put Earth, then the name of the country.

Uncle Denys tried to explain what a country was and how they started.

That was why he got her the *History of Earth* tape. She wanted to do that one again. It had a lot of really strange pictures. Some were scary. But she knew it was just tape.

She went to tapestudy. She studied biology and botany, and penmanship and history and civics this week. She got Excellent on her exams and uncle Denys gave her a nice holo that was a Terran bird. You turned it and the bird flapped his wings and flew. It came all the way from Earth. Uncle Giraud had got it in Novgorod.

But there was only Nelly for playschool. And it was boring doing the swings and the puzzlebars with just Nelly. So she didn't go every day anymore. She got tired of going everywhere with Nelly, because Nelly worried about everything and Nelly was always worrying about her. So she told uncle Denys she could go to tapestudy by herself, and she could go to library by herself, because people knew her, and she was all right.

She took a lot of time getting back from tapestudy. Sometimes she stopped and fed the fish, because there was a Security guard right at the door and uncle Denys had said she could do that. Today she went down the tunnel because there had been a storm last night and you had to stay indoors for a few days.

So she got to thinking how she and maman had come this way once when she went to see ser Peterson. You took the elevator. Dr. Peterson was boring as Seely was; but that hall was where Justin's office was.

Justin would be interesting, she thought. Maybe he would at least say hello. And so many people had Disappeared that she liked to check now and again to see if people were still there. It always made her feel safer when she found they were. So if she got a chance to see an old place, she liked to.

She took the lift up to the upstairs hall, and she walked the metal strips she remembered: that was nice too, like once upon a time, when maman had been down the hall in that very office; but it made her sad, too, and she stopped it and walked the center of the hall.

Justin's office door was open. It was messy as the last time. And she was happy of a sudden, because Justin and Grant were both there.

"Hello," she said.

They both looked at her. It was good to see someone she knew. She really hoped they would be glad to see her. There weren't many people who would talk to her that weren't uncle Denys's.

But they didn't say hello. Justin got up and looked unfriendly.

She felt lonely all of a sudden. She felt awfully lonely. "How are you?" she asked, because that was what you were supposed to say.

"Where's your nurse?"

"Nelly's home." She could say that now about uncle Denys's place without it hurting. "Can I come in?"

"We're working, Ari. Grant and I have business to do."

"Everybody's working," she complained. "Hello, Grant."

"Hello, Ari," Grant said.

"Maman went to Fargone," she said. In case they hadn't heard.

"I'm sorry," Justin said.

"I'm going to go there and live with her."

Justin got a funny look. A real funny look. Grant looked at her. And she was scared because they were upset, but she didn't know why. She sat there looking up and wishing she knew what was wrong. Of a sudden she was real scared.

"Ari," Justin said, "you know you're not supposed to be here."

"I can be here if I want. Uncle Denys doesn't mind."

"Did uncle Denys say that?"

"Justin," Grant said. And gently: "Ari, who brought you here?"

"Nobody. I brought myself." She pointed. "I came from tapestudy. I'm taking a shortcut."

"That's nice," Justin said. "Look, Ari. I'll bet you're supposed to go straight home."

She shook her head. "No. I don't have to. Uncle Denys is always late and Nelly won't tell him." She kept getting this upset-feeling, no matter how she tried to be cheerful. It was not them being bad to her. It was not a mad either. She tried to figure out what it was, but Grant was worried about Justin and Justin was worried about her being there.

Hell with Them, maman would say. Meaning the Them that kept things messed up.

"I'm going," she said.

But she did it again the next day, sneaked up and popped sideways around the doorframe and said: "Hello."

That scared them good. She laughed. And came out and was nice then. "Hello."

"Ari, for God's sake, go home!"

She liked that better. Justin was mad like maman's mad. She liked that a lot better. He wasn't being mean. Neither was Grant. She had got them and they were going to yell at her.

"I did Computers today," she said. "I can write a program."

"That's nice, Ari. Go home!"

She laughed. And tucked her hands behind her and rocked and remembered not to. "Uncle Denys got me a fish tank. I've got guppies. One of them is pregnant."

"That's awfully nice, Ari. Go home."

"I could bring you some of the babies."

"Ari, just go home."

"I have a hologram. It's a bird. It flies." She pulled it out of her pocket and showed how it turned, and came inside to do it. "See?"

"That's fascinating. Please. Go home."

"I'll bet you haven't got one."

"I know I don't. Please, Ari, —"

"Why don't you want me here?"

"Because your uncle is going to get mad."

"He won't. He never knows."

"Ari," Grant said.

She looked at him.

"You don't want us to *call* your uncle, do you?"

She didn't. It wasn't very nice. She frowned at Grant.

"Please," Justin said. "Ari."

He was halfway nice. And she was out of tricks. So she went outside, and looked back and smiled at him.

He was sort of a friend. He was her secret friend. She wasn't going to make him mad. Or Grant. She would come by just a second every day.

But they were gone the next day: the door was shut and locked.

That worried her. She figured they had either figured out she was coming at the same time every day or they were truly Disappeared.

So she sneaked over on her way to tape the next morning and caught them.

"Hello!" she said. And scared them.

She saw they were mad, so she didn't laugh at them too much. And she just waved them goodbye and went on.

She caught them now and again. When her guppy had babies she brought them some in a jar she had. Justin looked like that made him feel better about her. He said he would take care of them.

But when she took the lid off they were dead. She felt awful.

"I guess they were in there too long," she said.

"I guess they were," Justin said. He smelled nice when she leaned on the desk near him. A lot like Ollie. "I'm sorry, Ari."

That was nice anyway. It was the first time he had really been just Justin with her. Grant came and looked and he was sorry too.

Grant took the jar away. And Justin said, well, sometimes things died.

"I'll bring you more," she said. She liked coming by the office. She thought about it a lot. She was leaning up by Justin's desk now and he had stopped having that bad feeling. He was just Justin. And he patted her on the shoulder and said she had better go.

He had never been that nice since a long, long time ago. So she was winning. She thought he would be awfully nice to talk to, but she wasn't going to push and make everything go wrong. Not with him and not with Grant. He was her friend. And when maman sent for her she would ask him and Grant if they wanted to go with her and Nelly.

Then she would have all the special people and she would be all right on the ship, because Justin was a CIT and he was grown-up and he would know how to do everything you had to do to get to Fargone.

She had a birthday coming. She had not even wanted a kids' party. Just the presents, thank you.

Even that hadn't made her happy. Until now.

She skipped down the hall, playing step-on-the-metal-line. And got Nelly's keycard out of her pocket and used it on the lift.

Because she knew how Security worked.

"You damn fool," Yanni yelled, and threw the papers at him. And Justin stood there, paralyzed in shock as the sheets of his last personal project settled on the carpet around them. "You damned *fool*! What are you trying to do? We give you a chance, we do everything we fucking *can* to get you a chance, I sweat my *ass* off on my own fucking *time* working up critiques on this shit you dream up to prove to a hardheaded juvenile-fixated *fool* that his brilliant junior study project was just that, a fucking *junior study project* that Ari Emory would have dismissed with a *Thanks, kid, but we tried that*, if she hadn't been interested in getting her hands on your juvenile body and fucking over your *father*, son, *which you've just done all by yourself, you damned fool! Get this shit out of here! Get yourself back to your office, and you keep that kid out, you hear me?"*

It hit him in the gut, and paralyzed him between wanting to kill Yanni and believing for a terrible moment that it was over, that a little girl's spite had ruined him, and Jordan, and Grant.

But then he heard it all the way to the end and realized it was not entirely that, it was not doomsday.

It might as well be.

"What did she say?" he asked. "What did she say about it? *The kid brought me a damn jar of fish, Yanni, what am I going to do, throw her out of the office? I tried!"*

"Get out of here!"

"What did she *say?"*

"She asked her uncle Denys to invite you to her fucking *birthday* party. That's all. That's all. You've got yourself a *situation*, son. You've got yourself a real situation. Seems she's been coming by the office a lot. Seems she's been dodging Security through the upstairs, seems she's been using her azi's keycard to get up and down the lift, seems she's just real attracted to you, son. What in hell do you think you're doing?"

"Is this a psych? Is that it? Denys asked you to run a psych and see what falls out?"

"Why didn't you report it?"

"Well, hell, I have a few reasons, don't you think?" He got his breath back. He got his balance back and stared at Yanni hard and straight. "It's your security she outflanked. How am I to know Reseune Security can't track a seven-year-old kid? I'm not going to be rude to her. No, thanks. I don't want any part of it. *I* don't want to be the one to ring up Denys Nye and tell him he's lost track of his ward. You want a kid to get determined about something, you just tell her I'm forbidden territory. No, thanks. Denys said be polite, make nothing of it, avoid her where I can—hell, I started shutting my office when I knew she was due back from tape, what else can I do?"

"You could report it!"

"And get in the middle of it again? Get myself yanked in for another inquisition? I followed orders. I figured you were bugging my office. I *figured* Security knew where she was. I *figured* you knew exactly what I said, which was nothing. *Nothing*, Yanni, except Go home, Ari. Go home, Ari. *Go home, Ari.* And I got her out. It's a juvenile behavior. She's found an adult to tease. She's being an ordinary brat kid. For God's sake, you make something out of this, you'll *fix* it, Yanni, does a damned juvenile-fixated *fool* have to tell you calm down with this kid and just let her pull her little prank? She can read you. She can read the tension you're pouring on her, I know damned well she can, because I have to fight like hell to keep her from reading *me* in the two or three minutes she comes past and says hello, and you and Denys must be doing real well, the way you're coming through to me. Get off her! Just let the whole thing *alone*, for God's sake, or what in hell are you trying to *do*, push her at me till it *takes*?" A second pause for breath, while Yanni just stood there and stared at him in a way that raised the hair on his neck. "Is that what you're trying to *do*? Is that what's behind this? Are you helping her do this?"

"You're paranoid."

"Damned right. Damned *right*, Yanni. What are you trying to do to me?"

"Get out of here! Get the fuck out of here! I got you off. I got you off with Administration. I spent the fucking morning on you, *Petros* wasted a day covering your ass, and you're damn right this is a psych and you just flunked it, son, you just flunked it! I don't trust you. I don't trust you further than I can see where you are. You walk a tight line, a damned tight line. If she shows up again you get her out of there and you phone Denys before her steps are cool!"

"What about Jordan?"

"Now you want favors."

"*What about Jordan?*"

"I don't hear anything about them cutting the phone calls. But you're playing with it, son. You're really playing with it. *Don't* push. Don't push any further."

"What are you putting in that report?"

"That you're not real casual around that kid. That you've got yourself some real hostilities about that kid."

"*Not* about that kid! About the lousy things you're doing to her, Yanni, about your whole damned *program*, your whole damned *project*! You're going to drive her crazy, shooting her full of stuff and jerking everything human away from her, Yanni. You're not a human being any longer!"

"And you've lost your perspective, boy, you've damned well lost your professional perspective! You're feeding your own damn insecurities into the situation. You're *interpreting*, son, you're not observing, you're not functioning, you've lost your objectivity, and you're off the project, son, you're *off the project* until you come back here with your head back together. Now get out of here! And don't bother me with these damn play-time projects of yours until you *get* your problem fixed. *Get out!*"

"I don't know what I could have said."

He was shaking. He was shaking all over again when Grant came over to the couch and handed him a glass. The ice rattled. He drank a gulp, and Grant settled down beside him with the tablet.

Give it a few days. Yanni explodes. He calms down.

He shook his head. Made a helpless gesture with the glass and rested his eyes against his hand a moment while the whiskey hit his bloodstream and the cold hit his stomach. "Maybe," he said finally, "maybe Yanni's right. Maybe I'm what he said, an assembly-line designer making an ass out of myself."

"That's not so."

"Yanni ripped me to shreds the last two designs. He was *right*, dammit, the whole thing would have blown up, they'd have had suicides."

Grant grabbed the tablet next to him, and wrote:

Don't give up. And went on writing: *Denys said once Ari didn't fake your Aptitudes. You've taken it as an article of faith that she did. You've always thought you belonged in Education. You do. But Ari wanted you in Design. I wonder why.*

His gut went queasy when he read that.

Grant wrote: *Ari did a hell of a lot to you. But she never refused to look at your work.*

"I'm off the project," he said. Because that was no news to Security and their eavesdroppers. "He says I hate the kid. It's not true, Grant. It's not true. It's not true."

Grant gripped his shoulder. "I know it. I know it, they know it, Yanni knows it, it's what he does—he was psyching you. He was getting you on tape."

"He said I flunked, didn't he?"

"For God's sake, that's part of it, that's part of the psych-out, don't you understand it? You know what he was doing. The test wasn't over yet. He wanted a reaction, and you gave it to him."

"I'm still pulling up what I said." He took a second drink, still shaking. "I can remember what I meant. I don't know if I can figure Yanni well enough to know what he heard."

"Yanni's good. Remember that. *Remember that.*"

He tried to. He wrote: *The question is, whose side is he on?*

--------------------------------- **xii** ---------------------------------

Horse dipped his head and took grain from Florian's palm. "See," he said to Catlin, "see, he's friendly. He just worries when it's strangers. You want to touch him?"

Catlin did, very carefully. Horse shied back.

Catlin outright grinned as she jerked her hand back. "He's smart."

The pigs and chickens had not impressed Catlin at all. She had just looked at the chicks in disgust when they piled up against the wall, and retreated from the piglets in some alarm when they rushed up to get the food. Then she had said they were stupid, and when he explained how smart they were about what they ate, she said they wouldn't be bacon if they were smarter about where they got what they ate.

The cows she said looked strong, but she was not very interested.

But Horse got the first real grin Florian had ever seen from Catlin, and she climbed up on the rail and watched while Horse played games with them and snorted and threw his head.

"We aren't going to eat Horse's babies," Florian said, climbing up beside her. "He's a working animal. That means they're not for food."

Catlin took that in the way she took a lot of things, with no comment, but he saw the nod of her head, which was Catlin agreeing with something.

He liked Catlin. That took a lot of deciding, because Catlin was hard to get hold of, but they had been through the Room a lot of times, and only once had he been Got and that was because they had Got Catlin first, and there had just been a whole lot of the Enemy, all Olders. Catlin had been Got twice in all, but the second time she had yelled Go! and given him time to blow a door and get through, which was his fault: he had been slower than he ought; so she Got all the Enemy but the one that Got her, and he Got that one, because *he* had a grenade, and the Enemy didn't expect him to have because he was a tech with his hands full. Catlin had been real proud of him for that.

He was just glad it was a game, and he told the Instructor it was his fault, not Catlin's. But the Instructor said they were a team, and it didn't matter.

He gave them half their Rec time.

Which was enough time to come over here. And this time he talked Catlin into coming with him and meeting Andy and seeing all the animals.

He was not sure Andy and Catlin got along. But Catlin said Horse was special.

So he got Andy to show Catlin the baby.

"She's all right," Catlin said, when she saw the girl Horse, and it played dodge with them, her tail going in a circle and her hooves kicking up the dust of the barn. "Look at her! Look at her move!"

"Your partner's all right, too," Andy said, with a nod of his head toward Catlin.

Which was something, coming from Andy. Florian felt happy, really happy, because all things he liked fell into place that way, Catlin and Andy and everything.

He remembered then, though, that they had to get back before curfew, which meant they had to hurry.

"Time," he said, and to Andy: "I'll be back as soon as I can."

"Goodbye," Andy said. "Goodbye," Florian said with a little bow, and: "Goodbye," Catlin said, which was very unusual, Catlin usually letting him do the talking when they dealt with anybody but Security.

They had to walk fast. He had showed Catlin the shortcuts on the way and she knew all of them on the way back, which was the way with Catlin.

She was also longer-legged than he was, and she could pick him up. He had thought boys were supposed to be taller and stronger. The Instructor said not when you were seven.

So he felt a little better about it. And he walked fast keeping up with Catlin, breathing harder than she was when they got to Green Barracks.

But when they checked in there was a stop on both of them at the desk. The azi there looked at his machine and said:

"Report to the Super, White section."

That was clear across the Town. That was Hospital. That meant tape. Instead of going to their quarters. "Yes," Catlin said, taking her card back and clipping it to her shirt. He took his back.

"Same instruction," the azi said.

"I wonder why," he said when they went back out onto the walk, headed for White.

"No good wondering," Catlin said. But she was worried, and she walked fast. He kept up with little extra efforts now and again.

The sun had gone behind the Cliffs a long time ago. The sky was going pink now and the lights were going to be on before they could get back. The walks and the roads were mostly deserted because most everyone was at supper. It was a strange time to be going to take tape. He felt uneasy.

When they got to the Hospital the clerk took their cards and read them; and told them each where to go.

He looked at Catlin when she went off her own way. He felt afraid then, and didn't know what of, or why, except he felt like he was in danger and she was. If you took tape you went to Hospital in the daytime. Not when you were supposed to be having dinner. His stomach was empty and he had thought maybe it was going to be a surprise exercise: they did that to the Olders, hauled them out of bed and you could hear them heading down the hall in the middle of the night, fast as they could run.

But it was not a Room when they got there, it was truly Hospital. You couldn't do anything except what you were told, and you didn't *think* in Hospital, you just took your shirt off and hung it up, then you climbed up on the table and sat there trying not to shiver until the Super got there to answer your questions.

It was a Super he had never had before. It was a man, who turned on the tape equipment before he even looked at him; and then said:

"Hello, Florian. How are you?"

"I'm scared, ser. Why are we getting tape now?"

"The tape will tell you. Don't be scared." He picked up a hypo and took Florian's arm and shot him with it. Florian jerked. He had gotten nervous about noises like that. The Super patted his shoulder and laid the hypo down. And held on to him because that was a strong one: Florian could feel it working very fast.

"Good boy," the Super said, and his hands were gentle even if he didn't talk as nice as some Supers. He never let him go, and swung him around and helped him get his legs up on the table, and his hand was always there, under his shoulders, on his shoulder or his forehead. "This is going to be a deep one. You aren't afraid now."

"No," he said, feeling the fear go away, but not the sense of being open.

"Deeper still. Deep as you can go, Florian. Go to the center and wait for me there. . . ."

xiii

"I don't *want* a party," Ari said, slouching in the chair when uncle Denys was talking to her. "I don't want any nasty party, I don't like any of the kids, I don't want to have to be nice to them."

She was already in bad with uncle Denys for borrowing Nelly's keycard, because Nelly, being Nelly, had told uncle Denys and uncle Giraud the whole thing when uncle Denys asked her. Nelly didn't want to get her in trouble. They had caught her anyway. Nelly had been awfully upset. And uncle Denys had had a severe Talk with her and with Nelly about security and safety in the building and going where she was supposed to.

Most of all he had said he was mad at Justin and Grant for not calling him and telling him that she was where she wasn't supposed to be, and they were in trouble too. Uncle Denys had sent them an angry message; and now they were supposed to report her if she came by there instead of the halls she was supposed to be in.

Ari was real mad at uncle Denys.

"You don't want the other kids," uncle Denys said, like a question.

"They're stupid."

"Well, what about a grown-up party? You can have punch and cake. And all of that. And have your presents. I wasn't thinking of having the whole Family. What about Dr. Ivanov and Giraud—"

"I don't like Giraud."

"Ari, that's not nice. He's my brother. He's your uncle. And he's been very nice to you."

"I don't care. You won't let me invite who *I* want."

"Ari, —"

"It's not Justin's fault I took Nelly's keycard."

Uncle Denys sighed. "Ari, —"

"I don't want an old party."

"Look, Ari, I don't know if Justin *can* come."

"I want Justin and I want Grant and I want Mary."

"Who's Mary?"

"Mary's the tech down in the labs."

"Mary's azi, Ari, and she'd feel dreadfully uncomfortable. But if you really want to, I'll see about Justin. I don't promise, mind. He's awfully busy. I'll have to ask him. But you can send him an invitation."

That was better. She sat up a little and leaned her elbows on the chair arms. And gave uncle Denys a lot nicer look.

"Nelly isn't going to have to go to hospital, either," she said.

"Ari, dear, Nelly *has* to go to hospital, because you made Nelly awfully upset. It's not *my* fault. You put Nelly in a hard place and if Nelly has to go to rest a while, I'm sure I don't blame her."

"That's nasty, uncle Denys."

"Well, so is stealing Nelly's card. Nelly will be back tomorrow morning, Nelly will be just fine. I'll call Justin and I'll tell Mary you thought about her. She'll be very pleased. But I don't promise anything. You be good and we'll see. All right?"

"All right," she said.

She was still mad about having to stay in the downstairs hall on her way back and forth to tape; and she tried and tried to think how she could get around that, but she hadn't figured it out yet.

So they were not going to have a party in the big dining room downstairs this year because uncle Denys said there was so much work lately anyway that a lot of people couldn't come. So they were going to have just a little one, in the apartment, but the kitchen was going to do the food and bring it up; and there would be just a few grown-ups, and they would have a nice dinner and have punch and cake and open her presents. She would get to plan the dinner with Nelly and sit at the head of the table and have anything she wanted. And Justin and Grant might be able to come, Denys said.

So they did.

Justin and Grant came to the door and Justin shook uncle Denys's hand.

Then the scared feeling shot clear across the room. Justin was scared when he came in. Grant too. And everyone in the room was stiff and nasty and trying not to be.

It was her party, dammit. Ari got up with the upset going straight to her stomach, and ran over and was as friendly as she could be. You didn't get anywhere by telling people to be nice. You just got their attention and shook them up until they fixed on you instead of what they had fixed on, and then you could do things with them. She didn't have time to work out who was doing what—she just went for Justin: he was the key to it and she knew that right away.

Uncle Giraud was there, and Giraud's azi Abban; and Dr. Ivanov and a very pretty azi named Ule, who was his. And Dr. Peterson and his azi Ramey; and her favorite instructor Dr. Edwards and his azi Gale, who was older than he was, but nice: Dr. Edwards was one of her invites. Dr. Edwards was a biochemist, but he knew about all sorts of things, and he worked a lot with her after her tape. And there was uncle Denys, of course, who was talking to Justin.

"Hello!" she said, getting in the way.

"Hello," Grant said, and gave her their present. She shook it. It wasn't heavy. It didn't rattle. "What is it?" she asked. She knew they wouldn't tell her. Mostly she wanted to get hold of them. And they were looking mostly at her.

"You have to wait to open it, don't you?" Justin said. "That's why it's wrapped."

She bounced over and gave it to Nelly to put with all the others that were stacked around the chair in the corner. It was like the whole room took a breath. She let it go a minute to see what the grown-ups were going to do now that they knew for sure that Justin and Grant were her invites.

The grown-ups had drinks and got to talking, and everyone was being nice. It was going to be nice. She would make it nice even if uncle Denys was getting over a mad with Justin. It was *her* party and *her* say-so, and she intended to have it, and to have a good time. No one was going to spoil it; or she would get them good.

Giraud was the nasty one. She was watching him real close, and she caught his eye when no one else was looking, and gave him a real straight look, so he knew that. Then she bounced back over and took Justin's hand and had him look at all her pile of presents, and introduced him and Grant to Nelly, which embarrassed Nelly, but at least you knew Nelly was going to be nice and not make things blow up.

She went into her suite and brought out some of her nicest and most curious things to show everyone. She got everyone fixed on her. Pretty soon everybody was being a lot nicer, and people started talking and having a good time, having a before-dinner drink. But she didn't. She didn't want to spoil dinner.

It was different than parties she had had before, with the kids. She had a blue blouse with sparkles. A hairdresser had come in the afternoon and done her hair up with braids. She was very careful of it, and careful of her clothes when she sat on the floor. She was very pretty and she felt very grown-up and important, and she smiled at everybody now that they were being nice. When Seely said it was time to eat and the kitchen staff was going to be bringing the food in, she had Justin sit by her on one side at the table and Dr. Ivanov sat down next to him on the other, with Dr. Edwards across from him, so he was safe from Giraud, especially since Dr. Peterson sat down next to Dr. Edwards. Which left uncle Denys and uncle Giraud farthest away. You weren't supposed to have an odd number at table. But they did. She had wanted Grant to be there, but uncle Denys said Grant would enjoy the party more with the other azi, and even Nelly said, while she was helping her get dressed, that Grant would be embarrassed if he had to be the only azi at the table where the CITs ate. So since Nelly said it too, she decided uncle Denys knew what he was talking about.

She got to sit at the head of the table; and she got to talk to adults, who talked about the labs and about things she didn't know, but she always learned something when she listened, and she didn't mind it at all when the adults quit asking her questions about her studies and her fish and began talking to each other.

It was a lot better, she was sure now, than kid-parties, where everybody was nasty and stupid.

When Justin and Grant had come in everyone had acted just exactly the way the other kids acted when *she* came near them. She hated that. She didn't know why they did it. She had thought grown-ups were more grown-up than that. It was depressing to learn they weren't.

At least adults covered it up better. And she figured it was easier to deal with if you weren't the target of it. So she started figuring out where the problems were.

Uncle Giraud was the worst. He always was. Uncle Giraud was minding his manners, but he was still sulking about something, and talking about business to uncle Denys, who didn't want him to.

Justin wasn't saying anything. He didn't want to. Dr. Peterson was just kind of dull, and he was talking to Dr. Ivanov, who was bored and mostly trying to listen to what Dr. Edwards was saying about the problems with the algae project. Uncle Denys was watching everybody and being nice, and trying to get Giraud, who was next to him, to stop talking.

She knew about the algae. Dr. Edwards had told her. He showed her all these sealed bottles with different kinds of algae and told her what Earth's oceans had in them and what the difference was on Cyteen.

So she was trying to listen to that and she answered Dr. Peterson sometimes when he tried to talk to her instead of Dr. Ivanov.

It was still better than playing with Amy Carnath. And nobody was being nasty.

So when they got past cake and punch, and it was time for the adults to drink their drinks, she grabbed Justin by the hand and sat him in the circle of chairs right on the end next to uncle Denys. And, oh! that made Justin really nervous.

That was all right. That was because Justin was smart and knew if uncle Denys got mad at him everything was going to blow up. But she was too smart for that to happen. She opened uncle Denys' present first. It was a watch that could do most everything. A real watch. She was delighted, but even if she hadn't been she would have said she was, because she wanted uncle Denys happy. She went and she kissed uncle Denys on the cheek and was just as nice as she could be.

She opened uncle Giraud's present next, just to make uncle Denys *real* happy, and it was an awfully nice holo of the whole planet of Cyteen. You moved it and the clouds went round. Everybody was real impressed with it, especially Dr. Edwards, and uncle Giraud explained it was a special kind of holo and brand new. So uncle Giraud was a surprise: he had really tried hard to find her a nice gift and he really liked it himself. She had never known uncle Giraud liked things like that, but of course, he was the one who had given her the bird in the cube, too. So she understood something about Giraud that was different than him being nasty all the time. She gave him a big kiss and skipped off to open Dr. Ivanov's present, which was a puzzle box.

And Dr. Edwards', then, which was a piece of gold plastic until you put your fingers on it or laid something like a pencil on it, and then it made the shadow in different colors according to how warm it was, and you could make designs with it that stayed a while. It was real nice. She had known whatever he gave her would be. But she didn't make any more fuss over it than over Dr. Ivanov's puzzle and Dr. Peterson's book about computers, and certainly not more than over uncle Denys's watch or uncle Giraud's holo.

It was working, too. They were having a good time. She opened Nelly's present, which was underwear—oh, that was like Nelly—and then she opened Justin's; which was a ball in a ball in a ball, all carved. It was beautiful. It was the kind of thing maman would have had and said: *Ari, don't touch that!* And it was hers. But she mustn't fuss over it. No matter how much she liked it. She said thank you and got right into the huge pile of other things from people who hadn't come to her party.

There were things from the kids. Even nasty Amy sent her a scarf. And Sam gave her a robot bug that would really crawl and find its way around the apartment. It was expensive, she knew, she had seen it in the store; and it was awfully nice of Sam.

There were a lot of books and tapes and some paints and a lot of clothes: she thought uncle Denys probably told people the sizes because everybody knew. And there was clay to work and a lot of games and several bracelets and a couple of cars and even a roll-the-ball maze puzzle from Mary the azi, down in the labs. That was awfully nice. She made a note to send Mary a thank-you.

And Sam too.

Presents were good for making everybody feel happy. The grown-ups drank wine and uncle Denys even let her have a quarter of a glass. It was suspicious-tasting, like it was spoiled or something. All the adults laughed when she said that; even Justin smiled; but uncle Denys said it certainly wasn't, it was *supposed* to taste like that, and she couldn't have any more or she would feel funny and get sleepy.

So she didn't. She worked her puzzle-box and got it open while the grown-ups drank a lot and laughed with each other and while uncle Denys finally got her watch set with the right date. It was not a bad party at all.

She yawned and everybody said it was time to go. And they called the azi and wished her happy birthday while she stood at the door with uncle Denys the way maman would have and said goodbye and thank you for coming.

Everybody was noisy and happy like a long time ago. Denys was really smiling at Dr. Edwards and shook his hand and told Dr. Edwards he was really happy he came. Which made Dr. Edwards happy, because uncle Denys was the Administrator, and she wanted to get uncle Denys to like Dr. Edwards. And uncle Denys even was nice to Justin, and was really smiling at him and Grant when they left.

So *all* of her invites worked.

Everyone left, even uncle Giraud; and it was time to clean up the presents and all. But Ari figured it was not too late to get another point with uncle Denys, so she went and hugged him.

"Thank you," she said. "That was a nice party. I love the watch. Thank you."

"Thank *you*, Ari. That was nice."

And he smiled at her in a funny way. Like he was really happy for a lot of reasons.

He kissed her on the forehead and told her go to bed.

But she was feeling so good she decided to help Nelly and Seely pick up the presents, and she gave Nelly special instructions to be careful with her favorites.

She turned on Sam's bug and let it run around real fast. "What's that?" Nelly cried, and uncle Denys came out again to see what the commotion was.

So she clapped her hands and stopped it, and snatched it up and took it to her room.

Real fast. Because she was really trying to be good.

xiv

Ari waked in the morning with the Minder dinging away and told it shut up, she had heard it. She rubbed her eyes and really wished she could stay there, but she was supposed to go to tape, it was that day. And there was no more going by Justin's office either.

She had a lot of new toys in her bedroom, and a lot of new clothes; but mostly she would like to just lie here and go back to sleep, except pretty soon Nelly would be in telling her she had to move.

So she beat Nelly. She rolled over and slid over the side of the bed. And went to the bath and slid out of her pajamas and took her shower and brushed her teeth.

Usually Nelly was in the room by now.

So she put on the clothes Nelly had laid out for her last night and said: "Minder, call Nelly."

"Nelly isn't here," the Minder said. "Nelly's gone to the hospital."

She was scared then. But that could have been the old message. She said: "Minder, where's uncle Denys?"

"Ari," the Minder said, in uncle Denys's voice, "come to the dining room."

"Where's Nelly?" she asked again.

"Nelly's in the hospital. She's fine. Come to the dining room."

She brushed her hair fast. She opened the door and walked down the hall of her suite past Nelly's room. She opened the door to the main apartment and walked on into the sitting room.

Uncle Denys was at the table beyond the arch. She walked in, clipping her keycard on, and uncle Denys said she should sit down and have breakfast.

"I don't want to. What's the matter with Nelly?"

"Sit down," uncle Denys said.

So she sat. She wasn't going to learn anything till she did. She knew uncle

Denys. She reached for a muffin and ate a nibble dry. And Seely came and poured her orange juice. Her stomach felt upset.

"There," uncle Denys said. "Nelly's in hospital because she's getting some more tape. Nelly's not really able to keep up with you, Ari, and you're really going to have to be careful with her from now on. You're getting bigger, you're getting very clever, and poor Nelly thinks it's her duty to keep up with you. The doctors are going to tell her it's not her fault. There's a lot Nelly has to adjust to. But you do have to remember not to hurt Nelly."

"I don't. I didn't know the bug was going to scare her."

"If you'd thought, you would have."

"I guess so," she said. It was a lonely morning without Nelly. But at least Nelly was all right. She put a little butter on her muffin. It tasted better.

"One of the things Nelly has to adjust to," uncle Denys said, "is two more azi in the household, because there will be."

She looked at uncle Denys, not real happy. Seely was bad enough.

"They'll be yours," uncle Denys said. "They're part of your birthday. But you mustn't tell them that: people aren't birthday presents. It's not nice."

She swallowed a big gulp of muffin. She wasn't at all happy, she didn't want any azi but Nelly to be following her around, and if it was like a present, she didn't want to hurt uncle Denys's feelings, either, for a whole lot of reasons. She thought fast and tried to think of a way to say no.

"So you don't have to go to tapestudy today," uncle Denys said. "You go over to hospital and pick them up. And you can spend your day showing them what to do. They're not like Nelly. They're both Alphas. Experimentals."

A large gulp of orange juice. She didn't know what to think about that. Alphas were rare. They were also awfully hard to deal with. She was sure they were supposed to be watching her. That sounded an awful lot like uncle Denys was going to make it really hard for her to do *anything* she wasn't supposed to. She wasn't sure whether this present came from uncle Denys, or uncle *Giraud*.

"You go to the desk," uncle Denys said, "and you give your card to Security, and they'll register them to you. Effectively, you're going to be their Supervisor, and that's quite a lot different than Nelly. *I'm* Nelly's Supervisor. You're only her responsibility. This is quite different. You know what a Supervisor does? You know how responsible that is?"

"I'm a *kid*," she protested.

Uncle Denys chuckled and buttered another muffin. "That's all right. So are they." He looked up, serious. "But they're not toys, Ari. You understand how serious it is if you get mad at them, or if you hit them the way you hit Amy Carnath."

"I wouldn't do that!" You didn't hit azi. You didn't talk nasty to them. Except Ollie. And Phaedra. For different reasons. But they were both special, even Phaedra.

"I don't think you would, dear. But I just want you to think about it before you hurt them. And you can. You could hurt them very, very badly, a lot more than you can Nelly—the way only I could hurt Nelly. You understand?"

"I'm not sure I want them, uncle Denys."

"You need other children, Ari. You need somebody your own age."

That was true. But there wasn't anybody who didn't drive her crazy. And it was going to be awful if they did, because they were going to live-in.

"The boy is Florian, the girl is Catlin, and it's their birthday too, well, just about. They'll live in the room next to yours and Nelly's, that's what it was always for. But they'll have to go back to the Town for some of their lessons, and they'll do tapestudy in the House, just like you do. They're kids just like you, and they have Instructors they have to pay attention to. They're very quick. In a lot of things they're ahead of you. That's the way with azi, especially the bright ones. So you're going to have to work to keep up with them."

She was listening now. No one had ever said she wasn't the best at anything. She didn't believe they could be. They wouldn't be. There was nothing she couldn't do if she wanted to. Maman always said so.

"Are you finished?"

"Yes, ser."

"Then you can go. You pick them up and you show them around, and you stay out of trouble, all right?"

She got down from table and she left, out into the halls, past Security and the big front doors and across the driveway and along the walk to the hospital. She ran part of the way, because it was boring otherwise.

But she was dignified and grown-up when she passed the hospital doors and gave her card to hospital Security at the desk.

"Yes, sera," they said. "Come this way."

So they brought her to a room.

And they left and the other door opened. A nurse let in two azi her own age. The girl was pale, pale blonde, with a braid; the boy was shorter, with hair blacker than their uniforms.

And uncle Denys was right. Nobody ever looked at her that way when she had just met them. It was like friends right off. It was more than that. It was like they were in a scary place and she was the only one who could get them out of it.

"Hello," she said. "I'm Ari Emory."

"Yes, sera." Very softly, from both, almost together.

"You're supposed to come with me."

"Yes, sera."

It felt really, really strange. Not like Nelly. Not like Nelly at all. She held the door button for them and she took them out by the desk and said that she was taking them.

"Here are their keycards, sera," the man at the desk said. And she took them and looked at them.

There were their names. Florian AF-9979 and Catlin AC-7892. And the

Alpha symbol in the class blank. And the wide black border of House Security across the bottom.

She saw that and a cold feeling went through her stomach, a terrible feeling, like finding the Security guard in maman's apartment. She never forgot that. She had nightmares about that.

But she didn't let them see her face right then. She got herself straight before she turned around and gave them their cards, and they put them on.

And they had different expressions too, out here, very serious, very azi: they were listening to her, they were watching her, but they were watching everything.

You had to remember how they had been in the room, she thought. You had to think how they had looked in there, to know that that was real too, and that they were two things.

They were Security and they were hers, and it was other people they were watching like that, every little move that went on around her.

I wanted an Ollie, she remembered, but that was not what uncle Denys had given her. He gave her Security.

Why? she wondered, a little mad, a little scared. *What do I need them for?*

But they were her responsibility. So she took them out and down the walk to the House and checked them in with House Security. They were very correct with the officer on duty. "Yes, *sera*," they said very sharply to the officer, and the officer talked fast and ran through the rules for them in words and codes she had never heard. But the azi knew. They were very confident.

Uncle Denys hadn't said they had to come straight home, but she thought they should. Except she went by uncle Denys's office and uncle Denys was there. So she took them in and introduced them.

Then she took them home and showed them where they would live, and their own rooms; and explained to them about Nelly.

"You have to do what Nelly says," she said. "So do I, most of the time. Nelly's all right."

They were not quite nervous; it was something else. Especially Catlin, who had this way of looking at everything real fast. Both of them were very tense and very stiff and formal.

That was all right, they were respectful and they were being nice.

So she got out her Starchase game, set it up on the dining table and explained what the rules were.

None of the other kids ever listened the way they listened. They didn't tease or joke. She passed out the money and dealt out the cards and gave them their pieces. And when they started playing it got real tense.

She wasn't sure whether it was a fight or a game, but it was different than Amy Carnath, a lot different, because nobody was mad, they just went at it; and pretty soon she was leaning over the board and thinking so hard she was chewing her lip without knowing it for a while.

They *liked* it when she did something sneaky. They were sneaky right back, and the minute you got your pieces where you could get Florian in trouble, Catlin was moving up on the other side.

Starchase was usually real fast to play. And they were at it a long time, till she could get enough money to get enough ships built to keep Catlin off till she could get Florian cornered.

But then he asked if the rules let him join Catlin.

No one had ever thought of that. She thought it was smart. She got the rulebook out and looked.

"They don't say you can't," she said. And her shoulders were tired and she was stiff from sitting still so long. "Let's go put the board in my room so Seely won't mess it up and we'll have lunch, all right?"

"Yes, sera," they said.

They had a way of doing that to remind her they weren't just kids, every time she tried to make them relax.

But Florian carried the board in and he didn't spill it. And she thought she had rather go have lunch in North wing: uncle Denys let her go to the restaurant there, the little one, where the azi and the manager all knew her.

So that was where she took them, to *Changes*, down next to the shops, at the corner, where mostly Staff had lunch. She introduced them, she sat down and told them to sit down, and she had to order for them: "Sera," Florian whispered, looking awfully embarrassed after a moment of looking at the menu, "what are we supposed to do with this?"

"Pick out what you want to eat."

"I don't know these words. I don't think Catlin does."

Catlin shook her head, very sober and very worried-looking.

So she asked them what they liked, and they said they usually had sandwiches at lunch. She ordered that for them and for herself.

And thought that they were awfully nervous, and kept looking at everything and everyone that moved. Somebody banged a tray and their eyes went that way like something had exploded.

"You don't have to be worried," she said. They made *her* nervous. Like something was going to happen. "Calm down. It's just the waiters."

They looked at her, very sober. But they didn't stop watching things. Just as serious and just as sober as they were in the game.

The waiter brought their drinks and they looked at him, all over, real fast, so fast it was hard to see them do it, but she knew they were doing it because she was watching.

Nothing like Nelly.

Uncle Denys talked about being safe in the halls. And got her two azi who thought the waiter was going to jump them. "Listen," she said, and two serious faces turned toward her and *listened*, azi-like. "Sometimes we can just have fun, all right? Nobody's going to get us here. I know all these people."

They calmed right down. Like it was magic. Like she had psyched them exactly right. She let go a little breath and felt proud of herself. They sipped their soft drinks and when the sandwiches came with all the extra stuff that came with them they were real impressed.

They liked it. She could tell. But: "I can't eat this much," Florian said, worried-like. "I'm sorry."

"That's all right. Quit worrying about things. Hear?"

"Yes, sera."

She looked at Florian, and looked at Catlin, and all that seriousness; and thought of ways to un-serious them; and then remembered that they were azi, and it was their psychset to be like that, which meant you couldn't *do* a lot of things with them.

But they weren't stupid. Not at all. Alphas were like Ollie. And that meant they could take a lot that Nelly never could. Like in the game: she pushed them with everything she had, and they didn't get mad and they didn't get upset.

They were a big job. But not *too* big for her.

Then she thought, not for the first time that morning, that they were a Responsibility. And you didn't take on azi and then just dump them, ever. Uncle Denys was right. You didn't get people for presents. You got somebody who wanted to love you, and you couldn't ever just move away and leave them.

(Maman did, she thought, and it hurt, the way it always hurt when that thought popped up. Maman did. But maman didn't want to. Maman had been worried and upset for a long time before she went away.)

She would have to write and tell maman about them, fast, so maman would know she had to tell uncle Denys to send them with her. Because she couldn't just leave them. She knew what that felt like.

She wished she had gotten to pick them out, because her household was getting complicated; she would much rather have an Ollie for hers, and one and not two. She could have said no. Maybe she should have said no, and not let uncle Denys give them to her. She had thought she could sort of go along with it. Like everything else.

Till they looked at her that way over at the hospital, and they just sort of psyched her, not meaning to, except they wanted to go with her so much; and she had wanted somebody to be with her, just as bad.

So now they were stuck with each other. And she couldn't leave them by themselves.

Not ever.

Verbal Text from:
A QUESTION OF UNION
Union Civics Series: #3

Reseune Educational Publications: 9799-8734-3
approved for 80+

Union, as conceived in the Constitution of 2301 and developed through the addition and amalgamation of station and world governments thereafter, was structured from the beginning as a federal system affording maximum independence to the local level. To understand Union, therefore, one must start with the establishment of a typical local government, which may be any system approved by a majority of qualified naturally born inhabitants. Note: inhabitants, not citizens. The only segments of the population disenfranchised for such elections are minors and azi, who are not counted as residents for purposes of an Initial Ballot of Choice, although azi may later be enfranchised by the local government.

An Initial Ballot of Choice is the normal civil procedure by which any polity becomes a candidate for representation in Union. The Ballot establishes the representative local Constitutional Congress, which will either validate an existing governmental structure as representing the will of the electorate, or create an entirely new structure which may then be ratified by the general Initial Electorate. Second of the duties of the Constitutional Congress after the election is to assign citizen numbers and register legal voters, i.e., all voters qualified by age and citizen numbers to cast their ballots for the Council of Nine and for the General Council of Union. Third and final duty of the Congress is the reporting of the census and the voter rolls to the Union Bureau of Citizens.

Subsequent Ballots of Choice and subsequent Congresses can be held on a majority vote of the local electorate, or by order of the Supreme Court of Union after due process of law. In such a re-polling of the local electorate, all native-born residents and emigrated or immigrated residents are eligible in that vote, including azi who hold modified citizen status.

Within Union, the Council of Nine represents the nine occupational electorates of Union, across all Union citizen rolls. Within those occupational electorates, votes are weighted according to registered level of expertise: i.e., most voters in, say, the Science electorate are factored at one, but a lab tech with a certain number of years' experience may merit a two; while a scientist of high professional rating may merit as high as ten, depending on professional credentials achieved for this purpose—a considerable difference, since the factors are applied in a formula and each increment is considerable. An individual can always appeal his ranking to peer review, but most advances are virtually set with the job and experience.

When a seat on the Council of Nine falls vacant, the Secretary of the Bureau regulated by that seat will assume the position of proxy until that electorate selects a replacement; or the outgoing Councillor may appoint a different proxy.

Members of the Nine can be challenged for election at any time by the filing of an opposition candidate with sufficient signatures of the Bureau on a supporting petition.

Recently the rise of rival political parties has tended to make the vacancy of a seat the occasion of a partisan contention, and a challenge to a seat almost inevitably partisan. This has rendered the position of Secretary potentially more vulnerable, and increases the importance of the internal Bureau support structure and the administrative professionals which are necessary for smooth operation through changes in upper-tier administration.

The Councillor sets policy in a Bureau. The Secretary, who is appointed, frames guidelines and issues administrative orders. The various department heads implement the orders and report up the chain through the Secretary to the Councillor and through the Councillor to the Council of Nine.

The Council of Nine can initiate and vote on bills, particularly as touches the budget of the Bureaus, and national policy toward outsiders, but a unanimous vote by the delegation of any local unit can veto a law which applies only to that unit to the exclusion of others, which then will require a two-thirds majority in the General Council and a majority of the Council of Nine to override. The principle of local rule thus takes precedence over all but the most unanimous vote in Union.

A simple majority of the Nine is sufficient to pass a bill into law, unless overridden by a simple vote of the General Council of Union, which consists of one ambassador and a certain number of representatives from each world or station in the Union, according to population.

The Council of Nine presides in the General Council: the Council of Worlds (meaning the General Council without the Nine) can initiate and pass bills with a simple majority, until overridden by a vote of the Nine.

The Council of Worlds presently has seventy-six members, including the Representatives of Cyteen. When the Nine are present, i.e., when it is a General Council, the Representatives of Cyteen originally might observe but might not, until 2377, speak or vote, which was the concession granted by Cyteen as the seat of government, to run until the population of Union doubled that of Cyteen—a figure reached in the census of that year.

Certain entities within Union constitute non-represented units: these are Union Administrative Territories, which do not vote in local elections, and which are subject to their own internal regulations, having the same sovereignty as any planet or station within Union.

An Administrative Territory is immune to local law, is taxed only at the Union level, and maintains its own police force, its own legal system, and its own administrative rules which have the force of law on its own citizens. An Administrative Territory is under the oversight of the Bureau within which its principal activity falls; and is subject to Bureau intervention under certain carefully drawn rules, which fall within the Territorial charter and which may differ from Territory to Territory.

No discussion of the units of Union government could be complete without a mention of the unique nature of Cyteen, which has the largest concentration of population, which constitutes the largest section of any given electorate, which is also the site of Union government—over which, of course, Cyteen has no jurisdictional rights; and which is the site of three very powerful Administrative Territories.

Certain people argue that there is too much Union government on Cyteen, and that it cannibalizes local rights. Certain others say that Cyteen has far too much influence in Union, and point out that Cyteen has always held more than one seat of the Nine. Certain others, mostly Cyteeners, say that the whole planet is likely to become a government reserve, and that the amount of influence Cyteen has in Union is only fair, considering that Cyteen has become the support of the whole government, which means that Union is so powerful and the influence of the Nine so great on the planet, that everyone in Union has a say in how Cyteen is run.

Another point of contention is the use of Cyteen resources both by Union at large and by Administrative Territories, which pay no local tax and which are not within Cyteen authority. The Territories point out that their economic return to the Cyteen economy is greater than the resources they absorb; and that indeed, Cyteen's viability as a planet has been largely due to the economic strength of the several Territories on Cyteen. . . .

CHAPTER
7

The small jet touched down at Planys airfield and rolled to the front of the little terminal, and Justin unbuckled his safety belt, moving in the same sense of unreality that had been with him since the plane left the ground at Reseune.

He had thought until that very moment that some agency would stop him, that the game was giving him permission to travel and then maneuvering him or Jordan into some situation that would cancel it.

He was still scared. There were other possibilities he could think of, more than a psych of either one of them—like the chance of Reseune creating a situation they could use to harm Jordan or worsen his conditions. He tried to put thoughts like that in the back of his mind, where they only warned him to be careful; like the thoughts that armored him against the sudden recall, the sudden reversal of the travel permit, even this far into the matter.

One had to live like that. Or go crazy.

He picked up his briefcase and his bag from the locker while his Security escort were coming forward—it was the plane that shuttled back and forth between Reseune and Planys at need, a corporate plane with the Infinite Man symbol on its tail, not the red and white emblem of RESEUNEAIR, which carried passengers and freight over most of the continent and a few points overseas. Reseune Labs owned this one, even if it was a RESEUNEAIR crew that flew it; and the fact that this plane was, like *RESEUNE ONE*, private— kept its cargoes and its passenger lists from the scrutiny of the Bureau of Transportation.

A long, long flight from Reseune, over a lonely ocean. A plane with an airlock and a suction filter in the lock, and the need for D-suits and masks before they could go out there. He took his out of the locker, white, thin plastic, hotter than hell to wear, because the generic fits-everyone sort had no circulating system, just a couple of bands you put around your chest and shoulders to keep the thing from inflating like a balloon and robbing you of the air the helmet gave you.

The co-pilot took him in hand and checked his seals, collar, wrists, ankles and front, then patted him on the shoulder, pointing to the airlock. The generic suits had no com either, and you shouted or you signed.

So he picked up his baggage, likewise sealed in a plastic carry-bag, and looked to see if Security was going to let him out there.

No. One was going to lock through with him. That was how closely they were watching him.

So he went into the airlock and waited through the cycle, and went out down the ladder with the Security guard at his back, down where the ground crews, in custom-fitted D-suits, were attending the plane.

There was very little green in Planys. Precip towers did their best to keep the plants alive, but it was still raw and new here, still mostly red rock and blue scrub and woolwood. Ankyloderms were the predominant phylum of wildlife on this continent, as platytheres were in the other, in the unbridged isolation that had given Cyteen two virtually independent ecologies—except, always, woolwood and a few other windborne pests that propagated from virtually any fiber that got anywhere there was dirt and moisture.

Flora reinforced with absorbed silicates and poisonous with metals and alkaloids, generating an airborne profusion of fibers carcinogenic in Terran respiratory systems even in minute doses: the plants would kill you either in minutes or in years, depending on whether you were fool enough to eat a leaf or just unlucky enough to get an unguarded breath of air. The carbon monoxide in the air was enough to do the job on its own. But the only way to get killed by the fauna was to stand in its path, and the only way it ever died, the old joke ran, was when two of equal size met head to head and starved to death.

It was easy to forget what Cyteen was until you touched the outback.

And there was so profound a sense of desolation about this place. You looked away from the airport and the buildings, and it was Cyteen, that was all, raw and deadly.

Jordan lived in this place.

There was no taking the suits off until they got to Planys Annex, and the garage, and another airlock, where you had to brush each other off with some violence while powerful suction fans made the cheap suits rattle and flutter. You had to lift and stretch the elastic straps to get any fiber out of them, then endure a hosing down in special detergent, lock through, strip the suits and step up onto a grating without touching the outside surfaces—while the decontamination crew saw to your baggage.

Damn, he thought, anxious until the second door was shut and he and his escort were in a hall that looked more like a storm-tunnel at home—gray concrete, completely gray.

It was better on the upper floor: green-painted concrete, decent lighting. No windows . . . there was probably no window in all of Planys. A small concession to decor in a few green plastic hanging plants, cheap framed prints on the walls.

Building A, it said occasionally, brown stencil letters a meter high, obscured here and there by the hanging pictures. Doors were brown-painted metal. There was, anomaly, an office with curtained hallward windows. That was the one that said, in a small engraved-plastic sign: Dr. Jordan Warrick, Administrator, Educational Division.

A guard opened that door for him. He walked in, saw Paul at the desk, Paul, who looked—like Paul, that was all: he was dyeing his hair—who got up and took his hand and hugged him.

Then he knew it was real. "Go on in," Paul said into his ear, patting him on the shoulder. "He knows you're here."

He went to the door, opened it and went in. Jordan met him there with open arms. For a long, long while they just held on to each other without saying a word. He wept. Jordan did.

"Good to see you," Jordan said finally. "Damn, you've grown."

"You're looking good," Justin said, at arms' length, trying not to see the lines around the eyes and the mouth. Jordan felt thinner, but he was still fit and hard—perhaps, Justin thought, Jordan had done what he had done, from the day Denys had called him into his office and told him he had gotten a travel permit—run lap upon lap in the gym, determined not to have his father see him out of shape.

"I wish Grant could have come."

"So did he." It was hard to keep his composure. He got it back. And did not add that there was reason to worry, that Grant was more scared than Grant wanted to let on, being left alone at Reseune—azi, and legally under Reseune's authority. "Maybe some other trip."

This trip *had* to work. They *had* to make it as smooth and easy as possible, to get others in future. He had an idea every paper in his briefcase was going to be gone over again by every means Security had here; and that when he got back to Reseune they were going to do it all again, and strip-search him the way they had before he boarded the plane, very, very thoroughly. But he was here. He had the rest of the day and till noon tomorrow. Every minute he spent with Jordan, two high-clearance Security agents would be sitting in the same room; but that was all right, right as the cameras and the bugs that invaded every moment of his life and left nothing private.

So he walked over to the conference table with Jordan, he sat down as Paul came in and joined them, he said: "I brought my work. They'll get my briefcase up here in a bit. I'm really anxious for you to have a look at some of it."

It's a waste of time, Yanni had said, in Yanni's inimitable way, when he had begged Yanni to give him a clearance to bring his latest design with him.

And then cleared it by that afternoon. *This'll cost you,* the note Yanni sent him had said. *You'll pay me in overtime.*

"How have things been going?" Jordan asked him, asking him more than that with the anxiousness in his eyes, the way a son and a psych student could read and Security and voice-stress analyzers might possibly miss.

Is there some condition to this I don't know about?

"Hell," he said, and laughed, letting the tension go, "too damn well. *Too damn well,* all year. Last year was hell. I imagine you picked that up. I couldn't do anything right, everything I touched fell apart—"

A lot of problems I can't mention.

"—but it's like all of a sudden something sorted itself out. For one thing, they took me off real-time work. I felt guilty about that—which is probably a good indicator how bad it was; I was taking too long, I was too tired to think straight, just no good at it, that's all, and too tied up in it to turn it loose. Yanni thought I could break through, you know, some of my problems that way, I know damn well what he was trying to do; then he R&R'd me into production again. Until for some reason he had a change of heart and shoved me back into R&D, on a long, long lead-time. Where I do just fine, thanks."

They had talked so long in time-lag he found himself doing it again, condensing everything into packets, with a little worry about Security objecting in every sentence. But here he had more freedom. They promised him that. There was no outside eavesdropping to worry about and they could talk about anything—that offered no hint of escape plans or hidden messages to be smuggled outside Reseune.

Jordan knew about the Project. Both Projects, Ari and Rubin.

"I'm glad," Jordan said. "I'm glad. How's Grant's work?"

"He never was in trouble. You know Grant." And then he realized how far back that question had to go.

All those years. Grant in hospital. Himself in Security's hands. Jordan being whisked away to testify in Novgorod before they shipped him out to Planys.

His hand shook, on the table in front of him, shook as he carried it to his mouth and tried to steady himself.

"Grant—came out of it all right. Stable as ever. He's fine. He really is. I don't know what I'd have done without him. Have you been all right?"

"Hell at first. But it's a small staff, a close staff. They can come and go, of course, and they know my condition here, but it's a real difference—a real difference."

O God, be careful. Anything you say, anything you admit to needing, they can use. Watch what you say.

". . . We take care of each other here. We carry each other's loads, sometimes. I think it's all that desert out there. You either go crazy and they ship you out, or you get seduced by the tranquillity here. Even Security's kind of reasonable. —Aren't you, Jim?"

One guard had settled in, taken a chair in the corner. The man laughed and leaned back, ankles crossed.

Not azi. CIT.

"Most times," Jim the guard said.

"It's home," Jordan said. "It's gotten to be home. You have to understand the mentality out here. Our news and a lot of our music comes in from the station. We're real good on current events. Our clothes, our books, our entertainment tapes, all of that—get flown in when they get around to it, and books and tapes don't get into the library here until Security vets the addition. So there's a lot of staff silliness—you have to amuse yourself somehow; and the big new E-tape is *Echoes*. Which ought to tell you something."

Three years since that tape had come out. "Damn, I could have brought you a dozen."

"Listen, anything you can do for library here will be appreciated. I've complained. Everyone on staff has complained. The garrison snags everything. *Military* priority. And they do the luggage searches. I couldn't warn you. I hope to hell you haven't got anything in your overnight kit that's in short supply here, because they've got a censored number of soldiers over at the base really desperate for censored, censored, and censored. Not to mention toilet paper. So we're not the only ones."

He laughed, because Jordan laughed and Paul laughed, and Jim-the-guard laughed, because it was desperately, bleakly funny to think of, when there was so much that was not at all funny in this isolation; because it was so much relief to know Planys finally, not as a totally barren exile, but as a place where humanness and humor were valuable.

They talked and argued theory till they were hoarse. They went to the lab and Jordan introduced him to the staffers he had never met, always with Jim and his azi partner Enny at left and right of them. They had a drink with Lel Schwartz and Milos Carnath-Morley, neither one of whom he had seen since he was seventeen; and had dinner with Jordan and Paul—and Jim and Enny.

He had no intention of sleeping. Neither did Jordan or Paul. They had allotted him a certain number of hours to stay and he could sleep on the plane, that was all.

Jim and Enny traded off with two others at 2000 of the clock. By that time Jordan and Paul were both arguing ideas with him, criticizing his structures, telling him where he was wrong and teaching him more about sociological psych integrations than he had learned from all Yanni's books.

"Oh, God," he said, toward 0400 in the morning, in a break when they were all three hoarse and still talking, "if we could consult together—if you were there or I was here—"

"You're retracing a lot of old territory," Jordan told him, "but I don't call it a dead end. I *don't know*, you understand, and I don't say that too often, pardon my arrogance. I think it's worth chasing—not that I think you'll get where you're going, but I'm just curious."

"You're my father. Yanni says I'm crazy."

"Then Ari was."

He looked sharply at Jordan. And his gut knotted up just hearing Jordan name the dead without rancor.

"She told me," Jordan said, "when I suggested she'd rigged the Aptitudes—politely, of course—that it was your essay question cinched it. I thought that was her usual kind of snide answer. I'm not so sure, now, having seen where you've taken it. Did she help you with this?"

"Not this one. The first—" Few, he almost said. Till she died. Till she was killed. Murdered. He shuddered away from the remembrance. "You didn't take me seriously, then."

"Son, it was pretty bright for a youngster. Ari evidently saw something I didn't. Now so does Yanni."

"Yanni?"

"He wrote me a long letter. A long letter. He told me what you were working on. Said you were crazy, but you were getting somewhere. That you were getting integrations on deep-sets that he could see, and that he'd run them through Sociology's computers and gotten nothing—indeterminate, insufficient data, field too wide. That sort of thing. Sociology hates like hell to have its computers give answers like that; you can imagine how nervous it makes them."

Jordan started back to the table with the tea, and sat down. Justin dropped into his chair, shivering from too little sleep, too late hours. And leaned on his folded arms and listened, that was all.

"Ariane Emory helped map those sociology programs," Jordan said. "So did I. So did Olga Emory and James Carnath and a dozen others. You've at least handed them something that exceeds their projective range, that the computer's averaging can't handle. It's what I said. *I don't know* is a disturbing projection—when it comes from the machines that hold the whole social paradigm. Sociology, I think, is less interested in what you've done than in the fact that your designs refuse projection: Sociology's computers are very sensitive to negatives. That's what they're programmed to turn up."

He knew that.

"And there's either no negative in the run or it can't find it. It carried it through thirty generations and kept getting an *I don't know*. That may be why Administration sent you here. Maybe Reseune is suddenly interested. I am. They have to wonder if I'd lie—or lie to myself—because I'm your father. . . ."

Justin opened his mouth and stopped. So did Jordan stop, waiting on him; and there were the guards, there was every likelihood that they were being taped for later study by Security. And maybe by Administration.

So he did not say: *They can't let me succeed. They don't want me to call their Project into question by being anything like a success.* He clamped his mouth shut.

Jordan seemed to sense the danger. He went on quietly, precisely: "And I would lie, of course. I have plenty of motives. But my colleagues at Reseune wouldn't: they know there's something in this, Yanni says so, the Sociology computers say so, and they certainly don't have ulterior motives."

They could lock me away like you, couldn't they? What doesn't get out, doesn't breach Security. No matter what it contradicts.

Except—except I said it to Denys: if I go missing from Reseune, there are questions.

"I don't know if there's a hope in hell of getting you transferred to Planys," Jordan said. "But I'll ask you the question first: do you *want* to transfer?"

He froze then, remembering the landscape outside, the desolation that closed about him with a gut-deep panic.

He hated it. For all its advantages of freedom and relief from the pressure of Reseune, Planys afflicted him with a profound terror.

He saw the disappointment on Jordan's face. "You've answered me," Jordan said.

"No, I haven't. —Look, I've got a problem with this place. But it's something I could overcome. You did."

"Say I had a limited choice. Your choice is real. That's what you can't overcome. No. I understand. Your feelings may change with time. But let's not add that to the problems. We're certainly going to have Yanni in the loop. No way they're going to let us send anything anywhere without someone checking it for content. We'll just work on it—as we can, when we can. They're curious right now, I'm sure. They aren't so locked on their Project they can't see the potential in an unrelated idea. And that, son, is both a plus and a minus. You see how concerned they are for my well-being."

"Ser," the guard said.

"Sorry," Jordan said, and sighed, staring at Justin for a long while with somber emotions playing freely across his face.

Not free here, not as free as seems on the surface.

Succeed and gain protection; and absolutely protected, become an absolute prisoner.

He felt a lump in his throat, part grief, part panic. For a terrible moment he wanted to leave, now, quickly, before the dawn. But that was foolishness. He and Jordan had so little time. That was why they stayed awake and drove themselves over the edge, into too much honesty.

Dammit, he left a kid, and I'm not sure how he sees me. As a man? Or just as someone grown? Maybe not even someone he knows very well. I know him and he knows so little what I am now.

Damn them for that.

There's no way to recover it. We can't even say the things to each other that would let us know each other. Emotions are the thing we can't give away to our jailers.

He looked away, he looked at Paul, sitting silent at the table, and thought that their life must be like his with Grant—a pressured frustration of things they dared not say.

It's no different from Reseune, here, he thought. *Not for Jordan. Not really, no matter what the appearance they put on it. He can't talk. He doesn't dare.*

Nothing, for us, is different from Reseune.

ii

"Working late?" the Security guard asked, stopping in the doorway, and Grant's heart jumped and kept up a frantic beat as he looked up from his desk.

"Yes," he said.

"Ser Warrick's out today?"

"Yes."

"Is he sick?"

"No."

Where Justin was fell under Administrative need-to-know. That was one of the conditions. There were things he could not say, and the silence was irritating to a born-man. The man stared at him a moment, grunted and frowned and continued on his rounds.

Grant let go his breath, but the tension persisted, the downside of an adrenaline rush, fear that had only grown from the time Justin had told him he was going to Planys.

Justin was going—alone, because that was one of the conditions Administration imposed. He had brushed off Justin's worry about him and refused to discuss it, because Justin would go under whatever conditions, Justin had to go: Grant had no question about it.

But he was afraid, continually, a fear that grew more acute when he saw the plane leave the ground and when he walked back into Reseune alone.

It was partly ordinary anxiety, he told himself: he relied on Justin; they had not been apart since the incidents around Ari's death, and separation naturally brought back bad memories.

But he was not legally Justin's ward. He was Reseune's; and as long as Justin was not there to obstruct Administration and to use Jordan's leverage to protect him, he had no protection and no rights. Justin was at risk, traveling completely in the hands of Reseune Security—which might arrange an incident; but much more likely that they might take an azi down to the labs where they could question him or, the thing he most feared, run tape on him.

There was no good in panic, he told himself, since there was nothing, absolutely nothing he could do about it, nowhere he could hide and nothing he could do, ultimately, to stop them if that was what they intended.

But the first night that he had been alone with all the small lonely sounds of a very large apartment and no knowledge what was happening on the other side of the world, he had shot himself with one of the adrenaline doses they kept, along with knock-out doses of trank, in the clinical interview room; and taken kat on top of it.

Then he had sat down crosslegged at the side of his bed, and dived down into the innermost partitions he had made in himself, altering things step by step in a concentration that slicked his skin with sweat and left him dizzy and weak.

He had not been sure that he could do it; he was not sure when he exited the haze of the drug and the effort, that the combination of adrenaline and cataphoric would serve, but his heart was going like a hammer and he was able to do very little more after that than fall face down on the bed and count the beats of his heart, hoping he had not killed himself.

Fool was the word for a designer who got into his own sets and started moving them around.

Not much different, though, from what the test-unit azi did, when they organized their own mental compartmentalizations and controlled the extent to which they integrated new tape. It was a question of knowing one's own mental map, very, very thoroughly.

He turned off the computer, turned off the lights and locked the office door on his way out, walking the deserted hall to go back to that empty apartment and wait through another night.

Azi responses, dim and primal, said go to another Supervisor. Find help. Take a pill. Accept no stress in deep levels.

Of course doing the first was extremely foolish: he was not at all tempted. But taking a pill and sleeping through the night under sedation was very, very tempting. If he sedated himself deeply enough he could get through the night and go meet Justin's plane in the morning: it was only reasonable, perhaps even advisable, since the trank itself would present a problem to anyone who came after him, and if they were going to try anything at the last moment—

No, it was a very simple matter to delay a plane. They could always get more time, if they suddenly decided they needed it.

Mostly, he decided, he did not trank himself because he felt there was some benefit in getting through this without it; and that thought, perhaps, did not come from the logical underside of his mind—except that he saw value in endocrine-learning, which the constantly reasonable, sheltered, take-a-tape-and-feel-good way did not let happen. If it were an azi world everything would be black and white and very, very clear. It was the grays of flux-thinking that made born-men. Shaded responses in shaded values, acquired under endocrine instability.

He did not enjoy pain. But he saw value in the by-product.

He also saw value in having the trank in his pocket, a double dose loaded in a hypospray, because if they tried to take him anywhere, he could give them a real medical emergency to worry about.

iii

Nelly, Ari reflected, was still having her troubles.

"We have to be careful with her," Ari said to Florian and Catlin, in a council in Florian and Catlin's room, while Nelly was in the dining room helping Seely clean up.

"Yes, sera," Florian said earnestly; Catlin said nothing, which was normal: Catlin always let Florian talk if she agreed. Which was not to say Catlin was shy. She was just that way.

And Nelly had taken severe exception to Catlin showing Ari how to do an over-the-shoulder throw in the living room.

"You'll hurt yourself!" Nelly had cried. "Florian, Catlin, you should have better sense!"

Actually, it was Florian who was the one with the complaint coming, since Florian was the one on the floor. He was being the Enemy. Florian was all right: he could land and come right back up again, but Catlin wasn't teaching her what to do next, just first, and Florian was lying down being patient while Catlin was showing her how to make sure he wouldn't get up.

Nelly had heard the thump, that was all, and come flying in after Florian was down in the middle of the rug. Catlin was demonstrating how to break somebody's neck, but she was doing it real slow. If Catlin was really doing it and pulling it, she was so fast you could hardly see what she did. Catlin and Florian had showed her how to fall down and roll right up again. It was marvelous what they could do.

Sometimes they played Ambush, when they had the suite to themselves. You turned out the lights and had to find your way through.

She was *always* the one who was Got. That was all right. She was getting harder to Get and she was learning things all the time. It was a lot more fun than Amy Carnath.

Florian showed her a whole lot of things about computers and how to set Traps and do real nasty things with a Minder, like blow somebody up if you had a bomb, but they kept those down in the Military section. She knew about voice-prints and how the Minder knew who you were, and how handprint locks were linked into the House computer, along with retina-scans and all sorts of things; and how to make the electric locks open without a keycard.

Florian found out a lot of things, real fast. He said the House residential locks were all a special kind that was real hard to get past. He said that uncle Denys' apartment had a lot of interesting stuff, like really *special* special locks, that were tied in somewhere Florian couldn't trace, but he thought it was Security: he said he could try to find out, but he could get in trouble and they were Olders and he would do it only if she wanted.

He wouldn't tell her that until they were outside, because he and Catlin had found out other things.

Like the Minder could listen to you.

It was a special kind, Florian had told her: it could hear anything and see anything, and it was specially quiet, so you never knew; and specially shielded, with the tape functions somewhere outside the apartment. The lenses and the pickups could be small as pinheads, the lenses could be fish-eyed and the pickups could be all kinds, motion detection and sound. "They can put one of those in the walls," Florian said, "and it's so tiny and so transparent you can't see it unless you go over the walls with a bright light sort of sideways, or if you've got equipment, which is the best, but they have real good focus. Then they can digitalize and you can get it a lot tighter than that. Same with the audio. They can run a voice-stress on you. If they want something they can get it. That's if they want to. It's a lot of work. Most Minders are real simple and you can get into them. The ones in the House are all the complicated kind, all security, all built-ins, and it's really hard to spot all the pickups if they set them into the cement between stones and stuff."

That had made her feel real upset. "Even in the *bathroom*?" she had asked.

Florian had nodded. "Especially, because if you're setting up surveillance, they're going to try to go places they don't think they'll have a bug."

She had gone to uncle Denys then, and asked, worried:

"Uncle Denys, is there a bug in my bathroom?"

And uncle Denys had said: "Who told you that?"

"Is there?"

"It's for Security," uncle Denys had said. "Don't worry about it. They don't turn them on unless they have to."

"I don't want it in my bathroom!"

"Well, you're not a thief, either, dear, are you? And if you were, the alarm would go off in Security and the Minder would watch and listen. Don't worry."

"Yes, ser," she said; and had Florian go over the whole bathroom till he found the lenses and the pickups and put a dab of clay over them. Except the one in the wall-speaker. So she hung a towel over it, and Nelly kept moving it, but she always put it back.

Florian found the ones in the bedroom too, but uncle Denys called her in and told her Security had found the bathroom pickups dead in a regular test they ran, and he would let her cover up the bathroom ones, but the rest were apartment Security, and she had better not mess with them.

So they hadn't.

That wasn't the only Security, either. Catlin said Seely was Security. So was Abban, Giraud's azi. She could tell. Florian said he thought so too.

Catlin taught her things too: how to stand so still nobody could hear you, and where all the spots were that you ought to hit for if somebody attacked you.

So uncle Denys didn't need to worry so much about security all the time, and didn't need to worry about her being in the halls. And when maman's letter came—it had to come, soon; she had the months figured out—then she could take care of herself going to Fargone.

She was a lot more scared of going where there were strangers than she had ever been, since she had begun to understand there were a lot of people outside Reseune who wanted to break into places and steal and a lot who would kill you or grab you and steal *you*; but at least it was a scared that knew how to spot somebody being wrong; and she was learning how to handle nasty people more than by getting Hold of them and Working them.

She would really like to do it to Amy Carnath.

But that was where you stopped thinking about like-to and knew how wide that would go, all over the place, and Amy would really be dead, which meant something you couldn't take back and you couldn't Work and you couldn't get Hold of.

You got a lot more by Working people, if you had the time.

That was something she showed Florian and Catlin a little about. But not too much. First, they were azi, and you couldn't push them and it was hard to show them without *doing* it; and, second, she didn't want them learning how to do it at her.

For one thing she had to be best at it. She was their Super.

For another, they made her scared sometimes; sometimes she really wanted them, and sometimes she wished she didn't have them, because they made her mad and they made her laugh and they made her think sometimes, in the middle of the night, that she shouldn't like them that much, because maman might not let them come.

She didn't know why she thought that, but it hurt a lot, and she hated it when people made her scared; and she hated it when people made her hurt.

"We shouldn't get in trouble," she said to Florian and Catlin, when they were in the room after Nelly had scolded them; and finally, because it was on her mind, sneaked up on what she had been wanting to tell them for a long time, but it was hard to put words on it and it made her stomach upset. "I know a lot of people who aren't here anymore. You get in trouble and they get Disappeared."

"What's that?" Florian asked.

"They just aren't here anymore."

"Dead?" Catlin asked.

Her heart jumped. She shook her head, hard. "Just Disappeared. Out to Fargone or somewhere." The next was hard to talk about. She warned them with her face to be real quiet or she would be mad, because it wasn't Nelly she was going to talk about. "My maman and her azi got Disappeared. She didn't want to. Uncle Denys said she had real important business out on Fargone. Maybe that's so. Maybe it isn't. Maybe it's what they tell you because you're a kid. A lot of kids got Disappeared, too. That's why I'm real careful. You've got to be careful."

"If anybody Disappears us," Catlin said, "we'll come back."

That was like Catlin. Catlin *would*, too, Ari thought, or at least Catlin and Florian would do a lot of damage.

"My maman is real smart," she said, "and Ollie is real strong, and I'm not sure they just grab you. I think maybe they Work you, you know, they psych you."

"Who's our Enemy?" Florian asked.

It was the way they thought. Her heart beat hard. She had never, ever talked about it with anyone. She had never, ever thought about it the way the azi did, without being in the middle of it. Things suddenly made sense when you thought the way they did, straight and plain, without worrying. And when you thought: what if it *could* be an Enemy? She sat trying to think about who could do things like grab people and psych people and Disappear strong grown-up people without them being able to do anything about it.

She dragged Florian real close and whispered right into his ear between her two hands, the way you had to do if you really wanted something to be secret, because of the Minder—and if they were talking about an Enemy, you didn't know where you were safe. "I think it might be Giraud. But he's not a regular Enemy. He can give you orders. He can give Security orders."

Florian looked real upset. Catlin elbowed him and he leaned over and whispered in Catlin's ear the same way.

Then Catlin looked scared, and Catlin didn't do that.

She pulled Catlin close and whispered: "That's the only one I know could have Got my maman."

Catlin whispered in her ear: "Then you have to Get him first."

"He might not be it!" she whispered.

She sat and she thought, while Catlin passed it to Florian. Florian said something back, and then leaned forward and said to her:

"We shouldn't be talking about this now."

She looked at Florian, upset.

"An Older is real dangerous," Florian said. And in the faintest whisper of all: "Please, sera. Tomorrow. Outside."

They understood her, then. They believed her, not just because they were azi. What she said made sense to them. She tucked up her legs in her arms and felt shaky and stupid and mad at herself; and at the same time thought she had not put a lot of things together because she hadn't had any way of making it make sense. She had thought things just happened because they happened, because they had always happened and the world was that way. But that was stupid. It wasn't just things that happened, people made things happen, and Florian and Catlin knew that the way she should have known it if it hadn't always been there, all the time.

What's unusual? was a game they played. Florian or Catlin would say: What's unusual in the living room? And they timed how long it took you to find it. Once or twice she beat Catlin and once she beat Florian at finding it; a couple of times she set things up they had to give on. She wasn't stupid about things like that. But she felt that way about this.

The stupid part was thinking things had to be the way they were.

The stupid part was that she had thought when maman went away, that someone had made her go, but then she had just fitted everything together so that wasn't so important—if maman had had to go without her, it was because she was too young and it was too dangerous. And *that* was what she had been looking at, when the Something Unusual was sitting right in plain sight beside it.

The stupid part now was the way she still didn't want to think all the way to the end of it, about how if there was an enemy and he Got maman, she didn't really know whether maman was all right; and she was scared.

She remembered arguing with uncle Denys about the party last year. And her not wanting Giraud to come; and uncle Denys said: *That's not nice, Ari. He's my brother.*

That was scary too.

That was scary, because uncle Giraud might get uncle Denys to do things. Uncle Giraud had Security; and they might get into her letters. They might just stop the letters going to maman at all.

And that tore up *everything*.

Stupid. Stupid.

She felt sick all over. And she couldn't ask uncle Denys what was true. Denys would say: *He's my brother*.

---

iv

Giraud poured more water and drank, tracking on the reports, bored while the tutors argued over the relative merits of two essays, one out of archives, one current.

Denys, Peterson, Edwards, Ivanov, and Morley: all of them around a table, discussing the implications of vocabulary choice in eight-year-olds. It was not Giraud's field. It was, God help them, Peterson's.

"The verbal development," Peterson said, in the stultifying murmur that was Peterson in full display, "is point seven off, the significant anomaly in the Gonner Developmentals. . . ."

"I don't think there's any cause for worry," Denys said. "The difference is Jane and Olga, not Ari and Ari."

"Of course there is some argument that the Gonner battery is weighted away from concept. Hermann Poling maintained in his article in—"

It went on. Giraud drew small squares on his notepaper. Peterson did good work. Ask him a question, he had a pre-recorded lecture. Teacher's disease. Colleagues and strangers got the same as his juvenile subjects.

"In sum," Giraud said, finally, when the water was at half in his glass, and his paper was full of squares. "In sum, in brief, then, you believe the difference was Olga."

"The Poling article—"

"Yes. Of course. And you don't think corrective tape is necessary."

"The other scores indicate a very substantial correspondence—"

"What John means—" Edwards said, "is that she's understanding everything, she knows the words, but so much of her development was precocious, she had an internal vocabulary worked out that for her is a kind of shorthand."

"There may be a downside effect to insisting on a shift of vocabulary," Denys said. "Possibly it *doesn't* describe what she's seeing. She simply prefers slang and her own internal jargon, which I haven't tried to discourage. She does know the words, the tests prove that. Also, I'm not certain we're seeing the whole picture. I rather well think she's resisting some of the exams."

"Why?"

"Jane," Denys said. "The child hasn't forgotten. I hoped the letters would taper off with time. I hoped that the azi could make a difference in that."

"You don't think," Edwards said, "that the way that was handled—tended to make her cling to that stage; I mean, a subconscious emphasis on that stage of her life, a clinging to those memories, a refusal—as it were, to leave that stage, a kind of waiting."

"That's an interesting theory," Giraud said, leaning forward on his arms. "Is there any particular reason?"

"The number of times she says: 'My maman said—' The tone of voice."

"I want a voice-stress on that," Denys said.

"No problem," Giraud said. "It's certainly worth pursuing. Does she reference other people?"

"No," Edwards said.

"Not family members. Not friends. Not the azi."

"Nelly. 'Nelly says.' When it regards something about home. Sometimes 'my uncle Denys doesn't mind' this or that. . . . She doesn't respect Nelly's opinions, she doesn't respect much Nelly says, but she evidences a desire not to upset her. 'Uncle Denys' is a much more respectful reference, but more that she uses the name as currency. She's quite willing to remind you that 'my uncle Denys' takes an interest in things." Edwards cleared his throat. "Quite to the point, she hints her influence with 'uncle Denys' can get me a nicer office."

Denys snorted in surprise, and laughed then, to Edwards' relief. "Like the party invitation?"

"Much the same thing."

"What about Ollie?" Giraud asked.

"Quite rarely. Almost never. I'm being precise now. I'd say she used to mention Ollie right after Jane left. Now—I don't think I've heard that name in a long time. Maybe more than a year."

"Interesting. Justin Warrick?"

"She never mentions him. I did, if you recall. She was quite anxious to quit the subject. That name never comes up."

"Worth the time on the computers to run a name search," Denys said.

On all those tapes. On years of tapes. Giraud let his breath flow out and nodded. More personnel. More time on the computers.

Dammit, there was pressure outside. A lot of pressure. They were prepared to go public finally, to break the story; and they had an anomaly; they had a child far less serious than the first Ari, far more capricious and more restrained in temper. The azi had not helped. There was a little more seriousness to the child lately, a little gain in vocabulary: Florian and Catlin were better at essay than she was, but the hard edge was not there, maman was still *with* Ari in a very persistent sense, and the Warrick affair, Yanni's sudden revelation that young Justin had handed them something that stymied the Sociology computers—

Give it to Jordan, Denys had suggested. Send *him* to Jordan. The Warricks are far less likely to cause trouble with the Project if they're busy, and you know Jordan would work on the damned thing, no matter what it was, if it gave him a chance to see his son.

Which was trouble with Defense: they were jealous of Warrick's time. There was a chance Defense would take official interest in Justin Warrick: there was no way to run him past their noses unnoticed, and in the way of Defense, Defense wanted anything that might seem to be important, or useful, or suddenly anomalous.

Damn, and damn.

Ari wanted him, Yanni had said. *And, dammit, there's something there.*

There was the paradox of the Project: how wide the replication had to be. How many individuals, essential to each other? Thank God the first Ari's society had been extremely limited in terms of personal contacts—but it had been much more open in terms of news-services and public contact from a very early age.

"We've got to go ahead," Giraud said. "Dammit, we've got to take her public, for a whole host of reasons, Lu's out of patience and we're running out of time! We can't be wrong, there's no way we can afford to be wrong."

No one said anything. It was too evident what the stakes were.

"The triggers are all there," Petros said. "Not all of them have been invoked. I think a little more pressure. Academic will do. Put it on her. Frustrate her. Give her things she's bound to fail in. Accelerate the program."

That had consistently been Petros' advice.

"She hasn't met intellectual frustration," Denys said, "—yet."

"We don't want her bloody bored with school, either," Giraud snapped. "Maybe it *is* an option. What do the computers say lately, when they're not running Warrick's school projects?"

"Do we run it again?" Peterson asked. "I don't think there's going to be a significant change. I just don't believe you can discount the results we have. Accelerating the program when there's an anomaly in question—"

Petros leaned forward, jaw jutting. "Allowing the program to stagnate while the anomaly proliferates is your answer, is it?"

"Dr. Ivanov, allow me to make my point—"

"I *know* your damn point, we *know* your damn point, doctor."

Giraud poured another glass of water.

"Enough on it," he said. "Enough. We run the damn tests. We take the computer time. We get our answers. Let's have the query in tomorrow, can we do that?"

Mostly, he thought, the voice-stress was the best lead. All those lesson-sessions to scan.

The Project ate computer time at an enormous rate. And the variances kept proliferating.

So did the demands of the Council investigating committee, that wanted to get into documents containing more and more details of Science Bureau involvement in the Gehenna project, because Alliance was asking hard questions, wanting more and more information on the Gehenna colonists, and linking it to the betterment of Alliance-Union relations.

The Centrists and the Abolitionists wanted the whole archives opened. Giraud's intelligence reported Mikhail Corain was gathering evidence, planning to call for a Council bill of Discovery to open the entire Emory archives, charging that there were other covert projects, other timebombs waiting, and that the national security took precedence over Reseune's sovereignty: that Reseune had no right to the notes and papers which Ariane Emory had accrued while serving as Councillor for Science, that those became Union property on her death, and that a bill of Discovery was necessary to find out what was Reseune's and what of Emory's papers belonged to Union archives.

There were timebombs, for certain. The essential one was aged eight, and exposing her to the vitriol and the hostility in Novgorod—making her the center of controversy—

Everything came down to that critical point. They had to go public.

Before they ended up with a Discovery bill opening all Ari's future secrets into public view, where a precocious eight-year-old could access them out of sequence.

V

In mornings it was always lessons, and Ari took hers with Dr. Edwards in his office or in the study lab, but it was not just mornings now, it was after lunch in the library and the tape-lab, so there was a lot of follow-up and Dr. Edwards asked her questions and gave her tests.

Catlin and Florian had lessons every day too, their own kind, down in the Town at a place they called Green Barracks; and one day a week they had to stay in Green Barracks overnight. That was when they did a Room or did special drill. But most times they were able to meet her at the library or the lab and walk her home.

They did this day, both of them very proper and solemn in their black uniforms, but more solemn than usual, when they walked down to the doors and out to the crosswalk.

"This is as safe as we can find to talk," Catlin said.

"But you don't know," Florian said. "There's equipment that can hear you this far if they want to. You can't say they won't, you can just keep changing places so if they're not really expecting you to say something they want right then they won't bother. Set-up is a lot of work if your Subject moves around a lot."

"If they didn't hear us last night, I don't think they would be onto us," Ari said. She knew how to be nice enough not to get in trouble without being too nice and making people think she was up to something. But she didn't say that. She walked with them along toward the fishpond. She had brought food in her pocket. "What were you going to tell me?"

"It's this," said Catlin. "You should hit your Enemy first if you can. But you have to be sure, first thing, *who* it is. Then how many, where are they, what have they got? That's the next thing you have to find out."

"When your Enemy is an Older," Florian said, "it's real hard to know that, because they know so much more."

"If he's not expecting it," Catlin said, "anybody can be Got."

"But if we try and miss," Florian said, "they *will* try to Disappear us. So we're not sure, sera. I think we could Get them. For real. I could steal some stuff that would. They put it in Supply, and they're real careless. They ought to fix that. But I can get it. And we could kill the Enemy, just it's real dangerous. You get one chance with an Older. Usually just one."

"But if you don't know where his partners are," Catlin said, "they'll Get you. It depends on how much that's worth."

That made a lot of things she was thinking fall into place. Click. She walked along with her hands in her pockets and said: "And if you don't know all those things, it's more than getting caught; it's not knowing what one to grab next. There's things that run all over Reseune, there's what his partners are going to do, there's who's friends and who's not, and who's going to take Hold of things, and we can't do that."

"I don't know," Florian said. "You'd have to know those things, sera, we wouldn't. I know we could Get one, maybe two, if we split up, or if we could get the targets together. That's the main ones. But it's not near all the ones that would be after us."

They reached the fishpond. Ari knelt down at the edge of the water and took the bag of fish-food out of her pocket. Catlin and Florian squatted beside her. "Here," she said, passing them the bag to get their own, and then tossed a bit into the water for the white one that came up, from under the lilies. White-and-red was almost as fast. She watched the rings go out from the food, and from the strike, and the lilies swaying. "He's not easy," she said finally. "We can't Get everything. There are too many hook-ups. Connections. He's important; he's got a lot of people, not just in Reseune, and what he's got—Security, for one thing. I don't know what else. So even if he was gone—" It was strange and upsetting to be talking about killing somebody. It didn't feel real. But it was. Florian and Catlin really could do it. She was not sure that made her feel safer, but it made her feel less like things were closing in on her. "—We'd still be in trouble.

"Also," she said, "they could Get my maman and Ollie. For real." They didn't understand that part, she thought, because they had never had a maman, but they looked at her like they took it very seriously. "I'm afraid they could have. They're at Fargone. I sent letters. They should have got there by now. Now I'm not sure—" Dammit, she was going to snivel. She saw Florian and Catlin look at her all distressed. "—I'm not sure," she said in a rush, hard and mad, "they ever got sent."

They didn't understand, for sure. She tried to think of what she had left out they had to know.

"If there is an Enemy," she said, "I don't know what they want. Sometimes I thought maman left me here because it was too dangerous to go with her. Sometimes I thought she left me here because they made her. But I don't know why, and I don't know why she didn't tell me."

The azi didn't say anything for a minute. Then Florian said: "I don't think I'd try to say. I don't think Catlin can. It's CIT. I don't understand CITs."

"CITs have connections," she said. It was like telling them how to Work someone. She felt uneasy telling them. She explained, making a hook out of two fingers to hook together. "To other CITs. Like you to Catlin and Catlin to you and both of you to me. Sometimes not real strong. Sometimes real, real strong. That's the first thing. CITs do things *for* each other, sometimes because it feels good, sometimes because they're Working each other. And sometimes they do things to Get each other. A lot of times it's to protect themselves, sometimes their connections: connections are a lot more in danger, sometimes, if you don't let your Enemy be sure where *your* connections are, and whether some of them are to people he's connected to. Like building-sticks."

Wide, attentive stares. Anxious stares. Even from Catlin.

"So you can Work somebody to make them do something if you want to, if you tell him you'll hurt him or hurt somebody he's connected to. Like if somebody was going to hurt me, you'd react." While she was saying it she thought: *So it's maman they must want something out of, because maman's important. If that's true she's all right. They're Working her with me.*

It couldn't be the other way. They haven't told me they'd hurt maman.

Could that be?

But they're Olders, like Florian says, and they always know more and they don't tell you everything you need.

"That's one way to Work people," she said. "There's others. Like finding out what they want and almost doing it and then not, if they don't make you happy. But maman wouldn't leave me just for something she wanted."

Would she?

Is there anything she would want more than me?

Ollie?

"There's ways to Get someone that way," she said, "instead of just Working them. You get them to get in trouble. It's not real hard. Except you have to know—"

What can get Giraud in trouble?

What could I get instead if I could Work him like that?

"—you have to know the same things: who are they, how many are there, what have they got? It's the same thing. But you can find out by Working them a *little* and then watching what they do."

Their eyes never left her. They were learning, that was what, they were paying attention the way azi could, and they would never ask questions until she was done.

"Me," she said, thinking carefully about how much she was giving away, "I don't give anybody anything I don't have to. They take Nelly in and they ask her stuff and she'll tell them right off. I can't Work that. I wish I could. But if they try to take you, I'll Work them good. It's easier. Uncle Denys said you're mine. So if Security tells you to go to hospital, you go right to me first. That's an order. All right?"

"Yes, sera." One movement, one nod at the same time.

"But," Florian said, "we're not like Nelly. Nobody but you can give us orders. They'd have to go to you first and you have to tell us. That's the Rule, because otherwise we're supposed to Get them."

She had not known that. She had never even suspected that. It made her feel a lot better in one way, and feel threatened in another. Like everything had always been a lot more serious than she had thought. And they had always known. "If you come to me, I'll tell them no. But they're stronger than you are."

"That's so," Catlin said. "But that's the Rule. And they know it. Nobody else's orders."

She drew a long breath. "Even if uncle Denys is a Super."

"Not for us," Catlin said. "You told us mind him. And Nelly. We'll do that. But if it's any big thing we come to you."

"You come to me first after this, if it's anything more than a 'pick that up.' You don't go anywhere they tell you and you don't go with anybody they tell you, until after you tell me."

"Good. If you tell us that, that's the Rule."

"You be sneaky about it. Don't fight. Just get away."

"That's smart. That's real good, sera."

"And you don't ever, ever tell on me, no matter who asks. You lie if you have to. You be real smooth and then you come and tell me what they asked."

"Yes, sera." Both of them nodded, definitely.

"Then I'll tell you a big secret. I never tell anybody everything. Like on my exam this morning, I could have put down more. But I won't. You don't let anybody but me know what you really know."

"Is that a Rule?"

"That's a big Rule. There's a boy named Sam: I used to play with him. He's the one that gave me the bug. He's not real smart, but everybody likes Sam—and I figured out it's easier to *be* Sam most of the time. That way I can get a lot of people to be nicer: that way even stupid people can understand everything I need them to if I'm going to Work them. But they can't know you're not like that, you can't let them find out from anybody. So you do it all the time. I learned that from Sam and uncle Denys. He does it. He's smart, he always uses little words, and he's real good at getting points on people. That's one thing you do. You don't want them to know you're doing it unless that's part of the Working. And we don't. So here's what we do. We start being real nice to Giraud. But not right off. The first thing we do is shake him up. Then we let him yell, then we act like he yelled too much, then we get him to do something nice to make up for it. Then he won't be surprised when we start being nice, because he thinks he's Working *us*. That's how you Work an Older."

"That's sneaky," Catlin said, and actually grinned.

"I'll tell you another secret. I've been counting What's Unusuals. It's

Unusual that people Disappear. It's Unusual that maman didn't tell me she was going or even say goodbye. It's Unusual Nelly goes to the hospital all the time. It's Unusual a CIT kid has two azi to Super. It's Unusual I have to get my blood tested every few days. It's Unusual I go to adult parties and other kids don't. It's Unusual I'm so smart. It's Unusual you're on a job when you're still kids. I'm still counting the Unusuals. I think there's a lot of them. A whole lot. I want you to think and tell me all the ones you know. And tell what you can do to find out stuff without getting caught."

vi

The plane touched and braked and rolled toward the terminal, and Grant gave a sigh of profoundest relief, watching it from the windows.

There was still a lot to wait through: there was a Decon procedure for anything coming in from the other hemisphere, not just the passengers having to go through Decontamination, but the luggage had to be treated and searched, and the plane itself had to be hosed down and fumigated.

That was starting when Grant left the windows and walked over to the Decon section and stationed himself outside the white doors, hands locked between his knees, flexing and clenching—nervous tic, that. You have a lot of tension, a Supervisor would tell him, who saw it.

A Supervisor could say that about any CIT anytime, Grant reckoned. Flux-thinking bred it. Azi-mindset said: there's not enough data to solve the problem, and the sane and sensible azi filed it and blanked out to rest or worked on another problem. A CIT threw himself at a data-insufficient problem over and over, exploring the flux in his perceptions and shades of value in his opinions, and touching off his endocrine system, which in turn brought up his flux-capable learning—which hyped the integrative processes in the flux. He was doing too much of it lately for his liking. He hated the stress level CITs lived at.

And here he was sitting here worrying about four and five problems at once, simply because he had become an adrenaline addict.

The white doors opened. Part of the crew came out. They ignored him and walked on down the hall.

Then the doors opened again, and Justin came through. Grant got up, caught the relief and the delight in Justin's expression and went and hugged him because Justin offered him open arms.

"Are you all right?" Grant asked.

"I'm fine. Jordan's fine." Justin pulled him out of the way of more people coming out the doors, and walked with him behind them. "Got to pick up my briefcase and my bag," he said, and they walked to Baggage, where it was waiting, fogged, irradiated, and, Grant reckoned, searched and scanned, case and light travel bag alike.

"I'll carry them," Grant said.

"I've got them." Justin gathered everything up and they walked to the doors, to the waiting bus that would take them up to the House.

"Was it a good trip?" Grant said, when they were where no eavesdropper could likely pick it up, going out the doors into the dark.

"It was," Justin said, and gave the bags to the azi baggage handler.

Security was in the bus, ordinary passengers like themselves, from this point. They sat down, last aboard. The driver shut the doors and Justin slumped in the seat as the bus pulled out of the lighted portico of the terminal and headed up toward the house.

"I got to talk to Jordan. We stayed up all night. Just talking. We both wished you were there."

"So do I."

"It's a lot better there than I thought it was. A lot worse in some ways and a lot better. There's a good staff. Really fine people. He's getting along a lot better than I thought he would. And Paul is fine. Both of them." Justin was a little hoarse. Exhausted. He leaned his head on the seat-back and said: "He's going to look at my projects. He says at least there's something there that the computers aren't handling. That he's interested and he's not just saying that to get me there. There's a good chance I can go back before the year's out. Maybe you too. Or you instead. He'd really like to see you."

"I'm glad," Grant said.

There was not much they could say, in detail. He *was* glad. Glad when they pulled up in the portico of the House, checked in through the front door, and Justin doggedly, stubbornly, insisted to carry his own baggage, tired as he was.

"You don't carry my bags," Justin snapped at him, hoarsely.

Because Justin hated him playing servant in public, even when he was trying to do him an ordinary favor.

But Justin let him take them and put them over against the wall when they were inside, in their own apartment, and Justin took his coat off and fell onto the couch with a sigh. "It was good," he said. "All the way. It's hard to believe I was there. Or that I'm back. It's so damned different."

"Whiskey?"

"A little one. I slept on the plane. I'm out, already."

Grant smiled at him, Justin half-nodding with time-lag. He went and fixed the whiskey, never mind now that he was playing servant. He made two of them.

"How's it been here?" Justin asked, and there was a small upset at Grant's stomach.

"Fine," he said. "Just fine." The upset was more when he brought the drink and gave it into Justin's hand.

Justin took it. His hand shook when he drank a sip of it, and Justin looked up at him with the most terrible, weary look. And smiled with the same expression as he lifted the glass in a wry toast. There was no way for either of them to know, of course, whether the other had been tampered with.

But that was all right: there was nothing either of them could do about it, if Security had done anything. There was nothing, Grant thought, worth the fight for either of them if that was the case.

Grant lifted his glass the same way, and drank.

Then he went to the bedroom and pulled a note out from under Justin's pillow. He brought it back to him.

If I'm showing this to you, it said, *I'm in my right mind. If I didn't, and you just found it, I'm not. Be warned.*

Justin looked at him in frightened surmise. And then in earnest question.

Grant smiled at him, wadded up the note, and sat down to drink his whiskey.

vii

It wasn't hard at all to get out the kitchen way. They didn't go together. Catlin and Florian went first because they were Security and the kitchen staff wouldn't know they shouldn't: Security went everywhere.

Then Ari went in. She Worked her way through, made herself a pest to the azi who was mixing up batter, and got a taste, then went over to the azi chopping up onions and said it made her cry. So she went out onto the kitchen steps and dived right off and down, and ran fast to get down the hill, where the hump was Florian and Catlin told her about.

She slid down on her back and rolled over and grinned as they looked at her, lying on their stomachs too.

"Come on," Catlin said then. She was being Team Leader. She was the best at sneaking.

So they followed her, slithered down to the back of the pump building where she stripped off her blouse and her pants and put on the ones Florian gave her, azi-black. Getting shoes that fit was harder, so she had bought some black boots on uncle Denys' card that worked all right if nobody looked close. And she was wearing those. Florian got her card off her blouse and taped a black band across the bottom and a mark like the azi triangle in the CIT blank.

"Do I look right?" she said when she had clipped the card on.

"Face," Catlin said. So she made an azi face, very stiff and formal.

"That's good," Catlin said.

And Catlin slithered over, looked around the corner of the pump building, then got up and walked out. They followed Catlin as far as the road, and then they just walked together like they belonged there.

It was going to take them a while to miss her up at the House, Ari thought, and then Security was going to get real upset.

Meanwhile she had never seen the Town except from the House, and she wished they could walk faster, because she wanted to see as much as she could before they got caught.

Or before she decided to go back, somewhere around dark. It was going to be fun at the same time as it was not going to be: it was going to be a lot of trouble, but she really hoped they could sneak back up and get her clothes, and just sneak back in by the kitchen, when everyone was really in a panic. But that might look too smart, and that might make them watch her too close.

It was better to be Sam, and get caught.

That way she would say she made her azi do it, and that would work, because they had to take her orders, and everybody knew that. So they wouldn't get in any trouble. She would. And that was what she wanted.

She just wanted to have a little fun before they caught her.

viii

The problem was running, the computer working timeshare on a Beta-class design and going slow this morning, because Yanni Schwartz had the integrative set running: everyone else got a lower priority. So Justin leaned back, got up, poured himself a cup of coffee, and filled Grant's empty cup, Grant working away at his terminal in that kind of fixed concentration that was not going to lose that chain of thought if the ceiling fell around him.

Grant reached over without even looking away from the screen, picked up the coffee cup and took a sip.

Someone arrived in the door, brusque, abrupt, and more than one. Justin's ears had already registered that as he looked around, saw Security black, and had a man in his office, two others behind him.

Muscles tightened, gut tightened in panic.

"You're wanted in Security," the man said.

"What for?"

"No questions. Just come with us."

He thought of the hot coffee in his hands, and Grant *had* noticed, Grant was getting up from his chair, as another Security guard moved in behind the first.

"Let's go straighten this out," Justin said calmly, and put the cup down.

"Let me shut down," Grant said.

"Now!" the officer said.

"My program—"

"Grant," Justin said, articulate, he did not know how. It was happening, the thing he had been expecting for a long, long time; and he thought of doing them all the damage he could. But it could be something he could talk his way out of. Whatever it was. And there was, whatever else, enough force at Reseune Administration's disposal to take care of two essentially sedentary tape designers, however well-exercised.

The only thing he could hope for was to keep the situation calm, the way he had mapped it out in his mind years ago. He kept his hands in sight, he got himself and Grant peacefully out the door, he walked with the Security guards without complaint, to take the lift down to the basement storm-tunnel.

The lift door opened, they walked out as the guards directed. "Hands on the wall," the officer said.

"Grant," he said, catching Grant by the arm, feeling the tension. "It's all right. We'll sort it out."

He turned to the wall himself, waited while two of them searched Grant for weapons and put on the handcuffs, then took his own turn. "I don't suppose," he said calmly as he could with his face against the wall and his arms pulled behind him, "you people know what this is about."

"Come along," the officer said, and faced him about again.

No information. After that at least the guards were less worried.

Keep to the script. Cooperate. Stay calm and give absolutely no trouble.

Through a locked door into a Security zone, lonelier and lonelier in the concrete corridors. He had never seen this part of Reseune's storm-tunnels in all his life, and he hoped to hell they *were* going to Security.

Another locked door, and a lift, with the designation SECURITY 10N on the opposing wall: he was overwhelmingly glad to see that sign.

Up, then, with extraordinary abruptness. The doors opened on a hall he did know, the back section of Security, a hall that figured in his nightmares.

"This is familiar," he said lightly, to Grant; and suddenly the guards were pulling Grant off toward one of the side rooms and himself off down the hall, toward an interview room he remembered.

"Don't we get checked in?" he asked, fighting down the panic, walking with them on legs suddenly gone shaky. "I hate to complain, but you're violating procedures all the way through this."

Neither of them spoke to him. They took him into the room, made him sit down in a hard chair facing the interview desk, and stayed there, grim and silent, behind him.

Someone else came in behind him. He turned his head and twisted to see who it was. Giraud.

"Thank God," Justin said, half meaning it. "I'm glad to see somebody who knows the answers around here. *What* in hell's going on, do you mind?"

Giraud walked on to the desk and sat down on the corner of it. Positional intimidation. Moderate friendliness. "You tell me."

"Look, Giraud, I'm not in any position to know a thing. I'm working in my office, these fellows come in and haul me over here, and I haven't even seen the check-in desk. What's going on here?"

"Where did you go for lunch?"

"I skipped lunch. We both did. We worked right through. Come on, Giraud, what does lunch have to do with anything?"

"Ari's missing."

"What do you mean missing?" His heart started doubling its beats, hammering in his chest. "Like—late from lunch? Or *missing*?"

"Maybe you know. Maybe you know all about it. Maybe you lured her outside. Maybe she just went with a friend."

"God. No."

"Something Jordan and you set up?"

"No. Absolutely not. My God, Giraud, *ask the guards at Planys*, there wasn't a time we weren't watched. Not a moment."

"That they remember, no."

It *had* reached to Jordan. He stared at Giraud, having trouble breathing.

"We're going over your apartment," Giraud said calmly. "Never mind your rights, son, we're not being recorded. I'll tell you what we've found. Ari went out the kitchen door, all right. We found her clothes at the back of the pump station."

"My God." Justin shook his head. "No. I don't know anything."

"That's a wide shore down there," Giraud said. "Easy for someone to land and get in. Is that what happened? You get the girl out to a meeting, where you don't show up, but someone else does?"

"No. No. No such thing. She's probably playing a damn *prank*, Giraud, it's a damn kid escapade—didn't you ever dodge out of the House when you were a kid?"

"We're searching the shore. We've got patrols up. You understand, we're covering all the routes."

"I wouldn't hurt that kid! I wouldn't do it, Giraud."

Giraud stared at him, face flushed, with a terrible, terrible restraint. "You'll understand we're not going to take your word."

"I understand that. Dammit, I want the kid found as much as you do."

"I doubt that."

"I'll consent. Giraud, I'll give you a consent, just for God's sake let Grant be with me."

Giraud got up.

"Giraud, does it cost you anything? Let him be here. Is that so much? *Giraud, for God's sake, let him be here!*"

Giraud left in silence. "Bring the other one," Giraud told someone in the hall.

Justin leaned against the chair arm, broken out in cold sweat, not seeing the floor, seeing Ari's apartment, seeing it in flashes that wiped out here and now. Hearing the opening of doors, the shouts in distance, the echoes of footsteps coming his way. Grant, he hoped. He hoped to God it was Grant first, and not the tech with the hypo.

ix

Olders passed them on the sidewalk and Ari kept on being azi, did just what Florian and Catlin did, made the little bow, and kept going.

They were not the only kids. There were youngers who bowed to them, solemn and earnest. And one group hardly more than babies following an Older leader in red, the youngers all in blue, all solemnly holding each other's hands.

"This is Blue," Florian said as they walked along past the string of youngers. "Mostly youngers here. I was in that building right over there when I was a Five."

They took the walk between the buildings, going farther and farther from the road that ran through the Town.

They had already seen Green Barracks, outside, because it would be hard to get out without questions, Catlin said; and they had seen the training field; and the Industry section, and they walked up and looked in the door of the thread mill; and the cloth mill; and the metal shop; and the flour mill.

The next sign on the walk was green, and then white in green. It was real easy to find a place in the town: she knew how to do it now. She knew the color sequence, and how the Town was laid out in sections, and how you could say, like they were now, red-to-white-to-brown-to-green, and you just remembered the string. That meant you went *to* red from where you were, and then you looked for red with a white square, and so on.

The next was a huge building, bigger than the mills, and they had come to the very end of the Town: fields were next, with fences that went all the way to the North Cliffs and the precip towers.

So they stood right at the edge, and looked out through the fences, where azi worked and weeded with the sniffer-pigs.

"Are there platytheres out there?" Ari asked. "Have you ever seen one?"

"I haven't," Florian said. "But they're out there." He pointed to where the cliffs touched the river. "That's where they come from. They've put concrete there. Deep. That stops them so far."

She looked all along the fence to the river, and looked along the other way, toward the big barn. There were big animals there, in a pen, far away. "What are those?"

"Cows. They feed them there. Come on. I know something better."

"Florian," Catlin said. "That's risky."

"What's risky?" Ari said.

Florian knew a side door to the barn. It was dark inside with light coming from open doors at the middle and down at the far end. The air was strange, almost good and not quite bad, like nothing she had ever smelled. The floor was dirt, and feed-bins, Florian called them, lined either wall. Then there were stalls. There was a goat in one.

Ari went to the rail and looked at it up close. She had seen goats and pigs up by the House, but never up close, because she was not supposed to go out on the grounds. It was white and brown. Its odd eyes looked at her, and she stared back with the strangest feeling it was thinking about her, it was alive and thinking, the way not even an AI could.

"Come on," Catlin whispered. "Come on, they'll see us."

She hurried with Catlin and Florian, ducked under a railing when Florian did, and followed him through a door and through a dark place and out another door into the daylight, blinking with the change.

There was a pen in front of them, and a big animal that jangled tape-memory, tapes of Earth, story-tapes of a long time ago.

"He's Horse," Florian said, and stepped up and stood on the bottom rail.

So did she. She leaned her elbows on the top rail as Catlin stepped up beside her, and just stared with her heart thumping.

He snorted and threw his head, making his mane toss. That was what you called it. A mane. He had hooves, but not like the pigs and the goats. He had a white diamond on his forehead.

"Wait," Florian said, and dived off the rail and went back in. He came back out with a bucket, and Horse's ears came up, Horse came right over and put his head over to the rail to eat out of the bucket.

Ari climbed a rail higher and put out her hand and stroked his fur. He smelled strong, and he felt dusty and very solid. Solid like Ollie. Solid and warm, like nothing in her life since Ollie.

"Has he got a saddle and a bridle?" she asked.

"What's that?" Florian asked.

"So you can ride him."

Florian looked puzzled, while Horse battered away with his head in the bucket Florian was holding. "Ride him, sera?"

"Work him close to the corner."

Florian did, so that Horse was very close to the rail. She climbed up to the last, and she put her leg out and just pushed off and landed on Horse's back.

Horse moved, real sudden, and she grabbed the mane to steer with. He felt—wonderful. Really strong, and warm.

And all of a sudden he gave a kind of a bounce and ducked his head and bounced again, really hard, so she flew off, up into the air and down again like she didn't weigh anything, the sky and the fence whirling until it was just ground.

Bang.

She was on her face, mostly. It hurt and it didn't hurt, like part of her was numb and all her bones were shaken up.

Then Catlin's voice: "Don't touch her! Careful!"

"I'm all right," she said, tasting blood and dust, but it was hard to talk, her breath was mostly gone and her stomach hurt. She moved her leg and tried to get up on her arm, and then it really hurt.

"Look out, look out, sera, don't!" Florian's knee was right in her face, and that was good, because the pain took her breath and she fell right onto his leg instead of facedown in the dirt. "Catlin, get help! Get Andy! Fast!"

"I think I needed a saddle," she said, thinking about it, trying not to snivel or to throw up, because she hurt all through her bones, worse than she had ever hurt, and her shoulder and her stomach were worst. There was still dust in her mouth. She thought her lip was cut. "Help me up," she told Florian, because lying that way hurt her back.

"No, sera, please, don't move, your arm's broken."

She tried to move on her own, to get a look at what a broken arm looked like. But she was hurting worse and worse, and she thought she would throw up if she tried.

"What did Horse do?" she asked Florian. She could not figure that.

"He just flipped his hind legs up and you flew off. I don't think he meant to, I really don't, he isn't mean."

There were people running. She heard them, she tried to move and see them, but Florian was in the way until they were all around, azi voices, quiet and concerned, telling her the meds were coming, warning her not to move.

She wished she could get up. It was embarrassing to be lying in the dirt with everyone hovering over her and her not able to see them.

She figured Giraud was going to yell, all right; that part would work real well.

She just wished the meds would hurry.

X

Grant sat with his back braced against the padded wall, with a cramp in his folded legs gone all the way to pain under Justin's weight, but he was not about to move, not about to move even his hands, one on Justin's shoulder, one on Justin's forehead, that kept him stable and secure. No movement in the cell, no sound, while the drug slowly ebbed away.

Security would not leave them unattended. There were two guards in the soundproofed, glass-walled end of this recovery cell. Rules, they said, did not permit anyone but a physician with a detainee in recovery. But Giraud had not regarded any of the rules this far. He did whatever he wanted; and permission was easy for him, an afterthought.

Justin was awake, but he was still in that de-toxing limbo where the least sensation, the least sound magnified itself and echoed. Grant kept physical contact with him, talked to him now and again to reassure him.

"Justin. It's Grant. I'm here. How are you doing?"

"All right." Justin's eyes half-opened.

"Are you clearer now?"

A little larger breath. "I'm doing all right. I'm still pretty open."

"I've got you. Nothing's going on. I've been here all the time."

"Good," Justin murmured, and his eyes drifted shut again.

Beyond that Grant did not attempt to go. Giraud had limited the questioning to the visit with Jordan and the possibility of Justin's involvement in Ari's disappearance. To reassure Justin there would be no more questions would be dangerous. There might be. To encourage him to talk, when they were likely being taped—was very dangerous, tranked as he was.

Giraud had asked: "How do you feel about young Ari?"

And Justin had said, with all his thresholds flat: "Sorry for her."

There was motion in the glass-walled booth. Grant looked up, saw Denys Nye in the room with the guards, saw them exchange words, saw the guards come and open the door into the recovery cell to let Denys in.

Grant gave Denys a hard look, locked his arms across Justin, and bent close to his ear: "Justin. Ser Denys is here, easy, I have you, I won't leave."

Justin was aware. His eyes opened.

Denys walked very quietly for so large a man. He came close and stopped, leaning near, speaking very softly. "They've found Ari. She's all right."

Justin's chest moved in a gasp after air. "Is that true?" he asked. "Grant, is he telling the truth?"

Grant glared at Denys, at a round, worried face, and gave up a little of his anger. "I think he may be." He tightened his arms again so Justin could feel his presence.

"It's true," Denys said and leaned closer, keeping his voice very, very quiet. "Justin, I'm terribly sorry. Truly I am. We'll make this up to you."

Justin's heart was hammering under his hand. "Easy," Grant said, his own heart racing while he sorted Denys' words for content. And then because he had never felt so much unadulterated anger in his entire life. "How are you going to do that, ser?" he said to Denys softly, so softly. "The child is safe. What about the rest of Reseune's resources? You're *fools*, ser. You've risked a mind whose limits you don't even know, you've persecuted him all his life, and you treat him as if he were the perpetrator of every harm in Reseune—when he's never, *never*, in his entire life—done harm to any human being, when Yanni Schwartz could tell you they took him *off* real-time because he couldn't stand people suffering. Where's Reseune's vast expertise in psychology, when it can't tell that he isn't capable of harming *anyone*, not even the people who make his life *hell*?"

"Grant," Justin murmured, "Grant, —"

Denys' brow furrowed. "No," he said in a hushed voice, "I know, I know, I'm sorry is too little, and far too late. Grant is quite right. You're going home now, you're going home. Please. Believe me. We did find Ari. She's in hospital, she had a fall, but everything's all right. She ran away on her own, disguised herself—it was a childish prank, absolutely nothing you had anything to do with, we know that. I won't stay here, I know I have no business here, but I felt I had to tell you Ari's all right. I believed you'd want to know that because you *don't* want any harm to her, and God knows you deserve some courtesy after this. I mean it. I'll make this up somehow, I promise that. I let too much go on for *security's* sake, and it's not going to go on happening. I promise that, too." He put a hand on Grant's shoulder. "Grant, there's a group of meds coming here. They'll take him the tunnel route, over to your Residency, they'll take him home, if that's what he wants. Or he can rest here till he recovers. Whatever he wants."

"Home," Grant said. "Is that right, Justin? Do you want to go home now?"

Justin nodded faintly. "I want to go home."

Carefully enunciated. More self-control than a moment ago. Justin's arm twitched and lifted and he laid it on his stomach, in the same careful way, return of conscious control.

"I promise you," Denys said tightly. "No more of this."

Then Denys left, anger in the attitude of his body.

Grant hugged Justin and laid his head against Justin's, editing the tension out of his own muscles, because Justin could read that. Azi-mind. Quiet and steady.

"Was Denys here?" Justin asked.

"He just left," Grant said. "Just a little while and you're going home. I say it's true. They found Ari, it wasn't your fault, they know that. You can rest now. Wake up at your own speed. I'm not going to leave you, not even for a minute."

Justin heaved a sigh. And was quiet then.

xi

Ari rode back home in the bus, just for that little distance, and she argued with uncle Denys until he let her walk from the front door herself, holding his hand, with the other arm in a sling; but after the ride, it was almost longer, she thought, than she was going to be able to make. Her knees were getting weak and she was sweating under her blouse, that they had had to cut because of the cast, even to get it on.

She was not going to be out in public in her nightgown and her robe. She was going to walk, herself. She was determined on that.

But she was terribly glad to see the inside of uncle Denys' apartment, and to see Nelly there, and Florian and Catlin, all looking worried and so glad to see her. Even Seely looked happy.

She felt like crying, she was so glad to see them. But she didn't. She said: "I want my bed." And uncle Denys got her there, with the last strength that she had, while Nelly fluttered ahead of them.

Nelly had her bed turned down. Poo-thing was there where he belonged. The pillows were fluffed up. It felt so good when she lay down.

"Let me help you out of your clothes," Nelly said.

"No," she said, "just let me rest a while, Nelly." And uncle Denys said that was a good idea.

"I want a soft drink, Nelly," she said, while uncle Denys was leaving. "I want Florian and Catlin."

So Nelly went out; and in a little while Florian and Catlin came in, very quiet, very sober, bringing her soft drink.

"We feel terrible," Florian said. And they both looked it.

They had been with her at the hospital. They had been so scared, both of them, and they had stayed with her and looked like they could jump at anybody who looked wrong. But finally they had had to go home, because she told them to, uncle Denys said she should, they were so scared and so upset, and they needed to settle down. So she woke up enough to tell them it wasn't their fault and to send them home.

I'll be there in a little while, she had said.

So she was.

Dr. Ivanov said she was lucky she had only broken her arm, and not her head. And she felt lucky about it too. She kept seeing the sky and the ground, and feeling the jolt in her bones.

Uncle Denys said she was lucky too, that Horse could have killed her, and he was awfully upset.

That was true. But she told uncle Denys it wasn't Horse's fault, he just sort of moved. "Horse is all right, isn't he?" she had asked.

"Horse is fine," uncle Denys had said. "He's just fine. You're the one we're worried about."

That was nice. People generally weren't, not in any nice way. Dr. Ivanov was kind to her, the nurses gave her soft drinks, Florian and Catlin hung around her until she sent them away. The one thing she had not gotten out of it was uncle Giraud: uncle Giraud had not come at all, but she was too tired to want him there anyway, it was all too much work.

Now Florian and Catlin were back and she was safe in her bed and she really, truly, felt just sort of—away from everything. Quiet. She was glad people were being nice, not because she couldn't Work them, but because she was so tired and it took so much, and she just wanted to lie there and not hurt awhile, after she had drunk a little of her soft drink.

"It's not your fault," she said to Florian and Catlin. "It was my idea, wasn't it?"

"We shouldn't have let you," Florian said.

"Yes, you should have," she said, frowning real quick. "You do what I tell you and that's what I told you. Isn't that so?"

"Yes," Catlin said after a moment. "That's so."

They both looked happier then.

She slept all afternoon, with her arm raised in a sling the way Dr. Ivanov said she had to, to keep her hand from swelling. She didn't think that would work, because she always tossed around a lot, but it did: she went right off to sleep, waked up once when Nelly told her to take a pill, and went back to sleep, because it was her bed and her room, and the pills that kept her from hurting also made her very drowsy.

But Nelly woke her up for supper, and she had to eat with her left hand. Dr. Ivanov had said things about left-right dominance to her and said how she mustn't do any writing until she got out of the cast, but she could do everything else. Dr. Ivanov said she should have a Scriber to help her with her lessons, just like his, and she liked that idea.

He said that she ought to be in the cast about three weeks, because he had done a lot of special things to help it heal fast, and it was going to be good as new. He said she was going to do gym exercises after, to make her arm strong again. She agreed with that. Having a broken arm was an adventure, but she didn't want it to do anything permanent.

It was kind of interesting to have the cast and all, and to have everyone fussing over her. The way people changed when they were anxious was interesting. She thought a lot about it when she was awake.

She had her supper, things she could eat with her fingers, and she wanted Florian and Catlin to stay in her room, because she was awake now. But uncle Denys came in and said they could come in a little while, but right then he had to have a Talk with her.

"I don't want to," she said, and pouted a little, because she really hurt, and it wasn't fair of uncle Denys, uncle Denys had been nice all day, and now everybody was going to go back the other way before she was ready for it, she saw it coming.

"It won't be a long one," uncle Denys said, shutting the door, "and I'm not even going to mention about your going down to the Town."

That wasn't what she expected. So she was curious and uncomfortable at the same time, while he pulled Nelly's chair over: she was glad he wasn't going to sit on the bed, because she was just settled and he was so heavy.

"Ari," he said, leaning forward with his elbows on his knees and his face very anxious. "Ari, I want to tell you why everyone was so upset, but this isn't about the Town: it's about how important you are, and how there are people—there are people who might want to hurt you, if they got into Reseune. That's why you scared Security so bad."

That was serious. It clicked right in with the Safety in the Halls lecture and the fact that she was the only kid she knew who had two Security azi for company. She was interested and scared, because it was like it sent out little hooks into a whole lot of things. "So who are they?"

"People who would have hurt your predecessor. Do you know why they put PR on a CIT number?"

"Because they're a Parental Replicate."

"Do you know what that means?"

She nodded, definitely. "That means they're a twin to their own maman or their papa."

"Just any kind of twin?"

"No. Identical."

"Identical all the way down to their genesets, right?"

She nodded.

"You don't have a PR on your number. But you could have."

That was confusing. And scary. It didn't make sense at all.

"Pay attention. Don't think about it. Let me guide you through this, Ari. Your maman, Jane Strassen, had a very good friend, who died, who died very suddenly. Reseune was going to make another one of her, which, you know, means making a baby. Jane said that she wanted that baby, she wanted to bring it up herself, for her own, because she didn't want that baby to go to anybody else. She did it for her friend, who died. And when she got that baby she loved it so much it was hers. Do you understand me, Ari?"

There was a cold lump in her throat. She was cold all over, right down to her fingers.

"Do you understand me, Ari?"

She nodded.

"Jane *is* truly your maman. That's so, nothing can change that, Ari. Your maman is whoever loves you and takes care of you and teaches you like Jane did."

"*Why did she leave me?*"

"Because she had to do something only she could do. Because, next to the first Ari herself, Jane Strassen is the best one to do it. Also, Ari, Jane had another daughter—a grown daughter named Julia, who was terribly jealous of the time you took; and Julia had a daughter too, named Gloria Strassen, who's your age. Julia made things very hard for your maman, because Julia was being very difficult, and Julia was assigned to Fargone too. Your maman finally had to see about her other daughter, and her granddaughter, because they were terribly jealous and upset about her being your maman. She didn't want to, but that was the way it was. So she went to Fargone and she took them with her because she wasn't going to leave them here where they could be mean to you. She told me to take care of you, she told me she would come back if she could, but it's a terribly long way, Ari, and your maman's health isn't too good. She's quite old, you know, and it would be awfully dangerous for her now. So that's why your maman left, and why she knew she might not be able to come back: she'd done everything for her friend who died, to start with. And she knew she'd have to go away before you were grown. She thought it would be easy, when she started. But she really got to be your maman, and she got to love you not just because of the Ari who died, but because *you're* Ari, and you're *you*, and she loves you just because, that's all."

Tears started rolling down her face. She didn't even know she was crying till she felt that. Then she moved the wrong arm to wipe them and had to use the other hand, which was awkward.

"She can't have you at Fargone," uncle Denys said, "because, for one thing, she has Julia and Gloria there. And because you're *you*, you're Ari, and your genemother was what she was, and because you have enemies. You could grow up safe here. There were teachers to teach you and people to take care of you—not always the best; I know I'm not the best at bringing up a little girl, but I really have tried, Ari, and I go on trying. I just figure it's time I explained some things to you, because you're old enough to try to go places on your own, that's pretty plain, isn't it? You might run into people who might accidentally say the wrong thing to you, and most of all I didn't want you to hear any of this from some stranger down in the Town. A lot of people know who you are, and you're getting old enough to start asking questions—like why your name is Emory and not Strassen, to start with."

She *hated* to feel stupid. And that was a big one, a terribly, terribly big one. Of course people had different names, a lot of people had different names. She thought it was who maman picked to make her baby with.

You got into trouble, making up your mind why things were that grownups wouldn't tell you.

Why can't I be Strassen? she remembered asking maman.

Because you're Emory, maman had said, because, that's why. I'm Strassen. Look at Tommy Carnath. His maman is Johanna Morley. Grownups figure these things out.

Her stomach turned over, suddenly, and she felt sweaty and cold.

"Please," she said, "uncle Denys, I'm going to be sick. Call Nelly."

Denys did, real quick. And Nelly got her arm unhooked and got her to the bathroom, where she felt that way for a long time, but nothing happened. She only wished she could be, because she hurt inside and out.

Nelly got her a glass of fizzy stuff for her stomach, and it was awful, but she drank it. Then she felt a little better, and lay against her pillows while Nelly stroked her face and her hair a long, long time and worried about her.

Nelly was the same. Nelly was the way Nelly had always been to her. She guessed it was true maman was really still her maman, but she was not sure who *she* was anymore. She wanted to find out. Uncle Denys knew, and she wanted to ask him, but she was not sure she wanted any more yet.

Uncle Denys came back in finally, and he came and patted her shoulder, the good one. "Are you all right, sweet? Are you going to be all right?"

Maman called her that. Uncle Denys never had. Ari bit her lip till it hurt more than that did.

"Ari?"

"What other things was I going to notice?"

"That there was a very famous woman at Reseune who had the same name as you," uncle Denys said, and pulled the chair over, so Nelly got back, and took some stuff off the night-table and took it to the bath. "That you look just like her when she was a little girl, and her pictures are all through the tapes you really need to study. She was very, very smart, Ari, smarter than anyone. She wasn't your maman. You aren't her daughter. You're something a lot closer. How close we don't know yet, but you're a very extraordinary little girl, and I know Jane is very, very proud of you."

He patted her shoulder then. Nelly had come back through and left. Now he got up again. She didn't care. She was still thinking and it was like her brains were mush.

"Ari, I'm going to have Florian and Catlin stay all night in your room, if you want. I think you'd like that, wouldn't you?"

She didn't know how she was going to tell Florian and Catlin she had been that stupid. They wouldn't stop liking her: they were her azi, and they had to like her. But they were going to be upset. They were going to be upset by her being upset. So she swiped the back of her left hand across her face and tried to stop sniveling.

"Ari?"

"Does Nelly know?"

"Nelly knows. Nelly doesn't understand, but Nelly knows, she always has."

That made her awfully mad at Nelly.

"Nelly was your maman's, Ari. Your maman put an awfully heavy load on Nelly, telling her as much as she did, and telling Nelly she had to keep that secret. Nelly is very loyal to your maman. Of course she would."

"Ollie knew too."

"Ollie knew. Do you want me to send Florian and Catlin to spend the night? They can have pallets over in the corner. They won't mind at all."

"Do they know?"

"No. Only your maman's people knew. They're yours."

She felt better about that. At least *they* hadn't been laughing at her. "Does Amy Carnath know?"

Uncle Denys frowned and took a second about that. "Why does Amy Carnath knowing matter?"

"Because it *does*," she snapped at him.

"Ari, I'm in charge of your education. Your maman and I agreed that there are some questions I just won't answer, because they're for you to figure out. You'll be mad at me sometimes, but I'll have to stay by what I agreed with your maman. You're very, very bright. Your maman expects you to figure out some of these things yourself, just the way the first Ari would, because she knows how good you are at figuring things out. It's part of your growing up. There'll be a lot of times you'll ask me things—and I'll say, you have to figure that one, because you're the one who wants that answer. Just remember this: whatever you ask anyone—can tell them a lot. You think about that, Ari."

He closed the door.

Ari thought about it. And thought that uncle Denys was maybe doing what maman had said; and maybe again uncle Denys wasn't. It was hard to tell, when people could be lying to you about what maman had said.

Or even about what she was.

In a little while more Florian and Catlin came in, very quiet and sober. "Ser Denys says you have orders for us," Catlin said.

Ari made her face azi-like, very quiet. Her eyelashes were still wet. She figured her nose was red. They would pick all of that up, but she couldn't stop that, they had to be near her. "I've got something to tell you first. Sit down on the bed. I've found out some answers."

They sat down, one on a side, very carefully, so they didn't jostle her.

"First," she said, "uncle Denys says I'm not from maman's geneset at all, I'm a PR of somebody else, and she was a friend of maman's. That maman has a grown-up daughter and a granddaughter maman never told me about, and Nelly and Ollie both knew all about where maman got me. But he won't tell me a whole lot else. He says *I* have to find it out." She made the little sign with her fingers that said one of them should come close and listen. But she couldn't make it with the right hand. So it was Florian who got up and came clear around the bed to put his ear up against her mouth. "It might be uncle Denys Working me. I don't know. And I don't know why he would, except Giraud is his brother. Pass it to Catlin."

He did, and Catlin's eyebrows went up and Catlin's face got very thoughtful and still when she looked at her. Catlin nodded once, with a look that meant business.

So she was not sure whether she felt stupid or not, or whether it was true at all, or whether part of it was.

Florian and Catlin could track down a lot of things, because that was what they knew how to do.

It answered a lot of the What's Unusuals, that was what scared her most, except it didn't answer all of them.

Like why the Disappeareds and what Giraud was up to.

Like why maman hadn't written *her* a letter in the first place, or what had happened to it if maman had.

There were new ones.

Like it was Unusual that they didn't just tell her the truth from the start.

Like it was Unusual maman had gone all round the thing about her name, and told her her papa was a man named James Carnath. Which was still not where she got the Emory.

It was Unusual maman had dodged around a whole lot of things that maman had not wanted to answer. She had not wanted to ask very much when she was a little kid, because she felt it make maman real uncomfortable.

And when she thought about it, she knew maman had Worked her too, she could feel it happen when she remembered it.

That was what made her want to throw up.

She was scared, scared that nothing was true, not even what uncle Denys was telling her. But she couldn't let anybody know that.

That last uncle Denys had said was something she knew: what you asked told a whole lot to somebody you might not want to trust. So uncle Denys knew that too, and warned her not to ask him things.

Like maman, only uncle Denys did it a different way, straight out: don't give things away to me because you don't know whether I'm all right or not.

If uncle Denys wanted to Work her, he was doing something real complicated, and the pain medicine made her brain all fuzzy. If that was what he was doing he was starting off by confusing her.

Or taking her Fix off what she was trying to look at.

Dammit, she thought. Dammit.

Because she was stuck in this bed and she hurt and she couldn't think at all past the trank.

xii

Report to my office, the message from Yanni said, first thing that Justin read when he brought the office computer up; and he turned around and looked at Grant. "I've got to go see Yanni," he said; and Grant swung his chair around and looked at him.

No comment. There was nothing in particular to say. Grant just looked worried.

"See you," Justin said with a wry attempt at humor. "Wish you could witness this one."

"So do I," Grant said, not joking at all.

He was not up to a meeting with Yanni. But there was no choice. He shrugged, gave Grant a worried look, and walked out and down the hall, with his knees close to wobbling under him, it was still that bad and he was still that much in shock.

God, he thought, get me around this.

Somehow.

Grant had kept track, with Grant's azi-trained memory and Grant's professional understanding of subject, psychset, and what he was hearing, of everything that had gone on around him while he was answering Giraud's questions and of everything that had gone on around him in recovery, right down to the chance words and small comments of the meds that had taken him home. Playing all that back and knowing it was *all* that had gone on, was immeasurably comforting; having Grant simply *there* through the night had kept him reasonably well focused on here and now, and made him able to get up in the morning, adopt a deliberately short-sighted cheerfulness, and decide he was going to work.

I can at least get some of the damned records-keeping done, he had said to Grant, meaning the several towering mounds of their own reports that had been waiting weeks to be checked against computer files and archives and hand-stamped as Archived before being sent for the shredder. Can't think of a better day for it.

He could not cope with changes, and he reckoned on his way down the hall and up to Yanni's door that Security thought it had found something or suspected something in the interview, God knew what, and Yanni—

God knew.

"Marge," he said to Yanni's aide, "I'm here."

"Go on in," Marge said. "He's expecting you."

A flag on his log-on, that was what.

He opened the door and found Yanni at his desk. "Ser."

Yanni looked up and he braced himself. "Sit down," Yanni said very quietly.

Oh, God, he thought, gone completely off his balance. He sank into the chair and felt himself tensed up and out of control.

"Son," Yanni said, more quietly than he had ever heard Yanni speak, "how are you?"

"I'm fine," he said, two syllables, carefully managed, damn near stammered.

"I raised hell when I heard," Yanni said. "All the way to Denys' office *and* Petros *and* Giraud. I understand they let Grant stay through it."

"Yes, ser."

"Petros put that as a mandate on your charts. They better have. I'll tell you this, they *did* record it, not on the Security recorders, but it exists. You can get it if you need it. That's Giraud's promise, son. They're sane over there this morning."

He stared at Yanni with a blank, sick feeling that it had to be a lead-in, that he was being set up for something. Recorded, that was sure. Trust the man and he would come in hard and low.

"Is this another voice-stress?" he asked Yanni, to have it out and over with.

The line between Yanni's brows deepened. "No. It's not. I want to explain some things to you. Things are real difficult in Giraud's office right now. A lot of pressure. They're going to have to break the secrecy seal on this. The kid's timing was immaculate. I don't want to go into it more than that, except to tell you they've broken the news to Ari, at least as far as her not being Jane Strassen's biological daughter, and her being a replicate of somebody named Ariane Emory, who's no more than a name to her. So some of that pressure is going to be relieved real soon. She's got a broken arm and a lot of bruises. They threw the news at her while she was tranked so they could at least hold the initial reaction to the emotional level where they could halfway control it, get it settled and accepted on a gut level before she heads at the why of it with that logical function of hers, which, I don't need to tell you, is damned sharp and damned persistent. I'm telling you this because she's come your way before and she's going to be hunting information. If it happens, don't panic. Follow procedures, call Denys' office, and tell her you have to do that: that Security will get upset if you don't—which is the truth."

He drew easier breaths, told himself it was still a trap, but at least the business assumed some definable shape, a calamity postponed to the indefinable future.

"Do you have any word," he asked Yanni, "how Jordan came through this?"

"I called him last night. He said he was all right, he was concerned for you. You know how it is, there's so damned much we can't do on the phone. I told him you were fine; I'd check on you; I'd call him again today."

"Tell him I'm all right." He found himself with a deathgrip on the right chair arm, his fingers locked till they ached. He let go, trying to relax. "Thanks. Thanks for checking on him."

Yanni shrugged, heaved a sigh and scowled at him. "You suspect me like hell, don't you?"

He did not answer that.

"Listen to me, son. I'll put up with a lot, but I know something about how you work, and I knew damn well you hadn't had anything to do with the kid, it was Giraud's damn bloody insistence on running another damn probe on a mind that just may be worth two or three others around this place, never mind *my* professional judgment, *Giraud* is in a bloodyminded *hurry*, to hell with procedures, to hell with the law, to hell with everything in his way." Yanni drew breath. "Don't get me started. What I called you in here to tell you is, Denys just put your research on budget. Not a big one, God knows, but you're going to be seeing about half the load you've been getting off the Rubin project, and you're going to get computer time over in Sociology, not much of it, but some. Call it guilt on Administration's part. Call it whatever you like. You're going to route the stuff through me to Sociology, through

Sociology over to Jordan, and several times a year you're going to get some time over at Planys. That's the news. I thought it might give you something cheerful to think about. All right?"

"Yes, ser," he said after a moment, because he had to say something. The most dangerous thing in the world was to start trusting Yanni Schwartz, or believing when indicators started a downhill slide that it had been a momentary glitch.

"Go on. Take a break. Go. Get out of here."

"Yes, ser." He levered himself up out of the chair, he got himself out the door past Marge without even looking at her, and walked the hall in a kind of numb terror that somewhere Security was involved in this, that in the way they had of getting him off his guard and then hitting him hardest, he might find something had happened to Grant—it was the most immediate thing he could think of, and the worst.

But Grant was there, Grant was in the door waiting for him and worried.

"Yanni was polite," he said. The tiny, paper-piled office was a claustrophobic closeness. "Let's go get a cup of coffee." No mind that they had the makings in the office. He wanted space around him, the quiet, normal noise of human beings down in the North Wing coffee bar.

Breaking schedule, being anywhere out of the ordinary, could win them both another session with Giraud. Nothing was safe. Anything could be invaded. It was the kind of terror a deep probe left. He ought to be on trank. Hell if he wanted it.

He told Grant what Yanni had said, over coffee in the restaurant. Grant listened gravely and said: "About time. About time they came to their senses."

"You trust it?" he asked Grant. Desperately, the way he had taken Grant's word for what was real and what was not. He was terrified Grant would fail him finally, and tell him yes, believe them, trust everything. It was what it sounded like, from the one point of sanity he had.

"No," Grant said, with a little lift of his brows. "No more than yesterday. But I think *Yanni's* telling the truth. I think he's starting to suspect what you might be and what they might lose in their preoccupation with young Ari. That's the idea he may have gotten through to Denys. If it gets to Denys, it may finally get through to Giraud. No. Listen to me. I'm talking very seriously."

"Dammit, Grant, —" He felt himself ludicrously close to tears, to absolute, overloaded panic. "I'm not holding this off well. I'm too damned open, even wide awake. Don't confuse me."

"I'm going to say this and get off it, fast. *If* the word is getting up to them from Yanni, it's perfectly logical they're turning helpful. I'm not saying they're any different. I'm saying there may be some changes. For God's sake take it easy, take it quietly, don't try to figure them on past performance, don't try to figure them at all for a few days. You want me to talk to Yanni?"

"No!"

"Easy. All right. All right."

"Dammit, don't patronize me!"

"Oh, we *are* short-fused. Drink your coffee. You're doing fine, just fine, just get a grip on here, all right? Yanni's gone crazy, you're just fine, I'm just fine, Administration's totally off the edge, I don't know what's different."

He gave a sneeze of a laugh, made a furtive wipe at his eyes, and took a sip of cooling coffee.

"God, I don't know if I can last this."

"Easy, easy, easy. One day at a time. We'll cut it short today and go home, all right?"

"I want us near witnesses."

"Office, then."

"Office." He drew a slow breath, getting his pulse-rate back to normal.

And bought a holo-poster at the corner shop, on the way back, for the office wall over his desk.

Grant lifted an eyebrow, getting a look at it while he was handing the check-out his credit card.

It was a plane over the outback. FLY RESEUNEAIR, it said.

Verbal Text from:
A QUESTION OF UNION
Union Civics Series: #3

Reseune Educational Publications: 9799-8734-3
approved for 80+

In the years between 2301 and 2351, Expansion was the unquestioned policy of Union: the colonial fervor which had led to the establishment of the original thirteen star stations showed no sign of abating.

The discovery of Cyteen's biological riches and the new technology of jump-space travel brought Cyteen economic self-sufficiency and eventual political independence, not, however, before it had reached outward and established a number of colonies of its own. The fact that Cyteen was founded by people seeking independence from colonial policies of the Earth Company, however, provided a philosophical base important to all Union culture—the idea of a new form of government.

From the time the tensions between Cyteen and the Earth Company they had fled, led to the Company Wars and the Secession, we have to consider Cyteen as one planet within the larger context of Union. Within that context, the desire for independence and the strong belief in local autonomy; and second, the enthusiasm for exploration, trade, and the development of a new frontier—have been the predominant influences. The framers of the Constitution made it a cardinal principle that the Union government will not cross the local threshold, be it a station dock, a gravity well, or a string of stars declaring themselves a political unit within Union—unless there is evidence that the local government does not have the consent of the governed, or unless one unit exits its own area to impose its will on a neighbor. So there can be, and may one day be, many governments within Union, and still only one Union, which maintains what the founders called a consensus of the whole.

It was conceived as a framework able to exist around any local structure, even a non-human one, a framework infinitely adaptable to local situations, in which

315

local rule serves as the check on Union and Union as the check on local rule.

But, in the way of secessions, Union began in conflict. The Company Wars were a severe strain on the new government, and many institutions originated as a direct response to those stresses—among them, the first political parties.

The Expansionist party may be said to have existed from the founding of Union; but as the war with the Earth Company entered its most critical phase, the Centrist movement demanded negotiation and partition of space at Mariner. The Centrists, who had a strong liberal, pacifist and Reunionist leaning in the inception of the organized party, gained in strength rapidly during the last years of the War, and ironically, lost much of that strength as the Treaty of Pell ended the War in a negotiation largely unpopular on the home front. Union became generally more pro-Expansion as enormous numbers of troops returned to the population centers and strained the systems considerably.

From that time the Centrist platform reflected in some part the growing fears that unchecked Expansion and colonization would lead to irredeemable diffusion of human cultures—and, in the belief of some, —to war between human cultures which had arisen with interests enough in common to be rivals and different enough to be enemies.

But except for social scientists such as Pavel Brust, the principal proponent of the Diffusion Theory, the larger number of Centrists were those who stood to be harmed by further colonization, such as starstations which looked to become peripheral to the direction of that expansion, due to accident of position; and the war-years children, who saw themselves locked in a cycle of conflict which they had not chosen.

The Centrists received a considerable boost from two events: first, the peaceful transition within the Alliance from the wartime administration of the Konstantins to that of the Dees, known to be moderates; second, the discovery of a well-developed alien region on the far side of Sol. Sol, sternly rebuffed by the alien Compact, turned back toward human space, and it became a principal tenet of the Centrist Party that a period of stability and consolidation might lead to a reunification of humanity, or at least a period of peace. To certain people troubled by the realization that they were not only not alone, but that they had alien competitors, this seemed the safest course.

In 2389 the Centrists were formally joined by the Abolitionists, who opposed the means by which existing and proposed colonies were designed, some on economic grounds and others on moral grounds ranging from philosophical to religious, denouncing practices from mindwipe to psychsurgery, and calling for an end to the production of azi. Previously the Abolitionists had lacked a public voice, and indeed, were more a cross-section of opposition to the offworld government, including the Citizens for Autonomy, who wished to break up the government and make all worlds and stations independent of central authority; the Committee Against Human Experimentation; the Religious Council; and others, including, without sanction of the official party, the radical Committee of Man, which committed various acts of kidnapping and terrorism aimed at genetics research facilities and government offices.

To those who feared Sol's influence, and those who felt the chance of alien war was minimal, the Centrist agenda seemed a dangerous course: loss of momentum and economic collapse was the Expansionist fear. And at the head of the new Expansionist movement was a coalition of various interests, prominent among whom, as scientist, philosopher and political figure, was Ariane Emory.

Her murder in 2404 touched off a furor mostly directed at the Abolitionists, but the Centrist coalition broke under the assault.

What followed was a period of retrenchment, reorganization, and realignment, until the discovery in 2412 of the Gehenna plot and the subsequent investigations of culpability gave the Centrists a cause and an issue. Gehenna lent substance to Centrist fears; and at the same time tarnished the image of the Expansionist majority, not least among them Ilya Bogdanovitch, the Chairman of the Nine; Ariane Emory of Reseune; and admiral Azov, the controversial head of Defense, who had approved the plan.

The Centrists for the first time in 2413 gained a majority in the Senate of Viking and in the Council of Mariner; and held a sizable bloc of seats and appointed posts within the Senate of Cyteen. They thus gained an unprecedented percentage of seats in the Council of Worlds and frequently mustered four votes of the Nine.

Although they did not hold a majority in either body, their influence could no longer be discounted, and the swift gains of the Centrists both worried the Expansionist majority and made the uncommitted delegates on any given issue a pivotal element: delegates known to be wavering were courted with unprecedented fervor, provoking charges and countercharges of influence-trading and outright bribery that led to several recall votes, none of which, however, succeeded in unseating the incumbent.

The very fabric of Union was being tested in the jousting of strong interest groups. Certain political theorists called into question the wisdom of the founders who had created the electorate system, maintaining that the system encouraged electorates to vote their own narrow interests above that of the nation at large.

It was the aphorism of Nasir Harad, president of the Council, on his own re-election after his Council conviction on bribery charges, that: **"Corruption means elected officials trading votes for their own advantage; democracy means a bloc of voters doing the same thing. The electorates know the difference."**

CHAPTER 8

i

An announcement came through the public address in Wing One corridors—storm alert, Justin thought, ticking away at his keyboard on a problem while Grant got up to lean out the door and see what it was.

Then: "Justin," Grant said urgently. *"Justin."*

He shoved back and got up.

Everything in the hall had stopped, standing and listening.

". . . in Novgorod," the PA said, *"came in the form of briefs filed this morning by Reseune lawyers on behalf of Ariane Emory, a minor child, seeking a Writ of Succession and an injunction against any Discovery proceedings of the Council against Reseune. The brief argues that the child, who will be nine in five days, is the legal person of Ariane Emory by the right of Parental Identity, that no disposition of Ariane Emory's property can be taken in any cause without suit brought against the child and her guardians. The second brief seeks an injunction against the activities of the Investigatory Commission on the grounds that their inquiries invade the privacy and compromise the welfare and property rights of a minor child.*

"The news hit the capital as the Commission was preparing to file a bill requiring the surrender of records from Reseune Archives pertinent to the former Councillor, on the grounds that the records may contain information on other Gehenna-style projects either planned or executed.

"Mikhail Corain, leader of the Centrist party and Councillor of Citizens, declared: 'It's an obvious maneuver. Reseune has sunk to its lowest.'

"James Morley, chief counsel for Reseune, when told of the comment, stated: 'We had no wish to bring this suit. The child's privacy and well-being have been our primary considerations, from her conception. We cannot allow her to become a victim of partisan politics. She has rights, and we believe the court will uphold the point. There's no question about her identity. A simple lab test can prove that.' "Reseune Administration has refused comment. . . ."

---

ii

Ari thought she was crazy sometimes, because twice an hour she thought everyone was lying, and sometimes she thought they were not, that there really had been an Ari Emory before she was born.

But the evening when she could get out of bed and come in her robe to the living room with her arm still in a sling, uncle Denys said he had something to show her and Florian and Catlin; and he had a book filled with paste-in pictures and old faxes.

He had them sit at the table, himself on her left and Florian and then Catlin on her right, and he opened the book on the table, putting it mostly in front of her, a book of photos and holos, and there were papers, dim and showing their age. He showed her a picture of *her*, standing in the front portico of the House with a woman she had never seen.

"That's Ari when she was little," Uncle Denys said. "That's *her* maman. Her name was Olga Emory." There was another picture uncle Denys turned to. "This is James Carnath. That was your papa." She knew that. It was the picture maman had once showed her.

The girl in the picture looked just exactly like her, but it was not her maman; but it was the right name for her papa. It was all wrong. It was *her* standing there. It was. But the front doors were not like that. Not quite. Not now.

She felt her stomach more and more upset. Uncle Denys turned the page and showed her pictures of old Reseune, Reseune before the House was as big, before the Town was anything but old barracks, and the fields were real small. There were big buildings missing, like the AG barn, and like a lot of the mills and half the town, and *that* Ari was walking with her maman down a Town Road that was the same road, toward a Town that was very different.

There was that Ari, sitting in her same classroom, with a different teacher, with a kind of screwed-up frown on her face while she looked at a jar that was like her saying *Ugh*, she could feel it right in her stomach and feel her own face the way it would be.

But she never had a blouse like that, and she never wore a pin like that in her hair.

She felt herself all sick inside, because it was like it was all real, maman *had* tricked her, and she was stupid like she had been afraid she was, in front of Catlin and Florian, in front of everybody. But she couldn't *not* look at these things, she couldn't do anything but sit there with her arm aching in the dumb cast and herself feeling light-headed and silly being out here in the dining room in her robe and her slippers, looking at herself in a place that was Reseune a long, long time ago.

A *long* time ago.

That Ari had been born—that long ago. Her maman's friend, uncle Denys had called her; and she had not thought when he said that, just how old maman was.

A hundred thirty-four years. No. A hundred forty-one, no, *two*, she was real close to her ninth birthday and maman was that old now.

A hundred forty-two. . . .

She was close to her ninth birthday and maman's letter *had* to come, any day now, and maybe maman would explain some of these things, maybe maman would send her all the letters maman must have written too, all at once, like hers. . . .

"There's your maman," uncle Denys said, and showed her a picture of her and a bunch of other kids all playing, and there was this pretty woman with black hair, with her maman's mouth and her maman's eyes, only *young*, with *her*, but she was about five or six. A baby. Maman had had another Ari, *first*, a long, long time ago.

It hurt to see maman so pretty and not with her at all, not really, but with that other baby. It had stopped hurting until then. And it made her throat ache.

Uncle Denys stopped and hugged her head against his shoulder gently. "I know. I know, Ari. I'm sorry."

She shoved away. She pulled the book over so it was in front of her and she looked at that picture till she could see everything about it, what her maman was wearing, what that Ari was wearing, that proved it was not something she had forgotten, it was really not her, because everything about it was old-fashioned and long-ago.

"That's your uncle Giraud," uncle Denys said, pointing to a gangly boy.

He looked like anybody. He didn't look like he was going to grow up to be nasty as Giraud was. He looked just like any kid.

She turned the page. There was that Ari with her maman, and a lot of other grown-ups.

Then there was *her* with Florian and Catlin, but it was not them, they were all in the middle of old-time Reseune.

She felt another deep chill, like when she flew off Horse and hit the ground. She felt scared, and looked at Florian and Catlin for how they saw it.

They didn't ask. They wouldn't ask. They were being proper with uncle Denys and not interrupting, but she knew they were confused and they were upset, because they had both gone completely azi, paying real close attention.

She couldn't even reach to Florian to squeeze his hand, it was the side with the cast.

"Do you recognize them?" uncle Denys asked.

"Who are they?" Ari asked, angry, terribly angry of a sudden, because it was not making sense, and she was scared, she knew Florian and Catlin were scared, everything was inside out.

"You're not the only one who's come back," Denys said very softly. "There was one other Catlin and one other Florian: they belonged to that other Ari Emory. They protected her all their lives. Do you understand me, Florian? Do you, Catlin?"

"No, ser," Florian said; and: "No, ser," Catlin said. "But it makes sense."

"Why does it make sense?" uncle Denys asked.

"We're azi," Catlin said, the most obvious thing in the world. "There could be a lot of us."

But I'm a CIT, Ari thought, upset all the way through. *Aren't I?*

"You're Alphas," uncle Denys said, "and, no, it's not ordinary with Alphas. You're too difficult to keep track of. You change so fast. But you're still a lot easier to duplicate than a CIT, you're right, because azi start with very specific tape. Teaching Ari has been—ever so much harder."

Teaching me. Teaching me—what? Why?

But she knew that. She understood all across the far and wide of it, that uncle Denys was saying what she was, and not saying it to her, but to Florian and Catlin, because it was something she could not understand as easily as her azi could.

Do you know, maman had asked her, the day she saw the babies, *the difference between a CIT and an azi?*

I only thought I did.

Denys left that page open a long time. "Ari," he said. "Do you understand me?"

She said nothing. When you were confused, it was better to let somebody else be a fool, unless you were the only one who knew the question.

And uncle Denys knew. Uncle Denys was trying to tell her what he knew, in this book, in these pictures that weren't her.

"Your maman taught you," uncle Denys said, "and now I do. You're definitely a CIT. Don't mistake that. You're *you*, Ari, you're very exactly *you*, exactly the way Florian is Florian and Catlin is Catlin, and that's hard to do. It was ever so hard to get this far. Ari was a very, very special little girl, and you're taking up everything she had, everything she could do, everything she held and owned, which is a very great deal, Ari. That you hold Florian and Catlin's contracts is all part of that, because you all belong together, you always have, and it wouldn't be right to leave them out. You own a major share of Reseune itself, you own property enough to make you very, very rich, and you've already proved to us who you are, we haven't any doubt at all. But remember that I told you Reseune has enemies. Now some of those enemies want to come in here and take things that belong to you—they don't even know there *is* an Ari, you understand. They think she died, and that was all of her, and they can just move in and take everything that belonged to her— that belongs to *you*, Ari. Do you know what a lawsuit is? Do you know what it means to sue somebody in court?"

She shook her head, muddled and scared by what uncle Denys said, getting too much, far too much from every direction.

"You know what judges are?"

"Like in a court. They get all the records and stuff. They can send you to hospital."

"A civil suit, Ari: that's different than a criminal case. They don't send you to hospital, but they can say what's so and who owns what. We've lodged a suit in the Supreme Court, in Novgorod, to keep these people from taking everything you own. They can't, you understand, if somebody *owns* it, really owns it. The only thing is, people don't know you exist. You have to show up in that court and *prove* you're really Ari and that you have a right to Ari's CIT-number."

"That's stupid!"

"How do they know you're not just some little girl all made up and telling a lie?"

"I know who I am!"

"How do you prove it to people who've never seen you?"

She sat there trying to think. She had the shivers. "You tell them."

"Then they'll say we're lying. We can send the genetic records, that can prove it, beyond any doubt. But they could say we just got that out of the lab, because of course the Ari geneset is there, isn't it, because you were born out of the lab. They could say there isn't any little girl alive, and she hasn't got any right to anything. That's what could happen. That's why you have to go, and stand in that court, and tell the judges that's your genetic record, and you're you, Ariane Emory, and you own all that stuff these people in the Council want to take."

She looked at her right, at Florian and Catlin, at two pale, very azi faces. And back at uncle Denys. "Could they take Florian and Catlin?"

"If you don't exist, you can't hold a contract, can you?"

"That's *stupid*, uncle Denys! They're stupid!"

"You just have to prove that, don't you? Dear, I wish to hell I could have saved this till you felt better. But there isn't any time. These people are moving fast, and there's going to be a law passed in Council to take everything, *everything* that belongs to you, because they don't know about you. You've got to go to Novgorod and tell the judges it does belong to you and they can't do that."

"When?"

"In a few days. A very few days. There's more to it, Ari. *Because* you've been a secret, your enemies haven't known about you either. If you go to Novgorod they will know. And you'll be in very real danger from then on. Most of them would sue you in court and try to take what you've got, *that* kind of enemy; but some of them would kill you if they could. Even if you're a little girl. They're that kind."

"Ser," Catlin said, "who?"

"A man named Rocher, for one. And a few random crazy people we don't know the names of. We wish we did. If Ari goes to Novgorod she'll have a lot of Security with her. Armed Security. They can stop that kind of thing. But you have to watch out for it, you have to watch very closely, and for God's sake, leave any maneuvering to the senior Security people, you two. Just cover Ari."

"Do we have weapons, ser?"

"I don't think Novgorod would understand that. No. Just cover Ari. Watch around you. Keep her safe. That's all."

Ari drew a deep breath. "What am I supposed to do?"

"You talk to the judges. You go in front of the court, you answer their questions about when you were born, and where, and what your name and number are. Uncle Giraud will be there. Giraud knows how to argue with them."

She went cold and clammy all over. "I don't want Giraud! I want *you* to come."

"Dear, uncle Giraud is especially good at this. He'll show them all the records, and they won't have any trouble believing you. They may take a little cell sample. That'll sting a little if they do that, but you're a brave girl, you won't mind that. You know what that's for. It proves you're not lying. Everyone in the world has seen pictures of Ari Emory—you won't have any trouble with that. But there *will* be other people to deal with. People not in the court. Newspeople. Reporters. There'll be a lot of that. But you're a little girl, and they can't be nasty, they'd better not be, or your uncle Giraud will know exactly what to do with them."

She had never thought it could be a good thing to have uncle Giraud. But uncle Denys was right, uncle Giraud would be a lot better at that.

If he wasn't *with* the Enemy in the first place. Things were getting more and more complicated.

"Florian and Catlin are going for sure?"

"Yes."

"The judges can't just take them, can they?"

"Dear, the law can do anything; but the law *won't* take what belongs to you. You have to prove you're *you*, that's the whole problem. That's what you're going there for, and if you don't, nothing is safe here either."

So Ari sat in a leather seat in *RESEUNE ONE*, a seat so big her feet hardly reached the floor; and Florian and Catlin sat in the two seats opposite her, taking turns looking out the windows, only she had one right beside her, with the real outback under them for as far as you could see.

They would land at Novgorod, they would land at the airport there, but before they landed they were going to see the city from the air; they would see the spaceport, and the Hall of State and the docks where all the barges went, that chugged past Reseune on the Novaya Volga. They were going to see Swigert Bay and the Ocean. The pilot kept telling them where they were and what they were looking at, which right now was the Great West Sink, which was a brown spot on the maps and a brown place from the air with a lake in the middle. She could talk back to the pilot if she pushed a button by her seat.

"We're coming up on the Kaukash Range on the right side," the pilot said.

They had let her go up front for a little while. She got to see out past the pilot and the co-pilot, when they were following the Novaya Volga.

The pilot asked if she liked flying. She said yes, and the pilot told her what a lot of the controls were, and showed her how the plane steered, and what the computers did.

That was the best thing in days. She had him show Florian and Catlin, until uncle Giraud said she had better sit down and study her papers and let the pilot fly the plane. The pilot had winked at her and said she ought to, they were spilling uncle Giraud's drinks.

She wished she had her arm out of the cast, because that was a nuisance; and gave uncle Giraud an excuse to tell her she ought to stay belted-in in her seat.

Most of all she wished they were all through the court business and the reporters, and they could get to the things uncle Denys told her they were going to get to see while they were in Novgorod. That would be fun. She was going to have her birthday in Novgorod. She wanted to prove everything and then get to that part of it.

Most of all she was worried what would happen if uncle Denys was wrong.

Or if uncle Giraud *couldn't* prove who she was.

The court couldn't make a mistake, uncle Denys said, over and over. Not with the tests they had, and the law was the law: they couldn't take what belonged to somebody without suing, and then it was going to be real hard for them to sue a little girl. Especially because Giraud had a lot of friends in the Defense Bureau, who would classify everything.

That meant Secret.

The reporters are going to be a bigger problem than the court, uncle Denys had said. *The reporters will pull up a lot of the old pictures of the first Ari. You have to expect that. They'll talk about a little girl Reseune birthed a long time ago, a PR off Estelle Bok. It didn't work right. You've beaten all that little girl's problems. If they say you're like that other little girl they're being nasty, and you answer them that you're you, and if they doubt that they can wait and see how you grow up. I've no doubt at all that you can handle that sort of thing. You don't have to be polite if reporters start being nasty, but you can get a lot more out of them if you act like a nice little kid.*

It sounded like a fight. That was what it sounded like. She figured that. It was one of the only times uncle Denys had ever talked to her about Working people, but uncle Denys was good at it, and she was sure he knew what was what.

The Enemy cheats, Catlin always said.

It worried her, about whether the Court ever did.

"Sera," Catlin had come to whisper in her ear that night when they were all going to bed, Florian and Catlin on their pallets, and herself in her own bed with her arm propped up again, "sera, who's our side in this?"

Florian was usually the one who asked all the questions. That was one of Catlin's best ever.

And Catlin waited while she thought about it, and motioned Catlin up close and whispered back: "I am. I'm your side. That's all. You never mind what anybody says, that's still the Rule. They can't say I'm anybody else, no matter what."

So Catlin and Florian relaxed.

She looked at the papers uncle Giraud had given her to study about what the reporters and the judges could ask, and wished *she* could.

--------------------------------- iii ---------------------------------

There was very little work getting done in Wing One, or likely anywhere else in Reseune on this morning, and if there was a portable vid no matter how old not checked out or rented anywhere in the House and the Labs, it was well hidden.

Justin and Grant had theirs, the office door shut—some of the junior designers were clustered together in the lounge downstairs, but the ones in some way involved with the Project sealed themselves in offices alone or with closest associates, and nothing stirred, not even for phone calls.

The cameras were the official ones in the Supreme Court, no theatrics, just the plain, uncommentaried coverage the Supreme Court allowed.

Lawyers handed papers to clerks, and the Court proceeded to ask the clerk if there were any absences or faults in the case.

Negative.

There was a very young girl sitting with her back to the cameras, at the table beside Giraud, not fidgeting, not acting at all restless through the tedium of the opening.

Listening, Justin reckoned. Probably with that very memorable frown.

The news-services had been right on it when the plane landed, and a single news-feed from the official camera set-up at the airport reception lounge had given the news-services their first look at Ari Emory, no questions allowed, until after the ruling.

Ari had stood there with her good hand in uncle Giraud's, the other arm in a cast, wearing a pale blue and very little-girl suit, with black-uniformed Florian and Catlin very stiff and looking like kids in dress-up, overkill in mimicking elder Ari—until a piece of equipment clanked, and eyes went that way and bodies stiffened like the same muscle moved them.

"That'll send chills down backs," Justin had muttered to Grant. "Damn. That *is* them, no way anyone can doubt it. No matter what size they are."

The news-services had done archive filler after, brought up split-screen comparisons between the first and second Ari and Catlin and Florian, from old news photos; and showed a trio so much like them it was like two takes in slightly different lighting, Ari in a different suit, standing beside Geoffrey Carnath instead of Giraud Nye.

"My God, it's right down to mannerisms," he had murmured, meaning the frown on Ari's face. On both Ari-faces. The way of holding the head. "Have they *taught* her that?"

"They could have," Grant had said, unperturbed. "All those skill tapes. They could do more than penmanship, couldn't they? —But a lot of *us* develop like mannerisms."

Not in a CIT, had been his internal objection. *Damn, they've got to have done that. Skill tapes. Muscle-learning. You could get that off a damn good actress.*

Or Ari herself. No telling what kind of things Olga recorded. —Are they going that far with the Rubin kid?

He watched that still, attentive little girl at the table, in front of the panel of judges. They had not let Florian and Catlin sit with her. Just Giraud and the team of lawyers.

"Reseune declines to turn genetic records over to the court," the Chief Justice observed. *"Is that the case?"*

"I need not remind the Court," Giraud said, rising, *"that we're dealing with a Special's geneset. . . ."*

The Justices and uncle Giraud talked back and forth and Ari listened, listened very hard, and remembered not to fidget, uncle Giraud had told her not.

They were talking about genetics, about phenotype and handprints and retinal scan. They had done all the tests but the skin sample already, when she checked in with the court ID office.

"Ariane Emory," the Chief Justice said, "would you come stand with your uncle, please?"

She got up. She didn't have to follow protocols, uncle Giraud said, the Court didn't expect her to be a lawyer. She only had to be very polite with them, because they were lawyers themselves, the ones who solved all the most difficult cases in Union, and you had to be respectful.

"Yes, ser," she said, and she gave a little bow like Giraud's, and walked up to the railing, having to look up at them. There were nine of them. Like Councillors. She had heard about the Court in her tapes. Now she was here. It was interesting.

But she wished it weren't her case.

"Do they call you Ari?" the Chief Justice asked.

"Yes, ser."

"How old are you, Ari?"

"I'm four days from nine."

"What's your CIT number, Ari?"

"CIT 201 08 0089, but it's not PR." Uncle Giraud told her that in the paper she had studied.

The Justice looked at his papers, and flipped through things, and looked up again. "Ari, you grew up at Reseune."

"Yes, ser. That's where I live."

"How did you get that cast on your arm?"

Just answer that, Giraud had said, about any question on her accident. So she said: "I fell off Horse."

"How did that happen?"

"Florian and Catlin and I sneaked out of the House and went down to the Town; and I climbed up on Horse, and he threw me over the fence."

"Is Horse a real horse?"

"He's real. The labs birthed him. He's my favorite." She felt good, just remembering that little bit before she went over the fence, and the Justice was interested, so she said: "It wasn't his fault. He's not mean. I just surprised him and he jumped. So I went off."

"Who was supposed to be watching you?"

"Security."

The Justice looked funny at that, like she had let out more than she intended; and all the Justices thought so, and some thought it was terribly funny. But that could get out of control and make somebody mad, so she decided she had better be careful.

"Do you go to school?"

"Yes, ser."

"Do you like your teachers?"

He was trying to Work her, she decided. Absolutely. She put on her nicest face. "Oh, they're fine."

"Do you do well on tests?"

"Yes," she said. "I do all right."

"Do you understand what it means to be a PR?"

There was the trap question. She wanted to look at uncle Giraud, but she figured that would tell them too much. So she looked straight up at the Justice. "That means I'm legally the same person."

"Do you know what *legally* means?"

"That means if I get certified nobody can say I'm not me and take the things that belong to me without going through the court; and I'm a minor. I'm not old enough to know what I'm going to need out of that stuff, or what I want, so it's not fair to sue me in court, either."

That got him. "Did somebody tell you to say that?"

"Would you like it if somebody called you a liar about who you are? Or if they were going to come in and take your stuff? They can tell too much about you by going through all that stuff, and that's not right to do to somebody, especially if she's a kid. They can *psych* you if they know all that stuff."

Got him again.

"God," Justin said, and lifted his eyes above his hand, watching while Giraud got Ari back to her seat.

"She certainly answered that one," Grant said.

Mikhail Corain glared at the vid in his office and gnawed his lip till it bled.

"Damn, damn, *damn*," he said to his aide. "How do we deal with *that?* They've got that kid primed—"

"A kid," Dellarosa said, "can't take priority over national security."

"You say it, I say it, the question is what's the Court going to hold? Those damn fossils all came in under Emory's spoils system—the head of Justice is *Emory's* old friend. Call Lu in Defense."

"Again?"

"Again, dammit, tell him it's an emergency. He knows damn well what I want—you go over there. No, never mind, *I* will. Get a car."

". . . *watch the hearing*," the note from Giraud Nye had read, simply. And Secretary Lu watched, fist under chin, his pulse elevated, his elbows on an open folio replete with pictures and test scores.

A bright-eyed little girl with a cast on her arm and a scab on her chin. That part was good for the public opinion polls.

The test scores were not as good as the first Ari's. But they were impressive enough.

Corain had had his calls in from the instant he had known about the girl. And Lu was not about to return them—not until he had seen the press conference scheduled for after the hearing, the outcome of which was, as far as he was concerned, a sure thing.

Of paramount interest were the ratings on the newsservices this evening.

Damned good bet that Giraud Nye had leaned on Catherine Lao of Information, damned good bet that Lao was leaning on the newsservices—Lao was an old and personal friend of Ari Emory.

Dammit, the old coalition seemed strangely alive, of a sudden. Old acquaintances reasserted themselves. Emory had not been a friend—entirely. But an old and cynical military man, trying to assure Union's simple survival, found himself staring at a vid-screen and thinking thoughts which had seemed, a while ago, impossible.

Fool, he told himself.

But he pulled out a piece of paper and initiated a memo for the Defense Bureau lawyers:

Military implications of the Emory files outweigh other considerations; draft an upgrading of Emory Archives from Secret to Utmost Secret and prepare to invoke the Military Secrets Act to forestall further legal action.

And to his aide: *I need a meeting with Harad. Utmost urgency.*

Barring, of course, calamity in the press conference.

---

iv

"Ari," the Chief Justice said. "Would you come up to the bar?"

It was after lunch, and the Justice called her right after he had called uncle Giraud.

So she walked up very quiet and very dignified, at least as much as she could with the cast and the sling, and the Justice gave a paper to the bailiff.

"Ari," the Justice said, "the Court is going to certify you. There's no doubt who your genemother was, and that's the only thing that's at issue in this Court today. You have title to your genemother's CIT number.

"As to the PR designation, which is a separate question, we're going to issue a temporary certification—that means your card won't have it, because Reseune is an Administrative Territory, and has the right to determine whether you're a sibling or a parental replicate—which in this case falls within Reseune's special grants of authority. This court doesn't feel there's cause to abrogate those rights on an internal matter, where there is no challenge from other relatives.

"You have title to all property and records registered and accrued to your citizen number: all contracts and liabilities, requirements of performance and other legal instruments not legally lapsed at the moment of death of your predecessor are deemed to continue, all contracts entered upon by your legal guardian in your name thereafter and until now are deemed effective, all titles held in trust in the name of Ariane Emory under that number are deemed valid and the individuals within this Writ are deemed legally identical, excepting present status as a minor under guardianship.

"Vote so registered, none dissenting. Determination made and entered effective as of this hour and date."

The gavel came down. The bailiff brought her the paper, and it was signed and sealed by the whole lot of judges. *Writ of Certification*, it said at the top. With her name: Ariane Emory.

She gave a deep breath and gave it to uncle Giraud when he asked for it.

"It's still stupid," she whispered to him.

But she was awfully glad to have it, and wished she could keep it herself, so uncle Giraud wouldn't get careless and lose it.

The reporters were *not* mean. She was real glad about that, too. She figured out in a hurry that there weren't any Enemies with them, just a lot of people with notebooks, and people with cameras; so she told Catlin and Florian: "You can relax, they're all right," and sat on the chair they let her have because she said she was tired and her arm hurt.

She could swing her feet, too. Act natural, Giraud had said. Be friendly. Don't be nasty with them: they'll put you on the news and then everybody across Union will know you're a nice little girl and nobody should file lawsuits and bring Bills of Discovery against you.

That made perfect sense.

So she sat there and they wrote down questions and passed them to the oldest reporter, questions like: "How did you break your arm?" all over again.

"Ser Nye, can you tell us what a horse is?" somebody asked next, out loud, and she thought that was funny, of course people knew what a horse was if they listened to tapes. But she was nice about it:

"I can do that," she said. "Horse is his name, besides what he is. He's about—" She reached up with her hand, and decided that wasn't high enough. "Twice that tall. And brown and black, and he kind of dances. Florian knows. Florian used to take care of him. On Earth you used to ride them, but you had a saddle and bridle. I tried it without. That's how I fell off. Bang. Right over the fence."

"That must have hurt."

She swung her feet and felt better and better: she Had them. She liked it better when they didn't write the questions. It was easier to Work them. "Just a bit. It hurts worse now, sometimes. But I get my cast off in a few weeks."

But they went back to the written ones. "Do you have a lot of friends at Reseune? Do you play with other girls and boys?"

"Oh, sometimes." Don't be nasty, Giraud had said. "Mostly with Florian and Catlin, though. They're my best friends."

"Follow-up," somebody said. "Ser Giraud, can you tell us a little more about that?"

"Ari," Giraud said. "Do you want to answer? What do you do to amuse yourself?"

"Oh, lots of things. Finding things and Starchase and building things." She swung her feet again and looked around at Florian and Catlin. "Don't we?"

"Yes," Florian said.

"Who takes care of you?" the next question said.

"Nelly. My maman left her with me. And uncle Denys. I stay with him."

"Follow-up," a woman said.

Giraud read the next question. "What's your best subject?"

"Biology. My maman taught me." Back to that. News got to Fargone. "I sent her letters. Can I say hello to my maman? Will it go to Fargone?"

Giraud didn't like that. He frowned at her. *No.*

She smiled, real nice, while all the reporters talked together.

"Can it?" she asked.

"It sure can," someone called out to her. "Who is your maman, sweet?"

"My maman is Jane Strassen. It's nearly my birthday. I'm almost nine. Hello, maman!"

Because nasty uncle Giraud couldn't stop her, because Giraud had told her everybody clear across Union would be on her side if she was a nice little girl.

"Follow-up!"

"Let's save that for the next news conference," uncle Giraud said. "We have questions already submitted, in their own order. Let's keep to the format. Please. We've granted this news conference after a very stressful day for Ari, and she's not up to free-for-all questions, please. Not today."

"Is that the Jane Strassen who's director of RESEUNESPACE?"

"Yes, it is, the Jane Strassen who's reputed in the field for work in her own right, I shouldn't neglect to mention that, in Dr. Strassen's service. We can provide you whatever material you want on her career and her credentials. But let's keep to format, now. Let's give the child a little chance to catch her breath, please. Her family life is *not* a matter of public record, nor should it be. Ask her that in a few years. Right now she's a very over-tired little girl who's got a lot of questions to get through, and I'm afraid we're not going to get to all of them if we start taking them out of order. —Ari, the next question: what do you do for hobbies?"

Uncle Giraud was Working them, of course, and they knew it. She could stop him, but that would be trouble with uncle Giraud, and she didn't want that. She had done everything she wanted. She was safe now, she knew she was, because Giraud didn't dare do a thing in front of all these people who could tell things all the way to her maman, and who could find out things. She knew about Freedom of the Press. It was in her Civics tapes.

"What for hobbies? I study about astronomy. And I have an aquarium. Uncle Denys got me some guppies. They come all the way from Earth. You're supposed to get rid of the bad ones, and you can breed ones with pretty tails. The pond fish would eat them. But I don't do that. I just put them in another tank, because I don't like to get them eaten. They're kind of interesting. My teacher says they're throw-backs to the old kind. My uncle Denys is going to get me some more tanks and he says I can put them in the den."

"Guppies are small fish," uncle Giraud explained.

People outside Reseune didn't get to see a lot of things, she decided.

"Guppies are easy," she said. "Anybody could raise them. They're pretty, too, and they don't eat much." She shifted in her chair. "Not like Horse."

---

v

There was a certain strange atmosphere in the restaurant in the North corridor—in the attitude of staff and patrons, in the fact that the modest-price eatery was jammed and taking reservations by mid-afternoon—and only the quick-witted and lucky had realized, making the afternoon calls for supper accommodations, that thoroughly extravagant *Changes* was the only restaurant that might have slots left. Five minutes more, Grant had said, smug with success, and they would have had cheese sandwiches at home.

As it was, it was cocktails, hors d'oeuvres, spiced pork roast with imported fruit, in a restaurant jammed with Wing One staff spending credit and drinking a little too much and huddling together in furtive speculations that were not quite celebration, not quite confidence, but a sense of Occasion, a sense after hanging all day on every syllable that fell from the mouth of a little girl in more danger than she possibly understood—that something had resulted, the Project that had monopolized their lives for years had unfolded unexpected wings and demonstrated—God knew what: something alchemical; or something utterly, simply human.

Strange, Justin thought, that he had felt so proprietary, so anxious—and so damned personally affected when the Project perched on a chair in front of all of Union, swung her feet like any little girl, and switched from bright chatter to pensive intelligence and back again—

Unscathed and still afloat.

The rest of the clientele in *Changes* might be startled to find the Warrick faction out to dinner, a case of the skeleton at the feast; there were looks and he was sure there was comment at Suli Schwartz's table.

"Maybe they think we're making a point," he said to Grant over the soup.

"Maybe," Grant said. "Do you care? I don't."

Justin gave a humorless laugh. "I kept thinking—"

"What?"

"I kept thinking all through that interview, God, what if she blurts out something about: 'My friend Justin Warrick.'"

"Mmmn, the child has much too much finesse for that. She knew what she was doing. Every word of it."

"You think so."

"I truly think so."

"They say those test scores aren't equal to Ari's."

"What do you think?"

Justin gazed at the vase on the table, the single red geranium cluster that shed a pleasant if strong green-plant scent. Definite, bright, alien to a gray-blue world. "I think—she's a fighter. If she weren't, they'd have driven her crazy. I don't know what she *is*, but, God, I think sometimes, —God, why in *hell* can't they declare it a success and let the kid just grow up, that's all. And then I think about the Bok-clone thing, and I think—what happens if they did that? Or what if they drive her over the edge with their damn hormones and their damn tapes—? Or what if they stop now—and she can't—"

"—Integrate the sets?" Grant asked. Azi-psych term. The point of collation, the coming-of-age in an ascending pyramid of logic structures.

It fit, in its bizarre way. It fit the concept floating in his mind. But not that. Not for a CIT, whose value-structures were, if Emory was right and Hauptmann and Poley were wrong, flux-learned and locked in matrices.

"—master the flux," he said. Straight Emory theory, contrary to the Hauptmann-Poley thesis. "Control the hormones. Instead of the other way around."

Grant picked up his wine-glass, held it up and looked at it. "One glass of this. God. Revelation. The man accepts flux-theory." And then a glance in Justin's direction, sober and straight and concerned. "You think it's working—for Emory's reasons?"

"I don't know anymore. I really don't know." The soup changed taste on him, went coppery and for a moment unpleasant; but he took another spoonful and the feeling passed. Sanity reasserted itself, a profound regret for a little girl in a hell of a situation. "I keep thinking—if they pull the program from under her now— Where's her compass, then? When you spend your life in a whirlwind—and then the wind dies down—there's all this quiet—this terrible quiet—"

He was not talking about Ari, suddenly, and realized he was not. Grant was staring at him, worriedly, and he was caught in a cold clear moment, lamplight, Grant, the smell of geranium, in a dark void where other faces hung in separate, lamplit existence.

"When the flux stops," he said, "when it goes null—you feel like you've lost all contact with things. That nothing makes sense. Like all values going equal, none more valid than any other. And you can't move. So you devise your own pressure to make yourself move. You invent a flux-state. Even panic helps. Otherwise you go like the Bok clone, you just diffuse in all directions, and get no more input than before."

"Flow-through," Grant said. "Without a supervisor to pull you out. I've been there. Are we talking about Ari? Or are you telling me something?"

"CITs," Justin said. "CITs. We can flux-think our flux-states too, endless subdivisions. We tunnel between realities." He finished his soup and took a sip of wine. "Anything can throw you there—like a broken hologram, any piece of it the matrix evokes the flux. The taste of orange juice. After today— the smell of geraniums. You start booting up memories to recollect the hormone-shifts, because when the wind stops, and nothing is moving, you start retrieving old states to run in—am I making sense? Because when the wind stops, you haven't got anything else. Bok's clone became a musician. A fair one. Not great. But music is emotion. Emotional flux through a math system of tones and ratios. Flux and flow-through state for a brain that might have dealt with hyperspace."

"Except they never took the pressure off Bok's clone," Grant said. "She was always news, to the day she died."

"Or it was skewed, chaotic pressure, piling up confusions. *You're brilliant. You're a failure. You're failing us. Can you tell us why you're such a disappointment?* I wonder if anyone ever put any enjoyment loop into the Bok clone's deep-sets."

"How do you do that," Grant asked, "when putting it in our eminently sensible sets—flirts with psychosis? I think you teach the subject to enjoy the adrenaline rushes. Or to produce pleasure out of the flux itself instead of retrieving it out of the data-banks."

The waiter came and deftly removed the empty soup-bowls, added more wine to the glasses.

"I think," Justin said uncomfortably, "you've defined a masochist. Or said something." His mind kept jumping between his own situation, Jordan, the kid in the courtroom, the cold, green lines of his programs on the vid display, the protected, carefully stressed and de-stressed society of the Town, where the loads were calculated and a logical, humane, human-run system of operations forbade overload.

Pleasure and pain, sweet.

He reached for the wine-glass, and kept his hand steady as he sipped it, set it down again as the waiters brought the main course.

He was still thinking while he was chewing his first bite, and Grant held a long, long silence.

God, he thought, do I *need* a state of panic to think straight?

Am I going off down a tangent to lunacy, or am I onto something?

"I'm damn tempted," he said to Grant finally, "to make them a suggestion about Ari."

"God," Grant said, and swallowed a bite in haste. "They'd hyperventilate. —You're serious. *What* would you suggest to them?"

"That they get Ari a different teacher. At least one more teacher, someone less patient than John Edwards. She isn't going to push her own limits if she has Edwards figured out, is she? She's got a whole lot of approval and damned little affection in her life. Which would *you* be more interested in, in the Edwards set-up? Edwards is a damned nice fellow—damned fine teacher, does wonders getting the students interested; but if you're Ari Emory, what are you going to work for—Edwards' full attention—or a test score?"

Grant quirked a brow, genuine bemusement. "You could be right."

"Damn, I know I'm right. What in hell was she looking for in the office?" He remembered then what he had thought of when they made the reservations, that Security could find them, Security could bug the damned geranium for all he knew. The thought came with its own little adrenaline flux. A reminder he was alive. "The kid wants attention, that's all. And they've just given her the biggest adrenaline high she's had in years. *Sailing* through the interview. *Everyone* pouring attention on her. She's happier than she's been in her poor manipulated life. How can Edwards fight *that* when she gets back? What's he got to offer, to keep her interested in her studies, against that kind of rush? They need somebody who can get *her* attention, not somebody who lets her get *his*." He shook his head and applied his knife to the roast. "Damn. It's not my problem, is it?"

"I'd strongly suggest you not get into it," Grant said. "I'd suggest you not mention it to Yanni."

"The problem is, no one wants to be the focus of her displeasure," Justin said. "No one wants to stand in that hot spot, no more than you or I do. Ari always did have a temper—the cold sort. The sort that knew how to wait. I'm not sure how far it went, I never knew her that well. But senior staff did. Didn't they?"

<hr>

vi

They got out of the car with Security pouring out of the other cars, and Ari stepped up on the walk leading to the glass doors, with uncle Giraud behind her and Florian and Catlin closing in tight to protect her from the crush of their Security people and the reporters.

The doors opened. She could see that, but she could not see over the shoulders around her. Sometimes they frightened her, even if it was her they had come to see and even if it was her they were trying to protect.

She was afraid they were going to step on her, that was how close it was; and she was still bruised and sore.

They had driven around and seen the docks and the Volga where it met Swigert Bay, and they had seen the spaceport and places that Ari would have given a great deal to have gotten out to see, but uncle Giraud had said no, there were too many people and it was too hard.

Like at the hotel, where they had spent the night in a huge suite, a whole floor all to themselves; and where people had jammed up in the lobby and around their car. That had scared her. It scared her in the Hall of State when they were stopped in the doors and they started to close while she was in them; but Catlin shot out a hand and stopped them and they got through, all of them.

The Hall of State was the first thing they had really gotten to see at all, because there were all these people following them around, and all the reporters.

It was the way it looked in the tapes, it was huge and it echoed till it made you dizzy when you were looking around at it, with all the people up on the balconies looking down at them: it was real, the way the Court had been just a place in a tape, and now she knew what the room at the top of the steps was going to look like the moment uncle Giraud told her that was where the Nine met.

The noise died down. People were all talking, but they were not shouting at each other, and the Security people had put the reporters back, so they could walk and look at things.

Uncle Giraud took her and Florian and Catlin upstairs where she shook hands with Nasir Harad, the Chairman of the Nine: he was white-haired and thin and there was a lot of him that he didn't give away, she could tell that the way she could tell that there was something odd about him, the way he kept holding her hand after she had shaken his, and the way he looked at her like he wanted something.

"Uncle Giraud," she whispered when they were going through the doors into the Council Chamber, "he was *funny*, back there."

"Shush," he said, and pointed to the big half-circle desk where all the Councillors would sit if they were here.

It was funny, anyway, to be asking *Giraud* whether anybody was a friendly or not. She looked at what he was telling her, which seat was which, and where Giraud sat when he was on Council—that was Science, she knew that: they had driven past the Science Building, and Giraud said he had an office there, and one in the Hall of State, but he wasn't there a lot of the time, he had secretaries and managers to run things.

He had Security push a button that opened the wall back, and she stood there staring while the Council Chamber opened right into the big Council Hall, becoming a room to the side of the seats, with the Rostrum in front of the huge wall uncle Giraud said was made out of stone from the Volga banks, all rough and red sandstone, just like it was a riverside.

The seats all looked tiny in front of that.

"This is where the laws are made," uncle Giraud said, and his voice echoed, like every footstep. "That's where the Council President and the Chairman sit, up there on the Rostrum."

She knew that. She could tape-remember the room full, with people walking up and down the aisles. Her heart beat fast.

"This is the center of Union," uncle Giraud said. "This is where people work out their differences. This is what makes everything work."

She had never heard uncle Giraud talk like that, never heard uncle Giraud talk in that quiet voice that said these things were important. He sounded like Dr. Edwards, somehow, doing lessons for her.

He took her back outside then, where it was noisy and Security made room for them. Down the stairs then. She could see cameras set up down below.

"We're going to do a short interview," uncle Giraud told her, "and then we're going to have lunch with Chairman Harad. Is that all right?"

"What's going to be for lunch?" she asked. Food sounded good. She was not so sure about Chairman Harad.

"Councillor," an older woman said, coming up to them, and put her hand on uncle Giraud's sleeve and said: "Private. Quickly. *Please.*"

It was some kind of trouble. Ari knew it, the woman was giving it off like she was about to explode with worry, and Giraud froze up just a second and then said: "Ari. Stand here."

They talked together, and the woman's back was to them. The noise blurred everything out.

But uncle Giraud came back very fast, and he was upset. His face was all pale.

"Sera," Florian said, very fast, very soft, like he wanted her to say what to do. But she didn't know where the trouble was coming from, or what it was.

"Ari," uncle Giraud said, and took her aside, along by the wall, the huge fountain, and down to the other end where there were some offices. Security moved very fast, Florian and Catlin went with her, and nobody was following them. There was just that voice-sound, everywhere, murmuring like the water.

Security opened the doors. Security told the people inside to go into a back office and they looked confused and upset.

But: "Wait out here," uncle Giraud said to Florian and Catlin, and she looked at them, scared, uncle Giraud hurrying her into an empty office with a desk and a chair. They were going to follow her, not certain what to do, but he said: *"Out!"* and she said: "It's all right."

He shut the door on them. They were scared. Uncle Giraud was scared. And she didn't know what was going on with everyone, except he took her by the shoulders and looked at her and said:

"Ari, —Ari, there's news on the net. It's from Fargone. I want you to listen to me. It's about your maman. She's died, Ari."

She just stood there. She felt his hands on her shoulders. He hurt her right one. He was telling her something crazy, something that couldn't be about maman, it didn't make sense.

"She died some six months ago, Ari. The news is just breaking over the station net. It just got here. They're picking it up out there, on their comlinks. That woman—heard it; and told me, and I didn't want you to hear it out there, Ari. Take a breath, sweet. Ari."

He shook her. It hurt. And she couldn't breathe for a moment, couldn't, till she got a breath all at once and uncle Giraud hugged her against him and patted her back and called her sweet. Like maman.

She hit him. He hugged her so she couldn't, and just went on holding her while she cried.

"It's a damn lie!" she yelled when she got enough breath.

"No." He hugged her hard. "Sweet, your maman was very old, very old, that's all. And people die. Listen to me. I'm going to take you home. Home, understand? But you've got to walk out of here. You've got to walk out of here past all those people and get to the car, you understand me? Security's going to get the car, we're going to go straight to the airport, we're going to fly home. But the first thing you have to do is get to the car. Can you do that?"

She listened. She listened to everything. Things went past her. But she stopped crying, and he set her back by the shoulders and wiped her face with his fingers, and smoothed her hair and got her to sit down in the chair.

"Are you all right?" he asked her, very, very quiet. "Ari?"

She got another gulp of air. And stared through him. She felt him pat her shoulder, and heard him go to the door and call Catlin and Florian.

"Ari's maman has died," she heard him say. "We just found it out."

More and more people. Florian and Catlin. If all of them believed it, then it was truer and truer. All the people out there. Maman was on the news. The whole of Union knew her maman had died.

Uncle Giraud came back and got down on one knee and got his comb and very carefully began to comb her hair. She messed it up and turned her face away. *Go away.*

But he combed it again, very gentle, very patient, and patted her on the shoulder when he finished. Florian brought her a drink and she took it in her good hand. Catlin just stood there with a worried look.

Dead is dead, that was what Catlin said. Catlin didn't know what to do with a CIT who thought it was something else.

"Ari," uncle Giraud said, "let's get out of here. Let's get you to the car. All right? Take my hand. There's no one going to ask you any questions. Let's just walk to the car."

She took his hand. She got up and she walked with her hand in Giraud's out into the office and outside again, where all the people were standing, far across the hall; and the voice-sound died away into the distance. She could hear the fountain-noise for the first time. Giraud shifted hands on her, and put his right one on her shoulder, and she walked with him, with Catlin in front of her and Florian on her other side, and all the Security people. But they didn't need them. Nobody asked any questions.

They were sorry, she thought. They were sorry for her.

And she hated that. She *hated* the way they looked at her.

It was a terribly long walk, until they were going through the doors and getting into the car, and Florian and Catlin piling in on the other side, while uncle Giraud got her into the back seat and sat down with her and held her.

Security closed the back doors, one of them got in and closed the doors and the car started up, fast and hard, the tunnel lights flashing past them.

"Ari," Giraud said to her on the plane, moving Florian out of his seat to sit down across the little table from her, once they were in the air. "I've got the whole story now. Your maman died in her office. She was at work. She had a heart attack. It was very fast. They couldn't even get her to hospital."

"Where are my letters?" she asked, looking straight at him, looking him right in the face.

Giraud looked at her straight too. "At Fargone. I'm sure she read them."

"Why didn't she answer me?"

Giraud took a moment. Then: "I don't know, Ari. I truly don't know. I don't know if I can ever answer that. I'll try to find out. But it takes time. Everything between here and Fargone—takes a long time."

She turned her face away from him, to the window where the outback showed hazy reds.

She had not had her maman for six months. And she had never felt it. She had gone on as if nothing had happened, as if everything was still the same. It made her ashamed. It made her mad. Terrible things could have happened besides that, and it would take that long to know about them.

"I want Ollie to come home," she said to Giraud.

"I'll see about it," Giraud said.

"Do it!"

"Ollie has a choice too," Giraud said. "Doesn't he? He's your maman's partner. He'll have taken care of your maman's business. He'll have seen that things went right. He's not a servant, sweet, he's a very good manager, and he'll be handling your maman's office and handling her affairs for her. He'd want to do that. But I'll send and ask him what he wants to do."

She swallowed at the lump in her throat. She wished Giraud would go away. She didn't know what she thought yet. She was still putting it together.

She thought of that long walk and everybody in the Hall staring at her. And she had to do that again at Reseune—everybody staring at her, everybody knowing what was going on.

It made her mad. It made her so mad it was hard to think.

But she needed to. She needed to know where people were lying to her. And who would want to take things from her. And whether that *was* what had happened to maman.

Who are they, where are they, what have they got?

She looked at Giraud when he was not looking, just looked, a long time.

vii

The news played the clip over and over, the solemn, shaken girl in the blue suit, walking with Giraud and Florian and Catlin past the silent lines of newspeople and government workers, just the cameras running, and the quick, grim movement of Security flanking them as they passed through the hall.

Mikhail Corain watched it with his jaw clamped, watched the subsequent clips, some provided by Reseune, of Ari's childhood, of Jane Strassen's career, all interposed with the Court sequences, the interview after, and then back through the whole thing again, with interviews with the Reseune Information Bureau, with Denys Nye, with child psychologists—with solemn music and supered images and reportorial garbage making photo comparisons between the original Ariane standing solemnly at her mother's funeral, and the replicate's decorously pale, shock-stricken face in a still from the clip they played and played and played, dammit.

The whole of Cyteen was wallowing in the best damn theater Reseune could have asked for. That bitch Catherine Lao hardly had to bend any effort to key up the news-services, which had already been covering the Discovery bill—then the bombshell revelation that there was an Emory replicate filing for the right of Succession, no Bok clone, *brilliant*—then the court appearance, the interview—all points on the Expansionist side; Defense's invocation of the Military Secrets Act against the bill, a little coverage of Centrist objections, a possible gain against the tide—

Then Strassen's death, and the child getting the news, virtually on live cameras—

God, it was a circus.

A freighter docked at Cyteen Station and shot the content of its Fargone-acquired informational packet into the Cyteen data-sorters, the news-packet hit the Cyteen news-comp, the news-comp upgraded its information and scrolled it past the human watcher, and what might have been a passing-interest kind of story, the death of a Reseune administrator who was not even a known name to the average citizen, became the biggest media event since—

Since the murder at Reseune and the Warrick hearing.

The news had to be real: the data-storage of a starship—the whole system that carried news, electronic mail, publications, stockmarket data, financial records and statistics, ballots and civil records—was the entire data-flow of the last station visited, shot out of a starship's Black Box when it came to dock, as the current station's data spooled in. It was the system that kept the markets going and the whole of Union functioning: tampering with a Black Box was physically unlikely and morally unthinkable, and Fargone was six Cyteen months away, so there was no way in hell the information could have been timed for the impact it had—

God, he found himself sorting through every move he had made and every contact with Giraud Nye and Reseune he had had, wondering if there was any remotest chance he had been maneuvered into the Discovery bill at a time when Reseune was ready.

A lifetime of dealing with Emory, that was what made him have thoughts like that.

Like Strassen being murdered. Like the kind of ruthlessness that would use a kid the way they created and used this one—killing off one of their own, who was, God knew, a hundred forty-odd and already on the brink—

What was a life, to people who created and destroyed it as a matter of routine?

It was a question worth following up, quietly, by his own investigatory channels; but by everything he knew of RESEUNESPACE, existing in the same separate station as the Defense Bureau installation at Fargone with absolutely nothing to link them with Fargone Station except a twice-daily shuttle run, it was difficult to get at anything or anyone on the inside.

And the Centrist party could lose, considerably, by making the wrong move right now—by making charges that might not prove out, by going ahead with the bill that had to result in lengthy hearings and a court case involving the little girl who had turned seasoned reporters to emotional jelly and generated such a flood of inquiries the Bureau of Information had set aside special numbers for the case.

That was only the beginning. The ships that undocked from Cyteen Station this week were the start of a wave front that would go clear to Earth before it ran out of audience.

No way in hell to continue with the bill. *Anything* that involved drawn-out procedures could intersect with future events in very unpredictable ways.

While I consider the investigation ultimately necessary in the public interest, it seems inappropriate to proceed at this time. That was the sentence his speechwriters were still hammering out.

He was damned to look bad no matter what he did. He had thought of demanding an investigation into the child's welfare, and raising the issue of Reseune's creating the child precisely to shield those records.

The whole Centrist party suddenly found itself saddled with a serious position problem.

viii

Nelly helped her take the blouse off—it fastened on the bad shoulder, and the sleeve was cut and fastened back together, so it would come on and off over the cast. She had several of the same kind, and she wore things with jackets, that she could wear draped over the shoulder on the right side.

She felt better then. She had to take a shower with a plastic bag taped and sealed around her arm, and when she came out again, Nelly helped her take the tape off and get into her pajamas.

Nelly was upset, Ari could feel it, and she knew she shouldn't let her mad get loose with Nelly, she shouldn't let it get loose with anybody.

"I'm not going to bed yet," she said when Nelly wanted to put her there, and Nelly said:

"You're supposed to."

Which made her want to hit Nelly, or to cry, both of which were stupid. So she said, very patiently: "Nelly, let me alone and go to bed. Right now."

She had been to maman's memorial service today. She had gotten through it and not cried, at least she had not made a scene like Victoria Strassen, who had sniffed and hiccuped and finally Security had walked over and talked to her. She had never met aunt Victoria. She was already mad at her. Maman would have been mad at her, even if she was maman's half sister. Herself, she had sores on the inside of her mouth where she had bitten down to keep from crying, and she didn't mind, that was all right, it was better than aunt Victoria.

I want you to think about going, uncle Denys had said. *You don't have to, understand. I'm sure your maman wouldn't mind one way or the other: you know how she felt about formal stuff— She's gone to the sun at Fargone: that's a spacer funeral, and your maman was a spacer before she lived at Reseune. But here in the House we do things a little differently: we go out in the East Garden, where all the memorials are, if the weather's such we can, or somewhere—and your maman's friends will tell a few stories about your maman, that's the way we do. I don't want you to go if it's going to upset you; but I thought you might want to hear those things, and it might help you learn about your maman, who she was when she was young, and all the things she did. If you don't want to, don't go. If you want to go and then change your mind, all you have to do is pull at my sleeve and you and I will just walk out the gate and no one will think anything about it: children don't always go to these things. Not even all the friends do. It just depends on the person, whether they feel they need to, you understand?*

Florian and Catlin had not gone. They were too young and they were azi, uncle Denys said, and they didn't understand CIT funerals.

You don't want them to have to take tape for it, uncle Denys had said.

She was terribly, terribly glad it was over. She felt bruised inside the way she was outside, and uncle Denys kept giving her aspirin, and Dr. Ivanov had given her a shot he said would make her feel a little wobbly, but it would help her get through the services.

She wished he hadn't. She had wanted to hear some of it clearer, and it all rolled around in her head and echoed.

It still did, but she put Nelly out the door and told Nelly send Catlin and Florian and go to bed and take the tape Dr. Ivanov wanted her to have.

"Yes," Nelly said, looking miserable.

Ari bit her lip again. She wanted that badly to yell at her. Instead she went and fed her fish, and watched them chase after the food and dodge in and out of the weeds. There were a lot of babies. One of the big ones had had hers. And there was her prettiest male who was in the tank with all the ugly females, to see if the babies would be prettier. Florian could net him out for her and put him back in his regular tank: she was afraid of hurting him with the net, working with her left hand.

Tomorrow. She was not in the mood to do anything with them tonight.

Catlin and Florian came in, still in their uniforms, and looking worried, the way they had been constantly since they found out about maman. They didn't understand half how it felt, she knew that, but they were hurting all the same, because she hurt.

Florian had told her he felt terribly guilty about her arm and then her maman, and asked her if there was anything they could do.

She wished there were. But he couldn't be guilty, he just felt bad: she told him that, and asked him if he needed tape, the way she was supposed to if her azi came to her.

Uncle Denys had told her that.

"No," Florian had said, very quick, very definite. "We don't want to. What if you needed us, and we'd be in hospital? No. We don't want that."

Now:

"I want you to stay here tonight," she said when they came in.

"Yes, sera," Florian said; and: "We'll get our stuff," Catlin said, as if both of them were happy then.

She felt better when they were with her, when no one else was. It was hard to go out where there were people, like going out with no clothes on, like she was made out of glass and people would know everything inside her and find out everything she didn't want everyone to know. But she never felt that way with Florian and Catlin. They were her real friends, and they could sleep in the same room and sit around in just their pajamas together, even if Florian was a boy.

And with the door shut and with just them, she could stop having that knotted-up feeling that made her broken arm ache and made her feel sick at her stomach and tired, so tired of hurting.

"They said a lot of nice things about maman," she said when they had gotten their pallets made in the corner and gotten into their pajamas and settled down on the end of her bed.

A lot of the staff had really been maman's friends. A lot of them were really sorry and really missed her. Aunt Victoria was sorry and scared, when Security came and probably told her to stop crying or asked her to leave; then aunt Victoria had been really, really mad: so aunt Victoria had left the garden right after that, on her own, while Dr. Ivanov was telling how maman had run Wing One.

There were a lot of things she wished she could talk about out loud with Florian and Catlin. But she *was* going to tell them, that was no problem. It just took longer.

There had been a lot of upset people there, at the services, and it was strange how they Felt different than the reporters. The reporters had been sorry. Reseune was sorry too; but a lot of them Felt mad like her mad, which was maybe because it wasn't fair people had to die at all; but there had been so many different flavors of mad there, so many different flavors of being sorry, not at all like the reporters, but very strong, very complicated, all the way down past what she could pick up on their faces.

Justin and Grant had been there. Grant was one of the only azi.

A lot of grown people had said how maman had been their teacher, and they really loved her.

Dr. Schwartz had said maman and he used to fight a lot so loud that everybody in the halls could hear it, but that was because she never would take second best about anything; and he said whatever she set up at RESEUNESPACE was going to be all right, because that was the way maman always did things.

That made her remember her maman's voice echoing out of the bedroom, right through the walls: *Dammit, Ollie*— And made her feel warm all over, like maman was yelling at her: *Dammit, straighten up, Ari, don't give me any of that nonsense. That doesn't get anywhere with me.*

Like maman was back for a second. Like she was *there*, inside, just then. Or anytime she wanted to think about her. She wasn't at Fargone anymore.

Ollie was. And a lot of the Disappeareds might be.

She had thought on the plane coming home—who in the House just might know a lot of things.

And who she could scare into telling her.

"You're a damn fool," Yanni said, and Justin looked him in the eye and said:

"That's no news. It's all there in the memo. Probably you think I have ulterior motives—which isn't the case. Nothing against John Edwards. Nothing against anyone. I don't even know I'm right. Just—" He shrugged. It was easy to go too far with Yanni, and he had probably gone there, high and wide. Time to stage a retreat, he reckoned. Fast. "I'll go get back to *my* business," he said. "I'll have the GY project in tomorrow morning."

"Stay put."

He sank back into the chair, under Yanni's scowl.

"You think the kid doesn't have enough stress," Yanni said.

"I don't mean that. You know I don't mean that."

"Son, Administration is just a little wrought up just now. So am I. I appreciate the fact you don't hate the kid, you really think you see something— but you know, we're all tired, we're all frayed around the edges, and I really hope you haven't gone anywhere else with this."

"No. I haven't."

"You know what I think you're doing?"

Not a rhetorical question. Yanni left a long, deathly silence for his answer.

"What, ser?"

"Sounds like your own damn craziness, to me, the same damn sink you come back to like a stone falls *down*, that's what it sounds like to me. Motivations and reward structures."

"I think I have a point."

"And you put it in writing." Yanni picked up the three-page memo and slid it into a slot at the edge of his desk. A red telltale flashed, and a soft hum meant even the ash had been scrambled. "That's a favor, son. I'm not supposed to wipe documents that bear on the Project. I just broke a regulation. As it happens—there are those of us who think you're right on the mark with this. And I like one of your arguments . . . if you don't mind my borrowing it for the upcoming staff meeting."

"Whatever you like. I'd just as soon you didn't mention the source."

Yanni gave him a long slow look. "Sometimes you worry me."

"I haven't got any ulterior motives. I don't *want* my name on it."

Another long look. "Motivational psych. —You haven't *had* the Rubin data. Just the structures. I told you I'd keep you off real-time. But I'd like you to do something for me, son. A favor. A real favor. I'm going to dump all Rubin's data on you. The whole pile."

"He's, what, two?"

"Not the replicate. The original."

"Why?"

"I'm not going to tell you that."

"What do you want out of it?"

"I'm not going to tell you that either."

"I get the idea."

"All right." Yanni leaned on his elbows, hands locked in front of him. "You run the problem. I'll tell you what I think about it."

"Is this an exercise?"

"I'm not going to tell you that."

"Dammit, Yanni—"

"You're right about the kid. She's smarter than those scores. You leave that in my lap. You take care of your work. I'll take care of the Project. All right?"

X

Uncle Denys took another helping of eggs. Ari picked at hers, mostly just moved them around, because breakfast upset her stomach.

"We could go out to eat tonight," uncle Denys said. "Would you like that?"

"No," she said. "I'm not hungry."

It was her ninth birthday. She just wanted to forget it was her birthday at all. She didn't want to complain about her stomach, because then uncle Denys would call Dr. Ivanov, and that would mean another shot, and her head being all fuzzy.

"Is there anything you *do* want?" uncle Denys said.

I want maman, she thought, mad, mad until she felt like she could throw the dishes off the table and break everything.

But she didn't.

"Ari, I know it's a terrible time for you. There's nothing I can do. I wish there were. Is there anything you'd like to do? Is there anything you want that I can get you?"

She thought. There was no good throwing an offer like that away. If you could get something, you got it, and you might be glad later. She had figured that out a long time ago.

"There is something I want for my birthday."

"What's that, dear?"

She looked uncle Denys right in his eyes, her best wishing-look. "Horse."

Uncle Denys took in his breath, real quick. "Ari, sweet, —"

"You asked."

"I'd think a broken arm is enough. No. Absolutely not."

"I want Horse."

"Horse belongs to Reseune, Ari. You can't just *own* him."

"That's what I want, anyway."

"No."

That hurt. She shoved her plate away, and got up from the table.

"Ari, I think a broken arm ought to do, don't you?"

She felt like crying, and when she did that she went to her room. So she went that way.

"Ari," uncle Denys said, "I want to talk with you."

She looked back at him. "I don't feel good. I'm going to bed."

"Come here."

She didn't. She went to her hall and shut the door.

And went and cried like a baby, lying on her bed, till she got mad and threw Poo-thing across the room.

Then she felt like something had broken, because Poo-thing came from maman.

But he wasn't real, anyway.

She heard somebody open the hall door, and then they opened hers. She figured it was uncle Denys, and she turned over and scowled; but it was Catlin and Florian, come to see what was the matter with her.

"Ser Denys wants you," Florian said in a hushed voice.

"Tell him go to hell."

Florian looked distressed. But he would go do that and he would get in a lot of trouble for her, she knew he would.

"Yes, sera."

"No," she said, and wiped her eyes and got up. "I will." She wiped her eyes again and walked past him and Catlin, and went out to the living room.

It was a mistake to walk out on uncle Denys. When she did that, she let him Work her, and now she was having to walk back into the living room he owned and be nice.

Stupid, stupid, she told herself, and unraveled her mad and got a nicer expression on her face when she went to uncle Denys. Denys was in the dining room having his coffee and he pretended not to notice her for a second.

That was Working, too.

"I'm sorry, uncle Denys."

He looked at her then, took a quick sip of coffee, and said: "I did have a surprise planned for you today," he said. "Do you want some more orange juice?"

She moped over to the chair and climbed into it, hugging her cast with her good hand. "Florian and Catlin too," she said.

"Seely," uncle Denys said. And Seely came and got two more glasses and poured orange juice as Florian and Catlin quietly settled down across the table.

"Nelly's in hospital again," uncle Denys said. "Ari, you know it hurts her when you put her out and call somebody else."

"Well, I can't help it. Nelly fusses."

"Nelly doesn't know what to do with you anymore. I think it might be a good idea to let Nelly go work down in the Town, in the nursery. You think about that. But that's for you to decide."

She could not lose maman and Nelly in one week. Even if Nelly drove her crazy. She looked at the table and tried not to think about that.

"You think about it," uncle Denys said. "Nelly's the happiest when she has a baby to take care of. And you're not a baby. So you're making her unhappy—especially when you give her orders. But you just think about it. It's not like you couldn't see Nelly again. Otherwise she's going to have to take tape to re-train her and she'll have to do house management or something."

"What does Nelly want?"

"She wants you to be three years old. But that won't work. So Nelly's got to move or Nelly's got to change."

"Can Nelly have a job down in the baby lab? And live here?"

"Yes, she could do that. It's not really a bad idea." Uncle Denys set his cup down for Seely to pour more coffee, then stirred it. "If that's what you want."

"I *want* Horse."

Uncle Denys' brows came together. "Ari, you can't have what'll hurt you."

"Florian says there's a baby."

"Ari, horses are big animals. Nobody knows anything about riding them, not on Cyteen. We have them for research, not to play with."

"You could give me the baby one."

"God," uncle Denys said.

"Florian knows all about horses."

Uncle Denys looked at Florian and Florian went azi, all blank.

"No," uncle Denys said flatly. Then: "Let me talk to AG about it, Ari, all right? I don't know about horses. When you grow a bit, maybe. When you show me you're grown up enough not to *sneak* down there and break your neck."

"That's nasty."

"It's true, isn't it? You could have broken your neck. Or your back. Or your head. I don't mind if you do things: you'll fly a plane someday. You'll do a lot of things. But for God's *sake*, Ari, you don't sneak off and try to fly one of the jets, do you? You have to study. There's no second chance when the ground's coming at you. You have to know what can go wrong and how to deal with it, and you have to be big enough; and if you want to deal with a horse, you'd better be big enough to hold on to it, and you'd better show me you're grown up enough to be smarter than the horse is."

That was nasty too. But it was probably true.

"He surprised you," uncle Denys said, "because you didn't know what you were doing. So I suggest you study about animals. They're not machines. They think. And he thought: there's some fool on my back. And he was bigger and he got rid of her. Figure that one out."

She frowned harder. It sounded too much like what had happened. Only uncle Denys had gotten down to a Maybe about giving her Horse. That was something.

"I needed a saddle and a bridle."

"All right. So how do you make the horse wear it, hmmn? Maybe you'd better do some advance study. Maybe you'd better look some things up in library. Maybe you'd better talk to some people who might know. Anyway, you prove to me you know what you're doing and you prove to me you're responsible. Then we'll see about seeing about it."

That was halfway, anyway. For about two seconds she had forgotten how much she hurt, which threw her off for a moment when it all came back again, and she thought how she had been when maman went away to Fargone, and how she got over that.

It was awful to get over maman dying. But that was starting to happen. She felt it start. Like things were trying to go back the way they were, and uncle Denys was getting short with her and she was going to have to go back to classes and everything was going to be the way it was again.

She felt sad about feeling better, which was stupid.

She wished she could have told maman about Horse.

And then she still wasn't sure if maman had ever gotten her letters at all, no matter what they said, or if Ollie had. Thinking that made her throat swell up and the tears start, and she scrambled down from the table, ran for her hall and shut the door.

Then she stood there by Florian and Catlin's room and cried and pounded her fist on the wall and kicked it, and went in their room and got some tissue to wipe her eyes and blow her nose.

They came in. And just stood there.

"I'm all right," she said. Which probably confused hell out of them, maman would say.

"Ari," she heard uncle Denys calling her from the other room. The door was open. "Ari?"

She had given uncle Denys a hard morning. But that was all right, uncle Denys said; it was like getting well from something, sometimes you had aches and pains, and they got better, eventually. He wasn't mad at her.

"I've talked to AG," uncle Denys said at lunch. "As soon as they can schedule a tank, they're going to do a run for you."

"You mean a horse?"

"Don't talk with your mouth full. Manners."

She swallowed. Fast.

"Here's the work part. You have to go over all the data and write up a report just the way the techs do. You have to do it on comp, and the computer will compare your work against the real techs' input. And where you're wrong you have to find out why and write up a report on it. You have to do that from start to birth and then keep up with all the other stuff and all your other studies. If you want something born, you have to work for it."

That *was* a lot of work. "Do I get him, then?"

"Her, actually. We need another female anyway. Two males tend to fight. Some animals are like that. We're going to do another just like the one we have, instead of a new type, so we won't risk losing her. But if you don't keep up the work, you don't get the horse at all, because you won't have earned her. Understood?"

"Yes, ser," she said. Not with her mouth full. Horses grew up fast. She remembered that. Real fast. Like all herd animals. A year, maybe?

"They're real delicate," uncle Denys said. "They're a bitch to manage, frankly, but your predecessor had this notion that it was important for people to have them. Human beings grew up with other lifeforms on the motherworld, she used to say, and those other lifeforms were part of humans learning about non-humans, and learning patience and the value of life. She didn't want people on Cyteen to grow up without that. Her maman Olga was interested in pigs and goats because they were useful and they were tough and adaptable for a new planet. Ari wanted horses because they're a high-strung herd ungulate with a lot of accessible data on their handling: we can learn something from them for some of the other, more exotic preservation projects. But the other important reason, the reason of all reasons for having horses, she said, is that working with them does something to people. 'They're exciting to something in our own psych-sets,' those are her exact words: 'I don't want humans in the Beyond to grow up without them. Our ancient partners are a part of what's human: horses, cattle, oxen, buffalo, dolphins, whatever. Dogs and cats, except we can't support carnivores yet, or tolerate a predator on Cyteen—yet. Earth's ecology is an interlocking system,' she used to say, 'and maybe humans aren't human without input from their old partners.' She wasn't sure about that. But she tried a lot of things. So it's not surprising you want a horse. *She* certainly did, although she was too old to try riding it—thank God. —Does it bother you for me to talk about her?"

"No." She gave a twitch of her shoulders. "It's just—funny. That's all."

"I imagine it is. But she was a remarkable woman. Are you through? We can walk back now."

xi

Florian did the best he could. He and Catlin both.

He had even asked ser Denys if they were letting sera down somehow, or if there was something they ought to be doing to help her get well, and ser Denys had patted him on the shoulder and said no, they were doing very well, that when a CIT had trouble there were no tapes to help, just people. That if they were strong enough to take the stress of sera's upset without needing sera's help that was the best thing, because that was what CITs would do for her. "But don't let yourselves take damage," ser Denys had said. "That's even worse for sera, if something bad happened to you, too. You protect yourselves as well as her. Understand?"

Florian understood. He told Catlin, because they had agreed he would ask, she just wasn't good with CIT questions.

"We're doing right," he had said to her. "Sera's doing all right. We're doing what we're supposed to be doing. Ser Denys is happy with us."

"I'm not," Catlin said, which summed it up. Catlin was hurting worse than he was, he thought, because Catlin was mad about sera being hurt, and Catlin couldn't figure out who was responsible, or whether people were doing enough to help sera.

They were both relieved when sera had said she had an idea and a job for them to do. And when sera started back to classes and things started getting back to normal, they had classes then, down in the Town, ser Denys said they should and sera agreed. "Meet me after class," she said.

So they did.

And sera walked with them out to the fishpond and fed the fish and said: "We have to wait until a rainy day. That's next Thursday. I looked."

On the charts that showed when the weathermakers were going to try to make it rain, that meant. Usually the charts were good, when they were down to a few days. And sera told them what they had to do.

Catlin was happy then. It was an Operation and it was a real one.

Florian just hoped sera was not going to get herself into trouble.

Skipping study was easy: sera just sent a request down to Green Barracks and said they couldn't come.

Then they worked out a way to get to C-tunnel without going through the Main Residency Hall, which meant going down the maintenance corridors. That was easy, too.

So sera told them what she wanted, and they all set up the Operation, with a lot of variations; but the one that they were going to use, sera thought of herself, because she said it would work and it was simplest and she could handle the trouble if it went bad.

So Catlin got to be the rear guard and he got to be the point man because sera said nobody suspected an azi and Catlin said he was better at talking.

The storm happened, the students kept the schedule sera had gotten from Dr. Edwards' classbook, and sera whispered: "Last two, on the left," as the Regular Students came back from their classes over in the Ed Wing, right down the tunnel, right past them where they were waiting in the side tunnel that led to air systems maintenance. It was a good place for them: dark in the access, and noisy with the fans.

Florian let them get past just the way sera had said. They had talked about how to Work it. He let them string way out.

Then sera patted him on the back just as he was moving on his own: he went out in the middle of the hall just before the last few students could disappear around the corner.

"Sera Carnath!" he called out, and the last students all stopped. He held up his fist. "You dropped something." And just the way sera had said, several of the students walked on, disappearing at the turn. Then more did, and finally Amy Carnath walked back a little, looking through the things she had in her arms.

He jogged up to her. Just one girl was waiting with Amy Carnath. He did a fast check behind to make sure no one was coming.

No one was. Catlin was supposed to see to that, back at the other turn, having a cut hand and an emergency if she had to, if it was some Older coming and not a kid.

So he gave Amy Carnath the note sera had written.

Dear Amy, it said. That was how you wrote, sera said. *Don't say a thing about this and don't tell anybody where you're going. Say you forgot something and have to go back, and don't let anybody go with you. I want to talk with you a minute. Florian will bring you. If you don't come, I'll see something terrible happens to you. Sincerely, Ari.*

Amy Carnath's face went very frightened. She looked at Florian and looked back at her friend.

Florian waited. Sera had instructed him not to speak at all in front of any of the rest of them.

"I forgot something," Amy Carnath said in a faint voice, looking at her friend. "Go on, Maddy. I'll catch up."

The girl called Maddy wrinkled her nose, then walked on after the rest of them.

"Sera, please," Florian said, and indicated the way she should go.

"What does she want?" sera Carnath asked, angry.

"I'm sure I don't know, sera. Please?"

Amy Carnath walked with him. She had her library bag. She could swing that, he reckoned, but sera said sera Carnath didn't know how to fight.

"This way," he said, when they got to the service corridor, and sera Carnath balked when she looked the way he pointed, into the dark.

And when sera stepped out from behind the doorway.

"Hello, Amy," sera said; and grabbed Amy herself, by the front of the blouse, one-handed, and pulled her, so Florian opened the door to the service corridor.

As Catlin came jogging up and into their little dark space.

Amy Carnath looked at her. Terrified.

"Inside," sera said. And pushed sera Carnath, not letting her go. Sera Carnath tried to protect her blouse from being torn, but that was all.

"Let me go," sera Carnath said, upset. "Let go of me!"

Florian pulled the penlight from his pocket and turned it on; Catlin shut the door; sera pushed Amy Carnath against the wall.

"*Let me go!*" sera Carnath screamed. But the door was shut and the fans were noisy.

"I'm not going to hurt you," sera said very calmly. "But Catlin will break your arm if you don't stand still and talk to me."

There were tears on sera Carnath's face. Florian felt a little sick, she was so scared. Even if she was the Target.

"I want to know," sera said, "where Valery Schwartz is."

"I don't know where he is," sera Carnath cried, biting her lip and trying to calm down. "He's at Fargone, that's all I know."

"I want to know where Sam Whitely is."

"He's down at the mechanics school! Let me go, let me *go*—"

"Florian has a knife," sera said. "Do you want to see it? Shut up and answer me. What do you know about my maman?"

"I don't know anything about your maman! I swear I don't!"

"Stop sniveling. You tell me what I ask or I'll have Florian cut you up. Hear me?"

"I don't know anything, I don't know."

"Why am I poison?"

"I don't know!"

"You know, Amy Carnath, you know, and if you don't start talking we're going to go down deep in the tunnels and Catlin and Florian are going to ask you, you hear me? And you can scream and nobody's going to hear you."

"I don't know. Ari, I don't know, I swear I don't."

Sera Carnath was crying and hiccuping, and Ari said:

"Florian, —"

"I can't tell you!" sera Carnath screamed. "I can't, I can't, I can't!"

"Can't tell me what?"

Sera Carnath gulped for air, and sera pulled sera Carnath's blouse loose and started unbuttoning it, one-handed.

"They'll send us away!" sera Carnath cried, flinching away; but Catlin grabbed her from behind. "They'll send us away!"

Sera stopped and said: "Are you going to tell me everything?"

Sera Carnath nodded and gulped and hiccuped.

"All right. Let her go, Catlin. Amy's going to tell us."

Catlin let sera Carnath go, and sera Carnath backed up to a bundle of pipes and stood with her back against that. Florian kept the light on her.

"Well?" sera asked.

"They send you away," sera Carnath said. Her teeth were chattering. "If anybody gets in trouble with you, they can send them to Fargone."

"*Who* does?"

"Your uncles."

"Giraud," sera said.

Sera Carnath nodded. There was sweat on her face, even if it was cold in the tunnels. She was crying, tears pouring down her cheeks, and her nose was running.

"All the kids?" sera asked.

Sera Carnath nodded again.

Sera came closer and took sera Carnath by the shoulder, not rough. Sera Carnath thought sera was going to hit her, but sera patted her shoulder then and had her sit down on the steps. Sera got down on one knee and put her hand on sera Carnath's knee.

"Amy, I'm not going to hit you now. I'm not going to tell you told. I want to know if you know anything about why my maman got sent away."

Sera Carnath shook her head.

"*Who* sent her?"

"Ser Nye. I guess it was ser Nye."

"Giraud?"

Sera Carnath nodded, and bit her lips.

"Amy, I'm not mad at you. I'm not going to be mad. Tell me what the other kids say about me."

"They just say—" Sera Carnath gulped. "—They just say let you have your way, because everybody knows what happens if you fight back and we don't want to get sent to Fargone and never come back—"

Sera just sat there a moment. Then: "Like Valery Schwartz?"

"Sometimes you just get moved to another wing. Sometimes they take you and put you on a plane and you just have to go, that's all, like Valery and his mama." Sera Carnath's teeth started chattering again, and she hugged her arms around her. "I don't want to get sent away. Don't tell I told."

"I won't. Dammit, Amy! Who said that?"

"My mama said. My mama said—no matter what, don't hit you, don't talk back to you." Sera Carnath started sobbing again, and covered her face with her hand. "I don't want to get my mama shipped to Fargone—"

Sera stood up, out of the light. *Maman* and *Fargone* were touchy words with her. Florian felt them too, but he kept the light steady.

"Amy," sera said after a little while, "I won't tell on you. I'll keep it secret if you will. I'll be your friend."

Sera Carnath wiped her face and looked up at her.

"I will," sera said. "So will Florian and Catlin. And they're good friends to have. All you have to do is be friends with us."

Sera Carnath wiped her nose and buttoned her blouse.

"It's the truth, isn't it, Catlin?"

"Whatever sera says," Catlin said, "that's the Rule."

Sera got down beside sera Carnath on the steps, her casted arm in her lap. "If I was your friend," sera said, "I'd stand up for you. We'd be real smart and not *tell* people we were friends. We'd just be zero. Not good, not bad. So you'd be safe. Same with the other kids. I didn't know what they were doing. I don't *want* them to do that. I can get a lot out of my uncle Denys, and Denys can get things out of uncle Giraud. So I'm a pretty good friend to have."

"I don't want to be enemies," sera Carnath said.

"Can you be my friend?"

Sera Carnath bit her lip and nodded, and took sera's left hand when sera reached it over.

They shook, like CITs when they agreed.

Florian stood easier then, and was terribly glad they didn't have to hurt sera Carnath. She didn't seem like an Enemy.

When sera Carnath got herself back together and stopped hiccuping, she talked to sera very calm, very quiet, and didn't sound at all stupid. Catlin stopped being disgusted with her and hunkered down when sera said, and rested her arms on her knees. So did Florian.

"We shouldn't be friends right off," sera Carnath said. "The other kids wouldn't trust me. They're scared."

As if sera Carnath hadn't been.

"We get them one at a time," sera said.

xii

"Shut the door," Yanni said; Justin shut it, and came and took the chair in front of Yanni's desk.

Not *his* problem this time. Yanni's. The Project's. It was in those papers on Yanni's desk, the reports and tests that he had *not* scanned and run on the office computer, but on a portable with retent-storage.

He had not signed his write-up. Yanni knew whose it was. That was enough.

"I've read it," Yanni said. "What does Grant say, by the by?"

Justin bit his lip and considered a shrug and no comment: Yanni still made his nerves twitch; but it was foolish, he told himself. Old business, raw nerves. "We talked about it. Grant protests it's a CIT question—but he says the man doesn't sound like he's handling it well at all."

"We're six months down on this data," Yanni said. "We don't have a ship-call from that direction for another month and a half, we don't have anything going out their way till the 29th. Jane was worried about Rubin. If our CIT staff kept off Ollie he'll have tried to work on it, I'm sure of that, but he's azi, and he's going through hell, *damn* my daughter's meddling—she's a damn expert, *she* has to know CIT psych better than Ollie does, right?"

"No comment."

"No comment. Dammit, I can *tell* you what they've been doing these last few months. My daughter and Julia Strassen. I *never* wanted those two on staff. So they get a harmless job . . . on the Residency side, of course. With Rubin. Jane gets out there and gets a look at the Residency data and Jane and my daughter go fusion in the first staff meeting. I think it contributed to Jane's heart attack, if you want my guess."

Justin felt his stomach unsettled—Yanni's pig-stubborn daughter, thrown out to Fargone on an appointment she never wanted . . . and probably thought she would get promotion from, setting up RESEUNESPACE labs and administration along with Johanna Morley; then Yanni's old adversary-sometime-lover Strassen the Immovable suddenly put in as Administrator over her head the same as over her father's; *his* stomach was upset, and he figured what was going on in Yanni.

Dammit, Administration is crazy.

Crazy.

"I'd trust Strassen," he said quietly, since Yanni left it for him to say something.

"Oh, yes, damn right I'd trust Strassen. Jenna might be a good Wing supervisor, but hell if she's got her own life sorted out, and she's Alpha-bitch when she's challenged. So Jane dies. That means someone has to run things. Jenna listens to her staff, all right. But Rubin's mother is a complicated problem. A real power-high when Rubin got his Special status, a real resentment when Rubin got the lab facilities and a little power of his own. Rubin's psychological problems—well, you've got the list: depressions over his health, his relationship with his mother—all of that. Rubin acts like he's doing fine. Happy as a fish in water. While his mother wants to give network interviews till Jenna hauls her in. Stella Rubin didn't like that. Not a bit. That woman and the Defense Bureau go fusion from the start . . . and Rubin's situation has been an ongoing case of *can't live with her or without her*. Rubin plays the psych tests we give him, Rubin's happy so he can keep peace, *that's* what Jane estimated—not an honest reaction out of him since the Defense Bureau put the lid on mama. Six months ago, spacetime. That's why I wanted you to look at the series. And the bloodwork—"

"Considering what's going to arrive out there in another six months or so."

"Ari's interviews, you mean."

"He's a biochemist. He's aware they're running some genetic experiments on him. What if someone picks up on it?"

"Especially—" Yanni tapped the report on his desk. "This shows a man a hell of a lot more politically sophisticated than he started. Same with his mother."

"Reseune can do that, can't it?"

"Let me give you the profile I've got: Rubin isn't the young kid they made a Special out of. *Rubin's* grown up. Rubin's realized there's something going on outside the walls of his lab, Rubin's realized he's got a sexual dimension, he's frustrated as hell with his health problems, RESEUNESPACE goes into a power crisis at the top and Rubin's hitherto quiet, hypochondriac mother, who used to focus his health anxieties *and* his dependencies on herself, is carrying on a feud with Administration and the Defense Bureau *and* reaching for the old control mechanisms with her son, who's reacting to those button-pushes with lies on his psych tests and stress in the bloodwork, while *Jenna*, damn her, has torn up Jane's reassignments list and declared herself autonomous in that Wing on the grounds Ollie Strassen can't make CIT-psych judgments."

"Damn," Justin murmured, gut reaction, and wished he hadn't. But Yanni was being very quiet. Deadly quiet.

"I'm firing her, needless to say," Yanni said. "I'm firing her right out of Reseune projects and recalling her under Security Silence. Six months from now. When the order gets there. I'm telling you, son, so you'll understand I'm a little . . . personally bothered . . . about this."

What in hell am I in here for? He knew this. It didn't take me to see it. What's he doing?

"You have some insights," Yanni said, "that are a little different. That come out of your own peculiar slant on designs, crazed that it is. I talked your suggestions over with committee, and things being what they were—I *told* Denys what my source was."

"Dammit, Yanni, —"

"You happened to agree with *him*, son, and Denys has the say where it concerns Ari's programs. Giraud was his usual argumentative self, but I had a long quiet talk with Denys, about you, about your projects, about the whole ongoing situation. I'll tell you what you're seeing here at Reseune. You're seeing a system that's stressed to its limits and putting second-tier administrative personnel like my daughter in positions of considerable responsibility, because they don't have anyone more qualified, because, God help us, the next choice down is worse. Reseune is stretched too thin, and Defense has their project blowing up in their faces. If Jane had lived six months longer, even two *weeks* longer, if Ollie could have leaned on Jenna and told her go to hell—but he can't, because the damn regulations don't let him have unquestioned power over a CIT program and he can't fire Jenna. He's got a Final tape, he can get CIT status, but Jenna's reinstated herself over his head with the help of other staff, and Julia Strassen declaring she's Jane's executor—so Jenna and Julia are the ones who have to sign Ollie's CIT papers, isn't that brilliant on our part? Jenna's going to pay for it. Now Ollie's got his status, from *this* end. But *that* won't get there for some few months either, and *he* doesn't know it." Yanni waved his hand, shook his head. "Hell. It's a mess. It's a mess out there. And I'm going to ask you something, son."

"What?"

"I want you to keep running checks on the Rubin data as it comes in, in whatever timeframe. Our surrogate with the Rubin clone is Ally Morley. But I want you to work some of your reward loops into CIT psych."

"You mean you're thinking of intervention? On which one of them?"

"It's the structures we want to look at. It's the feedback between job and reward. Gustav Morley's working on the problem. You don't know CIT psych that well, that's always been one of your problems. No. If we have to make course changes, you won't design it. We just want to compare his notes against yours. And we want to compare the situation against Ari's, frankly."

He was very calm on the surface. "I really want to think you're telling the truth, Yanni. Is this a real-time problem?"

"It's no longer real-time. I'll tell you the truth, Justin. I'll tell you the absolute truth. A military courier came in hard after the freighter that got us this data, cutting—a classified amount of time—off the freighter run. Benjamin Rubin committed suicide."

"Oh, God."

Yanni just stared at him. A Yanni looking older, tired, emotionally wrung out. "If we didn't have the public success with Ari right now," Yanni said, "we'd lose Reseune. We'd *lose* it. We're income-negative right now. We're using Defense Bureau funds and we're understaffed as hell. You understand now, I think—we were getting those stress indicators on Rubin before the Discovery bill came up, before Ari's little prank in the Town. We knew then that there was trouble on the Project. We'd sent out instructions which turned out to be—too late. We had pressure on the Discovery bill; we knew that was coming before it was brought out in public. We knew Ari was going to have to go public—and we had all of that going on. You may not forgive Giraud's reaction, but you might find it useful to know what was happening off in the shadows. Right now, Administration is looking at you—in a whole new light."

"I haven't got any animosity toward a nine-year-old kid, for God's sake, I've proved that, I've answered it under probe—"

"Calm down. That's not what I'm saying. We've got a kid out at Fargone who's the psychological replicate of a suicide. We've got decisions to make—one possibility is handing him to Stella Rubin, in the theory she's the ultimate surrogate for the clone. But Stella Rubin has problems, problems of the first order. Leave him with Morley. But where's the glitch-up that led to this? With Jenna? Or earlier, with the basic mindset of a mother-smothered baby with a health problem? We need some answers. There's time. It's not even *your* problem. It's Gustav Morley's and Ally's. There's just—content—in your work that interests Denys, frankly, and interests me. I think you see how."

"Motivational psych."

"Relating to Emory's work. There's a reason she wanted you, I'm prepared to believe that. Jordan's being handed the Rubin data too. When you say you've got some clear thought on it—I'm sending you out to Planys for a week or so."

"Grant—"

"You. Grant will be all right here, my word on it. Absolutely no one is going to lay a hand on him. We just don't need complications. Defense is going to be damned nervous about Reseune. We've got some careful navigation to do. I'm telling you, son, Administration is watching you very, very closely. You've been immaculate. If you—and Jordan—can get through the next few years—there's some chance of getting a much, much better situation. But if this situation blows up, if anything—if *anything* goes wrong with Ari—I don't make any bets. For any of us."

"Dammit, doesn't anybody care about the *kid*?"

"We care. You can answer this one for yourself. Right now, Reseune is in a major financial mess and Defense is keeping us alive. What happens to her—if Defense moves in on this, if this project ends up—under that Bureau instead of Science? What happens to any of us? What happens to the direction all of *Union* will take after that? Changes, that much is certain. Imbalance—in the whole system of priorities we've run on. I'm no politician. I hate politics. But, damn, son, I can see the pit ahead of us."

"I see it quite clearly. But it's not ahead of us, Yanni. I live in it. So does Jordan."

Yanni said nothing for a moment. Then: "Stay alive, son. You, and Grant, —be damn careful."

"Are you telling me something? Make it plain."

"I'm just saying we've lost something we couldn't afford to lose. We. Everybody, dammit. So much is so damn fragile. I feel like I've lost a kid."

Yanni's chin shook. For a moment everything was wide open and Justin felt it all the way to his gut. Then:

"Get," Yanni said, in his ordinary voice. "I've got work to do."

xiii

Ari walked with uncle Denys out of the lift in the big hall next to Wing One, upstairs, and it was not the kind of hall she had expected. It was polished floors, it was a Residency kind of door, halfway down, and no other doors at all, until a security door cut the hallway off.

"I want to show you something," uncle Denys had said.

"Is it a surprise?" she had asked, because uncle Denys had never shown her what he had said he would show her; and uncle Denys had been busy in his office with an emergency day till dark, till she was *glad* Nelly was still with them: Seely was gone too.

"Sort of a surprise," uncle Denys had said.

She had not known there *were* any apartments up here.

She walked to the door with uncle Denys and expected him to ring the Minder; but:

"Where's your keycard?" he said to her, the way the kids used to tease each other and make somebody look fast to see if it had come off somewhere. But he was not joking. He was asking her to take it and use it.

So she took it off and stuck it in the key-slot.

The door opened, the lights came on, and the Minder said: *"There have been twenty-seven entries since last use of this card. Shall I print?"*

"Tell it save," uncle Denys said.

She was looking into a beautiful apartment, with a pale stone floor, with big furniture and *room*, more room than maman's apartment, more room than uncle Denys', it was huge; and all of a sudden she put together *last use of this card* and *twenty-seven* and the fact it was *her* card.

Hers. Ari Emory's.

"This was your predecessor's apartment," uncle Denys said, and walked her inside as the Minder started to repeat. "Tell it save."

"Minder, save."

"Voice pattern out of parameters."

"Minder, save," uncle Denys said.

"Insert card at console."

He did, his card. And it saved. The red light went off. "You have to be very careful with some of the systems in here," uncle Denys said. "Ari took precautions against intruders. It took Security some doing to get the Minder reset." He walked farther in. "This is yours. This whole apartment. Everything in it. You won't live here on your own until you're grown. But we are going to get the Minder to recognize your voice." He walked on, down the steps, across the rug and up again, and Ari followed, skipping up the steps on the far side to keep close to him.

It was spooky. It was like a fairy-tale out of Grimm. A palace. She kept up with uncle Denys as he went down the hall and opened up another big room, with a sunken center, and a couch with brass trim, and woolwood walls—pretty and dangerous, except the woolwood was coated in thick clear plastic, like the specimens in class. There were paintings on the walls, along a walkway above the sunken center. Lots of paintings.

Up more steps then, past the bar, where there were still glasses on the shelves. And down a hall, to another hall, and into an office, a *big* office, with a huge black desk with built-ins like uncle Denys' desk.

"This was Ari's office." Uncle Denys pushed a button, and a terminal came up on the desk. "You always have a 'base' terminal. It's how the House computer system works. And this one is quite—protective. It isn't a particularly good idea to go changing these base accesses around, particularly on my base terminal . . . or yours. Sit down, Ari. Log on with your CIT-number."

She was nervous. The House Computer was a whole different system than her little machine in her room. You didn't log-on until you were grown, or you got in a lot of trouble with Security. Florian said some of the systems were dangerous.

She gave uncle Denys a second nervous look, then sat down and looked for the switch on the keyboard.

"Where's the *on?*"

"There's a keycard slot on the desk. At your right. It'll ask for a handprint."

She turned in the chair and gave him a third look. "Is it going to do something?"

"It's going to do a security routine. It won't gas the apartment or anything. Just do it."

She did. The handprint screen lit up. She put her hand on it.

"*Name,*" the Minder said.

"Ariane Emory," she told it.

The red light on the terminal went on and stayed on.

The monitor didn't come up from the console.

"What's it doing?"

"Checking the date," he said. "Checking all the House records. It's finding out you've been born and how old you are, since it's found similarities in that handprint and probably in your voiceprint, but it knows it's not the original owner. It's checking Archives for all the Ari handprints and voiceprints it has. It's going to take a minute."

It *wasn't* like the ordinary turn-on. She had seen uncle Denys do that, just talking to his computer through the Minder. She looked at this one working, the red light still going, and looked at Denys again. "Who wrote this?"

"Good question. Ari would have asked that. The fact is, Ari did. She knew you'd exist someday. She keyed a lot of things to you, things that are very, very important. When the prompt comes up, Ari, I want you to do something for me."

"What?"

"Tell it COP D/TR comma B1 comma E/IN."

Take program: Default to write-files. "What's B1? What's IN?"

"Base One. This is Base One. Echo to Instore. That means screen and Minder output into the readable files. If I thought we could get away with it I'd ask it IN/P, and see if we could snag the program out, but you don't take chances with this Base. There!"

The screen unfolded from the desktop and lit up.

Hello, Ari.

Spooky again. She typed: *COP D/TR, B1, E/IN*

Confirmed. Hello, Ari.

"It wants *hello,*" uncle Denys said. "You can talk to it. It'll learn your voiceprint."

"Hello, Base One."

How old are you?

"I'm nine."

Hello, Denys.

She took in a breath and looked back at Denys.

"Hello, Ari," Denys said, and smiled in a strange way, looking nowhere at all, not talking to her, talking to *it.*

It typed out: *Don't panic, Ari. This is only a machine. I've been dead for 11.2 years now. The machine is assembling a program based on whose records are still active in the House computers, and it's filling in blanks from that information. Fortunately it can't be shocked and it's all out of my hands. You're living with Denys Nye. Do you have a House link there?*

"Yes," uncle Denys said, and when she turned around to object, laid a finger on his lips and nodded.

"Uncle Denys says yes."

The Minder could handle things like that. It just took it a little longer.

Name me the rivers and the continents and any other name you think of, Ari. I don't care what order. I want a voiceprint. Go till I say stop.

"There's the Novaya Volga and the Amity Rivers, there's Novgorod and Reseune. Planys, the Antipodes, Swigert Bay, Gagaringrad and High Brasil, there's Castile and the Don and Svetlansk. . . ."

Stop. That's enough. After this, you can just use your keycard in the Minder slot anywhere you happen to be before you log-on next, and state your name for the Minder. This Base is activated. I'm creating transcript continually. You can access it by asking the Minder to print to screen or print to file. If Denys is doing his job you know what that means. Do you know without being told?

"Yes."

Good. Log-on anytime you like. If you want to exit the House system just say log-off. Storing and recall is automatic. It will always find your place but it won't activate until you say hello. Denys can explain the details. Goodbye. Don't forget to log-off.

She looked at uncle Denys. Whispered: "Do I?" He nodded and she said: "Log-off."

The screen went dark and folded down again.

2415: 1/24: 2332

B/1: Hello, Ari.
AE2: Hello.
B/1: Are you alone?
AE2: Florian and Catlin are with me.
B/1: Anyone else?
AE2: No.
B/1: You're using House input 311. What room are you in?
AE2: My bedroom. In uncle Denys' apartment.
B/1: This is how this program works, Ari, and excuse me if I use small words: I wrote this without knowing how old you'd be when you logged-on or what year it would be. It's 2415. The program just pulled that number out of the House computer clock. Your guardian is Denys Nye. The program just accessed your records in the House data bank and found that out, and it can tell you that Denys ordered pasta for lunch today, because it just accessed Denys' records and found out the answer to that specific question. It knows you're 9 years old and therefore it's set a limit on your keycard accesses, so you can't order Security to arrest anybody or sell 9000 Alpha genesets to Cyteen Station. Remembering what I was like at 9, that seems like a reasonable precaution.

The program has Archived all the routines it had if you were younger or older than 9. It can get them back when your House records match those numbers, and it

360

can continually update its Master according to the current date, by adding numbers. This goes on continually.

Every time you ask a question it gets into all the records your age and your current clearance make available to you, all over the House system, including the library. Those numbers will get larger. When you convince the program you have sufficient understanding, the accesses will get wider. When you convince the program you have reached certain levels of responsibility your access will also get into Security levels and issue orders to other people.

There's a tape to teach you all the accesses you need right now. Have you had it?

AE2: Yes. I had it today.

B/1: Good. If you'd answered no, it would have cut off and said: log-off and go take that tape before you log-on again. If you make a mistake with your codes, it'll do that too. A lot of things will work that way. You have to be right: the machine you're using is linked to the House system, and it will cut you off if you make mistakes. If you make certain mistakes it'll call Security and that's not a good thing.

Don't play jokes with this system, either. And don't ever lie to it or enter false information. It can get you in a lot of trouble.

Now I will tell you briefly there is a way to lie to the system without causing problems, but you have to put the real information in a file with a sufficiently high Security level. The machine will always read that file when it needs to, but it will also read your lie, and it will give the lie to anyone with a lower Security clearance than you have. That means only a few people, mostly Security and Administration, can find out what you hid. This is so you can have some things private or secret.

Eventually you can use this to cover your Inquiry activity. Or your Finances. Or your whereabouts. That file can't be erased, but it can be added to or updated. When your access time in the House system increases and the number of mistakes you make per entry decreases to a figure this program wants, you'll get an instruction how to use the Private files. Until then, don't lie to the program, or you'll lose points and it'll take you a long time to get beyond this level.

You've probably figured out by now you can't question the program when it's in this mode. You can stop this tutorial at any point by saying: Ari, wait. You can go out of this mode and ask a question and come back by saying, Ari, go on.

Don't ever think that this program is alive. It's just lines of program like the programs you can write. But it can learn, and it changes itself as it learns. It has a base state, which is like a default, but that's only in the master copy in Archives.

Sometimes this program transcribes what I tell you for your guardian Denys. Sometimes not. It's not doing that now. I'm writing to files only you can access, by telling the Minder you want to hear the file from this session, by hour and date. This is an example of a Private file. Do you understand how to access it?

AE2: Yes.

B/1: If you make a mistake the program will repeat this information.

Never ask for a Private file in front of anyone but Florian and Catlin. Not even Denys Nye can see the things I tell you in Private files. If he tries to do this, this program will send an order to Security. This program has just sent a message to Denys' Base that says the same thing. Trust me that I have a reason for this.

Sometimes a file will be so Private I will tell you to be totally alone. This means not even Florian and Catlin. Never ask to review those files when anyone else is present. They won't print out either, because they involve things very personal to you only, that not even your friends should know about you.

Many of these things involve your studies and they will simply come out of my own notes.

A lot of times they will come simply because you've asked a question and the computer has found a keyword.

You carry my keycard, my number, and my name. My records exist only in Archives and yours are the current files. Don't worry about my being dead. It doesn't bother me at all at this point. You can call me Ari senior. There isn't any word in the language that says what we are to each other. I'm not your mother and I'm not your sister. I'm just your Older. I assume that word is still current.

Understand, Ari, there is a difference between myself, who say these words into a Scriber, —and Base One. Base One can use a language logic function to talk with you much more like a living person than I can, because it's real-time and I'm not, and haven't been since 2404.

That's the computer accessing my records, understand, to find out that date. Base One can answer questions on its own and bring up my answers to certain questions, and you can talk back and forth with it.

But never get confused about which one is able to talk back and forth with you directly.

Have you got a question now? Ask it the right way and Base One will start talking to you. If you make a mistake the program will revert to the instruction you missed. Or you can ask for repeat. Good night, Ari. Good night, Florian and Catlin.

AE2: Ari, wait.
B/1: I'm listening, Ari.
AE2: Are you Base One now?
B/1: Yes.
AE2: Who sent my maman Jane Strassen to Fargone?
B/1: Access inadequate. There is a reference from Ari. Stand by.
Ari, this is Ari senior.
This is the first time you've asked a question with a Security block on it. I don't know what the question is. It means something is preventing you from reaching that information in the House computers and your clearance isn't high enough. The most probable reason is: Minority status. End segment.

AE2: Ari, wait.
B/1: I'm listening, Ari.
AE2: Where is Valery Schwartz?
B/1: Access inadequate.
AE2: Where's Amy Carnath?
B/1: Amy Carnath checked into the Minder in U8899. U8899 is: apartment registered to Julia Carnath. There is no record of check-out in that Minder.
AE2: Then she's home.
B/1: Please be specific.

AE2: Then Amy Carnath is home, isn't she?
B/1: Amy Carnath is home, yes.

2315: 1/27: 2035

AE2: Base One: look up Ariane Emory in Library.
B/1: Access limited. Ari has a message. Stand by.
Ari, this is Ari senior.
So you've gotten curious about me. I don't blame you. I would be too. But you're 9 and the program will only let you access my records up to when I was 4. That gap will narrow as you grow older, until you're able to read into my records equal to and beyond your current age. There's a reason for this. You'll understand more of that reason as you grow. One reason you can understand now is that these records are very personal, and people older than 9 do things that would confuse hell out of you, sweet.
Also at 9 you're not old enough to understand the difference between my accomplishments and my mistakes, because the records don't explain anything. They're just things the House computer recorded at the time.
Now that you've asked, Base One will automatically upgrade the information once a week. I'd give it to you daily, because there's going to be a lot of it, but I don't want you to get so involved with what I did from day to day that you live too much with me and not enough in the real world.
You can access anything about anybody you want in Archives through 2287, when I was 4. If the person you want wasn't born by then, you won't get anything.
This gap will constantly narrow as you grow, and as your questions and your own records indicate to Base One that you have met certain criteria. So the harder you study in school and the more things you qualify in, the faster you get answers. That's the way life works.
Remember what you do is your own choice. What I did was mine.
Good luck, sweet.
Now Library will retrieve all my records up to the time I was 4 and store it for your access in a file named BIO.

2315: 4/14: 1547

B/1: Stand by for your Library request.
AE2: Capture.
B/1: Affirmative: document captured; copyrighted: I must dump all data in two days unless you authorize the 20-credit purchase price.
AE2: Scan for reference to horse or equine or equestrian.
B/1: Located.
AE2: How many references?
B/1: Eighty-two.
AE2: Compare data to data in study file: HORSE. Highlight and Tempstore additional information or contradictions in incoming data. Call me when you're done.

B/1: Estimated time of run: three hours.
AE2: Log-off.

2316: 1/12: 0600

B/1: Good morning, Ari. Happy birthday.
AE2: Is this Base One?
B/1: Ari, this is Ari senior. You're 10 now. That upgrades your accesses. If you'll check library function you can access a number of new tapes.

Your test scores are one point better than mine in geography, three points under mine in math, five points under mine in language. . . .

CHAPTER 9

i

Uncle Giraud called it the highest priced shop in the known universe, let alone Novgorod, and Ari loved it. She tried on a blouse that would absolutely *kill* Maddy Strassen: it was bronze and brown, it was satin, and it had a scarf around the throat with a topaz and gold pin—real, of course, at *this* place.

And she looked back at uncle Giraud with a calculated smile. It was a very grown-up smile. She had practiced it in the mirror.

The blouse cost two hundred fifty credits. It went into a box, and uncle Giraud put it on his personal card without saying a word.

She signed a picture of herself for the shop, which had a lot of pictures of famous people who shopped there: it had its own garage and a security entrance, and it was an appointment-only place, near the spaceport, where you couldn't just walk in.

Which was why uncle Giraud said it was a place they could go, the only place they could go, because of Security.

There was a picture of the first Ari. It was spooky. But she had seen those before. The first Ari was pretty even when she was almost as old as maman, and she had been a hundred twenty when she died. She had pretty, pretty eyes, and her hair was long and black (but she would have been on rejuv then and she would have dyed it) and parted in the middle the way Ari wore hers. She wanted to wear makeup like Ari senior, but uncle Denys said no, she could have a little, but not that much, and besides, styles changed.

Uncle Denys had given her cologne for last New Year's, that he said had been made especially for Ari by a perfumery in Novgorod. It smelled wonderful, like the greenhouse gardens when the tulips were blooming.

She was growing up, he said, and she knew that. All of a sudden one day a long time back Nelly had said she was getting too old to run around without her blouse on, and she had looked down and realized it was not that she was getting a little fat, but that something was changing.

At the time she had thought it was a damn nuisance, because she *liked* not having to wear a shirt.

By now she *definitely* was getting a shape, and even Catlin was, sort of. Nothing, of course, to match her cousin Maddy Morley-Strassen, who was a year older, transferred in from Planys with her maman Eva, who was aunt Victoria Strassen's daughter, and maman's niece; and a cousin of Amy Carnath through *Amy's* father Vasily Morley-Peterson, who was at Planys.

Maddy was—

An early developer, uncle Denys called it.

Maddy was not anybody she would want to be, but she was certainly not the sort to let get too comfortable.

So she bought a scarf for Maddy and a real gold pin for Amy and a pullover for Sam and one for Tommy, and *insisted* to carry them on the plane, besides the other things she got for everybody. It didn't matter that you could order a lot of it, she told uncle Giraud, it mattered it came from *Novgorod*, where the other kids didn't get to go, and she was too going to take it on the plane. She got a blouse for Catlin, for parties: black, of course, but gauzy; Catlin looked surprised when she saw herself in the mirror. And a shirt for Florian over on the men's side: black and satiny and with a high collar that was sort of like his usual uniform sweaters, but very, very elegant. And then the woman who owned the shop thought of a pair of pants that would fit Catlin, very tight and satiny. So that meant it was only fair Florian should get new pants too. And while they were doing that, *she* found a gunmetal satin pair of pants that just fit her, and that meant the sweater that went with them, which was bronzed lavenders on the shoulders shading down to gunmetal-sheen lavender and then gunmetal-and-black at the bottom. It was elegant. Uncle Giraud said it was too old for her before she put it on. When he saw her in it he said well, she *was* getting older.

She thought she could sneak some lavender eyeshadow when she wore it at Maddy's next party.

So take that, Maddy Strassen.

They brought so many packages out of *La Lune* that uncle Giraud and Abban had to put a lot of them in the security escort car, and she and Florian and Catlin had to sit practically on top of each other in the back seat.

Uncle Giraud said they were going to be into the next century going through Decon at Reseune.

That was the wonderful thing about Novgorod: because they had the Amity escarpment on the east and the terraforming had piled up the rock and put up towers to make the Curtainwall on the west, and because they had all those people and all that sewage and all that algae and the greenbelt and algae starting out even in the marine shallows, it was one of the few places in the world besides Reseune that people went out without D-suits and the only other airport besides Reseune where you could take your baggage right through without anything but a hose-down and an inspection.

There was an interview to go through, in the lounge at the airport, while Abban was supervising the baggage being loaded. But she knew a lot of the reporters, especially one of the women and two of the oldest men and a young man who had a way of winking at her to get her to laugh; and she didn't mind taking the time.

Ransom, uncle Giraud called it, for being let alone while she got to see the botanical gardens, except for the photographers.

"What did you do today, Ari?" a woman asked.

"I went to the garden and I went shopping," she said, sitting in the middle of the cameras and in front of the pickup-bank. She had been tired until she got in front of the cameras. But she knew she was *on*, then, and *on* meant sparkle, which she knew how to do: it was easy, and it made the reporters happy and it made the people happy, and it made uncle Giraud happy—not that Giraud was her favorite person, but they got along all right: she had it figured uncle Giraud was real easy to Work in a lot of ways, and sometimes she thought he really had a soft place she got to. He would buy her things, lots of things. He had a special way of talking with her, being funny, which he wasn't, often, with other people.

And he was always so nasty every time they had a party or anything in the House.

About Giraud and maman—she *never* forgot that. Ever.

"What did you buy?"

She grinned. "Uncle Giraud says 'too much.' " And ducked her head and smiled up at the cameras with an expression she knew was cute. She had watched herself on vid and practiced in the mirror. "But I don't get to come to the city but once a year. And this is the first time I ever went shopping."

"Aren't there stores in Reseune?"

"Oh, yes, but they're small, and you always know what's there. You can always get what you need, but it's mostly the same things, you know, like you can get a shirt, but if you want one different from everybody's you have to order it, and then you know what you're going to get."

"How are the guppies?"

Another laugh. A twitch of her shoulders. "I've got some green long-tails."

Uncle Denys had given her a whole lab. And guppies and aquariums were a craze in Novgorod, the first time in the world, uncle Denys said, that anybody had had pets, which people used to, on Earth. Reseune had gotten a flood of requests for guppies, ever since she had said on vid that they were something anybody could do.

And she got a place to sell her culls: uncle Denys said she should keep all the records on it, she would learn something.

Which meant that most every flight RESEUNEAIR's freight division made out, had some of her guppies on it, sealed in plastic bags and Purity-stamped for customs, and now it was getting to be an operation larger than the lab she did the breeding in: uncle Denys said it was about time she franchised-out, because guppies bred fast, and bred down, and the profit was in doing the really nice ones, which meant you had to get genesets. It was really funny, in some ways it was a lot easier to clone people than guppies.

"We hear," someone else said, "you've taken up another project. Can you tell us about the horse?"

"It's a filly. That's what you call a female baby horse. But she's not born yet. I had to study about her and help the techs get the tank ready; and I have to do a lot of reports—it's a *lot* of work. But she's going to be pretty just like her genesister. *She's* pregnant. She's going to birth not too long after my filly comes out of the tank. So we'll have *two* babies."

"Haven't you had enough of horses?"

"Oh, no. You have to *see* them. I'm going to ride mine. You *can*, they do it on Earth, you just have to train them."

"You're not going to break another arm, are you?"

She grinned and shook her head. "No. I've studied how to do it."

"How do you do it?"

"First you get them used to a saddle and a bridle and then you get them used to a weight on their back and then they don't get so scared when you climb on. But they're smart, that's what's so different, they're not like platytheres or anything, they *think* what they're going to do. That's the most wonderful thing. They're not like a computer. They're like *us*. Even pigs and goats are. You watch them and they watch you and you know they're thinking things you don't know about. And they feel warm and they play games and they do things just like people, just because they think of it."

"Could we get a clip of that?"

"*Could* we, uncle Giraud?"

"I think we could," Giraud said.

ii

Uncle Giraud was very, very happy with the session in Novgorod, Ari decided that on the flight back. She and Florian and Catlin sat up front in the usual spot and drank soft drinks and watched out the windows, while Giraud and the secretaries and the staffers sat at the back and did business, but there was a lot of laughing.

Which was why uncle Giraud bought her things, she thought. Which was all right. Sometimes she almost warmed up to Giraud. That was all right too. It kept Giraud at ease. And she learned to do that, be very nice to people she knew quite well were the Enemy, and even like them sometimes: it didn't mean you weren't going to Get them, because they were bound to do something that would remind you what they were sooner or later. When you were a kid you had to wait, that was all. She had told that to Catlin and Florian, and she got Catlin in front of a mirror and made Catlin practice smiling and laughing until she could do it without looking like she was faking it.

Catlin was ticklish right around her ribs. *That* was a discovery. Catlin was embarrassed about it and said nobody was supposed to get that close anyway. She didn't like her and Florian laughing at first. But then Catlin decided it was halfway funny, and laughed her real laugh, which was kind of a halfway grin, without a sound. The other was fake, because Catlin was good at isolating muscles and making them do whatever she wanted to.

Catlin had laughed her real laugh when she saw herself in the gauzy blouse, in the shop in Novgorod, and her eyes had lit up the way they would when Florian showed them something he had learned in electronics. *Catlin had a new skill.*

Then Catlin had turned around to the shop-keeper with her stage-manners on and acted just like Maddy Strassen, which was funny as hell, maman would say, right down to Maddy's slither when she turned around to look at the satin pants in the mirror. It was a Maddy-imitation. Ari had nearly gotten a stitch, inside, especially seeing Giraud's face. But Giraud was fast, especially when she winked at him and cued him in it was a prank.

Florian had stood over in the doorway to the men's side being just straight azi, which meant he was having a stitch too, because Florian never had to practice laughing. Florian just did; and stopping himself was the trick, before he gave Catlin away.

Things were a lot better in Novgorod, and there was a lot less pressure, Ari picked that up. Giraud said he thought there was a market for *tapes* about animals people couldn't own, that it was a real good idea, and that getting two hundred fifty credits for a fancy guppy meant there was a market for a lot of things, and hell if they were going to franchise it out: they could *hire* it done over in Moreyville, and maybe there was a market for koi, too, and the people who had been making aquariums and filter systems on special order for Reseune research labs might want to invest in a whole new division of manufacture.

"That's the way it works," he said. "Everything is connected to everything else."

There were miners clear out in brown little outback domes who were spending a fortune on guppy rigs, especially for the bright-colored ones, and for green *weed*, because they liked the colors and the water-sound, out where there was nothing but pale red and pale gray-blue. At Reseune people said it was the contact with a friendly ecosystem, and it was good for people: miners swore the air off the tanks made the environment healthier. Reseune said it just made people *feel* healthier and gave them a sense of connection to everything that was green and bright and Terran.

Giraud just said it made money and maybe they could look in the genebanks and the histories and see if there was something else they were missing.

Meanwhile it didn't hurt anything that people thought of her as the kid who made all that available to people. It made it hard for the people who had been the first Ari's enemies.

That was Giraud, all right. But she was doing the same thing when she practiced how to smile for the cameras. She had met the Councillor for Information, Catherine Lao, who wore a crown of braids just like Catlin, and was blonde like Catlin, but about a hundred years old: and Councillor Lao had been a friend of Ari senior's, and was so happy to see how she was growing up, the Councillor said, *so* pleased to see her doing so well.

Ari tried not to like people right off: that was dangerous, because you missed things that way that you ought to see—Ari senior had told her that, but it just clicked with something she already knew, down inside. All the same, she liked Councillor Lao a lot; and Councillor Lao was friendlier with her than with Giraud, no matter how hard the Councillor tried to hide it: *that* gave Ari a contrast to work with, which made anybody easier to read, and it made her think Councillor Lao really was someone she might like.

It didn't hurt at all that Catherine Lao was Councillor of Information, which meant the whole news-net, among other things, and libraries and publishing and archives and public education.

There was Admiral Gorodin too, who was Defense, and Defense had protected her stuff from people going through it; he was a lot different than Lao, kind of this way and that about a lot of things, not friendly, not hostile, just real interested and kind of prickly with Giraud, but coming at her like he had known her a long time.

She had even met Mikhail Corain, who was the Enemy, and said hello to him, and he tried his best to be nice. They had been in the Hall of State, in front of all the cameras. Councillor Corain had looked like he had indigestion, but he said he had a daughter about her age, and he hoped she enjoyed her trip to Novgorod, did she want to run for Council someday?

That was too close to ideas she had that she wasn't about to tell even Giraud or Denys, so she said she didn't know, she was busy with her schoolwork, which gave the reporters a stitch and made Corain laugh, a laugh like Catlin being Maddy, and he backed up and said the world had better look out.

So would he, she thought, a little worried about that: that had been a little nasty at the last, and she wished she could have thought of something else real fast to Get him in front of the cameras. But she didn't know what was going on that he could have been talking about, and uncle Giraud had said she had done exactly right, so she supposed she must have.

So it was the plane flight and touchdown at Reseune; and the reporters waiting for her at landing—so Amy and Tommy got to be on vid. She smiled for the cameras—they didn't have to do an interview, just there were some shots the news wanted, so they got them, and then the camera people folded up to catch their RESEUNEAIR flight back on up to Svetlansk, where they were covering a big platythere that had broken right through an oil pipeline— she would like to have *seen* that, she wanted to go, but uncle Giraud said she had been away from classes long enough, and she had *better* go see about her filly.

"Is she all right?" she asked, scared by that.

"Well, who knows?" uncle Giraud said, Working her for sure, but it was a good one. "You haven't checked on her in a week."

She didn't wait for baggage. She took the bus with uncle Giraud and Florian and Catlin and Amy and Tommy went too; and she didn't even go home first, she went straight over to the lab.

The filly was doing fine, the lab said; but the Super there gave her a whole packet of fiches and said that was what she had to catch up on.

It was a trap. She got a look at the filly on the monitor: she was looking less and less like a person and more and more like a horse now. That was exciting.

It was exciting when she went over to Denys' office and got permission to bring Amy and Tommy home with her, because her baggage was going to be there by now and she wanted to give them their presents.

"Don't mess the place up," uncle Denys said, because Nelly was working babies during the day and just showing up at night; and that meant Seely and Florian and Catlin had to do a lot of the pick-up. She didn't care about Seely, but she did about Florian and Catlin; so she was careful. "Give me a hug," uncle Denys said, "and be good."

She had forgotten to get something for uncle Denys. She was embarrassed. And made a note to order something from the gourmet shop in North Wing and put it on her own card, because she had an allowance.

Something like a pound of coffee. He would like that and he wouldn't care it didn't come from Novgorod.

Besides, she got to have some of that too.

So she told Base One to buy it and send it to his office when she got in, easy as talking to the Minder.

Amy and Tommy were real impressed.

They were real happy with their presents. She brought them out of her room and didn't show off the other things—it's not nice, uncle Denys would say, to advertise what you've got and others don't.

Uncle Denys was right. Also smart.

Tommy loved his sweater. He looked good in it.

Amy looked a little doubtful about the tiny box, like a little box like that wasn't going to be as nice a gift, until she opened it.

"It's real," she told Amy, about the pin. And Amy's face lit up. Amy was not a pretty girl. She was going to be tall and thin and long-faced, and she had to take tape to make her stop slouching, but for a moment Amy looked pretty. And felt pretty, she guessed, which made the difference.

She wished Amy had the allowance she did, to buy nice things.

Then she got an idea.

And made a note to ask uncle Denys if *Amy* could take over the guppy project, Amy knew all about it, and she was sharp about what to breed to what, and very good with numbers.

She had enough to do with the filly, and she wanted to go back to just having a few pretty fish in the aquarium in her bedroom, and not having to do in the ugly ones.

iii

Justin dumped his bags in the bedroom and went and threw himself facedown on the bed, aware of nothing until he realized he had a blanket over him and that he was being urged to tuck up onto the bed. "Come on," Grant's voice said to him. "You're going to chill. Move."

He halfway woke up then, and rolled over and found the pillow, pulling it up under his head.

"Rotten flight?" Grant asked, sitting on the edge of the bed.

"Damn little plane; they had a hell of a storm over the Tethys and we just dodged thunderheads and bounced."

"Hungry?"

"God, no. Just sleep."

Grant let him, just cut the lights, and let him lie.

Which he dimly remembered in the morning, hearing noise in the kitchen. He found himself in his clothes, unshaven.

And the clock saying 0820.

"God," he muttered, and threw the cover over and staggered for the bath and the kitchen, in that order.

Grant, in white shirt and plain beige pants, looked informally elegant, was having morning coffee at the kitchen table.

Justin raked a hand through his hair and fumbled a cup out of the cabinet without dropping it.

Grant poured him half his cup.

"I can make some," he protested.

"Of course you can," Grant said, humoring the incompetent, and pulled his chair back. "Sit down. I don't suppose you're going in today. —How's Jordan?"

"Fine," he mumbled, "fine. He really is." And sat down and leaned his elbows on the table to be sure where the cup was when he took a drink, because his eyes were refusing to work. "He's looking great. So is Paul. We had a great work-session—usual thing, too much talk, too little sleep. It was great."

He was not lying. Grant's eyes flickered and took on a moment's honest and earnest relief. Grant had already heard the word last night, at the airport, but he seemed to believe it finally, the way they always had to doubt each other, doubt every word, without the little signals that said things were what they seemed.

And then Grant looked at the time and winced. "Damn. One of us had better make it in. Yanni's hunting hides this week."

"I'll get there," Justin said.

"You're worthless. Stay here. Rest."

Justin shook his head. "I've got a report to turn in." He swallowed down the last of the coffee at a gulp. "God. You go on first. I'll get the papers hunted down. I'll get there. Message Yanni I'm coming, I just have to get the faxes together, they messed everything up in Decon."

"I'm going." Grant dumped the last of his coffee into Justin's cup. "You need it worse. It seems to be a vital nutrient for CITs."

Damn. He had crashed incommunicado last night when Grant had been waiting days for news, and now he stole Grant's coffee at breakfast.

"I'll make it up to you," he called to Grant in the next room. "Get a rez at *Changes* for lunch."

Grant put his head back in. "Was it that good?"

"Sociology ran the TR design all the way past ten generations and it's still clean. Jordan called it clean as anything they're running."

Grant pounded the doorframe and grinned. "Bastard! You could have said!"

Justin raised an eyebrow. "I may be a son of a bitch, friend, but the very one thing I can't possibly be is a bastard. And now even Giraud will have to own up to it."

Grant hurled himself out into the living room again, crying: "Late, dammit! This isn't fair!"

In a moment the front door opened and shut.

There flatly was no time to go over things in the morning, even working back to back in the same office. Grant ticked away at the keyboard with occasional mutters to the Scriber-input, a constant background sound, while Justin ran the fax-scanner on his notes and Jordan's and the transcription of the whole week's sessions, punched keys where it was faster and sifted and edited and wrestled nearly fourteen hundred hours of constant transcription into five main topics with the computer's keyword scanning. Which still might miss or misfile things, so there was no question of dumping it: he created a sixth topic for Unassigned and kept the machine on autoTab, which meant it filed the original locations of the information.

He had four preliminary work-ups and one report nearing turn-in polish before Grant startled him out of a profound concentration and told him they had ten minutes to get to the restaurant.

He ground the heels of his hands into his eyes, saved down and stretched and flexed shoulders that had been rigid for longer than he had thought.

"Nearly done on the Rubin stuff," he said.

But that was not what he and Grant talked about all the way downstairs and across to North Wing, through the door at *Changes* and as far as their table—small respite for ordering drinks, more report, another break for ordering lunch, and into it again.

"The next thing," he said, "is getting Yanni to agree to test."

Grant said: "I'd take it."

"The hell you will."

Grant lifted a brow. "I wouldn't have any worry about it. I'd actually be a damned *good* subject, since it couldn't put anything over on me I couldn't identify—I understand the principles of it a hell of a lot better than the Test Division is going to—"

"And you're biased as hell."

Grant sighed. "I'm curious what it feels like. You don't understand, CIT. It's quite, quite attractive."

"Seductive is what I'm worried about. *You* don't need any motivation, friend, —a vacation, maybe."

"A tour of Novgorod," Grant sighed. "Of course. —I still want to *see* the thing when you get through with it."

Justin gave him a calculated, communicative frown. They *still* had to worry about bugs; and telling Security how skilled Grant was at reading-absorption of a program was something neither one of them wanted to do.

That look said: *Sure you would, and if you internalize it, partner, I'll break your fingers.*

Grant smiled at him, wide and lazy, which meant: *You smug CIT bastard, I can take care of myself.*

A tightening of his lips: *Dammit, Grant.*

A wider smile, a narrowing of the eyes: *Discuss it later.*

"Hello," a young voice said, and Justin's heart jumped.

He looked at the young girl who had stopped beside their table, at a young girl in expensive clothes, clothes that somehow, overnight, seemed to have developed a hint of a waist; caught a scent that set his heart pounding in remembered panic, looked up into a face that was the child gone grave, shy— that had gotten cheekbones; dark eyes gone somber and, God, touched with a little hint of violet eyeshadow.

"Hello," he said.

"I haven't seen you in a while."

"No. I guess I've been pretty busy."

"I was back there." She indicated the area of the restaurant past the archway. "I saw you come in, but I was already started on my sandwich. I thought I'd say hello, though."

"It's good to see you," he said, and controlled his voice with everything he had, managing a cheerful smile: the kid could read people faster than any of Security's computers. "How's your classwork?"

"Oh, too much of it." Her eyes lit, kid again, but not quite. "You know uncle Denys is going to let me have a horse—but I have to birth it; *and* do all the paperwork. Which is his way of getting me to study." She traced a design on the table edge with her finger. "I had the guppy business—" A little laugh. "But I turned that over to Amy Carnath. It was getting to be too much work, and now *she's* drafted her cousin in on it. Anyway— What are *you* doing?"

"A government study. And some stuff of my own. I've been working hard too."

"I remember when you came to my party."

"I remember that too."

"What Wing do you work in?"

"I'm in Design."

"Grant too?" With a flash of dark eyes Grant's direction.

"Yes," Grant said.

"I'm starting to study that," she said. The finger started doing designs again. The voice was lower, lacking the little-girl pitch. It was a different, more serious expression, a different tone of voice than she gave the cameras. "You know I'm a PR, don't you?"

"Yes," he said calmly, oh, very calmly. "I knew that."

"My predecessor was pretty good at Design. Did you know her?"

God, what do I say? "I knew her, yes. Not very well. She was a lot older." *Best to create no mysteries.* "She was my teacher for a little while."

The eyes flashed up from their demure down-focus, mild surprise, an evident flicker of thought. "That's funny, isn't it? Now you know a lot more than I do. I wish I could just take a tape and know everything."

"It's too much to learn from one tape."

"I know." Another soft laugh. "I know where I can go if I get a question, don't I?"

"Hey, I can't help you dodge your homework, your uncle would have my skin."

She laughed, tapped the table edge with her finger. "Your lunch is getting cold. I'd better get back to the lab. Nice to see you. You too, Grant."

"Nice to see you," Justin murmured; and: "Sera," Grant murmured in courtesy, as Ari went her way.

Justin tracked her till he was sure she was out the door, then let out his breath and dropped his forehead against his hands. "God." And looked up at Grant. "She's growing up, isn't she?"

"It was a courtesy," Grant said. "I don't think it was more than that."

"No," he agreed, and got himself together, picked up his fork and prodded tentatively at a piece of ham, determined not to pay attention to the unease in his stomach. "Not a bit of malice. She's a nice kid, a damn nice kid." He took the bite. "Jordan and I talked about that, too. Damn, I'd like to see her test records."

Grant made a frightened move of his eyes toward the wall. *Remember the eavesdroppers.*

"They're using the other—" Justin went on doggedly: Rubin was not a word they could toss around in the restaurant. "—the other subject—to see what they *can* get away with. And we can't get the results, dammit, for fifteen years."

"A little late," Grant murmured.

A little late to do anything for Ari's situation, Grant meant; and gave him a brows-knit look that said: *For God's sake, let's not talk about this, here, now.*

It was only good sense. "Yes," Justin said, as if he were answering the former, and took another bite and a drink to wash it down. He was starved after the battering on the flight: food service had been limited. And sweating over the terminal had worked up an appetite nothing could kill.

"Talk to Yanni," Grant said when they were walking across the open quadrangle, on their way back to the office, "and call Denys, the way you're supposed to. For both our sakes."

"I have every intention to," Justin said.

Which was the truth. What else he meant to say, he hesitated to mention. But it was in the transcripts from Planys.

His opinion, and Jordan's, both . . . for what little it was worth to an Administration worried about its own survival.

iv

Down into the tunnels, and, with Florian's little manipulation of the lock, down into the ventilation service area, from a direction that did *not* have a keycard access involved: they always had to be first, because nobody else could get the door to their meeting-place open; and the last, because Florian and Catlin were the sharpest when it came to cleaning up and making sure they left no trace at all for the workmen to find.

They used several of these little nooks. They had them coded, so Ari had only to say: number 3, and Amy passed the word to Tommy and Maddy, and Tommy got Sam up from the port school.

So they waited for the knock, and all of them came together: Amy and Tommy and Sam. Maddy was with them. And a girl named 'Stasi Morley-Ramirez, who was the reason they were meeting in a place they didn't use very often.

'Stasi was a friend of Amy's and Maddy's, but Maddy had opened her mouth, that was what had happened.

'Stasi was scared, coming in here, she was real scared, and Ari stood there with her hands on her hips, glaring at her with Catlin on her left and the flashlight on the shipping can in front of them, which made their shadows huge and their faces scary—she knew that. She had practiced that with the mirror, too, and she knew what she looked like.

"Sit down," she told 'Stasi, and Amy and Tommy sat her straight down on a big waterpipe they used to sit on here, while Florian came up and stood behind her. So 'Stasi was the only one sitting. That was a psych.

"When you come down here," Ari said, "that's it. We either vote you in or you're in a lot of trouble, 'Stasi Ramirez. You're in a whole lot of trouble, because we don't like to lose a meeting-place. And if you tell Security, *I'll* fix you good, I'll see you and your maman get shipped out of here and you won't ever come back. Say you understand."

'Stasi nodded. Emphatically.

"So you tell us why you want in."

"I know all of them," 'Stasi said desperately, twisting around where she sat to look at Amy and Maddy and the rest.

"You don't know Sam."

"I know him," 'Stasi said. "I know him from the House."

"But you don't know him like friends. And Maddy can't vote, she's the one bringing you. And Amy and Tommy can't, they're friends of yours. So it's me and Sam and Florian and Catlin who get to say. —What do you think, Catlin?"

"What can she do?" Catlin asked in her flat way.

"What *can* you do?" Ari asked.

"Like what?" 'Stasi asked anxiously. "What do you mean?"

"Like can you wire locks or memorize messages or get past a Minder or get stuff out of the lab?"

'Stasi's eyes got wider and wider.

"Catlin and Florian can do all that. They can kill people, for real. Take your head off with a wire. Pop. Just like that. Sam can get tools and wire and stuff. Maddy can get office stuff." And eyeshadow. "Tommy can get all kinds of stuff and what Amy and I do, you don't need to know about. What can you get?"

'Stasi got a more and more desperate look. "My mama and my dad manage *Ramirez's*. A lot of stuff, I guess. What do you need?"

She knew that already. *Ramirez's* was a North Hall restaurant.

"Mmmmn," she said. "Knives and stuff."

"I could," 'Stasi said earnestly. "Or food. Or most anything like that. And my uncle's a flight controller. All sorts of airline stuff—"

"All right. That part's good enough. Here's the rest. If you get in and you do anything stupid and get caught, you don't talk about us. You say it was just you. But you don't *get* caught. And you don't bring anybody here without asking. And you don't tell anybody about us. Hear?"

'Stasi nodded soberly.

"Swear?"

'Stasi nodded.

'Stasi didn't talk much. Like Sam. That was a good sign.

"I vote yes," Ari said. And Sam nodded, then. She looked at Florian and Catlin.

They didn't look like it was a bad idea. Catlin always frowned when she was considering somebody.

"They say all right," Ari said.

So everybody climbed over the pipe and sat down: it was clean. Florian and Catlin always made sure the sitting place was, because otherwise people could tell they were running around in dusty places.

And Florian and Catlin just squatted down when they were relaxing.

So they got down to business, which was her telling a lot about the trip to Novgorod—Sam had his new sweater on and so did Tommy, and Maddy wore her scarf, but Amy's pin was too good to wear to classes. Then they talked about the party Maddy was going to have, which *they* were all going to be invites to, and Maddy was happy, about 'Stasi getting in, and about being important for a while.

It was true Maddy was an early developer. The way Maddy sat and the way the light came up from their makeshift table showed that, real plain; and she was always slinking around and fluttering at the boys.

Tommy took it all right. It really bothered Sam: poor Sam had grown up big and he was in kind of a clumsy stage, because he grew so fast, Tommy said, but Sam was mostly always banging his head on things—like he was always misjudging how tall he was. He was quick as Florian when it came to fixing something, his fingers were so fast it was amazing to watch him, and he could figure out mechanical things very fast.

Sam also was in love with her, sort of, Sam always had been, like he wanted really truly to be a special friend, but she never let him, because she just didn't feel that close to Sam from her side; and it made her mad when she saw how he took Maddy seriously and worried about it, like he knew he wasn't really part of the House, and he lived down next to the Town. Maddy was rich and that wasn't ever going to come to anything, no more than Sam with her.

She had all this figured out, in a years-away mode, that none of them were really serious yet, but Sam was born serious, and Maddy was *on* ever since she learned there was a difference in boys and girls.

She knew. You didn't breed guppies and study horses without figuring out how *that* worked, and why all of a sudden boys and girls were getting around to teasing each other.

She wasn't terribly interested. She resented the whole process. It made everybody act stupid, and it was a complication when you were trying to set things up with people.

Then she saw Maddy fake a trip when they were going out and nudge Florian with her hip.

You didn't push Florian: people bumping him scared him. But he recovered fast and put his arm out and she grabbed it, lucky she hadn't landed against the wall, because Florian had learned in Novgorod not to react too suddenly when they were in crowds.

Maddy managed to put her hands on his shoulders and laugh and pretend to catch her balance before she got out the door.

What Maddy didn't see was the funny look Florian gave her retreating back.

But Ari did. He was still wearing it when he looked back at her, like he thought he had just been Got in some vague way and wasn't sure whether he had reacted right or not.

She didn't help him out either. And she doubted Catlin understood.

V

It was a long time since Justin had come into Denys Nye's office. The last visit came back all too strongly: the heavy-set man at the desk, every detail of the room.

Giraud Nye's brother. One never forgot that either.

"Yanni said," Justin began, at the door, "you were willing to talk with me."

"Certainly. Sit down."

He came and sat down, and Denys leaned forward, hands on the desk. There was a dish of pastilles. Denys took one, offered the dish across the desk.

"No, ser, thank you."

Denys popped one in his mouth, leaned back with a creak of the chair, and folded his hands on his stomach. "Yanni sent me your work. He says you want to go Test. You're pretty confident about this one, arc you?"

"Yes, ser. I am. It's a simple program. Nothing at all fancy. I don't think it'll have to run long."

"I don't think it's a problem that the Test Division can show us much about. Jordan says it'll run, it'll run without a glitch. The trouble with your work, after all, *isn't* what it does in generation one or even two. If it were, wc—wouldn't have a problem with it, would we? We could just install and go."

Grant had arguments for the run too, azi-view. *Grant* understood how the Testers worked: Grant could do what the Testers did. But it was the last place he was going to say anything on that score, not if it cost him his chance, not if it was the one and only chance he would ever have.

Nothing—was worth Grant's safety.

"I value the Testers' opinion," he said quietly. "And their experience. They have a viewpoint the computers can't give me; that's why we go to them last, isn't it?"

"That's why their time is more valuable. But they still can't answer thc multi-generational problem."

"I don't know, ser, I have a great deal of confidence in their emotional judgment. And the run would give me a lot if it could turn up anything, *any* sort of input. Jordan is saying it should run. He isn't saying that just because he's my father, ser. Not to me. Not on something that important."

Denys gave a slight, sad smile, and sighed. The chair creaked as he leaned forward and leaned his elbows on the table. And pushed a button. The bone-deep hum of the Silencer enveloped them, afflicting the nerves and unsettling the stomach. "But the problem is beyond a twenty-year study even if we gave you a full run with a geneset. That's the crux of it. Ultimately, proving whether you're right or wrong would take a Gehenna-style run. Twenty *generations*, not twenty years. We're just damn shy of planets to hand you. And what do we do with the culture that turns out if you're wrong? Nuke it? That's the scale you work on, son."

He heard *no* coming, in a slow, sarcastic way, and bit his lip and controlled his temper. "Kind of like Emory," he said, bitterly. Ultimate hubris, in Reseune. And almost said: *if your committee had had to vet her projects we'd still be a damn production farm.*

But then he was in no wise sure what Emory had done twenty or thirty generations down, or how far, or whether Union itself worked. Denys' Gehenna-reference chilled him.

"Kind of like Emory," Denys said slowly, without inflection. "I'll tell you, Sociology has been mightily upset with your designs—the suggestion that they might have turned up a flaw in the projection programs, you know. You've given the programmers over there some sleepless nights. And quite honestly, we haven't spilled the fact to Defense. You know how excited they get."

"I've never thought of going to them."

"Never?"

"No, ser. I don't see any percentage in doing it. Reseune—has its advantages. More than Planys does."

"Even if Defense might promise you residency with Jordan."

He took a breath and felt the unease of the Silencer to the roots of his teeth. It was hard to ignore. "I *have* thought of that. I hope to get him back here, ser, not—not put both of us there. He understands. He hopes for the same thing. Someday. Or we could have leaked this to Defense. Neither of us has."

"Jordan never has *liked* Defense," Denys said. "They certainly didn't help him at his hearing."

"You've counted on that," Justin said quietly. "He could have talked to them. He didn't. Not that I ever know of."

"No, you're quite right. He doesn't trust them. But mostly the consideration of your career. And Grant's. Let's be frank. We know—how far he could push us . . . and why he won't. Let me go on being honest with you. He has every motive to lie to us and to you: to convince us you're valuable in your own right, to make sure you're protected—if he gets careless. You're very naive if you think he wouldn't do that."

He ignored the body blows and kept his face unmoved. "He values Grant too," he said. "And I do. You always have a hostage. All you have to do is keep him untouched."

"Of course. That's why Grant doesn't travel."

"But once—alone—even for a few hours—-that trip would be worth it to Grant. And to my father. What's a hostage worth, if the one you're holding him against—forgets his value?"

Denys gave a heavy sigh. "Son, I don't enjoy this situation; and I had far rather have peace with the Warrick clan, God knows how, without making a slip that gets someone hurt. I'm being utterly honest with you, I'm telling you my worries in the matter. I still believe in you enough to have you in on the Project on Yanni's say-so. We're solvent again, but we're sure as hell not taking chances or spending wildly, and you're asking for a major amount of effort here, on something that's already been a headache to Sociology—"

"You say yourself, if those projections are wrong, if Sociology is working on flaws, then Defense ought to be interested. I'd call that a major matter, ser, I don't know what more it takes to qualify."

Denys frowned. "I was about to say, young friend, —'but, over all, a benefit.' All right, you get your test subject. Six-month run."

"Thank you, ser." Justin drew a whole breath. "I appreciate your honesty." *Like hell.* "And I hope—from my side—you understand the meeting yesterday—"

"Absolutely," Denys said. "I do. I appreciate the call. Ari has lunch in there now and again. You can't stay in hiding. You handled it exactly right."

"I told her Ari was my instructor. Since she asked about my knowing her. I figured—I'd better say how I knew her—early."

"That falls in an area she can't research. But yes, I see your reasoning. I have no objection to it. Sometimes you have to make fast assessments with her—God knows. You should *live* with her." Denys chuckled, and leaned back again. "She's a challenge. I know that, believe me."

"I—" God, it was an opening. It was lying in front of him. "The other thing I wanted to talk with you about: the Rubin sets, ser, I wish—wish you'd take a look at that, yourself; and my arguments. Working with Ari, the way you do, —I thought you—could give me a viewpoint—I don't have."

"On the Rubin case? Or regarding Ari?"

"I—see one bearing on the other. Somewhat. Ser."

Denys rocked his chair back and forth and lifted his brows. "Yanni told me."

"I just wonder if you'd take a look at the latest paper."

"I *have* looked at it. Yanni sent it over. I'll tell you, a lot you're doing is quite, quite good. I'm aware of your personal profile. I know what a strain it is for you to work real-time, or anything close to it, and I appreciate the stress you've undertaken—for that boy on Fargone. I know it's hard for Morley to appreciate how much pressure you're under . . . your tendency to internalize these cases. Damn bad thing for a clinical psychologist. About Ari, let me tell you, of *course* the cases are linked and of *course* your worry for the Rubin boy is going to spill over in worry about Ari, your personal mindset guarantees it. —But we *can't* hand you the whole of both projects, you do understand that, Justin, no more than we can find you a planet to test with."

"I just—" He had had enough people calling him a fool in his life he should be less sensitive; but Denys didn't bludgeon, Denys was stinging and unexpected as a paper-cut. "—just hoped—if you had time, ser, you might want to consider contingencies."

Riposte to Denys.

Denys rocked forward again, leaned on the desk. "We're working an emergency course change with the Rubin baby. You're giving us a useful perspective on the Rubin case, because we *have* a problem, but we sure as hell aren't in that situation with Ari—"

"*Rubin* worked till the thing blew up, forgive me if I misunderstand, but the matter went deeper than Jenna Schwartz and Stella Rubin—"

"Let me tell you, Justin, I *do* worry about someone who's so sure he's right he can't conceive of being wrong. I know Yanni's talked to you about that problem."

"*I'll send you my project papers. I'll pay for them. Enough for your damn committee. Point of information—is that interference?*" He drew a breath. "I happen to think it's *sane* to consider related data in a case where a committee is running an untested program. I'm not asking you for data; I'm not asking you even for data on the Rubin case that I damn well need to work with, because I know I haven't got a chance in hell of getting it. But I can hand it to you, at my own expense, since Reseune can't afford the faxes, in the theory you ought to have it available. I don't call that interference. Shred it if you like. But at least I'll have tried!"

Denys rubbed his lip, and picked up another pastille. Popped it into his mouth. "Damn, you're persistent."

"Yes, ser."

Denys looked at him a very long time. "Tell me. Does your own experience—as Jordan's replicate—bear on your confidence that you understand the Project?"

The question he had not wanted asked. Ever. His heart hit bottom. "I don't know. Everything bears on my ideas. How can I sort it out?"

"It's interesting to me. You were never aware of yourself as a replicate—until you were—how old?"

"Six. Seven. Something like. I don't remember."

"Always in Jordan's shadow. Always willing to take Jordan's opinion over your own. I think there *is* something in you . . . possibly a very important something. But sometimes I see other things: Jordan's stubbornness; his tendency to be *right* beyond all reason." Denys shook his head and sighed. "You have a hell of a way of applying for finance. Attack the people who can give it to you. Just exactly like Jordan."

"If politics matters more than what *is*, —"

"Damn, more and more like your father."

Justin shoved the chair back and got up to leave. Fast. Before he lost his temper altogether. "Excuse me, then."

"Justin, Justin, —remember? Remember who *funded* your research time? That was out of *my* budget, at a time we could hardly afford it. I take everything you've said as an honest intent to help. I assure you. I have your report; I'll have my secretary fax it for the committee. And any other material you want to send."

He was left, on his feet, with the anger still running through him. It made a tremor in his muscles. He jammed his hands in his pockets to hide their shaking. "Then thank you, ser. What about my Test request?"

"God," Denys sighed. "Yes, son. You have it. No change in that. Just—do us all a favor. *Don't* intrude any further into the Project. Keep on being prudent as you have been. Ari's handling everything very well. She's accepted being Ari's replicate, taken everything in stride. But she likes you. And she doesn't know how her predecessor died. Her time-frame on Ari is constantly lagged. The Ari she knows is five going on six, and beyond that, she's seen only a few pictures. Remember that."

"When *will* she know?"

"I'm not sure," Denys said. "I tell you that honestly. We make decisions real-time on this side of the Project; there's no way for me to answer that question. But believe me—I will warn you, when it becomes—immediate. That's one of the things we worry about as much as you do."

---

vi

It was *shots* again. Ari winced as the hypo popped against her arm, not one hypo, but three, besides the blood tests she had had every few days of her life.

Nothing wrong with you, Dr. Ivanov had told her repeatedly. *We just do this.*

Which was a lie. Dr. Ivanov had finally said so, when she found out she was a replicate and asked whether the first Ari had had something wrong with her: *No, but the first Ari had tests just like yours, because her maman knew she was going to be somebody special, and because tests like these are valuable information. You're a very bright little girl. We'd like to know if something special goes on in your bloodstream.*

But the shots made her dizzy and sick at her stomach and she was tired of getting shots and having needles in her arm.

She frowned at the nurse and thought where she would like to give the nurse a hypo, right when her back was turned. But she took the thermometer under her tongue a second till it registered, then took it out and looked at it.

"A point under," she told the nurse. Who insisted to look at it. "I always am. Do I get to go now?"

"Wait here," the nurse said, and went out, leaving her sitting in the damn robe and a little cold, the way the hospital always was, people could *freeze* to death in this place.

In a moment Dr. Ivanov came in. "Hello, Ari. Feeling fine?"

"The shot made me sick. I want to go get an orange or something."

"That's fine. That's a good idea." He came and took her pulse again. And smiled at her. "A little mad?"

"I'm tired of this. I've been in here twice this week. I'm not going to have any blood left."

"Well, your body is going through some changes. You're just growing up, sweet, that's all. Perfectly normal. You know a lot of it. But you're going to take a tape this afternoon. If you have any questions you can call me or Dr. Wojkowski, whichever you'd rather—she might be a little better at this."

She wrinkled her nose, not with any clear idea, really, what he was talking about, except she was embarrassed sitting there in the robe, which was more than she used to sit there in, and suspecting that it had to do with sex and boys and that she was going to be embarrassed as hell if she had to listen to Dr. Ivanov explain to her what she had already figured out.

Do you understand? he would ask her every three lines, and: *Yes,* she would say, because he would not get through it without that.

But he didn't mention it. He just told her go on to library, she had the tape to do.

They gave it to her to take home to use, on the house machine, so it wasn't one of the skill ones, that she had to take with a tech.

It certainly wasn't, she decided, when she saw the title. It said *Human Sexuality*. She was embarrassed in front of the librarian, who was a man, and tucked it into her bag and took it fairly straight home, very glad that Seely was out and Nelly was at her day job and there wasn't anyone around.

She applied the patch over her heart and lay down on the couch in the tape lounge and took the pill. When the pill began to work she pushed the button.

And was awfully glad, in a vague, tape-dazed way, that she hadn't had to take this one with any tech sitting by her.

There *were* things she hadn't known, things a lot different than horses, and things the same, and things Dr. Edwards had sort of hit on in biology, but not really explained with pictures and in the detail the tape had.

When it was over she lay there recovering from the pill and feeling really funny—not bad. Not bad at all. But like something was going on with her she could not control, that she sure as hell didn't want uncle Denys or Seely to know about.

It certainly had to do with sex. And it was hard to get up finally and get her mind off it. She thought about doing the tape again, not that she was not going to remember, but because she wanted to try out the feeling again, to see if it was the way she remembered it.

Then she thought it might not feel the same, and she didn't want it not to. So she put the tape back in her bag and because she didn't want the thing lying around her room where Nelly would find it and look at her funny, she had a glass of orange juice to get her blood moving again and walked all the way back to the library to drop it in the turn-in slot.

Then she went to lunch and went to class, but her concentration was shot to hell. Even Dr. Edwards frowned at her when he caught her woolgathering.

She did her write-up on the filly. It was a long day, because people were mostly busy, uncle Denys and Seely and Nelly and everybody, because Florian and Catlin were off since three days ago on a training exercise that was not going to finish till the end of the week.

She went over to the guppy lab to see if Amy was there. Tommy was. Tommy was not who she wanted to see, but she sat and talked with him a little while. Tommy was doing some stuff with the reds that she could give him some information on.

She went home to do more homework. Alone.

"Ari," uncle Denys said, on the Minder, when she had had dinner and she was still doing homework in her room. "Ari, I want to talk with you in my study."

Oh, God, she thought. Uncle *Denys* was going to ask her about the tape. She had rather die.

But it was even more embarrassing to make a fuss about it. So she got up and slunk in and stood in uncle Denys' doorway.

"Oh. Ari. There you are."

I'm going to die. Right here. On the spot.

"I want to talk with you. Sit down."

God. I have to look at him.

She sat, and held on to the arms of the chair.

"Ari, you're getting older. Nelly's really fond of you—but she's really not doing much but housework anymore. She really lives with the lab babies. And she's awfully good at that. I wonder if you've thought any more whether you'd like—well, to see Nelly go over to lab full-time. It's the nature of nurses, you know, the babies grow up."

That was all it was. She drew a long breath, and thought about her room, and how she *liked* Nelly, but she liked Nelly better when she wasn't *with* Nelly, because Nelly always had her feelings hurt and was always upset when she wanted to spend more time with Florian and Catlin, and was constantly tweaking at her hair, her clothes, straightening her collar—sometimes Nelly made her want to scream.

"Sure," she said. "Sure, if *she's* all right. I don't think she's very happy."

She felt guilty about that, sort of, because Nelly had been maman's, because Nelly had been hers—because Nelly was—Nelly—and never would understand the way she was now.

And because she was so glad it was about that and not about the other thing she just wanted to agree and get out of there.

She was guilty the next morning when Nelly went to hospital not knowing what they were going to do with her tape this time.

"I'm really not upset," Nelly protested to uncle Denys at the door, with her overnight kit in her hand. "I don't think I need to."

"That's fine," uncle Denys said. "I'm glad. But I think you're due for a check."

A Super said anything that he had to say, to keep an azi from being stressed.

So Nelly came and kissed her goodbye. " 'Bye, Nelly," Ari said, and hugged her around the neck, and let her go.

She was able to do that, because letting Nelly know would scare Nelly to death. Only when the door shut she bit her lip hard enough to bleed and said to uncle Denys:

"I'm going on to class."

"Are you all right, Ari?"

"I'm fine."

But she cried when she got out in the hall, and straightened her face up and wiped her eyes and held it in, because she was not a baby anymore.

Nelly was not going to get hurt; Nelly was going to hospital where they would slide her right over to a job she was happy at, and tell her she had done a wonderful job, her first baby was grown, and she had a whole lot of others that needed her.

It was foolish to cry. It was foolish to cry when it was just part of growing up.

The apartment was going to be lonely until suppertime. She went over to Amy's to do her homework, and told Amy about Nelly leaving, because she was finally able to talk about it.

"She was in the way anyway," she said. "She was always sniping at Florian and Catlin."

Then she felt mean for saying that.

"How are you feeling?" uncle Denys asked her again at dinner. "Are you all right with Nelly?"

"I'm fine," she said. "I just wish Florian and Catlin would get back."

"Do you want to call them home?"

Right at the end of one of their Exercises. It was very serious to them. So was she, but it was like taking something away from them. "No," she said. "They really like the overnights. Not—*like*, because they come back all scraped up; but, *like*, you know—they enjoy telling me about it. I don't need them that bad."

"I'm proud of you," uncle Denys said. "A good Super has to think that way."

She felt a little better then. And went to do her homework ahead, because she could, and she had rather do it and have something to fill her time and have it over with when Florian and Catlin got home.

Except she had a message from the computer when she went in her room. "Ari," the Minder said. "Check Base One."

"Go ahead," she said, and looked at the screen.

Ari, this is Ari senior.

Sex is part of life, sweet. Not the most important part, but this is your coming-of-age lecture. I don't know how old you are, remember, so I have to keep it simple. Library says you've checked out Human Sexuality. *Have you had it?*

"Yes. Yesterday."

Good. You're 10 years old. This program is triggered by your medical records. You're about to start your monthly cycles, sweet. Welcome to a damn unfunny fact of life. Housekeeping has been notified. You're going to have the appropriate stuff in your cabinet. Hell of a thing to get caught without. You've also had a shot that means you'll reject any pregnancy. So you don't have to worry about that, at least . . . because without that, your body's perfectly capable of it now.

I'm going to leave the what-to and what-with to the tape program, sweet. I figure you know. Probably it's given you some ideas. I know. I had it too. They're not bad ideas. I want you to listen to what I'm going to say next with everything you've got, like it was tape. This is private, it's about sex, and it's one of the most important things I'll ever have to tell you. Are you alone?

"Yes."

All right.

The ideas you have, sweet, are perfectly natural. Is your pulse a little elevated?

"Yes."

You feel a little flushed?

"Yes."

That's because you're thinking about sex. If I asked you to do complicated math you'd probably make a mistake right now. That's the important lesson, sweet. Biology interferes with logic. There's two ways to deal with it—do it and get it out of your head, because that feeling explodes like a soap bubble once you've done sex—or if it's somebody you really like, or somebody you don't like, who upsets you and makes you feel very, very strong reactions, you'd better think a whole lot about doing it, because that kind explodes all right, but it keeps coming back and bothering you. When you get into bed with somebody, you're not going to be thinking with your brain, sweet, you'll be thinking with the part of you that doesn't have anything but feeling, and that's damned dangerous.

When adults meet, sweet, and start getting to know each other, this is one of the main things that's different than kids. Kids are quite logical in some ways adults aren't. That's why they seem to see character so clearly. But when adults deal with each other, this feeling you've begun to get, gets right in the middle of their judgment.

Now there are some people who just let it take over. And the thing about this feeling is that it's playing totally off the emotional level, out of memories, out of what we're set up to believe is handsome or sexy, a whole lot of things that haven't got a damn thing to do with truth.

There are some people who learn early that they're very good-looking and that they can make anybody have this feeling about them—and they use it to get what they want. This doesn't mean they have any feeling inside at all. That's one reason to watch out who you go to bed with and who you let affect you that way.

There are other times when you get that feeling about somebody who doesn't have it for you, and that's one of the hardest things in the world to deal with. But you have to stop it then and let your brain take over, because you don't get everything you want in this world, and it's not fair to the other person at all. If you think about it you'll know how they'd feel, first if they didn't care for you as a friend and then if they did, and you kept insisting on having your way.

You can see how messy that gets.

Sometimes it happens the other way around. And if you don't see it happening or if you're too soft-hearted to say no, you can hurt somebody worse than if you say: I'm sorry, this won't work, *right off.*

Sometimes it works right on both sides, and watch out then too, sweet, because sex isn't the only thing in life, and if you let it be, that's all you'll ever have.

I'll tell you what the most important thing is, in case you haven't figured it out: It's being able to do what makes you the happiest the longest, and I don't mean sex and I don't mean chocolates, sweet, I mean being able. *Able means just exactly having the time, the money, the ability, and a thing to do that makes your life worth living long enough to get it done.*

You aren't going to have a clear sight of that thing until you've had a look at the world as it is, and had a chance to figure out what the world could be if you worked at it.

So when you get that feeling, you think real clearly whether you can afford to give in to it and whether you're able *to handle it without getting your whole life slanted in some direction that isn't smart. The time to give in to that feeling is when you can afford to, just the same as you don't spend money you haven't got, promise things you don't have time to do, or get involved in projects you can't finish. If it's a minor thing and nobody can get hurt, fine, do it. If it's got complications, don't do it until you know damn well you can handle it, and know how far the complications can possibly extend. At 10, you can't see everything. I was there. Believe me, I know. I got involved with somebody once, and I really liked him; unfortunately, he wasn't as smart as I am, and he wanted to tell me what to do and how to run my life, because he sensed I really was hooked on him, and he really liked ordering people around. So do I, of course. So when I got that figured out, which took longer than usual, because neurons work logic problems a hell of a lot faster than glands—I'm being facetious—anyway, I told him off, I reversed what was going on, and he hated it like hell. Hated me after that, too. So not only did the feeling go away, I lost a friend who would have stayed a friend if I hadn't let him do a power-move on me. I'm telling you about it now because you can learn about fire two ways: put your hand in it and understand it with the neurons below your neck or listen to me tell you about it and understand it with the ones up in your head. Your brain is the operations center that has to keep your hand out of the fire in the first place, so if you can believe me, and use the sense you were born with, you can save yourself all the pain and embarrassment of a real lesson.*

Brains and sex fight each other to control your life, and thank God brains get a head start before sex comes along. Sex is when you're the most vulnerable you'll ever be. Brains is when you're least. Brains have to win out, that's all, so they can make a safe time for sex to happen. Remember that.

Now, don't mistake: it's not bad to be vulnerable sometimes, but it's stupid to walk around that way: there are too many people just waiting for that chance. It's stupid to miss sex altogether for fear someone will take advantage of you—use the brain, sweet, and find somebody and some place and some time safe. Brains are nature's way of making sure you live long enough to spawn—if you were a frog. But you're better than a frog. So plan to live longer.

And for God's sake, don't ever use sex to get your own way where brains won't work. That's the dumbest thing in the world to do, because then you're operating without brains at all, aren't you? That's as plain as I can make it.

I want you to come back to this more than once, till you've understood what I'm saying.

If I could have learned this one thing early enough, I'd have been happier. Good luck, Ari. I hope to hell you learn this part.

She thought about that a long time into the night, into a very lonely night, because Nelly was gone and Florian and Catlin were away; and she felt awful the next morning.

Then she found out why she felt awful and why her gut hurt, and mostly she just wanted to kill something. But she found the stuff in the bathroom, all right, read the instructions and got it all figured out: Dr. Wojkowski had given her a booklet with the package, which was very plain and echoed a lot of things the tape had said.

It was more biology than she wanted in one week, dammit. And she was embarrassed and mad when the Minder said uncle Denys was waiting breakfast.

"I'll get there when I can," she yelled at it.

And took her pill and got herself in order and went out to breakfast.

"Are you all right?" Denys asked.

She glared at him, figuring he damn well knew, everybody else did. "I'm just fine," she said, and ate without another word while he read his morning reports.

Florian and Catlin came home late, sore and tired and with bandages on Catlin's hand; and full of stories, what the Exercise had been, how Catlin had gotten her hand cut getting a piece of metal fixed for a trap, but it had worked, and they had survived all the way through the course. Which youngers didn't do.

She wished she had something better than losing Nelly to tell them. And she wasn't about to tell them why she was sulking in her bedroom and feeling rotten.

Certainly not Florian, anyhow. But she got Catlin apart from Florian and told Catlin what the trouble was. Catlin listened and made a face and said well, it happened: if you were on an Operation you could take stuff so it came early or later.

Never take azi-pills, maman had said, but it sure sounded attractive.

It was worth asking Dr. Wojkowski about. Damned if she was going to ask Dr. Ivanov.

It was also a damned nasty come-down from all the *interesting* stuff about sex. Not fair, she thought. Not fair.

Just when her friends were getting home.

And one of them was a boy, and azi, and she was his Super, which meant she had to be responsible.

Dammit.

Maman had had Ollie. She thought about Ollie a lot, when she thought about boys. Ollie was administrator of RESEUNESPACE, doing maman's job. But Ollie never wrote. And she figured he would if he wanted to. Or maman had never gotten the letters. Or never wanted them.

That hurt too much to think about. She knew what she thought: maman had never gotten them. Giraud had stopped them. And Giraud would stop any letters from getting to Ollie.

So she tried not to think about that part. Just Ollie, how nice he had been, how he had always been so patient and understood maman; and how maman could be down, and Ollie would come up and put his hand on her shoulder, and maman felt better, that was all.

There was Sam. Sam was going to be big and strong as Ollie. But Sam was one of those people Ari senior was talking about that liked you without you liking them that way.

She felt good about having figured that out before she ever heard it from Ari senior, like it proved her predecessor was giving her good advice.

She felt about the same about Tommy: Tommy was all right to work with, but he was stubborn, he was all right being Amy's cousin, and number two behind Amy; and that meant doing anything with Tommy was going to mess up things with Amy. That part of the first Ari's advice made that make sense, too: complications.

There were older boys—Mika Carnath-Edwards, Will Morley, Stef Dietrich, who were worth thinking about. But Mika was a lot older, that was no good; Will was just dull; and Stef was Yvgenia Wojkowski's, who was his age.

She sighed, and kept circling back to the same thought, and watching Florian when Florian wasn't watching her.

Florian was smarter and more fun than any of them. Even Sam.

Florian was so damned nice-looking, not baby-faced like Tommy: not clumsy like Sam. She found herself just watching him move, just staring at the way his jaw was, or his arms or—

Whatever.

He had a figure the others didn't, that was what, because he worked so hard. He could move the way they couldn't, because he had muscle Tommy didn't and he was limber like Sam wasn't. And he had long lashes and dark eyes and a nice mouth and a jawline with nothing of baby about it.

He was also Catlin's partner. He was part of two, and they had been together forever, and they depended on each other in ways that had to do with things that could get you killed, if that partnership got messed up.

That was more serious than any hurt feelings. And they trusted her and depended on her in ways nobody else ever would, as long as she lived.

So she played Ari senior's advice over and over when she was alone in her room, silent, because of the Security monitoring, and told herself there had to be somebody safe, somewhere, somebody she couldn't hurt or who wouldn't mess things up.

Sex wasn't fun, she decided, it was a damned complicated mess, it gave you cramps and it tangled things up and made grown-ups not trust each other. And if you really fouled up you got pregnant or you got your best friends mad at each other.

No fair at all.

vii

Spring happened. The eleventh. And the filly was getting restless in her tank, a knot of legs and body, for a long time now too big for the lens to see all of.

Florian loved her, loved her the moment she began to look like a horse and sera had brought him to the lab and let him look into the tank. And when it came to birthing her, which sera said felt like *she* had been pregnant all these months, she had to work so hard for her, and do all that paperwork—Florian knew who was the best person down in AG to help out with that, and who was strong enough to handle the filly and keep her from hurting herself, and who knew what to do.

He told sera, and sera told the staff in the AG lab, taking his advice right off. So up came Andy, a very pleased Andy, who shyly shook sera's hand and said in his quiet way, thank you, sera; because Andy loved Horse and all Horse's kind, and sera loved them in spite of the fact Horse had broken sera's arm . . . which was probably the worst moment of Andy's whole life.

So it was a very, very happy Andy who came up to the AG lab, and knew it was true what Florian had come down to the barns to tell him, that sera wasn't put out with Horse, sera loved him too, and sera wanted more of his kind, sera was working to birth another female, and was going to ride her, and show everybody what Horse and his kind could do.

"Sera," Andy said, bowing low.

"Florian says you're the best there is," sera said, and Andy knew then, Florian was sure, that his m'sera was the finest, the best, the wisest m'sera in all Reseune. And maybe farther.

"I don't know," Andy said, "sera. But I'll sure take care of her the best I can."

So the labor started in the evening, and they just watched, watched while the foal slid down the chute into the bed of fiber; and watched while the AG techs got the cord; and Andy took sponges and towels and dried the filly all over and got her up on her wobbly legs.

Sera got to touch her then, for the first time. Sera patted her and helped dry her, and Florian helped, until Andy said that was enough and picked the filly up—Andy was very strong, and he said there was no way any truck was going to take the filly down to the barn, he could carry her.

"I want to see her," sera said.

"We can walk down," Florian said, and looked at Catlin, who stood by all this, taking it in—he knew how Catlin thought—but a great deal bewildered by all the fuss, by babies, and by sera's worry over the filly—

It was healthy, it was all right. he could read Catlin's mind that well; so why was sera worried? Babies happened. They were supposed to be studying. They had an Exercise coming up.

"I'll go," he said to Catlin. "Sera and I will be back in about an hour."

"All right," Catlin said. Because Catlin had a lot of study to do. Because if he did that, Catlin was the one who was going to save them, he knew he was going to foul up, unless Catlin could brief him fast and accurately.

But for sera, for the filly, too, who was not at fault—no animal could choose its time to be born—he had not the least hesitation: training was training, and sera was—everything.

So Andy carried the filly down the hill to the horse barn, and Florian walked with sera, happy the way she was, *because* she was, and because now there were three horses in the world, instead of two.

Andy set the little filly down in a warm stall, and got the formula they had ready and warm, and let sera give it to the baby, which stood on shaky legs and butted with her nose as if that could get more milk faster. Sera laughed and backed up, and the filly wobbled after. "Stand still, sera," Andy called out. "Just hold it."

Sera laughed, and held on.

Down the way, in her stall, the Mare called out, leaning over the rail.

"I think she smells the baby," sera said. "That could be trouble. Or she might take up with her. I don't know."

"I don't either," Andy said.

"There being just three," sera said, "everything's like that, isn't it? The books don't say about a horse who never saw but one other horse in the world."

"And she's pregnant," Andy said in his quiet way, shy around a CIT, "and she's got milk already. And animals are like CITs, sera, they have their own ways, it's not all one psychset, and there isn't any tape for *them*."

Sera looked at him, not mad, just like she was a little surprised at all that out of Andy. But it was true, Florian knew it. One pig was trouble and its birthsisters weren't. It just depended on a lot of things, and when babies happened the way they did with pigs, with a boar and a sow, you were dealing with scrambled genesets and didn't know what you had—like CITs, too.

At least, with the filly, it was likely to be a lot like its genesister the Mare, which meant she was going to be easy to handle.

Bang! on the rails from down the row. The Mare called out, loud. And the azi who were standing in the barn to watch the new baby went running to get the Mare.

"This is all complicated," sera said, worried.

"Animals are like that," Andy said. "She's all right. It would be good if she would accept the baby. Animals know a lot. Some things they seem to be born knowing."

"Instinct," sera said. "*You* should cut a tape. I bet you know more than some of the damn books."

Andy grinned and laughed, embarrassed. "I'm a Gamma, sera, not like Florian. I'm just a Gamma." As one of the other AG-techs came running down to say the Mare was fine, they were going to move her to the little barn and get her out of here.

"No, do that, but pass her by here," Andy said. "But hold on to her. Let's see what she does. Sera, if she makes trouble, you better be ready to climb up over those rails to the side there and get into the other stall. Florian and I can hold the baby, and the boys can hold the Mare, but we sure don't want you to break another arm."

"I can help hold her."

"Please, sera. We don't know what will happen. Just be ready to move."

"He's the best," Florian said. "Andy's always out here; the Supers are always in the offices. Andy's birthed most everything there is. You should do what he says, sera."

"I'll move," sera said, which was something, from sera. But she *liked* Andy, and she realized right off that Andy had good sense, that was the way sera was. So she stood there watching anxiously as the techs led the Mare past, two of them, each with a lead on her.

The Mare pulled and they let her stop and put her head over the stall door. She snuffed the air and made a strange, interested sound.

The baby pricked up her ears, and stood there with her nose working hard too.

"Put the Mare in the next stall," Andy told the techs holding the Mare. "Let's just watch this awhile."

That was the way Andy worked. Sometimes he didn't know. Sometimes no one knew because no one in the world had ever tried it. But Andy didn't let his animals get hurt and he had a way of figuring what they were going to do even if Andy had never read a book in his life.

"She's *talking* to her," sera said, "that's what she's doing."

"They sure teach something," Andy said. "Animals sort of do tape on each other."

"They're a herd animal," sera said. "It's got to be *everything* to do with how they act. They want to be together, I think."

"Well, the little girl will fix on people," Andy said. "They're that way, when they're born from the tank. But the Mare could help this little horse. She's getting milk, already. And milk from a healthy animal is a lot healthier than formula. I'm just worried about how she'll act when hers comes."

"Politics," sera said. "It's always politics, isn't it?" Sera was amused, and watched as the Mare put her head over the rail of the next stall. "Look at her. Oh, she wants over here."

"Somebody's going to sit all night with the Mare, too," Andy said. "When we've got something we don't know about, we just hold on to the ropes and stay ready. But there's a chance the Mare will want this baby. And if she does, she's the best help we could get."

They were *very* late getting back up the hill. Florian wouldn't trade the time with sera and the filly for his own sake, but he was terribly sorry when he got back to the room, in a dark and quiet apartment, and said to Catlin: "It's me," when he opened the door.

"Um," Catlin said, from her bunk, and started dragging herself up on an arm. "Trouble?"

"Everything's fine. The baby's doing real well. Sera's happier than I've ever seen."

"Good," Catlin said, relieved. So he knew Catlin had been worrying all this time.

"I'm *sorry*, Catlin."

" 'S all right. Shower. I'll tell you the stuff."

He shut the door, asked the Minder for the bathroom light and started stripping on his way to the bath while Catlin got herself focused. He hardly ran water over himself and pulled on clean underwear and came out again, cut the light and sat there on his bed while Catlin, from hers, a calm, coherent voice out of the dark, told him how they were going to have one bitch of a problem tomorrow, they had to break past a Minder and get a Hostage out alive.

They said there were going to be three Enemies, but you never knew.

394 · C.J. Cherryh

You never knew what the Minder controlled, or if there wasn't some real simple, basic wire-job on the door, which was the kind of trap you could fall into if you got to concentrating too much on the tech stuff.

They had to head down the hill at 0400. It was drink the briefing down, fix what could happen, and sleep for whatever time they could without getting there out of breath, because you never knew, sometimes they threw you something they hadn't told you about at all, and you had to cope with an Enemy attack before you even got to the Exercise.

Catlin never wasted time with what and where. She had showed him a lot in the years they had worked together, about how to focus down and think narrow and fast, and he did it now with everything he had, learning the lay of the place from maps he scanned by penlight, not wanting to shine light in Catlin's eyes, learning exactly how many steps down what hall, what the distance was and what the angles and line of sight were at any given point.

You hoped Intelligence was right, that was all.

It was eighty points on the Hostage, that was all they were saying. That meant in a hundred-point scale at least one of them was expendable. They could do it that way if they had to, which meant him, if it had to be: Catlin was the one who had the set-up best in her head and she was the one who would most likely be able to get through the final door, if he could get it open. But you didn't go into anything planning what you could give away. You meant to make the Enemy do the giving.

He did the best he could, that was all.

viii

It was Catlin on the phone. *Catlin* made a phone call; and Ari flew out of Dr. Edwards' classroom and down the hall to the office as fast as she could run.

"Sera," Catlin said, "we're going to be late. Florian's in hospital."

"What happened?" Ari cried.

"The wall sort of fell," she said. "The hospital said I should call, sera, he's real upset."

"Oh, God," she cried. "Catlin, dammit, how bad?"

"Not too. Don't be mad, sera."

"Catlin, dammit, report! What happened?"

"The Enemy was holding a Hostage, we had to get in past a Minder, and we did that; we got all the way in, but the Hostage started a diversion while they were trying to Trap the door. The Instructor is still trying to find out what happened, but their charge went off. The whole wall went down. It wouldn't really do that, it would blow out, but this was a set-up, not a real building, and it must have touched off more than one charge."

"Don't they *know*?"

"Well, they're dead. Really."

"I'm coming. I'm coming to the hospital right now. Meet me at the front door." She turned around and Dr. Edwards was there. So she told him. Fast. And told him call uncle Denys.

And ran.

"He thinks it's his fault," Catlin said, when she got there, at the front door, panting and sick at her stomach.

"He didn't tell me you had an Exercise today," Ari said. That was what she had thought all the terrible way down the hill. "He didn't tell me!"

"He was fine," Catlin said. "He didn't make a mistake. They shouldn't have been where they were, that's first." She pointed down the hall, where a man in black was talking to the doctors. "That's the Instructor. He's been asking questions. The Hostage—he's a Thirteen, he's the only one alive. It's a mess. It's a real mess. They're asking whether somebody got their charges mixed up, where the explosives kit was sitting, they think it was up against the wall right where they were working, and they hadn't Trapped everything they could have, so that was two charges more than they were using on the door. The whole set-up came down. Florian kind of threw himself backward and covered up, or he could have been killed too. Lucky the whole door just came down on him before the blocks did."

Ari walked on past the desk with Catlin, down where the doctors were talking with the Instructor, and past, where Florian was, in the hall, on one of the gurneys. He looked awful, white and bruised and bleeding on his shoulder and on his arms and hands, but they had cleaned those up and sprayed them with gel.

"Why is he out here?" Ari snapped at the med who was standing there.

"Waiting on X-ray, sera. There's a critical inside."

"I'm all right," Florian muttered, eyes half-opening. "I'm all right, sera."

"You—" *Stupid*, she almost said. But a Super couldn't say that to an azi who was tranked. She bit her lip till it hurt. She touched his hand. "Florian, it's not your fault."

"Not yours, sera. I wanted to go. With the filly. I could have said."

"I mean it's *not your fault*, hear me? They say something blew up." She went over where the doctors and the Instructor were, right up to them. "It wasn't Florian's fault, was it?" Her voice shook. "Because if it was, it was mine, first."

"This is sera Emory," Dr. Wojkowski said to the frowning Security Instructor who looked at her like she was an upstart CIT brat. "Florian and Catlin's Supervisor."

The man changed in a hurry. "Sera," he said, Catlin-like, stiff. "We're still investigating. We'll need to debrief both of them under trank."

"No," she said.

"Young sera, —"

"I said no. Let them alone."

"Sera is correct," a hard voice said, from a man in ordinary clothes, who had come up on the other side of the group, a man a little out of breath.

It was Seely. She never thought she would be that glad to see Seely in her whole life.

Uncle Denys couldn't run. But Seely had, clear from Administration. And Florian and Catlin were right: Seely was Security, she knew it the minute he launched into the Instructor.

It was a *lot* better. Florian had had a piece of metal driven into his leg, that was the worst, but they had gotten that out, and he had sprains and bruises, and he was going to be sore, because they had pulled a lot of building blocks off the door that had fallen on him.

"Fools," was what Seely said when Ari asked him what he had found out, talking to Catlin and talking to the Instructor and the Hostage, when he came around, what little he could. When she heard it she drafted Seely into the room where Florian was starting to come around. "Tell *him*," she said, while Catlin came into the room behind Seely and stood there with her arms folded.

So Seely did. "Are you hearing me?" Seely asked Florian.

"Yes," Florian said.

"The Instructor is under reprimand. The amount of explosives allotted exceeded the strength of the set-up. The Hostage attempted a distraction according to his orders, while the team inside was Trapping the door. The Hostage doesn't know what happened at that point. He took out one team member. Apparently the two working with the door had set their kit close to them, probably right between them, and possibly the distraction, or the third boy falling against them—dropped the charge they were working with into two others they had in the kit."

"They didn't start Trapping the door they were behind until we got in past the Minder," Catlin said, walking close to the bed. "They thought they could get out and score points, because there was a third team coming in at our backs. They didn't tell us that. They were working with the Enemy and they were supposed to hit us from behind. But they were sticking to the Instructor's timetable and we got past the Minder too fast. . . ."

"Too *fast*?" Florian murmured, with a flutter of his eyes. "That's crazy. What was I supposed to do?"

". . . so the other team tried to improvise and tried to Trap the door when they knew we were ahead of what they expected. And the Hostage followed his orders, kicked the guard, but the guard fell into the two at the door and they dropped the charge right into their kit. Wasn't your fault. We couldn't fire into the room because of the Hostage. He was supposed to be on our side and cause *them* trouble. It was a double-team exercise. So it was the set-up that went wrong."

"You didn't Trap the door," Seely asked Florian.

"I can't remember," Florian said. Then, blearily: "No. I wouldn't. No reason. Not in the plan."

"You didn't," Catlin said. "I was covering your back, in case the third Enemy was behind. You were going to blow the door and gas the room, remember?"

Florian grimaced as if it hurt. "I can't—remember. It's just gone. I don't even remember it blowing."

"Happens," Seely said, arms folded, just like Catlin. Ari sat there in a straight chair and listened. And wondered at Seely. "You may never get those seconds back. The shock jolted you. But you're all right. It wasn't your fault."

"You don't put your charges—" Florian said thickly, "under where you're working."

"You don't exceed your building limits with the charges in a training exercise, either, or set up a double-team course with a Murphy-factor in it like that in a dead-end room. You exceeded expectations. The other team fell below. End report. You'll be back in training next week. They won't."

"Yes, ser," Florian said quietly. "I'm sorry about them, though."

"He needs tape," Seely said, looking at Ari. "He shouldn't feel that way. That'll give him trouble in future."

That made her mad; and shouldn't. Seely was trying to help. "I'll decide," she said, afraid he was going to say that to uncle Denys too.

Seely nodded, very short, very correct. "I have business," he said, "if that's all, sera. You're doing everything right here."

"Thank you, Seely. Very much. Tell uncle Denys I might be over here for supper."

"Yes, sera."

Seely left.

Catlin walked over to the chair, arms still folded, and sat down.

"Catlin," Ari said. "Did *you* get hit?"

"Not much," Catlin said. "Most of my end of the hall was still standing." She flexed her left arm and wrist. "Sprain from moving the blocks. That's all."

"I went too *fast*," Florian said, like he was still a little tranked. "That's crazy. It was an old-model Minder."

"They made the mistake," Catlin said firmly, definite as the sun in the sky. "We didn't."

Ari bit her lip. *Florian* got to use the House library. Florian got into the manuals for the House systems. Florian knew a lot of things they didn't, down in the Town, because Florian and Catlin never stopped learning.

She went out in the hall, got permission for the phone, and called uncle Denys herself.

"Uncle Denys," she said, "Florian worked the course too fast. That's what they're saying. He got hurt for being better. That's lousy, uncle Denys. He could have gotten killed. Three people *did*. Aren't there any better Instructors down there?"

Uncle Denys didn't answer right off. Then he said: "I've got Seely's report up now. Give me a while. How is he?"

"He's damn sore," she said, forgetting not to say *damn* to uncle Denys. And told him what Dr. Wojkowski had said and what Seely and Catlin had said.

"I agree with you. If that's borne out in the report, we're going to have to do something. Do you want to spend the night down there, or is he going to need that?"

"I want to do it. With Catlin."

"All right," uncle Denys said, without arguing at all. "Make sure you get something to eat. Hear?"

Uncle Denys surprised her sometimes. She went back to the room, feeling a little like she had been hit with something too. Everything had been so good, and then everything went so bad. And then Seely and Denys both got reasonable, when she least expected it.

"They're going to fix things," she said to Catlin, because Florian's eyes were shut. "I just called uncle Denys. I think there's a foul-up somewhere higher up than the Instructor. I think you know too much for down there."

"Sounds right," Catlin said. "But it makes me mad, sera. They keep saying we're a little better than they expect. They wasted those azi. They were all right. They weren't the best in Green, but they didn't need to get killed. They lived right across the hall from us."

"Dammit," she said, and sat down with her hands between her knees. Cold all over and sick at her stomach, because it was not a game, what they did was never a game, Catlin was right from the start.

<hr>

ix

Florian was still limping a little, but he was doing all right when he came into the barn with Catlin and Amy and the other kids. Ari watched him, watched a smile light his face when he saw the Mare and the filly—two fillies. One with a light mane and tail, that was Ari's; and one with black—that was Horse's daughter.

"Look at her!" Florian exclaimed. And forgot all about his limp; and came and patted the Mare on the shoulder, and hugged her around the neck. Which impressed hell out of the kids. Except Catlin, of course, who knew Florian wasn't scared of horses.

The Mare deserved it in Ari's estimation. The Mare mothered both babies, the one she had birthed and the one who was her genesister, which of course the Mare could not understand, except the Mare was just generous and took care of both of them.

"She's so big," Amy said.

They were a little scared of the fillies too. It was the first time they had ever been close to animals, and they were still afraid they were going to get knocked down—good guess, because they tended to spread out and get too close and dodge into each other's and the horses' way when the horses shied. Even Catlin, who backed up and tucked her hands behind her, stiff and azi, when 'Stasi nearly bumped into her. Maddy yelped and nearly got it from the Mare's backside, and Ari just dropped her face into her hands and looked up again, with the horses all off across the big barn arena and the kids looking a little foolish.

"You have to go a little slower," Andy said from behind them. "They don't want to step on you. But you smell funny to them."

The kids looked at Andy as if they thought he was joking or they had just been insulted.

"Come on," Ari said to Florian. "Let's see if we can get her."

"Wait, sera, I can," Florian said, and walked after her.

It was strange finally to come out in the open, and pretend they were mostly friends of Amy's, that everyone knew was her friend, and who, she figured, was safer from Disappearing than anybody else because her mama was a friend of uncle Denys and uncle Giraud. She didn't think it would happen anymore, but the kids worried; and that was the set-up she had worked out with Amy—because the kids were still worried.

But, she told them, they could go to places like seeing the new babies together and not have anybody get onto the fact she had friends, the same way she could buy things for people and not have uncle Giraud know they saw each other more than at parties. Andy wasn't in the House circuit, so Andy wouldn't tell everything he saw and neither would the azi in the barn. So they felt safer.

Florian caught the Mare with no trouble. He brought her back and the fillies came right along. That impressed the kids too.

It was strange how the kids looked at Florian and Catlin now, too, since Florian had come back still a little stiff and sore, and she had had Florian and Catlin tell what had happened down there in the Exercise—it was all right to tell them, she had explained to Florian and Catlin, because they were CITs and they were in the House, except Sam, and Sam was all right. So Florian had started telling it, but when he got to the part where he went down the hall, he couldn't remember past that point, and Catlin had to tell it, and about the hospital and everything.

It was the first time either one of them had said more than a sentence or two at a time to the kids, and it was something to get Catlin to tell a story; but once Catlin got warmed up, Catlin knew enough gory stories to get them all going, and all of a sudden the kids seemed to figure out that Florian and Catlin were real. That a whole lot of things were. That they had seen dead people. That they really could do what she said.

—Not, really, she thought, that they had ever doubted her, but that they had had no way to understand what it was like to walk down a hall toward an Enemy, carrying explosives which, thank God, had not gone off . . . or even that there were Enemies who could come right up on Reseune's grounds and try to blow things up or shoot people.

They started wondering why, that was one thing that was different. They wanted to know what went *on* in the Council and why people had wanted to take things from her in Court—and they got to questions where she couldn't give them all the answers.

"That's something I'm still trying to figure out," she had told them. "Except there are people who don't want azi to be born and they'd like to shut Reseune down."

"We do more than azi," Sam had said.

"Florian and Catlin wouldn't like not to be born," Amy had said.

"They might be born," Ari said, "but they'd bring them up like CITs and teach them like CITs. They wouldn't like it."

"Would you?" Amy had asked them, because they had started asking Florian and Catlin questions that didn't go through her.

"No," Florian had said, very quiet, while Catlin shook her head. Ari knew. Florian was too polite to say what he had said to her when she had talked with them about it before: that he didn't like most CITs, because they were kind of slow about things; a lot of CITs, he had said, worked harder trying to make up their minds *what* to do than they did doing what they'd decided, and he hated to be around people like that. And Catlin had said, a depth of thought which had surprised her, that she figured CITs had made azi to run things like Security because they knew they couldn't trust each other with guns.

"Do you *like* being azi?" 'Stasi had gotten far enough to ask, that time down in the tunnels.

Florian had gotten a little embarrassed, and nodded without saying a thing.

"I think he's sexy," Maddy had said outright, in school, not in Florian or Catlin's hearing. "I wish *I* had him." And giggled.

I'm glad you don't, had been Ari's thought.

That popped into her head again while Florian was leading the horses back: he was so neat and trim in his black uniform, you couldn't see he was a kid if you didn't know the Mare's height. Florian and Catlin—were enough to make you jealous you couldn't walk like that and look like that and be like that.

Because CITs didn't take care of themselves like that, she thought, they ate too much and they spent too much of their time sitting down and, face it, she told herself, nature dealt Amy eyes that had to be corrected and made Tommy just average-looking, and didn't give Maddy any sense.

While Florian and Catlin looked like that and were so good at what they did that they were out of Green and into House Security, because they were just better than their predecessors—because they were taught *after* the War, Denys had said, using modern-day stuff that made them work harder and use what they had, and because she was right, they had learned a lot of classified stuff up in the House that the Instructors down in Green didn't even know about, that was different since sometime in the War, too. All of which came down to the fact that they started doing their tape in House Security, and that after this no Exercise with them involved could use a double-blind situation.

Like adult Security. Because their reactions had gotten so fast and so dangerous there was no way to make it safe if they got surprised, and they could push other teams past all their training.

She was damned glad Maddy *didn't* have their Contracts. Damned glad Maddy didn't have her hands on Florian and didn't have any chance to mess with that partnership, because she understood now beyond any doubt that it was life-and-death business with them. She had made Florian late for one study-session, Florian and Catlin had thrown everything they had into their Exercise, afraid they were going to fail it; and that had made them overrun the course and push another team to the point it got rattled and made a mistake, that was what had happened, so that three azi had gotten killed was, at least remotely, her fault. Not blamable fault, but it was part of the chain of what had happened, and she had to live with that.

She was terribly glad she hadn't done anything with Florian that would have put any more strain on him. Because he could just as well have been dead, and it would have been her fault, really, truly her fault.

Maddy was right. He was so damned pretty. She wanted so much to do with him exactly what Maddy wanted to do.

And Maddy would have no idea in her head why she couldn't.

She wished to hell Ari senior *could* talk back and forth, because she had tried to ask Base One if Ari had anything to say about Florian being in hospital or about whether it was safe to do sex with her azi, if they were Security. But Base One had said there was no such information.

She was so desperate she even thought about getting Seely off in a corner somewhere and asking *him* that question. But Seely was as much Seely as he had ever been—and not even sex could make her *that* desperate.

Yet.

X

Her twelfth birthday, she had a big party—a dance in the Rec hall, with every kid in Reseune who was above nine and under twenty—uncle Denys begged off and said he had work, but that was because he hated the music.

He missed something, because Catlin learned to dance. Catlin got the idea of music—it's a mnemonic, Ari said, when Catlin looked puzzled at the dancing: the variations on the pattern are the part that makes it work.

Florian had no trouble at all picking it up—but he was too self-conscious to clown with it in public: that was the funny thing; and it was *Catlin* who shocked everybody, by trying to teach Sam a step he couldn't get—an azi out on the floor with a CIT. Everybody got to watching, not mad, just amazed, and Catlin, in a gauzy black blouse that covered just about what it had to with opaque places, and black satin pants that showed off her slim hips like everything, —smiled, did three or four fast steps and showed what you could *do* if you could isolate muscle groups and keep time with the music.

After that every boy in the room wanted to have one dance with Catlin, and it was funny as hell, because all the girls in the room didn't know whether to be jealous of an azi or not.

So Maddy Strassen flounced over and asked Florian, and the other girls started asking him, and the few older CIT kids who had azi their own age began showing them the steps, until the thing got all over the House by the next morning.

"You know," uncle Denys said about it at breakfast, "there *are* azi that could bother. You really ought to be careful."

"Seely was there," she said, tweaking uncle Denys just a bit. "And a lot of Security. They could have stopped it, anytime."

"Probably the music paralyzed their judgment. They were there to stop Abolitionists with grenades. They needn't have worried. They couldn't get past the noise."

"Well, none of the azi got pushed. Some would dance, some wouldn't, nobody pushed anybody. Florian said Catlin thought it was interesting. She's supposed to protect me, right? And she's not as social as Florian. But she can imitate anything physical and she can *act* like anybody. So she was having a great time out there. She was psyching everybody and getting the feel of how they moved and they never knew what she was doing. Want to know what she said?"

"What?"

"She said they were all soft and they were generally real vulnerable in their balance. That she could take out any one of them with an elbow."

Uncle Denys sneezed into his orange juice.

---

xi

More shots. They brought her period on. She swore she was going to get Dr. Ivanov. A call at his door at night and blam! a gift from Florian.

He probably had enough of her blood to transfuse most of Novgorod.

"I think I want a different doctor," she said to uncle Denys.

"Why?" uncle Denys asked, over his reports, at the supper table, which was the only place she saw him—at breakfast and at supper.

"Because I'm tired of getting stuck with needles. I'm going to be anemic."

"Dear, it's a study. It got started when you were born and it's a very valuable study. You just have to put up with it, I don't care what doctor you have; and you'd hurt Petros' feelings. You know he's very fond of you."

"He smiles very nice, right before he gives me something that makes me want to throw up."

"You know, you have to watch, dear, your voice does tell what's going on with your cycles. That's something you don't want to make that public, isn't it?"

"I don't know why not! I don't know why they don't put it on the news! Why don't you hand the news-services the tapes from my bedroom? I bet I can give them some real thrills if I work at it, I bet the Security techs just love it!"

"Who said we were taping? That's a Security system."

"Florian and Catlin are House Security, remember?"

Uncle Denys put down his reports, suddenly very serious.

So was she, not having intended to bring it up. Yet. Till they found out some other things. But he was off his balance: she had her opening; she Got him with it.

Good.

"Dear, all right—yes. There are tapes. They go into Archive, no one accesses them. They're just a historical record."

"Of me having my period."

"Ari, dear, don't be coarse."

"I think it's coarse! I think it's a damn coarse thing to do to me! I want that system shut *down*, uncle Denys! I want it off, I want those tapes destroyed, I want Florian and Catlin to rip out that entire unit, *at the control board*."

"Dear me, they *are* observant, aren't they?"

"Damn right they are."

"Ari, dear, *don't* swear. You're not old enough."

"I want that unit *off*! I want it *out*! I want those tapes *burned*! I want to move up to *my* apartment and I want Florian and Catlin to go over *that* and have access to all the control boards in all the secret little rooms in Security!"

"Ari, dear, calm down. I'll have them turn it off."

"The hell! You'll just relocate the board somewhere else you think Florian and Catlin can't find it."

"Well, then, you'd have a problem, wouldn't you? You have to believe me."

"No, I don't, because I'll know if that unit is running."

"How?"

"I'm not going to tell you. Ask Seely. I'm sure he can explain it."

"Ari, dear, your temper is running a bit high today, I'm sure you've noticed. And I really, really don't want to discuss things with you when you're *on* like this. I'm very, very fond of you, but no one likes to listen to a cultured twelve-year-old swear like a line soldier, and no one likes to be called a liar—as you once said in a very public place. So do you think you could lower the volume a little and discuss this rationally, or shall we say I'm sure Seely is still a little ahead of Florian? —If I wanted to continue the surveillance against your wishes. I appreciate the fact you're not a little girl anymore. I know there are very good reasons why you don't want to be taped in your bedroom, and the fact that you've objected is enough. We can't get any value out of a study if the subject is acting for the cameras, now, can we? So the taping will stop, not because you have the power to take out the units, but because it loses its value."

"I want the tapes burned!"

"I'm sorry, not even we can get at them. They've gone into the Archive vault, under the mountain out there, and they're irretrievable as long as you're active in the House computer."

"You mean while I'm logged in?"

"No, as long as you're an active CIT-number in the files. As long as you live, dear. Which is going to be a long, long time, and then you won't care, will you, whether somebody has a tape of a twelve-year-old girl in her underwear?"

"You've seen those tapes!"

"No, I know the twelve-year-old, that's quite enough. The taping will shut down. Florian can verify it, if you like, and Florian can remove the unit himself, with, I trust, some reasonable care not to damage the rest of the system."

"Today."

"Today." Uncle Denys looked very worried. "Ari, I *am* sorry."

He was acting with her. Working her. The way he had been Working the whole situation and trying to get her to believe him. The way she Worked him.

He was probably good enough to spot that too. If Seely was ahead of Florian, uncle Denys was still ahead of her, she thought. Maybe.

But she could Work him right back by using her upset and letting it go on long enough to let him do the Shift on her, and do it a couple of times so he thought he Had her.

Then she could do what he was trying to get her to do and see where it led, without *being* led.

"I'm sorry, Ari."

She glared at him.

"Ari, this is a very bad time for this. I wish you'd come to me earlier."

Dammit, he wanted her to ask. She wanted to Work him to have to tell her whatever he was up to, but that would give it away for sure that she was onto him Working her. Which he might know anyway: you never knew how many layers there were with uncle Denys.

"You know there's a bill up to extend you the first Ari's Special status."

"I know."

"You know it's going to pass. There's not going to be any problem with it. There's no way the Centrists can stop it."

"That's nice, isn't it?"

"It was the one thing the Court didn't hand you with Ari's rights. The one thing they held back. So you'll have that. You'll have everything. You know Reseune is so proud of you."

Flattery, flattery, uncle Denys.

"You *are* going to be on your own in a few years. You'll leave this apartment and move to yours, and I won't be with you: I'll go back to being a fat old bachelor and see you mostly in and out of the offices and at parties."

Saying bad things on himself; humor; trying to get her to think about missing him.

She would. So you didn't let people Hook you, not when they were uncle Denys.

She didn't say a thing. She just let him go on.

"I worry, Ari. I really hope I've done all right with you."

Trying to scare her. Trying to talk like something was going to change. Another maman-event. Damn him anyway.

I hope you do *Disappear, uncle Denys.*

That wasn't quite the truth, but it was a real low move uncle Denys was doing and she wasn't about to show how mad it made her.

"We get along all right," she said.

"I'm very fond of you."

God. He's really pushing it.

"Ari? Are you mad?"

"I sure am."

"I'm sorry, sweet. I really am. Someday I can tell you why we do these things. Not now."

Oh, that's a hook, isn't it?

"You know Amy's mother invited you and Florian and Catlin to come over this evening."

"I didn't know that. No."

"Well, she did. Why don't you?"

"Because I feel lousy. And Amy didn't say anything about it."

"It's a surprise."

The hell.

"I think you've been studying too hard. I think an evening out would do you a world of good."

"I don't want to go anywhere! I feel lousy! I want to go to bed!"

"I really think you should go to Amy's."

"I'm not going to Amy's!"

Uncle Denys didn't look happy at all, and began getting up. "I'll call Dr. Ivanov. I think maybe he *did* give you something that's bothering you. Maybe he can send you something."

"The hell he can! I don't want any more shots, I don't want any more blood tests, I don't want any more cameras in my bedroom, I don't want any more people messing with me!"

"All right, all right. No medicine. Nothing. I'll talk to Petros." He frowned. "I'm really upset about this, Ari."

"I don't care." She got up from the table. She was wobbly from anger. It was out of control. She was. She hated the feeling, *hated* whatever they did to her.

"I mean I'm worried," uncle Denys said. "Ari, —you're using the computer tonight, aren't you?"

"What has that got to do with anything?"

"Just—when you do—remember I love you."

That hit her. Uncle Denys saying *I love you*? It was a Trap, for sure. It hurt, because it was about the lowest try yet.

"Sure," she said shortly. "I'm going to my room, uncle Denys."

"Hormones," he said, as shortly. "It's hormones. Adolescence is a bitch. I'll be glad when you're through this. I really will."

She walked out, and shut the door between her hallway and the living room.

Florian and Catlin stepped out their door the instant she did.

Saying *What's the matter?* with their faces.

"I'm fine," she said. "Uncle Denys and I had a discussion about the taping. You're going to take the unit out first thing tomorrow."

"Good," Florian said in a vague, stunned way.

"I'm going to my room," she said. "I'm all right. Don't worry about me. Everything's fine."

She walked past them.

She closed the door of her room.

She looked at the computer on the desk.

Exactly, she figured, what he wanted her to do. She should frustrate hell out of him. Make him worry. Not touch the thing for days.

Not smart. The best thing was find *out* what he was wanting. Then deal with it.

"Base One," she said. "Is there a message?"

"No message," Base One said through the Minder.

That was not what she expected.

"Base One, what *is* in the system?"

The screen lit. She went over to it. There was only one item waiting for her.

The regular weekly update. Second week of April, 2290.

She sat down in front of the screen. Her hands were shaking. She clenched them, terrified, not sure why. But something was in it. Something Denys wanted was in that week, that year.

Second week of April.

Second week of April. Five years ago.

She had been at school. In the sandbox. She had started home.

"Selection one."

It came up. It started scrolling at the usual pace.

Olga Emory.

Deceased, April 13, 2290.

Ari senior had been at school. When her uncle Gregory had come to get her and break the news.

"Dammit!" she screamed, and got up and grabbed the first thing she found and threw it. Pens scattered clear across the bed and the holder hit the wall. She grabbed a jar and threw it at the mirror, and both shattered and fell.

As Catlin and Florian came running in.

She sat down on her bed. And grabbed up Poo-thing and hugged him, stroked his shabby fur, and felt like she was going to throw up.

"Sera?" Florian said.

And he and Catlin came and knelt down by the side of the bed where she was sitting, both of them, even though she had been breaking things and they must think she was crazy. It was terribly scary for them; it was scary for her to have them come that close when she was already cornered. She knew how dangerous they were. And there was nothing she could trust.

"Sera?" Catlin said, and got up by her, just straightened up, solid muscle, and flowed onto the bed and touched her shoulder. "Sera, is there an Enemy?"

She could have taken Catlin with her elbow. She thought about it. She knew Catlin did. Florian put his hand on hers, on the edge of the bed. "Sera, are you hurt? Has something happened?"

She reached up with her other hand and touched Catlin's, on her shoulder. Florian edged up onto the bed on her other side, and she got her breath and got her arm behind Catlin and her hand locked onto Florian's and just sat there a moment. Poo-thing fell. She let him.

"They sent maman away," she said, "because Ari's mother died."

"What, sera?" Florian asked. "What do you mean? When did she die?"

"The same day. When Ari was the same age. Her uncle came to get her. Just like uncle Denys came for me." Tears ran out of her eyes and splashed onto her lap, but she wasn't crying, not feeling it, anyway; the tears just fell. "I'm a replicate. Not just genetic. I'm like you. I'm *exact*."

"That's not so bad," Catlin said.

"They sent my maman away, they sent her on a long trip through jump, it made her sick and she *died*, Catlin, she *died*, because they wanted her to!"

Catlin tapped her shoulder, hard, leaned up to her ear and whispered: "Monitors."

She felt the shock of that reminder in her bones and caught her breath, trying to think.

The scrolling stopped on the screen in front of them.

"Ari, check Base One," the Minder said.

She made a second gasp after air. Like she was drowning. She held onto Florian and Catlin.

"Ari, check Base One."

Uncle Denys had known what would come up.

Uncle Denys hadn't wanted her to go on-line tonight. Go to Amy's, he had said.

Then *told* her to check the computer.

"Ari, check Base One."

"Base One, dammit!" She disentangled herself from Florian and Catlin and thought it was Unusual that uncle Denys and Seely hadn't tried to get in to see about her when the mirror broke. And then she thought that it wasn't Unusual at all.

Not with the room monitored.

She sat down at the terminal, in front of the monitor.

Ari, it said. *This is Ari senior. By now you've gotten the update. By now you know some things you may not have figured out before. Are you upset?*

"Of course not." She felt Florian beside her. She grabbed his arm and held it, hard. "Go on, Ari."

Your access is upgraded. You are no longer on time-lag. Data is available through April 13, 2295.

She grabbed Catlin's shoulder, on the other side of her.

"Go on, Ari."

That's when I was 12. Updates will still be weekly.

Good night, Ari.

She clenched down until her fingers hurt; and then she realized what she was doing and let up. "Log-off," she said. And sat there shaking.

Catlin patted her shoulder and gave her the handsigns they had made up for Tomorrow, Outside.

Florian signed: Tonight. Take-out Monitor.

She shook her head, and signed: Stay.

And took them each by a hand.

Knowing that five more years of data were in the files. But she had an idea what was in it.

Exactly what was in it.

Dammit. Dammit. Dammit.

Security was still taping. "Florian," she said, "Catlin, we *are* going to Security. Right now."

Catlin made the sign for Seely.

"They won't stop us. Get your stuff. Come on. We're going to go kill that thing. *Hear that, uncle Denys?*"

He didn't answer. Of course not.

She went and washed her face while Florian was getting his small tool kit. While Catlin was getting whatever she thought she might need. Which probably included a length of fine wire.

They walked out into the living room. Uncle Denys was reading at the dining table beyond the arch. Like most evenings.

He looked at her.

She said: "We're going down to Security, in case you missed it."

"I'll advise them," uncle Denys said. "*Don't* break anything, Florian."

Seely was not in the room. Seely should have been. Maybe Seely was monitoring from the office.

She stood there and stared at uncle Denys a long, long while.

"Like your maman," uncle Denys said, "I've tried to help you."

"They could kill you."

"Yes. I know that. You know that. You could do that anytime, if you put your mind to it. We have to take chances like that. Because I'm your friend. Not your uncle. Not really. I've been your friend for as long as you've lived."

"*Which* how long?"

"As long as you've lived. You're Ari. One *is* the other. That's what this is about. Neither one of you betrayed the other one. You *are* the one who did all these things—in a very direct sense. Think about it."

"You're crazy! Everybody in this House is crazy!"

"No. Go see about Security. I'll tell them. Your accesses have upgraded considerably tonight. You *have* real authority in some things. You don't have to live here. You can take your apartment, if you want to. It'll be very large, for a young girl and two azi. But you have the key. If you want to go there, you can. Florian can access the Security system there, and vet it for you. Or you can come back here when you're through. Or you can go over to Amy's. Her mother won't ask any questions."

"Does everybody in Reseune know what I am?"

"Of course. Everybody knew the first Ari. And you began, at least on paper, the day after she died."

"Damn you."

"Same temper, too. But she learned to control it. Learned to *use* it, not let it use her. There's a lot of Cyteen history in those data files, too. A lot of Reseune history. A lot of things your education has just—avoided, until now. Once upon a time there was a man who could see the future. He began trying to change his life. But that *was* his future. Someday you'll access yours—as far as you want to. Think about it."

"I'm not doing anything you tell me from now on."

"Ask yourself why five years. Why not six? Why not four? Ask the computer what happened April 13, 2295."

"*You* tell me."

"You can look it up. You have the access."

"I want all my stuff up at my apartment."

"That's fine. Tell Housekeeping. They can do that first thing in the morning. You'd better pack at least the basics—for the apartment where you're going. Or buy it. *Necessaries* is open round the clock. If you need anything—like advice on how to fill out the paperwork, whatever, —call me. I certainly don't mind helping you."

Trust Denys to get to the mundane, the depressing workaday details of anything.

"I'll manage."

"I know you will, dear. I'm still here. If I can help you I want to. Florian, Catlin, don't let her hurt herself. Please. And take some pajamas."

"Dammit, uncle Denys, —"

"Dear, *somebody* has to take care of things. It's usually me. Do you want to go to your apartment, —or do you want to come back and live here for a little while, till you've figured out what it takes to *run* an apartment on your own?"

"No. No, I don't. I'll manage."

"I'll send Housekeeping *for* you. They can't go in up there. But I'll have a package waiting at your door, and send your things on tomorrow. Practical things, Ari. I'll fill out your supply forms for you, and your budget report, you have to have that, or you foul up accounting. I'll give you copies so you know how to set it up in your Base."

"Thank you."

"Thank you, Ari. Thank you for being reasonable about this. This is different from Ari senior, understand. She was fourteen when she moved out of this apartment. But you're overrunning your course too, by a little. Please. Take care of yourself. Can you give me a kiss?"

She stood there, frozen. *Out of this apartment.* She swallowed a lump of nausea. And shook her head. "Not right now. Not right now, uncle Denys."

He nodded. "Sometime, then."

She clenched her jaw and motioned to Florian and Catlin that they were leaving.

2418: 4/14: 0048

AE2: Minder, this is Ari Emory. Florian and Catlin are with me. Print out all entries since I was here last.

B/1: There are two messages.

Welcome to your own home. If you get scared and you want to call me or Security, please don't hesitate. But you're as safe there as here. Trust Florian and Catlin. Take their advice when it comes to your safety.

Drop by the office tomorrow if you feel like it. There's so much you need to know. I let you go because you're not a child, and I wouldn't bring your Security and mine into conflict: my bet would still be on Seely, but I truly don't want to put that to the test.

Attached to your Housekeeping list will be Security's standard recommendations and Seely's for basic Security set-up. Give it to Catlin and Florian. They'll understand. They probably don't need it, but a checklist never hurts even with experienced personnel.

Don't let Housekeeping in unless Florian or Catlin is watching, Seely always did that for us, in case you never noticed.

Refrigerate the eggs and use the ham immediately: it'll have thawed. I wasn't going to send perishables, but you haven't got any breakfast otherwise. I put in a box of cocoa.

You're responsible for everything now. But if it gets too much for you, please, call or come by the office.

You'll have to have an office now, in Wing One. You won't need it, but now that this apartment is active, you'll use at least one secretary and one clerk, which

410

you can request from the Wing One administrator, Yanni Schwartz. Do that, or you'll be diverting valuable time from your studies filling out silly forms, which, I'm sorry, are necessary. I've assigned you an office in I-244, and you'll need to set that up with Wing One Security. Again, let Florian read Security's recommendations on that.

I'm upping your personal allowance to 10,000 cr. per month. That may sound like a fortune, but you have to pay 1200 per month for the office and 5000 for the clerk and secretary. The rest will go fast, believe me, so you're going to have to keep track of that. Of course I'll help you if you need something special: but you should learn good habits.

Your secretary can manage the credit account, but should not have certain accesses. Again, let Florian and Catlin talk to Seely.

The first Ari's system of protections is still in Base One: for God's sake don't dismantle it until you've devised a better one. Florian will advise you there is a security problem with that: it's been in place when other people, mainly myself, could access some of the keyword functions from the top. But it's better than nothing at the bottom, where your secretaries will work.

Read the building safety recommendations relative to fire exits and storm drill. Your area has special protections, but there are special things to learn.

Never mind: just read everything I send you and pass it to Florian and Catlin if it involves security or safety of any kind.

I still love you. It's much more complicated than that, but I am glad you were here and would be more than glad to have you back. There were a lot of times I came to odds with Ari senior. But we were friends. As I am and will always be yours.

Everything in the apartment is exactly the way your predecessor left it the day she died. You will want to dispose of a great deal of the clothing. Styles change. Pack what you don't want and notify Housekeeping to remove it.

Your key will also work at my apartment until you're fourteen. That's only two more years. It seems impossible.

Meanwhile be good. Please keep your doctor appointments: it is necessary for your health, and you'll recall your maman saw you kept them, so it's not just me. You still have obligations, as everyone does who lives in Reseune, and your independent status doesn't excuse you, it only adds more of them, including obeying adult rules; and if medical says a Supervisor comes in for a check, they come in or they can lose their license. I'll add the obligation to keep your school schedule. I've indicated to Base One that you are extremely mature and responsible. Please don't make me a liar.

So many people have loved you. Jane loved you most of all. She never wrote to you because she felt that was best for you—she knew there was a time she had to cut the cord and let you go, for your own sake. So do I know that. So I wish you well, but I will still, because you are only twelve and because that apartment is very large and Reseune is much larger, be extremely concerned that you are well and taking care of yourself adequately. I know that you are much older than your chronological age, and that you have Base One to draw on, which is no small thing; you have handled Housekeeping and lab requisitions and finance; you have dealt with reports *and lab scheduling; you have lived with the security systems and the regulations of the House all your years; and you have two equally adept companions. I would trust the three of you to handle yourselves in a Security crisis; I am not, on the other hand, sure that you will not leave the oven on in the kitchen or have the watering system overflowing the garden. Ari, however much you disdain trivia and accuse me of obsession with it, I remind you again that clean laundry only happens when you remember to send it to Housekeeping.*

If this were Novgorod I could never countenance this move; but Housekeeping, like Security, is capable of coping with crises: and I am sure your mistakes will reach my desk. Reseune itself is my House, and you have elected to move to another of its Rooms.

Let me explain something further to you. I have encouraged you to this departure: I did so when I brought you here and told you that this would be yours.

You and I know the limits of your frustration, but Florian and Catlin do not, and neither, for that matter, does Seely. I believe you are emotionally mature enough to understand that the threats to your safety are real, and that indeed you are capable of giving an order which your companions will obey, which they must, I stress, obey—and they will kill, at your order, whether or not that order comes from a mature judgment.

I showed you this apartment because I felt that one day you would need this place to go to, a safety valve in a situation increasingly volatile and unpredictable. You are operating with a world-knowledge and maturity greater than many functioning adults, within a system of surveillance, interventions and monitoring which would stress an azi, with the internal emotional experience and stability of a pubescent child. I feared the explosion that has happened. I was glad to see it turn the direction it did. It is not unprecedented. I set you up for it. As you will see.

In 2295, when the first Ari was your age, I wasn't born yet. Giraud was four. Neither of us remembers that year, but Giraud does recall, when he was five, that the first Ari and her guardian Geoffrey Carnath had a spectacularly public argument at a New Year's party. Giraud doesn't himself remember what was said; Jane Strassen said it regarded Ari's showing up in makeup, but that was hardly an excuse for a screaming argument. Archives does say that Security had to mediate a severe problem between Ari and Geoffrey New Year's Day, when he ordered Florian and Catlin into detention for three days and Ari required unexplained medical treatment that may have included sedation.

There was, you will find, no taping on Geoffrey or the first Ari. We don't precisely know what happened. The public record of the problem involved Ari's demand to have a key to her own room. Years later, to me, she said Geoffrey had taken indecent liberties with Florian. Look that up, if you don't understand what I mean. Certainly Ari made certain things up. But while her early relationship with Geoffrey was friendly, it came to increasing stress and repeated altercations that finally resulted in a family council and Ari's being granted her own residency, independent of her legal guardian.

It's come true, hasn't it? Certainly not because of any such thing between myself and your staff, but because you're growing and you need more room. Perhaps that's the way it ought to be. Like your maman, I've done what I knew to do, the

best I knew. And that includes letting you go. We have offended against your dignity as far as you are justly willing to tolerate it; and hope that if Geoffrey could be
forgiven, so can we, in time.

Ari, incidentally, moved to a much more modest apartment: the present splendor, like much of Reseune, was her own creation. But you don't inherit her beginnings. You inherit what she held at the height of her power and intellect. In all
things. You will think about that statement later.

Be good. Be reasonable.

End message. Store to file or dump?

AE2: Store to file. Put that on the couch, Florian, is it clean?

Fl2: Yes, sera.

AE2: There's print coming you both need to read.

Fl2: Yes, sera. Are you upset, sera?

**AE2: Nothing. Go on. Stop worrying about me. You've got work to
do. Base One, continue.**

B/1: Second message.

Ari, this is Ari senior.

Welcome.

You're 2 years early.

This program is adjusting itself.

There's a Householding tape in the cabinet in the den. You need that.

*You are 12 years old. This program does not provide for that contingency. It
will treat you as if you were 14.*

A list of accesses and authorizations will print.

Recommended tapes will print.

*Base One access has been removed from your guardian's apartment. Security
monitoring has been redirected to Base One.*

*Lethal security measures have been disabled for your protection. When you are
16 you will have the option to reactivate them.*

*You may run a security check on any individual from Base One. Ask for Secu-
rity 10. The activity will not leave a mark on any file of lower security clearance
than your own.*

*I hope you are happy here. Your taste and mine may not coincide, but most
everything in this apartment is both real and handmade, from the tables to the vases
to the paintings on the walls. The paintings in particular are originals and they don't
truly belong to me or to you. They belong to the people of Union, someday, when
there are museums where they can be protected: they come from Earth, and from the
first starships, and from the beginnings of Cyteen as a human world. Guard them in
particular, whatever you feel or whatever you understand about me right now: if
you would harm any of these things you are a barbarian, and my geneset has gone
wrong in you; there are conditions of responsibility involved with your permissions
and accesses, and they will either expand or terminate. This program can protect
Reseune and itself against misuse.*

*You don't know me yet, as you don't know yet the good and the bad that you
are capable of reaching.*

I came to live on my own to escape an intolerable situation with my guardian, and because I was at that time a Special, I was given certain rights of majority. I maintained a speaking relationship with my guardian. We were never close, but once the situation was relieved, I saw that he was only a man, with human faults, some of which were considerable, and some virtues, once I was not living within his reach. The faults did not manifest until late. They were sexual in nature, and I need not go into them: your database now reaches to the year 2297. That will tell you as much as you need to know, perhaps more than you want to know, and I certainly hope your own experiences have been happier.

Whatever has happened, whether your parting from your guardian was amicable or otherwise, you are still a minor even at 14, and it would be foolish of you to do other than cooperate with Administration until you have the experience to outmaneuver it. I could not win against my situation except by protesting to Security and establishing an independent residency. If House Security has become corrupt you have a serious problem. Do you feel this is the case?

AE2: I don't know.

B/1: A list of precautions will print. This program will search all House activity and advise you of any actions which may involve yourself or your rights. The list will print. This option is also available under Security 10, which can read into House Security but which cannot be read by them.

Remember that a negative or a positive result in any single question itself means nothing. You have to interpret your own situation. Remember a person with a higher security clearance than yours can install false information in the House system.

Florian and Catlin have survived to be here with you. Good. Are they physically and mentally well?

AE2: Yes.

B/1: Do you believe their loyalty to you is absolute and without exception?

AE2: Yes.

B/1: Is there any condition under which they would disobey you?

AE2: No.

B/1: Beware of absolute answers. Would you like to reconsider?

AE2: No.

B/1: This program accepts them. Security 10 can revise any estimation. Do not permit Florian or Catlin to take tape outside your personal supervision, not for two seconds, outside your direct observation. You can obtain their drugs with your supervisor's clearance. Advise them of this. Under no circumstances must they take any drug you do not provide or permit any intervention without your presence. You must run an intervention to do this. You are not yet qualified in this procedure. A routine will print. Follow instructions meticulously. Read the cautions and observe them. So much as a chance sound could do them great harm.

Their instruction is the most necessary security measure you will take.

Now name the individuals at Reseune or elsewhere you would like investigated by the Security accesses of this program. I urge you begin with your closest friends and your known enemies, and add anyone else whose behavior is not ordinary. You may amend this list by Security 10. The program will provide you the security status of these individuals.

Name as many as you wish.

AE2: Florian and Catlin. Amy Carnath. Sam Whitely. Dr. John Edwards. Denys Nye. Giraud Nye. Madelaine Strassen. Tommy Carnath-Nye. Julia Strassen. Dr. Petros Ivanov. Dr. Irina Wojkowski. Instructor Kyle GK. AG tech Andy GA. Mikhail Corain.

Dr. Wendell Peterson. Victoria Strassen.

Justin Warrick. Grant, Justin Warrick's Companion. I don't know his prefix.

B/1: *Immediate security flag on Justin Warrick, Grant ALX, Julia Strassen. Your clearance is not adequate to access those records.*

AE2: Ari, wait. Define: security flag.

B/1: *Security flag indicates person with limited accesses in area queried.*

AE2: Ari, go on.

B/1: *Persons with security clearance exceeding yours: Denys Nye; Giraud Nye; Dr. John Edwards; Dr. Petros Ivanov; Dr. Wendell Peterson; Dr. Irina Wojkowski; Mikhail Corain.*

You will be messaged at any change in relative clearances.

Now before I finish I will tell you one other thing I did not then understand. My guardian Geoffrey Carnath behaved badly, but he did not intend me personal harm. He knew my value. Whoever has caused your birth surely must know yours. Geoffrey and I were cold but cordial and did not publicize our differences even within the House, certainly not outside, because it could harm Reseune.

Base One can now contact one point outside Reseune: are you now in any danger you yourself cannot handle?

AE2: No. I don't think so.

B/1: *Base One can call House Security or the Science Bureau Enforcement Division through Security 10. It will call both if it detects your voice raised in alarm on the keyword Mayday. The consequences of a false alert could be considerable, including political ones endangering your life or status. Never pronounce that word unless you mean it. You may set various emergency responses through the Security 10 keyword function.*

If absolutely no other means is available to you to reach the Science Bureau to apply for legal majority, use the Mayday function. Under ordinary circumstances a quiet note to Security or a phone call should be adequate and Reseune should assist you. I reached my legal majority at 16, by a tolerably routine application to the Science Bureau. You may apply at any time you think this has become advisable. I do not advise doing this before 16, except if your life or sanity is threatened. The ordinary age of majority is, as you should know by now, 18.

Cast off all emotional ties to Denys Nye.

Protect Reseune: someday it will be in your hands, and it will give you the power to protect everything else.

You are 14 years old. Time itself will bury any enemy you do not yourself make—as long as you don't make a mistake that lets them bury you.

I am your safest adviser. You are the successor I choose; I aim for your mental and physical safety from interests that may have gained power since my death, or who might want to profit from your abilities. You would not be wise to believe that of everyone in Reseune.

CHAPTER 10

Uncle Denys was right. It was a huge place. It was very quiet, and at the same time filled with strange noises—motors going on, expansion of metal in the ducts, or small sounds that might have been a step, or a breath, though the Minder would surely sound an alarm if there were a living presence.

If it had not been tampered with. If Base One itself was reliable.

Ari knew which bedroom had been the first Ari's. The closets were full of her clothes. The drawers had more clothes, sweaters, underwear, jewelry, real jewelry, she thought. And the smell of the drawers and the closet was the smell of home—the scent *she* wore. The same smell as permeated her closet at home—at uncle Denys' apartment.

There was a room which had belonged to the first Florian and another which had belonged to the first Catlin. There were uniforms in their closets which were a man's and a woman's. Which bore their numbers. And party clothes in satin and black gauze.

There were things in the bureau drawers—there were guns, and odd bits of electronics, and wire—as well as personal things.

"They were Older," Catlin said.

"Yes," Ari said, feeling a chill in her bones, "they were."

There were, constantly, the sounds, the small whisperings that the rooms made.

"Come on," she said, and brought them out of the first Catlin's room.

She kept telling herself the Minder would react to an intruder.

But what if one had already been there?

What if the Minder were in someone's control?

She took them back to Ari's bedroom, back at the far end of the house. They brought the guns that they had found, even though Catlin said they ought not to rely on charges that old. They were better than nothing.

"Stay with me," Ari said to them, and sat down on the bed and patted the place beside her.

So they got beneath the covers in their clothes, because the night seemed cold, and she was in the middle of the huge bed, Ari's bed, and Florian and Catlin were on either side of her, tucked up against her for warmth, or to keep her warm.

She shivered, and Florian put his arm around her on the right side and Catlin edged closer on her left, until she was warm.

She could not tell them the things they needed to know, like who the Enemy was. She did not know any longer. It was ghosts she imagined. She had read the old books. She was afraid of things she reckoned Florian and Catlin did not even imagine, and they were foolish to name.

No one had slept in this bed, on these sheets, since the first Ari died. No one had used her things or turned back the covers.

The whole bedroom smelled of perfume and musty age.

She knew it was foolish to be afraid. She knew that the sounds probably had to do with heating and cooling of metal ducts and unfamiliar, wooden floors. And the countless systems this place had.

She had read Poe. And Jerome. And knew there was no ghost to haunt the place. Things like that belonged to old Earth, which believed the nights were full of spirits with unfinished business, anxious to lay hands on the living.

They had no place in so modern a place, so far from old Earth, which had had so *many* dead: Cyteen was new, and they were only stories and silliness.

Except in the dark around their lighted rooms, in the unexplained noises and the start and stop of things that were surely the Minder doing its business.

She wanted to ask Florian and Catlin if they felt anything like that, in their azi way of looking at things: she wondered in one part of her, cold curiosity, if CITs could feel ghosts because of something in CIT mindsets— shades of value, her psych instructor said. Flux-thinking.

Which Florian and Catlin could do, but it was something they were just now learning to do.

Which meant if she told them about ghosts they could get very disturbed: Catlin was so literal, Catlin believed what she said, and if she started talking about Ari being dead and still *in* this place—

No. Not a good idea.

She tucked the sheets up around her chin and Florian and Catlin both tucked themselves up against her, warm and dependable and free of wild imagination, never mind the fact that Catlin also had a gun with her under the covers, which ought to make her more nervous than thumps in the night.

The whole thing was unreal. Uncle Denys had called her bluff, that was what he had done, and hoped she *would* foul up and come back.

No, Base One had altered itself. It kept saying she was fourteen. It complained she was low in her test scores. Dammit, she was twelve; twelve; twelve; she was not ready to grow up.

And here she was, in a mess because she did not know whether to believe Base One anymore; or where everybody was pushing her life.

By setting her free. It was crazy. They set her free; and she didn't have to listen to Base One, she could ignore it, she didn't have to read the data, she didn't have to know what happened to Ari senior between seven and fourteen, that was seven *years*, dammit, she was supposed to jump over.

She wanted to be a kid. She wanted to take care of the Filly and have her friends and have fun and be just Ari Emory, just nobody-Ari, not—somebody who was dead.

And they—the They who did things in Reseune, like uncle Denys and uncle Giraud and dead Ari—they shoved her into this huge, cold place and told her to live by herself with no maman and no uncle Denys and no Nelly or Seely, nobody to take care of anything if it went wrong.

It had started out feeling good, and then feeling like an adventure, and now, at 0300 and snuggled down in a strange, huge bed with two kid azi, it started feeling like a terrible mistake.

I wonder if I can get Base One to back up and say I'm twelve again.

Or have I gotten myself into a mess and I can't back up and I can't catch up with it, it's just going to keep going, faster and faster, until I can't handle it anymore.

If I say no, Base One will stop all my accesses and take my Super license, and if they take that, they'll take Florian and Catlin—

They can't do that. Everybody across Union knows me, knows Catlin and Florian, I could call Mayday—

Not if I lose those accesses. Base One has to do that.

I daren't lose them. If I lose that I lose everything. I stop being Ari. I stop being—

—Ari.

I've got to do good, I've got to hold on to this, I can't do those things uncle Denys said, I can't foul up. I'm going to look like a fool, I know I'm going to do something wrong the very first day out—

I wish—

I wish I knew whether I like Ari. I wonder what did happen to her?

Are they going to do it to me, the way they did everything else?

But in this place Base One is supposed to take care of me. If that's lying, then everything is lying and I'm in bad trouble.

I can't foul up tomorrow. I can't look like I've had no sleep. I've got to do better than I usually do, that'll Get uncle Denys, throw me out, dammit, bug my room, put tapes of me under the mountain. I bet he can get at them, I bet he can, I bet his Base can retrieve it.

That whole list of people with higher clearances than mine—can lie to the system and lie to me and I can't find it out.

Unless I get a higher clearance . . . and the way I get that is when I do something that gets Base One to do it.

Which means doing everything Ari wants.

Nothing Ari wants, me-Ari, myself, for me. If I'm not the same. If there is a me. If there ever was a me that isn't Ari. Or if she's not me.

If I was her, how old would I be? A hundred fifty and twelve, a hundred sixty-two. That's older than Jane, no, she was born—Jane was a teenager, Jane was a hundred forty-two when she died, and she held the first Ari when she was a baby, so if I'm twelve and Jane was my maman when she was a hundred thirty-four and I was born—and if uncle Denys is right and I was begun on paper the day after Ari died—

It could take more work than making the Filly. And that was tons of figuring. And I'm not an azi, I'm not a production geneset, so that's nothing fast. So say it was a year, and then nine, ten months, and everything works out that Ari was a hundred—twenty-something.

You can live longer than that. I wonder if that's when I'm going to die. I wonder what she died of.

Rejuv usually doesn't go till you're a hundred forty if you get it started early, and she was pretty, she was pretty when she was older, she was on it early, for sure—

That's depressing. Don't think of that. It's awful to know when you're going to die.

It's awful to read ahead what's going to happen to you. I don't want to read that stuff in the files. I don't want to know.

And it's real stupid not to.

There was a man who could see the future. He tried to change his. But that was his future.

That was his future.

Like changing it—can't work. Because then you go off what the Base wants and you're frozen, locked up, no accesses.

I have to do well. I have to do everything they want and then when I grow up I can Get them good.

Damn. That's exactly what Ari said I should do.

How do I get away from her?

Can I get away from her—and still be me?

ii

She was very careful to keep on time when the Minder woke her, shower fast, grab breakfast—Florian and Catlin cooked it: the eggs got too done, and the cocoa was lumpy, but it was food, and she swallowed it down and headed out for class . . . Florian and Catlin to clean up and then wait for the deliveries from Housekeeping and check them out and get their stuff installed in their rooms; and stay put, and debug the place, as soon as Housekeeping brought some batteries up for some of the first Florian's stuff. *They* had an excuse to miss classes today. She didn't, and there was no stopping by the fishpond this morning: she had to stop by the pharmacy, and she was going to walk through Dr. Edwards' door right on the minute.

Dr. Edwards was very relieved to see her: he said that without saying a word; and was uncommonly easy on her in the work—she noticed that and looked up sideways and gave him her wickedest grin. "I suppose uncle Denys told you what happened last night."

Oh, he didn't want to talk about that. "In a general kind of way. You know he'd be worried."

"You tell him I was on time and we didn't burn up anything in the kitchen."

"I'll tell him. Don't you want to tell him yourself?"

"No," she said cheerfully, and went back to her frog eggs.

She really put her mind to it in Designs, worked with no nonsense, blasted through two lessons and actually enjoyed it: she got Dr. Dietrich to give her a complete manual on one of the Deltas in Housekeeping management, so she could see the whole picture of a Design, because that was the way she liked to learn, get the idea what the whole thing looked like so that the parts made sense.

She *wanted* an Alpha set, but Dr. Dietrich said it was better to learn a more typical kind and then work on the exotic cases. That made sense.

Dr. Dietrich said it shouldn't be anybody she knew. That she wasn't ready for that.

Nice that she wasn't ready for *something*. It made her feel like there was at least a floor to stand on. She had learned a very good word in Dr. Dietrich's class.

Flux. Which fairly well said what she was caught in.

She didn't have class with any other kids until just before noon, when she had Economics with Amy and Maddy.

Amy and Maddy *hadn't* known about her moving out. They thought she was putting one on them. So she put her card in the nearest House slot in One A, and it started spitting out all these messages she hadn't known she was going to get, like Housekeeping asking for a verification on an order for a special kind of battery—she knew who had asked that, and punched yes—and a note from Yanni Schwartz telling her that her office in 1-244 was keyed to her card, and he had a secretary and a clerk going to set up in there, whose names were Elly BE 979 and Winnie GW 88690, and their living allowances were now on her card, along with the equipment requisition for another couple of terminals and on-line time on the House system; and a message from Dr. Ivanov that her prescription was waiting at the pharmacy.

That impressed Amy and Maddy, all right.

They looked like they still weren't sure she hadn't set this up to Get them, but she told them that tomorrow they were going to get a chance to see, she would take them up where she lived now, all on her own.

And they went funny then, like something was going different.

That was something she hadn't thought about.

She was thinking about it all the way to the pharmacy, and then she had that package to worry about, up past the Security guards into the lonely terrazzo hallway that was all hers down to the barrier-wall. She used her keycard on the door, and let herself in. The Minder told her that Florian and Catlin were there, and quick as that they showed up from the hall to the kitchen.

"Did Housekeeping get here?" she asked.

"Yes, sera," Florian said. "We've got everything put away. We went all over the apartment."

That meant the batteries Florian had wanted had gotten there. "Housekeeping was in order," Catlin said. "We made them set the boxes in the kitchen, no matter what they were, and we went over everything piece by piece before we put it away. We're warming up lunch."

"Good," she said. "Class was fine. No problems." She walked all the way back through the halls to her office to put down the carry-bag.

Her office, when she had automatically started for her bedroom. But now there was a room for everything. She unloaded the manual there; and took the carry-bag back past Florian and Catlin's rooms to her own bedroom.

Poo-thing was there, right on her bed where he always was. She picked him up and thought it would be really rotten if uncle Denys had bugged him. She picked him up and set him down again against the pillows.

And sat down and kicked off her shoes, and took out the pills from her carry-bag, the prescription pharmacy had fussed about until they nearly made her late for school, no matter what her keycard said and no matter what the House system told them she was authorized to have.

"75's," Florian said, looking at the pill-bottle, after lunch. Ham-and-cheese sandwiches. With nothing burned. "That's all right. That's right for a deep dose."

"Do you want to see what I have to tell you?" She had run out the print, and she had the paper in her lap. "I've told the Minder, no calls, no noises. I've got everything on the list. But I'd feel better if you looked at it."

She passed the printout over; they read it, one after the other.

"Sounds reasonable," Catlin said. "I haven't any trouble about it."

"I don't see any problem," Florian said. "It won't take half a minute. If there's no tape to do."

It still scared her. It scared her more than anything else.

But she did what it said. They took their pills and she followed what the paper said; and left them to sleep, then.

And went into her office, shut the door, and used the keyboard with Base One, because she wanted no noise in the apartment at all while they were that far down.

She told Base One the routine was run.

And Base One said: *This Base now recognizes their cards.*

She read, mostly, late, because she wanted them to wake up before she could rest. She scanned Ari senior's data, on the words *Geoffrey Carnath*. And she *had* understood uncle Denys in what he had said happened. She scanned it all the way to the end, when Ari moved out. She read the worst things and sat there feeling strange, just strange, like it was bad, but nobody had died, that was the worst, if somebody had died.

Then they might Disappear someone else.

And she was mad. Mad about things another Ari's guardian had done a long, long time ago, which weren't there, but the Security reports were, right up to when Ari had turned herself and Florian and Catlin over to Security, saying her uncle was abusing Florian.

That was the way Security wrote it. But she knew what had happened. Sort of. She couldn't make a picture in her mind, but she knew, all the same.

And Ari talked about getting along with her guardian.

I'd have killed him. Like I'd have killed uncle Denys if he'd gone after me. Because you don't play games with Security. Not with Seely, not with Denys. But then where would I be? In a lot of trouble.

In a lot *of trouble.*

Her stomach went upset. She had known she was in a corner, deep down. Geoffrey Carnath's security had gotten the better of the first Ari's. They must have had a fight. Something must have happened.

Florian and Catlin had gone to detention. Ari had gone to hospital.

Ari, hospital, she typed, for that date.

Sedation, it said. Geoffrey Carnath's order.

Florian, security.

A medic had seen him. He was hurt. So was Catlin. And they had run tapes on him and Catlin. She got the number on them.

She chased the case through files for an hour and chased the move-in order, and the Family council meeting—where senior staff, knowing what had happened, had given Ari senior a place of her own, with her own key and no one to watch over her, because that was what she demanded to have, because she was threatening to go to the news-services and Geoffrey Carnath was too much trouble for even the whole Family to fight him over the guardianship.

True. Everything true, as far as Base One went. Things like that had happened to the first Ari.

They had taken maman. But uncle Denys and uncle Giraud had never done what Geoffrey Carnath had done to the first Ari.

She sat there a long time staring at the screen, and then started looking up some of the words the report had used.

And sat there a long time after, feeling her stomach upset.

She was terribly, terribly relieved when Florian called to her on the Minder and said that he was awake, and all right, just a little sleepy yet.

"I'm here," Catlin said then, a little vaguely; but Catlin made it into the hall before Ari did. Leaning on the wall. "Is there a problem?"

"Nothing," Ari said, "nothing right now. Go sleep, Catlin. Everything's fine. I'm going to fix dinner myself. I'll call you."

Catlin nodded and went back into her room.

There were a lot of things in the apartment, once they started going through it—a lot of Ari senior's clothes that were very nice but too large yet.

Ari senior had been—a bit more on top. And taller. That was spooky too, figuring out in the mirror what size she was going to be. Someday.

There was jewelry. Terribly expensive things. Not near as much as maman's, mostly gold, a lot of what could be rubies, just lying in the chest on the bureau—all these years—but who in the House would steal?

There was a wine cabinet taller than she could reach, which wouldn't have spoiled, she knew that, it was probably real good by now; and there was whiskey and other things under the counter that wouldn't have been hurt by all these years of sitting there.

There was a big tape library. A lot were about Earth and about Pell. A lot were on technical things. A lot were Entertainment. And a *lot* of those . . . had a 20 Years and Over sticker. And titles that made her embarrassed, and uneasy.

Sex stuff. A lot of it.

It was like looking through Ari senior's drawers in her bedroom, like it was private, and she would hate if she were grown-up and dead, to have some twelve-year-old kid going through *her* drawers and finding out *she* had stuff like that in her library, but it was interesting too, and scary. The first Ari had said there was nothing wrong with the thoughts she had had, just that she was too young and shouldn't be stupid.

But it was all right when you were Older.

She remembered how the first tape felt. And she closed up the cabinet door and wondered what was in them, and whether they would be like the other one. They were just E-tapes. They weren't deep or anything like it. They couldn't hurt you.

If they were hers like everything else in the apartment, then she could do whatever she wanted with them—when she was settled in, when she was sure everything was safe.

It wasn't like being stupid with *people*, where sex could hurt you.

Kids were supposed to be curious. And there was no way anybody could find out she was using them. Just Catlin and Florian, and they wouldn't mess with her stuff. She could do private things now, real private, and uncle Denys couldn't know.

When she got settled in. You didn't do Entertainment tapes just anytime you wanted, no more than you had all the food you wanted. You got your regular work done.

Even if you thought about how interesting it would be, and what there was to find out, and how the teaching-tape had felt.

Meanwhile the cabinet stayed closed.

"It's all right, come on," she said, and brought Amy and Maddy past the Security guards and up the lift.

She used her keycard on the door and let them in. The Minder told her that Florian and Catlin were not there, they were off in classes doing make-up work, the way she had told them they should.

She saw Amy and Maddy look at each other and look around at the huge front room, real impressed.

Something said to her she ought not let anyone see *all* of where she lived, or know how things were laid out: she knew Catlin would worry about that. But she showed them the middle of it, which was the big room in front and the kitchen and the breakfast room with the glassed-in garden where nothing was growing yet—and back to the main front room and into the other wing, where there was the big sunken den and the bar and then her office, and her bedroom and the bedrooms that had been Florian's and Catlin's (and were again).

They had oh'ed over this and that at the start, when she said that there were rooms down past the kitchen, mostly offices and stuff. And over the garden. But when they got this far, into still another living room with more rooms yet to go, they just stared around them and looked strange.

That bothered her. She was used to figuring people out, and she couldn't quite figure what they were thinking, except maybe they were worried about there being something dangerous about this, or her, or uncle Denys.

"We don't have to meet down in the tunnels anymore," she said. "We can be up here and there's no way they can find out what we're doing, because Florian and Catlin have this place checked over so nobody can bug us. Not even uncle Denys."

"They can still find out who we are," Amy said. "I mean, they know me and Maddy, maybe Sam, but they don't know all of us."

That was it. She had wondered over and over how much to tell them—particularly Maddy. She worried about it. But there were things they had to know, before they got the wrong ideas. "It's all right," she said, then took a deep breath and made up her mind on a big secret. "Let me tell you: I've got it set up so if any of you or your families gets a Security action, I know it the second it goes in."

"How can you?" Maddy asked.

"My computer. The Base I've got. My clearance is higher than yours—maybe not higher than somebody who could put a flag on and keep me from finding out stuff, but I've got my Base fixed so if there's information I'm not accessing it tells me it's going on."

"How?" Maddy asked.

"Because I'm in the House system. Because I've got a real high Base and a lot of clearances a kid isn't supposed to have. They come with this place. Lots of things. You don't have to worry. I've got an eye on you. If anything goes into the system about you, it calls me right then."

"Anything?"

"Not private stuff. Security stuff. And I'll tell you something else." Another deep breath. She shoved her hands into her belt and thought very carefully what she was saying and how much she was giving away; but Amy and Maddy were the highest-up in the gang. "You tell this and I'll skin you. But you two don't have to worry anymore. None of my friends do. I know why the Disappearances happened, and I don't think it's going to happen anymore. Except if I asked it to. If there was somebody I really, really wanted not to see again. Which isn't any of you, as long as you're my friends."

"*Why* did they?" Amy asked.

"Because—" *Because things had to happen to me. Like Ari senior. That's too much, a whole lot too much about my business.* She shrugged. "Because I wasn't supposed to know things, because my uncles figured they'd tell."

They were quiet a long time. Then Amy said, very carefully: "Even your maman?"

A second shrug. "Maman. Valery. Julia Strassen." She wanted off the subject. "I know why they did it. That's all." *My maman agreed to go, but I'm not telling anybody that. They'd think she didn't like me. And that wouldn't be so.* "I know a lot of things. Now they have to watch out, because I know they can't do anything to me, because anything they do from now on, they know I'll hold a grudge. And I will, if they Get any of my friends . . . because I know who they are, and they know how far they can go with me."

"Then who are they?" Amy asked.

"My uncles. Dr. Ivanov. Lots of people. Because of me being a PR of Ariane Emory. That's what. This was her place. Now it's mine, because I'm a PR. Everything she had is mine. The way there used to be a Florian and a Catlin, too, and they died; and they replicated them for me."

That took some thinking on their part. They knew about the replicate bit. They knew about a lot of things—like Florian and Catlin. But they never knew how it fit.

"I'll tell you," she said while she Had them, "why they won't do anything that makes me mad. Reseune needs me, because if I'm a PR I have title to a whole lot of things they want real bad; and because if I'm a minor it's going to be a while before the first Ari's enemies can do anything against me, because of the courts, because if my uncles do any more to me than they've already done they're in a lot of trouble, because they know I'm onto them. I don't forget about maman. I don't forget a lot of things. So they're not going to bother my friends. You can figure on that."

They looked at her without saying anything. They were not stupid. Maddy might be silly and she had no sense, but she was not at all stupid when it came to putting things together, and Amy was the smartest of all her friends, no question about it. Amy always had been.

"You're serious," Amy said.

"Damn right I'm serious."

Amy grunted and sat down on the big couch with her hands between her knees. And Maddy sat down. "This isn't any game," Amy said, looking up at her. "It's not pretend anymore, is it?"

"Nothing is pretend anymore."

"I don't know," Amy said. "I don't know. God, Ari, you could park trucks in this place. —Isn't there *any*body here at night, or anything? Aren't you scared?"

"Why? There's nothing I can't order from Housekeeping, same as being at uncle Denys's. There's Security watching us all the time. We cook our food, we clean up, we do all that stuff. We can take care of ourselves. The Minder would wake us up if there was any trouble."

"I'll bet somebody comes in at night," Maddy said.

"Nobody. The Minder isn't easy to get by; not even Housekeeping gets in here without one of us watching them every minute. That's how the security is here. Because my Enemies are real too. It's not pretend. If somebody sneaks in here, they're dead, for-real dead." She sat down, at the other side of the corner. "So this is mine. All of it. And they can't bug it. Florian and Catlin have been over it from end to end. We can have our meetings up here often as we like and we don't have to worry about Security. We can do a lot of stuff up here, with no Olders to get onto us."

"Our mothers will know," Amy said. "Security's going to tell them."

"It's safe," Ari said.

"They still might not like it," Amy said.

"Well, they wouldn't like the tunnels either, would they? That didn't scare you any."

"This is different. They'll *know* we're here. They *know* people can get in trouble, Ari, my mama is worried about me getting in too much with you, she's real worried, and she didn't want me to take on the guppy business, remember?"

"She said it was all right, then."

"She still worries. I think somebody talked to her."

"So she'll let you. She won't mind."

"Ari, this is—real different. She's going to think you can get in trouble up here without any Olders. And then we could be. They could say it was us. And we'd all be at Fargone. Bang. That fast."

So she got an idea of the shape of what was wrong with Amy and Maddy, then, even if she couldn't see all of it.

"We're not going to get in any trouble," she said. "We'd get in a lot more if they caught us in the tunnels. I'm telling you I can *tell* if something's going on in Security. And Florian and Catlin *are* Security. They find out a lot of things, like stuff that doesn't go in the system."

"Not really Security," Maddy said. "They're kids."

"Ever since those kids got killed, they're Security, that's where they take their lessons. That's what their keycards say. And they work office operations a lot of the hours they're there. Real operations. They can come in and out of there and they find out a lot of things."

Like about taping in my apartment. But she wasn't about to tell them that either.

"Our mothers don't know about the tunnels," Amy said, "but they're going to know about us coming here."

"Not if you don't tell them right off. Security's not going to run to them the first day, are they? Then you can say you've *been* doing it, it's all right. How else do you get away with stuff? Don't be stupid, Amy."

They still looked worried.

"Are you my friends?" she asked them, face on. "Or aren't you?"

"We're your friends," Amy said. The room was quiet. Real quiet.

And she felt a little cold inside, like something *was* different, and she *was* older, somehow, and was getting more and more that way, faster than Amy, faster than anybody she knew. Overrunning the course, she thought, remembering Florian going down that hallway too soon, too fast for the other team.

Who had had about a quarter of a second, maybe, to realize it had stopped being an Exercise and they were about to die for real.

I've got to be nice, she thought. *I don't want anybody to panic. I don't want to scare them off.*

So she talked with them like always, she bounced up to get them all soft drinks and show them the bar and the icemaker.

And all the stuff in the cabinet that opened up. The wine and everything.

"God," Maddy said, "I bet we could have a party with this."

"I bet we can't," Ari said flatly. Because that cabinet of wine was expensive stuff, and Maddy wasn't going to pay for it out of *her* allowance, that was sure; besides, she thought, a drunk Maddy Strassen squealing and clowning around Base One was a real scary thing to think about. Not mentioning the other kids, like the boys Maddy hung around.

Maddy thought that was a shame.

Amy said their mamas would smell it on them and they'd be in real trouble and so might Ari, for giving it to them.

Which was the difference between Maddy and Amy.

That night there was a message from uncle Denys on Base One. It said: "Of course I was checking up on you, Ari. You've done very well. I hoped you would."

"Message to Denys Nye," she answered it. "Of course I knew you were watching. I'm no fool. Thanks for sending my stuff over. Thanks for helping out. I won't be mad, maybe by next week. Maybe two weeks. Recording me was a lousy trick."

That would Work him fine. Let him worry.

---

iii

The Tester's name was Will, a Gamma type, a warehousing supervisor what time he was not involved in test-taking, plain as midday and matter-of-fact about internal processes Gamma azi were not usually aware of.

Phlegmatic of disposition, if he were a CIT: older, experienced. And stubborn.

"I want to see you in my office," the message from Yanni had said, and Justin had gathered his nerve and gone in with his notes and his Scriber to sit listening while Will GW 79 told him and Yanni what he had told the Testing Super.

It was good news. *Good* news, no matter how he turned it over and looked at all sides of it.

"He said," Justin reported to Grant when he got back to the office, Grant listening as anxiously as he had: "Will said he got along with it fine. Why Yanni called me in—it seems Will's told his super he wants to take it all the way. He *likes* it. His medical report is absolutely clean. No hyper reactions, no flutters. His blood pressure is still reading like he was on R&R. He wants to Carry the program. Committee's going to consider it."

Grant got up from where he was sitting and put his arms around him for a moment. Then, at arm's length: "Told you so."

"Not saying the Committee's going to approve." He tried desperately hard to keep his mental balance and not go too far in believing it was working. Discipline: equilibrium. Things didn't work so well when the ashes settled out. There were always disasters, things not planned for; and Administration's whims. He found the damnedest tendency in his hands to shake and his gut to go null-G, every time he thought about believing it was going to work. He wanted it too badly. And that was dangerous. "Damn, now *I'm* scared of it."

"I told you. I told you *I* wasn't scared of it. You ought to believe me, CIT. What did Yanni say?"

"He said he'd be happier if the Tester was a little less positive. He said addictions feel fine too . . . up to a point."

"Oh, *damn* him!" Grant threw up his hands and stalked the three clear paces across the cluttered office. "What's the matter with him?"

"Yanni's just being Yanni. And he's serious. It *is* a point he has to—"

Grant turned around and leaned on his chair back. "*I'm* serious. You know that frustrates hell out of me. They aren't going to know anything a Tester can't tell them; they've had their run in Sociology, let them believe what the man's saying."

"Well, it frustrates me, too. But it doesn't mean Yanni's going to go down against it. And it's had a clear run. It's had that."

Grant looked at him with agitation plain on his face. But Grant took a deep breath and swallowed it, and cleared the expression away in a transition of emotions possible only in an actor or an azi. "It's had that, yes. They'll clear it. They have to use sense sooner or later."

"They don't have to do anything," he admitted, feeling the pall of Grant's sudden communications shutdown. "They've proved that. I just have some hope—"

"Faith in my creators," Grant repeated quietly. "Damn, it deserves celebrating." The last with cheerfulness, a bright grin. "I can't say I'm surprised. I knew before you ran it. I told you. Didn't I?"

"You told me."

"So be happy. You've earned it."

One tried. There was a mountain of work to do and the office was not the place to discuss subtleties. But walking the quadrangle toward dark, an edge-of-safety shortcut with weather-warnings out and a cloud-bank beyond the cliffs and Wing Two: "You started to say something this afternoon," Justin said. He had picked the route. And the solitude. "About Yanni."

"Nothing about Yanni."

"Hell if there wasn't. Has he been onto you for something?"

"Yanni's conservatism. That's all. He knows better than that. Dammit, he knows it's going through. He just has to find something negative."

"Don't blank on me. You were going to say something. Secrets make me nervous, Grant, you know that."

"I don't know what about. There's no secret."

"Come on. You went 180 on me. What didn't you say?"

A few paces in silence. Then: "I'm trying to remember. Honestly."

Lie.

"You said you were frustrated about something."

"That?" A small, short laugh. "Frustrated they have to be so damn short-sighted."

"You're doing it again," Justin said quietly. "All right. I'll worry in private. No matter. Don't mind. I don't pry."

"The hell."

"The hell. Yes. What's going on with you? You mind telling me?"

More paces in silence. "Is that an order?"

"What the hell is this 'order'? I asked you a question. Is there something the matter with a question?" Justin stopped on the walk where it crossed the sidewalk from Wing Two, in the evening chill with the flash of lightning in the distance. "Something about Yanni? *Was* it Yanni? Or did *I* say something?"

"Hey, I'm glad it worked, I *am* glad. There's nothing at all wrong with me. Or you. Or Will."

"Addictions. Was that the keyword?"

"Let's talk about it later."

"Talk where, then? At home? Is it that safe?"

Grant gave a long sigh, and faced the muttering of thunder and the flickering of lightnings on Wing Two's horizon. It was a dangerous time. Fools lingered out of doors, in the path of the wind that would sweep down— very soon.

"It's frustration," he said. "That they won't take Will's word on it. That they know so damn much because they're CITs."

"They have to be careful. For Will's sake, if nothing else. For the sake of the other programs he tests, —"

"CITs are a necessary evil," Grant said placidly, evenly, against the distant thunder. "What would we azi possibly do without them? Teach ourselves, of course."

Grant made jokes. This was not one of them. Justin sensed that. "You think they're not going to listen to him."

"I don't know what they're going to do. You want to know what's the greatest irritation in being azi, Supervisor mine? Knowing what's right and sane and knowing they won't listen to you."

"That's not exactly an exclusive problem."

"Different." Grant tapped his chest with a finger. "There's listening and listening. They'll always *listen* to me, when they won't, you. But they won't *listen* to me the way they do you. No more than they do Will."

"They're interested in his safety. *Listening* has nothing to do with it."

"It has everything to do with it. They won't take his word—"

"—because he's in the middle of the problem."

"Because an azi is always in the middle of the problem, and damn well outside the decision loop. *Yanni's* in the middle of the problem, he's biased as hell with CIT opinions and CIT designs, does that disqualify him? No. It makes him an *expert*."

"I listen."

"Hell, you wouldn't let me touch that routine."

"For your own damn—good, —Grant." Somehow that came out badly, about halfway. "Well, sorry, but I care. That's not a CIT pulling rank. That's a friend who needs you stable. How's that?"

"Damn underhanded."

"Hey." He took Grant by the shoulder. "Hit me on something else, all right? Let's don't take the work I'd test my own sanity on and tell me you're put out because I won't trust my judgment on it either. I'd give you anything. I'd let you—"

"There's the trouble."

"What?"

"Let me."

"*Friend*, Grant. Damn, you're flux-thinking like hell, aren't you?"

"Ought to qualify me for a directorship, don't you think? Soon as we prove we're crazy as CITs we get our papers and then we're qualified not to listen to azi Testers either."

"What happened? What happened, Grant? You want to level with me?"

Grant looked off into the dark awhile. "Frustration, that's all. I—got turned down—for permission to go to Planys."

"Oh, damn."

"I'm not his son. Not—" Grant drew several slow breaths. "Not qualified in the same way. Damn, I wasn't going to drop this on you. Not tonight."

"God." Justin grabbed him and held on to him a moment. Felt him fighting for breath and control.

"I'm tempted to say I want tape," Grant said. "But damned if I will. *Damned* if I will. It's politics they're playing. It's—just what they can do, that's all. We just last it through, the way you did. Your project worked, dammit. Let's celebrate. Get me drunk, friend. Good and drunk. I'll be fine. That's the benefit of flux, isn't it? Everything's relative. You've worked so damn long for this, we've both worked for it. No surprise to me. I knew it would run. But I'm glad you proved it to them."

"I'll go to Denys again. He *said*—"

Grant shoved back from him, gently. "He said maybe. Eventually. When things died down. Eventually isn't now, evidently."

"*Damn* that kid."

Grant's hands bit into his arms. "Don't say that. Don't—even think it."

"She just has lousy timing. *Lousy* timing. *That's* why they're so damn nervous. . . ."

"Hey. Not her timing. None of it's—her timing. Is it?"

Thunder cracked. Flashes lit the west, above the cliffs. Of a sudden the perimeter alarm went, a wailing into the night. Wind was coming, enough to break the envelope.

They grabbed each other by the sleeve and the arm and ran for shelter and safety, where the yellow warning lights flashed a steady beacon above the entrance.

iv

"Dessert?" uncle Denys asked. At *Changes*, at lunch, which was where she had agreed to meet him; and Ari shook her head.

"You can, though. I don't mind."

"I can skip it. Just the coffee." Denys coughed, and stirred a little sugar in. "I'm trying to cut down. I'm putting on weight. You used to set a good example."

Fifth and sixth try at sympathy. Ari stared at him quite steadily.

Denys took a paper from his pocket and laid it down on the table. "This is yours. It did pass. Probably better without you—this year."

"I'm a Special?"

"Of course. Did I say not? That's one reason I wanted to talk with you. This is just a fax. There was—a certain amount of debate on it. You should know about that. Catherine Lao may be your friend, but she can't stifle the press, not—on the creation of a Special. The ultimate argument was your potential. The chance that you might *need* the protection—before your majority. We used up a good many political favors getting this through. Not that we had any other choice—or wanted any."

Seventh.

She reached out and took the fax and unfolded it. Ariane Emory, it said, and a lot of fine and elaborate print with the whole Council's signatures.

"Thank you," she said. "Maybe I'd like to see it on the news."

"Not—possible."

"You were lying when you said you hated the vid. Weren't you? You just wanted to keep me away from the news-services. You still do."

"You've requested a link. I know. You *won't* get it. You know why you won't get it." Uncle Denys clasped his cup between two large hands. "For your own health. For your well-being. There are things you don't want to know yet. Be a child awhile. Even under the circumstances."

She took the paper and carefully, deliberately slowly, folded it and put it in her carry-bag, thinking, in maman's tones: *Like hell, uncle Denys.*

"I wanted to give you that," uncle Denys said. "I won't keep you. Thank you for having lunch with me."

"That's eight."

"Eight what?"

"Times you've tried to get me to feel sorry for you. I told you. It was a lousy thing to do, uncle Denys."

Shift and Shift again. Working only worked if you used it when it was time. No matter if you were ready.

"The taping. I know. I'm sorry. What can I say? That I wouldn't have done it? That would be a lie. I *am* glad you're doing all right. I'm terribly proud of you."

She gave him a nasty smile, fast and right into a sulk. "Sure."

" 'To thine own self be true'?" With a smile of his own. "You know who planned this."

She ran that through again. It was one of his better zaps, *right* out of the blind-side, and it knocked the thoughts right out of her.

Damn. There weren't very many people who could Get her like that.

"I wonder if you can imagine how it feels," uncle Denys said, "to have known your predecessor—my first memories of her are as a beautiful young woman, outstandingly beautiful; and having the same young woman arriving at the end of my life—while I'm old—is an incredible perspective."

Trying to Work her for sure. "I'm glad you like it."

"I'm glad you accepted my invitation." He sipped at his coffee.

"You want to do something to make me happy?"

"What?"

"Tell Ivanov I don't *need* any appointment."

"No. I won't say that. I can tell you where the answer is. It's in the fifteenth-year material."

"That's real funny, uncle Denys."

"I don't mean it to be. It's only the truth. Don't go too fast, Ari. But I am changing something. I'm terminating your classes."

"What do you mean, terminating my classes?"

"Hush, Ari. Voices. Voices. This is a public place. I mean it's a waste of your time. You'll still see Dr. Edwards—on a need-to basis. Dr. Dietrich. Any of them will give you special time. You have access to more tapes than you can possibly do. You'll have to select the best. The answer to what you are is in there—much more than in the biographical material. Choose for yourself. At this point—you're a Special. You have privileges. You have responsibilities. That's the way it always works." He drank two swallows of the coffee and set the cup down. "I'll put the library charges to my account. It's still larger. —You can see your school friends anytime you like. Just send to them through the system. They'll get the message."

He left the table. She sat there a moment, figuring, trying to catch her breath.

She *could* go to classes if she wanted to. She could request her instructors' time, that was all.

She could do anything she wanted to.

Shots again. She scowled at the tech who took her blood and gave them to her. She did not even *see* Dr. Ivanov.

"There'll be prescriptions at pharmacy," the tech said. "We understand you'll be using home teaching. Please be careful. Follow the instructions."

The tech was azi. It was no one she could yell at. So she got up, feeling flushed, and went out to the pharmacy in the hospital and got the damned prescriptions.

Kat. At least it was useful.

She got home early: no interview with Dr. Ivanov, no hanging around waiting. She put the sack in the plastics bin and read the ticket and discovered they had billed her account thirty cred for the pills and probably for Florian and Catlin's too.

"Dammit," she said out loud. "Minder, message to Denys Nye: Pharmacy is your bill. *You* pay it. I didn't order it."

It made her furious.

Which was the shot. It *did* that to her. She took half a dozen deep breaths and went to the library to put the prescription bottles in the cabinet under the machine.

Damn. It was nowhere near time for her cycle. And she felt like that. She felt—

On. Like she wished she had homework tonight, or something. Or she could go down and see the Filly, maybe. She had been working too hard and going down there too little, leaving too much of the Filly's upbringing to Florian, but she didn't feel like that, either. The shots bothered her and she hated to be out of control when she was around people. It was going to be bad enough just trying not to be irritable with Catlin and Florian when *they* got home, without going around Andy, who was too nice to have to put up with a CIT brat in a lousy, prickly mood.

She knew what was going on with her, it had to do with her cycles, damn Dr. Ivanov was messing with her again, and it was embarrassing. Going around other people, grown-ups, likely they could *tell* what was going on with her, and that made her embarrassed too.

The whole thing was probably on Denys' orders. She bet it was. And she tried to think of a way to get them to stop it, but as long as Ivanov had the right to suspend her Super's license if she dodged sessions—she was in for it.

Dammit, there wasn't anything in the world those shots and those check-ups had to do with her dealing with azi, not a thing—but she couldn't prove it, unless maybe she could do what the first Ari had done and call Security, and get them to arrange a House council meeting.

God, and sit there in front of every grown-up she knew in the whole House and explain about the shots and her cycles? She had rather die.

Don't go up against Administration, Ari senior had told her, out of the things she had learned.

Except it was Ari senior doing it to her as much as it was Denys.

Damn.

Dammit, dammit, dammit.

She opened the tape cabinet, looking for something to keep her mind busy and burn some of the mad off. One of the E-tapes. Dumas, maybe. She was willing to do that tape twice. She knew it was all right.

But it was the adult ones that she started thinking about, which made her think about the last sex tape she had had, which was a long time back. And it was just exactly what she was in the mood for.

So she pulled one out that didn't sound as embarrassing as the others, *Models*, it was called; and she took it to the library, told the Minder to tell Florian and Catlin when they came in that she was doing tape and might be fifteen more minutes—she checked the time—by the time they got the message.

And locked the tape-lab door, tranked down with the mild dose you did for entertainment, set up and let it run.

In a while more she thought she should cut it off. It was different than anything she had thought.

But the feelings she got were interesting.

Very.

Florian and Catlin were home by the time the tape ran out. She ought not, she thought, stir about yet; but it was only a tiny dose, it was not dangerous, it only made her feel a little tranked, in that strange, warm way. She asked the Minder was it only them—silly precaution—before she unlocked the door and came out.

She found them in the kitchen making supper. Warm-ups again. "Hello, sera," Florian said. "Did it go all right today?"

Lunch with Denys, she realized. And remembered she was still mad, if she were not so tranked down. It was strange—the way things went in and out of importance in the day. "He stopped my classes," she said. "Said I didn't have to go to class anymore except just for special help. Said I had too many tapes to do."

So what do I start with? That *stupid thing. Like I had all kinds of time.*

"Is it all right, sera?" Catlin was worried.

"It's all right." She shoved away from the doorframe and came to put napkins down. The oven timer was running down, a flicker of green readout. "I can handle it. I will handle it. Maybe he's even right: I've got a lot to go through. And it's not like I was losing the school." She leaned on a chair back. The timer went. "I'll miss the kids, though."

"Will we meet with them?" Florian asked.

"Oh, sure. Not that we won't." She grabbed her plate and held it out as Florian used the tongs to get the heated dinner from the oven. She took hers and sat down as Florian and Catlin served themselves and joined her.

Dinner. A little talk. Retreat to their rooms to study. It was the way it always had been—except she had her own office and they had their computer terminals and their House accesses through the Minder.

She went to her room to change. And sat down on the bed, wishing she had left the cabinet alone and knowing she was in trouble.

Bad trouble. Because she was good at saying no to herself when she saw a reason for it . . . but it got harder and harder to think of the reasons not to do what she wanted, because when she did refuse she got mad, and when she got mad that feeling was there.

She went and read Base One . . . long, long stretches of the trivial housekeeping records Ari senior had generated, just the way they themselves were doing, until she ran them past faster and faster. Who *cared* whether Ari senior had wanted an order of tomatoes on the 28th September?

She thought about the tape library, about pulling up one of the Recommendeds and getting started with it. And finally thought that was probably the thing to do.

"Sera." It was Florian's voice through the Minder. "Excuse me. I'm doing the list. Do you want anything from Housekeeping?"

Bother and damnation.

"Just send it." A thought came, warm and tingly, and very, very dangerous. Then she said, deliberately, knowing it was stupid: "And come here a minute. My office."

"Yes, sera."

Stupid, she said to herself. *And cruel. It's mean to do, dammit. Make up something else. Send him off on a job.*

God. . . .

She thought about Ollie. The way she had thought about him all afternoon. Ollie with maman. Ollie when he had looked young and maman had. Maman had never had to be lonely . . . while Ollie was there. And Ollie never minded.

"Sera?" Florian said, a real voice, from the doorway.

"Log-off," she told Base One, and turned her chair around, and got up. "Come on in, Florian. —What's Catlin doing?"

"Studying. We have a manual to do. Just light tape. It—isn't something you need to Super, —is it? Should I stop her?"

"No. It's all right. Is it something really urgent?"

"No."

"Even if you were late? Even if you didn't get to it?"

"No, sera. They said—when we could. I think it would be all right. What do you want me to do?"

"I want you to come to my room a minute," she said, and took him by the hand and walked him down the hall to her bedroom.

And shut the door once they were inside and locked it.

He looked at that and at her, concerned. "Is there some trouble, sera?"

"I don't know." She put her hands on his shoulders. Carefully. He twitched, hands moved, just a little defensive reaction, even if he knew she was going to do it. Uneasiness at being touched, the way he had reacted with Maddy once. "Is that all right? Do you mind that?"

"No, sera. I don't mind." He was still disturbed. His breathing got faster and deeper as she ran her hands down to his sides, and walked around behind him, and around again. Maybe he thought it was some kind of test. Maybe he understood. Another twitch, when she touched his chest.

She knew better. That was the awful thing. She was ashamed of herself all the way. She was afraid for Catlin and for him and none of it mattered, not for a moment.

She took a hard grip on his shoulder, friend-like. "Florian. Do you know about sex?"

He nodded. Once and emphatically.

"If you did it with me, would Catlin be upset?"

A shake of his head. A deep breath. "Not if you said it was right."

"Would *you* be upset?"

Another shake of his head. "No, sera."

"Are you sure?"

A deep nod. Another breath. "Yes, sera." Another. "Can I go tell Catlin?"

"Now?"

"If it's going to be a while. She'll worry. I think I ought to tell her."

That was fair. There were complications in everything. "All right," she said. "Come right back."

V

He left sera to sleep, finally—he had slept a little while, but sera was restless. Sera said she was a little uncomfortable, and he could go back and sleep in his own bed, she was fine, she just wanted to sleep now and she wasn't used to company.

So he put his pants on, but he was only going to bed, so he carried the rest, and slipped out and shut the door.

But Catlin's room had the light on, and Catlin came out into the hall.

He stopped dead still. He wished he had finished dressing.

She just stood there a moment. So he walked on down as far as her room, past his own.

"All right?" she asked.

"I think so," he said. Sera was in a little discomfort, he had hurt sera, necessarily, because sera was built that way: sera said go on, and she had been happy with him, overall. He hoped. He truly hoped. "Sera said she wanted to sleep, I should go to bed. I'll do the manual tomorrow."

Catlin just looked at him, the way she did sometimes when she was confused, gut-deep open. He did not know what to say to her. He did not know what she wanted from him.

"How did it feel?"

"Good," he said on an irregular breath. Knowing then what he was telling her and how her mind had been running and was running then. Partners. For a lot of years. Catlin was curious. Some things went past her and she paid no attention. But if Catlin was interested this far, Catlin wanted to figure it out, the same way she would take a thing apart to understand it.

She said finally—he knew she was going to say—: "Can you show me? You think sera would mind?"

It was not wrong. He would have felt a tape-jolt about it if it were. He was tired. But if his partner wanted something, his partner got it, always, forever.

"All right," he said, trying to wake himself up and find the energy. And came into her room with her.

He undressed. So did she—which felt strange, because they had always been so modest, as much as they could, even in the field, and just not looked, if there was no cover.

But he was mostly the one who was embarrassed, because he had always had sex-feelings, he understood that now—while Catlin, who was so much more capable than he was in a lot of ways, missed so much that involved what sera called flux-values.

"Bed," he said, and turned back the covers and got under, because it was a little cold; and because bed was a comfortable, resting kind of place, and he knew Catlin would feel more comfortable about being up against him skin against skin in that context.

So she got in and lay on her side facing him, and got up against him when he told her she should, and relaxed when he told her to, even when he put his hand on her side and his knee between hers. "You let me do everything first," he said, and told her there was a little pain involved, but that was no more than a don't-react where Catlin was concerned. You didn't surprise her in things like that.

"All right," she said.

She *could* react, he found that out very fast, with his fingers.

He stopped. "It gets stronger. You want to keep going with this? Does that feel all right?"

She was thinking about it. Breathing hard. "Fine," she decided.

"You let that get started again," he said, "then you do the same with me. All right? Just like dancing. Variations. All right?"

She drew a deep, deep breath, and she took his advice, until he suddenly felt himself losing control. "Ease up," he said. "Stop."

She did. He managed all right then, finding it smoother with her than with sera—but of course it would be. Catlin would listen, even when it was hard to listen, and he had a far better idea this time what he was doing.

He warned her of things. She was as careful with him as he was with her, not to draw a surprise reaction: he had more confidence in her in that way too.

She did not put a mark on him. Sera had, a lot of them.

He finished; and said, out of breath: "Most I can do, Catlin. Sorry. Second round for me. I'm awfully tired."

She was quiet a minute, out of breath herself. "That was all right." In the thoughtful way she had when she approved of something.

He hugged her, on that warm feeling. She didn't always understand why he did things like that. He didn't think she had understood this time, just that it was temporary reflex, a sex thing, but when he kissed her on the forehead and said he had better get back to his own bed:

"You can stay here," she said, and sort of fitted herself to him puzzle-fashion and gave him a comfortable spot it was just easier not to leave.

They had to get up before sera anyway.

vi

Ari woke up at the Minder-call, remembered what she had done last night, and lay there for a minute remembering.

A little scared. A little sore. It had not been quite like the tapes—like real-life, a little awkward. But someone had said—the tape, she thought—that happens; even sex takes practice.

So they were twelve pushing thirteen real hard. Which was young. Her body wasn't through growing, Florian's wasn't. She knew that made a difference.

The tape had said so. "Does Ari have any reference on sex?" Ari asked Base One.

But Base One only gave her the same thing it had always given, and she had read that so often she had it memorized.

She had been irresponsible, completely, last night, that was what kept eating at her. She could have hurt them, and the worst thing was she still could: this morning she was still *on*, —a whole lot cooler and calmer, but sex was just like the tape, hard to remember what it felt like the minute it was over, a damn cheat, leaving just a curiosity, something you kept picking at like a fool picking at a scab to see if it hurt—again.

It was hard to remember a whole lot of things when *that* got started.

Like responsibility. Like people you cared about.

Like who *you* were.

Ari senior was right. It messed up your thinking. It *could* take over. Real easy.

Sex is when you're the most vulnerable you'll ever be. Brains is when you're least.

Damn those shots! They're Working me, that's what they're doing, they're Working me and I can't stop it, Dr. Ivanov can pull my license if I don't take them, and I know what they're doing, dammit!

That stuff is still in my bloodstream. I can still feel it. Hormones gone crazy. And I still want to pull Florian in and try it again like a damn fool.

Fool, fool, fool, Ari Emory!

"Are you all right?" she cornered Florian to ask, before breakfast, in the hallway. Carefully. *Care* about things. It was the only antidote.

"Yes, sera," Florian said, looking anxious—perhaps for being pulled alone out of the kitchen and far down the hall and backed against the wall, perhaps thinking they were going to go through it again.

Calm down. Don't confuse him. You've done enough, fool. She could

hear maman, could hear maman clear when she did something stupid—
Dammit, Ollie! "You're sure. I want you not to try to make me feel good,
Florian. If I did something wrong, tell me."

"I'm fine." He took a deep breath. "But, sera, —Catlin and I—she—I—
Sera, I slept with her last night. We—did sex too. It felt all right—then. It *was*
all right, —wasn't it?"

Surge of hormones. *Bad* temper. Panic. She found her breath coming
hard and folded her arms and turned away, looking at the stonework floor a
moment until she could jerk herself sideways and back to sense.

Stupid, Ari. Real stupid. Look what's happened.

*She's his partner, not me, what in hell am I being jealous for? I did a nasty
thing to him and he doesn't even know it's not right.*

Oh, dammit, Ari. Dammit!

*Flux. That's what sex sets loose. A hell of a flux-state. Hormones. That's
what's going on with me.*

I wonder if I could write this up for one of Dr. Dietrich's damn papers.

"But she's all right," she said, looking around at Florian—at a painfully
worried Florian. "She *is* all right this morning, isn't she? I mean, you don't
think it's messed anything up between you. *That's* what I'm worried about."

His face lightened, a cloud leaving. "Oh, no, sera. No. Just—we got to
thinking about it— Sera, Catlin was just curious. You know how she is. If it
was there she wants to know about it, and if it involved me—she—really
needs to know, sera, she really needs to understand what's going on." The
frown came back. "Anything I do—is her, too. It has to be."

She put her hand on his arm, took his hand and squeezed it hard. "Of
course it does. It's all right. It's *all right*, Florian. I'm only upset if you two
are. I don't blame you. I don't care what you did. I only worry I could have
hurt you."

"No, sera." He believed everything. He would do anything. He looked
terribly relieved. She took his arm through hers and held on to his hand,
walking him back down the hall toward the kitchen where rattles and closings
of doors said Catlin was busy.

"But Catlin's not as social as you. And sex is a hell of a jolt, Florian, an
awful hormone load." *But it's the flux-values it goes crazy with. Flux and feedback loop, brain and hormones interacting. That's what's going on with me. CIT
processing. The whole environment fluxing in values. Even Florian doesn't flux-
think that heavy.* "It didn't bother her—really?"

"I really don't think so. She said it—was sort of like a good workout."

A little laugh got away from her, just surprise on top of the angst, that
left her less worried and more so, in different directions. "Oh, damn. Florian.
I don't know everything I ought to. I wish I was azi, sometimes. I do. *Keep* an
eye on Catlin. If her reactions aren't up to par, or yours aren't, I want to know
it, I want to know it right then—call me if you have to stop an Exercise to do
it, hear?"

"Yes, sera."

"I just worry—just worry because I'm responsible, that's all. And experimenting around with us makes me nervous, because I can't go and ask, I just have to try things and I really need you to tell me if I do wrong with you. You object, hear me, you *object* if you think I'm doing something I shouldn't."

"Yes, sera." Automatic as breathing.

They reached the kitchen. Catlin was setting out plates. Catlin looked up at them, a little query in the tension between her brows.

"No troubles with me," Ari said. "Florian told me everything. It's all right."

The tension went away, and Catlin gave one of her real smiles.

"He was real happy," Catlin said, the way she could go straight to the middle of something.

Of course Florian had been happy. His Super took him to bed and told him he was fine; sent him away in a heavy flux-state to deal with a Catlin fluxed as Catlin could get—her Super locking her out of the room and doing something emotional and mysterious with her partner.

So they wake up with *that* load on them.

Fool, Ari. Upset them twice over, for all the wrong reasons. Can I do anything right?

They ate breakfast. Pass the salt. More coffee, sera?—While her stomach stayed upset and she tried to think and look cheerful at the same time.

Then: "Florian," she said, finally. "Catlin."

Two perfectly attentive faces turned to her, open as flowers to light.

"About last night—we're really pretty young yet. Maybe it's good to get experience with each other, so we don't get fluxed too badly if we do it with other people, because it's a way people can Work you. But the last thing we need to do is start Working each other, not meaning to, even if it is fun, because it sure gets through your guard. It got through mine."

It was Catlin she was talking to, most. And Catlin said: "It does that." With her odd laugh, difficult to catch as her true smile. "You could use that."

"You sure could," she said finally, steadier than she had been. The flux diminished, steadily, now that she knew her way. "But it's hard for CITs. *I'm* having flux problems . . . nothing I can't handle. You'll have to get used to me being just a little *on* now and again; it doesn't last, it doesn't hurt me, it's part of sex with CITs, and I know I'm not supposed to discuss my psych problems with you—but now I'm onto it, I've got my balance. Nothing at all unnatural for a CIT. You know a little about it. I can tell you a lot more. I think maybe I should—use *me* for an example, to start with. You aren't used to flux—" Looking straight at Catlin. "Not real strong, anyway. You did fine when Florian got hurt. But that's something you knew about. This is all new, it feels good, and it's an Older thing. Like wine. If you feel uneasy about it, you tell Florian or you tell me, all right?"

"All right," Catlin said, wide-open and very serious. "But Florian's had tape about it already, so he's all right. If he doesn't get a *no* with me it's just something he's the specialist at, that's all. But I can learn it all right."

Trust Catlin. Ari paid earnest attention to her eggs, because Catlin was real good at reading her face, and she came near laughing.

Hormones were still crazy. But the brain was starting to fight back.

The brain has to win out, Ari senior had said. But the little gland at the base of the brain is the seat of a lot of the trouble. It's no accident they're so close together: God has a sense of humor.

---

vii

"We're giving permission," Yanni said, "for Will to assimilate the routine. *I* think—and the board thought—he'd already done it to a certain extent, from the time it started working. With its touch with deep-set values, it's not at all surprising . . . and I agree with the board: it's cause for concern."

Justin looked at the edge of Yanni's desk. Unfocused. "I agree with that," he said finally.

"What do you think about it?"

He drew a breath, hauled himself back out of the mental shadows and looked at Yanni's face—not his eyes. "I think the board's right. I didn't see it in that perspective."

"I mean—what's your view of the problem?"

"I don't know."

"For God's sake, wake *up*, son. Didn't think, don't know, *what in hell's* the matter with you?"

He shook his head. "Tired, Yanni. Just tired."

He waited for the explosion. Yanni leaned forward on his arms and gave a heavy sigh.

"Grant?"

Justin looked at the wall.

"I'm damn sorry," Yanni said. "Son, it's temporary. Look, you want a schedule? He'll get his permit. It's coming."

"Of course it is," he said softly. "Of course it is. Everything's always coming. I know the damn game. I've had it, Yanni. I'm through. I'm tired, Grant's tired. I know Jordan's getting tired." He was close to tears. He stopped talking and just stared, blind, at the wall and the corner where the shelves started. A Downer spirit-stick, set in a case. Yanni had some artistic sense. Or it was a gift from someone. He had wondered that before. He envied Yanni that piece.

"Son."

"Don't call me that!" He wrenched his eyes back to Yanni, breath choking him. "Don't—call me that. I don't want to hear that word."

Yanni stared at him a long time. Yanni could rip him apart. Yanni knew him well enough. And he had given Yanni all the keys, over the years. Given him a major one now, with his reaction.

Even that didn't matter.

"Morley's sent a commendation on your work with young Benjamin," Yanni said. "He says—says your arguments are very convincing. He's going to committee with it."

The Rubin baby. Not a baby now. Aged six—a thin, large-eyed and gentle boy with a lot of health problems and a profound attachment to young Ally Morley. And in some measure—his patient.

So Yanni started hitting him in the soft spots. Predictably. He was not going to come out of this office whole. He had known that when Yanni hauled him in.

He stared at the artifact in the case.

Non-human. A gentle people humans had no right to call primitive. And of course did. And threw them into protectorate.

"Son—Justin. I'm telling you it's a temporary delay. I told Grant that. Maybe six months. No more than that."

"If I—" He was cold for a moment, cold enough at least to talk without breaking down. "If I agreed to go into detention—if I agreed to cooperate with a deep probe—about everything that's ever gone on between myself and Jordan—would that be enough to get Grant his permit?"

Long silence. "I'm not going to give them that offer," Yanni said finally. "Dammit, no."

He shifted his eyes Yanni's way. "I haven't got anything to hide. There's *nothing there*, Yanni, not even a sinful thought—unless you're surprised I'd like to see Reseune Administration in hell. But I wouldn't move to send them there. I've got everything to lose. Too many people do."

"I've got something to lose," Yanni said. "I've got a young man who's not a Special only because Reseune wouldn't dare bring the bill up—wouldn't dare give you that protection."

"That's a piece of garbage."

"I gave you a chance. I've taken risks with you. I didn't say I thought Will's got a problem. I'm saying that testing your routines—may have to absorb Test subjects. By their very nature. Once they've run, it takes mindwipe to remove them. That doesn't mean they're not useful."

Defense Bureau.

Test programs with mindwipe between runs—

"Justin?"

"God. God. I try to help the azi—and I've created a monstrosity for Defense. My God, Yanni—"

"Calm down. Calm down. We're not talking about the Defense Bureau."

"It *will* be. Let them get wind of it—"

"A long way from Applications. Calm down."

It's my work. Without me—they can't. If something happened to me—they can't—not for a long while.

Oh, damn, all the papers, all my notes—

Grant. . . .

"Reseune doesn't give away its processes," Yanni said reasonably, rationally. "It's not in question."

"Reseune's in *bed* with Defense. They have been, ever since Giraud got the Council seat."

Ever since Ari died. Ever since her successors sold out—sold out everything she stood for.

God, I wish—wish she was still alive.

The kid—doesn't have a chance.

"Son, —I'm sorry, Justin. Habit. —Listen to me. I see your point. I can see it very clearly. It worries me too."

"Are we being taped, Yanni?"

Yanni bit his lip, and touched a button on his desk. "Now we're not."

"Where's the tape?"

"I'll take care of it."

"Where's the damn tape, Yanni?"

"Calm down and listen to me. I'm willing to work with you. Blank credit slip. Let me ask you something. Your psych profile says suicide isn't likely. But answer me honestly: is it something you ever think about?"

"No." His heart jumped, painfully. It was a lie. And not. He thought about it then. And lacked whatever it took. Or had no reason sufficient, yet. *God, what does it take? Do I have to see the kids walking into the fire before I feel enough guilt? It's too late then. What kind of monster am I?*

"Let me remind you—you'd kill Grant. And your father. Or worse—they'd live with it."

"Go to hell, Yanni."

"You think other researchers didn't ask those questions?"

"Carnath and Emory built Reseune! You think ethics ever bothered that pair?"

"You think ethics didn't bother Ari?"

"Sure. Like Gehenna."

"The colony lived. Lived, when every single CIT died. Emory's work, damned right. The azi survived."

"In squalor. In abominable conditions—like damned *primitives*—"

"*Through* squalor. Through catastrophes that peeled away every advantage they came with. The culture on that planet is an azi culture. And they're unique. You forget the human brain, Justin. Human ingenuity. The will to live. You can send an azi soldier into fire—but he's more apt than his CIT counterpart to turn to his sergeant and ask what the gain is. And the sergeant had better have an answer that makes sense to him. You should take a look at the military, Justin. You have a real phobia about that, pardon the eetee psych. They do deal with extreme stress situations. The military sets will walk into fire. But an azi who's too willing to do that is a liability and an azi who likes killing is worse. You take a look at reality before you panic. Look at our military workers down there. They're damned good. Damned polite, damned competent, damned impatient with foul-ups, damned easy to Super as long as they think you're qualified, and capable of relaxing when they're off, unlike some of our assembly-line over-achievers. Look at the reality before you start worrying. Look at the specific types."

"These are survivors too," Justin said. "The ones who outlived the War."

"Survival rate among azi is higher than CITs, fifteen something percent. I have no personal compunction about the azi. They're fine. They like themselves fine. Your work may have real bearing on CIT psych, in behavioral disorders. A lot of applications, if it bears out. We deal with humanity. And tools. You can kill a man with a laser. You can save a life with it. It doesn't mean we shouldn't have lasers. Or edged blades. Or hammers. Or whatever. But I'm damned glad we have lasers, or I'd be blind in my right eye. You understand what I'm saying?"

"Old stuff, Yanni."

"I mean, do you *understand* what I'm saying? Inside?"

"Yes." True. His instincts grabbed after all the old arguments like he was a baby going for a blanket. About as mature. About as capable of sorting out the truth. Damn. Hand a man a timeworn excuse and he went after it to get the pain to stop. Even knowing the one who handed it to him was a psych operator.

"Besides," Yanni said, "you're a man of principle. And humans don't stop learning things, just because they might be risky: if this insight of yours is correct you're only a few decades ahead of someone else finding it on his own. And who knows, that researcher might not have your principles—or your leverage."

"Leverage! I can't get my brother a visit with his father!"

"You can get a hell of a lot if you work it right."

"Oh, *dammit*! Are we down to sell-outs, now? Are we through doing morality today?"

"Your brother. Grant's a whole lot of things with you. Isn't he?"

"Go to hell!"

"Not related to you. I merely point out you do an interesting double value set there. You're muddy in a lot of sensitive areas—including a little tendency to suspect every success you have, a tendency to see yourself perpetually as a nexus defined by other people—Jordan's son, Grant's—brother, Administration's hostage. Less as a human being than as a focus of all these demands. *You* have importance, Justin, unto yourself. You're a man thirty—thirty-one years old. Time you asked yourself what Justin is."

"We *are* into eetee psych, aren't we?"

"I'm handing it out free today. You're not responsible for the universe. You're not responsible for a damn thing that flows from things you didn't have the capacity to control. Maybe you *are* responsible for finding out what you *could* control, if you wanted to, if you'd stop looking at other people's problems and start taking a look at your own capabilities—which, as I say, probably qualify you as a Special. Which also answers a lot of questions about why you *have* problems: lack of adequate boundaries. *Lack* of them, son. All the Specials have the problem. It's real hard to understand humanity when you keep attributing to everyone around you the complexity of your own thinking. You have quite a few very bright minds around you—enough to keep you convinced that's ordinary. Jordan's, particularly: he's got the age advantage, doesn't he, and you've always confused him with God. You think about it. You know all this with the Rubin kid. Apply it closer to home. Do us all a favor."

"Why don't you just explain what you want me to do? I'm real tired, Yanni. I give. You name it, I'll do it."

"Survive."

He blinked. Bit his lip.

"Going to break down on me?" Yanni asked.

The haze was gone. The tears were gone. He was only embarrassed, and mad enough to break Yanni's neck.

Yanni smiled at him. Smug as hell.

"I could kill you," Justin said.

"No, you couldn't," Yanni said. "It's not in your profile. You divert everything inward. You'll never quite cure that tendency. It's what makes you a lousy clinician and a damned good designer. *Grant* can survive the stress—if you don't put it on him. Hear me?"

"Yes."

"Thought so. So don't do it. Go back to your office and tell him I'm putting his application through again."

"I'm not going to. It's getting too sensitive. *He's* hurting, Yanni. I can't take that."

Yanni bit his lip. "All right. Don't tell him. Do you understand *why* it's a problem, Justin? They're afraid of the military grabbing him."

"God. *Why?*"

"Power move. You can tell him that. I'm not supposed to tell you. I'm breaking security. There's a rift in Defense. There's a certain faction that's proposing the nationalization of Reseune. That's the new move. Lu's health is going. Rejuv failure. He's got at most a couple more years. Gorodin is becoming increasingly isolated from the Secretariat in Defense. He may get a challenge to his seat. That hasn't happened since the war. An election in the military. There's the head of Military Research, throwing more and more weight behind the head of Intelligence. Khalid. Vladislaw Khalid. If you're afraid of something, Justin, —be afraid of that name. That faction could *use* an incident. So could Gorodin's. Fabricated, would serve just as well. You're in danger. Grant—more so. All they have to do is arrest him at the airport, claim he was carrying documents—God knows what. Denys will have my head for telling you this. *I* wanted to keep you out of it, not disrupt your work with it— Grant's not getting a travel pass right now. *You* couldn't get one. That's the truth. Tell Grant—if it helps. For God's sake—tell him somewhere private."

"You mean they *are* bugging us."

"I don't know. I can answer for in here. We're off the record right now."

"You *say* we are—"

"I *say* we are. If Gorodin survives the election we're sure is going to be called—you'll be safer. If not—nothing is safe. We'll lose our majority in Council. After that I don't lay bets *what* will stay safe. If we lose our A.T. status, so will Planys. You understand me?"

"I understand you." The old feeling settled back again. Game resumed. He felt sick at his stomach. And a hell of a lot steadier with things as-they-were. "If you're telling me the truth—"

"If I'm telling you the truth you'd better wake up and take care of yourself. Next few years are going to be hell, son. Real hell. Lu's going to die. It's an appointive post. Lu could resign, but that's no good. Whoever gets in can appoint a new Secretary. Lu's wrecking his health, holding on, trying to handle the kind of infighting he's so damn good at. Gorodin's in space too much. Too isolate from his command structure. Lu's trying to help Gorodin ride out the storm—but Lu's ability to pay off political debtors is diminishing rapidly, the closer he comes to the wall. He's balancing factions within his own faction. Question is—how long can he stay alive—in either sense?"

viii

The Filly made the circuit of the barn arena again, flaring her nostrils and blowing, and Ari watched her, watched Florian, so sure and so graceful on the Filly's back.

Beside her, arms folded, Catlin watched—so did Andy, and a lot of the AG staff. Not the first time any of them had seen Florian and the Filly at work, but it was the first time the AG staff and Administration was going to let *her* try it. Uncle Denys was there—uncle Giraud was in Novgorod, where he spent most of his time nowadays: they were having an election—a man named Khalid was running against Gorodin, of Defense, and everybody in Reseune was upset about it. *She* was, since what she heard about Khalid meant another court fight if he did what he was threatening to do. But an election took months and months for all the results to get in from the ends of everywhere in space, and uncle Denys took time out of his schedule to come down to the barn: he had insisted if she was going to break anything he wanted to be there to call the ambulance this time. Amy Carnath was there; and so was Sam; and 'Stasi and Maddy and Tommy. It made Ari a little nervous. She had never meant her first try with the Filly to turn into an Occasion, with so much audience.

Florian had been working the Filly and teaching her for months—had even gone so far as to make a skill tape, patched himself up with sensors from head to foot while he put the Filly through every move she could make, and kept a pocket-cam focused right past her ears—all to teach *her* how to keep her balance and how to react to the Filly's moves. It was as close to riding as she had come until today. It felt wonderful.

Uncle Giraud said, being uncle Giraud, that tape had real commercial possibilities.

Florian brought the Filly back quite nicely, to a little oh and a little applause from the kids—which upset the Filly and made her throw her head. But she calmed down, and Florian climbed down very sedately and held the reins out to her.

"Sera?" he said. Ari took a breath and walked up to him and the Filly.

She had *warned* everybody to be quiet. It was a deathly hush now. Everyone was watching; and she so wanted to do things right and not embarrass herself or scare anyone.

"Left foot," Florian whispered, in case she forgot. "I'll lead her just a little till you get the feel of it, sera."

She had to stretch to reach the stirrup. She got it and got the saddle and got on without disgracing herself. The Filly moved then with Florian leading, and all of a sudden she felt the tape, felt the motion settle right where muscle and bone knew it should, just an easy give.

She felt like crying, and clamped her jaw tight, because she was not going to do that. Or look like a fool, with Florian leading her around. "I've got it," she said. "Give me the reins, Florian."

He stopped the Filly and passed them over the Filly's head for her. He looked terribly anxious.

"*Please*, sera, don't let her get away from you. She's nervous with all these people."

"I've got her," she said. "It's all right."

And she was very prudent, starting the Filly off at a sedate walk, letting the Filly get used to her being up instead of Florian, when for months and months she had had to stand at the rail and watch Florian get to ride—and watch Florian take a few falls too, figuring out what nobody this side of old Earth knew how to do. Once the Filly had fallen, a terrible spill, and Florian had been out for a few seconds, just absolutely limp; but he had gotten up swearing it was not the Filly, she had lost her footing, he had felt it—and he had staggered over and hugged the Filly and gotten back on while she and Catlin stood there with their hands clenched.

Now she took the Filly away from him, for the Filly's really public coming-out, and she knew Florian was sweating and suffering every step she took—knowing sera could be a fool; the way Catlin was probably doing the same, knowing if anything went wrong it was only Florian stood a chance of doing anything.

She was fourteen today; and she had too much audience to be a fool. She was amazingly sensible, she rode the Filly at a walk and kept her at a walk, anxious as the Filly started trying to move—no, Florian had said: if she tries to break and pick her own pace, don't let her do that, she's not supposed to, and she's bad about that.

Florian had told her every tiny move the Filly tended to make, and where she could lose her footing, and where she tried to get her own way.

So she just stopped that move the instant the Filly tried it, *not* easy, no, the Filly had a trick of stretching her neck against the rein and going like she was suddenly half-*G* for a few paces: she was glad she had not let the Filly run the first time she was up on her; but the Filly minded well enough when she made her.

It was not, of course, the show she wanted to make. She wanted to come racing up at a dead run and give everyone a real scare; but that was Florian's part, Florian got to do that: *she* got to be responsible.

She passed her audience, so self conscious she could hardly stand it—she *hated* being responsible; and uncle Denys was probably still nervous. She came around to where Florian was standing by the rail, and stopped the Filly there, because he was walking out to talk to her.

"How am I?" she asked.

"Fine," he said. "Tap her once with your heels when she's walking, just a little. Keep the reins firm. That's the next pace. Don't let her get above it yet. Don't ever let her do it if you don't tell her."

"Right," she said; and started the Filly up, one tap, then a second.

The Filly liked that. Her ears came up, and she hit a brisk pace that was harder to stay with, but Ari found it. Her body suddenly began to tape-remember what to do with faster moves, found its balance, found everything Florian had given her.

She wanted to cut free, O God, she wanted to go through the rest of it and so did the Filly, but she kept that pace which the Filly found satisfactory enough and pulled up to a very impressive stop right in front of Andy and Catlin. The Filly was sweating—excitement, that was all; and stamped and shifted after she had gotten down and Andy was holding her.

Everyone was impressed. Uncle Denys was positively pale, but he was doing awfully well, all the same.

Amy and the rest wanted to try too, but Andy said it was best not to have too many new riders all at once: the Filly would get out of sorts. Florian said they could come when he was exercising the Filly and they could do it one at a time, if they wanted to.

Besides, Florian said, the best way to learn about horses was to work with them. The Mare was going to birth again and they were doing two completely different genotypes in the tanks; which would be seven horses in all—no longer Experimentals, but officially Working Animals.

Of which the Filly was the first. Ari patted her—good and solid: the Filly liked to know you were touching her; and got horse smell all over her, but she loved it; she loved everything; she even gave uncle Denys a hug.

"You were very brave," she said to uncle Denys when she did it, and on impulse, kissed him on the cheek and gave him a wicked smile, getting horse smell on him too. "Your favorite guinea pig *didn't* break her neck."

Uncle Denys looked thoroughly off his balance. But she had whispered it.

"Even her inflections," he said, putting her off hers. "God. Sometimes you're uncanny, young woman."

---

ix

"That's it," Justin said as the Cyteen election results flashed up on the screen, and: "Vid off," to the Minder. "Khalid."

Grant shook his head, and said nothing for a long while. Then: "Well, it's a crazy way to do business."

"Defense contractors in the Trade bureau, in Finance."

"Reseune has ties there too."

"It's still going to be interesting."

Grant bowed his head and passed a hand over his neck, just resting there a moment. Thinking, surely—that it was going to be a long while, a *long* while before either of them traveled again.

Or thinking worse thoughts. Like Jordan's safety.

"It's not like—" Justin said, "they could just ram things through and get that nationalization. The other Territories will come down on Reseune's side in this one. And watch Giraud change footing. He's damned good at it. He *is* Defense, for all practical purposes. I never saw a use for the man. But, God, we may have one."

X

It was one of the private, *private* parties, weekend, the gang off from school and homework, and the Rule was, no punch and no cake off the terrazzo areas, and if anybody wanted to do sex they went to the guest room or the sauna, and if they started getting silly-drunk they went to the sauna room and took cold showers until they sobered up.

So far the threat of showers had been enough.

They had Maddy, 'Stasi, Amy, Tommy, Sam, and a handful of new kids, 'Stasi's cousins Dan and Mischa Peterson, only Dan was Peterson-Nye and Mischa was Peterson—which was one brother set, whose maman would have *killed* them if she smelled alcohol on them, but that just made them careful; and two sets of cousins, which was Amy and Tommy Carnath; and 'Stasi and Dan and Mischa. Dan and Mischa were fifteen and fourteen, but that was all right, they got along, and they did everything else but drink.

In any case they were even, boys and girls, and Amy and Sam were a set, and Dan and Mischa both got off with Maddy, and 'Stasi and Tommy Carnath were a set; which worked out all right.

Mostly they were real polite, very quiet parties. They had a little punch or a little wine, the rowdiest they ever got was watching E-tapes, mostly the ones the kids' mothers would kill them for, and when they got a little drunk they sat around in the half-dark while the tapes were running and did whatever came to mind until they had to make a choice between the Rule and finishing the tape.

"Oh, hell," Ari said finally, this time when Maddy asked, "do it on the landing, who cares?"

She was a little drunk herself. A lot tranked. She had her blouse open, she felt the draft and finally she settled against Florian to watch the tape. Sam and Amy came back, very prim and sober, and gawked at what was going on next to the bar. While 'Stasi and Tommy were still in the sauna room.

Mostly she just watched—the tapes or what the other kids were doing; which kept Florian and Catlin out of it.

"You have a message," the Minder said over the tape soundtrack and the music.

"Oh, hell." She got up again, shrugged the blouse back together and walked up the steps barefooted, down the hall rug and into her office as steadily as she could.

"Base One," she said, when she had the door shut and proof against the noise outside in the den. "Message."

"Message from Denys Nye: Khalid won election. Meet with me tomorrow first thing in my office."

Oh, shit.

She leaned against the back of the chair.

"Message for Denys Nye," she said. "I'll be there."

The Minder took it. "Log-off," she said, and walked back outside and into her party.

"What was it?" Catlin asked.

"Tell you later," she said, and settled down again, leaning back in Florian's lap.

She showed up in Denys' office, 0900 sharp, no frills and no nonsense, took a cup of Denys' coffee, with cream, no sugar, and listened to Denys tell her what she had already figured out, with the Silencer jarring the roots of her teeth.

"Khalid is assuming office this afternoon," Denys said. "Naturally—since he's Cyteen based, there's no such thing as a grace period. He moves in with all his baggage. And his secret files."

Uncle Denys had already explained to her—what Khalid was. What the situation could be.

"Don't you think I'd better have vid access?" she asked. "Uncle Denys, I don't care *what* you think I'm not ready to find out. Ignorant is no help at all, is it?"

Uncle Denys rested his chins on his hand and looked at her a long time as if he was considering that. "Eventually. Eventually you'll have to. You're going to get a current events condensation, daily, the same as I get. You'd better keep up with it. It looks very much as if we're going to get a challenge before this session is out. They'll probably release some things on your predecessor—as damaging as they can find. This is going to be dirty politics, Ari. Real dirty. I want you to start studying up on things. Additionally—I want you to be damned careful. I know you've been doing a lot of—" He gave a little cough. "—entertaining. Of kids none of whom is over fifteen, at hours that tell me you're *not* playing Starchase. Housekeeping says my suspicions are—" Another clearing of the throat. "—probably well-founded."

"God. You're stooping, uncle Denys."

"Security investigates all sources. And my clearance still outranks yours. But let's not quibble. That's not my point. My point is—*ordinary* fourteen- and fifteen-year-olds don't have your—independence, your maturity, or your budget; and Novgorod in particular isn't going to understand your—mmmn, parties, your language—in short, we're all being very circumspect. You know that word?"

"I'm up on *circumspect*, uncle Denys, right along with *security risk*. I don't have any. If their mothers know, they're not going to object, because they want their offspring to have careers when *I'm* running Reseune. There are probably a lot of mothers who'd like to shove their kids right *into* my apartment. And my bed."

"God. *Don't* say that in Novgorod."

"Am I going?"

"Not right now. Not anytime soon. Khalid is just in. Let him make a move."

"Oh, that's a *wonderful* idea."

"Don't get smart, sera. Let him draw the line, I say. While you, young sera, do some catch-up studying. You'd better learn what an average fourteen-year-old is like."

"I know. I know real well. I might know better, if my friends hadn't Disappeared to Fargone, mightn't I?"

"Don't do this for the cameras. You think you're playing a game. I'm telling you you can really lose everything. I've explained nationalization—"

"I do fine with big words."

"Let's see how you do with little ones. You're not sweet little Ari for the cameras anymore, you're more and more like the Ari certain people remember—enough to make it a lot more likely you'll get harder and harder questions, and you don't know where the mines are, young sera. We're going to stall this as long as we can, and if we can get you another year, it's very likely you'll have to apply for your majority status. That's the point at which some interest will get an injunction to stop the Science Bureau granting it; and you'll be in court again . . . with a good chance of winning it: the first Ari did at sixteen. But that *won't* solve the problem, it'll only put the opposition in a bad light, taking on a fifteen-year-old who *has* to handle herself with more finesse than you presently have, young sera."

"I learn."

"You'd better. Age is catching up with us. Your predecessor's friend Catherine Lao, who's helped you more than you know—is a hundred thirty-eight. Giraud is pushing a hundred thirty. Your presence—your *resemblance* to your predecessor—is like a shot of adrenaline where certain Councillors are concerned, but you have to have more than presence this time. If you make a mistake—you can see Reseune sucked up by the national government, and Defense declaring it a military zone, right fast. They'll have a pretext before the ink is dry. You'll spend your days working on whatever they tell you to do. Or you'll find yourself in some little enclave with no access to Novgorod, no access to Council or the Science Bureau."

She looked at Denys straight on, thinking: *You haven't done that well. Or how else are we in this mess?*

But she didn't say it. She said: "Base One only lets me go so fast, uncle Denys."

"Let me try you on another big word," Denys said. "Psychogenesis."

That *was* a new one. "Mind-originate," she said, remembering her Greek roots.

"Mind-origination. Mind-cloning. Now do you understand me?"

She felt cold inside. "What has that got to do with anything?"

"The resemblance between you and Ari. Let me give you a few more words to try on your Base. Bok. Endocrinology. Gehenna. Worm."

"What are you talking about? *What do you mean, the resemblance—*"

The sound-shielding hurt her teeth.

"Don't shout," Denys said. "You'll deafen us. I mean just what I've always told you. You *are* Ari. Let me tell you something else. Ari didn't die of natural causes. She was murdered."

She took in a breath. "By who?"

"Whom, dear."

"Dammit, uncle Denys—"

"*Watch* your language. You'd better clean it up. Ari was killed by someone no longer at Reseune."

"She died *here?*"

"That's all I'm going to tell you. The rest is your problem."

2420: 10/3: 2348

AE2: Minder, this is Ari Emory. I'm alone. Give me references on psychogenesis.

B/1: Stand by. Retrieving.

Ari, this is Ari senior. Stand by.

The program finds you are 14 chronological years, with accesses for 16 years. This program finds you an average of 10 points below my scores overall.

Your psych scores are 5 points off my scores.

Your Rezner score has not been updated since age 10.

You are 5 points off qualification for access.

AE2: Base One: can my accesses reach data on Bok: keyword, clone?

B/1: Stand by. Retrieving.

Accesses inadequate.

AE2: Try endocrinology: keyword, psychogenesis. Gehenna: keyword, project. Worm: keyword, psych.

B/1: Accesses inadequate.

2420: 11/1: 1876:02

AE2: Minder, this is Ari Emory. I'm alone. Reference: psychogenesis.

B/1: Stand by. Retrieving.

Ari, this is Ari senior. Stand by.

The program finds you are 14 chronological years, with accesses for 16 years. This program finds you an average of 7 points below my scores overall.

Your psych scores are 1 point above my scores.

Your Rezner score has not been updated since age 10.

You are qualified to access files. Stand by.

Ari, this is Ari senior. These files can be read only from Base One Main Terminal. All relevant and resultant files are being stored in your personal archive under voice-lock.

You have used a keyword. You now have access to my working notes. I apologize in advance for their sketchy quality. They're quite fine when I was younger, but disregard a lot of the things dated pre-2312: they're useful if you want to see the evolution of thought: psychogenesis was something I was working on as early as 2304, but I didn't have the key studies in endocrinology until I had studied a good deal more; you can benefit from my study notes in those years, but I wasn't on the right track until 2312, and I didn't get the funds I needed until 2331. I benefited a great deal by Poley's work in that same decade: we disagreed, but it was an academic, not a personal difference. We exchanged considerable correspondence, also in the archives. By the year 2354, at the close of the Company Wars, my notes are much less coherent and a great deal more meaningful.

That you have accessed these notes means something has worked.

You have matched my ability. I hope to hell you have a sense of morality.

Your Base can now access all working notes. Good luck.

AE2: Base One: can my accesses reach data on Bok: keyword, cloning?

B/1: Stand by. Retrieving.

AE2: Try endocrinology: keyword, psychogenesis. Gehenna: keyword, project. Worm: keyword, psych.

B/1: Stand by. Retrieving.

B/1: The Bok clone failed because it was assumed genetics and training would create a genius. It was more than a scientific failure; it was a human tragedy. The project files are now available to your Base . . .

B/1: Endocrinology is a multitude of files. They are now available to your Base.

B/1: Gehenna is the name of a G5 star. Newport colony at Gehenna was a project I handled for Defense. This program is searching House Archives for outcome.

There is presently human life on the planet.

They have survived there for 65 years.

This indicates *some* chance it is a viable colony.

This was a Defense Bureau operation which I elected to undertake for reasons my notes will make clear to you. It was also, unknown to Defense, but within the parameters of their mission requirements, an experiment.

I designed a very simple program. The operational sentence was: You were sent from space to build a new world: discover its rules, live as long as you can, and teach your children all the things that seem important.

No further tape was sent. This was by design.

Integrating any individual of this population into mainstream cultures poses extreme risks. Examine the environment as well as the program. That was the aspect I could not adequately examine. Consult all files and understand what I have done before attempting any intervention.

Quarantine should be extended until results can be projected through 30 generations.

All relevant files are now available to your Base.

B/1: A worm is a deep-set-linked program which has the capacity to manifest itself in subsequent generations of a population without changing its character.

CHAPTER
11

---------- i ----------

The lenses crowded close on each other, a solid phalanx of cameras bristling with directional mikes like ancient spears. Behind that, the army of reporters with their Scribers and their individual and zealously securitied com-links.

Behind her, Florian and Catlin, and a miscellaneous assortment of what might be uncle Giraud's aides and staff; but eight of them were Reseune Security, and armed, under the expensive tailoring.

She had chosen a blue suit, recollecting the public image of the little girl with the cast, the little girl who had lost her mother and caught the sympathy of people the length and breadth of Union. She had thought about sweeping her hair up into Ari senior's trademark chignon; but she only parted it in the middle, the way it wanted to fall anyway, and swept it up on the sides and let it fall behind, with combs sprigged with tiny white quartz flowers to hold it. A minimum of makeup . . . just enough for the cameras: her face had lengthened, acquired cheekbones; acquired a maturity that she had consciously to lighten with a little smile at favorite reporters, a little deliberate flicker of recognition as her eyes found them—an intimation of special fondness.

So they might hold back some of the worst questions. People liked to have special importance, and those she favored were the ones who favored her; and old Yevi Hart, who had a hard-nosed reputation and who, in the year after she lost her mother, had turned halfway nice. She had been Working on him for years, a little special look, a little disappointment when he would ask the rough questions. This time she looked at him with a secret between-them

456

glance, knowing he had the first question. *All right, Yevi, go, we both know you're just doing a job: you're still an old dear.*

He looked at her and seemed to lose the thread of his question a split second. His dour face looked worried. He took another breath, wadded up his question-slip and shoved his hand in his coat pocket. "Young sera, —"

"I'm still Ari, Yevi." A tilt of her head, a little sad smile. "I'm sorry. Go on."

Third breath. "Ari, you're applying for majority. The Centrists are suing the Science Bureau to prevent the grant. How do you answer their charge that you've been deep-taught and primed to perform by Reseune staff, that you were created specifically as a legal device to give Reseune and your relatives control of Emory's property?"

She outright laughed. She *was* amused. "One: I've never had deep-tape at all; I learn like any CIT. Two: if—"

"Follow-up."

"Let me get just through these things, Yevi, and then the follow-up. Can I?"

A grim nod.

"Two," she said, holding up fingers, and smiled. "I think they must have meant I was primed for the specific answers to reporters' questions, because if we had tape that could teach me my courses just like that, it would be wonderful—we could sell it all over Union and that would give my relatives a *lot* of money; but the Centrists have to know that's not so, so they must mean primed for the questions, and that means you're letting Reseune see the questions at least a day in advance. That's not the case, is it?"

"Absolutely not." Yevi looked a little cornered. "But if—"

"Three." Another finger. A chorus of blurted questions. "Just a second, I don't want to skip a question. Ser Corain says my relatives created me as a puppet to let them control my predecessor's estate; they say I shouldn't have my majority because it's just a trick to maintain a cover-up about Emory's involvement in Gehenna. That's really two questions. A, if I get my majority I own the rights, my relatives don't, and that means they actually *lose* their control of them, legally; they will go on advising me, but any businessperson gets advice in technical things like investments and research, and that doesn't mean the advisers own him. There's more than my relatives at Reseune—there are thousands and thousands of people I need to listen to—the way my predecessor did even when she was sitting in Council. B, —"

"Ari, —"

"Just let me get the other part of the question. Then the follow-up. I want to do all of them. B, that getting me my majority is a trick to cover Emory's involvement in Gehenna. *I* have access to the Gehenna notes, and I'm perfectly willing to testify to the Council as soon as I *have* my majority. Until then I'm a minor and I can't. So it seems to me that the Centrists' suit is covering up things, because if they really want to know what I know, why are they trying to keep me from being able to go under oath? Those files are under my voice-lock, and not even computer techs could get them out without messing things up and maybe losing real important pieces of it, just gone, for good. Not even my relatives have read the Gehenna files. I'm the only one who has them, and ser Corain is filing suit to keep me from being able to testify."

The reporters all started yelling. She pointed at Yevi. "Yevi still has his follow-up."

Yevi said: "What would be the reason?" Which was not his original follow-up, and some of the other reporters objected.

"I wish I could ask ser Corain," she said. "Maybe there's something in there."

"Follow-up."

"Yevi, I *have* to get to this m'sera, she's been waiting."

"What keeps your uncles from reading the files?"

Ouch. Good question. "Me. I have a special program my predecessor left for me. My voice is a lot like hers, and my geneset *is* hers, so when I was old enough to identify myself to the computer, it opened up these areas; but it's got a lot of security arrangements, and it won't let me access if there's anybody else going to hear; and it can tell."

"*Follow-up!*" the woman yelled over the shouting. "Can't *you* record it with a tape or something?"

Another good question. Remember this woman and be careful. "I could if I was going to allow it, but I'm not going to. My predecessor went to a lot of trouble about security and she warned me right in the program that I had to take that very seriously, even about people I might trust. I did, even if I didn't understand, and nobody at Reseune tried to get me to tell what was there either. Now I think it was a good idea, because it seems to be something real important, and I think the Council ought to be the ones to decide who gets to hear it, not any fifteen-year-old kid and not just any one part of the government either, because there's too much fighting going on about it and I don't know how to decide who to tell. The Council is supposed to decide things like that. That's the way I understand it. —Ser Ibanez."

"Can you tell us if there's anything in the files that you think would damage the reputation of your predecessor?"

"I can tell you this, because if anything happened to me it's terribly important people should know it: Gehenna has to stay quarantined. My predecessor was under Defense Bureau orders, but it scared her; and that was why she left things sealed for me. —Ser Hannah."

Chaos broke out. Everyone was shouting.

"Wasn't that irresponsible of your predecessor—if it was that important? Why did she keep it secret?"

"It was a Defense secret and it *was* quarantined. She *did* tell some people. But a lot of them are dead, and some of them probably don't understand what she did. *I* don't know it all yet. That's the bad thing: you have to be as smart as she was before you can work with the problem. She's dead and nobody else understands what she understood. That's why they made me. I'm *not* a Bok-clone situation. I *am* a Special, and someday I'm going to be able to understand what happened there. Right now nobody does. But she did leave instructions, and I'm not giving them to anybody until Council asks me under oath, because I'm not going to muddy up the waters by talking until I *can* swear to what I'm saying and the whole universe knows I'm an adult and I'm not lying. If I did it any other way, people could question whether I was telling the truth or whether I knew what I was doing."

They shouted and pushed and shoved each other. She felt Florian and Catlin move up on either side, anxious.

But she Had them. She was sure of it. She had gotten out exactly what she wanted to say.

---

ii

"Release the damn broadcast!" Corain yelled into the securitied phone, at Khalid's chief of staff, who swore Khalid was not available. "God! I don't care if he's in *hell*, get hold of him and get that release, you damn fool, it's gotten to my office, and thirty-five top reporters sent it downline—what do you mean security hold?"

"This is Khalid," the Councillor cut in, displacing the aide. "Councillor Corain, in light of the content of the interview we've requested a security delay of thirty minutes for the child's own protection. We seem to have a major problem."

"We *have* a major problem. The longer that hold stays on, the more that *hold* is going to become news, Councillor, and the longer it stays, the more they're going to ask why. We *can't* stop that broadcast."

"Assuredly we can't. There were too many news-feeds. I told you not to allow the interview. A minor child is making irresponsible charges on extremely sensitive matters, with international implications. I suggest we answer this with a categorical denial."

"It would have been foolhardy *not* to allow it. You can't keep the news-services away from the kid, and you saw what she can do with innuendo."

"She's obviously well-instructed."

"Instructed, *hell*, Khalid. *Take that damned hold off!*"

There was long silence on the other end. "The hold will go off in fifteen minutes. I strongly suggest you use the time to prepare an official statement."

"On *what*? We have nothing to do with these charges."

Again a silence. "Neither have we, Councillor. I think this will require investigation."

It was a securitied line. *Any* communication could be penetrated if one could get access to the installers; or to the other end of the transmission.

"I think it will, Admiral. There will be a Centrist caucus in one hour. I hope you will be prepared to explain your position."

"It's completely without substantiation," Khalid said to the cameras, on the office vid, while Corain rested his chin on his hand, glancing between the image on the screen and the news-feed that an aide slipped under his view: *NP: DEFENSE BUREAU SPOKESMAN DECLINES COMMENT ON ACTION* and *CP: KHALID CALLS CHARGES FABRICATION.*

". . . nothing in those files to substantiate any continued quarantine order. It's exactly what I say: Giraud Nye has come up with a piece of fiction, an absolute piece of fiction, and tape-fed it to a minor child who is in no wise fit or competent to understand the potential international repercussions. This is a reprehensible tactic which seeks to use the free press to its own advantage—utterly, utterly fabricated. I ask you, consider whether we will *ever* see documentation of the child's representations—files which a fifteen-year-old girl *maintains* she alone has seen, which she cannot—I say *cannot* produce—unless others produce these putative files *for* her—files which an impressionable fifteen-year-old child maintains were left for her by her predecessor. I will tell you, seri, I have grave suspicions that no such secret files *ever* were made by Ariane Emory, that no such *program* was ever created by Ariane Emory to give ghostly guidance to her successor. I suspect that any such *program* was written much closer to hand, that the child has been *programmed*, indeed, programmed—a process in which Reseune is absolutely expert, and in which Councillor Nye himself is an acknowledged authority—in fact a Special who gained his status as a result of his expertise in that very field. The child is a pawn created by Reseune to place legal and emotional obstacles in the way of matters of paramount national interest, and callously used and manipulated to maintain the privilege of a moneyed few whose machiavellian tactics now bid fair to jeopardize the peace. . . ."

Reporters were waiting at the hotel. "Are you aware," someone shouted, "of Khalid's accusations, Councillor Nye?"

"We heard them on the way over," uncle Giraud said, while Security maintained them a little clear space in the foyer, while cameramen jostled each other.

"*I* have an answer," Ari said, ignoring Florian's arm as he tried, with other Security, to get her and uncle Giraud on through the doors. "I *want* to answer him, can we set up in a conference room?"

". . . Thank you," the girl said, made a very young-girl move with both hands getting her hair back behind her shoulders, and then grimaced and shaded her eyes as a light hit her face. "Ow. Could you shine that down? Please?" Then she leaned forward with her arms on the conference table, suddenly businesslike and so like Emory senior that Corain's gut tightened. "What's your question?"

"What do you think about Khalid's allegations?" some reporter yelled out over the others.

Chaos. Absolute chaos. The light swung back into the girl's face and she winced. "Cut it off," someone yelled, "we don't need it."

"Thanks." As the light went off. "You want me to tell what I think about what the admiral says? I think he knows better. He used to be head of Intelligence. He sure *ought* to. It's not real smart either, to say I'm programmed. I can write psych designs. *He's* trying to run a psych on everybody, and I can tell you where, do you want me to count it off for you?"

"Go ahead," voices yelled out.

The girl held up one finger. "One: he says there's nothing in the files about a quarantine. He says he doesn't *know* what's in the files in Reseune: that's what he's complaining about. Whichever way it is, he's either trying to trick you or he's lying about what's in the files.

"Two: he says my uncle tape-fed me the stuff. He doesn't know any such thing. And in fact it's not true.

"Three: he says I don't understand what it could mean in international politics. Unless he knows what's in those files, he doesn't know as much as I do what it could mean.

"Four: he makes fun of the idea my predecessor left a program for me. That's a psych. Funny stuff breaks your concentration and makes you not think real hard about what he's really saying, which is that it's impossible. It's *certainly* possible. It's a simple branching program with a voice-recognition and a few other security things I don't want to talk about on vid, and I could write it, except for the scrambling, and that's something my own security understands—he's fifteen too. I'm sure Councillor Khalid does, if he was in Intelligence, so it's a pure psych.

"Five: he says my uncles write all the stuff. That's a psych like the first one, because he can just say that and then everybody wonders. I can give you one just exactly like it if I said Khalid won the election because he made up the rumor Gorodin was against the military retirement bill, and because of the way news goes out to the ships in space, and it being right before the vote, the vote was already coming back and being registered by the time Gorodin's saying it wasn't true even got to a lot of places. I heard that on the news. But I guess people forget who it is that makes up lies."

"Oh, my God. . . ." Corain murmured, and rested his head against his hands.

"I think that's done it," Dellarosa said. "I'd advise, ser, we hold a caucus *without* Defense. I think we need to draw up a position on this."

Corain raked his hand through his hair.

"Dammit, he can't even sue her for libel. She's a minor. And that went out live."

"I think the facts are, ser, the military may have had real practical reasons for preferring Khalid in spite of the rumor. But I think he's taken major damage. *Major* damage. I wouldn't be surprised if we don't see a challenge from Gorodin. We need to distance ourselves from this. We need a position statement on these supposed secret files. We need it while this broadside barrage is still going on."

"We need—" Corain said, "we *need* to call for a Science Bureau select committee to look into this, *past* Giraud Nye, to rule on the girl's competency. But, dammit, you *saw* that performance. The girl *got* Khalid, extemp. He played a dirty little in-Bureau game he'd have gotten away with because no one could pin it on him *or* his staff—but no one's going to forget it in *that* context."

"Nye told her."

"Don't make that mistake. Khalid just did. And he's dead. Politically, he's dead. He can't counter this one."

"She could charge anyone with being in those damn files!"

"She could have charged Khalid. But she didn't. Which probably means they exist and she's going to produce them. Or she's keeping her story clean . . . that she's waiting on Council. I'll tell you the other problem, friend. Khalid's going to be a liability in that office."

"Khalid's got to resign."

"He won't! Not that one. He'll fight to the bloody end."

"Then I suggest, ser, before we even consider Gorodin, who's stuck with the two-year rule, we explore who else might be viable for us inside that Bureau. How long do you think this is going to go? One bit of garbage floats to the surface—and other people start talking to the press. One more—and it becomes a race to the cameras."

"Dammit."

He had insisted Khalid take the hold off the news releases.

And there was no practical way to answer the charges, except to stall with the Bureau hearings. Which Nye could rush through at lightning speed. More exposure of the girl to the news-services.

No way. Withdraw opposition.

Then the girl got herself a full Council hearing.

And the repercussions of revelations on Gehenna went to the ambassadors from Alliance and from Earth.

The girl was *not* bluffing.

"One thing," he said as Dellarosa was leaving, "one thing she absolutely beat him on. *Find* somebody in Defense who makes speeches people can *understand*, for God's sake."

iii

Justin watched and watched, every nuance, every shift in the replay. He had missed the whole afternoon, buried in the sociology lab; and he watched it now, once and twice, because the keyword response in the vid recorder had gotten all the references to the hearings, to Ari, to all the principals.

He shook his head, hands under chin, elbows on knees.

"Remarkably accurate retention," Grant said, beside him on the couch. "For a CIT. She hit every point she wanted to make, certainly. And confused them about the rest."

The tape reached Khalid's second refutation, the cold, passionless statement that Ari had been prompted with that accusation by Giraud Nye, that Giraud used her as his voice because it was otherwise actionable.

Justin shook his head again. "He may have given it to her. But the kid's sense of timing is impeccable."

"Khalid mistook his opponent," Grant said. "He thought that it was Giraud all along."

"Vid off," Justin said, and there was silence in the room.

Grant reached across and shook at his knee. "Do you think Khalid—is capable of harming her?"

"I think that man is *capable* of anything. I don't know. He won't move on—won't move on *her*. She's too hard a target. I'm going to call Denys."

"*Why?*"

"CIT craziness. Politics. She's too hard a target. *Jordan* works for Defense."

Grant's face went expressionless. Then showed shock.

"I don't think we should put that through the Minder. We should *go* to him."

"How in hell do we get an interview with Denys at this hour? There's no way he'll open the door to us."

"Security," Grant said after a moment. "We ask him to meet us in Security."

"I appreciate your concern," Denys said, the other side of the desk from them, themselves in two hard chairs, Seely standing by the wall, in the interview room.

Justin remembered the place—too well. "Ser, I—don't call it an irrational fear. Order him not to answer any calls from the base."

"We don't need any moves against Defense on record," Denys said. "That in itself—could call unwelcome attention to your father. Possibly you're being alarmist . . ."

"Khalid has reason to want an incident, ser. And my father is sitting there without protection. They can *tell* him damned well anything. Can't they?"

Denys frowned, thick fingers steepled, then interlocking. "Seely. Move on it. Now."

"Yes," Seely said, and left.

Grant rose from his chair, following Seely with his eyes. *Then* the thought came; and Justin stood up, suddenly facing two armed guards in the doorway.

"What is he going to do?" Justin asked, looking at Denys. "That wasn't an instruction. *What is he going to do?*"

"Relax," Denys said. "Relax, son. Sit down. Both of you. There are contingency plans. You're not the first one to think of these eventualities. Seely understands my meanings perfectly well."

"*What contingencies?*"

"Dear God, we certainly don't intend any harm to your father. Sit down. Please. You have a very active imagination tonight."

"What is he going to do?"

"He's simply going to go to the front desk and they'll transmit a code, which you don't need to know, which simply advises Planys lab to go on extreme alert. That means Reseune Security trusts no one who is not Reseune Security. And no one comes in or goes out who's *not* Reseune Security. We simply claim a laboratory incident. Very simple. Since Jordan has the highest-level Security flag at Planys—rest assured, he's not available to any calls, except from us. Sit down."

Justin sat, and Grant did.

"There," Denys sighed. "Thank you. I appreciate your level of paranoia, Justin. It's finely honed, God knows. I never undervalue a good set of nerves. Storm-sense. Seely—never needs the weather warnings. Isn't that an odd thing—in a mind so rational? —What did you think of her?"

Off the flank and unforeseen. Justin blinked, instantly wary—and that in itself was a reaction he did not want. "Of Ari? Ari was brilliant. What else could she be?"

"I have a little pride invested in her," Denys said. "You know she brought up her psych scores six points in less than a month, when the rascal got the notion she had to. I told the committee exactly that. And they wouldn't believe she was laying back. Forgive me. I'm also extremely nervous until we get her back here safe, inside *our* perimeters."

"So am I. Honestly."

"I believe that. I truly do. I must tell you—our concern with your father has been in an entirely different context during this trip. I told you I would tell you—when Ari became aware of her predecessor's—death."

"You've told her, then."

Denys bit his lip and studied his hands. "Not all of it. Not yet." He looked up. "On the other hand—I sweated through that first interview. At one point I was sure Ari was going to say—in response to *why* the first Ari didn't make better provision for passing on the information—that Ari was murdered. And then the reporter would have keyed right onto the relationship of the murder to that information—no valid connection, of course. But I felt for a split second that was exactly where it was going—and then Ari changed course. Thank God. I really don't want her to hear the words 'the Warrick case' for the first time—in front of the cameras. Or in the hearings. She's flying home tonight. Totally unscheduled departure, Science Bureau chase planes with full radar coverage. You see we're likewise very paranoid. Giraud is, I think, going to break the news to her on the way. So I've warned you."

---

iv

"Ari," Giraud said, settling into the seat Florian had vacated for him, across from her, while *RESEUNE ONE* flew through the dark and there was nothing but stars out the windows—stars and the running lights of the planes Giraud said were flying with them.

Because they had to worry about electronic interference and all sorts of things that even Florian and Catlin frowned over. Because they had challenged a very dangerous, very desperate man who had all kinds of contacts, and because the world had crazy people in it who might try something and try to blame it on Defense.

She would be very glad, she thought, when she felt them touch down at Reseune. Enemies didn't much bother her, except the kind who might aim another plane at you or take out your navigation or who might be Defense trying to blame it on extremists or extremists trying to blame it on Defense.

"We're doing fine," uncle Giraud said. "Radar's perfectly clear. Our escort is enough to keep them honest. I imagine you're anxious for your own bed tonight."

Oh, damn, we've got the Minder checkout to go through when we get back to the apartment, and Florian and Catlin are tired as I am. I just want to go to bed. And I can't sleep.

"I did worry today," Giraud said, "about one thing I was afraid they were going to throw at you. That—we really haven't wanted to go into. But I think—and Denys thinks—I've talked with him on the Bureau system—that you need to know."

God, get to it!

"You know your predecessor was murdered. And that it was somebody in Reseune."

"Who?"

"A man named Jordan Warrick."

She blinked and felt the sting of exhaustion in her eyes. There was only one Warrick at Reseune *she* had ever met. "Who's Jordan Warrick?"

"A Special. The absolute authority in educational design. Justin Warrick's father."

She rubbed her eyes and slid up a little in her seat, looking at Giraud.

"I didn't want you to find that out in front of the cameras. I certainly don't want you to find it out from Council next week. Jordan and Ari had personal and professional difficulties; and political ones. He accused Ari of tampering with his work and taking credit from him—as he saw it. They quarreled— Do you want to hear this in detail?"

She nodded.

"Most likely, and he claims this was the case, it wasn't premeditated. They fought—a physical fight—and she hit her head—at which point he panicked and tried to cover up what had happened. It happened in the cold lab down in Wing One basement. The section is very old, the cryogenics conduits are completely uncovered; he created a break, blew the line, shut the door—it *still* swings, it has to do with the way the building settled, and the door is unfixable; but we've disabled the lock. In short, Ari froze to death in a release of liquid nitrogen from a pipe rupture. It was relatively painless; she was unconscious from the blow. Jordan Warrick—being a Special—had a Council hearing. It was an absolutely unprecedented case—Specials don't commit murder. And his mind—whatever his faults—is protected by law. He did agree to accept a transfer out of Reseune. He lives at Planys. Justin does visit him now and again."

"Did he know about it?"

"Justin didn't have any idea what was going to happen. He was only seventeen. He'd attempted—using resources of his father's—to smuggle Grant out of Reseune and into Novgorod—Jordan wanted to get the directorate at RESEUNESPACE, and Grant's status as an X-number meant it might have been hard to get him to go with them. But it went wrong, the contacts Justin used—friends of his father—happened to have ties to the Abolitionists, who attempted a very misguided intervention with Grant. I've always entertained a private suspicion that Grant figured in the argument Jordan had with Ari. Grant had to be rescued; he was in hospital that night, in very precarious shape—and Justin was visiting him about the time the murder happened, so there's no question about Justin's whereabouts. He had no idea his father was going to see Ari. He certainly had no notion what his father would do."

She felt a little sick at her stomach. "He's my *friend*."

"He was seventeen when all this happened. Just two years older than you are. None of it was his fault. He lives at Reseune—his father lives at Planys under a kind of perpetual arrest. You understand, I think, why we've been very anxious about your contacts with him. But he's never initiated them; he's been very careful to follow the rules that let him live at Reseune. He was able to finish his education; he's made a home at Reseune, he causes no one any trouble, and it didn't seem fair to punish him for something which absolutely was none of his doing, or to send him where he wouldn't have the facilities to pursue his work. He's very bright. He's a very troubled man, a very confused one, sometimes, but I hope he'll work out his own answers. Most of all we've worried about the chance he would do something or say something to hurt you—but he never has. Has he?"

"No." *Remember the source*, Ari senior would say, *had* said, advising her how to deal with deceptions. *Remember the source*. "Why didn't he go to Fargone? Valery did. Valery was only four years old and he never hurt anybody."

"Frankly we wanted Justin where we could see him," Giraud said, going right past the matter of Valery. Of course. "And we didn't want him in prolonged contact with any ship crew or within reach of outside communications. His father's friends—are Rocher and that crowd, the Abolitionists—who are one of the reasons we have that escort flying off our wings."

"I understand." She needed to think about it for a while. She had no desire to talk about it with uncle Giraud, not right now.

"We knew it would upset you," Giraud said, trying for a reaction out of her.

She looked at him and let the situation flow right through her, bland as could be, the night, the planes outside, the news about Justin, Giraud's evading the Valery question. So they could get blown up. So the whole world was crazy. But she had figured it was dangerous when she made up her mind she was going to mention the Gehenna things—when she had warned uncle

Denys and uncle Giraud what she was going to do, and they had been nervous about it. But one thing about Giraud—once things went inertial he had a cool head and he came across with the right things at the right time: if she had to pick somebody to be with her in Novgorod she figured Giraud was one of the best. And what he was saying had to be true: it was too easy to check out.

She sighed. "It does upset me," she said, "but I'm glad I know. I need to think about it, uncle Giraud."

He looked at her a moment, then fished in his pocket, and pulled out a little packet, reached and laid it on her side of the table.

"What's that?"

Giraud shrugged. "No shopping this trip," he said. "But I did remember this little thing in a certain shop. I had Security pick it up. They hadn't sold it."

She was bewildered. She picked it up, unwrapped the paper and opened the box. There was a pin with topazes of every shade, set in gold. "Oh," she said. "Oh!"

"So much jewelry came with Ari's estate," Giraud said, and got up to go back to his own seat at the back. "I thought you should have something that was only yours."

"*Thank* you, uncle Giraud." She was entirely off her balance.

And more so when she looked up at him. The way the light came down on him from the overhead in that second made his skin look papery and old; he walked by and put his hand on her arm and his hand showed deep creases. Old. Of course he was.

Something that was only yours. That rattled around in her head and found such a central place to light that she turned the thought over as often as she did the pin, turning all the facets to the light—whether Giraud had just Worked her or whether it was just that her uncle had this thing about young girls or maybe—maybe a single soft spot that had started back when she was little had just grown along with her, until he finally really had thoughts like that. After all the rotten things he had done.

He had Got her good, that was sure.

One thing that was truly hers. So very few things were.

"What is it, sera?" Florian asked, and: "It's pretty," he said.

"Nice," Catlin said, coming to take the seat beside her, and reached out a hand to touch it.

Of course they were hers. Ari and Ari blurred together and came separate and blurred together again, with very little discomfort nowadays. Ari senior had collected real trouble in her lifetime, but that was all right, she didn't like Ari's Enemies either. They had murdered Ari and now she had Security with her everywhere and planes flying beside just to be sure she got home, to Ari's bed and Ari's comforts and Ari's Rescue, in all—

She didn't mind being Ari, she decided. It was not a bad thing to be. It was a little strange. It was a little lonely a lot of the time, but that was all right, there were enough people to keep it from being *too* lonely. There was a lot to keep up with, but it was never boring. She would not be Maddy or 'Stasi, or even Amy—Amy, closest, maybe, but she had rather be Ari, all the same, and travel to Novgorod and have Catlin and Florian with her—not forgetting that: Amy had no company. Just her maman and her maman's staff, who were no fun.

Being Jane would have been all right. She thought about Ollie, suddenly, hurt because he never wrote; but Ollie wouldn't, Ollie was so correct when he had to be.

He might not even be alive anymore. People could die at Fargone and it took so long to find it out.

She put the pin back in the box. "Put that in my carry, will you?" she said to Florian. "I don't want anything to happen to it." When there was a chance she would wear it where Giraud could see it. He would like that.

"Are you tired, sera?" Catlin asked. "Do you want us to put out the lights?"

"No. I'm fine." But she felt after the lap robe, and tucked it up around her, listening to the drone of the engines.

She could write to Fargone. But it was not wise right now. Anything she did would make her Enemies nervous and maybe put other people in danger, like hanging a sign out over them saying: This is a friend of mine.

Her friends didn't have Security to protect them, if they came outside Reseune and Reseune's other holdings. She had to think about things like that now.

From now on.

V

Ari, this is Ari senior.

You've gained your majority. You are 15 chronological years. This program deals with you as 17. Your accesses have widened.

You may now access all working notes to the year of my death and all history up to 2362, which is the year I resigned as Reseune Administrator to take up the Council Seat for Science.

When I was 17, in 2300, Union declared itself a nation and the Company Wars began.

When I was 35, in 2318, I sat as Proxy Councillor for Science during the illness of Lila Goldstein, of Cyteen Station, who subsequently died.

When I was 37, in 2320, I yielded the seat to Jurgen Fielding, of Cyteen. The Special Status bill passed and I was one of 5 persons accorded that privilege.

When I was 48, in 2331, I became Director of Wing One at Reseune, on the death of Amelie Strassen; I went on rejuv in that year.

When I was 62, in 2345, I became Administrator of Reseune, on the death of my uncle Geoffrey Carnath. The Company Fleet in those years had succeeded in interdicting Union warships from all stations Earthward of Mariner, and attempted to blockade merchanters from dealing with Cyteen and Fargone and to destroy any merchanter registered to Cyteen. Heavy losses of ships and the need for workers and trained military personnel had brought Reseune into the war effort: from the years 2340 to 2354, Reseune increased in size over 400%.

Actions which I took during those years: franchising of production centers; automation of many processes; building of mills to relieve dependency on scarce transport; expansion of agriculture; establishment of Moreyville as a shipping center; establishment of RESEUNEAIR as a commercial carrier for the Volga area; establishment of Reseune's legal rights over franchised production centers; establishment of Reseune as legal guardian of all azi, no matter where produced; establishment of Reseune as sole producer of all tape above skill-level.

I consider the latter measures, which make it possible for Reseune to guide and oversee all azi throughout Union, to be among the most important things I have ever done—for the obvious reasons of the power it conveys, for moral reasons of the azi's welfare, and for two reasons less apparent . . . 1. that it gives us the leverage to terminate the production of azi at some future date, to prevent the establishment of a permanent institution of servitude in Union or elsewhere; 2. See file under keyword: Sociogenesis.

When I was 69, in 2352, Union launched its last major offensive of the war; and came to me with the outline of the Gehenna project.

See file under keyword: Gehenna, keyword: private file.

When I was 71, in 2354, the Company Wars ended with the Treaty of Pell.

When I was 72, in 2355, the Gehenna Colony was dispatched, as a contingency measure. My advice to the contrary was overruled by Adm. Azov, Councillor of Defense.

When I was 77, in 2360, I challenged Jurgen Fielding for the Science seat.

When I was 79, in 2362, final vote tabulations gave me the seat, which I hold at the time I am writing these notes.

It's one thing, young Ari, to study older people as a fact in psychology; it's quite another thing to be aware of the psychology of old age in yourself—because you do get old inside, even if rejuv holds your physical age more or less constant.

The difference rejuv has made in human psychology is a very profound difference: consider . . . without rejuv, the body begins to change by age 50 and specific deteriorations begin and grow acute enough within the next 20 to 30 years to cause disability. That is the natural aging process, which would lead to natural death between the ages of 60 and 110 at the outside, varying according to genetics and environment.

In individuals without rejuv, the 20-to-30-year period of decline in functions, followed by a period of diminished function and degenerative disease, works a considerable psychological change. In eras when no rejuv was possible, or in places such as Gehenna, where no rejuv is available, there are sociological accommodations to having a large portion of the population undergoing this slow diminution of physical and in a few cases mental capacity. There may be institutions and customs which provide support to this segment of the population, although, historically, such provisions were not always optimum or satisfactory to the individual faced with the psychological certainty that the process had begun. With rejuv, we contemplate natural death at, considering mere percentages, a little greater lifespan, ranging in my time between 100 and 140 . . . bearing in mind that rejuv is still a tolerably new phenomenon, and the figure may increase. But rejuv was a discovery on Cyteen, was available for the first time during my mother's generation, and the sociological adjustments were still extremely rapid during my early years: keyword: Aging, keyword: Olga Emory: keyword: thesis.

At the time I write these notes, the major change has not been so much length of life, although that has had profound effect on family structures and law, due to the fact most people now live near their parents for a century or more, and frequently enter into financial partnership in their estates, so that inheritance, as you have done with my estate, is quite rare: estates usually progress rather than leap from one individual to the other nowadays.

The major change has been the combination of advanced experience with good health and vitality. The period of decline is usually brief, often under 2 years, and frequently there is no apparent decline. Death has become much more of a sudden event; and one enters one's 140's with the expectation one will die, but faces it, not in the depressive effects of degenerative illness, but as an approaching time limit, a fearful catastrophe, or, quite commonly, with the I'm-immune attitude which used to characterize much younger individuals.

I digress with a purpose. I cannot predict for your time and your age what old age may be. I do know this, that the sense of limitations sets in early at Reseune, because of the very nature of our work, which is so slow, and involves human lifespans. By my 70's, I saw an experiment launched which I knew I might not see the end of. And you may not. But that knowledge is something foreign to you, at your age.

Remember this, when you read beyond 2345.

Changes happen. Therefore I have made access to certain keyword areas of my diary slower to access beyond the year 2362, based on a series of examinations this program will administer. I have fears for your psychological health if you attempt to deceive this program in this regard: expert as you may become at analyzing tests and guessing which answers are key to obtaining more information, I ask you to trust my mature judgment in this, remembering that I write this with the perspective of a woman who knows you in ways no one else does—even if you know how to trick the program, answer it with absolute honesty. If an emergency arises and you must get that information, your skill should enable you to lie to the test and get what you need; but bear in mind two things: first, as I once told you, this program is capable of protecting Reseune from abuse, and certain attitudes, even if they are pretended, may cause it to take defensive actions; of course this means if you are a scoundrel, you can perhaps lie in the other direction, but your psych profile does not presently indicate you are one, or you would not be getting this information right now. Second, I will withhold no part of my working notes, and there will be nothing in those hidden portions that you will need for anything but personal reasons.

Last of all I remind you of this: I am safely dead and incapable of shock. The program will draw a firm line between your fantasies and your real actions as observed through House records. Treat the program with absolute honesty. You will occasionally see a new question surface, as your actions within the House or your chronological age activates a new aspect of the test. Never lie, even if you suspect the truth may cause the program to react. It is designed to detect lies, deceptions, evasions, and various other contingencies, but then, I knew I would be dealing with a very clever individual—with my impulses, if I am correct.

I will tell you that I have caused deaths and hurt others in my life. I will tell you something terrible: I have a certain sadistic bent I try to control. Self-analysis is a trap and I have had to do more of it to write this program than I have liked to do. I will tell you that my sexual encounters with CITs have been unsatisfactory from my adolescence onward; that they have inevitably ended in professional antagonism and ended a few valuable friendships; that the events of my childhood, lurid as some of them were, contributed more to my sense of independence and my sense of responsibility toward others. That my uncle was cruel to me and my household taught me compassion.

But that my compassion made me vulnerable to others, all CITs, whose egos did not take well to my independence and my intellect, caused me great pain; in plain language, I fell in love about as often as any normal human being. I gave everything I had to give. And I got back resentment. Genuine hatred. I tried, God knows, not to trample on egos. But my mere existence challenges people, and I challenged everyone past their endurance. Nothing I could do was right. Everything I did fractured their pride. My azi could deal with me, as yours can with you. But I felt an essential isolation from my own kind, a sense that there was an area of humanity I would never adequately reach or understand—on a personal level, no matter my brilliance or my abilities. That is a painful understanding to reach—at nineteen.

That pain created anger; and that anger of mine helped me survive and create. It drove me into that other aspect of myself, my studies of human thought and emotion—challenging all my ability, in short, which in turn fed back into the other situation and exacerbated it with lovers yet to come. I think that that cycle of sexual energy and anger are interlocked in me to such an extent that I cannot control it except by abstinence, and as you are no doubt aware, abstinence is not an easy course for me.

I hesitate even to warn you, because that frustration had an important, even a beneficial effect on my work. I reached a point in my 70's when I had surpassed every mind around me. Jane Strassen, Yanni Schwartz, Denys and Giraud Nye, and of course Florian and Catlin, were among the friends who still challenged me. But I passed even them. I went more and more inward, and found myself more and more solitary in the personal sense. Then I confess to you that I was extremely happy in my professional work, and I was able to confine my sexual energies to a mere physical release, on a very frequent basis, which, with the satisfactions of my work and the company of a few reliable friends, kept me busy. In some ways I was very lonely, but in the main I was happy. It was a very productive period for me.

But now, above a century, I know that I am launched on projects none of which I will finish, that I am doing things that may save humankind or damn it, and I will never know the outcome.

Most of all that anger drives me now, impatience with the oncoming wall, impatience with time and the limits of those around me; there is no chance to stop and breathe, or rest. I can no longer travel freely, no longer fly, the dream I had of seeing space is something I have no right to indulge in, because security is so difficult and finishing this work is so important. Sex used to relieve the tensions; now it interlocks with them, because the anger is linked with it and with everything I do.

The most terrible thing—I have hurt Florian. I have never done that in my life. Worse than that—I enjoyed it. Can a child understand how much that hurt? Worst of all—Florian understands me; and forgives me. Whatever you do, young Ari, use the anger, don't let it use you.

Because the anger will come, the pain will come, because you are not like everyone else, no more than I could be.

You are not my life's work. I hope that does not touch you in your vanity, and that you will understand why I reactivated my psychogenesis study and devoted so much of my time to creating you. My life's work is not psychogenesis, but sociogenesis, and no one but you has ever heard that word in any serious context.

I have shifted the entire course of humanity by the things I have done. Your own unique perspective as a psychogenetic replicate can tell you something of the damage that might be done to Union if people became aware of what I have done. It had to be done, by everything that I saw.

But I worked increasingly alone, without checks, and without consultation with anyone, because there was no one who understood what I understand.

I can tell you in capsule form, young Ari, as I have told the press and told the Council repeatedly: but few seem to understand the basics of what I am saying, because it runs counter to short-term goals and perceptions of well-being. I have not been able to model simply enough the complex of equations that we deal with; and I fear demagogues. Most of all I fear short-term thinkers.

The human diaspora, the human scattering, is the problem, but Centrism is not the answer. The rate of growth that sustains the technological capacity that makes civilization possible is now exceeding the rate of cultural adaptation, and distance is exceeding our communications. The end will become more and more like the beginning, scattered tribes of humans across an endless plain, in pointless conflict—or isolate stagnation—unless we can condense experience, encapsulate it, replicate it deliberately in CIT deep-sets—unless psychogenesis can work on a massive scale, unless it can become sociogenesis and exceed itself as I hope you will exceed me. Human technology as an adaptive response of our species has passed beyond manipulation of the environment; beyond the manipulation of our material selves; beyond the manipulation of mind and thought; now, having brought us out of the cradle it must modify our responses to the universe at large. Human experience is generating dataflow at a rate greater than individuals can comprehend or handle; and the rate is still increasing. We must begin compression: we must compress experience in the same way human history compresses itself into briefer and briefer instruction—and events on which all history depended rate only a line in passing mention.

Ultimately only the wisdom is important, not the event which produced it. But one must know accurately what those things are.

One must pass the right things on. Experience is a brutal and an imprecise teacher at best.

And the time at which all humanity will be within reach, accessible to us—is so very brief.

You will see more than I could, young Ari. You may well be the only mind of your day able to grapple with the problem: I hope that events have handed you my power undiminished; but no matter, if I have fitted you to hold on to it I have also fitted you to acquire it. Most of all, govern your own self. If you survive to reach the power I have had, you will walk a narrow boundary between megalomania and divinity. Or you will let that anger reach humankind; or you will abdicate in cowardice.

If I have failed with you, I have failed in everything, and I may have created nothing worse than presently exists; or I may have doomed at least half of humanity to wars or to stifling tyranny.

If I have succeeded, there is still work to be done, to keep the hand on the helm. Situations change.

If I had done nothing at all, I foresaw a war that the human species might not survive: too much of it resides only on two planets and depends on too few production centers. We are too young in space; our support systems are still too fragile, and our value systems still contain elements of the stone ax and the spear.

That conviction is the only moral assurance I will ever have.

Study the Company Wars. Study the history of Earth. Learn what we are capable of.

Study Gehenna. This program has ascertained re-contact has been made. People have survived there. Its generations are shorter than ours. Gehenna is the alarm system.

Your Security clearance is now active in the Science Bureau with rank of: Department head, Reseune Administrative Territory.

Further explanation is filed in Reseune Security: access via Security 10, keyword: clearance.

---

vi

"No, ser," Ari said, hands folded on the table. The microphones picked up her voice and carried it, making it huge, a caricature of a young girl's voice. She sat by herself at a table facing the Nine. Uncle Giraud sat in the Science seat; there were Nasir Harad, and Nguyen Tien; Ludmilla deFranco; Jenner Harogo; Mikhail Corain; Mahmud Chavez; and Vladislaw Khalid—whose looks toward her were absolute hostility. Corain had asked the question.

"No, ser, I won't give you a transcript. I've said why. It wouldn't be all of it. And that's worse than nothing. I'm *telling* you the important things. Adm. Azov sent the colony even when Ari told him not; she didn't want it because it was too dangerous. And he went ahead.

"This is the important thing—let me say this—" she said, when Corain interrupted her. "Please."

"I doubt you would forget," Corain said dryly.

Harad's gavel came down. "Go on, young sera."

"This is important," Ari said. "This is the most important part. Adm. Azov came to my predecessor wanting a colony planted on that world because it was an Earthlike planet and it was right next to Pell. Defense wanted to make sure if Alliance got there in fifty years or a hundred they were going to find a planet full of Union people, or an ecological disaster that could contaminate the planet with human-compatible diseases . . ."

It disturbed the Council. Heads leaned together and the gavel banged down again.

"Let the girl finish."

"That was in the notes. They wanted Reseune to build those too. They wanted Ari to design tape so the azi they sent would always be Union, no matter what, and they would cause trouble and work from inside Alliance once Alliance picked them up off the world. Ari tried to tell them they were crazy. But they wouldn't listen.

"So Ari listened to everything they wanted, and she ordered some immunological stuff, I don't know what, but my uncle is going to talk about those. What they essentially did was use viruses to transfer material, and that was all done pretty much like we use for genetic treatment—and they picked some things they hoped would just help the colonists' immune systems; but there was another contractor Ari didn't trust and she didn't know what they might dump onto Gehenna that Reseune didn't know about."

"Do you know the name of that contractor?" Corain asked.

"It was Fletcher Labs. It was May of 2352. That's all she knew."

That made the Councillors nervous. An aide came up and talked to Khalid. Several others took the chance.

"But she was in charge of actually organizing the colony," Corain said then, when things settled down. "Describe what she did."

"She was in charge of picking the azi and training them; and she did the main instructional tape. They wanted her to do all this stuff you *can't* do. Like all these buried instructions. What she did, she made the primary instruction deep-tape; and she axed the azi's contracts in a way that meant if there weren't any CITs they were contracted to the world itself."

"She disregarded the Defense Bureau's instructions. That's what you're saying."

"If she'd done what the military wanted the whole colony would likely have died out; or if they lived past the diseases the third or fourth generation would be really dangerous—psychsets interact with environment. They didn't want to hear that."

"Time," Chairman Harad said. "Councillor Chavez of Finance."

"You consider you're qualified to pronounce on that," Chavez said, following up.

"Ser, that's a real basic."

"I don't care if it's a basic," Chavez said, "you're consistently reading in motives or you're attributing them to people only one of whom you know anything about, and you're not making it clear where you're quoting and where you're interpreting. I'm talking about your predecessor, young sera, who is the one whose notes you're supposed to be testifying to. Not your own interpretations of those notes."

"Yes, ser." Ari drew a long breath, and restrained her temper behind a very bland look. "I won't explain, then."

"I suggest you respect this body, young sera. You attained your majority last week; it means, young sera, that you are obliged to act as an adult."

She looked at Councillor Chavez, folded her hands again and sat there.

"Go on, young sera," Harad said.

"Thank you, ser Chairman. I'm sorry; I'll explain only if you ask. Ari wasn't technical about it: she said: quote: Defense insisted. I explained the hazards of environmental interactions in considerable detail. Their own psychologists tried to make them understand what I was saying; unfortunately the admirals had already made up their minds: the system of advancements in the military makes it damn near impossible for a Defense Bureau bureaucrat to back off a position. Even if—"

"Young sera," Chavez said. "The Council has limited time. Could we omit the late Councillor's profane observations?"

"Yes, ser."

"Go on."

"That was the answer."

"You didn't answer. Let me pose the question again. What, specifically, was Emory's argument to Defense?"

"I can't answer without explaining."

"What did Emory say?"

"She said they shouldn't do it because the environment would affect the psychsets and the tape couldn't be re-adjusted for the situation. And Defense couldn't tell her enough about the environment. That was the first reason she said they were crazy."

"She knew that when she made the original design. Why did she do it in the first place?"

"Because she did it during the War. If humanity had wiped itself out of space and gotten the planets too, it was one more place humanity might survive. It was real dangerous, but it wouldn't matter if they were the only ones."

"What was the danger?"

"You're going to get upset if I tell you again."

"Tell me."

"Letting a psychset run in an environment you don't know anything about. Do you want me to explain technically why that's dangerous?"

The Expansionists all laughed behind their hands. Even Tien, who was Centrist.

"Explain," Chavez said with a surprising lot of patience. She decided she liked him after all. He was not stupid. And he could back up when he got caught.

"Deep-tape is real simple and real general: it has to be. If you make aggression part of the set, and they're in an environment that threatens them, they'll expand the aggression all over everything, and it'll proliferate through the rest of the sets all the way to the surface; or if you put in a block *against* aggression, it could proliferate the same way, and they couldn't take care of themselves. Deep-tape gets all the way down to which way you jump when something scares you. It hits the foundation of the logic sets. And it almost has to be slightly illogical, because on pure logic, you don't move till you understand it. The deep-sets are a bias toward fight or flight. Things like that. And the Defense Bureau didn't give Ari senior any chance to design real deep-sets that might be a whole lot better for Gehenna. They came in and wanted her to program adult military-setted azi to colonize, and they wanted it in one year. She said that was garbage. She argued them into taking a mix of soldiers and farmers. So she composed a genepool of types that might have all the skills *and* the deep-sets she figured might hold *some* right answers to the environment, whatever it was."

"In other words she lied to the Bureau."

"She had to. They were going to go throw their own azi onto the world without her help, and they were telling their own psychology branch to break the law and try to run a deep-set intervention on them. Their own psych people said that was stupid, and some of them were threatening to talk to the Council, but Adm. Azov told one of them he could end up on Gehenna himself if he kept objecting. That's what that man told Ari. Then she thought about bringing it to Council, but she thought about the chance of the whole human race getting wiped out, and that was when she made up her mind to go along with it, but to do it safer than Defense was going to do it.

"She couldn't just go back and mindwipe all those azi and start over. That was another crazy suggestion the military had. Reseune didn't have enough facilities. And you don't recover from mindwipe that well that they could just dump them off on another planet and leave them there with no psych help. So she couldn't work with the deep-sets. She just studied all the deep-sets and worked up something real simple: she told the azi it was their planet and they had to take care of it and survive and teach their children what was important, that was all. As positive as she could. Because she didn't know how long Gehenna would be lost, and how much that would change.

"And that's the danger in it. Their generations are real short. There's already been a lot of change. Alliance is scared of them because they're afraid there's something on the planet like a secret base, that's the way I understand it; but if there's anything like that, it's not in the notes. Mostly I hear it's the azi that did survive, and there's not much left of CIT culture. That means the program did take.

"There's too many people to mindwipe—thousands and thousands. They'd have to mindwipe them all the way down, and that's a lot of psych work, and they haven't got a Reseune. Councillor Nye can tell you what it would take—"

"It would take a facility the size of Reseune," Giraud said, "doing nothing else, for at least ten years; and the re-integration of that many mindwiped individuals into ordinary society would tax anything *any* of us have. We're talking about thirty thousand individuals. Or more. They're still trying to estimate. No one has a place to disperse those people—they'd still cluster. Cluster means community; community means cultural identity. Alliance hasn't got the population base to absorb them. *We* don't. Don't even mention turning them loose on Earth."

"They probably can't find all of them," Ari said. "Anyway. So they can't get them off. They'll always be different; and they'll always be a problem. They're an azi population. They're *not* like CITs. They're just going to be crazy according to CIT thinking. Teaching their kids is part of their mindset; and if you bring them into the 25th century that's *another* environment that's going to hit that program and proliferate changes. That's Emory's word on it. If it's second generation, you could integrate them back, but there's even fourths now. Once it hits fourth, she said, you're into something real different. And they don't have rejuv. The Olders die off before they're a hundred. I've heard it's more like forty or fifty. That doesn't give them time to live with their kids or teach them much about being grown up. They're already more different from us than we are from Earth. That's Emory talking."

"I'm out of questions," Chavez said.

"We're going to recess for lunch," Harad said "And take ser Tien's questions after—are you holding up to this, young sera?"

"I'm doing all right," she said. "After lunch is fine. Thank you, ser."

"It vastly disturbs me, sera," Tien said, from the dais where the Nine sat. He spoke very quietly, very politely, which was the way the man talked. "I have to tell you I'm concerned with the security clearance the Science Bureau has given you—not, understand, that I think you're not an exceedingly mature young woman. But we're dealing with things that could mean war or peace, and things that have been thrust on you very prematurely. Do you ever talk to your friends about these things?"

"No, ser, absolutely not." It was a fair question. All along, Tien had been fair.

"Do you understand the importance of not talking to reporters about this?"

"Yes, ser. I do. The only people I've discussed this with are Denys Nye, Giraud Nye, and the Council, exactly; and my azi, but they're not in the room when I work with the System on this either, and they don't know everything. Certainly they don't talk: they're Reseune Security, and their psychset is against discussing anything about me, even little things."

"We understand that. Can you estimate how much of the data you're not telling us?"

Oh. Very good question. "My predecessor had some theories about what would happen on Gehenna." Try to answer without answering. "But they're complicated, and I can't report on those because they're all in design-structure, and they're something that's going to take me a long while to sort through. Science Bureau is going to provide us the Gehenna data as it comes in—"

"To you?"

"Ser, to whoever's working on this project, but likely to me, yes, since I'm the one with my predecessor's notes."

"Time," Harad said. "Adm. Khalid."

"Let's keep to the question of the notes," Khalid said. "And why those notes, if they exist, haven't been turned over to a competent researcher."

"She *is* technically rated as a Wing supervisor," Giraud said. "And she is competent."

"She has no business with the notes," Khalid said. "Or do we believe that Reseune is being steered by a fifteen-year-old and a dead woman? That raises more questions about the competency of Reseune's administration than it does about hers. I have no quarrel with the child. I do have with Reseune. I find evidence of gross mismanagement. *Gross* mismanagement. I think we have more than enough evidence to extend this investigation into Reseune's actions in creating this situation."

"You can do that," Giraud said, "but it won't get you those notes."

The gavel came down. Repeatedly.

"Young sera," Khalid said. "You *can* be held in contempt of a Council order. So can your Administrator and the other people who are prompting you."

Ari took a drink of water. When it was quiet she said: "You can arrest people, but what you want to know is science and you have to ask scientists, and we're it. Bucherlabs hasn't got anybody who can read it. Neither does Defense. I'm already telling you what's in the notes and what you'll find if you go to all that trouble. If you don't think I'm telling the truth now, are you going to believe me then?"

The gavel banged again. "Councillor. Sera. If you please. Councillor Khalid."

"We're dealing with an immature child," Khalid said, "who's being pushed into this position by Reseune Administration. I repeat, we need to widen this probe until we get at individuals who *are* responsible. This is a question of national security. The Military Secrets Act—"

"The Councillor is out of order," Giraud said.

"—requires an investigation of any mishandling of classified information. The mishandling that allowed a fifteen-year-old child to go in front of news cameras to leak information that *never* should have become public—"

Again the gavel. "Councillor, we operate under rules, let me remind you. This is not a debate."

"A diplomatic crisis is at issue. Our enemies have a pretext to break treaties, *including* the arms treaty, which is not to our advantage. They're talking about *plots*, seri, completely ignorant of what azi are and what they're capable of. This is the result of practicing diplomacy in the press."

"The Councillor is out of order," Giraud said.

"Admiral," Harad said, "your time is running. Have you a question for the witness?"

"I have. Under oath, young sera, and bearing in mind you *can* be prosecuted for perjury, how long have you known about these files?"

"About the Gehenna files? They surfaced when I used the keywords."

"When?"

"The day after you won the election."

"Where did you get the keywords?"

"Denys Nye suggested them." That was a bad thing to have to admit. "But—"

"Meaning they didn't exist until then. Thank you, young sera. That explains a great deal."

"That's a psych, ser. It doesn't prove anything. I had to know. My clearance—"

"Thank you, we've *had* your answer."

"No, you've made up one."

"The Council will not take disrespect, sera."

"Yes, ser. But I don't have to take being called a liar. You threatened us; I applied for my majority; that triggered—"

"It's not you who's lying, sweet. You've been deceived right along with the Council. Your uncle made those files. He's made them from the beginning. There's no secret, protected system. There are simply records Reseune doesn't want to release, for very clear reasons, and Reseune created *you* to stand between the Council and Reseune's mismanagement."

"No, ser, I'm under oath. I am and you're not. My getting my majority triggered the notes. So when you withdrew your suit, that did it. That's the truth. And *I'm* under oath."

There was a little shifting in seats. A snort from Catherine Lao.

"Your uncle made the files and prepped you for this whole business." The gavel banged. "That's enough, Councillor. Next question."

"I don't think we're listening to anything in this diplomatic fiasco," Khalid said, "but Denys Nye's constructions. Reseune is playing politics as usual, and it's held too much power too long."

"Do we mention the power in the Defense Bureau?" Giraud said.

"We have a clear case of conflict of interest on the Council. And we have embassies from Pell and Earth asking questions we had rather not answer."

"We have a clear conflict of interest as regards Defense," Giraud said. "Since your Bureau ordered this Gehenna mess over the protests of Science. *As* the witness has testified."

"Time," Harad said, and brought the gavel down.

"I'm due time to respond to that," Khalid said.

"Your time is up."

"I'd hate to accuse the Chairman of partisan politics."

Bang! "You are out of order, Councillor!"

Ari took another sip of water and waited while the Chair wrangled it out. Corain was making notes. So were Lao and a lot of the aides. Corain might have put Khalid up to it, making him the villain, since Khalid already had trouble. There was a challenge to Khalid's seat shaping up—already, a man named Simon Jacques. Much less flamboyant. Reseune had preferred Lu, but Lu's age was against him; and there was under-the-table stuff going on:

Corain had talked very secretly with Giraud and Jacques was a compromise they both could swallow, to get rid of Khalid. But that didn't mean Corain wouldn't let Khalid go after Reseune. It just meant that, under that table, Corain didn't want Reseune swallowed up by Defense any more than he wanted it to exist at all.

Meanwhile Khalid had broken off negotiations on a big Defense contract with Reseune. It was a fair-sized threat, but Khalid certainly wasn't doing any more than stalling, because there wasn't anywhere else to get tape from.

And the law that protected azi wound a civil rights issue right into Reseune's right of exclusivity on tape-production, because Reseune *was* the legal guardian of all azi, everywhere—Reseune *could* terminate all azi contracts with Defense—which they wouldn't do, of course, but, Giraud said, Defense had been fighting for years to get access to the birth-to-eighteen tapes for its soldiers, and Reseune would never give them up. That was why Khalid wanted to nationalize Reseune. Khalid said there had been mismanagement at RESEUNESPACE—meaning Jenna Schwartz; but he made it sound like it was present management, meaning Ollie, and that made her damned mad; Defense also said it was worried about something being buried in the training tapes; and Khalid was threatening to bring a bill to break Reseune's monopoly on tape and licensing—

Fine, Giraud said: Khalid didn't have the votes; Khalid's position was already unpopular with his own party—who didn't want *more* azi labs, they wanted fewer; so the whole Gehenna thing was a lever all sorts of interests were using. Corain would have liked to have used it much more, except Corain was worried about Khalid.

It was all very crazy. The stock markets were going up and down on rumors, Chavez, of Finance, was furious and sent a shut-down order on the wave of the rumors, so no ship could leave port for a few days, because they didn't want *that* market-dive information packet going off at trans-light across Union and clear to Pell and Earth, they wanted to get the market stable again before they let any ship leave; and that had the Trade Bureau upset and Information howling about trade censorship. It was a real mess. In fact everybody was getting anxious.

Council won't take this kind of stuff, Giraud had said. And grimly: this is getting very serious, Ari. Very serious.

There was, Giraud had said, a hard-line faction in the military that had been building up for years—a lot of them the old guard who blamed Gorodin and Lu for spending too much on the Fargone project and not getting the programs they wanted; *they* backed Khalid in the election, and they wanted more shipbuilding and more defense systems Sunward; but that was also along the Alliance corridors, and that made the Centrists nervous.

While everybody thought Jacques was a front for Gorodin and might resign and appoint Gorodin proxy if he got elected; and Lu's friends were mad about the double cross.

Crazy.

"We have this entire crisis," Khalid was saying, arguing with Harad, "because Reseune can sit in perfect immunity and level charges contained in documents only the Science Bureau can vouch for. Of *course* the Science Bureau is pure of Reseune influences!"

Giraud was right. Khalid was a disaster with the press, but he was fast on his feet and he was smart. You couldn't discount him.

But Harad brought down the gavel again. "Councillor Lao."

"The question is . . ." Thank God it was Lao's turn next. Uncle Giraud was out, because of conflict of interest. Harad of State was out because he was presiding. ". . . very simply, why a quarantine?"

"They're unpredictable, Councillor. That's the whole thing. We have huge computers that run sociology projections, when we work with psychsets: we try to balance populations so they end up with wide enough genepools and we check out the psychsets we use to make sure that we haven't put something together that's going to turn up social problems when everybody becomes CIT. This thing—this whole planet—is completely wild and it's all artificial, it's got no relation at all to Terran history—it's just Gehennan. We don't know what it is. That's what made Ari nervous. These azi-sets could have been under God-knows-what interventions while they still had kat and they knew they were in trouble; God knows what their Supervisors decided to tell them; or even if there were Supervisors at the last—" Tell them *that*, get them off the question about predictive sociology. "Take these people into the Alliance or into Union and they're *there* from now on, and they're *different*. Ari didn't say you should never do it. She said there's a period after which it's a lot better to let Gehenna alone and let it grow up, so you can see what it's going to do when it comes into the mainstream culture. Maybe it never will get along with us. Maybe it'll be something very good. We just don't know at this point."

"How *will* you know? Didn't she run those checks?"

"It changes with every generation. It relates to all those psychsets. It relates to the whole mix. Our sociology programs are always improving. Ari ran it every ten years or so until she died. But her data was all just the initial stuff; she was just testing it against the new Sociology programs. We've got to set up to run with the new data. We have to do all the sets with the master-program and then we have to integrate them—that's Sociology does that. Reseune is transferring data over right now to run it. But it's huge; it takes a lot of computer time. And we need up-to-date stats. We can tell Council a lot. But we can't do it overnight and there's nothing, sera, absolutely nothing that laymen can do with that kind of stuff, either, the only computers that can run it are ours. So the best thing, the thing Reseune wants, is to keep that planet exactly the way Alliance wants to—just as little contact as possible while we do the data-collecting. It's like trying to get a good level measure with somebody bouncing the instruments, if people keep meddling there. We have to input all the influences—because just the discovery team landing there had to have done something."

"This is not," Khalid said, "a playground for the Science Bureau."

"Nor for Defense, ser," Lao said sharply.

The gavel came down.

She lay flat on the bed in the hotel, limp, while Florian and Catlin rubbed the kinks out, and she went to sleep that way, unexpectedly, just out, pop, gone.

She woke up under the covers and Florian and Catlin had the light down very low, Catlin was stretched out on the other bed, and Florian was sitting in the chair in the corner.

"God," she said, which woke Catlin instantly. "Get to *sleep*. There's battalions of Security in the hall, aren't there?"

"Yes, sera," Florian said. Catlin said: "There are twenty-seven on duty."

"Well, *go to sleep.*"

Which was short, for people who loved her enough to stay awake after a day like this one, but she was still falling-over tired, and she did, just grabbed the pillow with her arm, tucked her head down and burrowed until she had a dark place.

Florian turned out the lights anyway; and she heard him cross the room and sit down on the other bed and start undressing.

She headed out again, then, a slow drift. Tomorrow morning was uncle Giraud's turn to testify. Then Secretary Lynch, of Science; Secretary Vinelli of Defense; Adm. Khalid—O God, Khalid, then her again, as soon as they got through. She hoped Giraud and Lynch did all right. But when Vinelli got up there, and Khalid, Giraud could cross-examine like everybody else.

Not saying, of course, that Khalid wouldn't go over uncle Giraud and Secretary Lynch the way he had headed at her.

It was going to be a long week.

Or two.

We're going to win about the quarantine, Giraud had predicted at the outset. There's no way Union can do anything like move in on Gehenna without bringing in warships, and there's no way we're going to go to war with the Alliance to get access to Gehenna. What we can lose is what position Union takes about those people on Gehenna—whether they regard them as Union citizens and use that as a lever with the Alliance; or whether they negotiate a joint protectorate with the Alliance; and the hawks have a real stake in that: it's Khalid's political clout that's at issue here—

The Centrist and the Expansionist coalitions were exactly that: coalitions. The hawks were trying to pull something different together by breaking off bits of both, *that* was what had surfaced in Khalid's rise. They were too high-up in the government to call them eetee-fringes. They were *real*: the whole thing that Ari senior had been worried about had come true, the old Earth territorial craziness had found itself an issue and a time to surface—

And here she was holding Ari senior's argument in both hands behind her back— *You know what it would do to Union if they found out what I've done,*

Ari senior had said. So she couldn't tell them: she couldn't get the things about Sociology even Sociology didn't know they had done—for Ari senior. She couldn't tell Council about the deep-set work Ari had done, or the fact that Ari had been planning—and installing—imperatives in the azi work crews, in the military, in a whole lot of places—including the deep-sets of the Gehenna azi.

The thing was already going on. By design, thirty percent of the azi Ari senior had designed and turned out of Reseune, and thirty percent of all the azi everywhere who used Reseune tape, would have kids and teach them, all across Union. A certain number of those azi had gotten their CIT papers as early as 2384, on Fargone, then in other places. A lot of them were in Science, a whole lot were in Defense: the Defense azi couldn't get CIT papers till they retired—but they were mostly male and they could still have kids or bring tank-kids up. A lot would do that, because *that* was in the deep-sets. The rest of those azi were scattered out through the electorates, heavy in Industry and Citizens, just exactly where the Centrists were strongest—a mindset that was biased right in its deep-sets, toward Ari senior's way of things.

And even other psych people wouldn't likely see what she had done— unless they were onto it—or unless they were as good as Ari senior, simply because what she did was a very accepted kind of program, a very basic kind of azi mindset. She had *showed* Council, she had even told them the program—and they couldn't see what it did with all those military psychsets, because the connections were so wide and so abstract—except when a living azi mind integrated them and ran with them in the social matrix.

That was what had scared Ari senior so bad.

There were thousands and thousands by now: not a whole lot yet proportionate to all of Union, but the program was running, and those tapes were still turning out azi. Even out of Bucherlabs and Lifefarms, in the simpler, gentle types they trained—there were attitudes designed to mesh with the psychsets of Reseune azi in very special ways.

Look up the word pogrom, *Ari had said, in her notes to her. And see why I am afraid for the azi if people find out too soon what I have done.*

Or too late.

I don't know what I have done. But the Sociology computers in my time can't see beyond twenty of our generations. I do. I've tried to devise logarithmic systems— but I don't trust them. The holes in my thinking could be the holes in the paradigms. Field Too Large is what the damned thing spits back on my wide runs.

I'm becoming emotional about those words.

I'll tell you: if anyone threatens to access these files but you—there is a program that will move them and re-key them in such ways that they will look like a whole lot of different kinds of records and continually lie about file sizes and other data so that searchers will play hob finding them.

But for God's sake don't use it until they're breaking the door down: it's terribly dangerous. It has defensive aspects.

I will give you the keywords now to disorganize the System.

It has three parts.

First keyword: the year of your birth.
Second keyword: the year of mine.
Third keyword: annihilate.
Then it will ask you for a keyword to re-integrate Base One. Have one in mind and don't panic.

It was a little comfort, knowing that was in there. Knowing she could hide what was going on.

But *she* wouldn't have had just one answer in the computer, to protect something that important.

She didn't think Ari had.

She tossed over on her other side and burrowed again.

And finally she said: "Florian. . . ."

---

vii

Ari stepped off the plane and into the safeway, and walked the long weary way to the terminal, to get her baggage. Just the briefcase and her carry-bag, that Florian and Catlin had.

Night-flight again, with the escort. Which was a news story unto itself, but all Giraud would say was 'precautions.'

And all the public got was: 'quarantine justified.'

There were people going to be filming here, too—Reseune Information gave a live feed to Cyteen Station, and the station distributed it everywhere. Ships were on their way, the whole of Cyteen commerce was moving again, and the world took a collective breath.

Not knowing all of it, but feeling things were steadier. They were. The markets were up on bargain-hunting and in some ways healthier, because there had been a lot of built-up war-scare that just burst like a bubble, Defense stocks were taking a beating, but diversifieds were doing fine, shipping stocks were soaring again, the futures market was shifting: the Cyteen market believed in peace again after a bad scare, and there was a lot of anti-hawk feeling coming to the surface in the Information polls, which encouraged the shyer voices to speak up and dragged the undecideds back to the peace camp.

After three bad weeks, you could say you wanted peace with the Alliance and sound like a responsible moderate—not a Universalist-eetee, who wanted all the human governments to build a capital in the Hinder Stars—never mind that Earth had over five thousand governments at last count; or a Pax agitator, the sort that had bombed a rush-hour subway car and killed thirty-two people last week in Novgorod.

The police were afraid there was some kind of a pipeline from the Rocher Abolitionists to the Paxers. They might have gotten the explosives from mine-camp pilferage or maybe just making the stuff: there were possible crime connections, everything from the illicit tape-trade to illegal drugs to the body trade, and a lot of the ones the police could get at were z-cases, just wipe-outs the real criminals used to do the work and take the hits.

The familiar walk from the plane to the safeway doors, the quiet, beige cord-carpet, the sight of Reseune Security guards *talking* with each other in more than coded monosyllables and moving easily, like there was more than a synapse-jump between a sudden noise and hosing-down the room—made her want to melt down on the spot and just sleep for a week, right there, right then, knowing she was safe.

But cameras met her at the exit into the terminal, Security reacted, the few reporters who had gotten passes shoved mikes at her and asked why Giraud had stayed—"He's still got some clean-up," she said. "Office things."

Some secret meetings, staff with staff, Secretary Lynch's staff with Chavez's staff, which was a pipeline from Corain, but that was, God knew, not for the reporters.

"Do you feel confidence in the decision?"

"I think people are going to do the right things now. I think I made them understand—everything's fine if they just treat those people all right—"

"The Gehennans, you mean."

"Yes, the Gehennans. The Science Bureau is going to advise the Alliance ambassador we need some real close communication—that's what's going on right now. But that's the Bureau and the Secretary; and Councillor Harad's office. I think everything's going to work out fine."

Time, well time, to calm the situation down: that was her job; and Giraud's; and Harad's.

"There's no truth to the rumor about a secret base on Gehenna."

She made a deliberate surprise-reaction. "Absolutely not. No. It's not about that at all. I *can* let something out: they're going to make an official statement tomorrow morning: there was some real illegal bacteriological stuff done there. It was our fault. It shouldn't have happened. And we don't need that stuff coming back."

The reporters got excited. They were supposed to. And it was absolutely true, it *was* one of the cautions, the one they could give out right away, and one of the most urgent ones. "What *sort* of bacteriological stuff?" they asked.

"Designed stuff. Viruses. It's not fatal to humans; the Gehennans tolerate it fine. But there are a lot of questions. They did some stuff back in the War that shouldn't have been done. I can't talk about more than that. Councillor Harad said I could say that; he's going to hold a news conference tomorrow morning. I'm sorry—I'm *awfully* tired, and they're signaling me come on—"

"One more question! Is the rumor accurate the Councillor is going to propose talks with Alliance?"

"I can't talk about that." Thank God Catlin just grabbed her by the arm and Florian body-blocked and adult Security and uncle Denys' staff got there, Seely in plain-clothes, like always, and Amy and Maddy and Sam closing in—doing the Family-homecoming number—getting her *out* of there—

Getting her all the way to the bus, where she could hug Amy and Maddy and Sam for a whole different reason, for real, because Giraud had let her in on the secret, that a Family reception at the airport was the best way in the universe to get a wedge in on the reporters, get her out, and still give the cameramen the kind of human-interest endshot that left the right kind of feeling with everybody—*who* showed up to do the airport-rescue depended on the kind of impression they wanted to give out.

So uncle Denys sent her the youngers, no official stuff, no indication to the outside world what Reseune's *official* reaction was, no high administrators who could get caught for follow-up by the reporters—just a real happy group of kids slipping in with the Security people, real Family stuff.

Damn, they carried it off smooth as Olders could have.

And left the reporters to guess who they were and to focus on something just human, about Reseune, about the fact Reseune wasn't long-faced and worried and just ordinary kids showed up to welcome her home, after they had seen so much of Reseune Security and asked questions about the chase planes.

Fade-out on happy kids.

People grabbed on to things like that real fast.

"I want to sleep," she said.

"Bad news," Amy said. "They're waiting for you in the front hall." Amy patted her shoulder. "Everybody wants to see you. Just to say welcome back. You were great, Ari. You were really *great*."

"Oh, God," she mumbled. And shut her eyes. She was so tired she was shivering all over. Her knees ached.

"What happened in the hearings?" Maddy asked.

"I can't say. Can't. But it was all right." Even her mouth had trouble working. The bus made the turn and started up the hill. She opened her eyes and remembered she had her hair against the seat back. She sat up and felt to see if it was mussed, and straightened it with her fingers. "Where's my comb?"

Because she was not going into the hall with her hair messed if people had come to see her.

Even if she was falling on her face.

Uncle Denys himself was at the door; she hugged him and kissed him on the cheek and said into his ear: "I'm so awful tired. Get me home."

But Florian had to go ahead to check the Minder before she could even have her bed. *Especially* now.

And she walked the hall through all the Family and the staff; and got hugs and flowers and kissed Dr. Edwards on the cheek and hugged Dr. Dietrich and even Dr. Peterson and Dr. Ivanov—him a long, long moment, because whatever else he had done, he had put her together right; and she had gotten mad at him, but she knew what he had done for her— "You and your damn shots," she said into his ear. "I held together fine in Novgorod."

He hugged her till her bones cracked and he patted her shoulder and said he was glad.

She got a little further. Then: "I've got to rest," she said finally to sera Carnath, Amy's mother, and sera Carnath scolded everybody and told them to let her through.

So they did; and she walked to the lift, went up and over to her hall, and her apartment, and her bed, clothes and all.

She woke up with somebody taking them off her, but that was Florian and Catlin, and that was all right. "Sleep with me," she said, and they got in, both of them, one warm lump, like little kids, right in the middle of the bed.

viii

The Filly loved the open air—there was a pasture bare of everything, where the horses could get a long run—good solid ground, and safe enough if you kept the Filly's head up and never let her eat anything that grew in the fields. Sometimes the azi that worked the horses when Florian was busy used her and the Mare's daughter to exercise the Mare instead of using the walker; but when the Filly was out with her or Florian on her back she really put on her manners, ears up, everything in her just waiting for the chance to run, which was what the Filly loved best.

It made uncle Denys nervous as hell when he got reports about her riding all-out.

Today she had Florian by her on Filly Two, both horses fretting at the bits and wanting to go. "Race you," she said, and aimed the Filly at the end of the field, to the kind of stop that had once sent her most of the way off, hanging on the Filly's neck—she had sworn she would *kill* Andy and Florian if they told; and she was very glad no one had had a camera around.

All the way there with both horses running nearly neck and neck; and it would have taken somebody on the ground to see who was first. Florian could try to be diplomatic. But the fillies had different ideas.

"Easier back," Florian said. The horses were breathing hard, and dancing around and feeling good. But *he* worried when they ran like that.

"Hell," she said. For a moment she was free as the wind and nothing could touch her.

But racing was not why they were out here, or down in AG, or why Catlin had special orders up in the House.

Not why Catlin was walking out of the barn now—a distant bit of black; with company.

"Come on," she said to Florian, and she let the Filly pick her pace, which was still a good clip, and with ears up and then back again as the Filly saw people down there too, and tried to figure it out in her own worried way.

ix

Justin stood still beside Catlin's black, slim impassivity, waiting while the horses brought Ari and Florian back—big animals, coming fast—but he figured if there were danger of being run down Catlin would not be standing there with her arms folded, and he thought—he was sure . . . that it was Ari's choice to scare him if she could.

So he stood his ground while the horses ran up on them. They stopped in time. And Ari slid down and Florian did.

She gave Florian her horse to lead away. She had on a white blouse, her hair was pinned up in Emory's way; but coming loose all around her face. The smell of the barn, the animals, leather and earth—brought back childhood. Brought back the days that he and Grant had been free to come down here—

A long time ago.

"Justin," Ari said. "I wanted to talk to you."

"I thought you would," he said.

She was breathing hard. But anyone would, who had come in like that.

Catlin had called his office, said come to the doors; he had left Grant at work, over Grant's objections. No, he had said; just—no. And gotten his jacket and walked down, expecting—God knew—Ari, there.

Catlin had brought him down here, instead, and no one interfered with that. But no one likely interfered much with anything Ari did these days.

"Let's go sit down," Ari said now. "Do you mind?"

"All right," he said; and followed her over to the corner where the fence met the barn. Azi handlers took the horses inside; and Ari sat down on the bottom rail of the metal fence, leaving him the plastic shipping cans that were clustered there, while Catlin and Florian stood a little behind him and out of his line of sight. Intentionally, he thought, a quiet, present threat.

"I don't blame you for anything," she said, hands between her knees, looking at him with no coldness, no resentment. "I feel a little funny—like I should have put *something* together, that there was something in the past—but I thought—I thought maybe you'd gotten crosswise of Administration. The family black sheep. Or something. But that's all history. I know nothing is your fault. I asked you to come here—to ask you what you think about *me.*"

It was a civilized, sensible question. It was the nightmare finally happening, turning out to be just a quiet question from a pretty young girl under a sunny sky. But his hands would shake if he was not sitting as he was, arms folded. "What I think about you. I think about the little girl at the New Year's party. About the damn guppies. I think about a sweet kid, Ari. That's all. I've had nightmares about your finding out. *I* didn't want what happened. I didn't want fifteen years of walking around the truth. But they couldn't tell you. And they were afraid I would. That I would—feel some resentment toward you. I don't. None."

Her face was so much Ari's. The lines and planes were beginning to be there. But the eyes were a young woman's eyes, worried—that rare little expression he had seen first that day in his office—over a jar of suffocated baby guppies. *I guess they were just in there too long.*

"Your father's at Planys," she said. "They say you visit him."

He nodded. A lump got into his throat. God. He was not going to break down and go maudlin in front of a fifteen-year-old.

"You miss him."

Second nod. She could feel her way to all the buttons. She *was* Emory. She had proved it in Novgorod, and the whole damn government had rocked on its pinnings.

"Are you mad at me about it?" she asked.

He shook his head.

"Aren't you going to talk to me?"

Damn. *Pull it together, fool!*

"Are you mad at my uncles?"

He shook his head again. There was *nothing* safe to say. Nothing safe to do. She was the one who needed to know. He knew everything. And if there was a way out for Jordan it was going to be in her administration—someday. If there was any hope at all.

She was silent a long time. Just waiting for him. Knowing, surely, that he was fracturing. Himself, who was thirty-four years old; and not doing well at all.

He leaned forward, elbows on knees, studied the dust between his feet, then looked up at her.

No knowledge at all of what the first Ari had done to him. Denys swore to that. And swore what he would do if he opened his mouth about it.

I won't, he had said to Denys. *God, do you think I want her into that tape? She hasn't got it*, Denys had assured him. *And won't get it.*

Yet—had been his thought.

There was nothing but worry in the look Ari gave him.

"It's not easy," he said, "to be under suspicion—all the time. That's the way I live, Ari. And I never did anything. I was seventeen when it happened."

"I know that," she said. "I'll talk to Denys. I'll make it so you can go visit when you like."

It was everything he had hoped for. "Right now—" he said, "there's too much going on in the world. The mess in Novgorod. The same reason they have you flying with an escort. There's a military base right next to Planys. The airport is in between the two. Your uncle Denys is worried they might try to grab my father; or me. I'm grounded until things settle down. I can't even talk to him on the phone. —And Grant's never even gotten to go. Grant—was like his second son."

"Damn," she said, "I'm sorry. But you *will* get to see him. Grant, too. I'll do everything I can."

"I'd be grateful."

"Justin, —does your father hate me?"

"No. Absolutely not."

"What does he say about me?"

"We stay off that subject," he said. "You understand—every call I make to him, every second I spend with him—there's always somebody listening. Talking about you—could land me back in Detention."

She looked at him a long time. Shock, no. But they had not told her that, maybe. There was a mix of expressions on her face he could not sort out.

"Your father's a Special," she said. "Yanni says you ought to be."

"Yanni says. I doubt it. And they're not even going to allow the question—because they can't touch my father—legally—so they don't want *me* unreachable. You understand."

That was another answer that bothered her. Another moment of silence.

"Someday," he said, "when things are quieter, someday when you're running Reseune—I hope you'll take another look at my father's case. You could do something to help him. I don't think anyone else ever will. Just—ask him—the things you've asked me." *But, O God, the truth . . . about that tape; about Ari; the shock of that—no knowing what that will do to her.*

She's not like her predecessor. She's a decent kid.

That tape's as much a rape of her—as me.

God, God, when's she going to get the thing? Two more years?

When she's seventeen?

"Maybe I will," she said. "—Justin, *why* did he do it?"

He shook his head, violently. "Nobody knows. Nobody really knows. Temper. God knows they didn't get along."

"You're his replicate."

He lost his breath a moment. And got caught looking her straight in the eyes.

"You don't have a temper like that," she said. "Do you?"

"I'm not like you," he said. "I'm just his twin. Physical resemblance, that's all."

"Did he fight with a lot of people?"

He tried to think what to say; and came up with: "No. But he and Ari had a lot of professional disagreements. Things that mattered to them. Personalities, mostly."

"Yanni says you're awfully good."

He wobbled badly on that shift of ground and knew she had seen the relief. "Yanni's very kind."

"Yanni's a bitch," she laughed. "But I like him. —He says you work deep-set stuff."

He nodded. "Experimental." He was glad to talk about his work. Anything but the subject they had been on.

"He says your designs are really good. But the computers keep spitting out Field Too Large."

"They've done some other tests."

"I'd like you to teach me," she said.

"Ari, that's kind of you, but I don't think your uncle Denys would like that. I *don't* think they want me around you. I don't think that's ever going to change."

"I want you to teach me," she said, "what you're doing."

He found no quick answer then. And she waited without saying a thing.

"Ari, that's *my* work. You know there *is* a little personal vanity involved here—" Truth, he was disturbed; cornered; and the child was innocent in it, he thought, completely. "Ari, I've had little enough I've really done in my life; I'd at least like to do the first write-up on it, before it gets sucked up into someone else's work. If it's worth anything. You know there *is* such a thing as professional jealousy. And you'll do so much in your life. Leave me my little corner."

She looked put off by that. A line appeared between her brows. "I wouldn't steal from you."

He made it light, a little laugh, grim as it was. "You know what we're doing. Arguing like the first Ari and my father. Over the same damn thing. You're trying to be nice. I know that—"

"I'm not trying to be nice. I'm asking you."

"Look, Ari, —"

"I won't steal your stuff. I don't *care* who writes it up. I just want you to show me what you do and how you do it."

He sat back. It was a corner she backed him into, a damned, petulant child used to having her way in the world. "Ari, —"

"I *need* it, dammit!"

"You don't *get* everything you need in this world."

"You're saying I'd steal from you!"

"I'm not saying you'd steal. I'm saying I've got a few rights, Ari, few as they are in this place—maybe I want my name on it. *And* my father's. If just because it's the same last name."

That stopped her. She thought about it, staring at him.

"I can figure that," she said. "I can *fix* that. I promise you. I won't take anything you don't want me to. *I don't lie*, Justin. I don't tell lies. Not to my friends. Not in important things. I want to learn. I want you to teach me. Nobody in the House is going to keep me from having any teacher I want. And it's you."

"You know—if you get me in trouble, Ari, you know what it can do."

"You're not going to get in any trouble. I'm a wing supervisor. Even if I haven't got a wing to work in. So I can make my own, can't I? You. And Grant."

His heart went to long, painful beats. "I'd rather not be transferred."

She shook her head. "Not really *move*. I've got a Wing One office. It's just paper stuff. It just means my staff does your paperwork. —I'm sorry." When he said nothing in her pause: "I *did* it."

"*Damn* it, Ari—"

"It's just paperwork. *And* I don't like having stuff I'm working on lying around your office. —I can change it back, if you like."

"I'd rather." He leaned his arms on his knees, looking her in the eye. "Ari, —I told you. I've got little enough in my life. I'd like to hang on to my independence. If you don't mind."

"They're bugging your apartment. You know that."

"I figured they might be."

"If you're in my wing, I can re-route the Security stuff so I get it, same as uncle Denys."

"I don't *want* it, Ari."

She gave him a worried, slightly hurt look. "Will you teach me?"

"All right," he said. Because there was no way out of it.

"You don't sound happy."

"I don't know, Ari."

She reached out and squeezed his hand. "Friends. All right? Friends?" He squeezed hers. And tried to believe it.

"They'll probably arrest me when I get back to the House."

"No, they won't." She drew her hand back. "Come on. We'll all walk up together. *I've* got to get a shower before I go anywhere. But you can tell me what you're working on."

X

They parted company at the quadrangle. He walked on, heart racing as he walked toward the Wing One doors, where the guard always stood, where—quite likely, the guard was getting an advisement over the pocket-com; or sending one and getting orders back.

He had seen enough of Security's inner rooms.

He walked through the door, looked at the guard eye to eye—offering no threat, trying without saying a thing to communicate that he was not going to be a problem: he had had enough in his life of being slammed face-about against walls.

"Good day, ser," the guard said, and his heart did a skip-beat. "Good day," he said, and walked on through the small foyer into the hall, all the way to the lift, all the time he was standing there expecting to get a sharp order from behind him, still expecting it all the way down the hall upstairs. But he got as far as his office, and Grant was there, unarrested, looking worried and frayed at the edges.

"It's all right," he said, to relieve the worst of Grant's fears. "Went pretty well. A lot better than it could have." He sat down, drew a breath or two. "She's asked me to teach her."

Grant did not react overmuch. He shrugged finally. "Denys will put the quietus on that."

"No. I don't know *what* in hell it is. She got us transferred. I," he said as Grant showed alarm, "got us transferred *back* to Yanni's wing. But right now—and until she gets it straight with Security—we're not Wing One. That's how serious it is—if she's telling the truth; and I haven't a reason in the world to doubt it. She *wants* me to work with her. She's been talking with Yanni about my work, Yanni told her—damn him—he thinks I'm on some kind of important track, and young sera *wants* what I know, wants me to show her everything I'm working on."

Grant exhaled a long, slow breath.

"So, well—" Justin swung the chair around, reached for his coffee cup and got up to fill it from the pot. "That's the story. If Security doesn't come storming in here— You want a cup?"

"Thanks. —Sit down, let me get it."

"I've got it." He retrieved Grant's cup and gave him the rest of the pot and a little of his own. "Here." He handed Grant the cup. "Anyway, she was reasonable. She was—"

Not quite the little kid anymore.

But he didn't say that. He said: "—quite reasonable. Concerned." And then remembered with a flood of panic: *We're in her administration at the moment; if there's monitoring going on, it's not routed just to Denys, it's going straight to her. My God, what have we said?*

"We'll be under her security for a little while," he said with that little Remember the eavesdroppers sign, and Grant's eyes followed that move.

Trying to remember what he had said, too, he imagined, and to figure out how a young and very dangerous CIT could interpret it.

2421: 3/4: 1945

AE2: Base One, enter: Archive. Personal.

I think I ought to keep these notes. I feel a little strange doing it. My predecessor's never told me to. But they archived everything I did up to a few years ago. I imagine everything on Base One gets archived. Maybe I should put my own notes in. Maybe someday that'll be important. Because I think I *am* important.

That sounds egotistical. But that's all right. They wanted me to be.

I'm Ari Emory. I'm not the first but I'm not quite only the second either. We've got so much in common. Sometimes I hate my uncles for doing what they did to me—especially about maman. But if they hadn't—I don't know, I wouldn't want to be different than I am. I wouldn't want to not be me. I sure wouldn't want to be other people I could name. Maybe the first Ari could say that too.

I know she would. I know it even if she never told me.

I'd say: That's spooky.

She'd say: That's damned dangerous.

And I know what she'd mean. I know exactly what she'd mean by that and why she'd worry about me—but I know some things she didn't, like how I feel and whether the way I think about her is dangerous, or whether being a little different from her is dangerous. I'm pretty sure I'm all right, but I don't know if I'm close enough to her to be as smart as she was or to

494

take care of the things she left me, and I won't know the things that made me smart enough until I'm good enough to look back on how they made me and say—they needed that. Or, they didn't.

I'm riding about fifteen to twenty points above her scores in psych—at the same chronological age. And I'm two points ahead of her score two years from now. Same in most of my subjects. But that's deceptive because I've had the benefits of the things she did and the way she worked, that everybody does now. That's spooky too. But that's the way it'd have to be, isn't it? Tapes have gotten better, and they've tailored so much of this for me, specifically, off her strong points and weaknesses, it's no wonder I'm going faster. But I can't get smug about it, because there's no guarantee on anything, and no guarantee I'll stay ahead at any given point.

It's spooky to know you're an experiment, and to watch yourself work. There's this boy out on Fargone, who's like me. Someday I'm going to write to him and just say hello, Ben, this is Ari. I hope you're all right.

Justin says they're easier on him than on me. He says maybe they didn't have to be so rough, but they couldn't take chances with me, and when I'm grown maybe I can figure out what they really could have left out.

I said I thought that was damned dangerous, wasn't it? Doing psych on yourself—is real dangerous, especially if you're psych-trained. I'm always scared when I start thinking about how I work, because that's an intervention, when you really know psych, but you don't know enough yet. It's like—my mind is so hard to keep aimed, it wants to go sideways and inside and everywhere—

I told Justin that too. He said he understood. He said sometimes when you're young you have to think about things, because you're forming your value-sets and you keep coming up with Data Insufficient and finding holes in your programs. So you keep trying to do a fix on your sets. And the more powerful your mind is and the more intense your concentration is, the worse damage you can do to yourself, which is why, Justin says, Alphas always have trouble and some of them go way off and out-there, and why almost all Alphas are eccentric. But he says the best thing you can do if you're too bright for your own good is what the Testers do, be aware where you got which idea, keep a tab on everything and know how your ideas link up with each other and with your deep-sets and value-sets, so when you're forty or fifty or a hundred forty and you find something that doesn't work, you can still find all the threads and pull them.

But that's not real easy unless you know what your value-sets are, and most CITs don't. CITs have a trouble with not *wanting* to know that kind of thing. Because some of them are real eetee once you get to thinking about how they link. Especially about sex and ego-nets.

Justin says inflexibility is a trap and most Alpha types are inward-turned because they process so fast they're gone and thinking before a Gamma gets a sentence out. Then they get in the habit of thinking they thought of everything, but they don't remember everything stems from input. You may have a new idea, but it *stems* from input somebody gave you, and that could be wrong or your senses could have been lying to you. He says it can be an equipment-quality problem or a program-quality problem, but once an Alpha takes a falsehood for true, it's a personal problem.

I like that. I wish I'd said it.

And once an Alpha stops re-analyzing his input and starts outputting only, he's gone completely eetee. Which is why, Justin says, Alpha azi can't be tape-trained past a certain point, because they don't learn to analyze and question the flux-level input they get later, and when they socialize too late, they go more and more internal because things actually seem too fast and too random for them, exactly the opposite of the problem the socialized Alphas have—too fast, though, only because they're processing like crazy trying to make more out of the input than's really there, because they don't understand there *is* no system, at least there's no micro-system, and they keep trying to make one out of the flux they don't understand.

Which is why some Alphas go dangerous and why you have trouble getting them to take help-tapes: some start flux-thinking on everything, and some just go schiz, de-structure their deep-sets and reconstruct their own, based on whatever comes intact out of the flux they're getting. And after that you don't know what they are. They become like CITs, only with some real strange logic areas.

Which is why they're so hard to help.

I think Yanni is right about Justin. I think he's awfully smart. I've asked my uncle Denys about him, about whether they don't make him a Special because of politics; and Denys said he didn't know whether Justin qualified, but the politics part was definitely true.

Ari, Denys said, I know you're fond of him. If you are, do him and yourself a favor and don't talk about him with anybody on staff—especially don't mention him in Novgorod.

I said I thought that was rotten, it was just because of what his father did, and it wasn't his fault any more than it was mine what my predecessor and his father were fighting about.

And then uncle Denys said something scary. He said: No. I'm telling you this for his sake. You think about it, Ari. He's very bright. He's possibly everything you say. Give him immunity and you give him power, Ari, and power is something he'd have to use. Think about it. You know Novgorod. You know the situation. And you know that Justin's honest. Think about what power would do to him.

I did think then, just like a flash, like lightning going off at night, and you can see everything, all the buildings you know are there, but you forget—you forget about the details of things until the flash comes—and it's gray and clearer than day in some ways. Like there could be color, but there's not quite enough light. So you can see everything the way you can't see it in daylight.

That's what it is when somebody throws light on what you've got all the pieces of.

His father is at Planys.

That's first.

Then there are all these other things—like him being my teacher. Like—we're best friends. But it's like Amy. Amy's my best friend but Florian and Catlin. And we couldn't get along till Amy knew I could beat her. Like she was going to *have* to do something about me until she knew she couldn't. Then we're all right.

Power stuff. Ari was right about that too—about us being territorial as hell, only territory is the wrong word. Territory is only something you can attach that idea to because we got used to the root concept when we were working with animals.

That's what Ari called science making itself a semantic problem. Because if you think territoriality you don't realize what you're really anxious about. We're not bettas.

The old Greeks talked about moira. Moira means *lot* in Greek. Like your share of things. And you can't grab somebody else's—that's stealing; you can't not do your own; that's being a coward. But figuring out what yours is would be a bitch, except other people and other animals help you define what your edges are when they react back: if they don't react back or they don't react so you can understand them you get anxiety reactions and you react with the fight or flight bias your psychset gives you, whether you're a human being or a betta. I got that from Sophocles. And Aristotle. And Amy Carnath and her bettas, because she's the first CIT friend I ever had I worked that out with, and she breeds fighting fish.

It's not territory. It's equilibrium. An equilibrated system has tensions in balance, like girders and trusses in a building.

Rigid systems are vulnerable. Ari said that. Equilibrated systems can flex under stress.

The old Greeks used to put flex in their buildings, moving joints, because they had earthquakes.

I'm leading up to something.

I think it has to do with me and Justin.

I don't trust too much flex any more than too little. Too much and your wall goes down; too little and it breaks.

I'm saying this for the record. If I was talking to Justin or Yanni or uncle Denys I'd say:

Non-looping paths don't necessarily have to be macro-setted on an individual level.

Except then—

—then you have to macro-set the social matrix, which you can do—

—but the variables are real killers to work out—Justin's proved that.

God, talking with yourself has some benefits.

That's what Ari meant by macro-values. That's what she was talking about. That's how she could be so damned careless about the random inputs with her designs. They all feed into a single value: the flux always has to reset off the central sets. That's what Justin was trying to explain to me: flux re-set functions.

Gehennans identify with their world. That's the whole center of what Ari did with that design. And no flux-thinking can get at that.

But where does that go?

Damn! I wish I could tell it to Justin. . . .

Define: world. There's the worm. God! It could be one, if you could guide that semantic mutation.

Pity we have to input words instead of numbers. Into a hormone-fluxed system.

Justin says.

Justin says semantics is always the problem; the more concrete a value you link the sets to, the better off your design is with the computers—but that's not all of it. The link-point has to be a non-fluxing thing—Justin says—

No! Not non-flux. Slow-flux. Flux relative or proportional to the rest of the flux in the sets—like a scissors-joint: everything can move without changing the structure, just the distance down the one axis—

No. Not even that. If the flux on the macro-set has a time-lag of any kind you're going to increase the adaptive flux in the micro-sets in any system. But if you could work out that relevancy in any kind of symbological matrix—then you can get a numerical value back.

Can't you?

Doesn't that do something with the Field Size problem? Isn't that something like a log, if the internal change rates in the sets could be setted; and then—

No, damn, then your world is fine until it gets immigrants; and the first random inputs come in and give you someone who doesn't share the same values—

Immigration—on Gehenna—

Could change the definition of *world* . . . couldn't it?

Damn, I wish I could ask Justin about these things. Maybe I know something. Even if I am sixteen. I know things I can't tell anybody. Especially Justin. And they could be terribly dangerous.

But Gehenna's quarantined. It's safe—so far. I've got time. Don't I?

Justin resents what I did, when I made him be my teacher. I know he does. He frowns a lot. Sometimes Grant looks worried about the situation. Grant's mad at me too. He would be. Even if both of them try to be nice. And not just nice. They *are* kind. Both. They're just upset. Justin's been arrested every time I got in trouble. A lot of things that weren't fair at all. I know why they did it. Like what my uncles did to me. But they were never fair to him.

So it's not like I blame him for his mad. And he keeps it real well: I can respect that. I have one of my own that I'll never forgive. Not really. He knows it's not my fault about his father and all. He knows I'm not lying when I say he and Grant can both go see his father when all this political mess clears up, and I'll help him every way I can.

But he's still hurting about his father. Maman was clear away on

Fargone and I never even heard from her again, but she was far away, out of reach, and after a while it didn't hurt so awful much. *His* father is on Cyteen, and they can talk, but that's bad too, because you'd always have to be thinking about how close that is. And now they can't even talk by phone and he's worried about his father, I know he is.

Then I go and tell him he's going to give me his research, that he's been working on with his father and he hopes could help his father—that's something I did, me. People have been terrible to him all his life and every- thing he's got he's fought to have, and some kid comes in and wants every- thing he's done—and *I'm* the one who gets him in trouble— That's my fault, I know it is, but I've got to have his stuff. It's important. But I can't tell him why and I can't tell him what I want. So he just goes azi on me. That's the only way I can describe it—just very cool and very proper.

We work in his office mostly. He says he wants witnesses when he's around me. The Warricks have had enough trouble, he says.

He gives me some real work, because he says I'm not bad, and I can do the frameworks. And then I catch him sometimes, because when I'm really, really doing my best, and especially when I come up with something all the way right, he forgets his mad for a second or two and he loosens up and something shines out of him, that's a hell of a precise description, isn't it? But he gets interested in what we're doing and the ice thaws a bit, and he's just—all right with me. For about two or three minutes, until he re- members that everything he teaches me is going away from him and into me. And I think he thinks I'm going to rob him of everything. And I wish I could make him understand I'd like to help him.

Because I do. I hurt when he's cold with me. It feels so good when he's happy.

Hell if I can give him what's mine, but I don't need to take what's his. And he's a lot like me, everybody's messed with his life.

If I could figure out something, if I could figure out something of Ari senior's that I *could* give him, maybe that would make it fair. Because I know so much, but I don't know enough to make it worth anything. And maybe I'm sitting still with something I think is a real little piece, but that would be worth a lot to him.

Because, oh, he's smart. I know, because when he tells me his reasons for what he does, he has a lot of trouble, because he just *knows* some of these things. He said once I'm making him structure his concepts. He said that's good. Because we *can* talk, sometimes Grant gets into it, and once, it was the best day we ever worked together, we all went to lunch and talked and talked about CIT and azi logic until I couldn't sleep that night, I was still going on it. It was one of the best days I ever remember. And they were happy, and I was. But it sort of died away, then, and everything got back to normal, things just sort of got in the way and Justin came in kind of down, the way he does sometimes, and it was over. Like that.

I'm going to Get him one of these days, though. I'm going to Get both of them. And maybe this is it.

Maybe if I just run through everything I've got on this model thing, maybe it won't work, I guess if it did someone would have thought of it—

No, dammit, Ari, Justin said—I should never tell myself that.

Don't cut ideas off, he says, till you know where they go.

If I could do something *real*, —

What would he do, —get mad, because then I'd be getting closer to what he's working on, and he'd resent that?

Or get mad, because he'd want it all to be his idea?

Maybe he would.

But maybe he'd warm up to me and it could be the way it is sometimes—all the time. That's what I wish. Because so much bad has happened. And I want to change that.

CHAPTER 12

There were new tapes. Maddy brought them. Maddy did the ordering of things like that, because her mother didn't mind, and uncle Denys said that it would be a scandal if it were on *her* account: which Maddy might have figured out, Maddy was not really stupid, but it pleased Maddy to be involved in intrigue and something she truly did best.

So that was a point Maddy got on her side. That kind of favor was something Maddy could use for blackmail, Ari thought, except there was no percentage in it. If Maddy ever wanted to use it in Novgorod, that was all right, she would be grown then and people would not see the sixteen-year-old—just a grown woman, who was, then, only like her predecessor—whose taste for such things was quietly known. Strange, Ari thought, how people were so little capable of being shocked in retrospect: old news, the proverb ran.

And Maddy could be free as she liked with sex, because Maddy was just Maddy Strassen, and the Strassens had no power to frighten anyone—outside Reseune.

It was a quiet gathering. The Kids. Period. Mostly she just wanted to relax, and they sat around watching the tape quite, quite tranked, except Florian and Catlin, and drinking a little—except Florian and Catlin. Sam spilled a drink—he was terribly embarrassed about it. But Catlin helped him mop up and took him to the back bedroom and helped him in another way, which was Catlin's own idea, because Sam and Amy were having trouble.

God, life got complicated. *Amy* had a fix on Stef Dietrich; and that was hopeless. Sam had one—well, on herself, Ari reckoned; and that was the trouble, that Amy got seconds on a lot of things in life. And Amy was interested in a lot of things Sam wasn't. And vice versa. She wished to hell Sam would find somebody. Anybody.

But he didn't. And Sam was the main reason why she didn't go off to the bedroom with Tommy or Stef or anyone who came to the apartment; but he wasn't the only reason. The main one was what it had always been, the same reason that she was best friends with Amy and Sam and Maddy and kept everyone else at arm's length—because Sam was always in the way to get hurt, there was no way to shut him out, nor was it fair, and yet—

And yet—

Of all the boys he was the only one who really liked just *her*, herself, from before he ever knew she was anybody.

And that made her sad sometimes, because all the others would be thinking about themselves and what it meant to them, and how she was a Special and she was rich and she was going to be Administrator someday, and making her happy was very, very important—

Which was a lot different than Sam, who loved her, she thought, who really truly loved her. And she loved him—what time she was not frustrated that he existed, frustrated that he had to love her *that* way, frustrated that he was the focus of all her other frustrations and never, ever, deserved them—

Because she would not sleep with Stef Dietrich if there never had been a Sam. That was still true.

For one thing it would kill Amy. Amy could stand to be beaten by Yvgenia, but not by her—in this. No matter that Amy was still gawky and awkward, and never *worked* at her appearance . . . until she took after Stef, and then it was almost pathetic. Amy, with eyeshadow. Amy, fussing with her hair, which was loose now, not in braids. After Stef, who was so damned handsome and so sure of it.

While Sam was a little at loose ends, not quite betrayed, but a lot at a loss. And if Stef had antennae for anything, he knew damned well he had better walk a narrow line between Yvgenia and Amy.

And it left her, herself, to watch the tapes and afterward, after Florian and Catlin had showed everyone out, to lie on the couch and stare at the ceiling in a melancholy not even they could relieve.

"Come to bed, sera," Florian said.

Worried about her.

Worried and absolutely devoted.

The ceiling hazed in her sight. If she blinked the tears would run and they would see them.

But the tears spilled anyway, just ran from the outside edge of her eye, so she blinked, it made no difference.

"Sera?" There was profound upset in Florian's voice. He wiped her cheek, the merest feather-touch. And was certainly in pain.

Dammit. Damn him. Damn him for that reaction.

I'm smarter than Ari senior. At least I haven't fouled up things with Sam and Amy. They've fouled it up with each other.

I don't understand CITs. I really truly don't understand CITs.

Azi are so much kinder.

And they can't help it.

"Sera." Florian patted her cheek, laid a hand on her shoulder. "Who hurt you?"

Shall we kill him? she imagined the next question. For some reason that struck her hysterically funny. She started laughing, laughing till she had to pull her legs up to save her stomach from aching, and the tears ran; and Florian held her hands and Catlin slid over the back of the couch to kneel by her and hold on to her.

Which only struck her funnier.

"I'm—I'm sorry," she gasped finally, when she could get a breath. Her stomach hurt. And they were so terribly confused. "Oh. I'm sorry." She reached and patted Florian's shoulder, Catlin's leg. "I'm sorry. I'm just tired, that's all. That damn report—"

"The *report*, sera?" Florian asked.

She caught her breath, flattened out with a little shift around Catlin and let go a long sigh. "I've been working so hard. You have to forgive me. CITs do this kind of thing. Oh, God, the Minder. I hope to God you didn't re-arm the system—"

"No, sera, not yet."

"That's good. Damn. Oh, damn, my sides hurt. That thing—calling the Bureau—would just about cap the whole week, wouldn't it? Blow an assignment, miss the whole damn point. Amy's making a fool of herself and Sam's walking wounded—CIT's are a bitch, you know it? They're a real pain."

"Sam seemed happy," Catlin said.

"I'm glad." For some reason the pain came back behind her heart. And she sighed again and wiped her eyes. "God, I bet that got my makeup. I bet I look a sight."

"You're always beautiful, sera." Florian wiped beneath her left eye with a fingertip, and wiped his hand on his sleeve and wiped the other one. "There."

She smiled then, and laughed silently, without the pain, seeing two worried faces, two human beings who would, in fact, take on anyone she named—never mind their own safety.

"We should get to bed," she said. "I've got to do that paper tomorrow. I've got to do it. I really shouldn't have done this. And I don't even want to get up from here."

"We can carry you."

"God," she said, feeling Florian slip his hands under. "You'll drop me— Florian!"

He stopped.

"I'll walk," she said. And got up, and did, with her arms around both of them, not that she needed the balance.

Just that she needed someone, about then.

Ari bit her lip, perfectly quiet while Justin was reading her report. She sat with her arms on her knees and her hands clenched while he flipped through the printout.

"What is this?" he asked finally, looking up, very serious. "Ari, where did you get this?"

"It's a world I made up. Like Gehenna. You start with those sets. And you tell them, you have to defend this base and you teach your children to defend it. And you give them these tapes. And you get this kind of parameter between A and Y in the matrix; and you get this set between B and Y, and so on; and there's a direct relationship between the change in A and the rest of the shifts—so I did a strict mechanics model, like it was a fluxing structure, but with all these levels—"

"I can see that." Justin's brow furrowed, and he asked apprehensively: "This *isn't* Gehenna, is it?"

She shook her head. "No. That's classified. That's my problem. I built this thing with a problem in it, but that's all right, that's to keep it inside a few generations. It's whether all the sets change at the same rate, that's what I'm asking."

"You mean you're inputting the whole colony at once. *No* outsiders."

"They can get there in the fourth generation. Gehenna's did. Page 330."

He flipped through and looked.

"I just want to talk about it," she said. "I just got to thinking about whether some of the problems in the sociology models, you know, aren't because you're trying to do ones that work. So I'm setting up a system with deliberate problems, to see how the problems work. I changed everything. You don't need to worry I'm telling you anything you don't want to know. I just got to thinking about Gehenna and closed systems, and so I made you a model. It's in the appendix. There's a sort of a worm in it. I won't tell you what, but I think you can see it—or I'm not right about it." She bit her lip. "Page 330. One of those paragraphs is Ari's. About values and flux. You tell me a lot of things. I looked through Ari's notes for things that could help you. That's hers. So's the bit on the group sets. It's real stuff. It's stuff out of Archive. I thought you could use it. Fair trade."

It was terribly dangerous. It was terribly close to things that people weren't supposed to know about, that could bring panic down on the Gehennans; and worse.

But everybody in Reseune speculated on the Gehenna tapes, and people from inside Reseune didn't talk to people outside, and people outside wouldn't understand them anyway. She sat there with her hands clenched together and her stomach in a knot, with gnawing second thoughts, whether he would see too much—being as smart as he was. But he worked on microsystems. Ari's were macros—in the widest possible sense.

He said nothing for a long while.

"You know you're not supposed to be telling me this," he said in a whisper. Like they were being bugged; or the habit was there, like it was with her. "Dammit, Ari, you *know* it— What are you trying to do to me?"

"How else am I going to learn?" she hissed back, whispering because he whispered. "Who else is there?"

He fingered the edges of the pages and stared at it. And looked up. "You've put in a lot of work on this."

She nodded. It was why she had blown the last assignment. But that was sniveling. She didn't say that. She just waited for what he would say.

And he *did* see too much. She saw it in his face. He was not trying to hide his upset. He only stared at her a long, long time.

"Are we being monitored?" he asked.

"My uncles," she said, "probably." Not saying that *she* could. "It might go into Archive. I imagine they take every chance to tape *me* they can get, since I threw them out of my bedroom a long time ago. Don't worry about it. It doesn't matter what they listen to. There's no way they'll tell *me* no, when it comes to what I need to learn. Or give you any trouble."

"For somebody who held off the Council in Novgorod," Justin said, "you can still be naive."

"They won't do it, I'm telling you."

"Why? Because you say so? You don't run Reseune, your uncles do. And will, for some years. Ari, —my *God*, Ari—"

He shoved his chair back and got up and walked out.

Which left her sitting there, with Grant on the other side of the cluttered little office, staring at her, not quite azi-like, but very cold and very wary, like something was her fault.

"Nothing's going to happen!" she said to Grant.

Grant got up and came and took the report from Justin's desk.

"That's his," she said, putting a hand on it.

"It's yours. You can take it back or I can put it in the safe. I don't think Justin wants to teach you any more today, young sera. I imagine he'll read it very carefully if you leave it here. But you've grounded him. I don't doubt you've grounded me as well. Security would never believe I wasn't involved."

"You mean about his father?" She looked up at Grant, caught in the position of disadvantage, with Grant looming over her chair. "It doesn't make any difference. Khalid's not going to hold on to that seat. Another six months and there won't be any problem. Defense is going to be sensible again and there won't be any problem."

Grant only stared at her a moment. Then: "Free Jordan, why don't you, young sera? Possibly because you *can't*? —Please go. I'll put this up for him."

She sat there a moment more while Grant took the report and took it to the wall-safe and put it inside. Then Grant left.

Just—left her there.

So she left, and walked down the hall with a lump in her throat.

He was better, at home, with a drink in him. With the report in his lap—he had gotten it from the safe, and when Grant said that it was dangerous to carry about, he had said: So let them arrest me. I'm used to it. What the hell?

So he sat sipping a well-watered Scotch and reading the paragraph on 330 over and over again. "God," he said, when he had gone through it the second time, sifting through the limitation of words for the precious content. It was valuable—was like a light going on—in a small area, but there was nothing small or inconsequential where ideas had to link together. "She's talking about values here. The interlock of the ego-net and the value sets in azi psych and the styles of integration—why some are better than others. I needed this—back at the start. I had to work it out. Damn, Grant, how much else I've done—is already in Archives, just waiting there? That's a hell of a thought, isn't it?"

"It isn't true," Grant said. "If it was, *Ari* would have been doing the papers."

"I think I know why I interested her," he said. "At least—part of it." He took another drink and thumbed through the report. "I wonder how much of this is *our* Ari's. Whether it's something Ari senior suggested to her to do— and gave her the framework on—or whether Ari just—put this together. It's a graduation project. That's what it is. A thesis. And I can see how Ari must have looked at mine—when I was seventeen and naive as hell about design. But there's a lot more in this. The model work is first rate."

"She's got a major base in the House computers to help her," Grant said. "She can pull time on nets you couldn't even consult when *you* were her age—"

"On facilities I didn't know existed when I was her age. Yes. And I hadn't had her world-experience, and a lot of other things— I was younger—in a lot of ways—than she is right now. Damn, she's done a lot of work on this. And typically, she never said a thing about what she was working on. I think it *is* hers. This whole model is naive as hell, she's planted *two* major timebombs in the center-set, which is overkill if she's trying to get a failure—but she's likely going to run it with increasing degrees of clean-up. Maybe compare one drift against the other." Another drink and a slow shake of his head. "You know what this is, it's a bribe. It's a damn bribe. Two small windows into those Archived notes, and both of them completely unpublished material— And I'm sitting here weighing what else could be there—that could make everything I'm doing obsolete before it's published—or be the key to what I *could* do—what I could have done—if Ari hadn't been murdered—And I'm weighing it against losing years of contact with Jordan. Against the chance neither one of us might ever—"

He lost his voice again. Took a drink and gazed at the wall.

"Because there's no choice," he concluded, when he had had several more swallows of whiskey and he was halfway numb again. "I don't even know why, or what part of this report is real, or how much of Gehenna is in here." He looked at Grant; and hated himself for the whole situation he was in, because it was Grant's chances of Planys that had been shot to hell, equally as well as his. Grant had sat at home waiting on all his other visits—because the whole weight of law and custom and the practical facts of Grant's azi vulnerabilities to manipulation and his abilities to remember and focus on instruction—had barred him from Planys thus far.

Now their jailers had the ultimate excuse, if they had ever needed one.

"I had no idea," he said to Grant, "I had *no* idea what she was working on, or where this was going."

"Ari is not entirely naive in this," Grant said. "If Gehenna is what she's working on—and she wants to work on it with you—she knows that won't sit well in some circles; *and* that you'll understand right through to the heart of the designs and beyond. Ari is accustomed to having her way. More than that, Ari is convinced her way is all-important. Be careful of her. Be extremely careful."

"She knows something, something that's got to do with Gehenna, that hasn't gotten into public."

Grant looked at him long and hard. "Be careful," Grant said. "Justin, for God's sake, be careful."

"Dammit, I—" The frustration in Grant's voice got to him, reached raw nerves, even past the whiskey. He set the glass down and rested his elbows on his knees, his hands on the back of his neck. "Oh, God." The tears came the way they had not in years. He squeezed his eyes shut, tried to dam them back, aware of painful silence in the room.

After a while he got up and added more whiskey to the ice-melt, and stood staring at the corner until he heard Grant get up and come over to the bar, and he looked and took Grant's glass and added ice and whiskey.

"Someday the situation will change," Grant said, took his glass and touched it to his, a light, fragile clink of glass on glass. "Keep your balance. There's no profit in anything else. The election count will be over by fall. The whole situation may change, not overnight, but change, all the same."

"Khalid could win."

"A meteor could strike us. Do we worry about such things? Finish that. Come to bed. All right?"

He shuddered, drank the rest off and shuddered again. He could not *get* drunk enough.

He slammed the glass down on the counter-top and pushed away from the bar, to do what Grant had said.

---

ii

Ari, Justin's voice had said on the Minder, *be in my office in the morning.*

So she came, was waiting for him when he got there, and he said, opening the door—he had come alone this time, almost the only time: "Ari, I owe you an apology. A profound apology for yesterday." He had her report with him and he laid it down on his desk and riffled the pages. "You did this. Yourself. It was your idea."

"Yes," she said, anxious.

"It's remarkable. It's a really remarkable job. —I don't say it's right, understand, but it's going to take me a little to get through it, not just because of the size. Have you shown this to your uncle?"

She shook her head. It was too hard to talk about coherently. She had not slept much. "No. I did it for you."

"I wasn't very gracious about it. Forgive me. I've been that route myself, with Yanni. I didn't mean to do that to you."

"I understand why you're upset," she said. "I do." Grant was likely to come in at any time and she wanted to get this out beforehand. "Justin, Grant took into me. He was right. But I am too. If Reseune is safe again you can travel. If it isn't, nothing will help, and this won't hurt—in fact it makes you safer, because there's no way they can come at you *or* your father without coming at me, because your father's worked on your stuff, and that means he's working with you and you're working with me, and all he has to do, Justin, all he has to do, if he wants my help—is not do anything against me. I don't even care if he likes me. I just want to work things out so they're better. I *thought* about the danger in working with you, I did think, over and over again—but you're the one I need, because you work long-term and you work with the value-sets and that's what I'm interested in. I'm not a stupid little girl, Justin. I know what I want to work on and Yanni can't help me anymore. Nobody can. So I have to come to you. Uncle Denys knows it. He says—he says—be careful. But he also says you're honest. So am I—no!" —As he opened his mouth. "Let me say this. I *will not* steal from you. You think about this. What if we put out a paper with your name and mine *and* your father's? Don't you think that would shake them up in the Bureau?"

He sat down. "That would have to get by Denys, Ari, and I don't think he'd approve it. I'm sure Giraud wouldn't."

"You know what I'd say to my uncles? I'd say—someday I'll have to run Reseune. I'm trying to fix things. I don't want things to go the way they did. Let me try while I have your advice. Or let me try after I don't."

He scared her for a moment. His face got very still and very pale. Then Grant showed up, coming through the door, so he drew a large breath and paid attention to Grant instead. "Good morning. Coffee's not on. Yet."

"Hint," Grant said, and made a face and took the pot out for water.

"Ari," Justin said then, "I wish you luck with your uncles. More than I've had. That's all I'll say. Someday you'll find me missing if you're not careful. I'll be down in Detention. Just so you know where. I'm rather well expecting it today. And I'm not sure you can prevent that, no matter how much power you think you have in the House. I hope I'm wrong. But I'll work with you. I'll do everything I can. I've got a few questions for you to start off with. Why did you install two variables?"

She opened her mouth. She wanted to talk about the other thing. But he didn't. He closed that off like a door going shut and threw her an important question. And Grant came back with the water. They were Working her, timing everything. And he had said what he wanted to say.

"It's because one is an action and one is a substantive. *Defend* will drift and so will *base*. And there's going to be no enemy from offworld, just the possibility of one, if that gets passed down. And they're not going to have tape after the first few years: Gehenna didn't."

Justin nodded slowly. "You know that my father specializes in educational sets. That Gehenna has political consequences. You talk about my working with him. You know what you're doing, throwing this my way. You know what it could cost me. And him. If anything goes wrong, if anything blows up—it comes down on us. Do you understand that?"

"It won't."

"*It won't.* Young sera, do you know how thin that sounds to me? For God's sake be wiser than that. Not smarter. *Wiser.* Hear me?"

God. Complications. Complications with Defense. With politics. With him. With everything.

"So," he said. "Now you do know. I just want you to be aware. —Your idea about semantic drift and flux is quite good—but a little simple, because there's going to be occupational diversity, which affects semantics, and so on—"

Another shift of direction. Firm and definitive. "They stay agricultural."

He nodded. "Let's work through this, step by step. I'll give you my objections and you note them and give me your answers. . . ."

She focused down tight, the way Florian and Catlin had taught her, mind on business, and tried to hold it, but it was not easy, she was not azi, and there was so much *to* him, there was so much complication with him, he was always so soft-spoken, Yanni's complete opposite. He could come off the flank and surprise her, and so few people could do that.

He could go from being mad to being kind—so fast; and both things felt solid, both of them felt real.

She felt Grant's disapproval from across the room. There was nothing she could gain there: win Justin and eventually she won Grant, it was that simple. And she had made headway with Justin: she added it up in its various columns and thought that, overall, complicated as he was, he had given her a great deal.

---

iii

"He was nice about it," she said to Florian and Catlin at dinner. "He truly was. I think it was real."

"We'll keep an eye on him," Florian said.

They did much less of their work at the Barracks nowadays. Just occasionally they went down to take a course, only for the day. They had taken one this day. Catlin was sporting a scrape on her hand and a bruise on her chin, but she was pleased with herself, which meant pleased with the way things had gone.

Mostly they did their study by tape. Mostly things were real, nowadays. And they watched the reports they got on the Defense Bureau, and all the comings and goings of things in the installations that bordered on Reseune properties.

There had been a lot of dirty maneuvers—attempts to create scandal around Reseune. Attempts to snare Reseune personnel into public statements. Khalid was *much* better behind the scenes than in front of the cameras, and he had gained ground, while Giraud told her no, no, there's no percentage in debating him. He can make charges. The minute you deny them you're news and the thing is loose again.

But she had rather have *been* news so she could throw trouble into Khalid's lap.

There had been a scare last week when a boat had lost its engines and come ashore down by precip 10: some CITs had taken offense at the level of security they ran into, and said so, which a Centrist senator from Svetlansk had used to some advantage, and proposed an investigation of brutality on the part of Reseune Security.

Never mind that the CIT in question had tried to repossess from Security a carry-bag that had turned out to contain a questionable number of prescription drugs. The CIT claimed they were all legitimate and that he had a respiratory ailment which was aggravated by stress. He was suing for damages.

There was a directive out to Security reaffirming that Reseune stood by the guard. But Florian worried about it; and Catlin did, when Florian pointed out that it could be a deliberate thing, and if someone hadn't thought of creating an incident with Reseune Security in front of cameras, someone surely would now, likely Khalid, and likely something in Novgorod.

Let me tell you, she had said, when they brought it up with her, *don't* worry about it. If that was engineered, *that's* a fallout that could benefit our enemies. *Don't* doubt your tape; react, and react on any level your tape tells you. If I'm alive I can handle whatever falls out—politically. Do you doubt that?

No, they had said solemnly.

So she slammed her hand down on the table and they jumped like a bomb had gone off, scared white.

"Got you," she said. "You're still fast enough. That was *go* and *stop*, wasn't it? Damn fast."

Two or three breaths later Florian had said: "Sera, that was good. But you shouldn't scare us like that."

She had laughed. And patted Florian's hand and Catlin's, Catlin all sober and attentive, the way Catlin got when she was On. "You're *my* staff. Do what *I* say. Not Denys. Not your instructors. Not anyone."

So when Florian said, *We'll keep an eye on him*, there was a certain ominous tone to it.

"He's my friend," she said, reminding them of that.

"Yes, sera," Catlin said. "But we don't take things for granted."

"Enemies are much easier to plan for," Florian said. "Enemies can't get in here."

It was sense they gave her. They were things she had known once, when they were children, in uncle Denys' apartment.

"Hormones," she said, "are a bitch. They do terrible things to your thinking. Of course you're right. Do what you have to."

"Hormones, sera?" Florian asked.

She shrugged, feeling uncomfortable. But there was no jealousy about it. Just worry. "He's good-looking," she said. "That gets in the way, doesn't it? But I'm not crazy, either."

She felt strange about that, after. Scared. And she thought of times when she had had a lot less flux going on.

So she thought of Nelly; and thought that it had been much too long since she had seen her; and found her the next morning, a Nelly a little on the plump side, and very, very busy with her charges in the nursery.

Nelly had a little trouble focusing on her, as if the changes were too sudden or the time had been too long. "Young sera?" Nelly said, blinking several times. "Young sera?"

"I got to thinking about you," she said to Nelly. "How are you doing? Are you happy?"

"Oh, yes. Yes, young sera." A baby began crying. Nelly gave it a distracted look, over her shoulder. Someone else saw to it. "You've grown so much."

"I have. I'm sixteen, Nelly."

"Is it that long?" Nelly blinked again, and shook her head. "You were my first baby."

"I'm your oldest. Can I buy you lunch, Nelly? Put on your coat and come to lunch with me?"

"Well, I—" Nelly looked back at the rows of cribs.

"I've cleared it with your Super. Everything's fine. Come on."

It was very strange. In some ways Nelly was still only Nelly, fussy with her own appearance—fussy with hers. Nelly reached out and straightened her collar, and Ari smiled in spite of the twitch it made about self-defense, because there was no one else in the universe who would do that now.

But she knew before lunch was half over that the small wistful thought she had had, of bringing Nelly back to the apartment, was not the thing to do.

Poor Nelly would never understand the pressures she stood—or, God knew, the tape library.

Nelly was only glad to have found one of her babies again. And Ari made a note to tell the nursery Super that Nelly should have reward tape: that was the best thing she could do for Nelly—besides let her know that her eldest baby was doing well.

That her eldest baby was—what she was . . . Nelly was hardly able to understand.

Only that Nelly straightened her collar again before they parted company, Ari treasured. It made a little lump in her throat and made her feel warm all the way down the hall.

She went out to the cemetery, where there was a little marker that said Jane Strassen, 2272-2414. And she sat there a long time.

"I know why you didn't write," she said to no one, because maman had gone to the sun, the way Ariane Emory had. "I know you loved me. I wish

Ollie would write. But I can guess why he doesn't—and I'm afraid to write to him because Khalid knows too much about people I'm fond of as it is.

"I saw Nelly today. Nelly's happy. She has so many babies to take care of—but she never cares what they'll be, just that they're babies, that's all. She's really nice—in a way so few people are.

"I know why you tried to keep me away from Justin. But we've become friends, maman. I remember the first time I saw him. That's the first thing I remember—us going down the hall, and Ollie carrying me. And the punch bowl and Justin and Grant across the room; and me. I remember that. I remember the party at Valery's after.

"I'm doing all right, maman. I'm everything all of you wanted me to be. I wish there was something you'd left me, the way Ari senior did. Because I wish I knew so many things.

"Mostly I'm doing all right. I thought you'd like to know."

Which was stupid. Of course maman knew nothing. She only made herself cry, and sat there a long time on the bench, and remembered herself with her arm in the cast, and aunt Victoria, and Novgorod and Giraud, and everything that had happened.

She was lonely. That was the problem. Florian and Catlin could not understand flux the way she felt it, and she wished when it grew as bad as it was, that there had been maman to say: Dammit, Ari, what in hell's the matter with you?

"Mostly I'm lonely, maman. Florian's fine. But he's not like Ollie. He's mostly Catlin's. And I can't interfere in that.

"I wish they'd made an Ollie too. Somebody who was just mine. And if there was, Florian would be jealous—but of him being another azi and close to me, not—not about what a CIT would be jealous of.

"I'm not altogether like Ari senior. I've been a lot smarter about sex. I haven't fouled up my friends. They've fouled each other up. 'Stasi's not speaking to Amy. Over Stef Dietrich. And Sam's hurt. And Maddy's just disgusted. I hate it.

"And I'm fluxing so badly I could die. I want Florian and I know it's smart to stay to him. But I feel like there's something in me that's just—alone all the time.

"And I feel bad about thinking it, but Florian doesn't touch the lonely feeling. He just feels good for a while. And even while we're doing it, you know, sometimes everything's all right and sometimes I feel like I'm all alone. He doesn't know all my problems, but he tries, and he'll never tell me no, I have to tell myself no for him. Like I always have to be careful. *That's* the trouble.

"I think it's like floating in space, maman. There's nothing around me for lightyears all around. There's times that I'd rather Florian than anybody, because there's no one understands me like he does when I'm down or when I'm scared. But there's a side of me he just can't help, that's the problem. And I think he knows it.

"That's the awful thing. He's starting to worry about me. Like it was his fault. And *I* don't know why I'm doing this to him. I'm so mad at myself. Ari talked about hurting Florian—her Florian. And that scares hell out of me, maman. I don't ever want to do that. But I am, when I make him feel like my problems are his fault.

"Did you ever have this with Ollie?

"Maybe I should just go down to the Town and try it with some of the azi down there, that do that kind of thing. Maybe somebody like a Mu-class, who knows? A grown-up one. Somebody I can't mess up.

"But that kind of embarrasses me. Uncle Denys would have a fit. He'd say—O God, I couldn't discuss that with him. Besides, it would hurt Florian's feelings. Florian would be a little disgusted if I did it with Stef, but he wouldn't be *hurt*.

"Some azi from the Town, though—I couldn't do that to him. I don't think Ari senior ever did anything like that. I can't find it in any records. And I looked.

"I think I'm being silly. I love Florian, truly I do. If there's trouble it's *my* trouble, not his. I should go back and be twice as nice to him and quit being selfish, that's what I ought to do. Lonely is all in my head, isn't it?

"Mostly. Mostly, I guess it is.

"Damn, maman, I wish you'd written. I wish Ollie would.

"He's CIT now. He's Oliver AOX Strassen. Maybe he thinks it would be presumptuous, to write now, like I was his daughter.

"Maybe he's just turned that off. He'll never stop being azi, down in his deep-sets, will he?

"I thought about having the labs make another of him.

"But you taught him the important things. And I'm not you, and I can't make him into Ollie. Besides, Florian and Catlin would be jealous as hell, like Nelly was, of them. And I'd never do that to them.

"Wish you were here. Damn, you must have wanted to strangle me sometimes. But you did a good job, maman. I'm all right.

"Overall, I'm all right."

---

iv

"It won't work," Justin said. "Look. There's going to be an increase in flux in the micro-sets. I can tell you what will happen."

"But it could be proportional. That's what I'm asking. If it's proportional, that's what I'm saying, isn't that right?"

He nodded. "I know what you're saying. I'm saying it's more complicated. Look here. You've set up for matrilineal education. That means you've got the AJ group, there, that's going to go with PA—there's your trouble, you've got a fair number of Alphas, maybe more than you ought to have. God knows what they're going to make out of your instructions."

"I asked Florian and Catlin how they'd interpret that instruction to defend the base. Florian said you just build defenses around the perimeter and wait if you're sure you're the only intelligence there. Catlin said that was fine, but you train your people for the next generation. Florian agreed with that, but he said they couldn't all be specialists, somebody had to see to the other jobs. But their psychsets aren't in the group. Ask Grant."

"Grant?"

Grant turned his chair around and leaned back. "I'd tend to agree with them, except everybody will have to be trained to some extent or you can't follow your central directive and you'll have some who aren't following it except by abstraction. Once you get that abstraction, that growing potatoes is defense, then you've got a considerable drift started. *Everything* becomes interrelated. Your definition of *base* may or may not drift at this point, and if I were in charge, I'd worry about that."

That was a good answer. She drew a long breath and thought about it.

And thought: *Damn, he's smart. And social. And in his thirties. Maybe that's the trouble, with me and Florian. Florian and Catlin are still learning their own jobs. And so am I. But Grant—*

Grant's a designer. That's one difference.

"I've handled that abstraction," she said, "so that there is a change like that. Because they're not stressed and there isn't an Enemy early on. But I think you're right, two variables is going to blow everything full of holes."

"*Maintain* would have been a more variable word than *defend*," Justin said, "but *defend* brings all sorts of baggage with it, *if* any of your group are socialized. And you say three are. The AJ, the BY and one of the IUs. Which means, you're quite right, that you've got three who are likely going to do the interpretation and the initial flux-thinking; which means your value-sets are going to come very strongly off these three points. Which is going to hold them together tolerably well to start with, because they're all three military sets. And they're likely going to see that 'defend the base' is a multigenerational problem. But your Alpha is likely to be less skilled at communication than the Beta. So I'll reckon that's your leader. The Beta."

"Huh. But the Alpha can get around her."

"As an adviser. That's my suggestion. But the smarter the Alpha is, the less likely his instructions are going to make any immediate sense. He'll dominate as long as it's a matter of azi psychsets. But he'll lose his power as the next generation grows up. Won't he? Unless he's more socialized than the Beta."

"They don't have rejuv. It's a hard life. They're going to die around fifty and sixty. So the kids won't be much more than twenty or so before they're going on just what they could learn."

"Your Beta's instructions are likely to be more near-term, less abstract, more comprehensible to the young ones."

"My Alpha founds a religion."

"God. He'd have to be awfully well socialized. And machiavellian. Besides, it's not an azi kind of thing to do."

"Just practical."

"But, given that he does, would the kids *understand* the value of the instruction? Or wouldn't it just go to memorizing the forms and ritual? Ritual is a damned inefficient transmission device, and it generates its own problems. —I think we'd better start working this out in numbers and sets, and get some solid data, before we get too far into speculations. I'm not sure your Alpha can win out over the Beta in any sense. You're likely to lose virtually all his input. And you're likely to end up with a matrilinear culture in that instance—and a very small directorate if it's by kinships. The question is whether kinships are instinctive or cultural . . . I'm cheating on that, because I've read the Bureau reports on Gehenna. But they're not going to resolve it, because there were CITs in the Gehenna colony."

She had lunch with Maddy; and heard the latest in the Amy-'Stasi feud. Which made her mad. "I could kill Stef Dietrich," Maddy said.

"Don't bother," Ari said. "I'll bet Yvgenia's already thought of that."

Mostly she thought about the colony-problem, around the edges of the Amy-'Stasi thing. And thought: *Damn, the minute anything goes CIT, everybody's crazy, aren't they?*

The office was shut when she got back. She waited at the door and waited, and finally Justin showed up, out of breath.

"Sorry," he said, and unlocked. (Although she could have had Base One do it, through Security 10, but that was overkill, and made Security records, and meant papers. So she didn't.)

"Grant's got some stuff over at Sociology," he said. "He's running a paper for me. I *do* get work done outside of this—"

He was in a good mood. It cheered her up. She took the cup of coffee he made for her and sat down and they started at it again. "Let's assume," he said, "that whether or not kinships are instinctual, your socialized azi are likely to replicate the parent culture."

"Makes sense," she said.

"Likely quite thoroughly. Because they'll place abstract value on it, as the source of the orders."

She had never noticed the way he bit at his lip when he was thinking. It was a boyish kind of thing, when mostly he looked so mature. And he smelled good. A lot like Ollie. A *lot* like Ollie.

And she couldn't help thinking about it.

He and Grant were lovers. She knew that from gossip in the House. She couldn't imagine it.

Except at night, when she was lying in the dark looking at the ceiling and wondering what made them that way and whether—

—whether he *had* any feelings about her, and whether it was all just worry about Security that made him want Grant there all the time. Like he needed protection.

She liked being close to him. She always had.

She knew what was the matter finally. She felt the flux strong enough to turn everything upside down, and felt a lump in her throat and outright missed his next question.

"I—I'm sorry."

"The second-generation run. You're assuming matrilineal."

She nodded. He made a note. Tapped the paper. She got up to see, leaning by the arm of his chair. "You should have had an instructional tape in the lot to cover family units. Do you want to input one?"

"I—"

He looked over his shoulder at her. "Ari?"

"I'm sorry. I just lost things a minute."

He frowned. "Something wrong?"

"I—a couple of friends of mine are having a fight. That's all. I guess I'm a little gone-out." She looked at the printout. And felt sweat on her temples. "Justin, —did you ever—did you ever have trouble with being smart?"

"I guess I did." A frown came between his brows and he turned the chair and leaned his arm on the desk, looking up at her. "I didn't think of it like that, but I guess that was one of the reasons."

"Did you—" O God, this was scary. It could go wrong. But she was in it now. She leaned up against the chair, against him. "Did you ever have trouble with being older than everybody?" She took a breath and slid her hand onto his shoulder and sat down on the chair arm.

But he got up, fast, so fast she had to stand up to save herself from falling.

"I think you'd better talk this over with your uncle," he said.

Nervous. Real nervous. Probably, she thought, uncle Denys *had* said something to him. That made her mad. "Denys doesn't have a thing to say about what I do," she said, and came up against him and held on to his arm. "Justin, —there's nobody my own age I'm interested in. There *isn't* anybody. It doesn't hurt, I mean, I sleep-over with anybody I want. All the time."

"That's fine." He disengaged his arm and turned and picked up some papers off his desk. His hands were shaking. "Go back to them. I engaged to teach you, not—whatever."

She had trouble getting her breath. That was a *hell* of a reaction. It was scary, that a man reacted that way to her. He just gathered up his stuff, went to the door.

As the door opened and Grant stood there taking in what he saw, with small moves of his eyes.

"I'm going home," Justin said. "Closing up early today. How did the run go?"

"Fine," Grant said, and came in and laid it down, ignoring her presence, ignoring everything that had gone on.

"The *hell*," Ari said, and to Justin: "I want to talk to you."

"Not today."

"What are you doing? Throwing me out?"

"I'm not throwing you out. I'm going home. Let's give us both a little chance to cool off, all right? I'll see you in the morning."

Her face was burning. *She* was shaking. "I don't know what my uncle told you, but *I* can find something to tell him, you just *walk* out on me. Get out of here, Grant! Justin and I are talking!"

Grant went to the door, grabbed Justin's arm and shoved him out. "Get out of here," Grant said to him. And when Justin protested: "*Out!*" Grant said to him. "Go home. Now."

They had the door blocked. She was scared of a sudden—more scared when Grant argued Justin out the door and closed her in the office.

In a moment Grant came back. Alone. And closed the door again.

"I can call Security," she said. "You lay a hand on me and I'll swear Justin did it. You watch me!"

"No," Grant said, and held up a hand. "No, young sera. I'm not threatening you. Certainly I won't. I ask you, please, tell me what happened."

"I thought he told *you* everything."

"What did happen?"

She drew a shaken breath and leaned back against the chair. "I said I was bored with boys. I said I wanted to see if a man was any different. Maybe he hit me. Maybe he grabbed me. Who knows? Tell him go to hell."

"Did he do those things?"

"He's screwed everything up. I need him to teach me, and all I did was ask him to go to bed with me, I don't think that was an insult!" Damn, she hurt inside. Her eyes blurred. "You tell him he'd *better* teach me. You tell him he'd *better*. I need him, damn him."

Grant went azi then, and she remembered he *was* azi, which it was easy to forget with him; and she was in the wrong, yelling at him and not at Justin; she had a license that said responsibility, and she wanted to hit him.

"Young sera," he said, "I'll tell him. Please don't take offense. I'm sure there won't be any problem."

" 'There won't be any problem.' Hell!" She thought of working with him, day after day, and shook her head and lost her composure. "Dammit!" As the tears flooded her eyes. She pushed away from the chair and went for the door, but Grant stopped her, blocking her path. "Get out of my way!"

"Young sera," Grant said. "Please. *Don't* go to Security."

"I never asked for this. All I asked was a polite question!"

"*I'll* do whatever you want, young sera. Any time you want. I have no objection. Here, if you want. Or at your apartment. All you have to do is ask me."

Grant was tall, very tall. Very quiet and very gentle, as he reached out and took her hand. And there was very little space between her and the desk. She backed into it, her heart going like a hammer.

"Is that what you want, young sera?"

"No," she said, finding a breath.

And did, dammit, but he was too adult, too strange, too cold.

"Sera is not a child. Sera has power enough to have whatever she wants, by whatever means. Sera had better learn to control *what* she wants before she gets more than she bargained for. Dammit, you've cost him his father, his freedom, and his work. What else will you take?"

"*Let me go!*"

He did then. And bowed his head once politely, and went and opened the door.

She found herself shaking.

"Any time, young sera. I'm always available."

"Don't you take that tone with me."

"Whatever sera wishes. Please come tomorrow. I promise you—no one will bring the matter up if you don't. Ever."

"The hell!"

She got out the door, down the hall. Her chest hurt. Everything did.

Like the part of her that was herself and not Ari senior—had just fallen apart.

I fell in love about as often as any normal human being. I gave everything I had to give. And I got back resentment. Genuine hatred.

. . . isolation from my own kind. . . .

She caught her breath, reached the lift, got in and pushed the button.

Not crying. No. She wiped the underside of her lashes with a careful finger, trying not to smear her makeup, and was composed when she walked out in the hall downstairs.

She knew what the first Ari would tell her. She had read it over and over. *So, well, elder Ari, you were right. I'm a fool once. Not twice. What now?*

V

Grant walked into the cubbyhole of the second floor restroom and found Justin at the sink washing his face. Water beaded on white skin in the flickering light second floor had been complaining about for a week. "She's gone home," Grant said, and Justin pulled a towel from the stack and blotted his face with it.

"What did she say?" Justin asked. "What did *you* say?"

"I propositioned her," Grant said. "I believe that's the word."

"My *God*, Grant—"

Grant turned on the calm, quiet as he could manage, given the state of his stomach. "Young sera needed something else to think about," he said. "She declined. I wasn't sure that she would. I was, needless to say, relieved. Very fast work for young sera. I was so sure you were safe for an hour."

Justin threw the towel into the laundry-bin and folded his arms tight about his ribs. "Don't joke. It's not funny."

"Are you all right?"

"I'm having flashes. Oh, God, Grant, I— *Dammit!*"

He spun about and hit the wall with his hand and leaned there, stiff, hard-breathing, in that don't-touch-me attitude that absolutely meant it.

But Grant had ignored that before. He came and pried him away and folded him in his arms, just held on to him until Justin got a breath and a second one.

"I—lost—my sense of where I was," Justin said finally, between small efforts after air. "God, I just—went away. I couldn't navigate. She's—God knows. God knows what I said. It just blew up—she—"

"—she *needed* a firm no. It's doubtless a new thing for her. Calm down. Now is now."

"A damn *kid*! I—had—no finesse about it, absolutely none, I just—"

"You were expressing a polite and civilized no when I walked in. That young sera doesn't recognize the word isn't your fault. Young sera may call Security and young sera may lodge charges, I have absolutely no idea. But if she does, you have a witness, and I have no trouble about going under probe. Young sera needs favors from *you*. I politely suggested she consider the trouble she's caused and show up tomorrow with a civilized attitude—at which time *I'm* going to be there; at all times hereafter, I assure you." He pushed Justin back at arm's length. "She's sixteen. Personalities aside, she's quite the other end of the proposition—a year younger than you were. A great deal more experienced, by all accounts, but not—not in adult behavior. Am I right? She has no idea what she's dealing with. No more than you did."

Justin blinked. Rapid thought: Grant knew the look. "Go back to the office."

"Where are *you* going?"

"To make a phone call."

"Denys?"

Justin shook his head.

"Good God," Grant said. And felt as if the floor had sunk. "You're not serious."

"I'm going alone, if she'll see me. Which is far from likely at this point."

"No. Listen. Don't do this. If you're having flashback, for God's *sake* don't do this."

"I'm going to straighten it out. Once for all. I'm going to tell her what happened—"

"No!" Grant seized his arm and held on, hard. "Administration will have your head on a plate—*listen to me*. Even if she took your side she hasn't got the authority to protect you. She hasn't got anything, not really. *Not* inside *these* walls."

"What in hell do we do? What do we do when they take us in and they trump up a rape charge—what happens when we end up in a ward over in hospital under Reseune law? All they need is a statement from her. . . ."

"And you're going to go over to her apartment and talk to her. No."

"Not her apartment. I don't think I can handle that. But somewhere."

vi

Justin took a sip of Scotch as the waiter at *Changes* brought the three to their table—Ari in an ice-green blouse with metallic gray beading, Florian and Catlin in evening black.

Evening at *Changes* was a dress occasion. He and Grant had taken pains, both of them in their best. Dress shirts and jackets.

"Thank you," Ari said, when the waiter pulled the chair back. "Vodka-and-orange for the three of us, please."

"Yes, sera," the waiter murmured. "Will you want menus?"

"Give us a while," Justin said. "If you will, Ari."

"That's fine." She settled in her chair and folded her hands on the table.

"Thank you for coming," Justin said as soon as the waiter left. "I apologize for this afternoon. For Grant and myself. It was me. Not you. Absolutely not you."

Ari shifted back in her seat, her lips pressed to a thin line.

And said not a thing.

"Has your uncle Denys called you?"

"Have you called him?"

"No. I don't think he wants to hear what happened. I don't know to what extent he can come back on you—"

"Only because he's the Administrator," Ari said. "There's nothing he'll do to me."

"I wasn't sure." He saw the waiter coming back with the drinks, and waited during the serving.

Ari sipped hers and sighed. "Whose credit is this on?"

"Mine," Justin said. "Don't hesitate." As the waiter discreetly took himself off. It was a private corner, quite private: a sizeable addition to the bill assured it. "I want to assure you first of all—I'm perfectly willing to go on working with you. I want to tell you—what you're doing—is full of problems. But it's not empty exercise. You've got some ideas that are—fairly undeveloped right now. I still don't know to what extent you've modeled this on reality—or borrowed from your predecessor. If it's considerable borrowing—it would be remarkable enough that someone so young is working integrations at all. If any portion of it is original—I have to be impressed; because there is a center of this that, if I were going faster, and not taking the time to demonstrate your problems—I would simply throw into research, because I think it's a helpful model."

"You can do that, if you like." Not spitefully. Reasonably. Quietly.

"Perhaps I'll do both. With your permission. Because I'm very afraid it's classified."

"Grant can do it."

"Grant could do it. With your permission. And Yanni's. We work for him."

"Because you refused to be transferred. I can still do that."

He had not expected that. He took a drink of Scotch. And was aware of Grant beside him, subject to whatever mistakes he made. "I wouldn't think," he said, "that you'd be thinking about that after the scene this afternoon."

Redirect. Shift directions.

She sipped at the vodka-and-orange. Sixteen, and fragile—in physiology. In emotions that the alcohol could flatten or exacerbate. Flux-thinking at its finest, Grant was wont to say. Puberty, hormones run wild, and ethyl alcohol. *Oh, God, kid, back off it: it did me no favors.*

Power. Political power that was still running in shockwaves across Union; threats of assassination. And all the stress that went with it.

"I'm glad you want to talk about it," Ari said, on a slight sigh following the vodka. "Because I need you. I study my predecessor's notes—on kat. I *know* things. I've talked to Denys about putting the stuff into print.

Organizing everything. I said I wanted you to do it and he didn't want that. I said the hell with that."

"Ari, *don't* swear."

"Sorry. But that was what I said. I could have sat down and said I wouldn't budge. But it's real good, politically, if the Bureau gets it about now. Sort of proof that I'm real. So you'll know pretty soon what's mine and what's Ari's. I'll tell you something else you can guess: not *all* the notes are going out. Some aren't finished. And some are classified." She took another sip. The glass hardly diminished. "I've thought about this. I've thought real hard. And I've got a problem, because you're the one who's working on deep-sets, you're the one who could teach me the actual things I need— Giraud's very bright; but Giraud's not down the same track. Not at all. I don't *want* to do the things he does. Denys is bright. He's very near-term and real-time. Do you want to know the truth? Giraud isn't really a Special. *Somebody* had to have it, to get some of the protections Reseune needed right then. The one who is, is Denys; but Denys wouldn't have it: it would make him too public. So he arranged it to get Giraud the Status."

He stared at her, wondering if it *was* true, if it *could* be true.

"It's in Ari's notes," Ari said. "Now you know something on Denys. But I wouldn't tell him you know. He'd be upset with me for telling you. But it's why you should be careful. I've learned from uncle Denys for years. I still do. But the work I really want is macro-sets and value-sets. You're the only one who's working on the things Ari *wanted* me to do. I listen to her."

"Listen to her—"

"Her notes. She had a lot to tell me. A lot of advice. Sometimes I don't listen and I'm generally sorry for it. Like this afternoon."

"Am I—in the notes?"

"Some things about you are. That she talked Jordan into doing a PR. That she and Jordan did a lot of talking about the Bok clone problem and they talked about the psych of a PR with the parent at hand—and one like the Bok clone, without. It's interesting stuff. I'll let you read it if you want."

"I'd be interested."

"Stuff on Grant, too. I can give you that. They're going to hold that out of the Bureau notes, because they don't want it in there, about you. Because your father doesn't want it, uncle Denys says."

He took a mouthful of Scotch, off his balance, knowing she had put him there, every step of the way.

Not a child. *Wake up, fool. Remember who you're dealing with. Eighteen years asleep. Wake up.*

"You didn't walk in here unarmed," he said. "In either sense, I'll imagine."

She ignored that remark, except for a little eye contact, deep and direct. She said: "Why don't you like me, Justin? You have trouble with women?"

A second time off his balance. Badly. And then a little use out of the anger, a little steadiness, even before he felt Grant's touch on his knee. "Ari, I'm at a disadvantage in this discussion, because you *are* sixteen."

"Chronologically."

"Emotionally. And you shouldn't have the damn vodka."

That got a little flicker. "Keeps me quiet. Keeps me from being bored with fools. Drunk, I'm about as eetee as the rest of the world."

"You're wrong about that."

"You're not my mother."

"You want to talk about that?" *Off* the other topic. "I don't think you do. Shows what the stuff's doing to you."

She shook her head. "No. Hit me on that if you like. I threw that at you. So you're being nice. Let's go back to the other thing. I want just one straight answer—since you're being nice. Is it women, is it because I'm smarter than you, or is it because you can't stand my company?"

"You want a fight, don't you? I didn't come here for this."

Another shake of the head. "I'm sixteen, remember. Ari said adolescence was hell. She *said* relations with CITs always lose you a friend. Because people don't like you up that close. Ever. She said I'd never understand CITs. Myself—for my own education—once—I'd like to have somebody explain it to me—why you don't like me."

The smell of orange juice. Of a musky perfume.

This is all there is, sweet. This is as good as it gets.

Oh, God, Ari.

He caught his breath. Felt his own panic, felt the numbing grip on his wrist.

"Sera," Grant said.

"No," he said quietly. "No." Knowing more about the woman eighteen years ago than he had learned in that night or all the years that followed.

And reacting, the way she had primed him to react, the way she had fixed him on her from that time on—

"Your predecessor," he said, carefully, civilized, "had a fondness for adolescent boys. Which I was, then. She blackmailed me. And my father. She threatened Grant, to start running test programs on him—on an Alpha brought up as a CIT. Mostly, I think—to get her hands on me, though I didn't understand that then. Nothing—absolutely nothing—of your fault. *I* know that. Say that I made one mistake, when I thought I could handle a situation when I was about your age. Say that *I* have a reluctance when I'm approached by a girl younger than I was, never mind you have her face, her voice, and you wear her perfume. It's nothing to do with you. It's everything to do with what she did. I'd rather not give you the details, but I don't have to. She made a tape. It may be in your apartment for all I know. Or your uncle can give it to you. When you see it, you'll have every key you need to take me apart. But that's all right. Other people have. *Nothing* to do with you."

Ari sat there for a long, long time, elbows on the table. "Why did she do that?" she asked finally.

"You'd know that. Much more than I would. Maybe because she was dying. She was in rejuv failure, Ari. She had cancer; and she was a hundred twenty years old. Which was no favorable prognosis."

She had not known that. For a PR it was a dangerous kind of knowledge—the time limits in the geneset.

"There were exterior factors," he said. "Cyteen was more native when she was young. She'd gotten a breath of native air at some time in her life. That was what would have killed her."

She caught her lip between her teeth. No hostility now. No defense. "Thank you," she said, "for telling me."

"Finish your drink," he said. "I'll buy you another one."

"I knew—when she died. Not about the cancer."

"Then your notes don't tell you everything. I will. Ask me again if I'm willing to take a transfer."

"Are you?"

"Ask Grant."

"Whatever Justin says," Grant said.

vii

"We've got a contact," Wagner said, on the walk over to State from the Library, "in Planys maintenance. Money, not conscience."

"I don't want to hear that," Corain said. "I don't want you to have heard it. Let's keep this clean."

"I didn't hear it and you didn't," Wagner agreed. A stocky woman with almond eyes and black ringleted hair, Assistant Chief of Legal Affairs in the Bureau of Citizens, complete with briefcase and conservative suit. A little walk over from Library, where both of them happened to meet—by arrangement. "Say our man's working the labs area. Say he talks with Warrick. Shows him pictures of the kids—you know. So Warrick opens up."

"We're saying what happened."

"We're saying what happened. I don't think you want to know the whole string of contacts. . . ."

"I don't. I want to know, dammit, is Warrick approachable?"

"He's been under stringent security for over a year. He has a son still back in Reseune. This is the pressure point."

"I remember the son. What's he like?"

"Nothing on him. A non-person as far as anything we've got, just an active PR CIT-number. Defense has a lot more on him. Doppelganger for papa, that's a given. But apparently either Warrick senior or junior has pressured Reseune enough to get a travel pass for the son. He's thirty-five years old. Reseune national. Reseune had so much security around him when he'd come into Planys you'd have thought he was the Chairman. There's an azi, too. An Alpha—you remember the Abolitionist massacre over by Big Blue?"

"The Winfield case. I remember. Tied into Emory's murder. That was one of the points of contention—between Warrick and Emory."

"He's a foster son as far as Warrick is concerned. They don't let him out of Reseune. We can't get any data at all on him, except he is alive, he is living with the son, Warrick still regards him as part of the family. I can give you the whole dossier."

"Not to me! That stays at lower levels."

"Understood then."

"But you can get to Warrick."

"I think he's reached a state of maximum frustration with his situation. It's been, what, eighteen years? His projects are Defense; but Reseune keeps a very tight wall between him and them, absolutely no leak-through. The air-systems worker—we've had him for—eighteen months, something like. What you have to understand, ser, Reseune's security is very, very tight. But also, it's no ordinary detainee they're dealing with. A psych operator. A clinician. Difficult matter, I should imagine, to find any guard immune to him. The question is whether we go now or wait-see. That's what Gruen wants me to ask you."

Corain gnawed at his lip. Two months from the end of the Defense election, with a bomb about to blow in that one—

With Jacques likely to win the Defense seat away from Khalid and very likely to appoint Gorodin as Secretary.

But Jacques was weakening. Jacques was feeling heat from the hawks within Defense—and there were persistent rumors about Gorodin's health—and countercharges that Khalid, who had been linked to previous such rumors—was once more the source of them.

But Khalid *could* win: the Centrist party had as lief be shut of Khalid's brand of conservatism—but it could not discount the possibility in any planning. The Jacques as Councillor/Gorodin as Secretary compromise Corain had hammered out with Nye, Lynch, and the Expansionists—was the situation Corain had rather have, most of all, if rumors were true and Gorodin's health was failing, because Gorodin was the *Expansionists'* part of the bargain.

Wait—and hope that a new hand at the helm of the military would enable them to work *with* Defense to get to Warrick in Planys; or go in on their own and trust to their own resources. And risk major scandal. That was the problem.

If Khalid won again—Khalid would remember that his own party had collaborated in the challenge to his seat. Then he would owe no favors.

Then he could become a very dangerous man indeed.

"I think we'd better pursue the contact now," Corain said. "Just for God's sake be careful. I don't want any trails to the Bureau, hear?"

viii

"I didn't know I was going to do that," Justin said, and tossed a bit of bread to the koi. The gold one flashed to the surface and got it this time, while the white lurked under a lotus pad. "I had no idea. It just—she was going to find out about the tape, wasn't she? Someday. Better now—while she's naive enough to be shocked. God help us—if it goes the other way."

"I feel much safer," Grant said, "when you decide these things."

"*I* don't, dammit, I had no right to do that without warning—but I was in a corner, it was the moment—it was the only moment to make the other situation right. . . ."

"Because of the tape?"

"You do understand it, then."

"I understand this is the most aggressive personality I've ever met. Not even Winfield and his people—impressed me to that extent. I'll tell you the truth: I've been afraid before. Winfield, for instance. Or the Security force that pulled me out of there—I thought that they might kill me, because those might be their orders. I've tried to analyze the flavor of this, and the flux was so extreme in me at that moment in the office doorway—I can't pin it down. I only know there was something so—violent in this girl—that it was very hard for me to respond without flux." Grant's voice was clinical, cool, soft and precise as it was when he was reasoning. "But then—that perception may have to do with my own adrenaline level—and the fact the girl *is* a Supervisor. Perhaps I misread the level of what I was receiving."

"No. You're quite right. I've tried to build a profile on her . . . quietly. Same thing her predecessor did to me. The choices she makes in her model, the things she'd do if she were in the Gehenna scenario—she's aggressive as hell, and self-protective. I've charted the behavior phases—menstrual cycles, hormone shifts—best I can guess, she's hormone-fluxed as hell right now; I *always* watch the charts with her. But that's never all of it." He broke off another bit of bread and tossed it, right where the spotted koi could get it. "*Never* all of it with her predecessor. That mind is brilliant. When it fluxes, the analog functions go wildly speculative—and the down-side of the flux integrates like hell. I've watched it. More, she *originated* the whole flux-matrix theory; you think she doesn't understand her own cycles? *And* use them? But *young* Ari made me understand something I should have seen—we deal with other people with such precision, and ourselves with such damnable lack of it—Ari is having difficulties with ego-definitions. A PR does, I should know; and it can only get worse for her. That's why I asked for the transfer."

"Fix her on us?"

He drew several long breaths. Blinked rapidly to clear away the elder Ari's face, the remembrance of her hands on him.

"She's vulnerable now," he said on a ragged breath. "She's looking for some sign of the human race—on whatever plane she lives on. That's the sense I got—that maybe she was as open then as I was—then. So I grabbed the moment's window. That's what I thought. That she's so damn self-protective—there might only be that chance—then—in that two seconds." He shuddered, a little, involuntary twitch at the nape of the neck. "God, I hate real-time work."

"Just because you hated it," Grant said, "doesn't mean you weren't good at it. I'll tell you what this azi suspects—that she would *regret* harm to one of us. I don't think that's true with a CIT. If she ever does take me up on my proposition— No," Grant said as he took a breath to object; Grant held up a finger. "One: I don't think she will. Two: if she does—trust me to handle it. Trust me. All right?"

"It's not all right."

"No, but you'll stay back: do the puzzling thing, and trust me to do the same. I think you're quite right. The puzzling thing engages the intellect—and I had far rather deal with her on a rational basis, I assure you. If you can commit us to your judgment in the one thing—trust me for mine and don't make me worry. I wouldn't have been in half the flux I was in, except I wasn't sure you weren't going to come back into the office and blow everything to hell, right there. I can't think and watch my flank when it's you involved. All right? Promise me that."

"Dammit, I can't let a spoiled kid—"

"Yes. You can. Because I'm capable of taking care of myself. And in some things I'm better than you. Not many. But in this, I am. Allow me my little superiority. You can have all the rest."

He gazed a long time at Grant, at a face which had—with the years—acquired tensions azi generally lacked. He had done that to him. Life among CITs had.

"Deal?" Grant asked him. "Turn about: trust *my* judgment. I trust yours about the transfer. So we can both be perturbed about something. How much do you trust me?"

"It's not trusting *you* that's at issue."

"Yes, it is. Yes. It is. Azi to Supervisor . . . are you hearing me?"

He nodded finally. Because whatever Ari could do—*he* could hurt Grant. He lied, of course. Maybe Grant knew he did.

ix

"There's a tape," Ari had said to Denys, in his office, and told him *which* tape.

"How did you find out about it?" he had asked.

"My Base."

"*Nothing* to do with dinner at *Changes* last night."

"No," she said without a flicker, "we discussed cultural librations."

Denys hated humor when he was serious. He always had. "All right," he said, frowning. "I certainly won't withhold it."

So he sent Seely for it. And said: "*Don't* use kat when you see this, don't expose Florian and Catlin to it, for God's sake *don't* put it where anyone can find it."

She had thought of asking him what was in it. But things were tense enough. So she talked about other things—about her work, about the project, about Justin—without mentioning the disagreement.

She drank a cup and a half of coffee and exchanged pleasant gossip; and unpleasant: about the elections; about the situation in Novgorod; about Giraud's office—and Corain—until Seely brought the tape back.

So she walked home with it, with Catlin, because she was anxious all the time she had it in her carry-bag; she was anxious when she arrived home and contemplated putting it in the player.

Her insecurity with the situation wanted Florian and Catlin to be beside her when she played it—

But that, she thought, was irresponsible. Emotional situations were *her* department, not theirs, no matter that sera was anxious about it, no matter that sera wanted, like a baby, to have someone with her.

I wouldn't have advised this, Denys had said—distressed, she picked that up. But not entirely surprised. *But I know you well enough to know there's no stopping you once you start asking a question. I won't comment on it. But if you have questions after you've seen it—you can send them to my Base if you find them too personal. And I'll respond the same way. If you want it.*

Meaning Denys wasn't putting any color on the situation.

So she closed the door on the library and locked it; and put the tape into the player—*not* taking a pill. She was no fool, to deep-study any tape blind and unpreviewed, and without running a check for subliminals.

She sat down and clenched her hands as it started—fascinated first-off by the sight of a familiar place, familiar faces—Florian and Catlin when they would have been a hundred twenty at least; and Justin—the boy was clearly Justin, even at the disadvantage of angle—he would be seventeen; and Ari herself—elegant, self-assured: she had seen newsclips of Ari this old, but none when Ari was not simply answering questions.

She listened—caught the nervousness in Justin's voice, the finesse of control in Ari's. Strange to *know* that voice so well, and to feel inside what it was doing—and to understand what kat would do to that experience, for someone skilled at tape-learning: she felt a little prickle down her back, a sense of hazard and involvement—*conditioned response*, a dim, analytical part of her thoughts said: the habits of this room, the physiological response of the endocrine system to the habit of taking kat here, and the lifelong habit of responding to tape— Azi must do this, she thought. And: The emotional context is kicking it off. Thank *God* I didn't trank down for this.

As muscles felt the sympathetic stimulus of nerves that *knew* what it felt like to walk and sit, and speak, and a brain that understood in all that context that Ari was On, and that her pulse was up, and that the target of her intentions was a Justin very young, very vulnerable, picking up the signals Ari was sending and reacting with extreme nervousness—

Back off, she told herself, trying to distance herself from the aggression Ari was radiating. *Disinvolve.*

The switch was beside her. She only had to reach to it and push it to cut it off. But the sexual feeling was too strong, toward an object otherwise out of reach—toward a Justin not quite real, not the man she knew, but Justin all the same.

She saw the glass fall—realized then what Ari had done to him, and that he was in terrible danger. She was *afraid* for him; but the muscles she felt move in response to that falling glass were Ari's, the impulse she felt through the heat of sex was concern for the orange juice spill on the damned upholstery— *Her* couch—

Oh, God, she should shut this off. Now.

But she kept watching.

X

It was a simple computer-delivered *See me: my office, 0900. —Denys Nye.* —-that brought him to the administrative wing, and to the door that he dreaded.

So she had the tape, Justin thought; so Denys knew about the dinner at *Changes.*

He had *not* expected Giraud with Denys. He froze in the doorway, with Seely at his back, then walked in and sat down.

"Let's dispense with what we both know," Denys said, "and not bicker about details. What in hell do you think you're doing?"

"I thought about coming to you," he said, "but she was embarrassed as well as mad. I figured—if I did—come to you—she might blow. I thought you wanted to avoid that."

"So you took a wide action. On your own judgment."

"Yes, ser." Denys was being reasonable—too reasonable, with Giraud sitting there staring at him with hostility in every line of his face. "And knowing you'd call me."

"She has the tape," Denys said. "That surprised me, Justin, that truly surprised me."

Giraud's not the Special. Denys is. . . .

"I'm flattered, ser. I don't expect to surprise you. But that wasn't why I did it. I wish you'd *let* me explain. Ari—"

"I don't need your explanation. Neither of us does."

"It's a simple adolescent infatuation—"

"She's been sexually active since she was thirteen. At least. And this fascination is thoroughly in program. We're not worried about that. Her predecessor had a pattern of such things. That you're young, male, and working at close quarters with her— No question."

"I haven't encouraged it!"

"Of course not. But you've tried to manipulate her by that means."

"That's not so. No."

"Sins of the heart, if not the intellect. You took her on, you've taught her, you've tried to steer her—admit it."

"*Away* from that kind of thing—"

Denys leaned forward on folded arms.

"That," Giraud said, "is intervention, in itself."

"Not to harm her," Justin said, "or me." Giraud had only to speak and reactions started running through him, kat-dream, deep as bone. He could not help that flutter of nerves, could not forget the whip-crack that voice could become . . . in his nightmares. He looked at Denys, feeling a tremor in his muscles. "I tried to keep it all low-key, non-flux."

"Until yesterday," Denys said, "when you decided to handle a situation yourself. When you exacerbated a situation—and decided to handle it . . . by handing her a major key. That is an intervention, you're an operator, you knew exactly what you were doing, and I want you to lay that out for me in plain words—consciously and subconsciously."

"Why should I?" His heart was slamming against his ribs. "Duplication of effort, isn't it? Why don't we just go over to Security and save us all time and trouble?"

"You're asking for a probe."

"No. I'm not. But that's never stopped you."

"Let's have a little calm, son."

Jordan. Oh, God.

He means me to think about that.

"Answer the question," Giraud said.

"I did it to save my neck. Because she's a damned dangerous enemy. Because she could as well blow up in your direction. What in hell *else* was charged enough to knock her back and make her reassess?"

"That's a tolerably acceptable answer," Denys said. Confusing him. He waited for the redirect and the flank attack. "The question is—what do you think you've induced? Where is your intervention going? What's her state of mind right now?"

"I hope to God," he said, his voice out of control, "I hope to God—it's going to make her careful."

"And sympathetic?"

"*Careful* would do."

"You're courting her, aren't you?"

"God, no!"

"Yes, you are. Not sexually, though I imagine you'll pay that if you have to—if you can gain enough stability to handle the encounter. But you'd much rather avoid it. 'Hell hath no fury'? Something like that in your considerations? Politics may make strange bedfellows, but bedfellows make deadly politics."

"I just want to survive here."

"In her administration. Yes. Of course you do. Protect yourself—protect Grant. The consequences of enmity with us—have only a few years to run, is that what you're thinking? A couple of old men—weighed against the lifespan of a sixteen-year-old whose power is—possibly adequate to work for you if you could maneuver your way into her considerations. A very dangerous course. A *very* dangerous course, even for a man willing to sell—what you were willing to sell her predecessor—"

Temper. Temper is . . . only what he wants here.

"—but then, your choices *are* limited."

"It doesn't take a probe," Giraud said, his deep voice quite gentle, "to know what your interests are. —And the latest business on my desk—I think you'll find quite—amusing in one sense. Alarming, in the other. The Paxers—you know, the people who blow up Novgorod subways, have decided to invoke your father's name—"

"He hasn't a thing to do with it!"

"Of course not. Of course not. But the Novgorod police did find some interesting documents—naming your father as a political martyr in their cause, stating that *the new monstrosity in Reseune* is a creation of the military—that assassinating Ari and creating maximum chaos would lead to a Paxer government—"

"That's crazy!"

"Of course it is. Of course your father knows nothing about it."

"He doesn't! My God, —"

"I said—of course. Don't let it upset you. This has been going on for years. Oh, not the Paxers. They're comparatively new. All these organizations are interlocked. That's what makes them so difficult to track. That and the fact that the people that do the bombing are z-cases. Druggers and just general fools whose devotion to the cause involves letting themselves be partial-wiped by amateur operators. *That* kind of fools. I thought I should tell you—there are people in this world who don't care anything for their own lives, let alone a sixteen-year-old focus of their hostilities. And they're using your father's name in their literature. I'm sorry. I suppose it *doesn't* amuse you."

"No, ser." He was close to shivering. Giraud did that to him. Without drugs. Because in not very long, there would be, he knew that; and not all the skill in the world could prevent it. "I'm not amused. I know Jordan wouldn't be, if he heard about it, which he hasn't, unless you've told him."

"We've mentioned it to him. He asked us to say he's well. Looking forward, I imagine, to a change of regime in Defense. —As we all are. Certainly. I just wanted to let you know the current state of things, since there are ramifications to the case that you might want to be aware of. That your father murdered Ari—is not quite old news. It's entered into threats against her successor's life. And Ari will be aware of these things. We have to make her aware—for her own protection. Perhaps you and she can work it out in a civilized way. I hope so."

What is he doing? What is he trying to do?

What does he want from me?

Is he threatening Jordan?

"How does your father feel about Ari? Do you have any idea?"

"No, ser. I don't know. Not hostility. I don't think he would feel that."

"Perhaps you can *find* out. If this election goes right."

"If it does, ser. Maybe I can make a difference—in *how* he feels."

"That's what we hope," Giraud said.

"I wouldn't, however," Denys said, "bring the matter up with Ari."

"No, ser."

"You're a valuable piece in this," Giraud said. "I'm sorry—you probably have very strong feelings about me. I'm used to them, of course, but I regret them all the same. I'm not your enemy; and you probably won't believe that. I don't even ask for comment—not taxing your politeness. This time I'm on your side, to the extent I wish you a very long life. And the committee is agreed: thirty-five is a little young for rejuv—but then, it seems to have no adverse effects—"

"Thank you, no."

"It's not up for discussion. You have an appointment in hospital. You and Grant both."

"No!"

"The usual offer. Report on schedule or Security will see you do."

"There's no damn sense in my going on rejuv—it's my decision, dammit!"

"That's the committee's decision. It's final. Certainly nothing you ought to be anxious about. Medical studies don't show any diminution of lifespan for early users—"

"In the study they've got. There's no damn sense in this. Ari's on the shots, damn well sure she is—"

"Absolutely."

"Then why in hell are you doing this?"

"Because you have value. And we care about you. You can go on over there. Or you can go the hard way and distress Grant—which I'd rather not."

He drew a careful breath. "Do you mind—if I go tell Grant myself? Half an hour. That's all."

"Perfectly reasonable. Go right ahead. Half an hour, forty-five minutes. They'll be expecting you."

xi

Another damned wait. Justin lay full-length on the table and stared at the ceiling, trying to put his mind in null, observing the pattern in the ceiling tiles, working out the repetitions.

Full body scan and hematology work-up, tracer doses shot into his bloodstream, more blood drawn. Dental checks. Respiration. Cardiac stress . . . *you have a little hypertension,* Wojkowski had said, and he had retorted: *God, I wonder why.*

Which Wojkowski did not think was amusing.

More things shot into his veins, more scans, more probings at private places and more sitting about—lying down for long periods, while they tried to get him calm enough to get accurate readings.

I'm trying, he had said, the last time they had checked on him. *I'm honestly trying. Do you think I like waiting around freezing to death?*

Complaining got him a robe. That was all. They finally put him on biofeedback until he could get the heart rate down, and got the tests they wanted.

Why? had been Grant's first and only question—a worried frown, a shrug, and a: *Well, at least we do get it, don't we?*

Which, for an azi, could be a question. He had never thought that it was, never thought that Reseune could go so far as to deny him and Grant rejuv when it was time for them to have it or vengefully postpone it beyond the point when they should have it, to avoid diminished function.

Thinking of that, he could be calmer about it. But he had sent a call through to Base One: *Ari, this is Justin.*

Grant and I have been told to report to hospital. We've been told we're to go on rejuv, over our protests. I want you to know where we are and what's happened. . . .

Which got them nothing. Base One took the message. No one was reading it. They could try for admission to Ari's floor, but open confrontation with Administration was more than Ari could handle. *No one answering,* he had said to Grant.

It's only one treatment, Grant had said.

Meaning that one could still change one's mind. It took about three to eight weeks of treatments for the body to adjust—and become dependent.

Nothing permanent, yet.

"You're going to be coming here for your treatments," Wojkowski had said.

"For *what?*" he had said. "To have you watch me take a damned pill? Or what are you giving me?"

"Because this was not elective. You understand—going off the drug has severe consequences. Immune system collapse."

"I'm a certified paramedic," he had snapped back. "Clinical psych. I assure you I know the cautions. What I want to know, doctor, is what else they're putting into the doses."

"Nothing," Wojkowski had said, unflappable. "You can read the order, if you like. And see the prescriptions . . . whatever you like. Neantol. It's a new combination drug: Novachem is the manufacturer, I'll give you all the literature on it. Hottest thing going, just out on the market. Avoids a lot of the side-effects."

"Fine, I'm a test subject."

"It's safe. It's safer, in fact. Avoids the thin-skin problem, the excessive bleeding and bruising; the calcium depletion and the graying effect. You'll keep your hair color, you won't lose any major amount of muscle mass, or have brittle bones or premature fatigue. Sterility—unfortunately—is still a problem."

"I can live with that." He felt calmer. Damn, he wanted to believe what Wojkowski was saying. "What are *its* side-effects?"

"Dry mouth and a solitary complaint of hyperactivity. Possibly some deleterious effect on the kidneys. Mostly remember to drink plenty of water. Especially if you've been drinking. You'll tend to dehydrate and you'll get a hell of a hangover. We *don't* know what the effects would be of switching off the regular drug and onto this. Or vice versa. We suspect there could be some serious problems about that. It's also expensive, over ten thou a dose and it's not going to get cheaper anytime soon. But especially in the case of a younger patient—definitely worth it."

"Does Grant—get the same?"

"Yes. Absolutely."

He felt better, overall, with that reassurance. He trusted Wojkowski's ethics most of the way. But it did not help get his pulse rate down.

Ten thousand a dose. Reseune was spending a lot on them, on a drug Reseune could afford—and he could not.

Not something you could find on the black market.

Substitutions contraindicated.

A dependency Reseune provided, that Reseune could withhold—with devastating effect; that nothing like—say, the Paxers or the Abolitionists—could possibly provide.

An invisible chain. Damn their insecurities. As if they needed it. But it took something away, all the same: left him with a claustrophobic sense that hereafter—options were fewer; and a nagging dread that the drug might turn up with side-effects, no matter that lab rats thrived on it.

Damn, in one day, from a young man's self-concept and a trim, fit body he had taken pains to keep that way—to the surety of sterility, of some bodily changes; not as many as he had feared, if they were right; but still—a diminishing of functions. Preservation for—as long as the drug held. A list of cautions to live with.

A favor, in some regards, if it did what they claimed.

But a psychological jolt all the same—to take it at someone else's decision, because a damned committee decided—

What? To keep a string on him and Grant? In the case they tried to escape and join the Paxers and bomb subways and kill children?

God. They were all lunatics.

The door opened. The tech came in and asked him to undress again.

Tissue sample. Sperm sample. "What in hell for?" he snapped at the tech. "I'm a *PR*, for God's sake!"

The tech looked at his list. "It's here," the tech said. Azi. And doggedly following his instructions.

So the tech got both. And left him with a sore spot on his leg and one inside his mouth, where the tech had taken his tissue samples.

Likely his pulse rate was through the ceiling again. He tried to calm it down, figuring they would take it again before they let him out, and if they disliked the result they got, they could put him into hospital where he was subject to any damn thing *anyone* wanted to run, without Grant to witness it, where neither of them could look out for the other or lodge protests.

Damn it, get the pulse rate down.

Get out of here tonight. Get home. That's the important thing now.

The door opened. Wojkowski again.

"How are we doing?" she asked.

"We're madder than hell," he said with exaggerated pleasantness, and sat up on the table, smiled at Wojkowski, trying not to let the pulse run wild, doggedly thinking of flowers. Of river water. "I'm missing patches of skin and my dignity is, I'm sure, not a prime concern here. But that's all right."

"Mmmn," Wojkowski said, and set a hypogun down on the counter, looking at the record. "I'm going to give you a prescription I want you to take, and we'll check you over again when you come in for your second treatment. See if we can do something about that blood pressure."

"You want to know what you can do about the blood pressure?"

"Do yourself a favor. Take the prescription. Don't take kat more than twice a week—are you taking aspirin?"

"Occasionally."

"How regularly?"

"It's in the—"

"Please."

"Two, maybe four a week."

"That's all right. No more than that. If you get headaches, see me. If you have any light-headedness, see me immediately. If you get a racing pulse, same."

"Of course. —*Do you know what goes on in the House, doctor? —Or on this planet, for that matter?*"

"I'm aware of your situation. All the same, avoid stress."

"Thanks. Thanks so much, doctor."

Wojkowski walked over with the hypo. He shed the robe off one shoulder and she wiped the area down. The shot popped against his arm and hurt like hell.

He looked and saw a bloody mark.

"Damn, that's—"

"It's a gel implant. Lasts four weeks. Go home. Go straight to bed. Drink plenty of liquids. The first few implants may give you a little nausea, a little dizziness. If you break out in a rash or feel any tightening in the chest, call the hospital immediately. You can take aspirin for the arm. See you in August."

There was a message in the House system, waiting for him when he got to the pharmacy. *My office. Ari Emory.*

She did not use her Wing One office. She had said so. She had a minimal clerical staff there to handle her House system clerical work, and that was all.

But she was waiting there now. Her office. Ari senior's office. He walked through the doors with Grant, faced a black desk he remembered, where Florian sat—with a young face, a grave concern as he got up and said: "Grant should wait here, ser. Sera wants to see you alone."

The coffee helped his nerves. He was grateful that Ari had made it for him, grateful for the chance to collect himself, in these surroundings, with Ari behind Ari senior's desk—not a particularly grandiose office, not even so much as Yanni's. The walls were all bookcases and most of the books in them were manuals. Neat. That was the jarring, surreal difference. Ari's office had always had a little clutter about it and the desk was far too clean.

The face behind it—disturbing in its similarities and disturbing in its touch of worry.

Past and future.

"I got your message," Ari said. "I went to Denys. That didn't do any good. We had a fight. The next thing I did was call Ivanov. He didn't do any good. The next thing I could do, I could call Family council. And past that I can file an appeal with the Science Bureau and the Council in Novgorod. Which is real dangerous—with all the stuff going on."

He weighed the danger that would be, and knew the answer, the same as he had known it when he was lying on the table.

"There could be worse," he said. His arm had begun to ache miserably, all the way to the bone, and he felt sick at his stomach, so that he felt his hands likely to shake. It was hard to think at all.

But the Family council would stand with Denys and Giraud, even yet, he thought; and that might be dangerous, psychologically, to Ari's ability to wield authority in future, if she lost the first round.

An appeal to the Bureau opened up the whole Warrick case history. That was what Ari was saying. Opened the case up while people were bombing subways and using Jordan's name, while the Defense election was in doubt, and Ari was too young to handle some of the things that could fall out of that kind of struggle—involving her predecessor's murderer.

They might win if it got to Bureau levels—but they might not. The risk was very large, while the gain was—minimal.

"No," he said. "It's not a matter of pills. It's one of the damn slow-dissolving gels, and they'd have the devil's own time getting the stuff cleared out."

"Damn! I should have come there. I *should* have called Council and stopped it—"

"Done is done, that's all. They say what they're giving us is something new; no color fade, no brittle bones. That kind of thing. I *would* like to get the literature on it before I say a final yes or no about a protest over what they've done. If it's everything Dr. Wojkowski claims—it's not worth the trouble even that would cause. If it costs what they say it does—it's not a detriment; because *I* couldn't afford it. I only suspect it has other motives—because I *can't* afford it, and that means they can always withhold it."

Her face showed no shock. None. "They're not going to do that."

"I hope not."

"I got the tape," she said.

And sent his pulse jolting so hard he thought he was going to throw up. It was the pain, he thought. Coffee mingled with the taste of blood in his mouth, where they had taken their sample from the inside of his cheek. He was not doing well at all. He wanted to be home, in bed, with all his small sore spots; the arm was hurting so much now he was not sure he could hold the cup with that hand.

"She—" Ari said, "she went through phases—before she died—that she had a lot of problems. I know a lot of things now, a lot of things nobody wanted to tell me. I don't want that ever to happen. I've done the move—you and Grant into my wing. Yanni says thank God. He says he's going to kill you for the bill at *Changes*."

He found it in him to laugh a little, even if it hurt.

"I told uncle Denys you were going on my budget and he was damn well going to increase it. And I had him about what he did to you, so he didn't argue; and I put your monthly up to ten *with* a full medical, *and* your apartment paid, for you and Grant both."

"My God, Ari."

"It's enough you can pay a staffer to do the little stuff, so you don't have to and Grant doesn't have to. It's a waste of your time. It's a lot better for Reseune to have you on research—and teaching *me*. Denys didn't say a thing. He just signed it. As far as I'm concerned, my whole wing is research. Grant doesn't have to do clinical stuff unless he wants to."

"He'll be—delighted with that."

Ari held up a forefinger. "I'm not through. I asked uncle Denys why you weren't *doctor* when you'd gotten where Yanni couldn't teach you anymore, and he said because they didn't want you listed with the Bureau, because of politics. I said that was lousy. Uncle Denys—when he pushes you about as far as he thinks he can get away with, and you push back, you can get stuff out of him as long as you don't startle him. Anyway, he said if we got through the election in Defense, then they'd file the papers."

He stared at her, numb, just numb with the flux.

"Is that all right, what I did?" she asked, suddenly looking concerned. Like a little kid asking may-I.

"It's—quite fine. —Thank you, Ari."

"You don't look like you feel good."

"I'm fine." He took a deep breath and set the cup down. "Just a lot of changes, Ari. And they took some pieces out of me."

She got up from behind the desk and came and carefully, gently hugged his shoulders—the sore one sent a jolt through to the bone. She kissed him very gently, very tenderly on the forehead. "Go home," she said. Her perfume was all around him.

But through the pain, he thought it quite remarkable her touch made not a twitch—no flashback, nothing for the moment, though he knew he was not past them. Maybe he escaped it for the moment because it hurt so much, maybe because for a moment he was emotionally incapable of reacting to anything.

She left, and he heard her tell Florian he should walk with them and make sure they got home all right, and get them both to bed and take care of them till they felt better.

Which sounded, at the moment, like a good idea.

xii

B/1: Ari, this is Ari senior.

You've asked about Reseune administration.

My father set it up: James Carnath. He had, I'm told, a talent for organization. Certainly my mother Olga Emory had no interest in the day to day management of details.

Even the day to day management of her daughter, but that's a different file.

I mention that because I fit somewhere in between: I've always believed in a laissez-faire management, meaning that as long as I was running Reseune, I believed in knowing what was going on in the kitchens, occasionally, in the birth-labs, occasionally, in finance, always.

An administrator of a facility like Reseune has special moral obligations which come at the top of the list: a moral obligation to humankind, the azi, the public both local and general, the specific clients, and the staff, in approximately that order.

Policies regarding genetic or biological materials; or psychological techniques and therapies are the responsibility of the chief administrator, and decisions in those areas must never be delegated.

Emphatically, the administrator should seek advice from wing supervisors and department heads. All other decisions and day to day operations can be trusted to competent staff.

I devised a routine within the House system coded MANAGEINDEX which may or may not be in use. Go to Executive 1 and ask for it, and it will tell you the expenses, output, number of reprimands logged, number of fines, number of requests for transfer, number of absences, medical leaves, work-related accidents, antimanagement complaints, and security incidents for any individual, group of individuals, office, department, or wing in Reseune, and use that data to evaluate the quality of management and employees on any level. It can do comparisons of various wings and departments or select the most efficient managers and employees in the system.

It will also run a confidential security check on any individual, including a covert comparison of lifestyle data with income and output.

It operates without leaving a flag in the system.

Remember that it is a tool to be used in further inquiry and interview, and it is not absolutely reliable. Personal interviews are always indicated.

I was a working scientist as well as chief Administrator, which I found to be generally a fifteen-hour-a-day combination. A pocket com and an excellent staff kept me apprised of situations which absolutely required my intervention, and this extended to my research as well as my administrative duties. Typically I was in the office as early as 0700, arranged the day's schedule, reviewed the emergencies and ongoing situations via Base One, and put the office in motion as the staff arrived, left on my own work by 0900, and generally made the office again briefly after lunch, whereupon I left again after solving whatever had to be done.

I had a few rules which served me quite well:

I did my own office work while no one was there, which let me work efficiently; I had Florian and Catlin sworn to retrieve me from idle conversations—or from being accosted and handed business. Florian, I would say, handle this. Which usually meant it went to the appropriate department head; but sometimes Florian would check it out, and advise me personally. As he still does. Now that I'm Councillor for Science, it's much the same kind of thing. I absolutely refuse to be bogged down by lobbyists. That's what my staff is for. And they're to hand me investigative reports with facts and figures; which I then have cross-checked by Reseune security, and finally, finally, if there seems to be substance that interests me, I'll have my full staff meet with the interest group; and I will, if the reports are reasonable—but not in other than a businesslike setting and with a firm time limit for them. It's quite amazing how much time you can waste.

Delegate paperwork. Insist the preparers of reports include a brief summary of content, conclusion and/or recommended action; and that they follow strict models of style: this will appear petty, but I refuse to search a report for information which should have been prominently noted.

Give directions and reprimands early and clearly: an administrator who fails to make his expectations and his rules clear is inefficient; an administrator who expects a subordinate to pick up unspoken displeasure is wasting his time.

Learn a little bit about every operation. On one notorious occasion I showed up in the hospital and spent two hours walking rounds with the nurses. It not only identified problems up and down the line, but the whole MANAGEINDEX of Reseune shifted four points upward in the next two weeks.

Most of all, know your limits and identify those areas in which you are less adept. Do not abdicate authority in those areas: learn them, and be extremely careful of the quality of your department heads.

This program finds you have the rank of: wing supervisor.

You are seventeen years old; you have held your majority for: 1 year, 4 months.

You have a staff of: 6.

You have one department head: Justin Warrick, over Research.

He has a staff of: 2.

This program is running MANAGEINDEX.

There have been 0 complaints and 0 reprimands.

There have been 0 absences on personal leave.

There have been 2 medicals in Research.

Your Research department staff has a total of 187 Security incidents, 185 of which have been resolved. Do you wish breakdown?

AE2: No. I've read the file. None of these occurred in my administration.

B/1: Projects behind schedule: 0.

Projects over budget: 0.

Project demand: 12.

Project output: 18.

Projects ongoing: 3.

Wing expenses, 3 mo. period: C 688,575.31.

Wing earnings, 3 mo. period: C 6,658,889.89.

This wing has the following problems:

1. security flag on: 2 staff in: Research: Justin Warrick, Grant ALX.

2. security watch on: 1 staff in Administration, Ariane Emory.

3. security alert: flag/watch contacts.

Status: Reseune Administration has signed waiver.

Your wing has an overall MANAGEINDEX rating of 4368 out of 5000. MANAGEINDEX congratulates you and your staff and calls your high achievement to the attention of Reseune Administration.

Your staff will receive notification of excellent performance and will receive commendations in permanent file.

—————————————————————— xiii ——————————————————————

The vote totals ticked by on the top of the screen and Giraud took another drink. "We're going to make it," he said to Abban.

After-dinner drinks in his Novgorod apartment. Private election-watch, with his companion Abban, who very rarely indulged. But Abban's glass had diminished by half since the Pan-paris figures had started coming in. Pan-paris had gone for Khalid in the last election. This time it went for Jacques by a two percent margin.

"It's not over," Abban said, dour as usual. "There's still Wyatt's."

The stars farther off the paths of possible expansion were very chancy electorates for any seat. The garrisons tended to be local, resisting amalgamation into other units, and voted consistently Centrist.

But Pan-paris augured very well . . . coming out of the blind storage on Cyteen Station: the computers spat up the stored results of other stations as Cyteen polls closed simultaneously, on-world and up at Station, and the tallies began to flood in.

"I told you," Giraud finally felt safe to say. "Not even with Gorodin's health at issue. Khalid's far from forming a third party. He certainly can't do it with support eroding inside his own electorate. Then we only have Jacques to worry about."

"Only Jacques," Abban echoed. "Do you think he'll keep a bargain? I don't."

"He'll appoint Gorodin. He knows damn well what reneging on that deal would do for him. All we have to hope is that Gorodin stays alive." He took a drink of his own. "And that he hurries and makes an appearance. *Hope* he's not going to wait overlong on proprieties."

The moderate do-nothing Simon Jacques for Councillor; Jacques to appoint Gorodin as Secretary of Defense, then Jacques to resign and appoint Gorodin proxy Councillor, back to his old seat—after which there was bound to be another round with Khalid.

But by then they had to have a viable Expansionist candidate ready to contend with Khalid. The two-year rule applied: meaning Khalid, having lost the election, could not turn around and re-file against the winner until two years had passed; which meant Jacques could hold the seat for two years without much chance of challenge—but if Jacques resigned directly after election, it would be a race to file: whoever filed first, Gorodin or Khalid, could preclude the other from filing because they were each a month short of the end of the prohibition from the election that had put *Khalid* in: which was sure to mean a Supreme Court ruling on the situation—the rule technically only applying to losers, but creating a window for an appeal on the grounds of legal equity.

That meant it was wiser to leave Jacques in office for as long as the two-year rule made him unassailable—while Gorodin—the health rumors were *not* fabricated this time—used what time he had to groom a successor of his own . . . because the one thing no one believed was that Gorodin would last the full two years.

A successor whom of *course* Jacques was going to support. Like hell. Jacques knew himself a figurehead, knew his own financial fortunes were solidly linked with Centrist-linked firms, and the next two years were going to be fierce infighting inside Defense, while Khalid, stripped of his Intelligence post, still had pull enough in the military system to be worrisome. The estimate was that Lu, tainted with the administrative decisions Gorodin's war record to some extent let him survive, had a reputation for side-shifting that did not serve him well in an elected post; and he was old, very old, as it was.

"We're running out of war heroes," Abban said. "Doubtful if Gorodin can find any of that generation *fit* to serve. This new electorate—I'm not sure they respond to the old issues. That's the trouble."

Seventy years since the war—and the obits of famous names were getting depressingly frequent.

"These young hawks," Giraud said, "they're not an issue, they're a mindset. They're pessimistic, they believe in worst-cases, they feel safe only on the side of perceived strength. Khalid worries me more as an agitator than as a single-electorate hero. He appeals to that type—to the worriers of all electorates, not just the ones who happen to be in Defense. It's always after wars—in times of confusion—or economic low spots, exactly the kind of thing a clever operator like Khalid *can* find a base in. There are alarming precedents. Lu would be the best for the seat, still the best for the seat and the best for the times—but this damned electorate won't vote for a man who tells them there are four and five sides to a question. There's too much uncertainty. The electorate doesn't want the truth, it wants answers in line with their thinking."

"One could," Abban said, "simply take a direct solution. I don't understand civs, I especially don't understand civ CITs. In this case the law isn't working. It's insanity to go on following it. Eliminate the problem quietly. Then restore the law." Abban *was* a little buzzed. "Take this man Khalid out. I could do it. And no one would find me out."

"A dangerous precedent."

"So is losing—dangerous to your cause."

"No. Politics works. When the Expansionists look strong, these pessimist types vote Expansionist. And they'll turn. We had them once. We can have them again."

"When?" Abban asked.

"We will. I'll tell you: Denys is right. Young Ari's image has been altogether too sweet." Abban's glass was empty. He filled Abban's and topped off his, finishing the bottle. "When our girl took into Khalid in front of the cameras—that threw a lot of Khalid's believers completely off their balance, but you mark me, they blamed the media. Remember they always believe in conspiracies. They weren't willing to accept Ari as anything solid—as *anything* that can guarantee their future. And *won't*, until she makes them believe it."

"Which alienates the doves."

"Oh, yes. When she went in front of those cameras head to head with

Khalid—it was damned dangerous. She pulled it off—but there was a downside. I argued with Denys. Her insistence on bringing Gehenna out public again—I'm sure inflamed the hawks and scared the hell out of a few doves—enough to bring the Paxers out in force. She may have attracted the few peace-pushers who aren't more scared of her than him, and may have lost him a few of his, but she didn't gain any of *his* people. It's Gorodin they're re-electing. Gorodin's an old name, a safe name. They're not about to go with a young girl's opinion. Not the worry-addicts."

More figures ticked by. Widening margin, Jacques' favor.

"I'll tell you what worries me," Giraud said, finally. "Young Warrick. He's going to be very hard to hold. How's our man doing—the one with the Planys contact?"

"Proceeding."

"We document it, we find some convenient link to the Rocher gang or the Paxers and that's all we need. Or we create one. I want you to look into that."

"Good."

"We need to leave the Centrists with very embarrassing ties— There have to be ties. That will keep Corain busy. *And* keep young Warrick quiet, if he has any sense at all."

"Direct solutions there are just as possible," Abban said.

"Oh, no. Jordie Warrick himself can be quite a help. We keep putting off the travel passes. Start a security scandal at Planys airport. That should do. Leak the business about young Warrick going on rejuv. Our Jordie's damned clever. Just keep the pressure on, and he'll get reckless—he'll throw something to the Centrists; and our man just funnels it straight to the Paxers. Then we just turn the lights on—and watch them run for cover."

"And *young* Warrick?"

"Denys wants to salvage him. I think it's lunacy. At least he took my advice—in the case we *have* a problem. The Paxers have handed us a beautiful issue. The doves hate them because they're violent—the hawks hate them for the lunacy they stand for. Let our Ari discover the Paxers are plotting to kill her, and that Jordan Warrick is involved with them; and watch those instincts turn on in a hurry. Watch her image shift then—on an issue of civil violence and plots. Absolutely the thing we need. Attract the peace-party *and* the hawks—and cultivate enemies that can only do her political good."

"Mark *me*, young Warrick is a danger in that scenario."

"Ah. But we've been very concerned with his welfare. Planning for his long life. Giving him rejuv puts that all on record, doesn't it? And if Ari's threatened—she'll react. If Jordan's threatened—so will young Warrick jump. You give me the incident I need, and watch the pieces fall. And watch our young woman learn a valuable lesson." A moment he stared at the screen and sipped at the wine. "I'll tell you, Abban: you know this: she matters to me. *She's* my concern. Reseune is. Damned if Jordie Warrick's son is going to have a voice in either. Damned if he is."

Cyteen Station results flashed up, lopsided.

"That's it," Abban said. "He's got it now."

"Absolutely. I told you. Jacques is in."

---

xiv

Catlin brought sera coffee in the home office, while sera was feeding the guppies in the little tank she had moved in from the garden-room—sera was quite, quite calm, doing that: it seemed to *make* her calm, sometimes, a sort of focus-down. Catlin could figure that. She also knew that it was a bad time, sera was waiting for answers from a protest she had filed with Administration; sera—outward evidence to the contrary—was in a terrible temper, not the time that Catlin wanted at all to deal with her. But she tried.

"Thank you," sera said, taking the mug and setting it on the edge of the desk, and fussing with the net and a bit of floating weed.

Sera never even looked her way. After a while Catlin decided sera was deliberately ignoring her, or was just thinking hard, and turned and walked out again.

Or started to walk out. Catlin got as far as the hall, and found herself facing her partner's distressed, exasperated look.

So Catlin stopped, drew a large breath, and went back to stand beside sera's desk, doggedly determined that sera should notice.

She had, she thought, rather have run a field under fire.

"What is it?" sera said suddenly, breaking her concentration.

"Sera, —I need to talk to you. About the Planys thing. Florian said—I was the one who heard. So it's mine to say."

It took a moment, sometimes, for sera to come back when she was really thinking, and especially when she was mad, and she brought some of that temper back with her. Because she was so smart, Catlin thought, because she was thinking so hard she was almost deep-studying, except she was doing it from the inside.

But that was a keyword—Planys. That was precisely what sera was mad about; and sera came right back, instantly, and fixed on her.

"What *about* Planys?"

Catlin clenched her hands. *You're* best at explaining things, she had objected to Florian. But Florian had said: You're the one heard it, *you* should tell it.

Because Florian came to pieces when it came to a fight with sera.

And it could.

"This Paxer group in Novgorod," she began.

There had been another subway bombing in Novgorod. Twenty people killed, forty-eight injured.

"What's *that* to do with Planys airport?"

"In security. They're—" She never could go through things without detail. She never knew what to leave out with a CIT, even sera, so she decided to dive straight to the heart of it. "Sera, they're pretty sure there is some kind of contact. The Pax group—they're the violent part. But there's a group called the Committee for Justice—"

"I've heard about them."

"There's overlap. Security is saying that's definite. One is the other, in a major way. They're doing stickers in Novgorod, you understand—someone just walks through a subway car and puts one up. Most of them say Committee for Justice. Or Free Jordan Warrick. But a few of them say No Eugenics and Warrick Was Right."

Sera frowned.

"It's very serious," Catlin said. "Security is terribly worried."

"I understand how serious it is, dammit. —What does this have to do with Planys airport security?"

"It's complicated."

"Explain it. I'm listening. Give me all the details. *What* does Security know?"

"The Novgorod police know the Paxer explosives are homemade. That's first. There's probably just a handful of people—real Paxers—in Novgorod. The police are pretty sure they're a front for Rocher. But they can't find Rocher. So they're sure he's living on somebody else's card. That's not hard to do. Nothing's hard to do, when there are that many people all crowded up in one place. There's probably a lot of connection between the Committee and the Paxers and Rocher—everybody. So the Novgorod police got the Cyteen Bureau to get Union Internal Affairs on it, on the grounds it's a problem that crosses the boundaries between Reseune and—"

"I know Reseune Security is on the case. But tell it your way."

"—and Cyteen. Which lets the Justice Bureau call on us to help the Novgorod police. They can't do the kind of stuff we'd like to—Novgorod is just too big. The police are *talking* about card-accesses on every subway gate, but that just means they'll always have somebody else's keycard, and they'll kill people to get them. A lot of things they could do to stop the bombings are real expensive, and they'd slow everybody down and make them take hours getting to and from work. They say Cyteen Station is getting real nervous and they *are* doing keycard checks and print-locks and all of that. So they've decided the only real way to get the Paxers is to infiltrate them. So they have. You just send somebody inside and you get good IDs and you start searching the keycard systems on *those* markers and you start taking a few of them out, you aggravate whatever feuds you find—make them fight each other and keep increasing your penetrations until you can figure their net out. *That's* the way they're working it."

"You mean you know they're already doing it."

Catlin nodded. "I'm not supposed to know. But yes, sera, they are. And they know the airports are one of the places where some of the illegal stuff they get is getting through security, and that's how it's going to spread *outside*

Novgorod, which is what the rumor is. That there's going to be a hit somewhere else. *That's* what's going on out there."

"They're not grounding traffic, are they?"

"No, sera. People don't know it's going on. They don't need to know.
But they're most worried about Planys and Novgorod. Novgorod because it's
biggest and there's the shuttleport. And Planys because they think there's a
problem there."

Sera closed the lid on the tank and laid the net down. "Go on. Take your
time."

"They're terribly worried," Catlin said. "Sera, they're not talking about
Jordan Warrick in the posters. It's against *you*. People are scared about the
subways. That's the Paxers' job. People aren't being very smart. They have all
these signs to tell them to watch about people leaving packages, and there's a
rumor out that the police have installed this kind of electronics at the subway
gates that'll blow any explosives up when it passes through that point, but
that's not so. People are calling the city offices and asking about more ped-
ways, but that's stupid—you can leave a package in a ped-tunnel that can kill
just as many people. So all they can do is put up with it, but people are getting
really upset, that's what they're saying, and when they're upset enough, the
Committee comes out more and agitates with some lie they'll make up about
you when they need it. They're not sure even this isn't something Khalid's
behind, but that's just something Security wishes they could prove. But *that's*
why they're doing all this stuff with the airports, and that's why Justin can't
get a pass. And that's not the worst, sera. There *is* somebody who's getting
stuff in and out of Planys. It's connected to Jordan Warrick. That's what's
going on. That's why they're stopping Justin and Grant from going there."

Sera stayed very still a moment. Mad. Terribly mad and upset.

It was not hard to figure why sera partnered with Justin Warrick: Catlin
knew the reasons in that the way she had known, after she had seen Florian
attack a problem, that Florian was everything she needed in the world.

And when somebody was your partner, you felt connected to them, and
you had rather anything than think they could fail you.

A long time sera stood there, and finally she sat down at her desk. "I
don't think they know," sera said.

"Not unless there's somebody working inside Reseune, sera. And that's
not likely. But not everybody at Planys is Reseune staff. That's where the hole
is. And they're not going to plug it. They're going to see what's going on first.
Jordan Warrick is linked to the Abolitionists. And maybe to respectable people. Nobody knows yet. They're trying to find out if those groups are doing
this."

Sera's face had gone terribly white, terribly upset.

"Sera?" Catlin said, and sat down in the interview chair and put her hand
on her sera's knee. "Florian and I will go on trying to find things out, if you
don't tell Denys about us knowing. That's the best thing. That's what we
need to do."

Sera's eyes seemed to focus. And looked at her. "There's not a damn thing Justin knows about it."

"They're going to let him talk to his father, sera. They're going to monitor that—very closely. They're going to give his father a lot of room, actually let up the security—"

"To trap him, you mean. God, Catlin, to *push* him into it, what do they think people are made of?"

"Maybe they will," Catlin said. "I'm not worried about that. I'm worried about Justin being *here*. I'm worried because he's going to be upset when he can't go to his father. Sera, —" This was terribly hard to say. She had it in her hands of a sudden, the whole picture that had been worrying her and she made a violent gesture, cutting sera off, before she lost the way to say it. "The trouble is in Novgorod. With people who hate you. And Jordan Warrick was with these people a long time ago. It doesn't matter whether it's his fault or their fault—what matters is they're making him a Cause. And that's power. And when he's got that—"

"He's got to do something with it," sera said.

Catlin nodded. "And Justin's real close to you, sera. Justin's inside. And his father's a Special in psych—and he's your Enemy. That's real dangerous. That's terribly dangerous, sera."

"Yes," she said, very quiet. "Yes, it is." And after a moment more: "Dammit, why didn't Denys *tell* me?"

"Maybe he thought you might talk to Justin, sera."

"I could *fix* this," sera said. "I could fix this— Damn, I'd—"

"What would you do, sera?" That sera might have an idea did not surprise her at all. But it disconcerted her to see sera's shoulders fall, and watch sera shake her head.

"Politics," sera said. "Pol-i-tics, Catlin. Dirty politics. Like our friends who aren't speaking to each other. Like *fools*, Catlin, who won't tell anyone the truth about what they want—like people want Reseune destroyed for a whole lot of reasons, and some of them are sane and some of them are crooked as hell. Like crazy people who blow up subways for peace. What does reason matter?"

Catlin shook her head, confused.

"I want to know who these people are," sera said in a hard voice. "I want to know, Catlin, whether any of them are of azi ancestry. Whether any of them are azi or whether this is a CIT craziness Reseune didn't have anything to do with." And a moment later: "I've got to think about the other. I've got to think about it, Catlin."

"Sera, *please* don't go to Justin with this. Don't tell him."

A long silence. "No," she said. "No. That's not the thing to do."

2423: 11/5: 2045

AE2: Base One, what data do you have on: keyword: assassination: keyword: Ariane Emory: keyword: death?

B/1: Ari senior has a message.

Stand by.

Ari, this is Ari senior.

You've asked about assassination.

This program will assess your current security problems while this message plays.

Most of all, beware the people you know. The others you would in no wise allow to approach you.

You've asked about death. First, don't mistake my limits for your own.

I don't know how much time there is as I write this. I know, at least, that rejuv is failing. So does Petros Ivanov, who is sworn to secrecy.

How do I face death? With profound anxieties. Anxieties because I know how much there is yet to do.

God, if I could have another lifetime.

But that's yours, sweet. And I'll never know, will I?

Base One has completed its assessment.

You are 17 years old. You are legally adult.

The indices this program uses in Security records indicate a troubled period. Do you think this is an accurate statement?

AE2: Yes.

B/1: Is your life in danger?

AE2: Yes.

B/1: Is the threat internal or external to Reseune?

AE2: I don't know.

B/1: Do you think you can trust the Science Bureau?

AE2: I don't know. I need more information. I want my clearance raised, Base One.

B/1: Working.

Describe the things you want to know.

AE2: Everything. I want this program to do everything it did for Ari senior and I want it to do it without leaving any flags in the system.

B/1: Your request is being processed.

Ari senior has a message.

Stand by.

Ari, this is Ari senior.

You've asked for Base One to assume full operation. The program is assessing your psychological profile, your current test scores, the state of House offices and departments.

Have you considered that the security wall this will create in the House system may be detected by other Bases? Are you knowledgeable enough to create cover?

AE2: Yes.

B/1: I can't foresee your situation when you make this request. I can't advise you in specific. The program, however, is biased to grant this expansion on your request, on a complex weighting of: the length of time you have held your legal majority, the amount and nature of covert activity in other bases, your own test scores and psychological profiles, and a number of other factors you may explore at your leisure.

I had thought about dividing the power of Base One, making it possible for you to acquire information first—without giving you the power to take certain actions through Base One's accesses, this for your protection, and Reseune's.

I decided against that . . . simply because I could not foresee your circumstances. But the program is running as it is because you are asking for a House system rating exceeding that of the present administrators of Reseune.

This may be necessary. It may be a grievous mistake.

Before you proceed, consider that the larger your real power grows, the more it makes you a danger to others. This move of yours, if detected, may increase the number and energy of persons working against you.

Do you still wish to proceed?

AE2: Yes.

B/1: I earnestly advise you, don't use Base One's interactive functions beyond the limits you have used already, until you have a political base to back you: I mean specifically covert actions on a level shutting out Denys Nye, Giraud Nye, Petros Ivanov, Yanni Schwartz, Wendell Peterson, or John Edwards, because they are very likely to catch you at it real-time, in ways that have nothing to do with the House system. You may be brilliant as I was, young Ari, but you are inexperienced at this level. Consider whether a 17-year-old is a match for the experience and political savvy of these people.

It's perfectly safe, however, to use the information-gathering functions of the new level: use that to learn what's going on in the House, by all means, just don't do anything about it until you know damn well you can keep your actions completely covert or until your position is overwhelmingly stronger than any opposition inside Reseune—or the Bureau, or wherever. I am not at all convinced that an inexperienced person can conceal actions within this system.

I am, as you have detected, extremely uneasy about this step. In my day Reseune knew secrets that could mean war or peace.

I did not wield Base One fully until I was 62. I estimate that I had the ability to have handled it when I was 30. But I would have taken it up then with precisely the same caution and by the same degrees I advise you to use at 17. If you cannot survive on wits and knowledge alone, either the situation is worse than mine, or you are not as clever as I was.

Do you wish to proceed, against all these cautions?

AE2: Yes.

B/1: Be aware that this request will begin your assumption of authority over Reseune. Consider the situation inside and outside Reseune, and ask yourself what could result and whether you are ready and able to handle it.

Be aware that others may have anticipated this move and covered their traces. But until you order it to take actions—or until, mark me well, you let slip that you know something you could only have known through a higher Base, you will not create traces. Use that secrecy as long as you can.

Study carefully how others lie to the system, so that when you do it, you will be too good for them to catch.

I have taken only one precaution which will remain in the system until you have control of Administration. Base One will read-only information with no additional prompt, and advise you which information would have been inaccessible to you prior to this expansion.

It will advise you where lies have been planted in the system and show you both sets of information.

I have installed a fail-safe specifically for you, if you should request this power before assuming the administration of Reseune. The system will stop and ask for a special prompt before acting on any level possible as a result of this expansion . . . in plain terms, it will go on acting as it did before, but it will identify and tag certain kinds of information to make you aware what other people think is hidden from you; and it will prevent your accidentally taking actions that would overrun the parameters they believe exist. The key to release the system for action is: Havoc. You may re-set the keyword to suit you. But you should also think about that word—and the consequences of ignoring my advice, no matter how hot the fire gets under your feet.

Second thoughts can generally be amended with judicious action; injudicious actions can seldom be recovered with second thoughts.

Do you understand me, Ari?

AE2: I understand, Base One.

B/1: Your access has been upgraded. This Base is now fully operational. Base One now outranks all other Bases in all Reseune systems.

AE2: Retrieve all previously hidden medical and security records on all individuals under my surveillance.

B/1: Working.

File: Justin Warrick
Emory I
2404: 11/5: 2045

Warrick, Justin.

Estim(ated) Res(ner Index of) 180+ comp(ares) favorab(ly) w(ith) pat [father] (but) lo(w) aggr(e)s(sion level) ref(erence to) presence dom(inant) g(ender)-i(dentical)-p(arent) ergo [I ordered production of] G(rant)ALX [as Justin Warrick's companion]. . . .

File: Justin Warrick
Emory II
2423: 11/10: 2245

Warrick, Justin.
Ref: psychogenesis.

On every evidence I've found in files so far, Justin Warrick was a test case from his conception.

Ari I claims she psyched Jordan into having a PR done. She said things like: "I'm not temperamentally suited to bringing up my own"—I think she meant her own PR. And she said: "Jordan's a loss." Meaning something I don't understand, either that she couldn't work with him, or that she didn't think his slant on his work was what she wanted. I think it was more of the second. But there was ability there, complementary to her own. I think that's what she saw.

She used to work with Jordan. They worked real well at first. But Jordan's upbringing made him a dominant, and she was, and the two of them had a lot of problems which bounced off a sexual encounter they had had when he was 17 and she was 92. That was his only heterosexual relationship, and what went wrong with it had more to do with the fact that he was not hetero to begin with and he had, at 17, begun working with Ari as a student—the whole pattern identical to what happened with Justin.

But in Jordan's case, he had applied to work with Ari, probably because of a genuine admiration for her work. He was young, he was attractive, and Ari's proclivities and his admiration led to a disillusioning experience.

But here's the thing no one's looking at: Jordan Warrick's index increased 60 points during the next ten years. He already had a respectable score. But no one knew what he was until he was working with Ari—because of the publicity and the chance to work *with* her, is the general opinion these days. But the fact is he wasn't Jordan Warrick SP then. He was just damn bright and he was Ari's student.

So I looked back at Jordan's parents. Jordan's mother didn't want him after he was born. She was a researcher. She wanted the bonus you got back then to have a baby in Reseune. But she didn't want a baby. She just picked its father, got pregnant about as clinically timed as you can and still have sex, birthed Jordan and handed him to his father to bring up. His father was an Ed psych specialist who practiced every theory he had on his kid. Pushed him into early learning. And tended to give him things—*lots* of expenditure on things for Jordan. Doted on him.

Anyway, that was Jordan Warrick—not to leave out his companion, Paul, whom he requisitioned a year after his encounter with Ari, and while he was still working with her—but after he had moved out of his father's residence.

After that, his scores came up a lot.

I think Ari intervened with him continually. Ari helped him requisition Paul. Ari claims she talked him into having a PR done when he was about 30, the year after his father died in a seal failure—which was the only family Jordan had except an aunt. So she certainly worked with him. She certainly was dealing with a man who'd just lost someone he loved a great deal, and it's true that the same week they started Justin Warrick, *she* started Grant ALX. Things were pretty good between her and Jordan during that period, and she told Jordan a couple of years later that she had an Alpha test subject she wanted socialized, and would he like to do it and incidentally provide a playmate for his own son.

Jordan agreed. But Ari had picked Grant very carefully, and she had done some very slight corrective work with his set on a couple of things that are easy fixes, nothing beyond that—more than anything, any change in the original Special geneset meant she didn't have to go to Council to get permission and it also meant Grant would be classed as an Experimental, which means Reseune will always hold his contract, no private person can. Ari did Grant's early tape. Ari used Base One to pull up everything she could on Jordan's past and Jordan's father, right around the time she was doing all the search-up for Grant's geneset and all the prep for him. And if Grant was ever part of any other research project, it wasn't in the records or in her notes.

She did have one note that Jordan was a dominating male, but that if he'd been reared by one he'd have curled up and gone under, because that was what he was set to respond to. And something about plants and taller plants getting all the sun. Meaning if Justin was a PR he couldn't turn out *like* his father, because his teacher wasn't Jordan's father, Martin. Martin wasn't a dominant, but he brought up a strong, self-centered dominant who still had his father's tendency to give his son an abundance of affection and material things. *This* was what was going to bring Justin up. And Jordan was much brighter than Martin Warrick, was professionally skilled at manipulation, but with a peculiar emotional blind spot that revolved around his son as an extension of himself—meaning his son was going to *be* himself, and avoid the Bok clone problem that's haunted every PR of a bright parent.

Ari said about Justin, on his school paper: As long as you confuse your father with God you won't pursue this, which would be a shame. I'm requesting you into my wing. It'll do you good, give you a different perspective on things.

I don't know how much of what happened was planned but a lot of it was calculated. She encouraged him in the essay paper. When he did it she approved it, even as much as it duplicated things already tried. She encouraged him; she snagged him into her wing, into her reach, and she ran an intervention on him.

I've seen the tape (ref. tape 85899) and I know that it was an intervention. She knew she was dying. She had maybe a couple of years. Justin Warrick was the test that would tell her whether or not I would exist—as I do.

She always made such precise procedural steps for people to look at; but when she operated, she always seemed to violate her own rules. That's because she tended to cluster steps and combine operations, because she could pick up on flux-states better than anyone I've ever seen.

The tape of her with Justin bothers me in a lot of senses. But I keep coming back to it because there are a handful of tapes of her doing clinical interventions, scattered through her life, under controlled conditions. But knowing as much as I do about Justin, and about psychogenesis—that tape, terrible as it is, is Ari going without tape, without a clinical situation, without any safeguards; and, here's the eerie part, knowing exactly what the situation was, knowing her reactions from the inside, I can see exactly what she sees, how fast she picks up on flux and how fast she can change an entire program—

Because I've got her notes on what she was going to do, and I can read her body language like no one else.

Justin worked . . . not the way he would have if she'd been able to go on working with him. I know that. I also think I know why my uncles opposed him.

Leaving her work in the hands of a young researcher like Justin Warrick is so in character for Ari, exactly in character with that intervention in the tape. She took chances when she was working that would scare hell out of an ethics board. That—scare me less than they should, maybe, because I can see at least some of what she saw. And I know the reasons she wanted someone to follow her—someone with a special kind of sensitivity and a special kind of vision. It was her macro-system interventions that scared her—that scare me, that make me more and more afraid, and drive me beyond what I can stand, sometimes.

I need him. And I can no more explain to my uncles than Ari could. If I told them in plain language about the macro-system interventions: Listen to me, Denys: Ari put a Worm in the system, it's real, it's working, and I need computer time and I need Justin Warrick's work—I can hear him say: even Ari had her out-there notions, dear, and there's no way you can focus an integration over that range. It just won't happen. And Giraud would say: Whatever it does, we make our money off short-term.

—that's exactly what I'd get.

And Giraud would say to Denys after I was out of the room: We've got to do something about Justin Warrick.

CHAPTER 13

The landing gear extended as they made their approach at Planys and Grant looked out the window while the blue-grays and browns of native Cyteen passed under the right wing. His heart beat very fast. His hands were sweating and he clenched them as the wheels touched and the plane braked.

He was traveling with Reseune Security: Reseune Security flew with everyone who came and went from Planys, they had told him that. But he was still afraid—afraid of nameless things, because his memory of plane flights involved suspicion, Winfield and Kruger, the crazy people who had tried to reprogram him, and an utter nightmare when Reseune Security had pulled him out, drugged and semiconscious, and flown him away to hospital and interrogations.

Twelve hours in the air, and chop and finally monotony over endless ocean in the dark—had calmed him somewhat. He had not wanted to tell Justin—and had not—what an irrational, badly fluxed anxiety he had worked himself into over this trip.

Transference, he told himself clinically, absolutely classic CIT-psych transference. He had gathered up all his anxieties about Justin's safety at home, about his own vulnerability traveling alone into Planys and about knowing no matter what Justin and Jordan insisted, he was not the one of them Jordan wanted most to see—and the plane flight was a convenient focus.

The plane would go down in the ocean. There would be sabotage. There were lunatics who would attempt to shoot it down— The engines would simply fail and they would crash on takeoff.

He had spent a great deal of the flight with his hands clenched on the armrests as if that levitation could hold the plane in the air.

He had been nervous in flight when he had been seventeen, but he had not had cold sweats—which showed that, over the years, he had become more and more CIT.

Now, with the wheels on the ground, he had no more excuses. The anxieties had to attach where they belonged, on meeting Jordan, and the fact that, azi that he was, he did not know what to say to the man he had once called his father; and who had been, whatever else, his Supervisor all during his childhood.

The thought of disappointing Jordan, of *being* that disappointment—was almost enough to make him wish the plane had gone down.

Except there was Justin, who loved him enough to give him the chance to go, who had fought for it and held out for it through all the contrived delays, the breaks in communication—everything, so that when permission came to travel again—*he* could go first. They hoped there would be another chance directly after. But there was no guarantee, there was never a guarantee.

Please, he had said to Jordan, in that last phone call before the flight. I really feel awkward about this. Justin should come first.

Shut up, Justin had said over his shoulder. This time is yours. There'll be others.

I *want* you to come, Jordan had said. Of course I want you.

Which had affected him more than was good for him, he thought. It made a little pain in his chest. It was a CIT kind of feeling, pure flux, which meant that he ought to take tape and go deep and let Justin try to take that ambivalence away before it disturbed his value-sets. But Justin would argue with him. And that curious pain was a feeling he wanted to understand: it seemed a window into CIT mentality, and a valuable thing to understand, in his profession, in the projects he did with Justin. So he let it fester, thinking, when he could be more sensible about it: maybe this is the downside of the deep-set links. Or maybe it's just surface-set flux: but should it make such physiological reactions?

The plane rolled up to the terminal: Justin had said there was no tube-connection, but there was, and there was a good long wait while they got the plane hosed down and the tube-connect sealed down.

Then everyone began to get up and change into D-suits, the way Justin had said they would.

He did as the Security escort asked him. He put on the flimsy protection over his clothes and walked out into the tube and through into Decontamination.

Foam and another hose-down, and a safety-barrier, where he had to strip the suit off and step out, without touching its exterior—

In places he had been, like Krugers', if one had to make a fast transfer, one held one's breath, got to shelter, held an oxy mask tight to one's face with one hand and stripped with the other under a hosing-down that was supposed to take any woolwood fiber down the drain.

Planys was terrifyingly elaborate, a long series of procedures that made him wonder what he had been exposed to, or whether all this was just to make people at this desolate place feel safer.

"This way, ser," one of the Decon agents said, and took him by the elbow and brought him aside into a small alcove.

Body-search. He expected this too, and stripped down when they told him and suffered through the procedure, a little cold, a little anxious, but even Reseune Security people got this treatment going in or out of Planys. So they said.

Not mentioning what they did to the luggage.

"Grant," Jordan said, in person, meeting him in the hall, and:

"Hello, ser," he said, suddenly shy and formal, the surface-sets knowing he should go and embrace Jordan, and the deep-sets knowing him as a Supervisor, and knowing him from his childhood, when all instruction had come from him, and he was God and teacher.

This was the man Justin would have become, if rejuv had not stopped them both a decade earlier.

He did not move. He could not, suddenly, cope with this. Jordan came and embraced him instead.

"My God, you've grown," Jordan said, patting him on the back. "Vid didn't show how tall you'd grown. Look at the shoulders on you! What are you doing, working docks?"

"No, ser." He let Jordan lead him to his office, where Paul waited—Paul, who had doctored his skinned knees and Justin's. Paul embraced him too. Then the reality of where he was began to settle through the flux and he began to believe in being here, in being welcome, in everything being all right.

But there were no guards in the office. That was not the way Justin had warned him it would be.

Jordan smiled at him and said: "They'll send the papers up as soon as they've been over them—Justin did send that report with you, didn't he?"

"Yes, ser. Absolutely."

"Damn, it's good to see you."

"I thought—security would be more than it is." *Are we monitored, ser? What's going on?*

"I told you it's been saner here. That's one of the things. Come on, we're closing up the office. We'll go home, fix dinner—not as fancy as Reseune, but we've got real groceries. We bought a ham for the occasion. Wine from Pell, not the synth stuff."

His spirits lifted. He was still anxious, but Jordan, he thought, was in charge of things; he relaxed a bit into dependency, azi on Supervisor, which he had not done with Justin—

—had not done since he was in hospital, recovering from Giraud's probes. Had never done, after, because he was always either Justin's caretaker or Justin's partner.

It was like years of pressure falling away from him, to follow Jordan when he said Come, to sink into azi simplicity with someone he could trust— someone, finally, besides Justin, who would not harm him, who knew the place better than he did, and whose wishes were sane and sensible.

It was finally, one brief interlude in all these years, *not* his responsibility.

Only when he thought that, he thought: *No, I can't stop watching things. I can't trust anything. Not even Jordan—that far.*

He felt exhausted then, as if just for a few weeks he would like to go somewhere and do mindless work under someone's direction, and be fed and sleep and have responsibility for nothing.

That was *not* what he could do.

He walked with them to the apartment they had; and inside, and looked around him— *Things are very grim there*, Justin had said. *Very primitive.*

It was certainly not Reseune. The chairs were plastic and metal; the tables were plastic; the whole decor was plastic, except a corner full of real geraniums, under light, and a fish-tank, and a general inefficient pleasantness to the place that had all the stamp of CITs in residence . . . what Justin called a homey feeling, and what he thought of as the CIT compulsion to collect things charged with flux and full of fractals. A potted geranium represented the open fields. The fish were random, living motion. The water was assurance of life-requirements in abundance; and made a fractally repetitive sound which might be soothing to flux-habituated, non-analytical minds. God knew what else. He only knew Justin had let all the plants die after Jordan left, but when things started to go well, Justin began to fuss with a few plants, which always died back and thrived by turns—in time to the rise and fall of Justin's spirits.

Healthy plants, Grant reckoned, were a very good sign among CITs.

Things *felt* safe here, he thought as he gave his jacket up and let Paul hang it in the closet, people were tolerably happy here.

So the improvements in the world, the changes that had made this last couple of years more livable, even happy—had gotten to Planys too, despite the frustrations of the Paxer scare. All the same he wished Jordan knew even a few of the multitudinous signals he and Justin had worked out, the little indicators whether a thing was to be believed.

Maybe Jordan picked up his nervousness, because Jordan looked at him, laughed and said: "Relax. They monitor us from time to time. It's all right. Hello, Jean!" —to the ceiling.

"We know each other," Jordan said then. "Planys is a very small establishment. Sit down. We'll make coffee. God, there's so much to talk about."

---

ii

It was very lonely, the apartment without Grant. There was ample justification for worry, and Justin swore he was not going to spend four uninterrupted days at it.

So he read awhile, did tape awhile, an E-dose only, a piece of fluff from library. And read again. Ari had given him an advance copy of Emory's *IN PRINCIPIO*, the first of the three-volume annotated edition of Emory's archived notes, which the Bureau of Science was publishing in cooperation with the Bureau of Information, and which was now selling as fast as presses could turn them out in the Cyteen edition and already on its way on ships which had bid fabulously for it, a packet of information destined for various stations which would in turn pay for the license, sell printout and electronic repros to their own populations and sell more rights to ships bound further on.

Even, possibly, more than possibly, to Earth.

While Reseune accounts piled up an astonishing amount of credit.

Every library wanted copies. Scientists in the field did. But it was selling in the general market with a demand that could only be called hysteria: a volume of extremely heavy going, illustrated, with annotations so extensive there were about three lines of Emory's notes to every page, and the rest was commentary, provided by himself and by Grant, among others: he was the JW and Grant was the GALX; YS was Yanni Schwartz; and WP, Wendell Peterson; and AE2 was Ari, who had gotten the original text out of Archive and provided reference notes on some of the most obscure parts. DN was Denys Nye; GN was Giraud; JE was John Edwards; and PI was Petros Ivanov, besides dozens of techs and assistants who served in editing and collation—each department head and administrator to read and vet the material from his own staff.

Dr. Justin Warrick, it said in the fine print in the table of contributors. Which, secretly, like a little child, he read over and over just to see it confirmed. Grant, they listed as Grant ALX Warrick, E.P., *emeritus psychologiae*, which meant an azi who should have a doctorate in psych, and would have, automatically, if he became CIT. It pleased Grant more than Grant would let on.

CIT silliness, Grant had said. *My patients certainly don't care.*

But it was there, in print. And meanwhile the general public was buying copies, long waiting lists at booksellers—the Bureau had figured on strong library interest, but *never* anticipated average citizens would buy them, and certainly was bewildered that they were selling at that rate at a pre-publication price of 250 cred per volume—until an embarrassed Bureau of Information cut the price to 120 and then to 75, based on advance orders; and that brought in an absolute flood of orders. There were precious few sales in fiche or tape, except to the libraries: the actual books, printed on permasheet, thank you, were status objects: one could hardly display a microfilm to one-up one's neighbors.

Young Ari avowed herself completely bewildered by the phenomenon.

People know, Justin had said to her, *that your predecessor did tremendously important things. They don't know* what *she did. They certainly can't understand the notes. But they feel like they ought to understand. What you ought to do, you know—is write a volume of your own notes: your own perspective on doing the volume. The things you've learned from your predecessor. You* ask *the BI if they'd be interested in the rights to* that.

Not surprisingly, Information jumped at the chance.

Now Ari was struggling to put her own notes in shape. And coming to him with: Do you think . . . and sometimes just chatter—about the hidden notes, about things as full of revelations as the books he had spent a year helping annotate with the barest explanations of the principles involved.

She had sent a copy of *IN PRINCIPIO* to Jordan.

"Because it has your name in it," Ari had said to him, "and Grant's."

"If it gets through," he had said. "Planys Security may not like it. Not to mention Customs."

"All right," she had said. "So I'll send it with Security. Let them argue with that."

She did thoughtful things like that. In a year and a half in her wing she had come through with every promise she had made, gotten him and Grant a secretary, taken the pressure off—

If something went wrong or something glitched, Florian was on the phone very quickly; and if Florian could not resolve it, it was—Wait, ser, sera will handle it—after which Ari would be on the line, with a technique that ranged rapidly between *This has to be mistaken*— to a flare that department heads learned to avoid. Maybe it was a realization Ari might remember these things in future. Maybe—Justin suspected so—it was because that voice could start so soft, go to a controlled low resonance uncommon at her age—then pick up volume in a punch that made nerves jump: that made his jump, for certain, and evoked memories. But she never raised that voice with him, never pushed him, always said please and thank you—until he found himself actually on the inside of a very safe circle and *liking* where he worked—with a small, niggling fear that he was losing his edge, becoming less worried, less defensive, relying too much on Ari's promises—

Fool, he told himself.

But he grew so tired of fighting, and the thought that he might have reached a situation where he could draw breath awhile, that he might actually have found a kind of safety, even if it meant difficulties to come . . . *later* was all right.

Ari was well aware of what came in and out of her wing, was aggressively defensive of her staff's time—her attention to pennies and minutes was, God, the living echo of Jane Strassen; so that, beyond the annotations which totaled about a hundred twenty pages between himself and Grant, and three months' intensive work, she accepted only design work for her wing, only troubleshooting after others had done the brute work, and it went, thank God, immediately *back* to junior levels in some other wing when he or Grant had provided the fix, no returns, no would-you-mind's? and no 'but we thought you could do that, we're running behind.'

So he critiqued Ari's work, answered Ari's questions, did the few fixes her wing ran, and had the actual majority of his time to use on his own projects—as Grant did, doing study of his own on the applications of endocrine matrix theory in azi tape, which Grant was going to get a chance to talk over with Jordan—Grant was very much looking forward to it.

They were, overall, happier than he remembered since—a long time; and it was the damnedest thing, waking up in the middle of the night as he did, with nightmares he could not remember.

Or stopping sometimes in the middle of work or walking home or wherever, overwhelmed by a second's panic, of nothing he could name except fear of the ground under his feet, fear that he was being a fool, and fear because he had no choice but be where he was.

Fear, perhaps, that he had not won: that he had in fact lost by the decisions he had made, and it would only take some few years yet to come clear to him.

All of which, he told himself severely, was a neurotic, compulsive state, and he resisted it—tried to weed it out when he found it operative. But take tape for it, he would not; not even have Grant run a little tranquilizing posthyp on him—being afraid of that too.

Fool, he told himself, exasperated at the track his thoughts tended to run, and marked his place and laid the book aside.

Emory for bedtime reading.

Maybe it was the fact he could still hear that voice, the exact inflection she would use on those lines he read.

And the nerves still twitched.

He rattled around an empty apartment in the morning, toasted a biscuit for breakfast, and went to the office—not the cramped, single office he and Grant had used for years, but the triple suite that Ari had leased—physically in the Ed Wing, which was back, in a sense, to where they had begun—simply because that wing had space and no one else did: an office apiece for himself and Grant, and one for Em, the secretary the pool had sent, a plump, earnest lad quite glad to get into a permanent situation where he could, conceivably, come up in rating.

He read the general advisories, the monthly plea from catering to book major orders a week in advance; a tirade from Yanni about through-traffic in Wing One, people cutting through the lower hall. Em arrived at 0900, anxious at finding the office already open, and got to work on the filing while he started on the current design.

That went on till lunch and during—a pocket-roll and a cup of coffee in the office; and a concentration that left him stiff-shouldered and blinking when the insistent blip of an Urgent Message started flashing in the upper left corner of the screen.

He keyed to it. It flashed up:

I need to talk to you. I'm working at home today. —AE.

He picked up the phone. "Ari, Base One," he told it.

Florian answered. "Yes, ser, just a second." And immediately, Ari: "Justin. Something's come up. I need to talk to you."

"Sure, I'll meet you at your office." *Is it Grant? God, has something happened?*

"Meet me here. Your card's cleared. Endit."

"Ari, I don't—"

The Base had gone off. Dammit.

He did not meet Ari except with Grant; except in the offices; except sometimes with Catlin and Florian, out to lunch or an early dinner. He kept it that way.

But if something had happened, Ari would not want to argue details over the phone; if something had happened with Grant—

He keyed off the machine, and got up and went, gathering up his jacket, telling Em to shut down and go home, everything was fine.

He headed over to the wing where Ari's apartment was, showed his card to Security at the doors and got a pass-through without question.

Dammit, he thought, his heart pounding, it had better be a good reason, it had better be business—

It had better *not* be because Grant was momentarily not in the picture.

"Come in," Florian said, at the door. "Sera is waiting for you."

"What does she want?" he asked, not committing himself. "Florian, —is this a good idea?"

"Yes, ser," Florian said without hesitation.

He walked in then, sweating, not only from the trip over. The room, the travertine floors, the couch—was a vivid flash of then and now. "Is it Grant?"

"Your jacket, ser? Sera urgently needs to talk with you."

"About what? —What's happened?"

"Your jacket, ser?"

He pulled the jacket off, jerked a resistant sleeve free, handed it to Florian as Ari arrived in the living room from the right-hand hall.

"What in hell's going on?" he asked.

She gestured toward the sunken living room, the couch; and came down the steps to take a seat there.

He came and sat down at the opposing corner. Not the private living room: thank God. He did not think he could have held together.

"Justin," she said, "thank you for coming. I know—I know how you feel about this place. But it's the only place—the only one I'm absolutely sure there's no monitoring but mine. I want you to tell me the truth, now, the absolute truth: Grant's safety depends on this. Is your father working with the Paxers?"

"My— God. No. No. —How in hell could he?"

"Let me tell you: I've got a report on my desk that says there are leaks out of Planys. That your father—has been talking with a suspect. Security is watching Grant very carefully. They fully expect Jordan to attempt an intervention with him—"

"He wouldn't! Not—not on something like that. He wouldn't do that to Grant."

"Your father could manage something like that without tape, without anything but a keyword, with someone of Grant's ability. I know what Grant's memory is like."

"He *won't* do it. It's a damned set-up."

"It may be," she said quietly. "That's why I wanted to talk to you, fast, before Security has a chance, because I'll do this: I'll look for all the truth. I'm the one it's against. And I've been aware of this—for a while; from long before Grant got that pass. Grant's gone into the middle of a Security operation that I don't want to agree with. I don't want to think that Grant could work against me, or that you could, but I have to protect myself—which is why I took this chance."

"I don't understand." He felt the old panic—too experienced to give way to it. Keep the opposition calm, keep the voices down, go along with things. He did not think Ari was at the head of whatever was going on, not with what he knew of where authority was in the House. "Ari, tell me what's going on."

"People who protect me . . . don't want me near you. That's why I waited and let Grant go—because I knew—I know very well that it's a set-up against you, which is why I called you to come here."

"Why is that? What do you want?"

"Because I have to know. That's first. And I know how you hate this place, but it's the only place, the only place I can trust." She reached into her left-hand pocket, and pulled out a little vial. Amber glass. "This is kat. It's a deep dose. You can help me or you can leave now. But this is the chance I have. You go in the tape lab and take this, and let me get you on tape—I promise, I *promise*, Justin, no lousy tricks. Just the truth on tape, for me to use. This is what I need. This is the kind of documentation I can use with the Bureau, if I have to go that far. This is the chance I have to believe you."

He flashed badly, totally disoriented, unable to think for a few breaths. Then he reached out for the vial and she gave it to him.

Because there was no choice. Not a thing he could do. He only thought— *God, I don't know if I can do this. I don't know if I can stay sane.*

"Where?" he said.

"Florian," she said; and he got up shakily and went after Florian as Florian indicated the hallway to the right.

An open door on the right again was the tape library, with a couch with all the built-ins for deep-study. He walked in and sat down there, set the vial down on the couch beside him and pulled off his sweater, feeling light-headed. "I want Ari here," he said, "I want to talk to her."

"Yes, ser," Florian said. "There's no lead, ser, it's just a patch, let me help you."

"*I want to talk to Ari.*"

"I'm here," she said at the door. "I'm right here."

"Pay attention," he said shortly. And uncapped the vial and took his pill, while the cardiac monitor flashed red with alarms. He looked at the flashes and concentrated, willing himself calmer. "Your patient tends to panic, sera, I hope to hell you remember that."

"I'll remember," Ari said, very quietly.

He worked with the monitor, staring at that, concentrating only on the rate of the flashes. A thought about his father leaked through, about Grant, a single second, and the light flickered rapidly; slow, he thought, that was all, while the numbness started and panic tried to assert itself. He felt a touch on his shoulder, heard Florian urging him: "Lie down, ser, please, just lean back. I've got you."

He blinked, thinking for a moment of the boy-Florian, spinning through the years to Florian grown strong enough to handle his weight, Florian bending over him—

"Be calm, ser," his gentle voice said. "Be calm. Are you comfortable?"

He felt an underlying panic, very diffuse. He felt the numbness growing, and his vision started going out. His heart began to speed, frighteningly, runaway.

"Calm," Ari said, a voice that jolted through his panic, absolute. "Steady down. It's all right. Everything's all right. Hear me?"

iii

"Has your father ever worked with these people?" Ari asked, sitting by the side of the couch, holding Justin's limp hand.

"No," he said. Which meant, of course, to the limit of Justin's knowledge. No, no, and no. She saw the cardiac monitor flash with a very strong rise in heart rate.

"Conspired with anyone against Reseune Administration?"

"No."

"Have you?"

"No."

Not conspiring with anyone. Against Reseune. Against Ariane Emory. Justin, at least, was not aware of any plot.

"Don't you ever get frustrated with Security?"

"Yes."

"Do you think things will ever change?"

"I—hope."

"What do you hope?"

"Keep quiet. Live quiet. People believe me. Then things change."

"Are you afraid?"

"Always."

"Of what?"

"Mistakes. Enemies."

He hoped if he could work with her—it would prove something about himself and his father, in a calmer world—

He was afraid for Grant more than Jordan. Jordan had his Special's status to protect him. Grant—if they interrogated him—would be subject to things they might try to impose on him, ideas and attitudes they might try to shape— Grant would resist it. Grant would throw himself into null and stay there: he had before. But if they kept working at him—

If *he* were arrested, here, in Reseune, if Reseune Administration was determined to make a case, then they could do that. He thought that could be the case—that politics always mattered more than truth. And more than a Warrick life—always.

"Jordan's not a killer," Justin said. "He's not like that. Whatever happened was an accident. He made his mistake in trying to cover it, that's what I know happened."

"How do you know it?"

"I know my father."

"Even after twenty years?"

"Yes."

He was close to the upturn, when the drug would fade. And she was all but hoarse from questions and from strain.

She thought: *I almost know enough to take on what Ari did. Almost. But he's not the boy she worked with.*

I could Work him to make him want me. So easily. So easily.

She remembered the tape, remembered it with sexual flashes that troubled her.

And thought, thinking of the possible intersections with so many, many knot-ups in his sets: *Damn, no.* Damn, *damn*, Ari, not so fast, not so reckless.

I could make him happy. I could take all of that away—

Politics is real and everything else takes second place, he *knows that—There's that on top of everything that's wrong in him.*

I could make him worry less. I can make him trust me more.

Is even that—fair? Or safe—in the world the way it is, or inside Reseune?

She got up, cut the recorder off and sat down on the edge of the couch beside him. She touched his face very gently, saw the monitor blips increase. "Hush, it's all right, it's all right—" she said, until she could get the monitor blips down again.

"Justin," she said when it was running even, "I believe you. You'd never hurt me. You'd never let me be hurt. I know all those things. I don't think they're going to make a move on Grant—not now that I've got you on record. I can tell my uncle what I have, and at the same time I'll tell him Grant's in my wing, and he'd better not move against him. That's what I'm prepared to do, because I believe you. Do you understand me?"

"Yes." A little flutter from the monitor.

"Don't be anxious about this place. This is my home. My predecessor isn't here anymore. That's all gone. That's all gone. You're safe here. I want you to remember these things. I can't get what I'd like out of hospital, without them knowing I'm doing this—but I want you to do the deep-fix for me, the way Grant could do it. Can you do that? Bear down hard, feel good, and remember this."

"Yes. . . ."

"I want you to think: I'm going to believe this forever. I promise you, if you trust me, if you come to me and if Grant comes to me when you need help, I'll do the best I can. You can rest now. You'll wake up feeling fine, and you'll be all right. Do you hear me?"

"Yes."

No flutter now, just a strong, steady beat. She got up, signaled Florian and Catlin to be very quiet, patted Justin gently on the shoulder. You stay with him, she signaled Florian.

And to Catlin, in the hall, she said: "What's the news?"

"Nothing more than we had," Catlin said.

"Stand by in case Florian needs you." She went to her own office and phoned Denys directly.

"Seely," she said, "I need Denys, right now." And when Denys came on: "Uncle Denys, how are you?"

"I'm quite well, Ari, how are you?"

"I wanted to tell you something. I've gotten very nervous about the situation, you know, with Grant being out and all, and Grant *is* vulnerable, so I asked Justin to talk with me about it—"

"Ari, this involves exterior Security. I strongly suggest you let this alone."

"I've done it already. I want an order, uncle Denys, for Grant to be immune to Security, I don't care if something should go on at Planys with Jordan, I have an agreement with Justin—"

"I'm sorry, Ari, this isn't at all wise. You don't *tie down your Security people. You have no business making promises to Justin, especially to Justin. I've talked to you about this."*

"This is the agreement, uncle Denys. Justin's agreed to take a probe with *my* security."

"Ari, you're interfering in a matter you have no expertise in whatsoever, that involves your safety. I won't have that."

"Uncle Denys, I've been thinking a lot. It runs like this: I'm getting a lot more grown-up. People couldn't ever make a campaign out of killing a cute kid. Paxers and all these groups haven't come out into the open all at once just by coincidence. They see me getting older, they know that I'm real, they know I'm going to be a lot of trouble to them someday, and they're going to throw everything they've got at me in the next few years. But you know what occurs to me, uncle Denys? That could be true on this staff too, inside Reseune. And I'm not going to have my staff tampered with by anybody except me."

"Ari, that's halfway prudent, but you're meddling with a kind of situation you're not equipped to deal with."

"I perfectly well am, uncle Denys. I'm not going to be reasonable on this. I want Grant back without any problems. Florian's going to meet the plane and bring him up here, and I'm going to talk to him, myself, *with* trank. If I find out anyone else has, I'm going to be real upset. I don't care if it's Jordan, or if it's Reseune Security, either one, I'm going to be real upset."

"Ari, —"

"I'm just telling you, uncle Denys. I know you don't like it. And I *don't* want to fight with you. Look at it from my point of view. You're getting up there in years, you could have a stroke or something—where would that leave me, if I don't have control of my own wing? I'd *have* to trust a lot of people all of a sudden, without knowing what's going on. And I don't ever want to be in that situation, uncle Denys."

"We've got to talk about this."

"We can. Only I want your promise that you're not going to let Security touch Grant even if you think Jordan did something to him: I'll tell you how Justin feels about it—if Jordan did something like that, Justin would be real mad. And that would mean Justin would be on my side about it. But if *you* did, then Justin would be mad at me. There's an old proverb about muddying up the water, do you know it? I'm getting old enough I don't want other people's notions of what's good for me muddying up the waters I have to swim in for the rest of my life, uncle Denys. That's exactly what it comes down to."

"I appreciate your feelings, Ari, but you'd better gather your data before you interfere with an operation, not after."

"We can talk about this as much as you like and you give me advice I know is going to be worth listening to. But then's then. Now is, I'm not going to have them messed with by anybody. They're in my wing and I've made promises I'm going to keep. If you do anything else, you cut me down with my own staff, and I'm not going to have that, uncle Denys. That's a promise."

There was a long silence on the other end. *"Have you discussed with Justin the chance that Grant might have been tampered with?"*

"He's afraid of it. He's the one brought it up with me. He's willing to trust *me* in this, uncle Denys, not Reseune Security, strange as that may seem —but then, by what he tells me Reseune Security isn't very polite. I've *got* his deposition that Grant went out of here clean, uncle Denys. I've got it under deep probe, and I'm quite sure of it. So we'll find out when Grant gets back, won't we? I'll be happy to lend you a transcript of the interview."

Another long silence. *"That's very kind of you. Dammit, Ari, Justin's got medical cautions, he's got major problems, I don't care if he thought this would be better, you're a seventeen-year-old kid—"*

"Eighteen in two months, which is going on twenty in the way Base One reckons. And damned good, uncle, *damned* good . . . or what's all your work good for, you want to answer me that one, uncle Denys? I've been running interventions on Florian and Catlin for more than five years, so I'm not really likely to slip up, am I?"

"I'm telling you, Ari, dammit, you've seen the tape Ari made, you know you're dealing with a man with a damn tenuous hold on sanity where you're concerned, and you want to go running interventions on him? We're talking about a thirty-six-year-old man who's lived half his life with a problem, and you want to meddle with it, alone, without any protection for yourself or him if he has a heart attack or slides over the mental edge. You want to know what you're meddling with, young sera, you could be working in your office, minding your own business someday, and have that young man come through the door with a knife, that's what you're playing with. We're dealing with a grown man a long time and a whole lot of business past that incident when he was your age—he's changed, what Ari planted

in him has had time to mutate unwatched, he won't go in for therapy, and like a fool, because I agreed with him, he had to become self-guiding, I let him decline therapy. Now it's turned out to be a major mistake. I had no idea my niece was going to let her glands interfere with her common sense, my dear, I certainly had no idea she was going to take this unstable young man to her bosom and make an adolescent fool of herself, no indeed, I didn't. And, my God! the kind of pressure you can put on this young man with your well-intentioned meddling— Don't you understand, child, Reseune has never intended any harm to Justin Warrick? We know his value, we've worked with him, we've done the best we could to secure his future and to prevent him from precisely the kind of blow-up you're courting with your meddling. And whose fault will it be then?"

"All that's very fine, uncle Denys, but I know what I'm doing, and my reasons stand."

A long silence.

"We'll talk about this," Denys said then.

"Yes. We will. But in the meantime you call Planys and call Security there and tell them be damned careful they don't lay a hand on Grant."

"All right, Ari. You get your way on this. We'll talk about it. But I don't just get that transcript. I get the tape of the session. You know what a transcript is worth. If you want my support in this let's try a little cooperation, shall we?"

"That's all I want, uncle Denys. You're still a dear."

"Ari, dammit, we're not talking about a little thing here."

"My birthday's coming up, uncle Denys. You know I'd like a party this year. I really would."

"I don't think this is the time to discuss it."

"Lunch, the 18th?"

Back, then, to Base One to be sure that call went the way uncle Denys said.

Be careful, Ari senior had said, using the information in the expanded base, because it was so easy to slip up and reveal what one should not have known—like exactly what Security was doing half a world away.

So one lied. One tried to get very good at it.

She went back to the library, because Catlin reported that Justin was coming out of it, quietly, still a little fuzzed—which was not a bad time to explain something.

So she sat down on the couch where Justin lay drowsing with the lights dimmed, with a light blanket over him and Florian keeping watch near him.

"How are you?" she asked.

"Not uncomfortable," he said, and a little line appeared between his brows as he tried to move. He gave that up. "I'm a bit gone yet. Let me rest. Don't talk to me."

On the defensive. Not the time with him, then. She laid her hand on his shoulder. "You can try to wake up a bit," she said. That was an intervention too, but a benign one. "Everything's fine. I knew you were all right. And I've talked to uncle Denys and told him keep hands off Grant, so Grant's going to be safe, but I do need to talk to you. Meanwhile you're going to stay in the guest room tonight. I don't think you ought to go back to your apartment till you're really awake."

"I can leave," he said.

"Of course you can, when you're able to argue, but not tonight. If you like, I'll have Florian guard your door all night, so it'll be very proper. It's completely in the other wing from my room. All right? As soon as you can walk all right, Florian will put you to bed."

"Home," he said.

"Sorry," she said. "I need to talk to you in the morning. You shouldn't leave before then. Go to sleep now."

That was, in his state, a very strong suggestion. His eyelids drifted lower, jerked, lowered completely.

"Guest bedroom," she told Florian. "Soon as he can. I do want you to stay with him, just to be sure he's safe."

---

iv

It was a strange bed, a moment of panic. Justin turned his head and saw Florian lying on his stomach on the second bed, fully dressed, boyish face innocent in the glow from the single wall-light. Eyes open.

He thought that he remembered walking to this room, that it was down a hallway he could remember, but he was still disoriented and he still felt a touch of panic at the remembrance of the drugs. He thought that he ought to be distraught to be where he was, flat-tranked as he was. He lay half-asleep, thinking that as the numbness let up he would suffer reactions. He was still dressed, except his sweater and his shoes. Someone had put a blanket over him, put a pillow under his head. It was, thank God, not Ari's bedroom.

"You're awake, ser?"

"Yes," he said, and Florian gathered himself up to sit on the edge of the other bed.

"Minder," Florian said aloud, "wake Ari. Tell her Justin is awake."

Justin shoved himself up on his hands, caught his balance, rubbed at his stubbled face.

"What time—?"

"Time?" Florian asked the Minder.

"0436," it said.

"We should start breakfast," Florian said. "It's near enough to the time sera usually gets up. There's a guest kit in the bath, ser. A robe if you like, but sera will probably dress. Will you be all right while I check on my partner?"

"Sera is almost ready," Catlin said, and poured him coffee, Catlin—whose blonde hair was for once unbraided, a pale rippled sheet past black-uniformed shoulders. "Cream, ser?"

"No," he said, "thank you."

Kids, he thought. The whole situation should be funny as hell, himself—at his age—virtually kidnapped, tripped, and finally solicitously fed breakfast by a pack of damned kids . . .

Not feeling too badly, he thought. Not as rough as one of Giraud's trips, in any sense. But he was wrung out, his lungs felt too open, and his limbs felt watery and altogether undependable.

Which they would, considering what a physiological shock that much cataphoric was; which was the reason for the mineral and vitamin pill Catlin put on a dish and gave to him, and which he took with his coffee without arguing.

It was a cure for the post-kat shakes, at least.

Ari arrived, in a simple blue sweater and blue pants, her black hair loose as she almost never wore it nowadays. Like Ari-the-child. Ari pulled back the chair at his right and sat down. "Good morning. —Thanks, Catlin." As Catlin poured coffee and added cream. And to him: "How are you feeling? Are you all right?"

"You said you had something important to say," Justin said.

"About Grant," Ari said, straightway. Then: "—We can make anything you want for breakfast."

"No. Thanks. Dammit, Ari, let's not do games, shall we?"

"I'm not. I just want to make sure you get something to eat. Have some toast at least. There's real honey."

He reached for it, smothering temper, patiently buttered it and put on a bit of the honey. An entire apiary set-up over in Moreyville, along with several other burgeoning commercializations. Fish. Exotics. Frogs. Moreyville was talking about expanding upriver, blasting out space on the Volga and creating new flats for agricultural use.

"This is the thing," Ari said, "I talked to uncle Denys last night and Denys pulled Security away from Grant. We had a bit of a fight about it. But I told him I couldn't trust having people in my wing gone over by people I don't know. It came down to that. So this is the deal we made. I run my own Security checks, and if I'm satisfied, that's all that gets done. What you have to do is agree that if there is a question, —I do an interview and get it settled."

He stared at the piece of toast in his hand, without appetite. "Meaning you run another probe."

"Justin, I hope there won't be any more questions. But this Pax thing is really dangerous. It's going to get worse—because they're seeing I'm serious. There aren't very many people anywhere I can trust. There aren't very many people anywhere you can trust either, because when politics gets thick as it's going to get—you know better than I do how innocent people get hurt. You remember you asked me to do something for your father. Well, I have: I probably stopped him from being arrested last night, at least on suspicion, and I know I stopped Grant from getting probed by Security. Probably your father won't even know how close it was, and if you'll take my advice, please don't tell him. Grant's going to get home all right. Your father's safe. And you're not any worse off this morning than yesterday, are you?"

"I don't know." *Shaken up, dammit, which I wasn't, yesterday. I don't know, I don't know, I don't know, and, God, where's a choice?*

"You don't want to deal with Security," Ari said. "Giraud doesn't like you, Justin, he really doesn't like you. I don't need professional psych to pick that up. I want you to stay; and that means everybody in the universe will know you could be a pressure point against me—they could put pressure on you, or Grant, or Jordan. Giraud certainly is going to put the pressure on and try to prove something against you or your father—if we don't have contrary evidence that you're working with me. That's what I need. I need it from you and I need it from Grant, and if you do that, then you'll be my friend and you'll have Security working to protect you. If you don't—I've got to put you and Grant out—outside, where you *can't* be trusted, because every enemy I've got will think of you and Grant and Jordan just as levers to be used. That's the way it is. And I think you know that. That's why you told me last night you hoped if you stayed close to me—you could make things better. You said that. Do you remember?"

"I don't remember. But I would have said that."

"I want you to be in my wing, I want you to work with me—but being on the inside of my Security means if I have the least idea something could be wrong, —I have to ask questions. That's the way it is."

"Not much choice, is there?" He took a bite of the toast, swallowed, found the honey friendlier to his stomach than he had thought it would be. "You expect me to order Grant to take a probe from a seventeen-year-old kid?"

"I don't want him to be upset. I wish you'd at least explain to him."

"Dammit, I —"

"He's safe, isn't he? When you see him off the plane, you'll know I kept my promise; and you can tell him why I'm doing it. Then you'll both be safe from anybody else. You won't have to worry about people making mistakes anymore, or blaming you for things. And I'm not a kid, Justin. I'm not. I know what I'm doing. I just don't have much real power yet. That's why I can't reach out of my wing to protect my friends, that's why I'm doing such a damn stupid thing as bringing you on the inside under *my* Security wall—you and a few others of my friends."

"Us. Grant and me. *Sure*, Ari. Sure, you are. Let's have the truth for a minute. Are you working some maneuver around your uncles—or did Giraud suggest this?"

"No. I trust you."

"Then you're damn stupid. Which I don't think you are."

"You figure it. You and Grant are the only adult help I can get that, first, I have to have, because I need you; second, that I can constantly check on, because there's nobody but you who needs something I can do, that only I'm willing to do. Sure I can hire help. So can my opposition."

"So can your opposition—threaten my father."

"Not—past my net. You're part of it. You'll tell me if you think he's threatened. And you figure it: are you safer on your own? Is Grant? Not at all. Besides which—if your safety is linked to mine—it's not really likely your father would make a real move against Reseune, is it?"

He stared at her, shocked; and finally shrugged and took another bite of toast and washed it down.

"You know, I tried this same move with your predecessor when I was seventeen," he said. "Blackmail. You know what it did for me."

"Not blackmail. I'm just saying what is. I'm saying if you go out that door and I put you out of my wing—"

"I get it from Giraud faster than I can turn around, I get it and Grant gets it, every time he finds an excuse. That's real clear. Thanks."

"Justin—Giraud might *make up* a case. I hate to say that. There's a lot good about Giraud. But he's capable of things like that. And he's dying. Don't tell that. I'm not supposed to know. But it's changed a lot of his motives. He and Jordan never got along—not personally, not professionally, not at all: they had a terrible fight when Jordan was working with Ari—really, terribly bitter. He disagrees with what he sees as a whole Warrick attitude—an influence toward a whole slant of procedure, a kind of interventionist way of proceeding that in his mind permeated Education and got out into the tapes through what he called 'Warrick's influence.' Which isn't so. Ari knew what she was doing. She knew absolutely what she was doing, and what Giraud hates so much was really Ari's—but you can't make him understand that. In Giraud's mind Jordan was the source of that whole movement—in fact, I think in Jordan's own mind Jordan was the source of the whole movement— which was never true. But Giraud won't believe it. He *wants* to settle the Centrists before he dies, because Denys is getting on in years too, and Giraud foresees a time when his generation will be gone and I'll still be vulnerable. He sees your father as a pawn the Centrists could use. He sees you as a reservoir of Warrick influence in Reseune, me as a kid thinking with her glands, and he's desperate to get you away from me. So I've not only got to convince myself you're clean-clearance, I've got to convince uncle Denys *and* Giraud I'm absolutely sure what I'm doing. I can handle them, however crazy I make it sound . . . because *I'm* going to tell them I've got Ari's notes on your case."

He swallowed hard.

"Have you?"

"That's what I'm going to tell them."

"I heard what you're going to tell them! I also know you just evaded me. You do have them, don't you?"

"You also know that whatever I say occasionally about what I'd *like* to be the truth, I do lie sometimes. Yanni says there are professional lies and they're all right. They're what you do for good reasons."

"Dammit—"

"I'm lying to protect you."

"To whom? You have *her* kinds of twists, young sera. I hope to hell it doesn't extend deeper."

"I'm your friend. I wish I were more than that. But I'm not. Trust me in this. If you can't—the way you say—who can you? I've kept you out of Detention. And I'll give you the session tape, I always will. With Grant too. I don't ever want you to doubt each other."

"Dammit, Ari."

"Let's be honest. That's an issue, and I'm disposing of it. Let's try another. You think I'll intervene with you—the way I'm going to tell Denys. You know—let's be plain about it—you're safer with me running unsupervised than with Giraud with all the safeguards there are. You're worried about trusting yourself and Grant to a kid. But I'm Ari's student. Directly. And Yanni's. I'm not certified . . . not just because I've never bothered to be. There are a lot of things I can do that I don't want on Bureau records yet. I confess to some very immature thoughts. Some very selfish thoughts. But I didn't do it. You woke up down the hall, didn't you?"

He felt his face go red. And expected a flash, in this place, under strained circumstances, but it was faint and almost without charge, just the older face, Ari getting ready for work, matter-of-factly, leaving him there with the kind of damage he had taken. . . .

He felt resentment, that was all . . . resentment much more than shame.

"You *did* something," he said to the seventeen-year-old. *His* seventeen-year-old.

"I told you calm down about this place," she said. "I figured it would bother you. I didn't think that was unethical."

"Ethics had nothing to do with it, sera. No more than with her."

She looked a little shocked, a little hurt. And he wished to hell he had kept *that* behind his teeth.

"Sorry," he said. "I didn't mean that. But, dammit to hell, Ari! If you've got to take these trips, stay off the peripheries with me!"

"It's embarrassing for you," she said, "because I'm so young, —isn't it?"

He thought about that. Tried to calm down. Temper. Not fright. And what she had said. "Yes, it's embarrassing."

"For me, too. Because you're so much older. I feel like you're going to critique everything I do, all the time. It makes me nervous, isn't that funny?"

"That's not the word I'd pick for it."

"I *will* listen to you."

"Come on, Ari, let's not do games, didn't I say? Don't play little-girl with me. You've stopped listening to everyone."

"I still listen to my friends. I'm not my predecessor. You'll remember me saying that too, —don't you?"

Another jolt at nerves. "I think that's only a question of semantics."

She reacted with a little flicker of the eyes, and a laugh. "Point. But there, you're pretty quick this morning. Aren't you?"

It was true. That self-analysis was what kept him from total panic. "You

have a lighter touch than Giraud," he said. "I give you that, young sera."
Young sera annoyed her. He knew it did. He saw the little reaction on that too.
A man didn't go to bed with *young sera*. And she was being honest. He saw the
little frown he expected, that, by all that was accurate about flux, said that she
was probably being straightforward this morning—or the reactions would
have showed. "But I want the tape of what you did. And I want to talk to
Grant."

V

It was riding with Amy that afternoon—herself on the Filly, Amy on the horse
they called Bayard—Amy had found that in a story, so the third filly had a
name, unlike goats and pigs who were usually just numbers, except a few who
were exceptional.

Filly's just the Filly, Ari had said. And the Mare's Daughter they called
the Daughter, or Filly Two, and Filly Two was Florian's even if he couldn't
own her: no CIT was ever to ride her. But the third was Bayard, and that was
Amy Carnath's horse; and the fourth and fifth and sixth belonged to Maddy
and Sam and 'Stasi, what time they were not doing little runs into the fields,
doing work, delivering items out where trucks would crush the plants and a
human walking was too slow.

There was going to be a stable and an arena just for the horses someday,
Ari had decided. Space in the safe zones was always at a premium and uncle
Denys called it extravagant and refused to allow it.

But *she* had notions of exporting to Novgorod, animals just to look at and
watch for a few years, but someday to sell use of, the way the skill tapes of
riding and of handling animals sold as fast as they could turn them out—to
people who wanted to know what pigs and goats and horses were like and how
they moved, and what riding a horse felt like. Spacers bought those skill
tapes, marketed as entertainment Sensatape. Stationers did. People from one
end of space to the other knew how to ride, who had never laid eye or hand on
a horse.

That more than paid for the stable and the arena, she had argued; *and* the
earth-moving and the widening of Reseune's flat-space: the horses did not
need the depth of soil that agriculture did, and the manure meant good
ground.

They eat their weight in gold, Denys had objected, with no, no, and no.

Grain is a renewable resource, she had said, nastily. It likes manure.

No, said Denys. We're not undertaking any expansions; we're not making any headlines with any extravagance in this political atmosphere; it's not
prudent, Ari.

Someday, she had said, defeated.

Meanwhile the horses were theirs, unique, and did their small amount of
work.

While out in the riding pen was the best place in Reseune besides her apartment to go to have a talk without worrying about security; and it had its own benefits, when it came to being casual and getting Amy Carnath to relax and talk about really sensitive things.

Because Amy was not happy lately. Sam had taken up with Maria Cortez-Campbell, who was a nice girl; Stef was back with Yvgenia; and Amy—rode a lot and spent a lot of time studying and tending the export business, which had sort of drawn her into a full sub-manager rating in the whole huge Reseune Exports division and a provisional project supervisor's rating in the Genetics Research division.

Amy was always the brightest. Amy was getting a figure, finally, at seventeen, at least something of a figure. She was getting pretty in a kind of long-boned way, not because she *was* pretty, but because she was just interesting-looking, and might get more so.

And Amy was too damned smart to be happy, because there just happened to be a shortage of equally smart boys in her generation. Tommy was the only one who came close, and Tommy was Amy's cousin, not interested in the same field, and mostly interested in Maddy Strassen anyway. *That* pair was getting halfway serious, on both sides.

"How are things?" she asked Amy when they were out and away from everyone, under a tranquil sky. And prepared herself for a long story.

"All right," Amy said, and sighed. That was all.

Not like Amy at all. Usually it was *damn Stef Dietrich*, and a long list of grievances.

She didn't know this Amy. Ari looked at her across the moving gap between the horses, and said: "It doesn't sound all right."

"Just the same old stuff," Amy said. "Stef. Mama. That's the condensed report."

"You'll be legal this month. You can do anything you damn please. And you've got a slot in my wing, I always told you that."

"I can't *do* any damn thing," Amy said. "Justin—he's *real*. I've got a pack of stuff in Exports. Merchandising stuff is all I do. That's all I use my psych for. That's not your kind of business. I don't know what you'd want me for."

"You've got a clean Security clearance, cleanest of all my friends. You're good at business. You'd be a good Super, you'd be good at most anything you wanted to take on, that's your trouble. You get small-focused into doing it instead of learning it; and I want you learning for a while. Remember when I snagged you into the tunnels and we started off the whole gang? That's why I asked you out here before I talked to anybody. You were always first."

"What are you talking about?" Amy suddenly looked scared. "First at what?"

"That this time it's for real. That this time I'm not talking about kid pranks, this time I'm talking about getting a position in the House. Things are shifting, they're shifting real fast. So I'm starting with you, the same way I did back then. Will you work for me, Amy?"

"Doing what?"

"Genetics. Whatever project you want to come up with for a cover. A real one. A put-together till you can make up your mind. I don't care. You go on salary, you get your share of your own profits—all that."

Amy's eyes were very large.

"I want you and Maddy in two different divisions," Ari said, "because I'm not going to put you two one over the other. That'd never work. But between you and me, you're smarter than she is, you're steadier, and you're the one I'd trust with the bad stuff. And there could be. Giraud is on the end of his rejuv. That's secret. A very few people know, but probably more and more will guess. *When* he dies, that's an election in Science. That's also about the time the Paxers and the rest of the people who want me dead—for real, Amy."

"I know it's real."

"You know why they made me and how they taught me, and you know what I am. And you know my predecessor had enemies who wanted her dead, and one who killed her. The closer I get to what she was, the more scared people get—because I'm kind of spooky, Amy, I'm real spooky to a lot of people who weren't half as afraid of my predecessor— Are you scared of me? Tell me the truth, Amy."

"Not—*scared* of you. Not really. *Spooky* is a good word for it. Because you're not—not the age you are; and you *are*, with us. Maddy and I have talked about it, sometimes. How we—sometimes just want to do something stupid, just for relief sometimes. Like sometimes—" Amy rode in silence a moment, patting Bayard's shoulder. "My mama gets so mad at me because I do spooky things, like she thinks I'm a kid and she worries about me, and she treats me like a kid. One time she yelled at me: Amy, I don't care what Ari Emory does or what Ari Emory says, you're my daughter—don't you look at me like that and don't you tell me how to bring you up. And she slapped me in the face. And I just stood there. I—didn't know what to do. I couldn't hit her. I couldn't run away crying or throw things. I just—stood there. So she cried. And then I cried, but not because she hit me, —just because I knew I wasn't what she wanted me to be." Amy looked up at the sky. There was a glitter of tears in the sunlight. "So, well, mama's got the notion I'm going to leave when I can, and she's sorry. We had a talk about it, finally. She's the one who's scared of you. She doesn't understand me and she thinks you're all to blame for me not having a childhood. That's what she says. You never got a chance to be a child. I don't know, I thought I had a childhood. We had a hell of a good time. Stuff mama doesn't know. But I don't like it anymore. I'm tired of *little* games, Ari, you know what I mean. I'm tired of Stef Dietrich, I'm tired of fighting with mama, I'm tired of going to classes and playing guessing-games with Windy Peterson on his damn trick questions and eetee rules and catch-you's. I think Maddy's about the same."

"Can you work with Sam?"

"Hell, he's got that airbrain of his—that's not nice to say, is it? I can't see what he sees in her."

"*Don't* mess him up, Amy."

"I won't. I'm through with all of it. You know what I want? I want exactly what you've got with Florian. No fuss. No petty spats. No jealousy. Moment I can afford it—"

"You want to take me up on the offer, I'll reckon you'd be a lot more efficient with an assistant. *My* feeling is you'd be frustrated as hell with anything but an Alpha and there's probably only a handful of those still unContracted. I'll give you a printout of all the numbers there are. Green Barracks is the most likely source. Which means somebody more like Catlin, but still, —you could fix that."

Amy just stared. And blushed a little.

"Someday," Ari said, "you'll be a wing Super yourself. That's what I intend. Someday I'll run Reseune, and we're not playing just-suppose now, we're dealing with long-term. I want you to have the kind of support you're going to need; I want you to have somebody capable of protecting you *and* of handling jobs you're too busy to do, and in your case, male and smart are two real necessities. Another female—you'd kill. Do I psych you right?"

Amy laughed suddenly, and colored a little. "I don't know. —I need time to think about this."

"Sure. You've got five minutes."

"No fair, Ari."

"Same thing as under the stairs. Same thing as then. I need my friends now, I need you first. And there's a real danger—if I'm a target, you could be too."

Amy bit her lip. "I don't mind that. I really don't. I mind the row it's going to make with mama. You know what I think? She wants to hang onto me. She sees you as more of an influence than she is, and she always planned me to go into Ed psych, never mind I'm better at other things."

"Hell, look at me. You think a PR doesn't have to figure out who's who?"

"I know that. But your—predecessor—isn't around to give you looks across the breakfast table."

"Whose life are you going to live? Yours or hers?"

Amy nodded finally. "Or mine or yours? I'm *mine*, Ari. I don't want you supporting me. If it's a real job, if it's *my money*, I'm fine."

"Deal."

"Deal," Amy said.

"So now we go get Maddy. And then we go for Sam. And Tommy."

" 'Stasi's all right," Amy said. "*I* don't mind her. But Stef Dietrich can go walk, for what I think."

"Stef's not in my crew," Ari said. "No hard feelings, but he's a troublemaker, and I don't need him." She stretched in the stirrups and settled again and said: "We get Maddy. Sam and Tommy. 'Stasi, I've got no objection to. But everybody comes in in just the same order they always did. Seniority. Something like that. I'll tell you: I've got one major problem, one major vulnerability, and one major help—and they're all Justin Warrick. He'll help us. But there's a lot coming at him. And he and Grant are the only ones *with* us who aren't *us*, you know what I mean."

"He's smart enough to be trouble," Amy said.

"I've thought about that. My uncles don't want him near me. The Warrick influence, they call it. They say he's poison. I know other things. I can tell you stuff, Amy, if you're in with me."

"I am."

"Denys is interested in Ari's notes—Ari's *notes* and the psychogenesis project—but I've held back on him. I put all the stuff in three blocs: one, I don't talk about. And the general notes—that's the published stuff, and the stuff that's going to be published. The Rubin project stuff: that's mostly secret, but that whole security wall is a farce—I'm public, and anybody who understands endocrine theory can figure a lot of what happened to me— You know one of the things they really want to keep secret? *Justin Warrick*. Because he's not Jordan, but he's sure not a Bok clone either, and he could become a voice inside Reseune—if they ever let him have a forum; because he's smart, he understands what I am, and he's a Special in everything but title, one of Ari's students—that's something they don't publicize either—another Special, PR of a Special, a lot more important than Rubin, no matter what they've sold the Defense department. Ari worked him like everything—but they don't tell Defense that either, because they're scared as hell of him and his influence. I think Denys is sure Ari worked with him. Denys is the one who's kept him from getting treatment—for things that really bother him, things Ari did with him—and her murder really messed him up, terribly, not just that his father did it, but that he needed her—so much."

"What did she do?"

"A real major intervention. Right before she was murdered. Something she never finished, something that pretty well set the pattern of Justin's life. Beyond that—it's personal to him, and I won't say. But it was rough."

"Like the stuff they did to you?"

She thought about that a moment. "A lot, yes. A lot. With some differences. *Jordan* wanted him to be like Jordan. He wouldn't have been. Ari knew what she wanted out of that geneset and she got it. That's the real story. She manipulated CIT deep-sets . . . with real accuracy."

Amy gave her a look.

"Psychogenesis can go two ways," Ari said, "just like any other kind of cloning. Either an identical—or a designer job. I'm as close an identical as you're likely to get. I told Justin I wasn't my predecessor and he said that was only a game of semantics. And I think he's right about that. There were real differences: my maman; Ollie; Denys—he wasn't Geoffrey Carnath, not by half, thank God. A lot of different things happened. But I had Florian and Catlin; I had no doubt the theories I was handed—worked. I could feel it work. I know what put me ahead of Ari. I had to work. I was scared. I couldn't just sink into out-there and survive on people taking care of me. I learned to focus-down and to work real-time, and to think out-there too.

That's the real lesson. Bok's clone never came in out of the dark, never owned anything, never *was* anything. You know what *I'd* have answered to the kind of questions that poor woman got? Go to hell! And if piano-playing was what I did, damn, I'd do it! And maybe I'd spit in the eye of math teachers who didn't teach me the kind of things Bok must have learned—like *being* in space, dammit! Like living like a spacer! Like knowing math is life and death! —Bok's clone got dry theory. She was creative, and they gave her dry dust. They cushioned her from everything. And *they* couldn't understand her music. She was a lousy pianist. She couldn't transcribe worth shit. But I wonder what kind of music she heard in her head, and why she spent more and more time there? I'm not sure she *did* fail. Maybe the damn geniuses couldn't talk to her. Maybe their notation didn't work for her. I wonder what the whole symphony was, and whether she was playing accompaniment. —Huh." She shook herself. "That's spooky, too, isn't it?"

"They ran her stuff through computer analysis. It came up neg."

"With Bok's theories. Yes. But she never knew her genemother."

"With her teachers' stuff?"

"Might be. Or something completely off in the beyond."

"I'd like to pull those files. Just to see what they tried."

"Do it. Do any damn thing you want. We're research, aren't we? You pull all your projects out of the other wings, you put them into our budget, and our credit balance will hold just fine for that kind of thing. The guppies and the bettas can buy a lot of computer time."

vi

The airport lobby was mostly deserted, RESEUNEAIR'S regular flights all departed, the passengers that came and went in this small public area of Reseune all on their way to Novgorod or Svetlansk or Gagaringrad. There was the usual presence of airport security, and a handful of black-uniformed Reseune Security down from the House, waiting to meet their comrades in from Planys. The same as he was there for Grant, Justin thought; nothing more.

But Florian had gone off into the deplaning area he had no admittance to, had assured him: "Sera Amy Carnath is just across the room, ser, and so is Sam Whitely, both friends of sera's: I've asked them keep their distance, so if you do get in trouble here, they have a pocket com and they can advise me, but I'm on the regular Security band—" This with a touch near the small button Florian wore next to his keycard. "I'll be monitoring Security. If anything should happen, go along with it and trust we can unravel it."

The two watchers kept to their side of the lounge, a big-boned, square-faced youth who was already huge, hard muscle and a way of sitting that said he was no accountant—Whitely was a Reseune name, but from the Town, not the House; Justin remembered seeing him in Ari's crowd. And Julia Carnath's girl Amy, Ari's frequent shadow, thin and bookish, and sharp, very sharp, by her reputation among the staff. Denys Nye's niece and a boy who looked like he could bend pipe barehanded—a combination that would give Security pause, at least, Security tending to abhor noisy incidents.

He felt safer with the kids there.

Damn, he had lived this long to be protected by children. To be co-opted by a child who was the same age as himself when he had fallen victim to her predecessor—that was the peculiarly distressing thing. Not that he had a chance, taking on Ari in the prime of her abilities, but that her successor reached out so easily, and just—swept him in and put him in this situation, with Grant on the other side of those doors likely wondering what Ari's personal bodyguard was doing involving himself in the baggage check and in the body search Florian was bound to insist on— Grant would start with a little worry in his look, an initial realization that something was amiss, and quietly go more and more inward, terrified, going through the motions because in that situation there was nothing to gain, nothing to do except hope to get through to his partner and hope that his partner was not already in Detention.

Florian had refused to take so much as a note: I'm sorry, ser; I have to follow regulations here. I'll get him through as quickly as I can.

Not knowing what was toward, not knowing what could have happened to his partner, and that partner waiting to tell him—

God, to tell him he was going up to Ari's floor. That he was going to have to take a probe. That it was all right—because his partner said so, of course, having just had one himself.

He thought it remarkable that he could sit through this nightmare, sit watching the guards in their small group, the two kids talking, listening to the ordinary sounds from the baggage department that meant they were active back there, probably lining up the luggage on the tables where Reseune Security would go through it and check everything item by item, nothing cursory on this one, he figured. Examination right down to the integrity of seams on one's shaving kit or the contents of opaque bottles.

He was used to packing for Security checks. No linings, everything in transparent bottles, transparent bags, as little clothing as possible, all documents in the briefcase only, and those all loose-leaf, so they could feed through the scanners.

Take sweaters. Shirts rumpled untidily in searches, and Security always questioned doubled stitching and double-thick collars.

He stretched his feet out in front of him, leaned back and tried to relax, feeling the old panic while the minutes went by like hours.

Sure, it's all right, Grant. I'm sure I wasn't tampered with.

Like hell.

But what have we got, else? Where can we go, except hope Ari's reincarnation isn't going down Ari's path?

If she's got those notes, dammit, she knows what her predecessor meant to do with me. She can change it—or she can finish it the way the first Ari would have, make me into what the first Ari planned. Whatever that is. I thought once that might have been the best thing—if Ari had lived. If there ever was a design. Now it's too imminent. Now it's not what Ari could have given me. I'm the adult. I've got my own work, I've got my own agenda—

And Grant, my God, Grant—what have I dragged him into? What can I do?

The doors opened, and Grant came out, carrying his own briefcase, Florian behind him with the luggage.

"Bus, ser," Florian said, waving a hand toward the doors as Justin stood up and started toward Grant.

Their paths in that direction intersected.

"I'm certainly glad to see you," Grant said. He had that slightly dazed look that went with a transoceanic flight and a complete turnabout of hours. Justin threw an arm about him, patted him on the back as they walked.

"How was the trip?"

"Oh, the ground part was fine, Jordan and Paul—everything's all right with them, I really enjoyed the time; just talk, really—a lot of talk—" Doors opened behind them, and Grant's attention shifted instantly, a glance back, a loss of his thought. "I—"

The doors ahead opened automatically, one set and the others, onto the portico where the bus waited.

"Are we all right?" Grant asked.

"Ari's being sure we are," Justin said, keeping a hand on Grant's back, cautioning him against stopping. Florian put the luggage right up onto the bus deck and got up after, giving a sharp instruction to the driver to start up as Grant stepped up onto the deck and Justin followed him on the steps.

"We've ten more passengers," the driver objected.

"I've a priority," Florian said. "—Get aboard, ser."

Justin crowded a step higher as Grant edged his way past, as Florian shut the door himself.

The driver started the motor and threw them into motion.

"You can come back down after the others," Florian said, standing by the driver as Grant sat down on the first bench and Justin sat down beside him.

"What are we doing?" Grant asked quietly, reasonably.

"We're quite all right," Justin said, and took Grant's wrist and pressed it, twice, with his fingers where the pulse was. Confirmation. He felt Grant relax a little then.

Florian came back and sat down across from them. "Catlin will hold the elevator for us," Florian said. "House Security at the doors will be just a little confused when the bus comes without the rest of the passengers. There's nothing really wrong. They'll probably move to ask the driver what's going on, and we just walk right on through—absolutely nothing wrong with what we're doing, ser, only we just don't need a jurisdictional dispute or an argument over seniority. If we're stopped, absolutely there's no problem, don't worry, don't be nervous, we can move very smoothly through it if you'll just let me do the talking and be ready to take my cues. Ideally we'll walk straight to the doors, through, down to the elevator—Catlin and I have double-teamed senior Security many a time."

"That'll take us up to Wing One residencies," Grant said quietly.

"That's where we're going," Justin said. "There's a little boundary dispute going on. Ari's coordinating this through the House systems so we *don't* end up with Giraud."

"Fervently to be wished," Grant said with a shaky little sigh, and Justin patted him on the knee.

"Terrible homecoming. I'm awfully sorry."

"It's all right," Grant murmured, as undone as Justin had seen him in many a year. Justin took hold of his hand and squeezed it tight and Grant just slumped back against the seat with a sigh, while the bus started the upward pitch of the hill.

Florian was listening to something through the remote in his left ear. He frowned a little, then his brows lifted. "Ah." A sudden twinkle in the eyes, a grin. "Security was complaining about the bus leaving. House Security just reported it's a request from sera; ser Denys just came on the system to confirm sera's authority to take Grant into custody. We're going to go through quite easily."

"We *are* in some trouble," Grant said. "Aren't we?"

"Moderately," Justin said. "Did you have trouble at Planys?"

"None," Grant said. "Absolutely none."

"Good," he said, and, considering they were within earshot of the azi driver, did not try to answer the look Grant gave him.

The lift doors let them out in the large, barren expanse of Ari's outside hall, baggage and all—which Catlin and Florian had appropriated, and Florian spoke quietly to empty air, advising Ari they were on the floor.

The apartment door opened for them, down the hall.

And Justin slipped his hand to Grant's arm as they walked. "We got into a bit of trouble," Justin said in the safety of Ari's private hall. "We have Giraud on our backs. They were going to plant something on you, almost certain. We've got a deal going with Ari."

"What—deal?"

He tightened his fingers, once, twice. "Take a probe. Just a handful of questions. It's all right, I swear to you."

"Same deal for you?" Grant asked. Worried. Terribly worried. Not: *do you promise this is all right?* But: *Are* you *all right?*

Justin turned Grant around and flung his arms about him, a brief, hard embrace. "It's all right, Grant. She's *our kid*, all right? No games, no trouble, she's just taking our side, that's what's going on."

Grant looked at him then, and nodded. "I haven't any secrets," Grant said. His voice was thin, a little hoarse. "Do you get to stay there?"

"No," he said. "Ari says—says I make her nervous. But I'll be in the room outside. I'll be there all the while."

Justin flipped pages in the hardprint Florian had been thoughtful enough to provide him—the latest *Science Bureau Reports*, which he managed to lose himself in from time to time, but the physics was hard going and the genetics was Reseune's own Franz Kennart reporting on the design of zooplankton, and he had heard Franz on that before. While a biologist at Svetlansk had an article on the increasing die-off of native Cyteen ecosystems and the creation of dead-zones in which certain anaerobic bacteria were producing huge methane pockets in valleys near Svetlansk.

It was not, finally, enough to hold his attention. Even the pictures failed, and he merely read captions and isolated paragraphs in a complete hodge-podge of data-intake and stomach-wrenching anxiety, old, old condition in his life—reading reports while waiting for arrest, doing real-time life-and-death design-work while awaiting the latest whim of Administration on whether he could, in a given month, get word of his father's health.

He flipped pages, backward and forward, he absorbed himself a moment in the diagrams of Svetlansk geology and looked at the photos of dead platytheres. There seemed something sad in that—no matter that it made room for fields and green plants and pigs and goats and humans. The photo of a suited human providing scale, dwarfed by the decaying hulk of a giant that must have lived centuries—seemed as unfeeling as the photos from old Earth, the smiling hunters posing with piles of carcasses, of tiger skulls, and ivory.

For some reason tears rolled down his face, startling him, and his throat hurt. For a damn dead platythere. Because he was that strung, and he could not cry for Grant, Grant would look at him curiously and say: *Flux does strange things, doesn't it?*

He wiped his eyes, turned the page and turned the page again until he was calm; and finally, when he had found nothing powerful enough to engage his attention, thought: *O God, how long can a few questions take?*

The first Ari did Grant's designs. She's got access to those. She's got the whole manual. The same as Giraud.

Giraud left him a z-case.

Has he gone out on her?

They'd call me. Surely they'd call me.

He laid the magazine on the table in front of him and leaned his elbows on his knees, ground the heels of his hands into his eyes and clasped his hands on the back of his neck, pulling against a growing ache.

Suppose that Jordan did plant something deep in him—Grant could do that, could take it in, partition it—

Jordan wouldn't do that. God, surely, no.

The door opened, in the hall; he looked up, hearing Ari's voice, hearing her light footsteps.

She came out into the front room, not distressed-looking. Tired.

"He's sleeping," she said. "No trouble." She walked over to the couch where he was sitting and said: "He's absolutely clean. Nothing happened. He's asleep. He was upset—of course he had reason. He was worried about you. I won't stop you from waking him. But I've told him he's safe, that he's comfortable. I'll give the tape to Giraud; I have to. Giraud's got a real kink in his mindsets on what he calls your influence. And you know what he'd think if I didn't."

"Whether you do or not, he's still going to think it. If that tape proved us innocent beyond a doubt—he'd find one."

She shook her head. "Remember I told Denys I've got Ari's working notes? I just tell him I'm quite well in control of the situation, that when I'm through it won't make any difference what Jordan did or didn't do, that if he's worried about the Warrick influence he can stop worrying, I'm working both of you."

It was credible, he thought; and of course it sounded enough like the truth under the truth to feed into his own gnawing worries and remind him of Emory at full stretch—layers upon layers upon layers of truth hidden in subterfuge and a damnable sense of humor. He rubbed the back of his neck and tried to think, but thoughts started scattering in panic—except the one that said: No choice, the kid's the only force in the House that ultimately matters, no choice, no choice, no choice.

. . . *Besides which*— he heard her saying over the breakfast table —*if your safety is linked to mine—it's not really likely your father would make a real move against Reseune, is it?*

"Let me tell you about Giraud," she said. "Sometimes I hate him. Sometimes I almost love him. He's absolutely without feelings for people he's against. He's fascinated by little models and microcosms and scientific gadgets. He views himself as a martyr. He's resigned to doing dirty jobs and being hated. He's had very few soft spots—except his feud with your father, a lot of personal anger in that; except me—except me, because I'm the only thing he's ever worked for that can put arms around him and give him something back. That's Giraud. We're on opposite sides of him. I don't say that to make you feel sorry for him. I just want you to know what he's like."

"I know what he's like, thanks."

"When people do bad things to you—it makes this little ego-net problem, doesn't it, isn't that what I learned in psych? There's this little ego-net crisis that says maybe it's your fault, or maybe everybody thinks you're in the wrong, —isn't that what goes on? And ego's got to restructure and flux the doubt down and go mono-value on the enemy so there's no doubt left he's wrong and you're right. Isn't that the way it works? You know all that. If you think about that mono-value it restarts all the flux and it hurts like hell. But what if you need to know the whole picture about Giraud, to know what you ought to do?"

"Maybe nobody ever gets that objective," he said, "when it's his ass in the fire."

"Giraud fluxed you. Fluxed you real good. Are you going to let him get away with it or are you going to listen to me?"

"You do this under kat, sera?"

"No. You'd feel the echo if I had, —wouldn't you? You're so fluxed on me you can't think straight. You're fluxed on me, on Giraud, on Jordan. On yourself. On everybody but Grant. That's who you'll protect. That's the deal, and I'm the only one who can offer it in the long run. Giraud's dying."

He stood there, adrenaline coursing through him, but the body got duller with overload. The brain did. And flux just straightened out, even when he knew she was Operating, even when he knew step by step what she was doing: even when he realized there had been deep-level tweaks that had prepared for this, even when he felt amazement that she did it from around a blind corner and improvising as she went.

The knot unkinked. He was wide-open as drugs could send him, for one dizzy instant.

"All right," he said. "That's got one little flaw: Grant's not safe when you can meddle with him."

"Grant would never do anything against you. That's as controlled as I need. I'd be a fool to meddle with the one stable point you've got—when what I want is to be sure where *you* are. You're the one I'd intervene with—if I was going to do it. But if Grant's safety is assured, you're going to remember—anytime you think about doing anything against me—that much as your father might want to, *he* hasn't got the power to protect himself, much less you; and I have. I'll never hurt Jordan. I'll never hurt Grant. I can't promise that with you. And right now you know exactly why—because you're my leverage on a problem that threatens a whole lot more than just me."

It was strange that he felt no panic. Deep-set work again. He felt that through a kind of fog, in which intellect took over again and said: *And you're my leverage. Aren't you?*

But aloud, he said: "Can I see Grant?"

She nodded. "I said so. But you will stay here—at least for a few days. At least till I get it straightened out with my uncles."

"It's probably a good idea," he said, quite calm, even relieved, past the automatic little flutter of alarm. Flux kicked back in. Defenses came up all the way. He thought about the chance that Giraud would arrest them even over Denys' objections.

Or arrange their assassination. Giraud was not a man who worried about his own reputation. A professional—in his own nefarious way—who served a Cause, Ari was right about that. Giraud would sacrifice even Ari's regard for him—to be sure in his own mind, that Ari was safe.

Giraud would do it dirty, too. It was Ari's regard for them he had to terminate. It was his ideas Giraud had to discredit.

There *had* been a plot to incriminate him through Grant. He was sure of that. Every trip to Planys was a risk. They were cut off again. *No* more visits. No chance to see Jordan. They were lucky to get Grant back unscathed. And if Giraud could work on Jordan, indirectly—

Jordan knowing his son and his foster-son had joined Ari's successor—

There was no end to the what-ifs, no way to untangle truth and lies. Anyone could be lying. Everyone had reason. Every move Jordan made in Planys—was a risk. Failing to get to them, Giraud might well move on Jordan to get leverage on them in Reseune, to create doubts in Ari's mind—

And Ari said—*I'm working both of you*—

God.

He went to the hall and to the open library door; and into the dim room where Grant lay on the couch, asleep and very tranked. Florian was there, shadow in the corner, just sitting guard. Catlin was not. Catlin was somewhere else in the apartment, in the case he had violated instructions to stay to the front rooms, he thought.

He laid his hand on Grant's shoulder and said: "Grant, it's Justin. I'm here, the way I said."

Grant frowned, and drew a deep breath and moved a little; and opened his eyes a slit.

"I'm here," Justin said. "Everything's all right. She said you're all right."

A larger breath. Eyes showing white and pupil by turns as Grant struggled up out of the trank and reached after him. He took Grant's hand. "Hear me?" Double press on the inside of the wrist. "It's all right. You want Florian and me to carry you? You want to go to bed?"

"Just lie here," Grant murmured. "Just lie here. I'm so tired. I'm so tired—"

His eyes closed again.

vii

"I'm doing quite well," Ari said, over a bite of salad; lunch, at *Changes*, the 18th December. "They're back in their own residency. Everyone's happy. There's no problem with Jordan, no lingering messiness. I just wasn't about to let them out where Giraud could get at them. You shouldn't worry. I can take care of myself. Is that enough said?"

"You know what I think about it," Denys said.

"I appreciate your concern. But," she said with a small quirk of her brow, a deliberate smile, "you probably worried about Ari senior this way too."

"Ari was murdered," Denys said.

Point.

And feeler? Denys was upset. Giraud was upset. Giraud *hated* disorder and his own impending death was creating maximum disorder: there were beginning to be rumors in the House—no leak: Giraud's own appearance, increasingly frail despite his large bones—was its own indicator of a man in failing health.

"One thinks she was murdered," Ari said. "Who knows? Maybe the pipe just blew. I've tried that door. A breath of air would disturb it, at certain points. A blown cryo line is just that. Isn't it? The line blows, she gets caught in the spray, falls, hits her head. The door closes quite naturally. Maybe murder was a useful story. *Murder* let you take fairly extreme measures."

"Is that what Justin says?"

"No. Dr. Edwards."

"*When* did John say a fool thing like that?"

"Not specifically. He just taught me scientific procedure. I never rule anything out. I just think some hypotheses are more likely than others."

"Confession makes it more likely, doesn't it?"

"I suppose it ought to. All things equal." She cut up a cucumber slice. "You know the kitchen's getting a little lazy. Look at this." She impaled a large lettuce rib. "Is that a way to serve?"

"Let's stay to business, dear, like why in hell you're being a fool about this man. Which has much more to do with glands than you want to admit. If you don't realize your vulnerability, I can assure you it's going to dawn on him, just as soon as the waves stop."

"Except one thing, uncle Denys: Justin's not Jordan. And he can't kill. He absolutely can't, for the same reason he can't work real-time. He'd freeze. He can't even hate Giraud. He feels other people's pain. Ari exacerbated that tendency in him. She leaned on it, hard. You see I *do* have those notes. I know something else, too: Jordan was hers. She just couldn't use his slant on things, so she conned Jordan into a replicate, and she took him, she absolutely took him. If she hadn't died, Justin would have slid closer and closer to her over the years—either healed the breach with Jordan or broken with him—because there's something very sad about his relationship to Jordan, and he would have learned it."

"What's that, mmmn?"

"That Jordan would have smothered him. Ari was never afraid of competition. Jordan was; and that relationship—Justin and his father—would have become more and more strained under Ari's influence. That's exactly what I project. Jordan is an arrogant, opinionated man who had intentions for his replicate, but they weren't going to work, because his son, with a good infusion of independence from Ari's side, was going to go head to head against him and make his life miserable; and I don't think Jordan's ego would ever let him see that."

"You don't even know Jordan Warrick."

"Ari did. It's my predecessor talking now. She set his whole life up. She provided Grant as an ameliorating influence on Justin, a partner of equal potential—Grant's predecessor was a Special, remember?—but deep-setted to be profoundly supportive of his Contract, which is exactly what a boy being pressured by his father to succeed—would rely on, wouldn't he, for the unqualified emotional support he'd need? Grant was always the leverage Ari would have to get Justin away from Jordan when the time was right; and now I have him. I'm going on Ari's instructions on this. She valued Jordan's abilities, she just wanted them to support her work—which, by what everyone tells me, is exactly the point where she and Jordan clashed: Jordan accused her of taking his ideas and claiming them. Justin's voiced similar reservations, of course. And he's confessed to resentments. But I've got that covered."

"How, pray tell?"

"I'm a little smarter than my predecessor. I've kept him out of my bed and dealt strictly with his *professional* qualifications."

"I'm relieved."

"I thought you would be. I know Giraud will be ecstatic. I *know* what he thinks went on while Justin was in my apartment. You can tell him not. I may have scared Justin out of good sense, but I've never scared him too much. I've behaved myself, I did a few psych-tweaks on Ari's intervention with him while he was under, and he's really glad I let him alone. Pretty soon, he'll be all the way over to grateful."

"You know, young sera, you're getting entirely too confident for your age."

"I'm a lot of things too much for my age, uncle Denys. Most people find that completely uncomfortable. I really appreciate it that I can be myself with you. And with Giraud. I really do. I appreciate it too that you can be sensible with me. You're not dealing with little Ari anymore. I'm much, much more like my predecessor. More than I've let on in public, which is exactly, of course, what she'd do in my position. My enemies think they've got more time than they do, which is one way of dealing with the problem. And positioning myself. —Which is why I've really, urgently got to talk to you about Giraud, uncle Denys."

"What about Giraud?"

"You're really very fond of him, aren't you? He's very much your right hand. And what are you going to do when he dies?"

Denys drew in his breath and rested his hand beside his plate. *Score one.* Denys looked as taken off guard as she had ever seen him. There was an angry frown, then a clearer expression. "What do you suppose I'll do?"

"I don't know. I wonder if you're thinking about it."

"I'm thinking about it. We're both thinking about it." Still the anger. "Your actions aren't helping. You know how volatile the situation in Council is going to be."

"I know Giraud's worried. I know how worried he is about me. 'The Warrick influence.' God, I've heard that till I'm deaf. . . . Let me tell you: Justin's *not* plotting against me." She saw the unfocusing of Denys's eyes, and rapped the table sharply with her knuckles. "*Listen* to me now, uncle Denys." The focus came back. "Stop thinking I'm a fool, all right? I need him for very specific, very *professional* reasons. He's working in an area I need, or *will* need, in future."

"Nothing you couldn't do, young sera."

"Maybe. But why should I, when I can have someone else do it, on his level, and save myself the time?"

"He'll like that."

"Oh, he'll get credit. I've told him. And unlike Jordan, Justin grew up number two in everything. He's got a good deal more flexibility than Jordan."

"What are you going to do with Jordan in your administration, pray tell?

Let him loose? That would be abysmally stupid, Ari. And that's exactly what your young man is going to ask of you—what he already *has* asked of you, why not be honest? I'm sure he has, just the same as he connived his way into your sympathy."

"He's asked. And I asked him if he thought Jordan himself would be safe—or whether Jordan could defend himself against people who'd want to use him. Like the Paxers."

"Young woman, you *are* meddling."

"It doesn't take *my* abilities, uncle Denys, to guess what kind of stuff Giraud would like to have planted on Grant and Jordan—about the time you break the news the Centrists are in contact with him. I'm sorry to mess Giraud up. I know he's furious with me. I'm sorry about that. But Giraud's messing up a much more important operation—mine. And I won't stand for it." She poured more wine. They had chased the waiter away and asked for him to respond only to the call-button. "You just don't give me enough credit, uncle Denys. Remember what I said about muddying the waters. I don't like that. I don't like it at all. Giraud's not thinking straight and I wish you'd straighten him out; he's tired, he's ill, and in this, I just don't know how to talk to him."

"I thought you knew everything."

"Well, say that I know enough to know he's not well, he's trying to hide that from the world, he doesn't want to admit it to me, and it's a guaranteed explosion if I try to reason with him. Excluding trank, which I'm not about to do to my uncle. You're the only one he'll listen to in this, you're the only one who can get him calmed down, because he knows you're objective and he won't believe that about me. And there's something else I want you to tell him. I want you to tell him . . . the Warrick influence isn't the only thing going in Reseune. He should believe . . . he should definitely believe . . . the Nye influence is terribly important to me. Indispensable to me . . . and to Reseune."

"That's gratifying."

"I haven't gotten to my point yet. This is terribly delicate, uncle Denys. I don't want you to take this wrong. And it's so hard to discuss with Giraud—but . . . Giraud's so hardheaded practical, and he's been such an influence—on me; on Reseune— What do you think he'd feel—about having a replicate done—like me?"

Denys sat still, a long, long moment. "I think he'd be amazed," Denys said. "He'd also point out that he's not documented to the extent you are."

"It's possible it'll work. It's even probable. All I'd need is the ordinary House stuff. Damn, this is so awkward! I don't know how to approach asking him. I don't know how he feels about dying. He's—never brought it up with me. I gather he doesn't want me to know. But I know a lot more about psychogenesis than you knew when you started; I know a lot I haven't written up—I know it from the inside, I know what matters and what doesn't and where you came close to a real bad mistake. And I really think I could run it with Giraud. If he'd let me."

"Dear, when one's dead, there's not a precious lot one can do to stop you from any damn thing, now, is there?"

"It matters what you want. And what Giraud wants, I mean, his opinion is the most important, because that has to do with his psychsets, and whether his successor would be comfortable with what he is. That's critical. And there's who would be the surrogates. You're not young yourself, to take on another kid. I thought about Yanni, Yanni's got the ability, and the toughness. Maybe Gustav Morley. But you'd be best, because you know things no one else *can* remember about your upbringing, and you can be objective, at least you could with me. But you weren't related to me. That's a difference to think about. That could be a lot of stress, and I'm not sure you want to cope with that now, with Giraud."

Denys had laid the fork down altogether. "I'd have to think about that."

"At least talk to him. Please make him understand—I *don't* want to fight with him. I need him, I'll need him in things I can't foresee yet. That's why I want to do this. Tell him—tell him I love him and I know why he's doing these things to stop me, but tell him I know something too and he should let me alone and let me operate. Tell him—tell him I understand all his lessons. I've learned from him well enough to protect myself. —And tell him if he wants to know what it's like to *be* a successor—I can tell him."

"I'd find that a point of curiosity too," Denys said after a moment, "what degree of integration there is. *Is* there identity?"

Gentle smile. "Profiles? Say they're real close. What it feels like, uncle Denys, what it feels like—is, you think,—*I'd never do that.* But eventually you would. You almost remember—*remember* things. Because they're part of the whole chain of events that lead to the point you go on from. Because you *are* a continuance, and what your predecessor did was important and the people she knew are still there, the enemies and the friends are still there for reasons of what she was and what she did—more, you *understand* what she felt about things and how it all fitted, from the gut, in your glands, in your bloodstream, and, oh, it makes more and more sense. You see yourself on an Archive tape and you feel this incredible—identity—with that person. You see a little slump; you straighten your own shoulders—*Stand straight, Ari, don't slouch.* You see a little upset—you feel personally threatened. You see anger. Your pulse picks up a bit. I *will* write a paper someday, when the subject's much more commonplace. But I don't think it's a thing I want to have in the *Bureau Reports* right now. I think it's one of those processes Reseune can bastardize for the other agencies that want to do it with easy types. But they'll always send the Specials to us, because they're going to be the real problem cases: Alphas always are. Even CITs. And that means more and more of the best talent—begins at Reseune."

Denys gazed at her a long time without speaking.

"I *am* very much the woman you knew," she said. "Never mind the kid's face. Or the fact my voice hasn't settled yet. There is a kind of fusion. Only I'm already working on Ari's final notes, not her starting hypotheses. Psychogenesis is a given with me. I'll do much more, much more than she did. Isn't that what you wanted?"

"Much—more than we expected."

She laughed. "Which way do I take that?"

"That we're very proud of you. I—personally—am very proud of you."

"I'm glad. I'm very glad. I'm very grateful to you, uncle Denys. And to Giraud. I always will be. You see: Ari was such a cold bastard. She learned to be, for very good reasons. But that part didn't have to be exact. I can love my uncles, and I can still be a cold bastard when I have to be, just because I'm very self-protective—because no matter what the advantages I've had, I'm a target and I know it. I won't be threatened. I'll be there first. That's the way I am. I want you to know that."

"You're very impressive, young sera."

"Thank you. So are my uncles. And you're both dears and I love you. I want you to think about what I want to do—about Giraud; and talk to Giraud, and tell me how he feels about it."

Denys cleared his throat. "I don't think—I don't think he'll turn you down."

Is there identity?

She knew damn well that Denys was asking for himself.

What's it like?

Will—I—remember? That was the really eetee one, which a sane man knew better than to wonder. So she flirted it right past him now; and made him sweat.

"I'll tell you where an interesting study might be, uncle Denys. Getting me and Giraud together someday and letting us compare notes. *I* have the illusion of memory. I wonder if he will."

Denys had not taken a bite in a half a minute. He sat there a helpless lump.

Shame on you, she thought to herself. *That's awful, Ari.*

But something in her was quite, quite satisfied.

What in hell's the matter with me?

I'm madder than hell, that's what. Mad that I'm young, mad that I'm dependent, mad that I'm trapped here and Denys is being Denys, and mad that Giraud's timing is so damn lousy, leaving me no way to get that seat. Dammit, I'm not ready for him to die!

Denys' fork rattled, another bite. He was visibly upset.

How can I enjoy doing that? My God. He's an old man. What's gotten into me?

Her own appetite curdled. She poked at the salad, extracting a bit of tomato.

She thought about it that night, listlessly dividing attention between a light sandwich Florian had made her, the evening news, and doing a routine entry on the keyboard—which she preferred to the Scriber when she was listening to something: the fingers were output-only, and what they were out-putting was in a mental buffer somewhere. Pause. Tick-tick-tick. Pause. While the visual memory played out lunch and uncle Denys and the logical function worked on the politics of it. *Is* there identity? —An eetee kind of question in the first place, never mind that she had eetee feelings about it— she knew how to explain them, in perfectly solid and respectable terms: she was used to deep-study, she could lower her threshold further by wanting to than most people could on E-dose kat, the tapes involved a person identical to her in the identical environment, and the wonder would be if the constant interplay of tape-flash and day-to-day experience of the same halls, the same people, the same situations—did not muddle together in a flux-habituated brain.

Denys understood that, surely, on the logical level.

People surely understood that.

Damn, *she* was not dealing well with that aspect of it. She dealt with massive movements in the populace. Microfocus failed her.

The average, harried, too-busy-for-deepthink Novgorod worker.

Listen and learn, Ari, sweet: ordinary people will teach you the truest, the most sane things in the world. Thank God for them.

And beware anyone who can turn them all in one direction. That one is not ordinary.

People were aware . . . of Reseune's power, of the power her predecessor had wielded.

IN PRINCIPIO was a phenomenon, Ariane Emory's basic theories and methodologies and the early character of Reseune, set almost within the most educated laymen's grasp, so that there was, in the public mind, at least the glimmering of what no demagogue could have made clear before that book aroused such strange, such universal interest in the popular market.

It had spawned eetee-fringe thinkers of its own, a whole new and trouble-some breed who took Emory for their bible and practiced experimental so-called Integrations on each other, in the idea it would expand their consciousness, whatever that was. There were already three cases down in the Wards, Novgorod CITs who had all drug-tripped their way to out-there on massive overdoses, run profound interventions on each other and now outraged staid old Gustav Morley by critiquing his methodology. A handful of admirers had outraged Reseune Security, too, by trying to leave the lounge down at the RESEUNEAIR terminal and hike up toward the House, proclaiming that they had come to see Ariane Emory—with the result that Reseune was urgently considering building a new terminal for commercial flights, *far* down from the old one where, in the old days, Family and ordinary through travelers using RESEUNEAIR had once mingled with casual indifference. A handful of would-be disciples had turned up over in Moreyville looking for a boat, until wary locals, thank God, had figured out what they were up to and called the police.

My God, what do I do if I meet one of these lunatics? What are they after?

It's a phase. A fad. It'll go. If it weren't this they'd be getting eetee transmissions on their home vids.

Why didn't *we see this?*

But of course we saw it. Justin saw it. There's always the fringe. Always the cheap answer, the secret Way—to whatever. Novgorod's in chaos, Paxers threatening people, wages aren't rising to meet spot shortages—

Danger signs. People yearning after answers. Seeking shortcuts.

Seeking them in the work of a murdered Special—

In the person of her replicate, as the Nyes fade, as the unstable period after that assassination births more instabilities, elections upon elections, bombings, shortages, and the Child—the Child verges on womanhood and competency in her own right, announcing herself with the recovery of Ari senior's legendary lost notes—

Damn well what I expected Science to understand—

But Novgorod's understanding it at a completely different level . . .

The children of azi's children—the constituency of Reseune: Ari's own creation, no theory in a Sociology computer. It's there. It's ready.

And Giraud, damn him, can't hold on to that seat long enough for me.

"Vid off," she said, and leaned back and shut her eyes, feeling that general pricklishness that meant her cycle was right on schedule.

Tomorrow I should work in, stay away from people.

I hurt Denys today. I Had him, I didn't need to take that twist. Why in hell did I do that?

What am I mad about?

Adrenaline high, that's what's going on. Not mentioning the rest of the monthly endocrine cocktail.

Damn, that was an underhanded shot I took. Denys didn't deserve that.

I know *what Ari came to. Her temper, her damnable temper—the anger she was always afraid to let out—*

Frustration with the irrational—with a universe moving too slow for her mind—

God, what's going on with me?

She tasted blood, realized she had bitten her lip, and unfocused.

She pressed her hands against her forehead, leaning back in the chair, shut her eyes . . . thinking about that tape, Justin's, thinking—

God, no. Not when she was fluxing this bad. Not when she could think of it as surrogate. Leave the damn thing in the cabinet, locked up, safe. Let it be.

It was—oh, God! not for entertainment—

Dammit, Ari, get off it!

Watch the damn fish. Watch the fish procreate and breed and spawn and live their very short lives, back and forth, back and forth in the tank beside the desk.

Sex and death. Breeding and devouring their own young if god did not take precautions and intervene with the net. How long can an ecosystem survive, inputting both the biomass of its own dead and its own births, and the artificial sunlight?

If you put them with big fish there won't be any blue fish at all. . . .
Do you know whether a fish sees colors? . . .
Breathing grew more even. Time reached a slower pace. Eventually she could sigh, bring the emotional temperature down, and postpone thinking. She got up and logged off and went to her bedroom, quietly, not to draw Florian and Catlin's notice.

She just wanted bed, that was all. But she sat staring at the dresser-top corner, where Poo-thing rested, well-worn and disreputable. No condemnation there.

She thought about putting him in the drawer. What if she had brought Justin to her room while he was here; and there was poor Poo-thing to laugh at?

That was the whole trouble—that there were no more games, there was no more give-and-take with friends, no more throwing a dart to see if it got one back, and having uncle Denys come back at her, hard-edged wit, a little sting to put her in her place. She tried to get a rise out of him and there was no bounce-back, no humor, nothing but the wary fencing of an old man who was no longer the power—just the threatened.

Floating-in-black-space.

Welcome to the real world. Poo-thing's worn out. Denys is a scared old man. And you're what he's scared of. People won't argue with you: who wants to lose all the time?

I could do any damn thing I want in Reseune. Like take anybody, anything, teach them what I could do—in one day, I could scare hell out of this place, make them understand I'm holding in—

Everybody'd love me then, wouldn't they?

Poo-thing stared, with wide black eyes.

I ought to take you to work, set you on the desk. You're the best conversationalist in Reseune.

Dammit, someone pull a prank on me, someone make me laugh, someone for God's sake answer me.

I can see all the star-stations, all the azi-sets, the whole thing in slow flux, so damned slow, and so dangerous—

Where's the advice, Poo-thing?

Amy, and Maddy and Tommy and Sam. Florian and Catlin. Justin and Grant. Yanni. And Andy down in AG.

It's talking, fool. The whole universe is talking. Listen and be amazed.

Nelly. Maman and Ollie. Denys. Giraud-present and Giraud-soon-to-be.

The static of the suns.

". . . Sera?"

She drew a long breath.

Short-focused again, black-clad figure in the doorway, tall and blond. Worried.

"I'm fine," she said; and discovered her legs asleep. Foolish predicament, gratefully foolish. She rubbed her aching thighs and levered herself up with absolute gracelessness, leaning on the headboard.

When she could stand she went over to the dresser, picked up Poo-thing and put him in the drawer.

Catlin looked at her strangely for that too. But she doubted Catlin had ever understood Poo-thing in the first place.

viii

Punch and sugary cookies. Ari nipped one off the table herself, ignoring the kitchen's more elaborate confections, savored the plain flavor, and took a drink of the green punch which she preferred, thank you, from the non-alcoholic bowl.

A little girl slipped up through the crowd of Olders and snatched a handful; and a second. Fast escape. That was Ingrid Kennart, aged six. Ari chuckled to herself, on a fleeting memory. And frankly could not recall for a second whether it was a flash off some Archive tape or out of her own past.

New Year's, God, of course it had been a New Year's. The music changed, live this year—a handful of the techs had a band, not bad, either. But the glitter was the same. And maman and Ollie—

She caught a flash of silver jewelry out of the corner of her eye and for a second saw a ghost—but it was only Connie Morley, who was tall and thin and wore her dark hair upswept and elegant—

She had a second of triste, no reason, just looked away across the floor where Olders were sitting—Denys: Giraud was in Novgorod this season. Petros Ivanov. Dr. Edwards. He could, she swore, never be *John* to her, no matter how old she got. And old Windy Peterson and his daughter, out dancing, Peterson *trying* to learn the new step.

Maddy Strassen was beautiful, really beautiful in silver-blue satin—no shortage of partners for her or 'Stasi, her faithful shadow. And Amy Carnath—Amy was out on the floor with a very correct, very confused-looking young azi who was, however, doing quite well with the step—blond, crewcut, and terribly handsome: Security, stiff as they came when Amy had gotten her hands on him, but loosening up a bit, to the amusement of all of them and the evident disquiet of Amy's mother. The lad was Alpha, and social as far as Green Barracks went—yes, sera! with a real snap in the voice. Quentin, his name was: Quentin AQ-8, who just *might* have ended up being Contracted to House Security or RESEUNESPACE, or outside, if any of a small handful of qualified agencies had wanted to pay the million and a quarter for his Contract, for an azi who had to be Supered directly from Reseune, and whose reflexes were dangerously fast. Quentin AQ would have found himself in someone's employment in another year.

Quentin was, Florian and Catlin reported, a very happy, if very over-anxious young man. And Amy was—

—in love, probably described it. At least it was a very healthy dose of infatuation, which made Amy Carnath insist Quentin was her partner, Quentin was going out onto the floor, fashions and customs changed, and people were forgetting *why* the old rules existed with the earliest azi: it had gotten to have completely different reasons, and it was going to stop. The youngers did it at their parties; the Olders could just accept it, so there: thus Amy Carnath.

Florian, Ari had said then, so Amy and Quentin were not out there alone. And after a while there were a few others.

But mostly Florian and Catlin shadowed her very closely, and Florian refused 'Stasi with an earnest: *I'm terribly sorry. I'm on duty.*

That was the way the world changed. In the House, Florian and Catlin were shadowing her with the attention they had used in Novgorod.

No relaxing. No let-down.

The Novgorod authorities were scared out of their minds about the New Year's crowds and the chance of an incident.

Hell of a thing. The Paxers were *not* Ari's design, she was more and more convinced. A cultural inheritance, an ugly little side-trip in the independence-prioritied mindsets that had founded Union. The grandsons and granddaughters of rebel scientists and engineers—blew up kids in subway stations, and wanted to run the government.

They talked about potential Worms in *Justin's* designs twenty, thirty generations down. Union had a few after three generations, real serious ones, and she was scared going into a controlled situation like New Year's with Family and staff, with Florian and Catlin to watch with a trained eye for anything Unusual. To have a Novgorod citizen's choice—kilometers of walking in ped-tunnels or twice daily percentaging the headlines and the mood of politics to decide whether to risk a ten-minute subway ride—not mentioning the chance of some ordinary z-case putting the push on you for your keycard—*hell* of a way to live. But Novgorod citizens hated the idea of a master-system for keycards: a danger to their freedom, they argued.

They had, she thought, a higher anxiety threshold than she did; but they were holding their own, that was the good part, hell with the Paxers, people held on; and she, Ari Emory, she followed the situation and wondered if there was perhaps merit in the idea of a major program to buy-off thousands of military azi still rejuvable, bring them back to Reseune for re-training, exactly the way they had done before she was born—

No question then of the bad precedent of having armed troops keeping order in Novgorod, but a loan of a civilian agency from Reseune Administrative Territory to the municipality of Novgorod. If these were the times they lived in, as well have a response for it, if it meant enforcement standing line-of-sight in every ped-tunnel and subway in Novgorod.

Manpower was the original reason Reseune existed; and she was working out the proposal to land on Denys' desk. And expected Denys to say no. Reseune was making profit again and Denys was determined to hold the line against what he called her out-there ideas.

She sighed, watching uncle Denys from across the room, and seeing a tired lump of a man who had some very strange turns: who had, she had discovered it in Denys' Base in the House system—a huge volume of unpublished work that she ached to talk with him about, work on inter-station economics that was bound to cause a ripple when it did come to light . . . *she* did not understand it, but it was very massive and very full of statistics; a huge work on the interaction of economics with the Expansionist theory of government that was absolutely fascinating; a massive study of the development of consumer society in azi-descended population segments, including specific tracing of psychsetted values in several generations of testing; a study of replicate psychology; a history of Reseune from its inception; and work on military systems, of a kind that looked very much like Giraud's work—until she put her finger on the telltale phrases and turns of speech and realized to her shock that Giraud did not write the things published under Giraud's name. They were Denys' writings. And this secret store of them, this absolute treasure-house of ideas, —kept in Archive? Never brought forward, just meddled with from time to time, adjusted—an enormous work-in-progress, from a man so obsessively retiring that he maneuvered his brother into a Special's status so that Giraud could have the reputation and do the public things, while Denys stayed in the background, appearing to devote himself exclusively to administrative work and the day-to-day decisions and approvals for R&D and implementations.

Besides bringing up a kid for a few years—letting *her* into that intense privacy, hosting birthday parties and putting up with Nelly and two junior Security trainees—while writing these things that never appeared, only grew and grew.

Strange man, she thought, objective about Denys for the first time in her life. Willing to take on Giraud's replicate—oh, yes. Beyond any doubt. And facing Giraud's death with—not quite grief: a sense of impending catastrophe.

No difficult question at all why Denys had been so willing to take her in, why he had thrown all Reseune into turmoil to recover Ariane Emory's abilities for Reseune: Denys was brilliant, Denys had the old problem with Alphas—that lack of checks, lack of boundaries, that floating-in-black-space problem, that meant no minds to bounce off, no walls to return the echo. Denys was brilliant, and quite eetee and self-defensive: and incapable, perhaps, of believing his work was finished—hence the perpetual adjustments. A mind working on a macro-system that only kept widening . . . a perfectionist, with the need to be definitive.

No need of people at all. Just a student of them.

And facing death—Giraud's and his own—with incredulity. Denys was the center of his own universe, Giraud his willing satellite, and of course Denys was interested in psychogenesis, Denys was so damned interested he had almost lost his balance with her, Denys wanted immortality, even without personal continuance—and she had only to hold out the promise: if Giraud was essential to the universe—who more than Denys?

She turned, set the cup on the edge of the table, and started, expecting the person behind her to be Florian, about to take the cup; but it was Justin; and she was chagrined in that half-second, at being that on-edge, and at being caught being foolish.

He took her hand, said: "I think I remember how," and offered the other hand.

She stared at him, thinking: *How much has he had?* and lifted her hand to his, fingers locked in fingers, the two of them moving out onto the floor to an older, slower number. He *had* been drinking, probably no few drinks, but he moved with some grace, surely as aware as she was of the fact other dancers broke step to gawk at them, that the music wobbled and recovered.

He smiled at her. "Ari never danced. But her dinners were always good for a week of office gossip."

"What in hell are you trying to do?"

"What I'm doing. What you did—with Florian—and young Amy. Good for you. Good for you, Ari Emory. Damned right. —I thought—a little social rehab—twice in a night—figuring you have a sense of humor—"

Other dancers were in motion, recovering their graces. And Justin's smile was thin, deliberately held.

"You're not in some kind of trouble, are you?"

"No. Just thinking—I've lost a big piece of my life—staying inconspicuous. What the hell. Why not?"

She caught a glimpse of Denys' chair, near the door. Vacant.

And thought: *God. Where are the edges of this thing?*

The music finished. People applauded. She stared a second at Justin, a second that felt all too long and public.

I've made a serious mistake.

Cover it, for God's sake, it's like the Amy/Quentin thing, people will take it that way with cue enough—

She walked with Justin hand-in-hand from the floor, straight for Catlin. "Here's the one to teach you the new steps. She's really amazing. —Catlin, *show* Justin, will you?"

As the band started up again, and Catlin smiled, took Justin by the hand and took him back to the floor.

Grant—was over by the wall, watching, with worry evident.

"Florian," she said, "go ask Grant what the hell Justin's up to."

"Yes, sera," Florian said, and went.

Denys was gone from the room. So was Seely.

Justin's linked himself with me—publicly. Not that everyone didn't know. But that I let it go—that, they'll gossip about.

She looked to the floor, where Justin made a brave and even marginally successful attempt to take up on Catlin. And to the corner of the room, where Florian and Grant were in urgent converse.

Denys—walked out.

Florian came back before the end of the dance. "Grant says: it's CIT craziness. I had no notion of this. Grant asked your help but he says if he intervenes it may be public and tense. He says Justin's been on an emotional bent ever since he and Grant went back to their own residency—Grant says he's willing to speak to you about it, but then he said: Sera intervened: ask sera if this is the result of it."

Ari frowned. "Dammit."

"Maddy," Florian said.

Which was a better idea than she had, fluxed as she was. "Maddy," she said. "Go." *Dammit, dammit! He's pushing, damned if this is innocent. Denys was here, the whole Family watching—*

She took a deep breath. *No more easy course. He's no kid. Denys isn't. Now they're not dealing with me as a kid either, are they? Grant thinks this is an emotional trip—or that's what Justin's told Grant to say.*

Damn, I should haul him in for a question-and-answer on this little trick, damn, I should.

And he'd never trust me, never be the same Justin, would he?

Catlin and Justin were leaving the floor. Maddy Strassen moved in with Maddy's own peculiar grace, said something to Catlin and appropriated Justin's arm, walking him over to the refreshments while the band took a break; and 'Stasi Ramirez was moving in from the other side.

Thank God.

She drew quieter breaths, sure that Denys had his spies in the room, people who would report to him exactly the way things went.

Like Petros Ivanov.

Which could only help, at this point.

Grant—stayed as unobtrusive as Grant's red-haired elegance could ever be, over in a corner of the room, having a bit of cake and a cup of punch. And talking to young Melly Kennart, who was twelve. Completely innocent.

Maddy partnered Justin through two dances. Ari took the second one with Tommy Carnath, who was looking a little grim. "Patience," Ari said, "for God's sake, we've got a problem."

"He's the problem," Tommy said. "Ari, he's moving on you. Your uncle's mad."

If Tommy saw it, so did a lot of other people.

And nothing could cover it. All she could do was signal she was not responding to the overture.

Embarrass him and send him off? He was vulnerable as hell to that. Laying himself wide open to it. Betting his entire career and maybe his life on that move, and *not* stupid, no, no way that a man who had run the narrow course he had run all his life suddenly made a thorough break with pattern on a flight of emotion. No matter if he was drunk. No matter what. Justin *had* thought about what he was doing.

And put her on the spot. Support me in front of the whole Family or rebuff me. Now.

I'll kill him.

I'll kill him for this.

<hr>

ix

"Ser Justin's here," Florian said, via the Minder, and Ari said, without looking up from her desk:

"Damn well about time. Bring him to the den. *Him*, not Grant."

"Grant's not with him," Florian said.

Florian had not let him in yet: the Minder always beeped in her general area to let her know when an outside access opened. It did then; and she waited to finish her note to the system before she stirred from her chair, told Base One log-off, and walked down the hall to the bar and the den.

Justin was there, in the room that held so many bad memories—walking the narrow margin behind the immense brass-trimmed couch, looking at the paintings. While Florian waited unobtrusively by the bar—unconscious echo on Florian's part: he and Catlin had never seen the tape.

She chose this place.

Favor for favor.

"I want to know," she said, to his back, across the wide expanse of the wood-floored pit, "what in *hell* you hoped to accomplish last night."

He turned to face her. Indicated the painting he had been looking at. "That's my favorite. The view of Barnard's. It's so simple. But it affects you, doesn't it?"

She took in her breath. *Affects you, indeed. He's Working me, that's what he's after.*

"*Grant* asked me for help," she said. "You've got *him* scared. I hope you know that. What are you trying to do? Unravel everything? It's damned ungrateful. I kept Giraud off your tail. I kept you out of Detention. I've taken chances for you—What do you expect I should do, shout across the room? I do you a favor. I do every damn thing I can to help you. What do you do for me? Push me in public. Put me in a situation. I *don't* think I'm that much smarter than you are, Justin Warrick, so don't tell me you were just going from the gut. I'll tell you you wanted me in a corner. Back you or not, on your damn timetable; and if Tommy Carnath saw it and Florian saw it and 'Stasi Ramirez saw it, you tell me whether Yanni Schwartz or Petros Ivanov or my uncle missed it."

He walked around the edge of the pit, to the front of the bar.

"I apologize."

"*Apologize* won't handle it. I want to know—simply and clearly—what you want."

"You can always ask that. Isn't that the agreement?"

"Don't push me. *Don't* push me. I'm still trying to save your butt, hear me?"

"I understand you." He leaned against the bar and looked at Florian. "Florian."

"Ser?"

"Scotch and water. Do you mind?"

"Sera?"

"My usual. His. It's all right, Florian." She walked down the steps and sat down on the couch, and Justin came down and sat. Put his elbow on the couch-back in the same way as all those years ago, unconscious habit or scene-following as deliberate as hers . . . she did not know. "All right," she said, "I'm listening."

"Not much to say. Except I trusted you."

"*Trusted* me! —For what, a damned fool?"

"It was just—there. That's all. What would I do? Work in your wing, be your partner another twenty years till Denys dies? Keep my head down and my mouth shut and attend all those damn parties, twenty lousy years of going through every social function, all the department functions, everything—with every CIT in the House feeling like he has to explain himself to Security or your uncle if he's spotted talking to me? Hell of a life, Ari."

"I'm sorry," she said shortly. Which was true: she had had a dose of it too, in growing up; and she had seen it happen to him and felt it in her gut. "But that still doesn't say why you did it. Why you had to wait for a damned sensitive time—I just got things smoothed over with Denys, I *just* got things settled, and you throw me a move like that."

"Sorry," he said bitterly.

"Sorry?"

"Times are always sensitive— Always. It's always something. I'm cut off from my father again, dammit, because of Giraud. I've got your word he's safe. That's all I've got."

His voice wobbled. Florian set the whiskey down by his hand, on the shelf behind the couch, and ghosted her direction, putting the vodka-and-orange by hers.

"Which," he continued, after a drink, "I don't doubt. But that's why. Others do doubt my father's safety. Giraud is one. So damned easy to have an incident—a confusion on the part of some poor sod of an azi guard—isn't it? Terrible loss—a Special. But as you say, —Giraud's dying. What can he care? You underestimate him—if you think he's not going to try to be rid of my father—except—except if he finds things *aren't* settled at Reseune, and I'm a threat he can't get at. Next to you. *Then* he'll doubt. And Giraud, scheming bastard that he is, —never makes precipitate, reckless moves. *I* want his attention. I want it on me until he's dead. It's that simple."

It made sense, it made a tangled, out-of-another-mindset sense, if you were Justin Warrick, if you knew Giraud, if you had no power and nothing to bluff with except Ari Emory and a potential for trouble.

"So," he said, "I just—saw a chance. I didn't thoroughly plan it. I just saw what you did with the Carnath girl—Amy—and thought—if you blew up, well, maybe I could patch it. If you covered me—it'd get to Giraud. Maybe it'd look like more than it was and worry hell out of him. I'm sorry if it's fouled *you* up; but I doubt it has; fouled up your plans to keep me pure in Security's sight, maybe; worried Denys, I'm sure; —but messed up anything for you, personally, I very much doubt it."

"Nothing like the mess you've made for yourself."

"Good. On both counts."

"You're a damned fool! You could *tell* me, you know, you could trust I can keep an eye to Jordan—"

"No, I can't trust that. I can't trust that, when you're *not* in contact with the military, when you're *not* in Giraud's position and you're not in Denys' chair either. I can't depend on your knowing what they're up to, I'm sorry."

He *didn't* know Base One's extent. Had no idea. And there was no telling him. Not on any account. She sipped her vodka-and-orange, set it down and shook her head.

"You could at least have consulted me."

"And put you on your guard? No. Now done's done. I'm being honest, since you've asked. I'm asking you one more thing: run a probe if you like, but *don't* give the tape to Denys."

"Who said I did?"

"I don't know. I just have my suppositions what would appease Denys. Don't give this one out. It can only harm my father. It sure won't make me look any better to either one of the Nyes."

"Except if I don't they'll be sure I'm going along with what you did."

"So you are turning the tapes over."

"The ones I admit to running. I've never let them have Ari's notes on you. I've never shown them what I did to settle some of the damage Ari left. The unresolved stuff. I've never shown them the little intervention that lets you be here, this close to me, without sweating."

"Without worse than that. Without much worse than that. I'm still getting tape-flash now and again. But most of the charge is gone. I only remember—at much more distance than I've ever had—or I never could have done what I did at the party; never could have come here; never could have contemplated—my real plan for irritating Giraud."

"That being?"

"Going to bed with you."

That jolted, hard. It was so matter-of-fact she was half embarrassed, only dimly offended at first blink.

"Not," he said, "that I thought of doing anything you hadn't flatly asked me—once and twice, and recently. Make you happy—make Giraud quite, quite unhappy. And not in a way that could hurt you . . . I never wanted that. To be honest, I wasn't sure I could. So I just—took a different course when it offered itself, that's all. I hope I don't offend you. And I wouldn't mention it, except I'd rather explain it with my wits about me, thank you, where I can at least string things together in my own defense. So there you are. That's why."

It was a deliberate move that made it psychologically harder for her to insist on a probe . . . quieten things down: defuse the situation. And tell enough of the truth to make everything reasonable.

Come in here without Grant, too. *That*, when he knew he was potentially in trouble.

Damn, possibilities multiplied ad infinitum when it involved motives and an unacknowledged Special whose stresses came from everywhere and everyone—not least the fact that she had Worked him under kat, grabbed hold of things which were profoundly important to him and tried, at least, to tie up the old threads—far as one could in a mind that had changed so much since Ari's notes; and considering the psychological difference of their reversed ages.

Very tangled. Very, very tangled.

"You've messed up work of mine," she said. "You've made me problems. I've got reason to be mad. And I supported you out there, dammit."

"Yes," he said. "Which I hoped you'd do."

"It's a damn mess." She swallowed down any assurances she could give of Jordan's safety. Or how she knew. Frustrating as it was to look like a fool, better that than be one. "Dammit, you've put me at odds with Giraud. I don't see why I should have to handle problems you've made me because you could betray my interests and trust I'd forgive you. That's a hell of a thing."

"I didn't have a choice."

"You damn well did! You could have told me."

He shook his head, slowly.

"You're really pushing me, Justin. You're damn well pushing me."

"I didn't have a choice."

"And now I've got to cooperate and keep Giraud's hands off you or he'll blow your whole little scheme, is that it?"

"Something like. What else can I say? I hope you will. I *hope* you will; and I don't hope for too much in my life."

"Thanks."

He nodded, once, ironically.

"So you get off cheap," she said. "You get everything you want and you don't even have to go to bed with me."

"Ari, I didn't mean that."

"I know. Not fair."

There was a deep-link in his sets—to Ari. And she knew that. Knew that it was active, in this place, at this time.

That it was double-hooked. He hoped to snare her into it—to irritate Giraud. He was still maneuvering: she knew where it was going.

But there were deeper hooks than he knew.

"You want me to?" he asked.

"I don't know," she said. Then: "No. Not like it was pay for something. There's a security wall down the hall. There's a guest accommodation on the other side. You go there. Florian will get you through. I'll call Grant to come up. Florian and Catlin will supervise Housekeeping, shutting down your apartment, packing up what you'll need. If they leave anything out, you can go back with them to get it."

He looked shocked.

"You want my help," she said, "it does cost. It costs you the apartment you have. It costs you your independence. It costs you convenience the way it costs me. But you're not going to go into Security and you're damn sure not going to spill what you know about me to Giraud either. Which is the other part of your threat, isn't it?"

"I don't know what I know—"

"I'm sure you could figure it. You come and go through that security door; your cards will admit you. You'll move into Wing One facilities, and I don't know who I'm going to have to bump to make room for you, but you're going inside Wing One security, and inside my security; and I don't want any argument about it."

"None," he said quietly.

X

"Grant is here," the Minder said, and Justin leapt up off the couch, was at the door almost before Grant could open it, as Grant came alone into the apartment.

"Are you all right?" Grant asked, first-off.

"Fine," Justin said, and embraced him. "Thank God. No trouble?"

Grant shook his head, and drew a breath. "I got the call, I told Em hold the office down—I walked out into the hall and Catlin picked me up. Walked me all the way to the lift. She said she'd go to the apartment and bring essentials and anything we call down for."

No questions, nothing. Habit of half a lifetime. "We can talk," Justin said, realizing that fact—that there was nothing, now, that could be secret if Ari wanted it, nothing that anyone *but* Ari was going to reach, here, in this place. It was a moment of vertigo, old cautions tumbling away into dark on either side. The thought shook him, left him lonely for reasons he could not understand. "God, it's not home, is it?"

Grant held on to him. He felt himself shivering, suddenly, he had no notion why, or what he feared, specifically, only that nothing seemed certain any longer . . . not even their habits of self-defense.

Not home. Not the place he had always lived, not the obscurity they had tried to maintain. They were closer and closer to the center of Reseune.

"No probe," he said. "Ari asked why—reasonable question. I told her. This is her notion of increased security. I've got to show you around this place. You won't believe it."

He got control of his nerves, turned Grant around and gave him the full perspective of the living room and dining room.

It was a huge apartment by any standards: a front hall mostly stone, roofed in plasticized woolwood; a sitting-room with a gray sectional, black glass tables; and beyond that a dining hall with white tile, white walls, black and white furnishings— *My God*, Justin's first thought had been, an emotional impact of stark coldness, an irrational: *one red pillow, anything, to save your sanity in this damn place—*

"It's—quite large," Grant said, —diplomatically, he thought: "isn't it?"

"Come on," he said, and took Grant the tour.

It was better in the halls, pastel blues and greens leading off to a frost-green kitchen and a white hall to a suite of rooms in grays and blues—a lot of gray stone, occasional brown. A sybaritic bath in black and silver, mirrored. Another one, white and frost-green glass.

"My God," Grant said, when he opened another door on the master bedroom, black and black glass and white, huge bed. "Five people could sleep in that."

"They probably have," Justin said. And suffered a moment of flashback, a bad one. "They promise us sheets and supplies. There's some sort of scanning system they run things through, even our clothes. It puts some kind of marker on it. If we pass the door with anything that hasn't gone through scan—"

"Alarm sounds. Catlin explained that. Right down to the socks and underwear." Grant shook his head and looked at him. "Was she angry?"

He did not mean Catlin. Justin nodded. "Somewhat. God knows she's got a right to be, considering. But she's willing to listen. At least—that."

Grant said nothing. But the silence itself was eloquent as the little muscle twitch in the eyes toward the overhead. *Do we worry about monitoring?*

Because Grant knew—Grant knew everything that he had confessed to Ari and then some, as far as their intention to divert Giraud. But there were things between himself and Ari he could not say where monitoring might exist, things she might go after under probe, but he could not bring them out, coldly, and have her know that Grant knew: the feeling he had had in that room in Ari's apartment, the shifting between then and now—

The gut-deep feeling—passing at every other blink between then and now; to look into Ari's eyes gone by turns young and old—knowing, for the first time since he was younger than she was now—that the sexual feelings that haunted every touch of other human beings, every dealing he had with humanity—had a focus, had always had a specific, drug-set focus—

He might have gone to bed with her. He could have gone to bed with her—in one part of his imagining. More, he had *wanted* to, for about two heartbeats—until he had flashed, badly, waiting on her answer, and known that he would panic; and was caught somewhere between a fevered hope of her and a sweating terror. As if she was the key.

Or the destruct.

God, what has she done to me?

What keys has she got?

"Justin?" Grant said, and caught his arm. "Justin, —"

He held to Grant's shoulder and shuddered. "O God, Grant. . . ."

"What's wrong?" Grant's fingers gripped the back of his neck, pressed hard. "Justin?"

His heart raced. He lost vision for a moment, broken out in sweat, feeling himself nowhere at all, if Grant were not holding to him.

That's what Ari wanted—all those years ago. Wanted me—fixed on her—
I've lost everything, dragged Grant and Jordan with me—
This is all there'll ever be, sweet—
Worm. Psychmaster. She was the best there ever was—
Pleasure and pain. *Deep-set links—*
His heart made a few deep, painful beats. But he could adjust to that, the way he adjusted to everything, always. Life *was*, that was all. One lived.

Even knowing that the worst thing that had been done to him all those years ago was not sexual. Sex was only the leverage.

Endocrine-learning and flux, applied full-force, the kind of wrench that could take a vulnerable, frightened kid and twist him sideways into another research, another path for his entire existence.

She saw to my birth.

One could live. Even with the ground dropping out from under one's feet. Even with black space all around.

"What did she do?" Grant asked him, a sane, worried voice out of that mental dark, a hard pressure around him, at the back of his neck. "Justin?"

"She gave me the keys a long time ago," he murmured. "I knew, dammit, I knew—I should have seen. . . ."

Things began to focus then. Vision came back, the edge of Grant's shoulder, the stark black and white room that was not home, the knowledge that, foreseeably, they would not go back to the friendly, familiar apartment with the brown stone and the little breakfast nook that had always seemed safe, no matter what they knew about Security monitoring. . . .

"She knew she was dying, Grant. She was the best damned analyst going— She could read a subject like no one I ever saw. D'you think she never knew Giraud?"

"Ari senior?" Grant asked.

"Ari. She knew Giraud was no genius. She knew who would follow her. Do you think she didn't know them better than we do? Ari said—I was the only one who could teach her. The *only one*. That she needs my work. And she's working off Ari's notes, doing what Ari told her to do . . . all down the line."

Grant pushed him back. He stared up into Grant's worried face, seeing it as a stranger would, in an objective way he had never looked at Grant, the unlikely perfection—Ari's handiwork too, from his genesets to his psychset.

Everything was, everything. No good, any longer, in fighting the design. Even Grant was part of it. He was snared, he had always been.

She wanted Jordan. Jordan failed her. She saw to my creation. Designed Grant.

Fixed me on her—in one damnable stroke—
Everything's connected to everything—
Field too large, field too large—
"Justin?"
God, is the kid that good, does she know what she's doing to me?

Whose hand was on the switch in there? Which Ari?

Does it even matter—that one could set a path that sure—that the other could operate, just take it up and go—

Grant seized his face between his hands, popped a light slap against his cheek. "Justin!"

"I'm all right," he said.

I'm scaring hell out of him. But I'm not scared. Just—

Cold as hell now. Calm.

Helps, when you know the truth, doesn't it?

"—I'm all right. Just—went a little sideways for a moment." He patted Grant's shoulder, distanced himself a few steps and looked down the hall, the strange, not-home hallway. "Like—I'd waked up. Like—for a moment—I could just shake it all off. Think right past it." He felt Grant's hand on his shoulder, and he acknowledged it with a pressure of his own—scared again, because he was alone where he was standing, and Grant wanted to be with him, but he was not sure Grant could be—that anyone could be. And Ari was out so far ahead of him, in territory that was hers and her predecessor's, in places that he could not reach.

Places Jordan had never been.

Ultimate isolation.

"Our poor kid," he murmured, *"is* Ari. Damn, she is. No one ever caught up to her. She's going out into that place no one else can get to and no one can really speak to. That's what's going to happen to her. Happening to me . . . sometimes." He blinked and tried to come back. To see the lights again. The damned stark decor. Black and white dining room down the hall. "God, Housekeeping's got to have a red vase or something, doesn't it? Pillows. Pictures. Something."

"What are you talking about?" Grant asked.

The Super's training tried to assert itself. *Get yourself together. You're scaring him.* "Flux. Not a damn thing human in this apartment. Until we get a few things up from ours. Things with color. Things that are *us.* God, this place is like a bath in ice water."

"Is that what's the matter?"

"Something like." He blinked rapidly, trying to clear his eyes of the fog and focus short-range. "Maybe just—thinking this was where we would have ended up, if Ari had lived a little longer. This would have been ours."

"Justin, what in hell are you talking about?"

"Common sense. Ari didn't want to ruin Jordan. She needed his abilities. She was dying. She knew the Nyes for pragmatic sons of bitches. Conservative as hell. She wasn't. And *they* were going to have her successor. Don't you think she worried about that? And if she'd had two more years, even six more months, I think—I damn well know—I wouldn't have been what she took in. I might have been able to fight Giraud. Might have had some input into Ari's upbringing. Might be in Administration, might be high in the Bureau, by now, maybe sitting in Peterson's chair, who knows?"

Now—I'm not that person.

But Ari's following her predecessor's program. Following her notes.

It's a dangerous course for her. If Ari hasn't the perspective to figure that out, to figure me *out—it's very dangerous.*

Not because I wish her harm.

Because I can't help it. I have ties—I can't shed.

"I don't want to hurt her, Grant."

"Is there a question of it?"

It was too much to say. Ari had sworn there was no monitoring, but that was only the truth she wished were so: her capabilities were another story. Ari would lie by telling what she wished instead of what she would do: Ari had confessed that to him—manipulative in that admission as in anything else she did. *Never take me for simple . . . in any sense.*

"No," he answered Grant. "Not by anything *I* want."

Are you listening, Ari?

Do you hear what I'm saying?

---

xi

"*Message,*" the Minder said, waking Ari out of sleep, and waking Florian.

"*Coded private, Base Three.*"

Giraud.

Giraud was in Novgorod. Or had been when she went to sleep.

"Damn," she said; and rolled out of bed and searched for her slippers and her robe.

"Shall I get up, sera?"

"Go back to sleep," she said. "It's just Giraud going through the overhead. What else did I expect? Probably one from Denys too. . . ."

She found one slipper and the other as she put her arms into the sleeves, found the sashes and lapped them. "A little light," she said, "dammit, Minder. Eight seconds. On in the hall."

The room light came up a little, enough to see her way to the door, while—a backward glance—Florian pulled the covers over his head and burrowed into the dark. Eight seconds. She opened the door to the outside, blinking in brighter light, rubbing her eyes, as the light faded behind her.

She shut the door, and saw Catlin in the hall, in her nightrobe, her hair loose. "Back to bed," she told Catlin. "Just Giraud."

Catlin vanished.

She wanted a cup of something warm. But she was not about to rouse either of them: they had worked themselves to exhaustion getting Justin packed and upstairs before the rest of House Security could get at Justin's belongings or Justin's notes, and getting enough essentials through the Residency scanners to give them a choice of clothing and the basics for breakfast and to put their working notes into their hands again—after which, she reckoned, Justin might be a good deal happier.

Giraud certainly would not be.

She went into her office, tucked up in the chair and said, "Minder, message. I'm alone."

"Message, Base Three to Base One. Ari, this is Giraud."

All right, all right. Who else?

"Abban's flying down with this tape and flying back again tonight. He'll probably be on his way back to the airport by the time the system's alerted you. I can't afford this time. He can't. But I expect you know what's got me upset."

Three guesses, uncle Giraud? Is this about the dance?

Or have you heard your niece's latest?

"I'm terribly worried, Ari. I've made multiple tries at recording this message. The first one wasn't polite. But I think I can understand at least the reasons behind your reasons.

"I'm not going to yell at you. Isn't that what you always used to say: if you're going to yell at me, uncle Giraud, I'm not going to listen.

"We're both too old for that, and this is much too important for temper to get into it. So please, listen to this all the way through. It's ephemeral in the system unless you capture and copy—which you may do. If you do, I leave it to your discretion whether to send it to Archive, but I advise otherwise for reasons which may occur to you. This message is cued only to Base One. Unless I am dangerously mistaken, that will assure you are the only recipient.

"There's been another bombing. You may have heard."

Damn. No.

"Major restaurant. Five dead, nineteen injured. New Year's Day crowds. That's what we're dealing with. Lunatics, Ari. People who don't care about their targets.

"Let me go through this point by point, as logically as I can, why what you've done regarding young Warrick isn't advisable.

"I advised you in the first place against coming to Novgorod. I foresaw a press furor that could well lead to more bombings, and the public is damn tense—putting up with it, surviving, but ready to find a focus for their problems, and I don't want that blood on you, understand. Certainly we don't need to make you a center of controversy.

"Your suggestion to lend enforcement and surveillance help under Reseune's aegis is a damned fine one. I'm ashamed not to have thought of the means: Novgorod city government's touchy and suspicious of anything that massive with Reseune's stamp on it, but they're desperate, and that gives them an alternative to the several other routes they don't want to go—they don't want the precedent of calling on the regular military; they don't have the funds to Contract more personnel. Reseune Security in the subways is bound to be a target, but no sitting target, either—and we can muster enough to handle it: borrow the transport and the weapons from the military, at a level where Novgorod doesn't have to be acutely aware of

that connection; shore up Jacques, too: the armed forces are chafing at what they call a do-nothing policy across the board. Success at something, success at anything, would make the whole administration of Union look a damned sight better.

"Which brings up another point, Ari. One I'm no happier talking about than you can imagine—but you and I both know that I'm on the downward slide."

Pity, uncle Giraud?

Shame on you.

"Just de-charge the situation and listen to me. I want you to start thinking clearly about what in hell you're going to do when I die, because I can assure you your enemies are planning for it.

"Khalid is beyond the two year rule. He could challenge Jacques again now. He could, but he hasn't filed. The Centrists are nominally backing Jacques. They're scared of Khalid: he's not someone they can control and Corain in particular sees Khalid as a clear danger to himself, someone who'd like to take the helm from him—and Corain's no young man any longer. Khalid calls Corain a tired old grandfather . . . behind closed doors, but that kind of thing gets passed along, in private circles.

"Me, he calls a dead man. Not particularly pleasant, but I'm getting used to the idea. He doesn't know yet how right he is."

My God, uncle Giraud. What a view of things!

"Look at Council, Ari. Catherine Lao's almost my age. That's your most valuable ally besides Harad and myself. I'm going. Jacques is a very weak figure and Gorodin's grooming a replacement in the senior end of the admiralty board, in a man named Spurlin, able, but very middle-of-the-spectrum, very strictly the interests of his own Bureau, blow anyone else. Are you following this?"

Too well. I'm ahead of you.

"I made a terrible mistake, Ari, when I moved against Warrick without consulting you. We crossed one another, and to your damage. I made a further mistake when I didn't level with you then. Now I have reason to suspect you've passed at least my Base . . ."

Oh. Dear.

". . . and possibly Denys' as well—either that or you have an uncanny timing.

"I confess that threw me. I didn't know then what to do. I'm old and I'm sick and I'm scared, Ari. But I'm not going to get maudlin. Just in that very bright mind of yours, you should realize that your uncles have human weaknesses. I should have taken immediate measures I failed to take. When I was younger I might have done better, but I'm not sure I would have. Doubts like that, you understand, are the bane of any reasoning mind. Do I not act because I see too much and the choices are too wide—or because I just can't make a choice?

"I'm making one now. A desperate one. I'm laying out the truth for you. Jordan Warrick is in direct contact with a man named McCabe, in air systems maintenance, who has direct links to Mikhail Corain's office. I'm appending the entire report into Base One . . ."

You're supposed to have put all the security reports into House systems, uncle Giraud. And this is totally new. How much else have you held out?

". . . along with all our current files on Planys security. It's quite a mass of information. Suffice it to say, quite honestly, Warrick is repeating an old pattern. You'll find in there a transcript from a meeting of Warrick with Secretary of Defense Lu, back in Gorodin's administration, a very secret transcript, that never came out at the hearings. Warrick was dealing, right before your predecessor's death, for his transfer out to Fargone, and all that goes with it. Warrick was discovered in his scheme. It collapsed. Everything went up in smoke. Ari caught him dealing with Corain and I imagine Ari told him the truth of what was going on with his son.

"Jordan Warrick saw that tape. I can attest to that. Exactly what his professional skills are capable of making out of it, with his own knowledge of his son, I don't know—but I know, you know, young Warrick knows, and I'm damned sure Jordan Warrick knows—that it was more than sexual gymnastics and more than a blackmail trip. He knew at that point that, A, Denys and I wouldn't let him get his son back in his hands to work with; and B, Ari had been working on him for a number of sessions he couldn't estimate. In Jordan Warrick's place, what would you conclude?"

My God, Giraud.

"Jordan Warrick is very well aware of his son's association with you. We've monitored very closely—to know what he does know. And what he can see is his son increasingly involved with you, with more and more to lose in any accident to you. That part of what you've done is instinctively correct, Ari. I tried to prevent it in the first place, afraid you were being an adolescent about the matter, but somewhere in the flux, your instincts are still quite true. And now I remember, as old men will, that Ari was very much the same. So I rely on that; and I warn you: Jordan has never trusted his son. Justin has never understood his father. Justin—is an idealist and an honest man, and as such, he is very useful as an instrument. But he is vulnerable to his father; and his father is your implacable enemy, your enemy on principle, your enemy in his opposition to Reseune and all it stands for. I worry less about your having sex with this man than about your public defense of him—your stripping away the political isolation we've placed him in. We've kept him powerless to harm you. That you might sleep with him is, at this point, an inconsequence. If it would cure the sexual infatuation I would be delighted.

"But bringing this man into prominence in Reseune—is deadly.

"Let me go afield a moment. I know you're able to compass this interconnection of facts.

"Gorodin's medical reports look worse than mine. I don't know about Lao's. I figure that I have, granted nothing goes catastrophically wrong, maybe this year in tolerable health. After that, Lynch is going to have to take more and more of the operations and leave me the decision-making. Which I plan to make you privy to, along with Denys.

"What will happen when I die   if I can prevail on my brother to leave Reseune, I'll appoint him proxy and he can stand for election. If. Denys is not taking my death well.

"I haven't thanked you properly for your—vote of confidence in me. Frankly,

I'm not sure what the proper response is to finding out I'll be replicated—a little flattered, I suppose, not exactly personally involved, except as it consoles Denys. I'm sure I won't know personally. I'm not even sure that it's true, or that I'm that important, although Denys is, and in the context of my value to him—I can well see there might be a point to it. But if it is true, for God's sake don't make it public. The public can accept the entity you call the cute kid. But I was always a sullen brat, your predecessor would have told you that; and I'm sure you can think what kind of furor it could stir up if my enemies could look forward to another round with Giraud Nye. I suppose Justin does know what you intend. He's altogether too close to your affairs; and I hope to hell he hasn't gotten that word to Jordan; because if he has, it's in Corain's office by now, and I can about swear that will be exactly the route.

"I don't want Denys to take guardianship of my replicate. Give that job to Yanni. He's at least as hardheaded as our father was; and I really want Denys in Novgorod, in office, and on the job, if any force can move him. You're not able to take Reseune Administration: you'll be at most twenty, and it needs a much more experienced hand. The logical candidate to administer Reseune is Yanni Schwartz. But you must above all else start taking a more public role and establishing a more professional image. You have to stand for that seat in your own right, at the right time.

"But don't count on your enemies standing still for that day. Khalid, I'm sure, has never forgotten what you and I did to him. I'm virtually certain, but I can't prove, that there is some very vague linkage among the Paxers, the Rocher party, the Abolitionists, and some allegedly respectable elements in the Centrist party, some of which links go perhaps very high indeed. I don't say that Khalid is bombing subways. I do think that he's prepared to use the whole issue of your existence and the Paxer movement against you—the fear of Reseune's power—all of that—

"The moment I'm dead, I figure there'll not only be the election in Science, but Khalid will challenge Jacques. We're caught in a situation in this. We're not enthusiastic about Gorodin's man Spurlin. Gorodin's health won't let him run again. Lu is disaffected, a bitter man. We're pressing Jacques to resign now and appoint Spurlin as proxy. He sees this as an Expansionist plot—correctly. But he doesn't admit that he can't beat Khalid again; and he won't look at his own polls that show him slipping badly. A case either of a man being pressured by Corain to hold on in hopes of a change in the polls; or a man being a fool. Corain tells me privately that he's urged Jacques to step down. He says Jacques refuses, that Jacques privately resents the label as a seat-warmer and a mouthpiece for Gorodin, Jacques is determined to hold the office in his own right, after Gorodin dies—a case of one man's vanity impinging on Union's future.

"What I'm afraid is going to happen is the following: two elections going, and no knowing how Gorodin's health will be. And in the wake of media interest in my death, and Denys' succession to the seat—that's precisely when I'm afraid Jordan Warrick is going to break his silence and come up with charges of his own, one of which is very likely going to be a claim of his own innocence and the claim that I blackmailed him into accepting blame for Ari's death. I think you can see the mess

you're about to create in rehabilitating his son. I hope you can see it. Your predecessor wouldn't fail me in this."

God. Dear God.

Is he innocent?

"There's no way in hell Jordan Warrick can testify or be questioned, without a major change in the law. He can make charges with the same immunity that he has in keeping silent. He can say anything. And this is a man who's waited two decades for this chance . . . who will have his chance, now, because we gave up our chance to have linked him to the Paxers. We still can, if you're willing to use your head. I'm afraid it wouldn't win you young Warrick's gratitude. But then again, you're much cleverer than I am, young sera. And maybe you can navigate those rocks.

"You have your predecessor's notes in Justin Warrick's case. You have run an intervention on him, I very much suspect, of what sort I will not speculate: I only know that the gesture he made at the party last night would once have been impossible for him. Having had him under probe a number of times, I know him and I know the nature of his problems, only some of which stem from that session with your predecessor—"

Damn you. *Damn* you, Giraud!

"Not to stand in the way of young love, Ari, sweet, but Justin's father put a damned heavy load on him. If you've got Ari's notes you know that. You count yourself expert enough to take on a case Petros and Gustav won't touch, I'll trust you can add up the stresses on Justin Warrick and figure out what's going on with him. And you can add up the stresses that will result if he hears his father claim he was framed and unjustly treated.

"I'm at the point where I have to surrender a good many things to young hands. I thought that, frankly, I could rid you of a very unpleasant decision. You've appropriated it to yourself by your maneuvers to forestall me and to prevent me from discrediting Jordan Warrick. I neither beg nor plead with you at this point. I'm accustomed to being the villain in the Family. I have no objection to bowing out in that role. If you would care to turn your back in the affair of Jordan Warrick, I could foresee that you could turn proof of his activities to your considerable personal advantage in dealing with Justin Warrick. I'm sure you understand me. If you decide on that course you have only to call on me.

"You assuredly know now why I have taken extreme precautions to prevent this tape from seeing Archives. It's potentially deadly. Never mind my reputation. Your own safety is in question, and if you use that famous wit of yours, you will look to that to the exclusion of all else.

"Above all, keep power out of the hands of people you would want to protect. Out of a hundred thirty-three years of living, love, that's the highest wisdom I can come to.

"I'll keep you posted. Abban may make many of these flights. I don't trust regular communications. Don't you

"Above all, take this for a storm-warning. I'm taking excellent care of myself. I've given up my few vices for your sake, to buy you time. Remember my offer.

Position yourself carefully, and don't be careless with your associates. Justice, guilt and innocence are irrelevant. Motivation and opportunity are the things you have to watch. Nothing else has any validity."

"Endit."

She sat still a long while.

"Log-off," she said finally.

And got up and went back to the bedroom.

Florian waked when she came in. Or had never been asleep.

She got in beneath the covers. And stared into the dark.

"Is there trouble, sera?"

"Just Giraud," she said, and rolled over and put her arm around him, burrowed down against his shoulder, smothering the anger, fighting it with all she had. "God. Florian. Do something, will you?"

2424: 2/3: 2223

B/1: Ari senior has a message.
Stand by.
Ari, this is Ari senior.
You've asked about power.
That's a magic word, sweet. Are you alone?
AE2: Yes.
B/1: You are 18 years old. You are legally adult. You have authority of: Wing Supervisor; Alpha Supervisor.

You have flagged for systems surveillance: Denys Nye; Giraud Nye; Petros Ivanov; Yanni Schwartz; Wendell Peterson; John Edwards; Justin Warrick; Jordan Warrick; Gustav Morley; Julia Carnath; Amy Carnath; Maddy Strassen; Victoria Strassen; Sam Whitely; Stef Dietrich; Yvgenia Wojkowski; Anastasia Ramirez; Eva Whitely; Julia Strassen; Gloria Strassen; Oliver AOX Strassen; and all their associations.

Additionally you have flagged for exterior surveillance and news-service monitoring: priority one: Mikhail Corain; Vladislaw Khalid; Simon Jacques; Giraud Nye; Leonid Gorodin; James Lynch; Thomas Spurlin; Ludmilla deFranco; Catherine Lao; Nasir Harad; Andrew McCabe; and all their households.

Do you wish to add or subtract?
AE2: Continue.
B/1: Ari, this is Ari senior.

You are monitoring inside and outside Reseune. You hold economic and administrative power inside Reseune with a rating of: excellent performance.

I advise against any move against Administration on the grounds of: chronological age.

NewsScan profile indicates No security anomaly within Reseune's internal surveillance. Do you disagree?

AE2: No.

B/1: You've asked about power. There are three parts to that. Taking it. Holding it. Using it. Taking it and holding it are very closely related: if you pay less attention to the second than to the first you are in trouble, because the same dynamics that put you in power will operate as well for someone else against you.

Let me tell you: physical force will only work on lower levels. Don't discount it. But the most effective way to power is through persuasion. This means psych, personally applied, and massively applied. If you have followed my work this far, you understand when I say that the press is one of the most valuable tools you will have to work with.

There are at least three possible situations with the press. A, Completely free; B, Free in some areas, controlled in others; C, Completely controlled. In the first instance, the press is vulnerable to direct manipulation; in the second, vulnerable to direct manipulation in some areas, but vulnerable to tactics which increase public distrust of official information; in the third state, rumor is potentially more powerful than the press, and with an efficient organization you can equally well turn that situation to your advantage. Which of the three do you estimate is the case?

AE2: The second.

B/1: Analysis indicates a period of unrest.

Intersection of data indicates reason for concern.

Your NewsScan profile is: low activity; predominantly favorable. Consider carefully the effects of a change in this profile at this time.

Always respect the power of public opinion. Need I say that to a Reseune-trained operator?

Remember that change in social macrosystems operates rarely like earthquake, more frequently like subsoil ice, deforming the terrain in general ways, by gravity and topological constraints. The potential for cataclysmic events is comparatively easy to figure: figuring the precise moment or trigger of fracture is not; while the temporal component in slow change is relatively easy to figure, the total direction of change is complex, involving more individual action. Politicians frequently ride the earthquakes; while Reseune has always operated best in the subsoil, slowly, with frequent small adjustments.

I distrust such models. But I trust I am giving them to an adult who understands me.

I urge you consider the changes in Novgorod and in Cyteen in your own lifetime, and in mine, and in Olga's. I predict they will be extreme, and I urge you watch several areas.

a) An early problem will be the pressure of CIT population increase, particularly in Novgorod, particularly on stations such as Esperance and Pan-Paris, which do not lie on the routes of proposed expansion: eventually CITs will find that jobs are not as easy to come by, and that will lead to increased power for the Abolitionists who call for the cessation of azi production.

b) Interstellar government having its capital resident in a world-based city is increasingly fraught with problems, however much the situation has been advantageous to Reseune. It may in your lifetime produce difficulties and threaten Union: placing the capital specifically at Novgorod instead of Cyteen Station exposed Union politics to Cyteen influence and to Cyteen economics in ways which I do not think healthy. Be alert for that sentiment. It will come, though perhaps not in your lifetime.

It is possible in the future that for reasons presently unforeseen, Novgorod may diminish in power and influence within Cyteen and consequently pose less problem, but I doubt it: geography favors it and the presence of Union government fattens it. I foresee it clinging to the government by every means possible, including dirty politics and gerrymandering which could threaten Union. Particularly beware the intersection of a) and b) or b) and c).

c) The discovery that Reseune has tampered with social dynamics at Gehenna and elsewhere could create widespread panic and distrust of Reseune's influence.

d) The mere potential for Earth's further intervention in Alliance affairs or outside human space, acts as a destabilizing force in Alliance-Union relations; an actual or perceived threat from that quarter could worsen relations.

e) The opportunity for major gains by political opposition during the interregnum of your guardians, and the death and defeat of various of my own allies in the interim, will likely effect the rise of major new political forces, some of whom may well be radically Abolitionist. I predict that within a decade or so of my death Mikhail Corain will be viewed as too moderate to control his own allies, and it is foreseeable that a more radical figure will unseat him, possibly changing the Centrists considerably. Particularly look to the effects of your own emergence into public life. I had enemies. You will face opposition which may have superstitious roots, in fear of the unknown, in fear of you as a political force, and in fear of what the science which brought you into being could mean—to a society only recently adapting to rejuv. Uncertainty of any sort creates demagogues.

f) A major new discovery of non-human intelligence might destabilize the situation I left, and might come at any time. I urge you press for expansion in safe areas and for necessary precaution against hostile contact. We do not know our time limits and we are scarcely stable enough in my time to deal with that eventuality.

g) There may be major divergences from my policies inside Reseune, and there exists the chance that you have either made personal enemies on-staff or that you are perceived as standing for policies others oppose.

h) A major breakdown could occur within a designed azi population, or there may be major difficulties in CIT-azi integrations within a given population. I hope this does not come to pass, but my best estimate of a problem area would be Pan-Paris, where economic constraints and military retirees may pose hardships; next most likely: Novgorod, in the third generation . . . where the old rebel ethos of the founders of Union may well find difficulty mixing with the Constitution-venerating descendants of the wartime worker-azi, and where population pressures and Cyteen's ability to terraform new habitat on that site may run a narrow race indeed.

I hope time has proven me wrong in some of these things.

But I urge you to study these situations and to prepare responses to them, before you make any move on your own.

Avoid precipitate action: by this I mean, don't be too quick to take what you're not ready for; don't be so late that you have to move hastily and without adequate groundwork.

Power of any kind lays heavy responsibility on you; and it changes your friends as it changes the way your friends regard you. Do not be naive in this regard. Do not assume. Do not overburden your friends with too much trust.

Above all remember what I said in the beginning: respect the power of public opinion.

NewsScan shows mention of you: 3 articles in last 3 months.

Mention of Giraud Nye: 189 articles in last 3 months.

Mention of Mikhail Corain: 276 articles in last 3 months.

Mention of Reseune: 597 articles in last 3 months.

Mention of Paxers: 1058 articles in last 3 months.

Continue?

AE2: Base One, give me the nature, location, and time of Ari senior's last entry into the House system.

B/1: Working.

Entry by TransSlate; 1004A, 2404: 10/22: 1808.

AE2: Give me the location and time of Ari senior's death.

B/1: Working.

1004A.

Autopsy ruling: 2404: 10/22: 1800 to 1830 approximate.

AE2: 1004A is the cold lab in Wing One basement. Correct?

B/1: Correct.

AE2: Who else has accessed this information?

B/1: No prior access.

AE2: Replay entry.

B/1: Working.

Order: Security 10: Com interrupt: Jordan Warrick, all outgoing calls. Claim malfunction. Order good until canceled.

AE2: Base One, is that the last entry from Ari from any source?

B/1: Working.

Affirmative.

AE2: Base One, at what time did Jordan Warrick enter Wing One basement security door on 10/22, 2404?

B/1: Working.

Wing One basement security door coded 14. Jordan Warrick's key accessed D14 at 1743 hours, that date.

AE2: Departure, same visit?

B/1: 1808 hours, that date: duration of visit: 25 minutes. . . .

AE2: Record current session to Personal Archive. Give me the full transcript, Autopsy, Ariane Emory; all records, Jordan Warrick, keyword: Emory, keyword: trial; keyword: murder; keyword, hearings; keyword: Council; keyword: investigation.

CHAPTER
14

"The first bill on the agenda is number 6789, for the Bureau of Trade," Nasir Harad said, "Ludmilla deFranco, Simon Jacques co-sponsors, proposing restructuring of the Pan-Paris credit system. Call for debate."

"Citizens," Mikhail Corain said, lifting his hand. "For the bill."

"Finance," Chavez said. "For the bill."

"Move to forgo debate," Harogo said, "in the absence of opposition."

Corain cast a look down the table, toward Nye, who had reached for his water glass.

It was a bargain, the time-saving sort. The acquiescence of the Expansionists in the move designed to take pressure off the ailing Pan-Paris central bank, the promise of military contracts, the private assurance that Reseune would grant more time on the considerable sum Pan-Paris owed—of course it would: Pan-Paris was Lao's central constituency and the bill was the first step in a long-proposed settlement on the Wyatt's Paradise–Pan-Paris loop that called for a fusion-powered station at Maronne Point, where there was only dark mass, but enough to pull a ship in.

There were four bills lined up, Expansionists falling all over themselves after decades of opposition, finally diverting funds from the slow construction of Hope to the more immediate difficulties of home space and a trade loop that had gotten, since the War, damnably short of exportable commodities.

Major construction, finally, beyond the rebuilding of stations damaged in Azov's desperate push in the last stages of the War; beyond the endless restructurings of debt and adjustments necessary when the merchanters associated into Alliance and left Union banks holding enormous debt.

Seventy years later, a policy shift to save that trade loop became possible only because the special interests that had blocked it suddenly discovered there was nothing left to do.

"Move to suspend debate," Harad said in his usual mutter. "Second?"

"Second," Corain said.

"Call for the vote."

A clatter from down the table. Nye had knocked the water glass over his papers, and sat there—sat there, with the water running across his notes, in a frozen pose that at first seemed incongruous, as if he were listening for something.

Then Corain's heart ticked over a beat, a moment of alarm as he saw the imminent collapse, as Lao, next to Nye, rose in an attempt to hold him, as of a sudden everyone was moving, including the aides.

But Giraud Nye was slumping down onto the papers, sliding from his chair, completely limp as the azi Abban shoved Lao aside and caught Nye in his fall between the seats.

The Council, the aides, everyone broke into tumult, and Corain's heart was hammering. "Get Medical," he ordered Dellarosa, ordered whoever would go, while Abban had Nye on the floor, his collar open, applying CPR with methodical precision.

It was quiet then, except the aides slipping from the chamber—strange that no one moved, everyone seemed in a state of shock, except a junior aide offering to spell the azi.

Medical arrived, running steps, a clattering and banging of hand-carried equipment, Councillors and aides clearing back in haste to let the professionals through, then waiting while more medics got a portable gurney through and the working team and Abban, clustered about Nye, lifted him and lifted the gurney up.

Alive, Corain thought, shaken: he could not understand his own reaction, or why he was trembling when Nasir Harad, still standing, brought the gavel down on Chairman's discretion for an emergency recess.

No one moved to leave for a moment. Centrists and Expansionists looked at each other in a kind of vague, human shock, for about a half a hundred heartbeats.

Then Simon Jacques gathered up his papers, and others did, and Corain signaled to his own remaining aides.

After that it was a withdrawal, increasingly precipitate, to reassess, to find out in decent discretion how serious it was, whether Nye was expected to recover from this one.

Or not.

In which case—in which case nothing was the same.

ii

". . . *collapsed in the Council chamber,*" the public address said, throughout Reseune, and people stopped where they were, at their desks, in the halls, waiting; and Justin stood, with his arms full of printout from the latest run on Sociology, with that vague cold feeling about his heart that said that, whatever Giraud was to him personally—

—there was far worse.

"He stabilized in the emergency care unit in the Hall of State and is presently in transit via air ambulance to the intensive care unit in Mary Stamford Hospital in Novgorod. There was early consideration of transfer to Reseune's medical facilities, but the available aircraft did not have necessary equipment.

"His companion Abban was with him at the time of the collapse, and remains with him in transit.

"Secretary Lynch has been informed and has taken the oath as interim proxy, for emergency business.

"Administrator Nye requests that expressions of concern and inquiries regarding his brother's condition be directed to the desk at Reseune hospital, which is in current contact with Stamford in Novgorod, and that no inquiries be made directly to Novgorod.

"Reseune staff is urged to continue with ordinary schedules. Bulletins will be issued as information becomes available."

"Damn," someone said, on the other side of the room, "here it goes, doesn't it?"

Justin took his printout and left, out into the hall beyond the glass partitions, where people lingered to talk in small groups.

He felt stares at his back, felt himself the object of attention he did not want.

Felt—as if the ground had shifted underfoot, even if they had known this was coming.

"It's the slow preparation," a tech said in his hearing. "He may already be dead. They won't admit it—till the Bureau has the proxy settled. They can't admit anything till then."

It was a dreadful thing—to go to Denys now. But a call on the Minder was too cold and too remote; and Ari faced the apartment door and identified herself to the Minder, with Florian and Catlin at her back, and nothing— nothing to protect her from the insecurity in front of her—an old man's impending bereavement, an old man facing a solitude he had never—Giraud himself had said it—never been able to come to grips with.

If Denys cried, she thought, if Denys broke down in front of her he would be terribly ashamed; and angry with her; but she was all the close family he had left, who did not want to be here, who did not want, today, to be adult and responsible, in the face of the mistake this visit could turn out to be.

But she had, she thought, to try.

"Uncle Denys," she said, "it's Ari. Do you want company?"

A small delay. The door opened suddenly, and she was facing Seely.

"Sera," Seely murmured, "come in."

The apartment was so small, so simple next her own. Denys could always have had a larger one, could have had, in his long tenure, any luxury he wanted. But it felt like home, in a nostalgic wrench that saw her suddenly a too-old stranger, and Florian and Catlin entering with her . . . grown-up and strange to the scale of this place: the little living room, the dining area, the suite off to the right that had been hers and theirs and Nelly's; the hall to the left that held Denys' office and bedroom, and Seely's spartan quarters.

She looked that direction as Denys came out of his office, pale and drawn, looking bewildered as he saw her.

"Uncle Denys," she said gently.

"You got the news," Denys said.

She nodded. And felt her way through it—herself, whom Union credited for genius in dealing with emotional contexts, in setting up and tearing down and reshaping human reactions—but it was so damned different, when the emotional context went all the way to one's own roots. Redirect, that was the only thing she could logic her way to. Redirect and refocus: *grief is a self-focused function and the flux holds so damn much guilt about taking care of ourselves. . . .* "Are *you* all right, uncle Denys?"

Denys drew a breath, and several others, and looked desperate for a moment. Then he firmed up his chin and said: "He's dying, Ari."

She came and put her arms around Denys, self-conscious—God, guilty: of calculation, of too much expertise; of being cold inside when she patted him on the shoulder and freed herself from him and said: "Seely, has uncle Denys still got that brandy?"

"Yes," Seely said.

"I have work to do," Denys said.

"The brandy won't hurt," she said. "Seely."

Seely went; and she hooked her arm in Denys' and took him as far as the dining table where he usually did his work.

"There's nothing you can do by worrying," she said. "There's nothing anyone can do by worrying. Giraud knew this was coming. Listen, you know what he's done, you know the way he's arranged things. What he'll want you to do—"

"I damned well *can't* do!" Denys snapped, and slammed his hand down on the table. "I don't intend to discuss it. Lynch will sit proxy. Giraud may recover from this. Let's not hold the funeral yet, do you mind?"

"Certainly I hope not." *He's not facing this. He's not accepting it.*

Seely, thank God, arrived with the brandy, while Florian and Catlin hovered near the door, gone invisible as they could.

She took her own glass, drank a little, and Denys drank, more than a little; and gave a long shudder.

"I can't go to Novgorod," Denys said. There was a marked fragility about the set of his mouth, a sweating pallor about his skin despite the cool air in the room. "You know that."

"You can do what you put your mind to, uncle Denys. But it's not time to talk about that kind of thing."

"I *can't*," Denys said, cradling the glass in his hands. "I've told Giraud that. He knows it. Take tape, he says. He knows damned well I'm not suited to holding office."

"It's not a question of that right now."

"He's *dying*, dammit. You know it and I know it. And his notions about my going to Novgorod—dammit, he knows better."

"You'd be very good."

"Don't be ridiculous. A public speaker? An orator? Someone to handle press conferences? There's no one less suited than I am to holding public office. Behind the scenes, yes, I'm quite good. But I'm much too old to make major changes. I'm not a public man, Ari. I'm not going to be. There's no tape fix for age, there's no damned tape fix to make me a speechmaker . . ."

"Giraud isn't exactly skilled at it, but he's a fine Councillor."

"Do you know," Denys said, "when I came down to the AG unit that time—that was the first time since I was nine, that I'd ever left these walls?"

"My God, uncle Denys."

"Didn't add that up? Shame on you. I came down to see my foster-niece risk her lovely neck, the way I watched from the airport remotes when your predecessor would come screaming in, in that damned jet. I hate disasters. I've always expected them. It's my one act of courage, you understand. *Don't* ask me to handle press conferences." Denys shook his head and leaned on his elbows on the table. "Young people. They risk their lives so damned lightly, and they know so little what they're worth."

He wept then, a little convulsion of shoulders and face, and Ari picked up the decanter and poured him more, that being the only effective kindness she could think of.

She said nothing for perhaps a quarter, perhaps half an hour, only sat there while Denys emptied another glass.

Then the Minder said: "*Message, Abban AA to Base Two, special communications.*"

Denys did not answer at once. Then he said: "Report."

"*Ser Denys,*" Abban's voice said, cold with distance and the Minder's reproduction, "*Giraud has just died. I'll see to his transport home, by his orders. He requested you merge his Base.*"

Denys lowered his head onto his hand.

"Abban," Seely said, "this is Seely SA. Ser thanks you. Direct details to me; I'll assist."

Ari sat there a very long time, waiting, until Denys wiped his eyes and drew a shaken breath.

"Lynch," Denys said. "Someone has to notify Lynch. Tell Abban see to that. He's to stand proxy. He's to file for election. Immediately."

iii

The Family filed into the East Garden, by twos and threes, wearing coats and cloaks in the sharpness of an autumn noon.

With conspicuous absences, absences which made Ari doubly conscious of her position in the forefront of the Family—eighteen, immaculate in mourning, and correct as she knew how to be—wearing the topaz pin on her collar, the pin Giraud had given her . . . *something that's only yours. . . .*

The funeral was another of those duties she would have avoided if she could have found a way.

Because Denys had made a damnable mess of things. Denys had fallen to pieces, refused the appointment as proxy Councillor of Science, and refused to attend the funeral. *Denys* was over at the old Wing One lab, supervising the retrieval and implantation of CIT geneset 684-044-5567 . . . precisely at this hour—at which Ari, even with compassion for his reasons, felt a vague shudder of disgust.

It left her, foster-niece, as nearest kin—not even directly related to Giraud, but ranking as immediate family, over Emil Carnath-Nye, and Julia Carnath-Nye, and Amy. She felt uncomfortable in that role, even knowing Julia's attachment to Giraud was more ambition than accident of blood. Hell with Julia: there was prestige involved, and she hated to move Amy out of her proper place, that was the uncomfortable part. The Carnath-Nyes stood, an ill-assorted little association of blood-ties far from cordial these days—Amy bringing Quentin as she had brought Florian and Catlin, for personal security in troubled times, not to flaunt him in front of the Family and her mother's disapproval; but that was certainly not the way Julia Carnath took it.

Julia and her father Emil resented having Abban standing beside them; and took petty exception to the man—*man*, dammit, who had been closer to Giraud in many ways than any next-of-kin, even Denys; who had held Giraud's hand while he died and taken care of notifications with quiet efficiency when no Family were there to do anything.

That attitude was damned well going to go: she had served notice of it and scandalized the old hands before now. Let them know what she would do when she held power in the House: hell with their offended feelings.

Amy was there; Maddy Strassen was in the front row, with aunt Victoria—maman's sister, and at a hundred fifty-four one of the oldest people alive anywhere who was not a spacer. Rejuv did not seem near failing Victoria Strassen: she was wearing away instead like ice in sunlight, just thinner and more fragile with every passing year, until she began to seem more force than flesh. Using a cane now: the sight afflicted Ari to the heart. *Maman would be that old now. Maman would be that frail.* She avoided Victoria, not alone because Victoria hated her and blamed her for Julia Strassen's exile to Fargone.

The Whitely clan was there: Sam and his mother; and the Ivanovs, the Edwardses; Yanni Schwartz and Suli; and the Dietrichs.

Justin and Grant were not. Justin had sent, all things considered, a very gracious refusal, and let her off one very difficult position. It was the only mercy she had gotten from Family or outsiders. Reporters clustered down at the airport press area, a half hour down there this morning, an appointment for an interview this afternoon, a half a hundred frustrated requests for an interview with Denys—

I'm sorry, she had said, privately and on camera. *Even those of us who work lifelong with psych, seri, do feel personal grief.* Coldly, precisely, letting her own distress far enough to the surface to put what Giraud would call the human face on Reseune. *My uncle Denys was extremely close to his brother, and he's not young himself. He's resigning the proxy to Secretary Lynch out of health considerations— No. Absolutely not. Reseune has never considered it has a monopoly on the Science seat. As the oldest scientific institution on Cyteen we have contributions to make, and I'm sure there will be other candidates from Reseune, but no one in Reseune, so far as I know, intends to run. After all—Dr. Nye wasn't bound to appoint Secretary Lynch: he might have appointed anyone in Science. Secretary Lynch is a very respected, very qualified head of the Bureau in his own right.*

And to a series of insistent questions: *Seri, Dr. Yanni Schwartz, the head of Wing One in Reseune, will be answering any specific questions about that. . . .*

. . . No, sera, that would be in the future. Of course my predecessor held the seat. Presently I'm a wing supervisor in Research, I do have a staff, I have projects under my administration—

Every reporter in the room had focused in on that, sharp and hard— scenting a story that was far off their present, urgent assignment: she had thrown out the deliberate lure and they burned to go for it despite the fact they were going out live-feed, with solemn and specific lead-ins and funeral music. She handed them the hint of a story they could not, with propriety, go for; and kept any hint of deliberate signal off her face when she did it.

But they had gone for it the moment they were off live-feed: to what extent was she actually in Administration, what were the projects, how were the decisions being made inside Reseune and was she in fact involved in that level?

Dangerous questions. Exceedingly dangerous. She had flashed then on bleeding bodies, on subway wreckage, on news-service stills of a child's toy in the debris.

Seri, she had said then, direct, not demure: with Ari senior's straight stare and deliberate pause in answering: *any wing administrator is in the process.*

Read me, seri: I'm not a fool. I won't declare myself over my uncle's ashes.

But don't discount me in future.

I came here, she had reminded them in that context, *as a delegated spokesman for the family. That's my immediate concern. I have to go, seri. I have to be up the hill for the services in thirty minutes. Please excuse me. . . .*

It was the first funeral she had attended where there was actually burial, a small canister of ash to place in the ground, and two strong gardeners to raise the basalt cenotaph up from the ground and settle it with a final thump over the grave.

She flinched at that sound, inside. So damned little a canister, for tall uncle Giraud.

And burial in earth instead of being shot for the sun. She knew which she would pick for herself—same as her predecessor, same as maman. But it was right for Giraud, maybe.

Emil Carnath called for speeches from associates and colleagues.

"I have a word," Victoria Strassen said right off.

O God, Ari thought.

And braced herself.

"Giraud threw me out of my sister's funeral," Victoria began in a voice sharper and stronger than one ever looked for from that thin body. "I never forgave him for it."

Maddy cast Ari an anguished look across the front of the gathering. *Sorry for this.*

Not your fault, Ari thought.

"What about you, Ariane Emory PR? Are you going to have me thrown out for saying what the truth is?"

"I'll speak after you, aunt Victoria. Maman taught me manners."

That hit. Victoria's lips made a thin line and she took a double-handed grip on her black cane.

"My sister was *not* your maman," Victoria said. "That's the trouble in the House. Dead is dead, that's all. The way it works best. The way it's worked in all of human society. Old growth makes way for new. It doesn't batten off the damn corpse. I've no quarrel with you, young sera, no quarrel with you. You didn't choose to be born. Where's Denys? Eh?" She looked around her, with a sweeping gesture of the cane. "Where's Denys?" There was an uncomfortable shifting in the crowd. "Sera," Florian whispered at Ari's shoulder, seeking instruction.

"I'll *tell* you where Denys is," Victoria snapped. *"Denys* is in the lab making another brother, the way he made another Ariane. *Denys* has taken the greatest scientific and economic power in human history and damned near run it into bankruptcy in his administration, —never mind poor Giraud, who took the orders, we all know that—damned near bankrupted us all for his eetee notion of personal immortality. You tell me, young sera, do you remember what Ariane remembered? Do you remember her life at all?"

God. It was certainly not something she wanted asked, here, now, in an argumentative challenge, in any metaphysical context. "We'll talk about that someday," she said back, loudly enough to carry. "Over a drink, aunt Victoria. I take it that's a *scientific* question, and you're not asking me about reincarnation."

"I wonder what Denys calls it," Victoria said. "Call your security if you like. I've been through enough craziness in my life, people blowing up stations in the War, people blowing up kids in subways, people who aren't content to let nature throw the dice anymore, people who don't want kids, they want little personal faxes they can live their fantasies through, never mind what the poor kid wants. Now do we give up on funerals altogether? Is that what everyone in the damn house is thinking, I don't have to die, I can impose my own ideas on a poor sod of a replicate who's got no say in it so I can have my ideas walking around in the world after I'm dead?"

"You're here to talk about Giraud," Yanni Schwartz yelled. "Do it and shut up, Vickie."

"I've done it. Goodbye to a human being. Welcome back, Gerry PR. God help the human race."

The rest of the speeches, thank God, were decorous—a few lines, a: *We differed, but he had principles*, from Petros Ivanov; a: *He kept Reseune going*, from Wendell Peterson.

It ascended to personal family then, always last to speak. To refute the rest, Ari decided, for good or ill.

"I'll tell you," she said in her own turn, in what was conspicuously her turn, last, as next-of-kin, Denys being exactly where Victoria had said he was, doing what Victoria had said, "—there was a time I hated my uncle. I think he knew that. But in the last few years I learned a lot about him. He collected holograms and miniatures; he loved microcosms and tame, quiet things, I think because in his real work there never was any sense of conclusion, just an ongoing flux and decisions nobody else wanted to make. It's not true that he only took orders. He consulted with Denys on policy; he implemented Bureau decisions; but he knew the difference between a good idea and a bad one and he never hesitated to support his own ideas. He was quiet about it, that's all. He got the gist of a problem and he went for solutions that would work.

"He served Union in the war effort. He did major work on human personality and on memory which is still the standard reference work in his field. He took over the Council seat in the middle of a national crisis, and he represented the interests of the Bureau for two very critical decades—into my generation, the first generation of Union that's not directly in touch with either the Founding or the War.

"He talked to me a lot in this last year: Abban made a lot of trips back and forth—" She looked to catch Abban's eye, but Abban was staring straight forward, in that nowhere way of an azi in pain. "—couriering messages between us. He knew quite well he was dying, of course; and as far as having a replicate, he didn't really care that much. We did talk about it, the way we talked about a lot of things, some personal, some public. He was very calm about it all. He was concerned about his brother. The thing that impressed me most, was how he laid everything out, how he made clear arrangements for everything—"

Never mind the mess Denys made of those arrangements.

"He operated during the last half year with a slate so clearly in order that those of us he was briefing could have walked into his office, picked up that agenda and known exactly where all the files were and exactly what had to be priority. He confessed he was afraid of dying. He certainly would have been glad to stay around another fifty years. He never expressed remorse for anything he'd done; he never asked my forgiveness; he only handed me the keys and the files and seemed touched that I did forgive him. That was the Giraud I knew."

She left it at that.

I have the files. That was deliberate, too. The way she had done with the press.

Not to undermine Lynch, damned sure. Denys refused the seat and someone had to hold it; Reseune was in profound shock. Certain people were urging Yanni to declare for the seat, challenge Lynch.

No, Denys had said, focused enough to foresee that possibility. No challenge to Lynch from anyone. He's harmless. Leave him.

What Yanni thought about it she was not sure. She did not think Yanni wanted that honor.

But Denys' refusal had jerked a chance at Reseune Administration out of Yanni's reach. And *that*, she thought, however much any of them in Reseune had suspected Denys would refuse the seat, that had to be a disappointment.

She made a point of going over to Yanni after the services, catching his arm, thanking him for his support and making sure the whole Family saw that.

Making sure that the whole Family knew Yanni was not out of the running in future, in her time. "I know what you're doing," she said fervently, careless of just who could hear, knowing some would. "Yanni, I won't forget. Hear?"

She squeezed his hand. Yanni gave her a look—as if he had not believed for a second it was more than a salve to his pride and then caught on that it was altogether more than that, in that subtle way such indicators passed in the Family.

Not a word said directly. But there were witnesses enough. And Yanni was profoundly affected.

Hers, she reckoned, when it came down to the line, in the same way Amy and Maddy and the younger generation were.

And others in the House would see the indicators plain, that she had declared herself on several fronts, and started making acquisitions, not on a spoils system for the young and upcoming, but for a passed-over senior administrator who enjoyed more respect in the House than he himself imagined.

Signal clearly that Yanni was hers and let Yanni collect his own following: Yanni took no nonsense and let himself be taken in by no one. *Yanni* had stripped his own daughter of authority when she had abused it, and favored no one except on merit: that was his reputation—when Yanni thought of himself as a simple hardnosed bastard.

Yanni had some reassessing to do. Figure on that.

Yanni was not going to be taken in by the bootlickers and the Stef Dietrichs in the House or elsewhere.

He had been one of maman's friends. She thought with some personal satisfaction, that maman would approve.

---

iv

She took the outside walk back to the House, around the garden wall, toward the distant doors: it was, thank God, quiet, after the pressure of the interviews. *Damn Victoria*, she thought, and reckoned that Maddy had wanted to sink out of sight.

"Do you wonder why we do such things?" she murmured to Florian and Catlin. "So do I."

They looked at her, one and the other. Catlin said, in Florian's silence: "It's strange when someone dies. You think they ought to be there. It was that way in Green Barracks."

Ari put her hand on Catlin's shoulder as they walked. Memories. Catlin was the one who had seen people die. "Not slowing down, are you?"

"No, sera," Catlin said. "*I* don't intend to be talked about."

She laughed softly. *Count on Catlin.*

Florian said nothing at all. Florian was the one who would have taken in every signal in the crowd; and work over it and work over it to make it make sense. Florian was the one who would worry about the living.

"He's gone," Ari said finally, at the doors. "Damn, that *is* strange." And looked at Florian, whose face had just gone quite tense, that listening-mode that said he was getting something attention-getting over the Security monitor. One or the other of them was always on-line.

"Novgorod," Florian said. "Jordan Warrick—has declared his innocence— He says—he was coerced. Reseune Security is issuing orders to place him in detention—"

Ari's heart jolted. But everything came clear then. "Florian," she said while they were going through the doors, "code J Red, go. We're on A; go for Q and we're Con2."

Make sure of Justin and Grant: Catlin and I are going for Denys; get home base secure and stay there; force permitted, but not as first resort.

That, before they were through the doors, while a Security guard whose com would not be set on that command-priority gave them a slightly puzzled look at their on-business split-and-go.

"They're not saying much," Catlin said as they went.

"Out to the news-services?"

"That, first," Catlin said. "Com 14 is loaded with incomings."

Reporters at the airport, at the edge of a major news event and hemmed in by an anxious, noncommunicative Security.

"Damn, is Denys on it? What in hell is he doing?"

Catlin tapped the unit in her ear. "Denys is still in the lab; Base One, relay Base Two transmission? —Affirmative, sera. He's sent word to defer all questions; he's saying the charges are a political maneuver, quote, ill-timed and lacking in human feeling. He says, quote, the Family is returning from the funeral and people are out of their offices: Reseune will have a further statement in half an hour."

"Thank God," she said fervently.

Denys was awake. Denys was returning fire.

Damned well about time.

V

It was a good day to stay home, Justin reckoned—given the situation in the House, given a general unsettled state in Security now that its chief was dead:

I don't want to be alarmist, Ari had said in a message left on the Minder, *but I'd be a lot easier in my mind if you and Grant didn't go anywhere you don't have to for the next few* days—*work at home if you can. I'm going to be busy; I can't watch everything; and Security is confused as hell—a little power struggle going on there. Do you mind? Feel free to attend the services. But stay where people are.*

I'll take your advice, he had messaged back. *Thank you. I know you have a lot to take care of right now. I don't think our presence at the services would be appropriate, or welcome to his friends; but if there should be anything Grant or I can do in the wing to take care of details, we're certainly willing to help.*

She had not asked anything of them—had more or less forgotten them, Justin reckoned, small wonder with the pressure she was under. The news was full of speculations about Denys' health, about the political consequences of Reseune yielding up the seat Reseune had held on Council since the Founding—about whether the Centrists could field a viable candidate inside Science, or whether Secretary and now Proxy Councillor Lynch had the personal qualifications to hold the party leadership which Giraud had held.

"There's nothing wrong with Denys' health," Grant objected, the two of them watching the news in the living room.

"I don't know what he's about," Justin said. And trusting then to the freedom Ari swore they had from monitoring: "But losing Giraud is a heavy blow to him. I think it's the only time I've ever felt sorry for Denys."

"They're doing that PR," Grant said; then: "Denys had to get Ari's backing, isn't that ironic as hell?"

"He's what—a hundred twenty-odd?—and that weight he carries doesn't favor him. He'd be lucky to see ten, fifteen more years. So he *has* to have Ari's agreement, doesn't he?"

"It's not going to work," Grant said.

Justin looked at Grant, who sat—they *had* found a scattering of red and blue pillows—in a nest at the corner of the couch, his red hair at odds with half of it.

"Denys *has* to set the pattern," Grant said, "has to give him that foundation or there's no hope for Giraud. I firmly think so. Yanni may have known their father in his old age, but Yanni's much too young to do for Giraud what Jane Strassen did—not mentioning how they've treated him—"

"He owes them damned little, that's sure enough."

"And there's always the question what's in and not in those notes Ari-younger got from her predecessor," Grant said. "I think Ari knows a lot she's not putting in those notes. I think *our* Ari is being very careful what she tells her guardians."

"Ari says sometimes—not everything was necessary."

"But whatever *is* necessary—is necessary," Grant said. "And Denys can't know—isn't in a position to know, that's what I think; and she's keeping it that way."

"The Rubin boy's going into chemistry, isn't he?"

"Fine student—test scores not spectacular, though."

"Yet."

Grant made a deprecating gesture. "No Stella Rubin. No one to tell him when to breathe. Hell is necessary for CITs, do we make that a given? You warned them not to let up on him too much—but the project is still using him for a control. Put the whole load on Ari; go easy on Ben Rubin; see what was necessary. . . . I'll bet you anything you like that Denys Nye had more to do with that decision than Yanni Schwartz did. *Yanni* never went easy on anyone."

"Except—Yanni's got a family attachment in the way. Rubin's suicide really got him, and Jenna Schwartz, remember, had some little thing to do with that. It could well be Yanni's going easy."

"But Rubin's still a control," Grant said. "And what he's proving—"

"What he's proving is, A, you can't do it with all genesets; B, some genesets respond well to stress and some don't—"

"Given, given, but in the two instances we have, —"

"And, C, there's bad match-ups between surrogate and subject. Don't discount the damage Jenna Schwartz did and the damage the contrast between Jenna Schwartz and Ollie Strassen did to the boy."

"Not to mention," Grant said, holding up a finger, "the fact Oliver AOX is male, and Alpha; and Stella Rubin is female and not that bright. I'd *like* to do a study on young Rubin. No edge to him, not near the flux swings. The instability goes with the suicide, goes with the brilliance—Among us, you know, they call it a flawed set."

"And do a fix for it."

"And lose the edge, just as often. —Which brings us back to young Ari, who's maybe given the committee all she knows—which I don't believe, if she's as much Ari as she seems, and our Ari—doesn't take chances with her security. I very much think access to those programs is a leverage of sorts—and do you know, I think Denys would have begun to guess that?"

Justin considered that thought, with a small, involuntary twitch of his shoulders. "The committee swears no one can retrieve from Ari's programs without Ari's ID. And possibly it's always been true."

"Possibly—more than that. Possibly that Base, once activated—can't be outmaneuvered in other senses. Possibly it's capable of masking itself."

"Lying about file sizes?"

"And invading other Bases—eventually. Built-in tests, parameters, —I've been thinking how I'd write a program like that . . . if she were azi. The first Ariane designed me. Maybe—" Grant made a little quirk of his mouth. "Maybe I have a—you'd say innate, but that's a mistake—in-*built* resonance with Ari's programs. I remember my earliest integrations. I remember—there was a—even for a child—*sensual* pleasure in the way things fit, the way the pieces of my understanding came together with such a precision. She was so very good. Do you think she didn't prepare for them to replicate her? Or that she'd be less careful with a child of her own sets, than with an azi of her design?"

Justin thought about it. Thought about the look on Grant's face, the tone of his voice—a man speaking about his father . . . or his mother. "Flux-thinking," he said. "I've wondered— Do you love her, Grant?"

Grant laughed, fleeting surprise. "*Love* her."

"I don't think it's impossible. I don't think it's at all unlikely."

"Reseune is my Contract and I can never get away from it?"

"Reseune is my Contract: I shall not want? —I'm talking about CIT-style flux. The kind that makes for ambivalences. Do you love her?"

A frown then. "I'm scared of the fact this Ari ran a probe. I'm scared because Ari's got the first Ari's notes—which include my manual, I'm quite sure. And what if—what if—This is my nightmare, Justin: what if—in my most fluxed imaginings, Ari planned for her successor; what if she planted something in me that would respond to her with the right trigger? —But then I flux back again and think that's complete nonsense. I'll tell you another nightmare: I'm scared of my own program tape."

Justin suffered a little sympathetic chill. "Because Ari wrote it."

Grant nodded. "I *don't* want to review it under trank nowadays. I know I could take enough kat to put me flat enough I could take it—but then I think—I can handle things without it. I can manage. I don't need it, God, CITs put up with the flux and they learn from it. And I do—learn from it, that is."

"I wish to hell you'd told me that."

"You'd worry. And there's no reason to worry. I'm fine—except when you ask me questions like that: *do I love Ari?* God, that's skewed. That's the first time I ever wondered about it in CIT terms. And you're right, there's a multi-level flux around her I don't like at all."

"Guilt?"

"Don't do that to me."

"Sorry. I just wondered."

Grant shifted position in the nest of pillows, against the arm. "Have you ever scanned my tape for problems?"

"Yes," Justin said after a little hesitation, a time-stretch of hesitation, that felt much too long and much too significant. "I didn't want to make it evident—I didn't want to worry you about it."

"I worry. I can't help but worry. It's too basic to me."

"You—worry about it."

Grant gave a small, melancholy lift of the brows, and seemed to ponder for a moment, raking a hand through his hair. "I think she asked something that jolted me—deep. I think I know where. I think she asked about my tape—which, admittedly, I have a small guilt about: I don't use it the way I'm supposed to; I think she asked about contact with subversives; and I dream about Winfield, lately. The whole scene out at Big Blue. The plane, and the bus with those men, and that room. . . ."

"Why didn't you tell me that?"

"Are dreams abnormal?"

"Don't give me that. Why didn't you tell me?"

"Because it's not significant. Because I know—when I'm not fluxed—that I'm all right. You want me to take the tape, I'll take it. You want to run a probe of your own—do it. I've certainly no apprehensions about that. Maybe you should. It's been a long time. Maybe I'd even feel safer if you did. —If,"

Grant added with a little tilt of the head, a sidelong glance, a laugh without humor. "If I didn't then wonder if *you* weren't off. You see? It's a mental trap."

"Because you got a chance to see Jordan. Because the damn place is crazy!" Of a sudden he felt a rush of frustration, an irrational concern so intense he got up and paced the length of the living room, looked back at Grant in a sudden feeling of walls closing in, of life hemmed around and impeded at every turn.

Not true, he thought. Things were better. Never mind that it was another year of separation from his father, another year gone, things no different than they had ever been—things were better in prospect, Ari was closer than she had ever been to taking power in her own right, and her regime, he sincerely believed it—promised change, when it would come.

They're burying Giraud today.

Why in hell does that make me afraid?

"I wish," Grant said, "you'd listened to me. I wish you'd gone to Planys instead."

"What difference? We'd have still been separate. We'd still worry—"

"What then? What's bothering you?"

"I don't know." He rubbed the back of his neck. "Being pent up in here, I think. This place. This—" He thought of a living room in beige and blue; and realized with a little internal shift-and-slide that it was not Jordan's apartment that had come back with that warm little memory. "God. You know where I wish we could go back to? *Our* place. The place—" Face in a mirror, not the one he had now. The boy's face. Seventeen and innocent, across the usual clutter of bottles on the bathroom counter, getting ready for an evening—

Tape-flash, ominous and chaotic. The taste of oranges.

"—before all this happened. That's useless, isn't it? I don't even want to be that boy. I only wish I was there knowing what I know now."

"It was good there," Grant said.

"I was such a damned fool."

"I don't think so."

Justin shook his head.

"I know differently," Grant said. "Put yourself in Ari's place. Wonder— what you would have been—on her timetable, with her advantages, with the things they did to her— You'd have been—"

"Different. Harder. Older."

"—someone else. Someone else entirely. CITs are such a dice-throw. You're so unintentionally cruel to each other."

"Do you think it's necessary? Can't we learn without putting our hand in the fire?"

"You're asking an azi, remember?"

"I'm *asking* an azi. Is there a way to get an Ariane Emory out of that geneset—or me—out of mine—"

"Without the stress?" Grant asked. "Can flux-states be achieved intellectually—when they have endocrine bases? Can tape-fed stress—short of the actual chance of breaking one's neck—be less real, leave less pain—than the real experience? What if that tape Ari made—were only tape? What if it had never happened—but you thought it had? Would there be a difference? What if Ari's maman had never died, but she thought she had? Would she be sane? Could she trust reality? I don't know. I truly don't know. I would hate to discover that everything until now—was tape; and I was straight from the Town, having dreamed all this."

"God, Grant!"

Grant turned his left wrist to the light, where there was always, since the episode with Winfield and the Abolitionists, a crosswise scar. "This is real. Unless, of course, it's only something my makers installed with the tape."

"That's not good for you."

Grant smiled. "That's the first time in years you've called me down. Got you, have I?"

"Don't joke like that."

"I have no trouble with reality. I *know* tape when I feel it. And remember I'm built right side up, with my logic sets where they belong, thank you, my makers. But flux is too much like dreams. Tape-fed flux—would have no logical structure. Tape-fed flux is too much like what Giraud did in the War, which I don't even like to contemplate—building minds and unbuilding them; mindwiping and reconstruction . . . always, always, mind you, with things the subject can't go back to check; and a lot left to the imagination. I honestly don't know, Justin. If there's a key to taping those experiences— *Giraud* could have had some insight into it, isn't that irony?"

It made some vague, bizarre sense, enough to send another twitch down his back, and a feeling of cold into his bones.

"Talking theory with Giraud—" But Giraud was dead. And yet-to-be. "It wasn't something we ever got around to."

"The question is, essentially, whether you can substitute tape for reality. I'm very capable, Justin; but I sweated blood on that flight to Planys, I was so damned helpless during the whole trip. *That's* what you give up: survivability in the real world."

Justin snorted. "You think I don't worry."

"But you could learn *much* more rapidly. Back to the old difference: you flux-learn; I logic my way through. And no aggregate of CITs is logical. Got you again."

Justin thought about it; and smiled finally, in the damnable gray apartment, in the elegant prison Ari appointed them. For a moment it felt like home. For a moment he remembered that it was safer than anywhere they had been since that fondly-remembered first apartment.

Then the apprehension came back again, the great stillness over Reseune, deserted halls, everything in flux.

There was sudden break-up on the vid, the news commentary thrown off in mid-word.

The Infinite Man appeared on screen. Music played. One never worried about such things. Someone kicked a cable, and Reseune's whole vid-system glitched.

Except it was also something Reseune Security did, for selected apartments, selected viewers.

My God, he thought, a sudden rush of worry, lifelong habit. *Were they monitoring? Have they gotten through her security? What could they have heard?*

---

vi

"Uncle Denys," Ari had relayed on the way, via Base One and Catlin's com unit, "I need to talk to you right away."

"Lab office," Seely had relayed back.

Shocked looks followed them through the labs from the time they had entered, techs who knew that things were already Odd with Denys, azi who were reading the techs if not the situation, and worried as hell; and now an unexplained break-in of conspicuous Family coming straight from the funeral, in mourning, and headed for lab offices at high speed—small wonder the whole lab stopped and stared, Ari thought; and at least she could freely admit to knowing as much as she knew, excepting what Planys was doing.

Past the tanks, the techs, the very place where she had been born, where likely by now half a dozen Giraud's were in progress—up the little stairs with the metal rail, to the small administrative office Denys had commandeered: Seely was evidently keeping a look-out through the one-way glass of the lab offices, because Seely opened the door to let them in before she had made the final turn of the steps.

Denys was behind the desk, on the phone—with Security, by what it sounded. Ari collected herself with a breath. "That's fine," she said, when Catlin whisked a chair to her back; she took off her gloves and her jacket, gave them to Catlin and sat down as Denys hung up the phone.

"Well, sera," Denys said, "we have the result of your baulking Security at Planys."

"Where is Jordan?"

"Under arrest at Planys. He and his companion. Damn him!"

"Mmmn, *Justin* is accounted for."

"Are you certain?"

"Quite. *Justin* is the one I want to talk to you about."

"Ser," Florian said when they had let him in, Florian in House uniform and without his coat, so Florian and therefore probably Ari had had time, Justin reckoned, to come in next door first.

But it made him anxious that it was not a call over the Minder, or a summons to Ari's apartment or her offices, just a Minder-call at the door, Florian asking entry.

And the vid still showed nothing on the news channel except that single logo.

"There's been an incident," Florian said, preface, and in the half-second of Florian's next breath: *O God*, Justin thought, *something's happened to Ari*; and was bewildered in the same half-second, that the fear included her, her welfare, which was linked with their own. "Your father," Florian said, and fears jolted altogether into another track, "—has gotten a message to the Centrists, claiming innocence."

"Of *what?*" Justin asked, still tracking on *incident*, not making sense of it.

"Of killing Dr. Emory, ser."

He stood there, he did not know how long, in a state of shock, wanting to think so, wanting to think—

—*but, my God, during Giraud's funeral—what's he doing? What's going on?*

"We don't know all the details yet," Florian said. "Sera doesn't want to admit to ser Denys just how far her surveillance extends, please understand that, ser, but she does know that your father is safe at the moment. She's asking you, please, ser, understand that there's extreme danger—to you, to her, to your father, no matter whether this is true or false: the announcement has political consequences that may be very dangerous, I don't know if I need explain them. . . ."

"God." *Ari's safety. Everything*— He raked a hand through his hair, felt Grant's hand on his shoulder. Florian—seemed older, somehow, his face utterly without the humor that was so characteristic of him, like a mask dropped, finally, time sent reeling. . . . *Could it be true?*

"She wants you to pack a small bag, ser. Sera's interim staff is on the way up to this floor, and sera asks Grant to stay here and put himself under their orders. . . ."

"Pack for *where?*"

Separate us? God, no.

"Sera wants you to go with her to Novgorod—to defuse this matter. To speak to the press. She wants to take the politics out of the question—for your father's sake, as much as her own. Do you understand, ser? There'll be a small question-and-answer at Reseune airport; that's safest. She's asking a meeting with Councillor Corain and Secretary Lynch. She earnestly hopes you won't fail her in this—"

"My God. God, Grant—" *What do I do?*

But Grant had no answers. *CITs are all crazy*, Grant would say.

Ari's out of her mind. Take me to Novgorod? They don't dare.

They need me. That's the game. My father under arrest. They want me to call him a liar.

Reseune Security doesn't need to kill him. They can use drugs. It takes time. Time I can buy them to operate on him—

Would Ari—do this to us?

Would Florian be here without her orders?

In front of those cameras—if I get that far— How can they stop me from any charges I can make?

Grant.

Grant—being here, in Ari's keeping. That's what they're offering me— Grant's sanity—or my father's.

He looked up into Grant's face—far calmer, he thought, than his own, Grant's un-fluxed logic probably understanding there was no choice in his own situation.

I have faith in my makers.

"Grant comes with me," he said to Florian.

"No, ser," Florian said. "I have definite instructions. Please, pack just the essentials. Everything will be inspected. Grant will be safe here, with sera Amy. There will be Security: Quentin AQ is very competent, and sera Amy will have her friends for help here. No way will any general Security come onto this floor or interfere with the systems. No way will sera Amy do anything to harm Grant."

A gifted eighteen-year-old, with a thin, earnest face and a tendency to go at problems head-on: an eighteen-year-old who, he had always thought, liked him and Grant. Honest. And sensible as an eighteen-year-old had any likelihood of being.

God, they *all* were. "It's a damn Children's Crusade," he said, and caught Grant's arm. "Do what they say. It'll be all right."

"No," he said in front of the cameras, in the lounge at Reseune airport. "No, I haven't been in contact with my father. I hope to get a call through— when we get to Novgorod. It's the middle of their night. They—" He tried, desperately, not to look nervous: *Don't look guilty,* Ari had said, before they left the bus. *Don't look like you're hiding anything. You can be very frank with them, but for God's sake think about the political ramifications when you do it. Be very careful about making charges of your own, they can only muddy things up, and we have to rely on uncle Denys—we can't offend him, hear me?*

"My father—is in Detention at the moment," he said, finding the pace of things too much, the dark areas too extensive. The truth seemed easier to sort out than lies were, if one kept it to a minimum. "All I can tell you—" No. *Can* meant dangerous things. "All I know how to tell you—is that there's an inquiry. My father told me—at the time it happened—exactly what he told the Council. But there were things going on at the time—that might have been a reason. That's why I'm going to Novgorod. I don't know—Ari herself doesn't know—who's telling the truth now. I want to find out. Reseune Administration wants to find out."

"I can assure you," Ari said, beside him, "I have a very strong motive for wanting to know the truth in this case."

"Question for Dr. Warrick. Are you presently under any coercion?"

"No," Justin said firmly.

"You are a PR. Are you—in any way—more than that?"

He shook his head. "Standard PR. Nothing extraordinary."

"Have you ever been subject to intervention?"

He had not expected that question. He froze on it, then said: "Psychprobe is an intervention. I was part of the investigation. There were a lot of them." They would question his sanity for that reason; and his reliability. He knew that. It would cast doubt on his license for clinical practice and cast a shadow on his research. He knew that too. The whole thing took on a nightmarish quality, the lights, the half-ring of reporters. He became quite placid, quite cold. "There was an illicit intervention when I was a minor. I've been treated for that. I'm not presently under drugs; I'm not operating under anyone's intervention. I'm concerned about my father and I'm anxious to get to Novgorod and answer whatever questions Council may have: I'm most concerned about my father's welfare—"

"Is he threatened in any way?"

"Ser, I don't know as much as you do. I'm anxious to talk with him. For one thing, I want to be sure what he did say—"

"You're casting doubt on his statement through Councillor Corain, as valid, or as coming from him."

"I want to be sure that he did send that message. I want to hear it from him. There are a lot of unanswered questions. I can't tell you what you want to know. I don't know."

"Sera Emory. Do you know?"

"I have ideas," Ari said, "but I'm being very careful of them. They involve people's reputations—"

"Living people?"

"Living and dead. Please understand: we're in the middle of a funeral. We've had charges launched and questions asked that depend on records deep in Archive, about things that are personal to me and personal to Justin—" She reached and laid her hand on his, clenched it. "We had come to our own peace with what happened. Justin's my friend and my teacher, and now we wonder what did happen all those years ago, and why Justin's father wouldn't have told *him* the truth, if there was more to it. We don't understand, either one of us. That's why we're going outside Reseune. We're going to handle this at the Bureau level—at Council level, since they're the ones who did the first investigation, if we have to go that far. But it's not appropriate for us to investigate this on a strictly internal level. Dr. Warrick has made charges; they need to be heard in the Bureau. That's where we're going—and I think we ought to get underway, seri, thank you. Please. We'll have more statements later."

"Dr. Warrick," a journalist shouted. "Do you have any statement?"

Justin looked at the man, blank for a fraction of a second until he realized that Dr. Warrick was the way the world knew him. "Not at the moment. I've told you everything I know."

Florian touched him as he got up, showed him a route through to the boarding area, for the plane that waited for them. *RESEUNE ONE.*

A solid phalanx of regular Security made a passage for them, an abundance of Security that clearly said: This is official; Administration is involved.

It answered to Ari. Giraud was a wisp of ash and a group of cells trying to achieve humanity; and meanwhile Ariane Emory was in charge, with all the panoply of Reseune's authority around her.

He went quickly through the doors, and down the corridor into the safeway and into the plane, where he stopped in confusion, until Florian took him by the arm and guided him to one of a group of leather seats, and settled him in.

"Would you like a drink, ser?"

"Soft drink," he said, while Ari was settling in opposite him, while the plane was starting engines and more Security was boarding.

"Vodka-and-orange," Ari said. "Thank you, Florian." And looking straight at him: "Thank *you*," she said. "You handled that very well."

He gazed back at her in a virtual state of shock, thoughts darting in panic to the Security around him, the fear that one of them could simply pull a gun and spray the cabin; fear for Grant back in the apartment, that, no matter what Florian said about general Security not having admittance to that level, an eighteen-year-old girl was in charge, along with a Security guard no older than she was, and anything could happen; fear that something might be happening with Jordan; or that Paxer lunatics might somehow have rigged a missile that could take the plane out of the sky—

There was not a damned thing he could do, except say what he was supposed to say, trust . . . God, that was the hard part. Let go all the defenses, do whatever Ari told him, and hope that another eighteen-year-old knew better than he did how to handle the situation.

"I was seventeen," he said to Ari, quietly, while the engines were warming up, "when I thought I knew what I was doing well enough to send Grant to Krugers. You *know* what that came to."

Ari snapped her seat buckle across, and reached up to take the drink Catlin handed her. "Warning taken. I know. But sometimes there aren't any choices, are there?"

vii

RESEUNE ONE made cruising altitude, and Ari took a sip of her drink and checked the small unit she had clipped to her chair arm, remote for the more complex electronics in the briefcase in its safety rack beside her seat, the first time she had ever carried it. She pushed the check button. It flashed a reassuring positive and beeped at her.

System up, link functioning.

Across from her, in his seat beside Justin, Florian nodded to her smile and nod at him. Florian had done the updating into the code system—of course it worked; and worked, so long as she made no queries, as a very thorough observer in Reseune's state-of-the-art net, simply picking up on all her flagged items and routing them to her as they came up in the flow.

Not even Defense had cracked that code-upon-code jargonesque flow Reseune Security used: one hoped.

Ari picked up her drink again and leaned back. "Everything's all right," she said to Justin. "No troubles we don't know about, and we're picking up our Bureau escort in about five minutes."

Justin looked from the window at his right toward her, truly looked at her, eye to eye across the low table that divided the seats. He had darted glances toward every movement in the plane, tense as Florian or Catlin when they were On; he was tracking even on the working of the plane's hydraulics, and the light from the window touched taut muscle in his jaw, mature lines of worry set into his brow and around his mouth: the years had touched him, no matter the rejuv. *He worries so much,* she thought. *He's too smart to trust anyone. Certainly not Reseune. Now, not even his father. He'll doubt Grant himself if he's gone too long.*

That's what he's trying to figure out—trying to estimate where I am in this, and whether Grant is safe, and how much I'm a young fool and how much I've got him fluxed and how much he can believe now of anything I say or do.

I'm not the kid he knew. He's begun to figure that; and he's started to wonder when it happened, and how far it's gone, and who was working on him while he was under kat. He's scared—and embarrassed about being scared of me; but he knows he has every right to be afraid now.

The brain has to rule the flux, Ari-elder; I think I've finally understood what you mean. Whether he slept with me or not, I'd have come round to this, I do think I would: you didn't bring up a fool, Ari-elder. Neither did maman and my uncles.

Ollie doesn't write because he values his neck, that's the truth. This universe is dangerous, and Ollie's just as upset as Grant is back there, alone, with strangers. He's trusted nothing since maman died. He works for Reseune Administration.

"We can talk now," she said, with a slide of her eyes toward the rear of the plane where the regular Security people sat. The engine noise was as good as any Silencer, given that Security did not have any unreported electronics back there; but the carry-bag at Florian's feet had its own array of devices, which one had to trust was up to what Florian vowed it was—and Florian's Base One clearance was quite adequate for him to find out whether it was up to date.

"An explanation would do," Justin said. "What are you doing?"

"I'd be ever so happy if I knew. I'm not choosing the timing on this. I'm afraid Councillor Corain is and it's not like him. I'm afraid the information has gotten to someone else, like Khalid, and he had to jump fast to be first—which is why it came out in the middle of the funeral, not tonight."

Justin looked taken off his balance. "You know about things like that. I'm sure I don't."

"You *know*, Justin, you know damn well, you just haven't had uncle Giraud's briefings; and it *still* caught us. Giraud knew there was a leak. He knew what your father would say; he warned me what your father would say if he got a chance. The question isn't even whether it's true. Let's assume it is."

He was going to slip her, she saw it coming, and she maintained his attention with an uplifted finger, exactly, *exactly* Ari senior's mannerism: she knew it. "*What* does it do for your father?"

"It gets him the hell out of Planys. It gets him clean, dammit, it gets him his standing with the Bureau—"

"All of which I'm not averse to—in my own time. My own time isn't now. It can't be now. *Think* about it, Justin; you can handle Sociology equations. Try this one, try this one near-term, like the next few years—tell me what's going to happen and what's going to result from it. *That's* first. That's the thing that matters. What does it do to him, what's going to happen? Second question: where does he stand, where does he think he stands, what side has he just taken—and don't tell me your father's naive, *no* one in Reseune is naive, just under-briefed."

He said nothing. But he was thinking, deep and seriously, *on* what she had said, and around the peripheries: who am I dealing with, what is she up to, has Denys choreographed this business? He was much too smart to take anything at one level.

"Did you leak it to Corain?" he asked.

Oh. That *was* a good one. It jolted a thought loose. "*I* didn't. But, God, Denys might have, mightn't he?"

"Or Giraud," Justin said.

She drew a long breath and leaned back. "Interesting thought. Very interesting thought."

"Maybe it's the truth. Maybe whoever leaked it is in a position to know it's the truth."

Florian was interested: Florian was watching Justin with utmost attention. She reckoned that Catlin was. God, Ari thought, and found herself smiling. He's not down, is he? I *see* how he's survived.

"Easier to answer that," she said, "if I had an idea what happened that night, but there's no evidence. I thought there might have been a Scriber record. There was just the TranSlate. There's nothing there. The sniffers were useless; there'd been too many people in and out before they thought about it. Psychprobe would have been the only way. And that didn't happen. And won't. It doesn't matter. Giraud talked about 'the Warrick influence.' Giraud made an enemy. Now what do we do about that enemy?"

A slower man, an emotional man, would have blurted out: *Let him go.* She sat watching Justin think, relatively sure of some of the tracks—the fact that Jordan's name was in Paxer graffiti; that Jordan's ideas had opposed her predecessor; that there was one election shaping up in Science and another virtually certain in Defense, both critical, both of which, if the Centrists won—could destroy Reseune, shift the course of history, jeopardize all Reseune's projects, and all her purposes. . . .

Perhaps three, four, minutes he sat there, deep focused and calm as kat could have sent him. Then, in with careful control:

"Have *you* run the projections of Jordan's input?"

She drew breath, as if one of a dozen knots about her chest had loosed.

There is *an echo*, she thought, imagining that dark place, that floating-in-null place. She took her own time answering. "Field too large," she said finally. "*I* don't aim at him. I want him safe. The problem is—he's quite intelligent, quite determined, and even if he didn't leak that message—what's he going to do if he gets in front of the news cameras? What's he going to do to every plan for solving this that I could have come up with?"

"I can solve it. Give me fifteen minutes on the phone with him."

"There's still a problem. He won't believe a word of it. Giraud said it: that tape was an intervention. Your father saw it—"

He reacted to that as if it had hit in the gut.

"You haven't," she said, "have you? Ever. You don't know what Ari did. You should have asked to see it. You should have gone over that damned thing as often as it took. It fluxed me too, fluxed me so I wasn't thinking straight: it took Giraud to point out the obvious. If *I* could see what Ari did, so could your father. Your father didn't see it as a seventeen-year-old kid, your father saw it as a psychsurgeon who had to wonder exactly how often and how deep Ari's interventions had been. He had to wonder how far they'd gone. You and Grant worry about each other when you've been separate three days. I know. You know they can't run an intervention on Jordan—but don't you think he has to wonder—after twenty years—just whose you are?"

Justin leaned forward and picked up his drink from the table, breathing harder: she marked the flare of his nostrils, the intakes and the quick outflow. And the little body moves that said he wanted out of that round. "Florian," he said, "would you mind terribly—I think I'd like something stronger."

She could read Florian too, instant suspicion: Florian distrusted such little distracting tactics, with thoughts engendered of lifelong training. He was not about to turn his back on an Enemy.

"Florian," she said, "his usual."

Florian met her eyes, nodded deferentially then and got up, not even looking at Catlin, who sat beside her: there was no question that Catlin was on, and hair-triggered.

"You can talk to your father," she said to Justin, "but I doubt he's believed you entirely for years. Not—entirely. He *knows* you were psychprobed, over and over again; and he doesn't believe in Reseune's virtue. If you try to reason with him—I'm afraid what he's going to think, do you see? And I'm not just saying that to get at you, Justin, I'm *afraid* what he's going to think, and I don't think you can do anything to stop him, not with reason."

"You forget one thing," he said, leaning back against his seat.

"What's that?"

"The same thing that keeps Grant and me alive. That past a certain point you don't care. Past a certain point—" He shook his head, and looked up as Florian brought the drink back. "Thank you."

"No problem, ser." Florian sat down.

"If he gets into public," Ari took up the thread of thought, "he can do himself harm, he can do me harm, of course—which I don't want. It's possible that your father has been psychologically—very isolate, for a very long time: insular and insulated from all the problems going on in the world. If he was protecting you against the release of that tape—which may be a real motive for him lying until now—he evidently believes you're capable of handling it or he's been told something by someone that makes him desperate enough to risk you as well as himself—*if* that message actually came from him, which is a question . . . but it doesn't really matter. What he'll do—that matters. And we have an image problem in all this mess, you understand me?"

Justin *was* understanding her, she thought so by the little motions of his eyes, the tensions in his face. "What is there to do?" he said. "You've left Grant back there; I don't know what they're doing to my father at Planys—"

"Nothing. They're not going to do anything to him."

"Can you guarantee that?"

She hesitated awhile over that answer. "That depends," she said. "That very much depends. That's why you're with me. *Someone* has to do something. I'd wanted to be inconspicuous for a while more, but I'm the only face the media knows and I'm the only one who has enough credit with them to patch this mess up—but I need you, I need your help. Possibly you'll double on me. I don't know. But whether it's true or false what they're saying, it's going to be terribly hard for your father to handle this or to back away from the cameras if he gets the chance. You're my hope of stopping that."

Another small silence. Then: "How did you get Denys's permission for this move?"

"The same way I've gotten you into my residency. I told Denys you're mine, that I ran a major intervention, that Grant is far more of a hold on you than your father is; that you'd choose him over your father if it came to a choice, because your father can take care of himself; while Grant—" She shrugged. "That kind of thing. Denys believes it."

That got through to him, just about enough threat to make sure he understood. Justin sat there staring at her, mad, very mad. And very worried. "You're quite an operator, young sera."

The compliment made her smile, though sadly. "Giraud died too soon. The Paxers aren't going to sit still in all this commotion. The elections are going to be chaos, there may be more bombings, more people dead—the whole thing is going to blow wide if we don't head it off. You know all of that. Your work is exactly in my field. That's one thing at stake. So you can put your father in a position where he has to do something desperate and put himself out front of something he can't control and I don't think he has any idea exists; or you can help me defuse this, calm him down and let me run a little game with Denys—put your father wise to it if you can, I don't mind; encourage your father to wait until I *do* run Reseune. We can double-team Denys, or you can blow everything to hell with the newsservices—by asking to get your father in front of the cameras; by doing things that make you look like you're under duress—"

"The truth, you mean."

"—or by doing things that give you a bad image. You can't look like a traitor to your own father. You're very good with bright people and design-systems; but you don't know where the traps are, you're not current with the outside world, you're not used to the press and you're not used to picking up on your own public image. For God's sake take advice and be careful. If you get stubborn about this you can lose every leverage you've got."

He stared at her a long time, and sipped his whiskey. "Tell me," he said finally, "exactly what sort of thing I should watch out for."

Grant watched, entranced by the precision, as the cards crackled into a precise shuffle in the girl's fingers. "That's amazing," he said.

"This?" Sera Amy looked pleased and did it again. "My mother taught me, God, I guess from the time my fingers were big enough." She shot a series of cards to her and to him. Quentin AQ was the silent presence in the room, a tall, well-built young man in Security uniform, who sat and watched—a young man altogether capable of breaking a neck in a score of different ways: Grant had no illusions about his chances if he made a move crosswise of Amy Carnath. He had looked to spend the time confined to his room at best and under trank or under restraint at worst; but young sera had instead made every attempt to reassure him: *It won't take long, they'll meet with the Bureau, I don't doubt they'll have everything straightened out in a couple of days*: and she had finally, after a mid-afternoon lunch, declared that she would teach him to play cards.

He was touched and amused. Young Amy was taking her recently-acquired Alpha license very seriously, and doing outstandingly well: the game did keep his mind off what, if he were half-tranked and locked in solitude, would have been absolute hell—a situation which was still hell, what time he let himself worry whether the plane had landed yet, whether Justin was safe, what was going on with Jordan in Planys.

He wished he were on that plane; but he figured he was actually doing more good for Justin as a hostage, being civil and cool-headed and not pouring fuel on the fires of juvenile excitement—or Administration paranoia.

Poker was also an interesting game, in which Amy said an azi had two considerable advantages, first, profound concentration, and second, the ability to conceal one's reactions. Sera was right. He very much wanted to try it with Justin.

When Justin got home.

It was the little thoughts like that, that sent panic rushing through him, with the thought that something could happen, that somehow an order could come through that sera Amy could not resist or that authorities elsewhere could take Justin into custody; and, Reseune holding his Contract, they might not meet again. Ever.

Then he might not sit placidly waiting for re-training. Then he might do something incredibly unlikely for an azi designer, and get his hands on a weapon: in a very fluxed way it seemed what a CIT might do and what was the best thing to do. At other moments—he was fluxing that wildly—he knew that his own personal CIT might fight to be free, but he would never turn a weapon on sera Amy, nor on Quentin AQ, and that Justin could never—he had told the truth to ser Denys—never harm any of the people who had harmed him. His CIT might threaten with a weapon, but pull the trigger—Justin could not, not even if it was Giraud, who was dead anyway.

No, when it came to it, Grant thought, studying the hand young sera had dealt him—he could not see himself surrendering to the hospital; but he could not see himself shooting to kill, either.

Young Amy told him that the secret of the game she was teaching him was to keep one's intentions and one's predicaments off one's face. Young Amy was very intelligent, and quite good at it herself, for a CIT. Possibly she was playing more than one game and trying to read more than what cards he held, the same way he was trying to read her for more information than she was willing to give.

So meanwhile he gambled for small markers, because one was supposed to play for money, but he owned none that was not Justin's; and he would not risk that, even at the minuscule levels young Amy proposed. He risked nothing that was Justin's, was very glad to have enough liberty in the apartment to know that Justin's papers were safe, and generally to catch what bits of information he could . . . dumb-annie was a role he still knew how to play. *I'll be all right*, Justin had said to him. And after all was said and done, he had to rely on that, like any azi—while he kept fluxing on Winfield and the Abolitionists and the fact that at thirty-seven he was legally a minor; and Amy Carnath at eighteen was legally an adult. *Dammit*, he wanted to shout at her, *take advice. Tell me what's going on and listen to someone with more experience than you have.*

But that was not likely to happen. Amy Carnath took Ari Emory's orders; and whether it was Denys Nye or Ari Emory managing things now—he could not at all figure.

viii

The airport stirred boyhood memories, himself in the terminal gift shop, begging a few cred-chits from Jordan for trinkets and gifts for home: Justin thought of that as they walked the safeway from the plane to the Novgorod terminal, with armed Security going ahead of them and crowding close behind.

No passage through the public terminal: Ari had explained that; no transfer to a car in the open. Things were too dangerous nowadays. They took a side door, hurried downstairs to a garage where cars waited with shielded windows.

There Security laid hands on him and took him apart from Ari and Catlin and Florian. Ari had warned him it would happen and asked him to do exactly what Security told him, but they were damned rough, and their haste and their force getting him into the car was more than it need have been.

He kept his mouth shut about it, sandwiched in between two guards in the back seat, and with a heavy hand on his shoulder as the doors locked.

Then the man let go of him and he settled back, watching as the first few cars left the garage. Their own driver joined the tight convoy, whisking out past *RESEUNE ONE*'s wing, along the edge of the field and out a guarded gate where they picked up more escort.

It was the sort of official protection, he thought, that must have attended Giraud Nye in these troubled years. He sat between the hard-muscled bodies of two of Reseune's senior House Security, with another, armed, in the front-seat passenger side, and one driving. He watched the road unfold to the river, the bridge and the drive—he remembered it—which led up to the government center, green crops growing in the interstices, a handful of trees which had prospered in the years since he had ridden this road at Jordan's side, taking the tour—

The Hall of State loomed up around a turn, suddenly filling the wind-shield; and he felt a chill and a sense of panic. "Aren't we going to the Bureau?" he asked his guards quietly, calmly. "I thought we were going to the Science Bureau."

"We follow the car in front of us," the one on the left said.

He figured that much. Damn, he thought, and sat and watched, wishing he had Grant's ability to go Out awhile. He wanted this day done with. He wanted—

God, he wanted to go home.

He wanted a phone, and a chance to talk to Jordan, and to find out the truth, but the truth, Ari had said it, was the least important thing.

He was numb, in overload, total flux. He tried to find answers and there was no information to give them to him, except the ones Ari herself led him through, bringing order where none existed—or finding the only way through, he did not know any longer. He had found himself agreeing to lie to the press, agreeing to deny his father's innocence—to which he himself could not swear—

He found himself doubting Jordan, doubting Jordan's motives, Jordan's love for him, everything in the world but Grant. Doubting his own sanity, finally, and the integrity of his own mind.

Not even Giraud did this to me. Not even Giraud.

Flux of images, the older Ari, the younger; flux of remembered panic, interview in Ari's office:

. . . *You make my life tranquil, sweet, and stand between me and Jordan, and I won't have his friends arrested, and I won't do a mindwipe on Grant, I'll even stop giving you hell in the office. You know what the cost is, for all those transfers you want.* . . .

. . . *I told Denys you're mine, that I ran a major intervention, that Grant is far more of a hold on you than your father is; that you'd choose him over your father if it came to a choice.* . . .

The convoy drew up under the portico at the side of the Hall of State. He moved when his guards flung the door open and hastened him out and through the doors—not so roughly this time: this time there were news cameras.

Ari stopped and took his arm. The thought flashed through his mind that he could shove her away, refuse to go farther, tell the cameras everything that had happened to him, shout out the fact that Reseune was holding Grant hostage, that they had worked on him to divide him from his father, that Jordan might well have spent twenty years in confinement for a lie—

He hesitated, Ari tugging at his arm, someone nudging him from behind.

"We're going to meet with Secretary Lynch," Ari said, "upstairs. Come on. We'll talk to the press later."

"Is your father innocent?" someone shouted at him out of the echoing chaos.

He looked at that reporter. He tried to think, in the time-stretch of nightmare, whether he even knew the answer or not, and then just ignored the question, going where Ari wanted him to go, to say whatever he had to say.

"You do this one alone," Ari told him when they reached the upstairs, turning him over to Bureau Enforcement. "I'll be getting the hearing on monitor, but nobody from Reseune will be there. The Bureau wants you not to feel pressured. All right?"

So he walked with blue-uniformed strangers still of Reseune's making, taught by Reseune's tapes—who brought him into a large conference room, and brought him to a table facing a triple half-ring of tables on a dais, where other strangers took their seats in a blurred murmur of conversation—

Strangers except Secretary-now-Proxy for Science Lynch: Lynch he knew from newscasts. He settled into his chair, grateful to find at least one known quantity in the room, at the head of the committee, he supposed. There was a pitcher of water in front of him, and he filled a glass and drank, trying to soothe his stomach. Ari's staff had offered him food on the plane, but he had not been able to eat more than the chips and a bite of the sandwich; and he had had another soft drink after the whiskey. Now he felt light-headed and sick. Damn fool, he told himself in the dizzying buzz of people talking in a large room, quit sleepwalking. Wake up and focus, for God's sake, they'll think you're drugged.

But the flux kept on, every thought, every nuance of everything Jordan had last said to him; everything Ari had said that might be a clue to what was going on or whether the threat was threat or only show for Denys and Security.

Secretary Lynch came up to the table where he was sitting, and offered his hand. Justin stood up and took it, felt the kindness in the gesture, saw a face that had been only an image on vid take on a human concern for him; and that small encouragement hit him in the gut, he did not know why.

"Are you all right?" the Secretary-Proxy asked.

"A little nervous," he said; and felt Lynch's fingers close harder on his. A little pat on his arm. Giraud's career-long associate, he suddenly remembered that with a jolt close to nausea, and felt the whole room go distant, sounds echoing in his skull in time with the beating of his heart. *Where does Ari stand with him? Is this choreographed?*

"You're inside Bureau jurisdiction now," Lynch said. "No Reseune staff is here. Three Councillors are in the city: they've asked to audit the proceedings: Chairman Harad, Councillor Corain; Councillor Jacques. Is there any other witness you want? Or do you have any objection to anyone here? You understand you have a right to object to members of the inquiry."

"No, ser."

"Are you all right?" It was the second time Lynch had asked. Justin drew in a breath and disengaged his hand.

"Just a little—" *Light-headed. No. God, don't say that.* He thought his face must be white. He felt the air-conditioning on sweat at his temples. "I was too nervous to eat. I don't suppose I could get a soft drink before we start. Maybe crackers or something."

Lynch looked a little nonplussed; and then patted his shoulder and called an aide.

Like a damned kid, he thought. Fifteen minutes, a pastry and a cup of coffee, that little time to catch his breath in an adjoining conference room, and he was better collected—was able to walk back into the hearing room and have Secretary Lynch walk him over to Mikhail Corain and to Simon Jacques and Nasir Harad one after the other, faces he recognized in what still passed in a haze of overload, but a less shaky one: God, he was fluxed. He had had nightmares about publicity, lifelong, felt himself still on the verge of panic—still kept flashing on Security—the cell—the Council hearings. . . .

Giraud's voice, saying things he could not remember, but which put a profound dread in him.

Wake *up*, dammit! No more time for thinking. Do!

"Dr. Warrick," Corain said, taking his hand. "A pleasure to meet you, finally."

"Thank you, ser."

When did that message actually come from my father? That was what he wanted to ask.

But he did not, not being a fool. *Audit*, Lynch had said: then the Councillors were not here to engage in questions.

"If you need anything," Corain said, "if you feel you need protection—you understand you can ask for it."

"No, ser. —But I appreciate your concern." *This is a man who wants to use Jordan. And me. What am I worth to him? Where would his protection leave me?*

Out of Reseune. And Grant inside.

Corain patted him on the arm. Simon Jacques offered his hand, introducing himself, a dark-haired, neutral kind of man with a firm grip and a tendency not to meet his eyes. "Councillor. . . . Chairman Harad." —as he shook Harad's thin hand, meeting a gray stare appallingly cold and hostile. *One of Reseune's friends.*

"Dr. Warrick," Harad said. "I hope you can clear up some of the confusion in this. Thank you for agreeing to appear."

"Yes, ser," he said. *Agreeing to appear. Who asked me? Who agreed in my name? How many things have gone out, in my name, and Jordan's?*

"Dr. Warrick," Lynch said, taking his arm. "If we can get this underway—"

He took his seat at the table; he answered questions: No, I have no way of knowing anything beyond my father's statements. He never discussed the matter with me, beyond the time—just before the hearing. When he was leaving. No, I'm not under drugs; I'm not under coercion. I'm confused and I'm worried. I think that's a normal reaction under the circumstances. . . . His hand shook when he picked up the water glass. He sipped water and waited while committee members consulted together, talking just under his hearing.

"Why do you believe," a Dr. Wells asked him then, "—or did you ever believe—your father's confession?"

"I believed it. He said so. And because—" *Bring out some of the sexual angle,* Ari had said on the plane. *It plays well in the press. Scandal always gets the attention, and you can work people en masse a lot easier if you've got their minds on sex:* everybody's *got an opinion on that. Just don't mention the tape and I won't mention the drugs, all right?* "Because there was a motive I could believe in— that everyone in Reseune believed in. Me. Ariane Emory blackmailed me into a relationship with her. My father found out."

The reaction lacked surprise. The interrogator nodded slowly.

"Blackmailed you—how?"

He slid a glance toward Mikhail Corain, though it was a committee member who asked the question. He said, watching Corain's reactions in his peripheral vision: "There was a secret deal for Jordan's transfer to RESEUNESPACE. Ari found out Jordan had pulled strings to get past her, and she made a deal with me—not to stop my father's transfer." Corain did not like that line of questioning. *So,* he thought, and looked back at the questioner. "She told me—that she intended me to stay in Reseune; that she meant to teach me; that she saw potential in my work she wanted developed, and that she wanted a guarantee Jordan wouldn't mess up the psychogenesis project. It looked like it would be a few years. Then she said she'd approve my transfer to go with him. Probably she would have. She usually kept her promises."

Slowly, slowly, there began to be consultation. *They knew,* he thought to himself. *They knew—the whole damn committee—even Corain— All these years; my God, the whole damn Council and the Bureau—there was no secrecy about me and Ari. But something I said—they didn't know.*

God! What am I into? What deals did Giraud make, what am I treading on?

"You wanted to keep the sexual relationship secret," Wells said. "How long did that continue?"

"A few times."

"Where?"

"Her office. Her apartment."

"Who initiated it?"

"She did." He felt the heat in his face, and leaned his arms on the table for steadiness. "Can I say something, ser? I honestly think, ser, the sex was only a means to an end—to make me guilty enough to drive a wedge between me and my father. It wasn't just the encounter itself. It was the relationship between her and my father. I'm a PR, ser. And she was not my father's friend. I thought I could handle the guilt. I thought it wouldn't bother me. From the other side of the event it looked a lot different; and she was a master clinician—she was completely in control of what was going on and I was a student way out of his limits. My father would have understood that part of it, when I couldn't, at the time. I didn't plan for him to find out. But he did."

A thought flashed up with gut-deep certainty out of the flux: *He didn't do it. He couldn't kill anyone. He'd have been concerned for me. He'd have wanted to work the situation, get me clear before he did anything—and I can't tell them that.* . . . —to change an instant later into: *Anyone can do anything under the right stress. If that was the right stress for him—the unbearable point—*

Lynch asked: "Did your father confront you with the discovery?"

"No. He went straight to her. I had a meeting with Ari for later that evening. I didn't know she was dead until they told me, after I was arrested."

Then—then the thing that had been trying to click into place snapped into lock, clear and plain, exactly where the way out was: *Disavow what Jordan's said—be the outraged son, defending his father: put myself in a position to be courted by both sides. That's the answer.*

Out of everything that Ari had said on the plane, exactly where she was trying to lead him. Her pieces, handed him bit by bit—*damn, she's an operator.* But there was a way to position all of it so he could step to either shore, play the emotional angle, the outrage—oppose Jordan and be won over; or win Jordan over—whichever worked, hell with Corain, hell with all the would-be users in this mess: he could maneuver if he could just get a position and focus everyone's efforts on him, to persuade *him.* It collected information, it collected a small amount of control, and he thought, he *thought* it possibly exceeded the perimeters where Ari had intended he should go—but only enough to worry her and keep her working on him and his position, *not* so long as he could tread a very narrow line between opposition and cooperation.

Under fire. When he always did his best thinking. He picked up the glass and took a second drink, and his hand was suddenly steady, his heart still pounding: *Damn, Giraud did a piece on me, didn't he? Shot my nerves to hell. But the mind works.*

"Were you aware of any other person who might have had a motive for murder?"

"I'm not aware of any," he said, frowning, and plunged ahead unasked. "I'll tell you, ser, I have a major concern about what's going on here."

"What concern?"

"That my father's being used. That if he did recant his confession—that can't be checked any more than the confession can be. No one knows. No one can know. He's a research scientist. He's been twenty years out of touch with current politics. He could make a statement. He could say anything. God knows what he's been told or what's going on, but I don't trust this, ser. I don't know if he's been told something that made him come out with this, I don't know if he's been promised something, but I'm extremely worried, ser, and I resent his name being caught up in politics he doesn't know anything about—he's being *used*, ser, maybe led into something, maybe just that people are taking this up that had absolutely nothing to say to help him twenty years ago and all of a sudden everyone's interested, *not* because they know whether he's guilty or innocent, but because it's a political lever in things my father's not in touch with, for reasons that don't have anything to do with my father's welfare. I'll fight that, ser."

There was silence for about two breaths, then a murmur broke out in the room.

Now the knives were going to come out, he thought. Now he had found his position and now he had built Jordan a defense no matter what he had said.

His hand was shaking nearly enough to spill the water when he took his next drink, but it was the after-a-fight shakes. Inside, he had more hope for himself and Jordan and Grant than he had had since he had known where they were taking him.

Corain bit his lip as young Emory courteously shook his hand during the mid-session recess, as she said earnestly, in the insulation of her personal Security and his: "It's politics, of course: Reseune understands that; but it's very personal with Justin. He's not political. He sees what happened to his father in the first place as political and now he sees it all starting up again now that Giraud's dead and there are elections on. I've advised him to tone it down; but he's terribly upset."

"You should advise him," Corain said coldly, "if that's his primary concern, he should stay away from the media, young sera. If he raises charges, they'll go before Council."

"I'll pass him that word, ser." With a little lift of the chin. Not Ari senior's smile, not that maddening, superior smile; just a direct look. "Possibly my predecessor slipped and fell. *I* have no idea. I'm interested in the truth, but I *really* don't think it's going to come out in this hearing."

If Ari senior had said that, it would surely have meaning under meaning. He looked this incarnation in the eye and was absolutely sure it did. Reseune was pulling strings in Science, damned right it was.

"I hate it," Ari Emory said, assuming a confidential friendliness, "that this has blown up now. Politics change, positions change—and develop common interests. I'll administer Reseune before too many years; there's a lot I can do then, and there are changes I want to make. I want you to understand, ser Corain, that I'm not welded to the past."

"You have a few years yet," Corain said. And thought: *Thank God*.

"A few years yet. But I've been in politics a long, long time. If my predecessor were alive right now, she'd look at the general situation and say something has to be done to calm it down. It's not good for either party. All it does is help Khalid."

Corain looked at the young face a long, long moment. "We've always maintained a moderate position."

"We absolutely overlap, where it comes to solving Novgorod's problems. And the Pan-Paris loop. All of that. I think you're entirely right about those bills—the way I know I'm right about Dr. Warrick."

"You don't have any power, young sera."

"I do," she said. "At least within Reseune. That's not small. Right now I'm here because I know people, and Justin doesn't; and because Justin's my friend and quite honestly, I don't think his father is any danger to me personally and neither does Reseune Administration. So it's psychology of a sort: I want people to know that I support Justin. He sees his father in danger of getting swept up in causes he knows his father wouldn't support; and that's where Reseune is going to insist on its sovereignty to protect its citizens, both him and his father. It can end up in court; and it can get messy. And that just helps the Paxers, doesn't it, that I don't think you like either. So is there a way out of this? You've got the experience in Council. You tell *me*."

"First off," Corain said, with a bitter taste in his mouth, "young Warrick has to back off the charges he's making."

She nodded. "I think that's a good idea."

"If I gave the committee the idea that I blame Councillor Corain," Justin said carefully, quietly, "I certainly want to apologize for that impression, that came to my attention at recess. I'm sure he has my father's welfare at heart. But I *am* afraid of violent influences that could have involved themselves in this—"

ix

It was after midnight before they made the hotel, via the underground entrance, the security lift straight to the upper floors that Reseune Security had made their own: Ari sighed with relief as the lift stopped on the eighteenth floor—a sprawling, single interconnected suite on this VIP level of the Riverside, and one that Giraud still had reserved for the month, in a hotel that Reseune Security knew down to its foundations and conduits.

Abban met her at the lift, and Ari blinked, surprised at first, then ineffably relieved to see Abban's competence handling what Florian and Catlin had had no opportunity to oversee, quietly on the job, no matter that they had buried Giraud that morning, no matter that Abban had been through hell this week. He had to have flown up from Reseune this afternoon, after the rest of the staff arrived.

"Young sera," Abban said. "Florian, Catlin, I've already made the checks: sera will want the master bedroom, I'm sure; ser Justin to the white room or the blue—as sera pleases."

The blue bedroom was far off across the suite, down a hall and past the tape studio; the white was next to the master suite, connected by a side door, if it was unlocked: white had lately been her room, when she had been in Novgorod with uncle Giraud. *I'd rather my old room,* was her thought; but that was too emotional a thing to say, Abban was not terribly social, even after all those years, and it was the pressure of the day and her exhaustion that made her wish she was a child again, with Giraud next door to handle all the problems. "He can take white," she said, and looked at Justin, who was altogether exhausted. "Go with Kelly, Justin, he'll see you settled—-is there anything to eat, Abban? Justin's starved."

"We thought meals might be short. Staff has a cold supper ready on call for any room; white wine, cheese and ham; or if sera prefers—"

"You're a dear, Abban." She patted his arm and walked wearily through the main doors of the VIP suite, Abban walking at her right, Florian at her left, and Catlin a little behind as they passed the guards into the long main hall of Volga sandstone. "I really appreciate your doing this. You didn't have to."

"Giraud asked me to close down his office and collect his personal papers. And ser Denys has asked me to oversee House Security, in somewhat Giraud's capacity, I hope on a tolerably permanent basis. It's only part of my job."

"I'm glad someone's looking after you. Are you all right, Abban?"

Abban was well above a hundred himself, having had one Supervisor for most of his life. He was very lost now, she thought, with Denys focused now on Giraud-to-come. Somebody had to take him—or give him Final tape and a CIT-number, which Abbban was ill suited for. All Abban had gotten since Giraud had died seemed to be snubs from the Family and responsibility for all the details, precious little grace for what he was suffering, and it made her mad.

"Perfectly well, thank you, scra. Ser Denys has offered me a place in his household."

"Good." She was surprised and relieved. "Good for Denys. I worry about you."

"You're very kind, young sera."

"I do. I know everything's in order; the staff's got it going. Go get some rest yourself."

"I'm perfectly fine, young sera, thank you: I prefer to stay busy." They stopped at the door of the master bedroom, a small suite within the suite, and Abban opened the door on manual. "I'll handle the staff and order your suppers—Florian and Catlin are staying right in your bedroom, aren't they? I'd advise that."

"Yes. Don't worry. It's all right." Abban would, she thought, have preferred Justin in the blue room, at the other end of the floor; and likely Giraud and therefore Abban had never believed there was no bed-sharing going on. "I assure you, *just* Florian and Catlin. Everything's fine. Get us our suppers and we'll all be in for the night."

"Remember even the main Minder is a limited system: you're on manual for the door. Please don't forget to lock it."

"Yes," she said. That would nettle Florian and Catlin—Abban's damned punctilious superiority, as if they were still youngers. She smiled, glad at least Abban had that intact. "Go," she said. "It's all right." And Abban nodded, gave her a courteous "sera" and left her to Florian and Catlin.

"He's doing fine," Florian said, with precisely that degree of annoyance she had figured. "*Abban* for head of Security. . . ."

Abban's nit-picking outraged Florian; Catlin found his reminders merely a waste of her time and treated them with cool disdain. That was the difference in them. Ari smiled, shook her head and walked on into the living area of the master suite, gratefully turned the briefcase over to Catlin and fell into a formfit chair with a groan, while Florian went straight to the Minder to read out the entries since Abban would have set it sometime today.

"God," she sighed, leaned back in the soft chair and let it mold around her, feet up. "How are we, clean enough?"

"Nothing's clean enough in this place," Catlin said. She set the briefcase on the entry table, opened it, pushed a button and checked the interior electronics. "Everything's real nervous," Catlin said. "I'll be glad to get out of here."

Florian nodded. "Minder was set up at 1747, only staff admitted since then."

"It was supposed to be set by 1500," Catlin said, cool disapproval.

"Abban did the set." Snipe. "Probably re-set it when he came in." Double snipe. "I'll ask him. —Sera, just sit here awhile. Let us go over everything."

"God," Ari moaned, and reached down and pulled off her shoes. "If there's a bomb I don't care. I want my shower, I want my supper, I want my bed, I don't care who's in it."

Florian laughed. "Quick as we can," he said, and left the Minder and went and looked at Catlin's readouts, then unpacked his own kit, laying out his equipment.

Carelessness was the one direct order they would never obey. No one checked out her residences except them and that was the Rule. Catlin had made it, years ago, and they all still respected it. No matter the inconvenience.

So she tucked her knees up sideways in the chair and shut her eyes, still seeing the cylinder going into the ground, the cenotaph slamming down; Abban's pale face; Justin's, across from her on the plane, so pale and so upset—

Damned long day. Damnable day. Corain was willing to deal but Corain was being careful, Corain was playing as hard and as nasty as he could. Corain had gotten to Wells, on the Bureau committee, and after the recess the questions had gotten brutal and detailed.

What is your present position in Reseune? Who approved it?

When was the last time you spoke to your father? What was his state of mind?

Have you ever had treatment for psychological problems? Who administered it?

You have an azi companion, Grant ALX-972. Did he come with you? Why not?

Have you ever been subject to a psych procedure you haven't previously mentioned to this committee?

Justin had held his ground—occasionally outright lying to the committee, or lying by indirection, a flat challenge to the opposition inside the Bureau to see if they had the votes to mandate another psychprobe: they don't have, she had assured him in the recess; but let's don't put that to the test, for God's sake.

He had held up, absolutely no fractures, till his voice began to give out: the temper built, the nerves steadied—he always did that, nervous as hell because politics gave him flashes, because that mind of his saw so many possibilities in everything, and sorted and collated over so wide a range he had trouble thinking of where he was and what was going on around him, but he had stalled off, found his equilibrium—she had recognized that little intake of breath, that set of the shoulders the instant she saw it on camera in the adjoining room, known that all of a sudden the committee was dealing with a Justin Warrick who was *in* that room, and starting onto the offensive.

Good, she had thought then, *good. They think they can push him. He hasn't even been here till now. Now he is. He's too smart to go over to Corain. He'll never follow anyone's lead who's making mistakes: he's got far too much impatience with foul-ups and he said it while he was under kat: No one helped my father then. Not one of his damn friends. He has a lot of hostility about that.*

They'll find out they're dealing with a Special, after he's made off with their keys and their cred-slips—damn, he's good when he cuts loose; everything they say his father has, including the temper—once you get it going, once you get him to stop analyzing and move. He's still learning these people and he hates real-time work with a passion. Field too large. He's never learned to average and extemp the way I have: Justin wants exactitudes, and you don't get that in real-time and you don't get it in politics. The same precision that makes him so valuable in design, that's why his designs are so clean—that's why he's so damn slow, and why he keeps putting embellishments on them—patches, for intersects he can see and the other designers, even Yanni, damned well can't—

Someday, when we get back, out of this, we've got to talk about that. . . .

There's got to be a search-pattern he's using that isn't in program, even if he's got total recall on those sets—

If he could explain it—

I can almost see it. There's something in the signature of the designers themselves—a way of proceeding—he's comprehending on a conceptual level. But he's carrying it into CIT work—

"They're sending a tray up," a strange voice said, and Justin, lying on the bed and almost gone, felt a jolt of panic: it should be Grant's voice; and it was not.

Kelly, the man's name was. Security. He passed a hand over his eyes, raked fingers through his hair and murmured an answer.

He was all right, he kept telling himself; he was safe. Kelly was on his side, there only to protect him.

He levered himself up off the bed, dizzy from fatigue, the down-side of the adrenaline high he had been on hour after hour. "I don't think I can eat."

"I have orders you should, ser," Kelly said, in a tone that said he would, bite by bite.

"Damn." A thought got to him. "I have a hospital appointment tomorrow. Rejuv. God." He thought of making the request through Kelly, but by his experience, nothing got done through lower levels. "Is Florian or Catlin still in the net?"

"Yes, ser."

"Tell them give me a call. Tell them I'm without my medication." He went into the bath and splashed water into his face and onto the back of his neck, worried now about Grant. He had no liking for taking medication from any random stock in Novgorod; he thought about Ari's elaborate security precautions around Grant and worried about the breach it could create, or whether there was any motive for anyone at Reseune to substitute drugs.

"Ser Justin?" Florian hailed him, from the wall-speaker. "This is Florian. Do you mean your prescription? We have that."

"Thanks. Have they made arrangements for Grant? He's on the same schedule."

"We thought of that. It's taken care of, ser. Do you need it tonight?"

"Thank you," he said, relieved. Trust Florian. *No* detail dropped. "No, I'm going to rest tonight, it sends me hyper—God knows I don't need it before bed." It also hurt like hell; and he was not looking forward to it. Could *not* go through tomorrow's hearings on pain-killer.

"Yes, ser. It's all right then. Have a good sleep."

"Endit," he said to the Minder. And heard the suite door open. His heart jumped.

Kelly, he told himself. Dinner was a little early. He toweled his face dry, hung the towel on the hook and walked out into the bedroom.

No Kelly.

Not *like* Security. "Minder," he said. "Minder, get Florian AF. Next door."

No sound.

"Minder, give me an answer."

Dead.

O my God.

"It's Abban, sera," the Minder said; and Ari levered herself out of the chair to manual the door herself, Florian and Catlin still being occupied about their checks in the bedroom.

"Sera!" Florian said sharply from behind her, and she stopped as he hurried to get the door himself. The Rule again. "I'll set supper out," he said quietly then, and with a little smile: "The shower's safe."

"I'm so glad." She started on her way, looked back as the door opened and Abban showed up with the catering staff.

As suddenly there was a pounding on the adjoining door from Justin's side. "Florian!" she heard him shout.

Then the whole wall blew outward, a sheet of bright fire, a percussion like a fist slamming against her; and she fell over a chair arm, complete tumble onto her knees and into the narrow wedge against the wall as flames shot up, as of a sudden a volley of gunshots exploded from her right, shells exploded to her left, and she stared in a split-second's horror, flinging up her arms as a flying body came at her, bore her over and cracked her head against the floor.

Second explosion, jolting the bones. "Sera!" Florian gasped into her ear, and she tried to move, cooperating by instinct as he tried to haul her along the floor behind the chair, with fire lighting the smoke and heat already painful. One more shot went off and exploded, and Florian fell on top of her, covering her with his body, protecting her head with his arms.

In a moment more there was a dreadful quiet, except the crackle of the fire that lit the lowering pall of smoke—then a sudden scrape of the chair pulled away and flung tumbling. Florian moved. She saw Catlin's stark, grim face upside down above her in the orange light, felt Florian's knee bruise her leg and his hand press her shoulder as he tried to get up and they tried to get themselves sorted out: he hauled himself up and got an arm around her with Catlin on the other side, Florian stumbling and catching himself on the wall.

A solid wall of fire enveloped the open door, a tumult of voices outside— *Theirs or ours?* Ari wondered desperately— The fire enveloped bodies on the floor, half-exploded, unrecognizable except the black Security uniforms— where Abban had been standing—and the heat burned her hands and her face—

Who's the Enemy? What's waiting out there? What's first? Can you run through fire that thick? Is it burning in the hall?

She felt the hesitation in Florian and Catlin, only a second; then Florian breathed, to someone not present: "Florian to Security Two—somebody's turned off the fire-systems. Re-engage, system two. That's an incendiary. Acknowledge."

"They're answering," Catlin said.

"Who's *they*?" Ari said, and choked on the smoke. The fire blinded, burned them with the heat, worse by the moment. "Dammit to hell, where's the hand extinguishers?"

As suddenly the fire-systems cut on with a wail of sirens.

There was fire: Justin was aware of that first, of blistering heat that drove him to move before he was fully conscious, of smoke that stung his nose and his throat and his lungs—deadly as the fire and harder to evade. He clawed his way up over debris of shattered structural panels and hot metal, felt one cut his leg as he went over, lost his balance and wormed through underneath the massive bureau that had come down onto the end of the bed—away from the fire, that was all he could think of at the moment, until his vision cleared and he could see the hallward door through the smoke, beyond the ruin of ceiling and wall-panels piled on the furniture.

There was a blank then. He came to on his knees, clinging to the door handle, trying to get to his feet again, finding fire on his left, the lights only clusters of suns in a universe gone to murk, to fire and shouts coming from somewhere. He pulled the manual latch, got the door unlocked, and pulled it open against the obstruction of debris around him.

Another blank. He was in the hall, dark figures rushed at him and one hit him, flinging him against the irregular stone of the wall. But that one stopped then, and hauled him up and yelled at him: "Get to the exit! That way—"

He felt the stiff material of a firesuit; felt a mask pressed to his face; felt himself dragged along while he inhaled cleaner air. Then he saw the emergency exit for himself, and tried to go under his own power—through the doors into clean air. The man yelled something at him, shoved him through—

Blank. Someone caught hold of him. There were people around him, in the stairwell.

"How far up is it?" someone shouted at him. "Where did you come from?"

He could not answer. He coughed and almost fell; but they helped him, and he walked.

X

"Kelly EK is dead," Catlin reported calmly, between listening to the net.

The rescue copters were still coming in at the pad outside Mary Stamford Hospital, and Ari angrily fended away the medtech who was trying to see if the lump on her head needed scan: "For God's sake, let me *alone*! Catlin, *where*, in the room?"

"In the hallway," Catlin said. "Alone. They identified him by his tags. —They're searching out on the far side of the building now, where the exit stairs let out: a lot of the guests went that way."

"God." Ari wiped a hand over her face—reflex: there was Neoskin on her hand and sweat stung.

The fire teams had it under control, the report ran. Explosions had gone off at several points on the floor, in the blue room and the white. *The explosives were rigged in White*, Florian had said, vastly chagrined. *A periphery scan wouldn't pick them up, but we'd have found them if we'd run the check from the top. But Abban psyched us. He had the trigger: I saw the flash from the briefcase on the table; and that rig was state-of-the-art.*

It had gone so fast, Justin's urgent shout through the connecting door, the split-second warning that had triggered Florian's something's-wrong reflexes and brought Catlin, armed, out that bedroom doorway the instant after the initial explosion, in a chain of thought that went something like:

explosions-can't-happen-with-adequate-checks; there's-Abban-who-ran-the-checks; *fire!*— about a nanosecond before Abban's fire came back at her a hair off. A good shot with a regular pistol and a better one with explosive rounds, that was what it had come down to, while Abban had hesitated one fatal synapse-jump between target A and target B.

Giraud's orders, Ari thought. Giraud ordered me killed. . . .

Rescue teams had gotten into Justin's charred room. They were searching through the wreckage; but from the time they had said that the heavy display cabinet had crashed down beside the connecting door and shielded that area from the force of the blast, and that they had found the hall door open, then she had believed Justin had to have gotten out. There were two dead of smoke inhalation that they had found; Kelly burned, evidently, beyond recognition, *not* with Justin, where he should have been; several severely burned trying to get to her—God help them; but Security from the floor below had gotten up there with emergency equipment and a unit captain with good sense had gotten Florian's advisement the fire systems were not operating and gotten to the control system to turn them on again—Abban had seen to that little detail too—while another had ordered all personnel who could not reach fire control equipment to get out, immediately . . . a damned good thing, because the majority were azi, who might well have tried to help her without fire-gear and died trying.

"*Damn!*" Astringent stung the wound on her head. They had already pulled a finger-wide fragment of plastic out of her shoulder. Florian was in worse shape, having caught several, and having bled profusely, in no condition to be running check-in, but Florian was at one door and a reliable guard was at the other, making sure badges got checked and that Reseune personnel were accounted for.

Abban and the two with him were dead. *I don't know if they were his,* Catlin had said. *There wasn't time to ask.*

An arriving ambulance jumped a curb, and Justin reeled back, stumbled and recovered himself in the dark, in the chaos of lights and firefighting equipment, announcements over loud-hailers, guests in night-robes and pajamas huddled together in the street outside and onto the gravel garden area. Firelight spread through smoke, smoke hazed the emergency lights and the floods around the entrance and down the drive.

He was on the street then. He did not know how he had gotten there, or where the hotel was. He was wobbling on his feet and he found a bench to sit on, in the dark. He dropped his head into his hands and felt clammy sweat despite the night chill.

He was blank for a time more. He was walking again, confronted with a dead end in the space between two buildings, and a stairway down. *Pedway,* the sign said.

Find a phone, he thought. *Get help. I'm lost.*

And then he thought: *I'm not thinking clearly. God, what if—*

It was someone on staff. Security had checked it.
Abban—had checked it.
Was it aimed at me? Was I the only one?
Ari—
He stumbled on the steps, caught himself on the rail, and made it to the bottom, to security doors that gave way to his approach, to a lighted tunnel that stretched on in eerie vacancy.

"Uncle Denys," Ari said; and of a sudden the load seemed too much— *Uncle Denys,* the way she had said in the hospital when she had broken her arm, when they had handed her the phone and she had had to tell Denys she had been a fool. Not a fool this time, she told herself that; lucky to be alive. But the report was nothing to be proud of either. "Uncle Denys, I'm all right. So are Florian and Catlin."

"Thank God for that. They're saying you were killed, you understand that?"

"I'm pretty much alive. A few scratches and some burns. But Abban's dead. Five others. In the fire." There was a limit to what they could say on the net, via the remotes Florian had set up with the mobile system. "I'm taking command of Security here myself. I'm issuing orders through the net. Security is compromised as hell, understand me. Someone got inside." Her hand started to shake. She bit her lip and drew in a large breath. "There've been two other bombings tonight—Paxers blew up some track in center city, they're claiming the attack on the hotel, and they're threatening worse; I'm in contact with the Novgorod police and all our systems—"

"Understood," Denys said, before she had to say more than she wanted. *"I'm relieved. We've got that on the net. God, Ari, what a mess!"*

"Don't be surprised by much of anything. It's all right, understand. Bureau Enforcement is moving on the hotel situation. Watch the net."

"Understood. Absolutely. We'd better cut this off. I'll up your priorities, effective immediately. Thank God you're safe."

"I plan to stay that way," she said. "Take care of yourself. All right?"

"You take care," Denys said. *"Please."*

She broke the contact, passed the handset back to Florian.

"We have confirmation," he said. "The plane has left the ground at Planys. They expect touchdown about 1450 tomorrow."

"Good," she said. "Good." From the fragile amount of control she had.

"Councillor Harad is waiting on-line; so is Councillor Corain. They've asked about your safety."

Strange bedfellows, she thought. But of course they would—Harad because he was an ally; Corain because, whatever he feared from her, he had more to fear from the Paxers, the radicals in his own spectrum; and the radicals in Defense.

"I'll talk to them. Have we got reporters down there?"

"Plenty."

"I'll talk to them."

"Sera, you're in shock."

"That's several of us, isn't it? Damn, get me a mirror and some makeup. We're in a war, hear me?"

The mirror in the ped-tunnel restroom showed a soot-streaked face that for a heartbeat Justin hardly knew for his own. His hands and arms were enough to raise question, the smell of smoke about his clothing, he had thought; and now he turned on the water full, took a handful of soap and started washing, wincing at bruises and burns.

The dark blue sweater and pants showed soot, but water and rubbing at least got the worst off and ground the rest in. He went through an entire stock of soap packets and dried his hair and his shoulders under the blowers, looked up again and saw a face shockingly pale. He was starting to need a shave. His sweater was burned and snagged, he had a tear above the knee and a gash where the tear was. Anyone who saw him, he thought, would report him to the police.

And that would catch him up in Cyteen law.

He leaned against the sink and wiped cold water across his face, clamping his jaws against a sick feeling that had been with him since he had come to. Thoughts started trying to insinuate themselves up to a conscious, emotional level: *It was Ari's wall; whoever did this was staff—whoever did this—*

Abban. Giraud's orders. But I'm only the incidental target. If she's dead—

The thought was incredible to him. Shattering. Ariane Emory had years to live. Ariane Emory had a century yet, was part of the world, part of his thinking, was—like air and gravity—there.

—someone else is in charge, someone else—wanting—someone to blame. Paxers. Jordan.

Amy Carnath waiting in the apartment, with Grant, with Security—if Ari's dead—what can anyone do—

They've got Jordan, got Grant—I'm the only one still free—the only one who can make them trouble—

Something was wrong. Grant heard the Minder-call in the other bedroom—they had given him Justin's, which was his own as well, out of courtesy, he thought, as the larger room, or perhaps because they had known. Florian had re-set the Minder to respond to Amy Carnath, so nothing of what it was saying got to him, but he reckoned that it was not minor if it wakened young sera in the small hours of the night. After that he heard both Amy and Quentin stirring about and talking together in voices he could not quite hear with his ear to the door.

He slammed the door with his open palm. "Young sera, is something wrong?"

No answer. "Young sera? Please?"

Damn.

He went back to the large and unaccustomedly empty bed, lay staring at the ceiling with the lights on and tried to tell himself it was nothing.

But finally sera Amy came on the Minder to say: "Grant, are you awake?"

"Yes, sera."

"There's been an incident in Novgorod. Someone bombed the hotel. Ari's all right. She's coming on vid. Do you want to come to the living room?"

"Yes, sera." He did not panic. He got up, got his robe, and went to the door, which Quentin opened for him. "Thank you," he said, and walked ahead of Quentin as far as his own living room, where Amy was sitting on the couch.

He took the other side of the U, Quentin took the middle, between him and Amy; and he sat with his arms folded against too much chill, watching the images of emergency vehicles, smoke billowing from breached seals on the hotel's top two floors.

"Were people killed?" he asked quietly, refusing to panic. Sera Amy was not cruel. She would not bring him out here to psych him: he believed that, but it was a thin thread.

"Five of Security," Amy said. "They say the Paxers got a bomb in. They aren't saying how. I don't know any more than that. We're not supposed to do things on the phones that give away where people are or what's going on or when they're going to be places. That's the Rule."

Grant looked at her past Quentin. Not panicking, not yet; but the adrenaline flood was there, threatening shivers, pure fight-flight conflict.

"I had a call from Dr. Nye warning me not to let you loose," Amy said. "He says he'd really like me to send you downstairs to Security, but I told him no. I lied to him. I said you were locked up."

"Thank you," Grant said, because something seemed called for.

And watched the vid.

Makeup covered the minor burns, but she left the visible bruise and the burn on her cheek; she put two pins in her hair, but she let it fly loose about her face. She had a clean sweater in her luggage that Security had rescued from the suite, but she chose to meet the cameras in what she was wearing, the tailored, gray satin blouse, with the blood and the burns and the soot, and the watermark the firefighting foam had made.

She was also sure, having stalled off twice, that the clips would hit the morning news with full exposure in Novgorod.

"They tried," she said grimly, in answer to the first question, which asked her reaction to what had happened; and she confronted the cameras with a rapid-fire series of answers that got around the fine question of who had done it and gave her the launching point that she wanted—

"We are very well, thank you. And I have a personal statement, which I'll give you first. Then questions.

"I don't know yet why this happened. I know part of it; and it was an attempt not quite to silence me, because I have no voice in politics—but to kill me before I do come of age enough to acquire one.

"It was a power move of some kind, because whoever did it wanted power without process. It cost the lives of brave people who tried despite fire and the dangers of more explosions, to rescue me and others; more, it was a clear attempt to destroy the political process, no matter who instigated it, no matter who perpetrated it. I don't think that the Paxers had anything to do with this. That they're anxious to claim they had is typical of the breed: and they hope to benefit from it—*benefit* from it, because that's exactly what's going on: that a handful of individuals too few to make a party and incapable of winning votes in debate thinks it can wear down the majority by terror—creates an atmosphere in which every fool with a half-conceived program can try the same thing and add to the confusion they hope to use. Let me tell you: whether this was the Paxers or one individual with a personal opinion he thinks outweighs the law, it's the peace under assault, it's our freedoms under assault, and every one of these attacks, no matter how motivated, makes the lawful rest of us that much more certain we don't want killers in charge of our lives and we damned well don't want their advice on how to conduct our affairs.

"Let me tell you also that within an hour of the disaster, Chairman Harad and members of the Council, Simon Jacques and Mikhail Corain, called me to express their profound outrage. *Everyone*, no matter what political party, understands what's threatened by actions like this. I don't need to say that to the people of Novgorod, who've held out against the tactics of the extremists and who've equally well held out against offers of help from the central government. I take my example from Novgorod. People can persuade me with ideas but there's no way in hell they're going to move me with violence or the possibility of violence.

"This isn't the first time in history someone's tried this; and by everything I've ever learned, the answer that works with them is exactly the kind of contempt Novgorod turns on them and their ideas—contempt, but no patience, *no* patience. Every time the Council sits to debate honest differences, *everybody* wins, precisely because civilization is working and the majority and the minority are trying to work out a fair compromise that protects the people they represent. That's why these types who want their own way above all have to destroy that; and that's precisely why the best answer is a consensus of all the elected bodies that ideas are valuable, peaceful voices deserve serious consideration, human needs have to be dealt with in a wise distribution of resources, and the principle of life itself has to be high on our list of values, just under our regard for the quality of life and the freedom to speak our opinions. Whoever did this, from whatever misguided notion of right above the law, he hasn't scared me into retreat, he's made me know how important law is; and I will run for office, someday; I'll run, and I'll respect the vote in my electorate, whatever the outcome, because an honest contest is one thing, but creating chaos to undermine the people's chosen representative isn't dissent, it's sabotage of the process, the same as the bombers are trying, and I'll have no part of that either."

Hear that, Vladislaw Khalid.

"If my electorate does think I should sit on Council I'll remember the cost it takes to *have* Council at all; and I'll remember that we have to have it, no matter the types who think they're above the law and so right they can take lives with impunity.

"That's the end of my personal statement. I've been very happy until now being as private as I could be; and I can't be now, because somebody decided to kill people to keep me from ever speaking out. So now I will speak up, loud and clear and often as there's something to say, because that's the best way I know to fight the ones who want me silenced.

"I'll take questions."

It was all right, she thought. She got off with a: "I'm sorry, my voice is going"; and a tremor in the hand she used to wipe a stray strand of hair—no need to pretend the latter: she had hid it until then, and got away from the cameras and had to sit down quickly, but she had gotten through it and said exactly what she had wanted to say.

"Is there any word?" she asked Catlin, who had been monitoring the net.

"No, sera," Catlin said.

She let go her breath and took the water Florian handed her. "Damn." Tears threatened, pain and exhaustion and the frustration of the situation. It was dawn. She had not slept since the morning of Giraud's funeral. Yesterday. God. "I'm going to make a phone call to Amy," she said in a controlled, quiet voice. "Ask Lynch to set up a very brief meeting with the Councillors and proxies at hand; and with the Bureau; I want to be at the airport by 0900."

"Sera, you haven't slept. Allow for that."

She sat a moment and thought about that. The blast kept replaying in her memory. The burned bodies. The smoke-filled halls, the lights shining out of haze.

She had no desire to shut her eyes at the moment, or to put food into her stomach, or to disturb her wounds by wrestling herself into the sweater she had brought: such little pains unnerved her, when there was so much worse to think about.

So one did not think about what-if and might-have-been. One handled things at the present, and trusted one's long-prepared decisions.

One Worked the whole of Union if that was what it took. One promised order where order did not exist; one held out the promise of moderation and rapprochement to shore up Corain, who was the opposition she preferred to Khalid.

One moved close to center for a while, to move the opposition closer to one's position—granted, of course, that they were trying to do the same: and granted at that point the clever and the quick would make the next jump out, leaving the opposition sitting bewildered at the new center.

Working the macrosystem, Ari senior would say.

While everything else went to hell and nothing that one wanted—stayed for long.

Except Florian and Catlin. Except the one flawless loyalty—the one thing that Ari's murderer had not dared to face.

Justin waked, winced at stiffened joints and the cramped position the thinly-padded bench in the restroom afforded; waked and tried to move in a hurry at the sound of the outer doors, to rake his hair into some kind of order and get to his feet before the intrusion passed the second doors; but he was only halfway up and off his balance before he faced two men in work-clothes, who stared at him half a heartbeat in surprise. He just turned to the sink, natural as breathing, turned on the water, wet his hands and ran them through his hair.

Except the two men showed up in the mirror, close behind him.

One moment he panicked. The next he thought: *Hell, they're not Reseune Security*, and turned around with a right elbow and all the strength he had— shocked as it connected, but still moving in the tape-taught sequence, full spin and a punch to the breastbone.

He stared a split-second at the result, one man flung backward against the corner, the other down—*God*, he thought, and then seeing the first man bracing to go for him, darted for the door and knocked it banging, went through the second the same way, and came out into a tunnel already beginning to fill with morning traffic.

What if I was wrong? That man could die. I may have killed someone.

Then: *No. I read it right.*

And: *I haven't studied that tape since I was a kid. I didn't know I could do that.*

He slowed to a fast walk, shaking in the knees and hurting in his shoulders and his back and knowing he was attracting attention with his unshaven face and his agitated manner; he tried to match the pace of the general traffic, put his hands in his pockets and tried to look more casual, all the while thinking that the men could be after him now with more than robbery in mind.

Damn, I'd have given them the keycard and wished them luck using it, let them lead the police on a chase—

God. No. Novgorod *doesn't have a check-system. There's no tracking system, they refused to put it in.*

He turned on one foot—his neck and shoulders were too stiff—caught his balance, looked back and moved on. He was not sure he could even recognize the men among the crowds—

More strangers than I've ever seen at once in my whole life—too many faces, too many people in clothes too much alike. . . .

People jostled him and cursed him: *Damn z-case*, a man said. He rubbed an unshaven chin and, since shutters were opening and shops were lighting up in this section of the tunnels, he found a pharmacy and bought a shaving kit; and a breakfast counter and bought a roll-up and a glass of synth orange. But the boy took an extra look at the keycard and made him nervous.

Justin Patrick Warrick, it said, *CIT 976-088-2355PR*, which was damning enough; but in faint outline behind that was the Infinite Man emblem of Reseune Administrative Territory.

"Reseune," the boy said, looking up, checking the picture, he thought—in case it was stolen. "Never seen one of those. You *from* there?"

"I—" He had not tried talking. His voice was hoarse and cracked. "I work in the city offices."

"Huh." The boy slid it into the register slot and handed it back with the cup and the roll on the lid. "You return the cup and lid we refund half." The number 3 was on both.

"Thanks." He went over to the counter, unlidded the drink, and took down the roll with huge gulps of the sugary, iced drink, no matter the rawness of his throat—uneasy on his stomach in the first few moments and then altogether equal to anything *Changes* could offer at twenty times the price. He leaned there a moment with his eyes watering, just breathing and letting his stomach get used to food.

Where in hell am I going? What am I going to do?

He wiped his blurring eyes, went back to the counter with the cup and the lid, among other customers, delayed a moment until they were served. "Where can you get the news?"

"They got a board down to the subway."

"Where?"

"Straight on, to your Wilfred tunnel, go right. —You been up to that fire at the Riverside?"

"Up all night with it," he said. "You hear anything—who did it, why?"

The boy shook his head, and served another patron. Justin waited.

"Emory was on vid this morning," the boy said; and Justin's heart skipped. "Madder'n hell."

"Emory's all right?"

"*She* was, yey." The boy broke off to take a card and pour a drink. "You *from* Reseune?"

Justin nodded. "Can I use a phone? *Please.*"

"I can't do that." Another customer. The boy yelled, pointing past the woman: "Down to the corner, public phone."

"Thanks!"

He went, walking fast, with the traffic, in the direction the boy had said, passing some casual walkers. *Call the Bureau. Ask for protection. They can't think I'm responsible. They can't blame anyone but Reseune Security—*

Abban, the head of it—

He saw the sign that said *Phone*, and kept his keycard in his hand. He knew the Bureau number: he had had it memorized for years—but he had never used a phone outside Reseune, and he picked up the receiver, reading instructions: *Lift receiver, insert card, key in or touch 0 and voice in. . . .*

"Ser."

He turned and saw a gray uniform, a tall, heavy-set body.

Novgorod police.

He dropped the receiver and hit the officer a glancing blow getting past him; and ran, desperately, through the crowds.

But his keycard, he realized to his horror, dodging past a group of workers and down a side tunnel—his keycard was still in the phone-slot.

_____ **xi** _____

". . . My own Security was remiss at best," Ari said, in what of a voice she had left, sitting at the table in the conference room where Justin had sat. "Reseune will be conducting an internal investigation. I will tell you this, seri, —" Her voice cracked, and she took a drink of water. She had gotten her clothes changed, her hair pinned up—Catlin and Florian had helped; and she had the shakes—even if they had gotten her a cup of coffee and a liquid breakfast, which was all she could stand on her smoke-irritated throat. "I'm sorry. The voice isn't much. —I was about to say: I'm functioning as temporary head of Reseune Security; I'm ordering transfers; I'm posting and making assignments. I'm prepared to continue in that post at least administratively if Family council confirms it, though I'm quite aware my age and experience in Security are at issue: my view of my position is as someone qualified to assess the individuals in charge of operations and to make sure communications go through. I feel—to put this delicately—that my uncle's death has left some disarray in the department; the death of the acting head in the fire—is extremely unfortunate."

"Do you feel," Lynch asked, "that there is a chance the attempt was entirely internal?"

She drew a breath and took another drink of water. "Yes. I don't discount that possibility. Reseune is in transition. Dr. Nye—my surviving uncle—is very much affected by his brother's death. There are questions about his own health. But there are certainly experienced administrators who can deal with the problems if Reseune's own council should give them that mandate."

"In short, you feel Reseune can handle the problems."

"I have no doubt."

"Internally," Dr. Wells said, Corain's voice in Science. "But there is, pardon me, sera Emory, some question in my mind, regarding Dr. Warrick's disappearance. You say he was lodged in the room next to yours—but you know he cleared that area."

"Yes."

"Do you consider there's a chance he ran?"

"I don't think that likely, no."

"Why? Because his father is detained by Reseune?"

"Because," she shot back, "of his testimony before this committee. The Paxers were damned—excuse me: were extremely quick to take advantage of the hotel bombing; I'm scared mindless that there may well have been Paxer agents hovering around the hotel because we were there, and that whether or not they were the ones who planted the bomb—they may have been in a position to recognize Dr. Warrick among the evacuees and to kidnap him."

"Certain people might suggest other agencies."

"We certainly have no motive to. We brought him here."

"His father remains in detention."

"Under protective guard, in view of a security breach that put him in contact with unauthorized personnel. We don't know *what* else could have gotten to him. The attempt on my life makes that more than a remote possibility. In the meanwhile I'm extremely worried about Justin Warrick's whereabouts and about his physical condition."

"While Dr. Jordan Warrick remains under arrest."

"You can call it what you like, ser; the facts are as I gave them."

"Under your direction of Security."

"Under my direction."

"From whom are you taking your orders?"

"I operate within the directives of Reseune Administration. I'm reviewing Jordan Warrick's security and I will be in communication with him; and with Reseune Administration; I'm not empowered to make changes without consultation."

"Is he aware of his son's disappearance?"

"No, ser. We hope to have better news for him. Justin's well aware of his personal danger—he may well have hidden somewhere until he can be sure of the situation. That's my best hope."

"Is there any likelihood," Lynch asked, "that one of the blasts was aimed at him?"

"The blast was incendiary and directional; they put it in his room because my security could have found it immediately if it had been inside. It was elaborately shielded, it was mounted, more than likely, my security tells me, behind the very large bureau—a floor-to-ceiling cabinet—against that wall." Her voice cracked. She took another drink. "Excuse me. Justin was at a connecting door at the time, right against that wall—he was trying to warn me or my staff of something: we don't know what. The wall blew; the bureau spun half about and fell against the bed between him and the blast; and the plastic fragments hit that and the far wall. He was protected. That's how we know he survived the blast and we know he made it out of that room. Possibly he had seen something *in* the room that shouldn't have been there. I want to ask him. I want to know why his personal guard was found dead down the hall, *not* in the room. There are a lot of unanswered questions revolving around Dr. Warrick."

"For the record, you don't consider any possibility that Dr. Justin Warrick was part of a conspiracy."

"Absolutely not. For the record, I'm worried about a problem inside our own staff, within the area of personnel attached to my late uncle—and I'm very hesitant to be more specific than that even with this distinguished committee and guests. I'm continuing to answer questions, but I'm *exceedingly* anxious to get to the airport and get home, to carry reports to members of the Reseune staff who may decide to take action. The attack proves well enough that lives may be in danger."

"From what source?" Wells asked.

"Again, ser, I don't feel I should make charges: the next step is internal investigation, after which appropriate authorities from my Territory will be in contact with the Bureau."

"You're extremely young to lecture this committee on judicial matters."

"I believe, ser, that I'm factually right; and I hold an administrative post within Reseune which requires legal expertise—I refer to my post as wing supervisor, ser. It is correct for me to bring my information before Reseune authorities: I can appeal to the Bureau only in a personal matter, and it would be irresponsible to treat this as a personal incident: its implications are far more extensive."

"Specifically?"

"The possibility that Reseune law is being violated. That security is compromised to the extent I can't be sure of my Administrator's security. Either his involvement—or his safety from persons who may be. I have to say that much, to make you understand it could cost lives if we delay in this committee, or if a message goes out of here to Reseune." *God. Let's not have a debate on this. We can't leak it that Jordan Warrick is on a plane, it's too damn vulnerable till it's on the ground; and after it is—*

It lands at 1500. God knows into what.

"Then perhaps Reseune should ask for Bureau Enforcement."

"Perhaps Reseune will. At the moment I ask you to realize that Reseune's internal stability is threatened. Its sovereignty is at issue. I hope to find I'm wrong. I'd *like* for this to have come entirely from outside. I don't see a reasonable possibility that it did."

"You talk about personnel attached to your late uncle, the Councillor. I have questions about that."

How many of the Bureau have ties to Giraud?

Lynch himself?

God, have I made a mistake?

"In consideration of sera Emory's health," Lynch said, "and request for consultation with her staff—"

"Mr. Chairman, —" Wells objected.

"—we'll take a recess at this time." The gavel came down. "Committee will re-convene at 1930 hours, sera Emory's health permitting."

She let go the breath she had been holding, and shoved back the chair from the table. "Thank you, ser Secretary," she said in what voice she had left; and looked to the side as Florian came up to her and cut the microphone off.

"Sera," he said in a low voice. "He's in the tunnels. Novgorod police almost had him. He left his keycard. They're sure it's him."

She almost had to sit down. She leaned on the table. "He's run?"

But they could not discuss it; Lynch was moving up on her other side. She turned and took his hand. "Thank you."

Lynch nodded. "Take care, sera."

Harad wished her much the same.

"Sera," Jacques said stiffly, non-committal.

And Corain: Corain gave her a long and wary look as he shook her hand.

xii

"Another, ser?" the guard asked, appearing by Jordan's seat.

"I could stand it," Jordan said. "Paul?"

"Yes," Paul said. And after the guard had walked down the aisle toward the bar: "You can't complain about the service."

"Sun off the right," Jordan observed. They were reaching cruising altitude again, after refueling at, he supposed, Pytho. In the dark. But the dawn-glow was visible ahead of the plane; and ever so slightly to the right.

From Pytho the plane could have gone to Novgorod or to Reseune. If it held course as they bore, it was Reseune—which was not, he was sure, any sort of good news.

Paul took his meaning. Paul was steady as ever, his support through the years; and now.

He wanted to see Reseune: it was strange that he could feel that way. But it was part of his life; it was civilization; and he was in some part glad to be going home. He hoped to see Justin.

He feared—much worse things.

"We've picked up a tailwind," one of the guards had said, in his better-than-average hearing. "We're going to beat our schedule."

The tunnels afforded few hiding places, only nooks, the dim recess of the news-shop; that took money to enter but the crowded doorway offered Justin a brief refuge and a vantage to scan the tunnel up and down. Then another public restroom, and a quick shave: he had kept the shaving kit and left the damned keycard; but he was afraid to stay there long—

The crowd in a restaurant, the general drift toward another corridor— another appeal to a shopkeeper: "Can I use your phone? I was robbed: I need to call my office—"

"Better call the police," the shop-owner said.

"No," Justin said; and seeing the look of suspicion on the man's face: "Please."

"Police," the man said into the receiver.

Justin turned and left, moving quickly into the crowds, dodging away, heart pounding. The strength the breakfast had lent him was gone. He felt the stiffness and the sprains, and his skull ached. He found himself farther down the corridor than he had thought, found another gap in his memory; and looked behind him in panic.

There were police at the intersection. He saw them look his way.

He turned back again and dived down a stairs: *Subway*, it said. He jostled past other walkers, came out at the bottom.

"Hey," someone yelled behind him.

He ran, out onto the concrete rim, evaded a headon collision and dodged around a support column.

People dived away from him, scrambled out of the way in panic: the whole strip was vacant. "Stop right there!" a voice thundered behind him, and screams warned him of a weapon drawn.

He dodged wildly aside and something slammed like a fist into his back; but he saw safety ahead—saw the black of Reseune Security, a man yelling: *"Don't shoot!"* and a gun in that man's hand too, aimed toward him.

But a numbness was spreading from his shoulder across his back, and balance went. He fell on the concrete, conscious, but losing feeling in his limbs.

"I'm Justin Warrick," he said to the black-uniformed officer who knelt down to help him. "Call Ari Emory."

And: "No," he heard the officer say, not, he thought, to him: "This man is a Reseune citizen. He's under our authority. File your complaints with my captain."

They wanted to take him to hospital. They wanted to take him to the Novgorod police station. They told him that it had not been a bullet but a high-velocity trank dart that had penetrated his shoulder: "I'm very glad to know that," he said, or tried to say, past the numbness of his mouth. And was equally relieved when the agent told him they had reached Ari, and that *RESEUNE ONE*, already on the runway, had turned back to hold for him.

---

xiii

"I'll walk," he said, and did, facing the climb up the passenger ramp; but Florian had come halfway down to help him and Ari was waiting at the top, in the doorway, with the frown he expected.

Ari put her arm around him when he made it through the doorway; so did Catlin, fending away other Security personnel; and steered him for the nearest seat. But he stopped, resisting their help for a moment, scanning the group of Security staff for Abban or for strangers. "Who's back there?" he asked. "Ari, who oversaw the plane, do you know?"

"The pilot and co-pilot," Ari said, in a voice only a little less hoarse than his. "And staff we're sure of."

"Abban—"

"Dead," Catlin said, and patted his shoulder. "We're onto it, ser. Come on."

He let go the seat then, eased himself into it, leaned back and stared at Ari in a dull, all-over malaise as she sat down opposite him. "Thanks for holding the plane," he said between breaths.

"Where in hell were you?"

"Went shopping," he said, as the door thumped to and sealed. For a moment he was disoriented. "Sorry." He knew her suspicions—and Florian's and Catlin's. He felt a dull surprise that they let him this close to her. "I wasn't anywhere. I got disoriented. Wandered off." The plane began to move, pale landscape swinging past the windows in the edge of his vision. "I just walked until I knew I was in the tunnels; and I found Security and I told them find you."

"That's not half of what I hear. Novgorod is real nervous about people acting odd around the subways."

He shut his eyes, just gone for the moment, exhausted, and the seat was soft, comfortable as a pillow all around him, while he was trying to organize his thoughts. The engines began to drown out sound, a universal white-out. Someone leaned near him and drew the belt over him. He looked up at Catlin as the catch snapped. The plane was gathering speed. Ari was belting in. Catlin and Florian dropped into the seats by him.

The takeoff had a peculiarly perilous feel. Maybe it was the drug that dizzied him; maybe it was the steep bank the pilot pulled, an abrupt maneuver unlike anything he had ever felt. He gripped the arms of the seat, remembering the chance of sabotage, remembering the fire—

"Wes, back there, is a class one medic," Ari said to him, raising her voice over the engine-sound. "He's got the equipment. When we level off we can get you an almost-real bed. How are you doing?"

"Fuzzed. They shot me with numb-out." He tried to focus on here and now, the list of things he wanted to ask her. "Giraud—Jordan—could be in danger."

"I'm head of Security at the moment," Ari said. "I'll tell you—I'm quite aware of our problems. I went to the Bureau, I laid the problems out, and when we land we're going to call Family council—that's why I desperately want you there. For one thing, you've a vote. For another, you can probably tell things I can't, about what's gone on all these years."

"You're challenging Denys?"

Ari nodded. "I'm bringing your father in. He's already left Pytho. *That* was for his protection, to get him home where there are witnesses. I could divert the plane. But that would tell too much. Say that I can hide certain orders from Denys. Not a whole plane. It's due in at 1500. We're projecting arrival about 1400. We're running that close. I can stall its landing, divert it to Svetlansk or somewhere, *after* we've landed. I hope to have Denys thinking I'm coming back for safety reasons. But he probably won't accept that."

He had thought he had had all he could take, already. He sat there with adrenaline pouring into his exhausted system and wondered why he was relatively calm. *We're going to die*, he thought. *Somewhere along this—they're going to get us. Somewhere in the networks of Security orders, the airport, the military—the Bureau—House Administration—*

"The first thing he'll move on," he said, "is my father and your friends. And they haven't got a way of finding it out."

"I sent Amy a very simple message this morning. It contained a codeword. There's a good chance she's been able to warn the others: she's on Base One right now, and that's a lot of defense in itself. Don't worry."

"God." He took several slow breaths. "Why are you trusting me?"

Ari gave a one-sided smile—her predecessor's expression, so like her it affected his pulse rate. "I could say, because you know how safe your father and Grant are with Denys right now. Or because you made your choice when you told them to call me. —But the real reason is, I always could read you—better than anyone in the House. You're my friend. I never forget that."

"You choose a damned peculiar way to show it."

The smile hardened. "I choose what works. I don't get my friends killed letting them run into a situation I can see and they don't. I don't argue about some things. I'm self-protective as hell. But you're special with me. You always have been. I hope we never come to odds."

He felt a profound unease at that. And reckoned she meant him to.

"I want to help your father," she said. "But you have to keep him from bringing this to Council. You have to get me the time. Give him time to know *me*, not the Ari he remembers."

"He'll do that for me."

"He won't trust you."

That hurt. It was also true. "But he'll give me the time. He won't betray his friends, but if I ask him I can get that from him. He *is* reasonable, Ari. And he does care what happens to me."

"That's clear too." She leaned her head back, turned her face toward Florian, beside her. "Tell Wes come help him. I'm going to trank out about half an hour. I've got to have it."

Justin thought the same. He unbuckled, levered himself out of his seat, and let the Security medic take his arm and steady him on his way aft.

xiv

Grant rested his head on his hands and wiped them back through his hair. "Here," Quentin said, and offered him a soft drink from their own kitchen.

"Thank you." He took it and sipped at it, sitting on the couch, while Amy Carnath pored over the output that they had linked up to the living room monitor.

Justin was all right; the plane was up. They were on their way back; the worst of their fears had not come true; but they were not home yet.

Ari had stalled the press conference till dawn, putting out bulletin after bulletin, each more appalling than the last, until she had come on herself and fueled a whole new set of speculations—*not* laying it indubitably to the Paxers, but by implication taking into Khalid, perhaps even intimating the existence of high-level complicity, virtually declaring for office—

Then, after the news conference, a message came through Base One to sera Amy, and Base One started pouring out instructions. . . .

Amy, this is Ari, via Base One. This is all pre-recorded, so you can't talk back and forth, just listen and do this.

Something's happened. I can't know what in advance, but if you're getting this, something drastic will have happened, and I'm either in hospital, dead, or somewhere outside Reseune and in trouble.

First thing, protect yourself.

Second, the warning flasher we talked is out over the House system now, so everybody knows to take precautions.

Help them if you can. Base One is now available for you to use on Florian's and Catlin's level, and that means you can get information and perform operations without leaving a flag even for Denys or Giraud. The Help function is under Tutor if you need it.

I don't think they'll go at you. They know Base One uses lethal force. I don't advise your taking other people up onto the floor, but use your discretion in extreme need.

Don't use Base One to request information outside Reseune. I can, but for various reasons I haven't incorporated that routine under this access—mostly that it's hard not to give yourself away. I've encoded every single contingency I can think of and if I've activated this, I've probably fired you off a list of pertinent items via a code transmission in the net to Base One.

As follows:

Assassination attempt; from inside Reseune; Jordan Warrick; not involved; Jordan Warrick moved; to Reseune; trust Grant; but; Justin Warrick; whereabouts uncertain; in Novgorod; watch out for; Denys.

Grant drank his soft drink and stared bleakly at the computer flow, codes, mostly, which he could not read, which, very likely, Amy could not read, but the advanced system which had annexed their home unit very probably did read, and Base One answered Amy's questions.

"Damn," Amy said.

Grant did not like that. He waited for illumination, and finally got up, but Quentin's instant, wary attention dissuaded him from taking a step in any direction.

"What's wrong?" he asked quietly. "Sera?"

"Oh, damn!" She spun her chair around. "Security's just gone off-line. The whole net is down."

"Denys is aware," Grant said with a cold feeling; and then saw the black screen come to life again.

This is the House System emergency function. Someone has attempted interrupt. The Bureau has been notified and the interrupt documented.

The System is now re-integrating. Source of the interrupt: Security main offices.

Control of the System has now passed to Ariane Emory.

All Security personnel, stand by further orders through normal channels: Security main offices are downgraded to: Unreliable; House Administrative offices downgraded to: Unreliable; control re-routed to: RESEUNE ONE.

"God," Grant breathed, and sat down.

"Well, Denys has done it," Ari said, and leaned back in her seat, watching the system-flow transit the briefcase flat-screen, Florian and Catlin reading over her shoulder.

"That sounds like my predecessor's work," Florian said.

"It might well be. And mine. —I'm surprised at Seely letting Denys try that."

"Seely is likely following orders," Catlin said. "Seely would have advised against it."

"Might not be there?"

"Might not," Catlin said, "but mostly, I think, they're preparing to defend the Administrative wing."

"Makes sense," Florian said. "The system may have downgraded his Base, sera, but I'm sure he's already gone to manual on those locks."

"Negotiation's what he's aiming for. He has absolutely nothing else to gain. *Denys* wants to be immortal. *Giraud* is down there in that tank, and Denys can't keep his hand on everything."

"Security won't like to be used against the House," Catlin said. "Abban I can understand. Seely I can. Some of the others—"

"Yakob?" Florian suggested.

"*Could* be odd tape. Could be odd tape on that whole senior wing. They've had twenty years to do it. I don't trust any of them."

"Don't count the Administrative systems as gone, sera," Florian said. "There could be a way—check and see if there's any order for Q system equipment credited to Administrative."

"Security 10: acquisitions: Administrative: computer equipment: search. —Why? You think that could have been the tamper in Security?"

Florian leaned on her seat-back, nodded vigorously as she looked up over her shoulder. "Acquisitions might not turn it up either," he said. "You can rig modules you could port in a suitcase, right down to the memory. Giraud could do it, easy. Right past Decon and everybody."

"Security 10: widen search, last item: computer equipment: twenty-year range: search. —You're right. Denys isn't stupid—even about the House systems. It makes damn good sense: divert Base Two to an alternate system, outflow without respecting any command-level inflow—like a one-way filter, to shut out the House system and still run it?"

"It's more complicated than that, but that's generally the idea. Your predecessor was full of tricks. He'd know there were protections—"

"He *does* know. What about airport defenses? Can we get in there?"

"As long as we have affirmative control while we're going in, and it's talking to us," Florian said, then shrugged. "Unless that system can do something I can't figure. It's always possible. Jeffrey BJ's supposed to be in charge at the airport, and I don't know there's anything wrong with him; but I'd say the best thing to do is check the flight schedules, make sure nothing's inbound, and then use the override to reorient and then lock down: that way if Denys' Base is going to touch anything off it won't hit anything."

"I can name you a handful," Catlin said, "who can make sure that power stays down."

"*You* two take it."

He came around and sat down carefully in the chair next to her, and took the microphone. Catlin perched on the leather arm of his chair; and for a few moments it was all their peculiar jargon and names she did not know, but Catlin and Florian did.

Meanwhile she watched the dataflow. Search negative. She was only moderately interested. It made thorough sense, what Florian suggested; and Giraud could well have gotten the equipment in years ago. They had had all her childhood to set it up, and make sure it functioned.

Kill the airport defenses first, get the plane on the ground; and then figure something could go wrong with the precip towers: envelope rupture would make things uncomfortable for anyone trying to get to the House; figure that Denys might simply have ordered the buses uphill and parked them.

Search: she keyed, *airport: bus, ser # ?; graph.*

The schematic of Reseune turned up both buses, at the front of the Administrative wing.

She keyed orders to the main boards at the precip towers. They were an hour away from the field.

Then she got up and went, herself, back where her Security staff sat talking together: they had heard the net go down and re-establish itself, each and every one of them who had been listening to the net, and that was all of them, she figured.

"We're doing all right," she said. "Stay seated: listen. Florian's taking the defenses down. Wes, Marco, you stay with me and Dr. Warrick, on the plane: we're going to be busy as hell and someone's got to coordinate whatever they can set for our protection. Dr. Warrick's a friendly, but he doesn't know the Rules: if so happen we have to move, you see he does what you tell him. The advance team is going to have to get into Administrative, and Florian and

Catlin are going to be leaders going in. Tyler, you're First after either one of them."

"Yes, sera," Tyler said, a smallish, wiry man, white-haired and crew-cut. Tyler had served as one of Ari senior's staff. Two of the others were retired marines, Wes was a Green Barracks instructor, and the rest ranged from diplomatic security to Marco, who was a systems programmer.

"We'll have a number of other Security on call-up," she said. "Take that advisement from Catlin: she's doing the organization, Florian's doing the special work, Catlin will brief you: we've kept this operation in ready-state for the last two years, not quite like we're improvising, all right? We just didn't know our target. Now we do. And we know right where the keys are. All right?"

"Yes, sera."

She patted Tyler's shoulder, walked back down the narrow aisle past the galley and the staff restrooms; and opened the door of the bedroom. Justin was asleep, completely out.

Burns and bruises, Wes had said. Memory gaps were the serious part; but, as Wes put it, you have one go off next to you, you drop a few things. Nothing unusual.

"Wake up," she said. "Justin. I need you up front."

XV

"They're in," Amy said. "That's the Tower. They're on the ground."

Grant, leaning on the back of the couch, breathed again.

Amy had confused hell out of Security, changing the whereabouts of everyone on her list for protection, lying with one output while she monitored the whereabouts of every Security unit in the buildings they could access, called Security personnel on the Approved list to Wing One, and secured the doors.

While Sam Whitely down at the motor pool arranged transport for Green Barracks personnel and Maddy Strassen and 'Stasi Ramirez and Tommy Carnath had simply gone missing to unlikely places as lies in the net persuaded any inquirers they had taken refuge in B lab and down in the Ag lab.

Call to Family council, the advisement flashed out on the net: *Ariane Emory, calling emergency session via House System, to consider the question: nomination of Dr. Yanni Schwartz to replace Denys Nye as Administrator of Reseune, meeting to be held at 1700 or as soon as practical.*

Grant stood back and folded his arms. *He* had no vote. He was following the scroll of activity on the monitor, that had accelerated markedly ever since RESEUNE ONE had entered approach. That last advisement came as a vast relief to more than himself, he thought: a calculated bit of psych, a tag of grim humor: Emory in full flower.

There were Security orders all over the system of a sudden, outpouring from Base One.

Ari did not look up from the screen; and Justin did not speak, following the flow on an auxiliary Florian had used. Occasionally she gave a voice input or pushed a key; and changes happened. Queries were incoming: *RESEUNE ONE*'s crew, forward, kept their posts, keeping the plane ready to move away and, if the airport seemed threatened, to take to the air again.

He had much rather stay on the ground; and he wished to hell he had some knowledge of the codes that might have told him where things stood.

"We're all right," Ari said. "Sam's got the trucks up from Green; they're going up the hill—no challenge yet. He's holding inside Administration, probably inside Security itself."

She made more changes.

She could, she said, open any doors that were not disabled or under an outlaw Base's control.

Makes it easier, Florian had said, stuffing the pockets of his jacket with various small components out of his own kit—probes and wire, mostly, with some sort of system evident. And Florian had taken a small bag from a locker, and another from a second locker; and handled those very carefully, while Catlin had arranged things with the Security agents aft.

They must be halfway up the hill now, Justin thought.

"*Sera,*" the intercom said suddenly, communication from *RESEUNE ONE*'s crew. "*We've got a phone relay from Administration. Dr. Nye, asking to speak with you personally, sera.*"

"Don't divert your attention," Justin muttered.

"Damn right. —Put it over the intercom; we're all intimate here. —Justin, punch that yellow button on your arm-rest and pass me the mike, will you? This one's engaged."

"*Ari,*" Denys' voice said over the intercom. "*I really think you're being a little excitable.*"

Ari laughed, never taking her eyes from the screen in front of her. She held out her left hand and Justin laid the mike-wand into it. "Are you hearing me, uncle Denys?"

"*I'm hearing you fine, dear. I wish you'd make clear exactly what's going on here, and call off your troops before they do serious damage to the wing.*"

"You want to unlock those doors, uncle Denys? We can talk about this. I promise you'll be safe. I'll even continue Giraud."

"*I don't know what happened in Novgorod: I'm sure it's more than you've told me. Can we talk about this?*"

"I don't mind."

"*I'm willing to resign. I want protection for myself and my people. I think that's reasonable.*"

"Perfectly reasonable, uncle Denys. How do we make that official?"

"*You stop your people. You guarantee me custody of Giraud's replicate. I'm perfectly willing to accept retirement. I have the means to make taking this place extremely expensive; but there's no need. I have the feeling you must blame me for the events in Novgorod—"*

Ari laughed again, with less humor, Justin thought. "I really don't know, uncle Denys. I don't entirely care. I've rather well overrun the course you set for me; and it's *my* time. The changing of the seasons. Perfectly natural. You can have a wing, you can have your comforts— I know that matters to you, uncle Denys. You can work on your books, — I do know about that. They're wonderful. You have so much valuable yet to do. . . ."

"You're very flattering, young sera. I want Seely."

Ari was silent a moment. "Under some restrictions. I can agree to that."

"You don't touch him!"

"I wouldn't hurt Seely, uncle Denys. We can work something out. I promise you. I won't file charges. Your life will be exactly the same. You don't travel anyway; and you'll have Giraud to occupy you and Seely, won't you? You were a damned good parent, you know; and very kind, really you were. You could have done a lot of things to me Geoffrey did to Ari senior; and you took a chance with the program and didn't. I really have quite a warm feeling for you about that, uncle Denys; and for Seely; and for Giraud. Giraud and I got to be really close at the last; and I really don't think he did it, I think it was a worm in Abban's tapes. I think it was something you put there. Maybe not. I may have an over-active imagination. —They're going to take those doors down, uncle Denys; and practically speaking, —you're running out of time."

"Stop them."

"Are you going to come outside, uncle Denys? With Seely?"

"All right. When you get up here. I want a guarantee of safety."

"You have it in my word, uncle Denys."

"I want you here to control your people. Then I'll open the doors."

Justin shook his head. Ari looked at him and said: "All right, uncle Denys. I'll be up there." She pointed at the button on Justin's seat. Justin pushed it, breaking contact.

"Ari?"

Ari pushed a button on her chair arm. "We're finished. Break contact."

"Ari," Justin said, "he wants you in range."

Ari watched the screen and said: "That might be, but he's in an awfully bad position." She picked up her own microphone. "We've got contact with Denys. He says hold off, he's just resigned. Confirm; pick it up. —Justin: *you* stay here."

"Dammit, Ari, —"

"I wouldn't be going up there, except I hope we can do this without a shot. I'm enough for Security to worry about; they don't need another one. If something goes badly wrong, this plane is going back to Novgorod, and you can tell the Bureau the whole damn mess, then do what you like. But I'd prefer you back in Reseune, running another of my sets. I'll even let you pick the surrogates."

He stared at her.

"I have a lot of unfinished business," Ari said, standing by the seat. "If I don't make it out of this—getting me back is a real priority. Gehenna is only *one* of the problems. And you need me the same as I need you."

She gathered up Marco, and Wes unsealed the door, and sealed it again after her.

It was true, he thought as that door closed. Everything else considered, —it was true.

Then he thought of what she had said: *only* one *of the problems*; and: *the same as I need you.* . . .

xvi

"I don't like this," Florian said, crouched close to Catlin, where the bus and the hill made a little cover a curve away from the glass main doors. His hands were cold, exposed to the air: he protected the left one under his arm and watched the data-flow on the hand-held monitor in his right.

"It's a case of What's he got," Catlin said, tucked down tight, chest against arms against knees.

"Seely isn't sera's kind of problem," Florian said.

Catlin looked at him, quick and hard. "Sniper or something bigger up there. You want those doors?"

"Grenade will handle that. They're doing final prep in there now, I'm sure of it, now sera's left the airport. This whole thing is a set."

"Go, then," Catlin said. "You time it. There's got to be a trigger in that hall."

Florian took a breath, flexed a stiffened hand and an injured shoulder. "Photocell, likely. Floor and body-height, with an interrupt, electric detonator, best guess—I'm first in on this one."

The shockwave shook the bus; and Ari was already ducking when Marco grabbed her and pulled them both down, but she fought to get a look as the bus made the turn.

Smoke billowed up from the area of the Administration Wing front doors. She could see the other bus parked on the slope. The black-uniformed group there was in sudden motion, running uphill.

Her driver stopped.

Marco pulled her flat and threw himself over her.

As the air shook and clods peppered the windows.

Florian picked himself up, wiped his eyes and staggered to his feet as someone helped him, he was not sure who, but it was from behind and it was friendly if it got him up again.

He saw Catlin ahead of him in the dim hall, saw her arm a grenade and wait, the thing live in her hand—because somebody like Seely could give it back to you.

She threw it, but a black blur came out that door.

Florian snapped his pistol up and fired; and the grenade blew the whole doorway to ruin. Catlin had fired too. She took another shot, point-blank, to be sure.

Florian leaned against the wall and caught his breath. The net was saying that the teams from Green Barracks had gotten into Security—up the lift shafts from the tunnel system: easy job, till they got to the traps and the defenses.

The whole hall was filled with bluish smoke. The fire alarms had gone off long since.

Catlin walked back to him, swinging her rifle to cover the hall beyond, while he kept a watch over her blind-side. "One more," she said.

He nodded.

He was not glad of this one. Denys had been kind to them. He remembered the dining room, remembered Denys laughing.

But it was sera's safety in question, and he had only a second's compunction.

Catlin had less.

The front doors were in ruins, the smoke still pouring out when Ari climbed off the bus; and Florian and Catlin both came out under the portico to meet her.

"Denys is dead," Florian told her first off. "I'm sorry, sera. It was a set-up."

"What about Seely?"

"Dead," Catlin said.

Ari walked up onto the porch and looked into the hall. Bodies lay scattered in the dim emergency lights, under a lowering canopy of smoke. She had known that place since childhood. It did not look real to her.

Denys gone. . . .

She looked back at Florian and Catlin. Catlin's expression was clear-eyed and cool. It was Florian who looked worried. Florian, who had a gash running blood down his temple and another on his cheek, not mentioning what he had had from Novgorod.

She did not ask. Not anywhere near witnesses.

xvii

The Reseune corporate jet touched smoothly, braked, and swung into a brisk roll toward the terminal and Decon—always a special treatment of plane and passengers, when a flight came in from overseas.

"It's going to take a while," Justin said, hand on Grant's shoulder; and they might have gone to sit down, then, in the comfort of the VIP and press room. But he watched it roll up to the safeway; watched the windows after it had come to rest. He could make out shadows moving inside, nothing more.

But one of them was Jordan and another was Paul.

Everything's all right, he had said, when *RESEUNE ONE* had let him speak to the incoming plane, when Grant was on the way down from the hill and Reseune was stirring to heal its wounds. *Don't worry. Yanni Schwartz is the new Reseune Administrator. Welcome home.*

He worried. He watched out the window mostly, while Decon did its work, hosing down the plane in foam. He and Grant exchanged stories in distracted bits and pieces, what they had known, and when, and what they had been in a position to pick up.

He worried until the doors opened and gave up two tired travelers.

After which they had the lounge to themselves, Ari had said, for as long as they wanted; and the sole surviving bus waiting out under the portico, to get them back up the hill.